VIA Folios 174

The Collected Stories
of Pietro Di Donato

Published by Bordighera Press, an imprint of the John D. Calandra Italian American Institute of Queens College, The City University of New York.

25 West 43rd Street, 17th Floor, New York, NY 10036

Library of Congress Control Number: 2024942523

The cover portrait of the author was done by the late Cam Price, a dear friend of Helen and Pietro.

A special thanks to RD for the curation of his father's works and the sustaining of his father's legacy. Thanks to Frank Trotta for his dedicated assistance in locating hard-to-find titles for this collection.

Editor's note: Changes to previous versions of the text appearing in this collection reflect the editor's notes, and attempts to correct errors in the originals. Quirks of the time, particular outlet, and Pietro di Donato, whether in grammar or spelling, have been otherwise maintained. If any other inconsistencies exist, the fault lies with the publisher.

VIA Folios 174
ISBN 978-1-59954-222-5

THE COLLECTED STORIES OF
PIETRO DI DONATO

Edited with a foreword
by Fred L. Gardaphé

BORDIGHERA PRESS

Table of Contents

Note on the Edition

Many of the works featured here were first collected in 1970 hardcover collection *Naked Author*, published by Phaedra. A subsequent paperback edition, *Naked, As An Auhor*, was published by Pinnacle in 1971. Previous to being collected in these editions, the works were featured in a number of diverse publications, listed below. The other previously uncollected works note their original sources in the table of contents.

Bluebook, for "A Gift from Dottie Ryan." August 1961.

Esquire, for "La Smorfia." December 1955.

Holiday, for "New York's Little Italy;" and "New York Chinese World." 1965.

Knight, for "The Pharaohs;" "The Broken Scaffold;" "Win a Kewpie Doll;" "And Your Sister Too!;" "Sugar, Spice and Everything Nice;" and "Lunch with President Kennedy." 1964-71.

Nugget, for "Sicilian Vespers;" "The Flesh, the Devil, and Santiago;" and "When Willy K. Vanderbilt Frolicked and I Shoveled His Snow." 1958-1968

Playboy, for "The Fireplace;" "The Overnight Guest;" "O'Hara's Love;" and "Tropic of Cuba." 1965-66.

Ramparts, for "Nude of an Author;" and "In the Wide Waste." 1966.

Foreword

Those who are familiar with the name Pietro di Donato usually begin and end their knowledge with his first novel, *Christ in Concrete* (1939), the fictionalized telling of his father's death in a building collapse close to the Brooklyn Bridge in lower Manhattan. As a result, young Pietro, being the oldest male, had no choice but to drop out of school in the seventh grade to support his seven brothers and sisters and his mother as an apprentice bricklayer under the watchful eye of his father's *paesani*.

Though he had little formal education, di Donato discovered both the American and European literary masters of the late nineteenth century when he was twenty-five years old. Inspired by the works of James Fennimore Cooper, Walt Whitman, Èmile Zola, and Leo Tolstoy, amongst others, he began to write, recounting the unusual and often brutal circumstances of the new life into which he had been violently thrust.

Not many of you may know that the novel was an extension of a short story di Donato first published in *Esquire* Magazine (1937), then the premiere men's magazine; it was included in Edward O'Brien's *Best American Short Stories* (1938). The novel focuses on bricklayer Geremio's eleven-year old son, Paul, and his single-minded battle (for each day on a merciless job was a literal battle) to become a working man molded in the image of his dead father. At an age when most kids are dealing with acne and awkward entries into social life beyond the home, Paul struggles to take his father's place on the scaffolds alongside hardened grown men, in addition to becoming the father-figure in the home. The novel dramatizes the toll the mythic American Dream takes on working immigrants as promised dreams turn into living American Nightmares.

The success of *Christ in Concrete*, (over 200,000 copies in initial sales and the Book of the Month Club selection over John Steinbeck's *Grapes of Wrath*), launched di Donato into commercial orbit as a top literary celebrity. Yet, after the initial earnings from the novel were spent spoiling his siblings and cavorting across the globe with the likes of Ernest Hemingway, di Donato was forced to return to laying bricks. During those years, via his kaleidoscopic memory of events, he generated short stories for his agent to submit to the top magazines. Fortunately they usually got published; otherwise, we wouldn't have this collection today. What you hold in your hands gathers for the first time an expansive collection of his short works.

Because he spent his life as a worker-writer, America's one true proletarian author, the short story has been the meat of di Donato's literary art, one could even argue that his novels are collections of interconnected stories, for with each one, he defies the traditional definitions of what a novel should be. These pieces began appearing in the mid 50s, in men's magazines such as *Nugget, Knight,* and *Blue Book.* As a counterweight to the racy periodicals, he had articles bordering on high literary appearing in *Esquire,* and *Holiday,* the glossy travel magazine of the era.

By 1962, the stories caught the attention and imagination of Hugh Heffner and a string of stories by the author would come out in *Playboy;* some even attracting national attention, like "The Tropic of Cuba," which sparked an anti-Castro riot in front of Playboy's Manhattan headquarters by exiled Cuban nationals decidedly unsympathetic to the authors equality-to-all message. With the 60s drawing to a close, *Penthouse, Ramparts,* and *OUI* magazines ushered in the 70s for the author with a terrific bang.

The collection opens with the never before published "Blood Cement." The author introduces us to Bob and Frankie, two bricklayers coming up the 55th St. west side subway steps—Bob, twenty years older, soft spoken, optimistic and sympathetic "with clumsy grace, dressed in heavy laboring wear." We like him immediately; while young, angry Frankie begins the day muttering, "Piss and vinegar, by Jesus, that's what life is!" On the job, fate has it that Frankie is suddenly promoted to foreman status. Overnight, he is in a position of power and the all-too-human nature of the working man, and the workplace hierarchy, springs to the fore. "Blood Cement," a variation on a theme, reverberates with the same cold realities of the working man's world that di Donato shocked America with his *Christ in Concrete* years earlier.

The ironic and amusing events surrounding his 1939 Book of the Month Club prize are recounted in "My Uncivilized Past." In it, on his way up to his publisher's office, an elegant older woman is in the elevator with him going to the same floor. An incident occurs and he pins the elevator operator to the wall snarling, "Listen, you little greaseball prick!" Minutes later the editors, falling all over the woman in greeting her, introduce him to Mrs. Woodrow Wilson.

Whether the author's treatment of Bernardo Bertolucci's father, the famous Italian poet Attilio Bertolucci, or his pampered protégé son and the then newly-released *Last Tango in Paris*, the author's unique Roman immersion pulls us in with writing only he was capable. After reading "The Roman Circus of Bernardo Bertolucci," an *OUI* magazine reader wrote to the editor, stating: "Pietro di Donato is the best writer I've read in years, as your profile of Bernardo Bertolucci (December, 1974) shows. It's been years since I've been to Rome, but the feel of the city I got from his piece was as fresh as the day I left—Di Donato takes you to surprising places in his prose and gives an impression that is incomparable in accuracy and texture. Congratulations on a superb piece."

Then there's "Ladies of the Roman Night," a sympathetic and very Italian treatment of the sub-culture existing alongside the chic and touristy world of Rome's Piazza di Spagna, circa the mid 70s. His observations and insights into twentieth-century life connect rich to the poor, and ancient to the contemporary like no other writer of his time. His bold and brash narratives reveal secrets of mafiosi and aristocrats alike, while becoming repositories for his own life's stories.

"Christ in Plastic," investigates the Aldo Moro kidnapping as no other journalist has, or ever will. Pietro Di Donato was the master of the short-story form, beginning with the 1937 *Esquire* story, and ending his long run of feature articles with this stunning account of the 1978 abduction, and subsequent execution weeks later, of the prime minister of Italy, Aldo Moro. Had the author miraculously penetrated a cell of the famous Brigate Rosse—the Red Brigades; or was the article the heart-wrenching account of the pawn Moro, sprung whole cloth from the genius of the author sent to Italy on an investigative assignment? We will never be fully sure of the answer. But what is fact is that the riveting piece won the prestigious Overseas Press Award for the year 1978.

The 1971 *Times*' article, "A Rinascimento on L.I.," is not only entertaining, but today we realize it to be an important piece documenting the migration of the Italian-American generations from the NYC boroughs, and the New Jersey Palisades, out through Nassau County and into Suffolk County on Long Island. There is much bitter irony to be found here: the very immigrants he had spent his youth defending, and uplifting, two and three generations later end up in the isles of the supermarkets and shopping malls, buying appliances, and consuming junk food and mindless entertainment. Towards the end of his life, he looks back, shakes his head, and concludes that the people he had given his life to had failed the test of integrity, miserably.

His accounts of New York's Italian enclaves, restaurants, bars, and social clubs after the turn of the century, his returns to Hoboken, Little Italy, and his insights into the growth of Chinatown, make you regret that you've never been there, or, if you had, you missed much. Via his stories you will feel his early traumas—traumas that shaped his world perspective and created obsessions that would haunt his life, and his writing, until his death.

What you will find here are imaginative, pithy, and passionate word renderings of life according to Pietro di Donato. In every story you'll feel the fierce, unfiltered sensuality of a writer who turns contempt into expression, body parts into poetry, transgressions into confessions, and experiences into the basis for his political stands.

Whether the publication was a men's magazine that gave him greater editorial freedom, or a mainstream periodical that projected more traditional moralities, this author gave his all by writing from his soul.

These stories appear in his characteristic and unique prose style— biblical and lyrical, historical, and hysterical. You'll find humor in his ironic juxtapositions of the sacred and profane, the weak and the strong, the virtuous and the vulgar. The writer takes everyone seriously, the fool, the hipster, the tepid and the hot, for his mission is to make you see through the illusions capitalism has created that lull you into mindless consumption.

His narrative ploy is to get you to see through his eyes, eyes that have seen it all; we sense through his body that has sensed it all, forcing us to question our own philosophical and moral foundations as he questions his. He doesn't care who his audience is; he writes literature as he believes it needs to be written, utilizing a variety of styles: journalistic, oral traditional, and high literary, passing along his antique Abruzzese folk wisdom so as to help us better understand our modern America.

The writing will take you to places you've never been and may have never wanted to visit. Through it all, though, he remains steadfast in seeking justice for the downtrodden—the unblighted innocents of the earth. We see this uncontrollable passion he had for the abused—the same passion which drove his *Christ in Concrete*, written in 1937—reach its climax with his final novel, *The American Gospels*. Begun in 1969 upon first seeing photos of the My Lai Massacre, the work would essentially consume the final twenty years of his life.

Ultimately, he had no choice but to create his own God, as he did in his *Gospels*—but not just one traditional Christ, the impotent Christ who failed him so in his childhood when his father was killed—he would go beyond by giving us *four* different Christs: two male and two female. It was the act of a man whose life was a morality play; or perhaps you might say it was a miracle play, given the virtual sainthood of his youth as savior to his eight surviving family members. In either case, it was a play he struggled through until the final scene of the final act.

Since his death in 1992, di Donato has been slowly resurrected through the attention given by literary scholars and the inclusion of excerpts from *Christ in Concrete* in anthologies. The novel has never gone out of print and is taught widely in college and university courses internationally. In academic circles, Pietro di Donato is recognized as the definitive Italian American writer of the twentieth century.

With this collection, both casual reader and scholar alike have the opportunity to better know Pietro di Donato, the worker, the writer, and the artist. Now we can discover new uses for the unique wisdom passed along by this most important and underrecognized writer of our time.

Fred L. Gardaphé

Blood Cement

"Piss and vinegar . . . !"

"Cheer up kid," said Bob, "you'll get used to it."

"Balls!"

Frankie's ambitious, uncertain expression, and Bob's pleasantly round face came up the 55th st. west side subway

Bob smiled sympathetically. Out on west 55th st. Frankie pulled up his coat collar and looked ahead sullenly. The bastardized detail of the cheap neighborhood projected into his feelings and he muttered, "Piss and vinegar, by Jesus, that's what life is!"

Bob whistled softly, That's just Monday morning, Frankie."

"Balls!"

"Ah, you'll be sour and blue until Wednesday; then you'll look forward to Saturday when the pay envelope comes and you'll swear again that buildin's the best racket goin'."

"It's so goddamn true."

"An' remember, you brickies get five bucks more a day then us helpers . . ."

Frankie didn't answer, but his head went a little higher. They came down 55th towards 11th; Bob, with clumsy grace, dressed in heavy laboring wear, and Frankie, in definitely more fashionable working clothes.

Frankie withdrew within himself . . . Piss and vinegar was piss and vinegar!

Bob knew when a man didn't feel like talking. He knew a few things. He was a good twenty years more than Frankie.

They were not far from 11th ave. when they noticed a long train of freight cars pulling past the job, preceded by a young man who galloped ahead on horse—back waving the red flag of danger.

Frankie burst, God—damn—it! Now we'll be late! Let's try to beat the train!"

Bob pulled him back. The train was already passing the job . . . too late. Nothing to do now but watch the cars jerk by.

"There goes the five minute whistle," groaned Frankie.

"Don't worry, kid, it's not the last one you'll hear."

Frankie jammed his fists further into his pockets. "By Jesus, I wouldn't weep if it was!'

They both looked over the heads of the rolling cars and took in the square gray bones of the job. Up on the tenth floor the swinging scaffold with its cabled—planked length skirted the cold new structure. 'Big ears' Baker, the labor boss, could be heard shouting his duty in professional rage . . . "Jack your dog up, Reuben! What the hell————— were you jackin' somethin' else over the weekend? Git it Reuben!"

Frankie's lip curled. "Listen to the big-eared sonofabitch. He'd break in half if he got a good day's work into him."

"You'd be no different than him, if you get the chance."

Frankie was silent. He dreamed of bettering himself. It was one thing to be gaffed, and another, to be the gaffer. He looked at Bob sideways. Bob had soft, sad, smiling eyes, was plump, and quite bald.

"What the hell are you always smilin' about, Bob?"

"Am I?"

"Aw balls . . . I wish this goddamn bunch of junk would roll outta the way. Look, the brickies are out on the scaffold already! Jeeze, there's old stone-eye Pitts up on the floor watching us!"

"We can't get over until the cars go by."

"That old bastard up there is givin' us the eye . . . just as though we ordered these trains to hold us up. Isn't he the sonofabitch. Some day I'm gonner dump a brick through his skull!"

Bob followed Frankie's gaze and saw old stone-eye, the head forman; his six-foot-four of buzzard perched at a point of vantage, inspiring awe, discipline, and production.

"Old Pitts is on the job aw-right."

"The bastard!"

"He's not bad."

"No——he's worse!"

"Take it easy, kid."

"Easy, hell! Why should I be here worrying about gettin' up there on the wall before eight! Why must he be the biggest thing in my life; the guy who I gotta respect and like it—the guy who can send me down the street talkin' to myself if I just don't strike him right . . . . ."

"If he doesn't do it, someone else will."

"Only a sonofabitch can be a boss! Say, don't you get excited *once* in a while? What the hell are you always smilin' about?"

"Half the year it's too hot and dry; the other half's too cold and wet. Ya look forward to getting' the job outta the cellar—ya plug the job to the roof and look forward to toppin' out so's you can get it behind you—and then, well, you just repeat the performance until you can't do it no more."

"Christ, that's rosy!"

"Ya take it up the old night-gown so much that the time comes when it don't make much difference whether it's hot, cold, wet or dry."

"I don't know what this hell you're talkin' about—sounds like you're talkin' in your sleep. Hey, Bob, the train's stopped; let's skip between."

They crept cautiously between two cars and ran to the jop. They checked in at the office, Bob went to the tool shed for his shovel, and Frankie raced into the bricklayers' shanty.

Bob made his way steadily up the stairway while Frankie hastily got into his overalls, jumper, and grabbed his tools.

The last whistle had just blown when Frankie came hot and panting up on the floor. Old stone-eye looked at his big round watch and then at Frankie.

"Up on the 55th st. corner, Frankie—and let 'er ride!"

"O.K., Mr. Pitts."

Frankie scrambled across the floor and hopped out into the scaffold. He hung his tool bag on the scaffold rail and laid his plumb rule on some terra cotta. It was piercingly cold and each frigid blast that swept up from the Hudson seemed to icen the marrow. Frankie jammed his trowel around in the mortar tub and when he pulled it out he noticed a slight freeze on the blade. Meanwhile, the sweat from running up the ten flights, cooled and formed chill sheet medal about his body.

Old stone-eye came over and looked significantly down the stretch of bricklayers who were waiting trowel in hand for the line to go up.

Frankie struggled furiously with his numb fingers to force a square cut nail into a frozen cross joint, for the purpose of giving the man the line which to work by. He hit the nail in with his brick hammer; it curled and fell from his fingers. He knew old stone-eye was watching. He took a small cold chisel from his bag and drove it into the cross joint. It held. He raised his voice in mad triumph and called to the corner man on the other end of the line. "Are you hump!"

"Yow!" re-echoed the call, and Frankie made fast.

Old stone-eye came closer and said, "You better get more than one course ahead of the line or the men'll be laughin' at you."

"O.K., Mr. Pitts." Frankie could've brained him. He troweled his mortar into flexibility, spread it skillfully, and set a one by two foot terra cotta block on his corner. The mortarslushed out from the bed joint as he tapped it plumb and level. With two swift scrapes of the trowel he shaved the joint clean. A quick automatic gaging with a squinted eye and he was assured of its trueness. Set into motion, trowel swinging, hammer tapping, and eye plumbing, his terra cotta corner soon mounted against the solid background of the concrete structure, and as soon as the men ran out the line he called the Tarzan-cry of the scaffolds, "Are you hump!"

After an hour, the wind left suddenly and the Sun came out strong. Frankie felt good. He was two courses ahead of the other corner man. His blood was up. Now was the time to screw the other guys and make a good showing. He ran the line up before the men were out.—Hell, better to screw than be screwed!

"Mor——tar!" He beat the tub with his trowel yelling, "Let's have it!"

Stone-eye sent Bob to supply him. Bob transferred some mortar from another tub.

"Worked all the piss and vinegar out, eh Frankie?"

"Yeah——throw some more of that mud here."

"I borrowed two bits from you last week. Here it is."

"O.K., Bob. Hand me that 'C' block of terra cotta. Have a good time over the weekend?"

"Fair."

"Same woman?"

"Same wife."

"Ohh, same wife. How many times did——say, bend your back Bob, here comes Pitts."

Old stone-eye came out on the scaffold.

"Reuben! Gus! Jack up this scaffold. Don't you know it cost twice as much when a man works above his waist? How many times must I tell you!"

Gus and Reuben, two of the best nigger scaffoldmen in the City, fitted their jack-handles into the cable winches and ho-ho-ed the scaffold up.

Stone-eye rested against the scaffold rail, folded his arms, and remarked diplomatically: "You swing a tasty blade, Frankie."

Frankie flushed. Old man Pitts certainly was a real skate!

"Wow, are you hump!" And the line shot up.

"Your corner block is lippin' a shade, Frankie."

"The block's kiln-twisted, Mr. Pitts; so I humored it a bit."

"Good boy. Remember what I told you on the first floor?"

"Yes, you bawled me out and said, 'Goddammit Frankie, a good bricklayer can lay anything!' and you showed me how."

"That's right Frankie."

"Don't take me long to learn——you either get a thing or you don't."

"That's the spirit. Remember, there's no stayin' still; you either go ahead, or fall behind——watch your line, boy."

"Are you hump——Yow! Yes, Mr. Pitts, I realize that. And I do wanna get somewhere in buildin's."

"How long have you been studyin' plans?"

"Two years, Mr. Pitts."

"Would you know how to hustle men, if you got the chance?"

Frankie's heart jumped. He tightened his jaws and said determinedly: "Nothin'd get by me if I can help it!"

Old stone-eye bestowed one of his rare, dainty smiles, cocked an eye, and walked away pursing his lips.

Frankie paused, his head swam sweetly. Was it possible that he might be promoted—be made a gaffer? Wasn't it rumored that ten more men were coming on because the company wanted to top out faster so's to get going on the other big job downtown, and wouldn't Pitts need an assistant forman? Why shouldn't he be chosen! he was a full-fledged journeyman—and could he hustle the men—boy, could he! Oh Christ, what he wouldn't do to get away from tools! To lay bricks, all you needed was a strong back and weak mind. He had nothing in common with the rest of the guys. He was ambitious. He should be a boss!

He moved like a timed machine. His worked jumped into place, and with automatic precision, his eyes, hands, and body mastered tool and material. He rushed the line and snapped the men. They stole black looks in his direction. He laughed. He felt superior. From a distance, old stone-eye beamed. The man on the other end of the line couldn't get his corner up fast enough. Frankie had run him into a hole, and he yelled, "Are you hump! Tie it on your leg if you got no corner!"

The men were sore, and Bob shook his head. Frankie caught their looks. To hell with the men. It's old stone-eye that matters!

At ten o'clock Pitts called Frankie down from the scaffold.

"Frankie, I'm going to make you my deputy-forman."

Frankie's eyes shone excitedly. "Yes, mister Pitts . . ."

"I want you to run the gang along this line. I've got a new gang comin' on in fifteen minutes and I want to break them in."

"Now see that your gang keeps movin'."

To Frankie, it was like hearing all this in his sleep, but he spoke. "When shall I take over?"

"Right now. You won't need any blueprints. Just follow up same as below.—Well, I hope you make good, Frankie." And once again he flashed his meaningful smile.

The big moment of Frankie's life had come. He was as nervous as a flock of scared pigeons. He was a boss now. He didn't have to do nothing but drive other men——and it meant more money, respect, higher position. There would be no turning back—he'd make a name for himself! He removed his overalls, smartened himself, and stepped out on the scaffold.

The men weren't told of the promotion, but the way he came out onto the scaffold was enough. Bob patted him on the back and said:

"Atta boy, Frankie."

Frankie frowned and said sternly, nervously: "Keep the boys supplied with plenty of mortar, Bob!" Bob smiled.

Frankie's fear cried, "Production! Production!" He was enraged that Bob had smiled. This was no time for friendships. He went along the scaffold and kept repeating in a low, aggravated voice, "Alright boys, on your toes—watch that line!" He felt worried and seriously important . . . His whole world was there on that scaffold. The change in the men was immediate. Within an hour the scaffold was jacked up three times. Frankie snapped the men frantically. They responded nervously and with sickly smiles . . . seeking his favor. He gloried in his new power.

He arrived. This new career was for him to have and to hold. The men raced along like overalled automations. Production was consciousness—consciousness was production . . . nothing else.

Only Bob moved along peacefully, rationally.

The scaffold was going up fast. At eight, it had been near the tenth; now, it was almost half-way to the 11th. Every man was on edge, and fighting his work; all but Bob were jerking and jumping about; he did his work without the benefit of false moves.

Frankie felt that Bob wasn't doing his best, that he should jump like the rest. Old stone-eye tapped him on the shoulder and beamed: "You're a natural, son. Old H.G. Pitts knows how to pick them!"

Frankie was thrilled with pleasure, and would have gladly died for H.G. Pitts right then and there.

Stone-eye continued: "It's 11:15. Do you think you can use another batch of mortar?"

"Send it up, mister Pitts. I want to reach the 11th by noon."

Stone-eye looked at him with the expression of a happy clam.

"H.G. can pick them!"

Going down the line, Frankie heard behind him: "Mister Pitts . . . He'll do!" He turned quickly but it was impossible to spot the speaker. "He'll do—He'll do—" and he glowed within. He could marry now, if he liked. He could brag. He'd have men hangin' around him ready to say 'yes' and ready to treat him. He'd buy a car, and join a lodge. He'll smoke cigars, and have goodlookin' whores. he'll talk boss-talk, and have a boss-face . . ."

"Put up that line! It isn't out yet? Well, why the hell isn't it!" No back talk—he can fire anybody—that puts the silencer on 'em.

Bob's smiling face was before him. He was wiping his wet forehead with the back of his glove. "Take it easy son, you'll last longer."

Frankie was infuriated. Justly so. "Never mind me, Bob. Get that new batch of mortar out on the scaffold!"

Bob's peaceful voice came back. "But Frankie, there's only twenty minutes to go . . ."

"Do you or don't you wanna get it out!"

The men weren't surprised that Frankie spoke that way . . . after all . . . he was a straw boss now.

Bob called Reuben over to hand him the mortar down from the 11th. Frankie was excited. How dare Bob talk back to him. He should have said 'yes' like the other men. Was Bob tryin' to crimp the works. By Jesus, you have to cut your friends dead first, if you want to get somewhere! He stood beside a mortar tub, leaned against the scaffold rail and watched Bob with squinted eyes.

Reuben, passing down the mortar from his barrow with a shovel to Bob, was jumpy and restless under Frankie's eyes.

Bob, standing at the edge of the scaffold, reached up between the planked top covering of the scaffold and the building, took the shovels of mortar as Reuben reached them down to him, and dumped the mortar into the tubs. He did his work gracefully and apparently without much effort.

Frankie was beside himself with rage. Everybody else was hoppin' it up, and Bob moves along in his own way and smiles. Did he think he was a wise guy, and Frankie a sucker? Did he think he could queer the show when a guy had to make good! Was he a fuckin' agitator!

Bob moved up to the tub near Frankie and passed mortar into it. At the second shovelful, a clump of mortar stuck to the shank of the shovel and Bob picked up a brick bat from the scaffold and proceeded to scrape it off.

Reuben jerked his black athletic frame about, and telegraphed to Frankie his nervous willingness to fight the work. As he jumped about, a knot of rage formed between Frankie's eyes. He was a boss now . . . didn't that mean anything to Bob! His fingers twitched on the scaffold rail.

Bob handed the cleaned shovel up to Reuben, and Reuben made much about scooping the barrow and handing the full shovel down. Bob reached up carefully for it, but just as he was about to get it he lowered his sight to secure his feet on the scaffold's edge, and then reached up carefully again for the shovel.

Frankie was convinced. Bob was out to jazz him! He jumped over the tub to snatch the shovel from Bob, and cried through his teeth, "Goddammit, you're as slow as the comin' of Christ!" Instead of grabbing the shovel from Bob's hands, he stumbles, pushed against him and fell back on the scaffold. Bob fell in towards the building with the shovel in front of him. The shovel hit the building and the hot lime mortar flew over his face. Blinded and off balance, he went off between the scaffold and the building, shovel in hand. The men watched the split-second action curiously, and as no one was within grabbing distance of him, they knew Bob was a dead man. He hit the window sill on the tenth, bounced out into the open and flew down with his face looking up at the scaffold and men. The men looked over the edge of the scaffold and watched Bob go. Frankie caught Bob's surprised and questioning expression as he looked up.

When the men got down to the bridge over the sidewalk, where Bob lay, the morgue car had pulled up to the job.

Bob's shovel had landed under him and cut clean through him, sticking up from his form . . . Through the mortar and blood, Bob's peaceful face smiled and dreamed.

As the men watched Bob's ceremony, they said without words:

"Better you than me."

Frankie felt weak and half drunk. He heard stone-eye say sweetly: "We've a lotta cement to use up this afternoon."

The men were talking in small groups, and some of them were removing their overalls. Frankie went over to them and said evenly: "Boys, we've a lotta cement to use up this afternoon."

They looked at him.

When the afternoon whistle blew., the man on the 55th st. corner yelled down the line, "Are you hump!" The other corner re-echoed "Yow!" and Frankie paced the scaffold with firm step and narrowed eyes.

The Pharaohs

As a little kid I dreamed of becoming a fast-drawing, Indian killing cowboy. I wrote a letter to Buffalo Bill, offering my services. Before I was eight years old I had headed for the far Wild West six times . . . . only to be tracked down by Mr. Lawn, the truant officer, or the police, and brought back to my slum home in the 'Dardanell's section of Hoboken.

To keep me off the streets and stop the runaway habit, my old man got me a job working after school and on weekends, in Florio's drugstore. Besides Mr. Popora, who was good to me (he was the prescriptionist), there was an optometrist, a girl at the soda fountain, a girl who sold stamps and tobacco, and the hippy first-aid nurse. I had to take orders from all of them.

Florio was a hearty, bearded, fat brute. On the first day, while sweeping, he watched me. I found a quarter on the floor, and gave it to him. I didn't know he had planted it there on purpose. When I turned he kicked my behind hard.

I tearfully asked what that was for. "Petey," he bellowed, "that's just a tiny taste of what you'll get if I catch you stealing!"

In those days child psychology was simply a man's pointed shoe that made a kid's butt ache. The cruel kick I got for nothing decided me to steal whatever struck my fancy. There was no quitting the drugstore, my father would have beaten me and made me return. I had to outwit Florio and keep away from his damned free-flying foot.

I was the jack of all trades and did the chores of three kids: running the ice cream machine in the dirty cellar, unpacking and storing, washing utensils, delivering, helping the nurse with accident cases, polishing lens for the optometrist, waxing the floor, making citrate of magnesia and Florio's phony cure-all tonics, salves and capsules. From the cellar I discovered holes in the floor where the nurse and the two other girls above were usually stationed. Being a natural eavesdropper, I saw bald-headed Mr. Porpora peeping up through the holes. At that tender age I was already curious about the mysteries girls had under their skirts. Standing on boxes, and crooking my neck, and using a flashlight, I almost ruined my eyesight straining to find out.

The cellar extended beneath the sidewalk. At the entrance to the store there was a glass vault light missing which afforded quite a private view of any woman who stood over it. Women often chatted there. I had fun poking a bamboo stick up through the hole, and hearing them yelp. They never knew where the jab came from.

Florio started me at twenty-five cents a week, and gradually and begrudgingly raised my salary to two dollars. He smugly thought he had me so fearful of him that I wouldn't dare pilfer. But I made his store compensate for his cheapness; as a matter of principle, every chance I had I took something. I became the generous big-shot of the fifth grade, giving out pistachio nuts, glass eyes, leeches, jock strops, cigarettes, sweets, smelly powders for stink bombs, laxative chewing gum, perfumes and pomades. I bought medicals books to school. During recess I gathered my pals to show them the colored illustrations of a woman's organs, which properly impressed them and horrified them and we snickeringly borrowed such terms as menstruation, vagina, rectum, and wrote notes to the girls.

On Sunday mornings when Florio was home I sneaked friends into the rear storeroom and let them see and handle the suspended human skeleton, and the big glass jar containing the freak two-headed fetus floating in liquid preservative.

At the beginning of the fifth term I had trouble with the teacher, Miss Mains, an old-fashioned red haired spinster. After rapidly finishing a test, I drew a dirty picture of her, and passed it around. The boys and girls laughed. She saw it handed back to me and demanded it. I crumpled it and put it in my mouth. She came to me and tried to force my mouth open. As I chewed and swallowed it she slapped me. She marched me to the front of the room, faced me to the class, and said, "Children, this is Peter di Donato, the perfect example of a cheat and show-off!" She kept me after school. "Miss Mains," I said, "the kids know I'm not a cheat. That paper had nothing to do with the test. On it was a picture I drew of you." She blushed, and permitted me to leave. From then on she favored me, and a strange, nice friendship developed between us. I enjoyed being near her, to smell her certain fresh fragrance. It was innocent affection. The kids said I was Miss Mains' pet. A jealous kid said I was a wop. I punched his nose. He bawled to Miss Mains and complained that I had called him an 'Irish fuck.' She told him there was no harm in being called an 'Irish fox,' and because he insisted otherwise, she made him write 'Irish fox,' a hundred times.

One of the fifth grade subjects was physiology. Physiology was my meat. I'd get up and recite the process of digestion, making the trip of a piece of bread through the system an odyssey. Miss Mains brought out the good in me and changed me from the problem boy of the class to the shining light. I liked her best in the morning when, following our pledge of allegiance to the flag, and singing *My Country 'Tis Of Thee,* she sat at her desk, and in a soft, fervent voice, read the twenty third psalm. I can still hear her, beginning: "The Lord is my shepherd; I shall not want: He maketh me to lie down in green pastures: he leadeth me beside the still waters . . ."

Florio was going to a druggists' convention. He and Mr. Popora were behind the cosmetic counter. They didn't notice me. Florio took out some white balloons from a drawer, put them in his pocket, and said chuckingly, "I ain't bringing home any presents to the wife."

"At the cathouse in Atlantic City I'm going to wash my feet with my socks on." Mr. Popora said, "Yeah, it doesn't pay to take chances."

I couldn't make head or tail out of their dialogue. I couldn't figure out the place of balloons in the drugstore. Intrigued, I saw further action. A woman would come in, say something into the nurse's ear, and the nurse would sell her balloons. A man would say something that could not be overheard to Mr. Popora, and Mr. Popora would sell him balloons. It seemed ridiculous. I investigated the drawer. It was full of neatly rolled white balloons in packages. All it said on the packages was, Pharaohs. I unrolled a balloon. It was sausage-shaped. I took a few packages.

At recess I stayed in the classroom, blowing into a balloon to see how big it would get before bursting. The thing expanded but wouldn't bust. Miss Mains looked up from her desk, and said, "Peter, that's a pretty balloon." I brought it to her. "It sure is made of tough rubber, Miss Mains," I said, "blew with all my might and couldn't break it." She examined it and commented, "It has a strong rim. I have never seen this kind of balloon. It must be a special foreign make."

When the kids came back I handed out balloons. They blew themselves dizzy and couldn't break one. We coaxed Miss Mains to try. Her balloons became enormous and finally burst.

She asked me where I had bought them. I pretended that my father had gotten them in New York for me. "The name on the package is *Pharaohs*," I said, "What does that mean?"

"Peter, the Pharaohs were the kings of Egypt, long, long ago."

She went into lyrical description of ancient Egypt with its deserts, camels, pyramids, crocodiles and mummies. So the kids concluded that the Pharaohs I bought were Egyptian balloons. The Egyptian balloons made me more popular than ever. We swatted them around, put a steel marble in them, tied the end and made them flop over and walk, and tested how much water they would hold.

Unloading a pharmaceutical supply truck I saw cartons of Pharaohs. When the driver went into the store to check the delivery list with Florio, I took a carton and cached it in the cellar.

It was two days to Christmas. All the classes were going to have a party in the assembly hall next to our room. What was I going to do with my hundreds of Egyptian balloons? I remembered how in parades, in the amusement park, and in festive movie scenes flocks of balloons were gaily released. I told Miss Mains my father had given me a carton of balloons, and that I thought it would be fun to have each kid in the class suddenly let go bunches of balloons at the end of the Christmas party.

She thought it would be great. By the morning of the day of the party, Miss Mains, the kids, and I improvised more ideas. There was an illuminating gas jet in the room. We attached a hose to the jet, filled the balloons with gas, and knotted the ends. When let go, a balloon would zoom right up to the ceiling. We decorated many of the balloons with water-color, painting faces and the names of the principal and teachers.

Many parents came to the party. On the dais were the principal, Mr. Carter, Santa Claus, and a minister. The speeches and songs were over. Santa Claus gave out boxes of candy. The minister said a prayer. Miss Mains got up and proudly announced that the fifth grade had a surprise ending for the party, arranged by 'Peter di Donato.' There was applause.

Our balloons were hidden in large paper bags. Miss Mains nodded to us. We ripped the bags and let the hundreds of balloons sail. It was spectacular. They bounced and clustered and went up in a white rubbery mass to the ceiling. But something went very wrong. The principal's face reddened. The adults whispered, muttered, arose, and angrily left. The teachers hastily dismissed their classes.

I was told to report to the principal. In his office Mr. Carter questioned me about the balloons. I told him the truth—that I had stolen them.

He said meanly, "You're an impossible, destructive boy. You disgraced Number Three School. We cannot have you in this school." I vowed that I would pay for the balloons. "My boy," he said. "There's more to it than that." I asked him what was I really being expelled for. He would not tell me the reason.

I was confused, and went to the drugstore. Mr. Carter had phoned Florio. Florio booted me and shouted, "Idiot, you fill the school with my condums? I'll kick your brains out!" Mr. Popora intervened. "Florio, the boy doesn't know what he's being punished for." Then he explained to me, "Petey, Pharaohs are 'condums'"—I shook my head incomprehensibly and said I thought they were balloons. "Petey, condums are used for—a—You know how babies are made?" I answered, "Of course, Mr. Popora." "Very well. You see—when a man wants to make love, and not have the woman get pregnant—well he puts a Pharaoh on his 'thing'—on his you-know-what—understand?"

I told him I understood then.

I returned to school to clear out my desk. Expulsion from public school meant I would go to parochial school. Miss Mains was emptying her desk too. She had resigned in shame. I told her I was terribly sorry.

She wept silently. I could hear the two janitors in the assembly hall, moving their tall ladders, and then puncturing the inflated Pharaohs, each going off with a bang.

La Smorfia

Mother was resolute; I was no longer to roam the streets of West Hoboken, the wandering, curious guttersnipe. She commanded me to don my "Sabbath vesture;" she had a new life arranged for me—a job in Florio's drugstore. "By the Saints," she vowed, "thou shalt not become an *Anima perduta* such as the children of the American barbarians! Thou art fully seven years old—the very age when thy father was learning the art of the *muratore*. Note this day for thou shall now commence to bear Christian responsibility.

On the way she paused in front of the barbershop next to the photographer Mastrobelangini's and decided that I should have a haircut. The barber, an Assyrian, was smoking his water pipe. Neither mother nor he spoke English; mother made a scissoring motion about my head; my hair was long, Buster Brown; she tried to tell him to trim it. Yes, yes, he understood. Then she left to see Mastrobelangini about the oft-discussed family portrait. The Assyrian had only one version of cutting children's hair. He clipped and shaved my head so that I was glistening bald, with every irregularity of my head exposed.

I clung to mother's side as she talked with Mr. Florio. He was florid and mustachioed. Gazing down me severely, he held out a gold watch. "What time is it?" I read the hour. "*Bene;* as of this minute you are in my employ." Then I received the catechism of my working hours: directly from school to the drugstore, off from six to seven for supper, quit at nine P.M.; all day Saturday; Sunday afternoons off.

Mr. Florio rubbed a heavy hand over my head and assured mother—as a special favor—he would make a man out of me, and perhaps some day "*dottore di farmacia.*" That was the Spring of 1917. His place, a corner store in a brick building, was not simply an apothecary's, but a multi-departmented establishment.

Upon entering to the left, was the soda fountain; in the center was an island rectangle featuring cigars, cigarettes, perfumes, and a caged stamp booth facing the apothecary counter, from which on either side were swinging doors leading to the prescription compound where there was a first-aid station, sinks and walls shelved with pharmaceuticals; a door led further back into the optometry room, and thence to a high-ceilinged combination lavatory and storeroom.

Making a man of me meant wiping sticky salves from spatulas and tablets with wood shavings; washing mortars and pestles, graduates, and myriad bottles from one ounce to ten gallons; making citrate of magnesia; packaging and labeling pills, camomile tea, bicarbonate, cream of tartar, salts, powders and unguents; bottling physics, oils, acids, syrups and chemicals; wiping lenses; sweeping, dusting, uncrating; sorting shelving; firing the coal furnace, hauling garbage and ashes; delivering prescriptions; changing the window display, and helping to make ice cream in the basement. My immediate superior was Mr. Florio's young brother, Tony, a semi-Mongoloid in his late twenties who still wore knee pants.

The optometry office was the clubroom for Dr. Florio's cronies: Dr. Poppora, the prescriptionist, Dr. Taprio, the psychiatrist, old tall dyspeptic Dr. Ciccione, and Padre Onorio, pastor of Saint Rocco's. They gathered on Sunday evenings for poker and philosophical gossip; I fetching cheroots, hero sandwiches, pastries and wine. I was witness also to an event that took place each Sunday evening which concerned a glass jar on the shelf in the lavatory; moronic. Tony initiated me into the mystery of its contents on my very first day at Florio's. He led me into the lavatory, switched on the light, made me solemnly sign the cross, then pointed to the glass jar and said: "That's Jesus Christ, and if you don't believe me you'll be struck dead, by God!" Floating in greenish formaldehyde was a seven-month male fetus; the nude miniature, large head, prominent lids, was cuddled with its finny hands on chest, tadpole legs tucked up, seeming to be patiently awaiting birthing from its vitreous and marine womb. Sunday evenings without fail, while doctors were at cards, two women came to visit the glass jar. They were Maddalena "La Smorfia" and her acolyte, Maria "La

Virgine," mother of the boy in the jar. I knew the forbidden black-shrouded woman with the twisted face, La Smorfia, a living legend among the *paesanos;* she had delivered me and my brothers and sisters; we thought she brought us to mother in the sack she carried under her dress. She was the high priestess of healing and the awesome Fattura, that shadowy region of the cabala from whence emanated the evil eye, portents, prophecy, the influencing of love and hate, and occult communion with the departed.

No one could tell when, where, how, or from whom the woman with the deep voice and paralyzed face had come to West Hoboken. It was said that La Virgine, when an orphaned girl preparing for the Vigil, had been criminally assaulted, that the shock unhinged her mind, and that she imagined her stillborn, premature issue, the veritable Divine Infant. She would appear in the wake of La Smorfia bearing a lighted candle and in white vestments similar to those worn by the Madonna as portrayed in the window of Saint Rocco's. They would enter the drugstore, walk past the doctors and Padre Onorio and go straight to the glass jar on the shelf in the lavatory. After these visitations the doctors would ruminate over La Smorfia, much to the discomfiture of Padre Onorio and the choler of Dr. Ciccione. "I've travailed for thirty years," said Dr. Ciccione, "to enlighten our illiterate paesanos, but that monster foils my efforts! She puts her grimy talons to every branch of surgery and medicine, but no one will co-operate with me to stop her. The prime culpability lies with the medieval, possessive, insanely jealous husbands who will not permit a man of science to even as much as touch with fingertips the precious 'persons' of their wives! The case of that stonemason beast Matteo Mezzanotte: his wife had an accident and was hemorrhaging in the private zone; not a serious matter but one requiring suture. Do you think he would let me see what I was doing? On pain of death! He covered his wife entirely with blankets—I had to ply needle gut in the dark with head averted as he stood over me with his stone-cutting hammer in hand! Naturally, with my shaking hands, the stitches went in the wrong place! After I left, there was trouble; he smashed the street window and bellowed for the fire department, the police and La Smorfia!"

The stories about La Smorfia were bruited in camera obscura

within which was the wed of hints and bone-chilling conjecture: she was a pagan immortal from the caves of Abruzzi; a defrocked nun who bartered her soul to Lucifer; a female Mephisto who gave birth to a horned, betailed, hoofed demon who scampered over the walls, into the coal stove, and escaped up the flue; nay, that she was not a woman, but shaved with a razor and had the appurtenances of a man!

What ranked Dr. Ciccione were the victories she scored over him. He treated Orlando's unmarried daughter for a tumor, but La Smorfia took over and delivered the tumor—a healthy ten-pound girl. The modern-minded wife of Placido, the baker, encouraged by Dr. Ciccione to give her baby plenty of fresh air, put the baby out in its carriage in subfreezing weather; La Smorfia chanced by, rubbed it with snow from head to foot and blew life back into the baby's mouth.

"Summon La Smorfia!" was the cry that resounded through West Hoboken when bodily woe or Fattura befell a *paesano*.

Dr. Taprio had had a brief career in medicine. His first case as a practitioner threw him into the safe and lucrative arms of psychiatry. He had been called to a home where the whole family was violently ill from having eaten home-canned peppers. As he floundered with diagnosis the ten members of the family promptly died from botulism. He took down his shingle, had himself psychoanalyzed, and embarked into the new field of mind over matter—even to writing books: *Who is Normal? The Power Of Positive Passion. Sexual Geometrics.*

In referring to La Smorfia he used such terms as: *psicologia della superstizione, ignoranza, paganesimo, della congiura.* Padre Onorio carefully avoided any entanglement with La Smorfia. He was content to nod, sigh, shrug his shoulders and lift his eyes to heaven. Dr. Poppora disdained to bother himself about the "peasant witch." While Dr. Florio admitted to sanguine admiration for La Smorfia: *"Un personaggio primitive e misterioso di molto interesse."* He attributed her uncanny power to the fact that she was epileptic. There live today in West Hoboken aged *paesano* woman who, beholding their progeny, long to embrace and kiss them but dare not because of an oath enjoined upon them under the celebrance of La Smorfia in the "Miracle of '17." "Diciassette," the numeral of dreaded recalling. The year of 1917 brought the strife of Institution versus Individual to a head, the undercurrent warfare of

Church and Science against the grim, solitary La Smorfia to climax. Who achieved the final victory? The answer remains locked in the breasts of the old *paesano* women. Prior to '17 the years of the lives of the *paesanos* unraveled in domestic, untoward sequence: fate and the will of the "children producers" could be ascertained as consonant; immigration, espousals, births, a passing here and there, love, feuds, problems and slumber went the clock.

The year '16 expired and '17 came on quiet foot; came softly, innocuously, incognito. I remember the lulling, dreamy, unseasonably warm spring. Mother would not let me discard my long underwear. "This *Primavera* is treacherous."

Perhaps the first indication that proved to be the harbinger of impending evil was the behavior of La Virgine. On Good Friday she walked up and down Central Avenue in front of Saint Rocco's in the full of the moon baying: "La Morte! La Morte! The murder on the Cross of my son Jesu brings soon the finite end of the world!" La Virgine's words disturbed the *paesanos*. The insane were not subject for scherzo. "This is a sign," said Mother. "Dio had a reason for removing her senses; He has a reason for everything. He had a difficult task forming us, but yet we are wont to chafe him even as a child disregards its parents. La Virgine, not knowing dexter from sinister, is given by *Dio* to speak the future." La Virgine traversed the streets night and day moaning her shivering cry: "La Morte! La Morte will find you!" The very air the *paesano* breathed was intangible fear, and they signed the cross at every turn.

I was in the third grade. One morning Mr. Carter, the principal, called assembly. He said our country declared war upon Germany. After we saluted the flag and sang *My Country, 'Tis of Thee* he dismissed school for the day. What was war? Something like cops and robbers, like cowboys and Indians. We ran out into the street in wild glee. Overnight, all talk was about "*La Guerra.*" Posters appeared everywhere: the Kaiser laughing as the *Lusitania* sinks; Uncle Sam rolling up his sleeves. Male foreigners were picked up and detained for clearance of their papers. We visited Father at the Union Hill jail where he was held for a day during the examinations. "Thank God," he said, "that my sons are too young. The fathers of those who are taken have sired tears."

The street world had a gala atmosphere: military music and parades and the tramping of marching men. In the saloons pianos played and people sang; *I Didn't Raise My Boy To Be a Soldier, Break The News To Mother,* and *Pack up Your Troubles In Your Old Kit Bag and Smile, Smile, Smile.* Summer uncoiled with a weighting, relentless heat. The glaring days baked the sidewalks and cobblestones; paint blistered, pedestrians fell prostrate, horses and dogs dropped frothing and had to be destroyed. The night air was not breathable; it was a turgid mass carrying the smell from the Secaucus refuse dumps and pig farms, stinging insects and mosquitoes from the Jersey swamps; with this followed a rash of itch measles and ringworm which made is scratch and bawl. The heat-wearied tried to find sleep on fire escapes, in parks and back yards. We made trips to the Jersey meadows and brought back bundles of cattails to light the night to ward off the insects. To add to the turmoil of our overcrowded flat my Aunt Giannina and her son Pasquale arrived from Italy, not without their ship having been torpedoed by a U-boat. Fires from spontaneous combustion occurred often. One night Mother was awakened by the caterwauling cats; the flat was smoke-filled. Father roused the children and guests, and we stumbled to the front-room windows and clamored: "Fire!" Within minutes the horse drawn engines arrived. We were carried down the ladders: mother was pregnant; we were virtually naked covered all over with a putrescent, luminous powder with which La Smorfia had been treating us for the itch.

The *paesano* women had an intuition of the supernatural, an osmotic feeling of the ominous. They read in La Virgine's insistent wail of "La Morte" an inevitable, moribund augury.

It was then the autumn with its sustaining, sinuous, sultry heat; the moon was red and enormously distended. Kids rumored that it was the beginning of the end of the world, and also that the Huns were going to land in West Hoboken and butcher us.

I was down in the cellar of the drugstore with Tony, mixing citrate of magnesia. Dr. Poppora called me upstairs. He was preparing a prescription that I was to rush to the house of La Regina. Doctors Florio and Ciccione were in conference. Dr. Ciccione was distraught. They were talking about his patient, Teodoro, the grown son of La Regina.

"It's a pulmonary disfunction. He came home ailing from work yesterday—today he is being consumed as with fire!" I raced on my bicycle with the medicine to the house of La Regina. My mother and other *paesanos* were grouped around Teodoro's bed I stayed by Mother and watched Teodoro die. Within a week there were many more cases throughout West Hoboken with the identical symptoms: sudden, raging fever and rapid death. It was named pulmo nipa espagnol—the Spanish flu. La Virgine's "La Morte" had arrived. There was a ditty among the street kids that ended with: *opened the window* and in-flew-Enza. The sad melodies of keening and the sight of bouquets on doorjambs and caskets became commonplace. And in the salons in the bright heat of afternoons men and women were unconscious from drink.

The *paesanos* knew that from birth they had been ordained for labor, poverty and war; with war one might see the enemy and fight for life— but how to fight against a silent, fatal germ? And the *paesanos* sought La Smorfia. She and La Virgine lived in a shed behind the Chinese hand laundry. The *paesanos* awaited her and as she and La Virgine came out into the street they beseeched her: "Maddalena—Maddalena! For the love of God have pity on us, come save my child—my husband—my wife—Maddalena!" The Black Angel struck capriciously and La Smorfia could not be everywhere. She went wheresoever La Virgine nodded. When I was stricken, in my delirium I felt La Smorfia hovering over me like a huge bat. She poured sugar and kerosene into my mouth, painted my throat with iodine, lay vinegar-soaked rags on my forehead, put alternate applications of steaming mustard poultices and ice on my chest, rubbed me with hot olive oil, and made me drink a bitterly acrid liquid from a dirty milk bottle within which was corn silk, worms and seaweed. After I recovered, everyone in the family had to eat raw garlic, garlands suspended around our necks in a cheesecloth bag with a lump of gell of camphor. From weeks of sleepless ministrations La Smorfia began to falter; she could hardly drag herself to the ill and dying. When La Virgine faded into her periodic catatonic state, La Smorfia remained with her in the shed, refusing to leave her. The epidemic of the Spanish Flu was to the *paesanos* a symbolic struggle between Death and La Smorfia. Now death had a free hand; it spared not the rich or poor, the young or old. Doctors and prayers were to no avail. Padre Onorio was helpless before the specter; his services for the dead had become meaningless. Hysteria rooted itself in the *paesanos*. With one mind they decided: a "sign" had presaged the Reaper, and a "countersign" could send him away. Only through the intercession of La Smorfia could the "countersign," the "Miracle." be drawn from La Virgine. And finally the stare left La Virgine and her face radiated and she spoke: "The worship of my son will banish La Morte!"

It was November the second, the night of All Souls'; the air was motionless, clouds invested the moon and stars. Mother and a band of *paesano* women and their children were stationed by the shed of La Smorfia; Father and the paesano men at a distance. The women had white shawls on their heads and in their hands held tapers and effigies of the Saints. La Virgine emerged in flowing white and wearing a crown of lighted candles. La Smorfia led the candlelit procession; the children behind the mothers, the fathers last. Crowds gathered along the way and followed in respectful amazement. At Iorio's drugstore La Virgine obtained the glass jar with her unborn. She held it ecstatically aloft. "Only through my son is your salvation!" The *paesanos* genuflected. Through the streets we trailed La Smorfia, La Virgine and the glass jar to Saint Rocco's Church. As we entered, a rushing wind swept down and distant constant rumblings drummed the shuttered sky. Padre Onorio was in bed with the flu and innocently unaware of the strange *Messa*.

La Smorfia reverentially placed the glass jar upon the altar. She put a votive flame and lit the incense lamps before the glass jar. In the lambent shadows she was a giantess in company with the looming statues of the Saints, more gaunt and her mouth more twisted. She circled La Virgine and swayed in a ritual unknown; she made the motions of a life-size Cross and said: "Bring wine of thy bread, the blood of thy children to the son of Maria!"

The mothers mercilessly pricked the arms of their children with needles and sucked the tiny lettings. The men stood open-mouthed as the children screamed with fright. Above the spire of Saint Rocco's the anxious autumnal storm sought release; dry lightning soundlessly flared up the stained-glass holy windows. With determined jaws the women fled to the altar and printed their bloody kisses upon the glass jar. They fell upon their knees and repeated after La Smorfia: "Oh, son of Maria, let our children live to be bearers of children, and for that we vow never more to embrace and kiss our children!" La Smorfia's eyes were burning, sweat dripped from her straining, tortured face. She threw out her arms to the glass jar and cried: "Son of Maria, send the *Spiritu Santa* to enter this flesh now! now! and purge the pulmonary death from our midst!!" She gasped and dropped with a convulsive seizure. Then arose the agonized chorus of the women cried; "*Salve! Salve!*" as they smote their breasts. The men and children joined. We chanted "*Salve! Salve!*" until we were exhausted, faint. The bursting clouds exploded with a precipitate roar and bolt upon bolt trembled Saint Rocco's.

Our fathers and mothers scuffled us home through the tearful, cooling beating, swirling cascading pour, the first true rain of '17. La Smorfia never regained consciousness; she died before Dr. Ciccione got to Saint Rocco's. The pestilential heat was shattered, and almost as if by magic the Spanish flu disappeared. La Smorfia was no more. Homeless, deserted, Maria La Virgine was picked up in raving madness at the grave of La Smorfia and committed to the asylum in Snake Hill.

Dr. Caprio characterized La Smorfia as a "singular example dementia praecox," that, had she lived, Snake Hill would also have claimed her.

Dr. Ciccione said La Smorfia died from an epileptic stroke. The *paesanos* shook their heads. They knew otherwise. In their hearts and souls they were convinced that on the night of the "Miracle of '17" Almighty God hearkened to her plea and sent her the *Spirito Santo* by hurling an invisible bolt of lightning upon Maddalena "La Smorfia."

The Cabala

"Petey is a pretty boy."

I heard that distinctly. Being alone in my New York Hotel room, I was startled.

"Come to me at midnight. I know you will come." It was the voice of my godmother, Corinne Williamson. Then her flesh smell like honey and lily of the valley surrounded me overpoweringly.

An author lives by imagination, But I know the difference between the conjured and the concrete.

It was the night before last and the beginning of Holy Week that godmother Corinne's unmistakable voice and smell came to me. I had total recall. She figured largely in my Eden childhood. Eden was an industrial town on the New Jersey side of the Hudson River that looked upon the Statue of Liberty and the towers of New York. We lived in the tenement slum section known as "The Dardenelles."

Corinne had a big white house in the silk-stocking district near the picnic park, "The Elysian Fields." People referred to her place as "The Garden of Eden" because of the many flower beds, bushes and trees about her house.

I was the only paesano kid with an American godmother. The paesanos said Corinne was a witch. They called her "The Cabala." She was my handsome young bricklaying father's lover. The paesanos contended that she held him in an accursed perverted spell.

Her tall, blonde, walrus-mustached, stout husband, Tom, was the much-feared chief of detectives. He treated Father as though Father was Prince Charming. That gave Father a decided social edge over the lowly paesanos. Corinne had a soft very feminine round pretty face and figure with brown hair, immense, warm brown eyes and a voluptuous mouth. She spoke with a lanquid Tennessee drawl. On the street she wore a great flowered hat, black neck band, high-heeled button kid shoes, a veil, lavender cape, and dresses of rich tones.

I looked forward to going with Father to her.

The white house with green shutters always looked as though it had just been painted. There was a picket fence with a hedge behind it around the property to the garage where she kept he Cadillac roadster. Between the hedge and the house was a perfect lawn lush with hydrangea and rhododendron bushes. Everything about the exterior was in purposeful order: screens on the windows, an enclosed area with neatly painted refuse cans, trim lines for drying clothes, a lean-to for garden implements, on the slate roof, a rooster weathervane, capped chimney and lightning rods. The porch steps and deck were a shiny maroon; there was a dog-shaped shoescraper, a coconut mat that said "Welcome" before the grainwood door, and on the jamb were a mailbox, a brass knocker and name plate. The vestibule had an umbrella vase, an oval looking glass and a rack with elks' feet for pegs.

The interior was grand with its affluent effects. there as a greeting of pleasant scents, the cleanliness of mopped floors, waxed furniture, varnished wainscoting and balustrade, Bon Ami-ed window panes, and incense.

Father was not like the squat, swarthy paesano run of men. He sought American speech, clothes, thinking and manners. There was the reason of blood: his father was a noblemen and his mother a peasant girl of Saracen strain. The nobleman was an Etrurian who summered his family on his estate in Vasto, Italy, on the Adriatic, Father's mother lived in a hut on the estate. When Father was born in secrecy, the noblemen gave him to the childless wife of a bricklayer, left his wife and family and took Father's mother to South America. They were never heard from again. At the age of seven Father was put in the craft of bricklaying. He had the deep-chested virile physique of the proletariat, and the haughty poise of the nobility. Until he came under the spell of Corinne Williamson he was the Don Juan, the cock pheasant of Eden. All he had to do was smile and grin to a woman. The women of the many races of Eden, the Jewish, Turkish, Irish, German, Swiss, Oriental, Slavish, and colored women, threw themselves at him.

When Father took me to Corinne's he would go upstairs with her with the pretense of receiving piano lessons, and I would have to stay downstairs with her husband.

Corinne's bedroom upstairs had a canopied bed with carvings of puttis and flowers. In the music room was a gilded piano, a Victrola with a horn, ferns in pots by the bay window, and on the piano a Spanish shawl and metronome. Tinkling Chinese glass curtains separated the music room from the parlor. The damask drapes of the parlor windows were drawn, and the floor lamp with its stained glass shade and beaded fringes was kept lit. There was a leather sofa, a love-seat, mounted birds, aquarium with tropical fish, cats, a wise parrot, and the table with the signs of the zodiac upon which Corinne read her cards of destiny.

The paesanos said that Corinne made love to Father "a la Franchese." I went up and peeked into the bedroom. Father and Corrine were in bed. I saw what the paesanos meant about "a la Franchese," and that scene never left me.

The last time I saw godmother Corinne was in the hospital the day after she had given birth to a son. I had gone there with Mother. The paesanos called Mother "La Giaconda" because of her resemblance to the Mona Lisa. Mother had long quietly suffered Father's double life with "The Cabala," but that day she blew up and brought things to a climax.

Corinne was in her hospital bed. As Mother wiped, oiled and powdered the baby she scrutinized him closely. The baby had Father's naturally polished long-shelled fingernails, dimples, twinkling black eyes, tight swift ears, with the top of the left ear elfin pointed, and the fourth toe of the left foot turned down and in. The baby was the image of Father. Corinne had named the baby Jerry, and Mother, pregnant, had planned to call her next boy Jerry.

Mother said, "This is my husband's baby. You have what you wanted. Is it enough. Are you content now?" Mother's face became a flame. She continued, "Fourteen years I have tethered my reproach. There is time to all things, a turning tide, a setting sun, a Last Supper, a time for 'stations' and the 'cross' time. Nothing remains unchanged, all transforms, except my love for God and my husband. If you do not break your spell over Jerry now I shall kill you!"

Corinne paled and nodded, and then said sadly, "Tell Jerry to be careful. The cards show this year ominous for him."

Mother answered, "It is not what your cards of the devil wills; it is what the good Christ wills."

Scenes of turning points in my life have been presaged by lucid conscious visions of the events to come in detail. At the moment of Father's fatal accident on a construction job, though he was miles away from me, I heard him whistle to me urgently, shatteringly, three times.

I cannot distinguish the tenses. To me time and space are indivisible, and the words, "past," "present," and "future," are nothing but words. The other day my hotel room was flooded with the sweetish smell of Corinne. Had Corinne's voice not repeated her message three times I would have doubted that I had heard her. After the third time I felt composed of involutions and anxieties and had hot and cold sensations. From my window I could see the lights of Eden across the river. Whether Corinne had communicated to me by occult means, clairvoyance or extra sensory perception, or a chamber of memory suddenly opened and brought her voice and smell, I nevertheless found myself going to Eden.

On the bus going through the tunnel I picked up a copy of the Eden Dispatch. there was an article about my bastard half-brother, Jerry Williamson. The heading read, "Jersey Cop and crook-killer, to have role of messiah in tomorrow's opening of the Passion Play."

I arrived in Eden at midnight. In the moonlight Corinne's white house, trees and gardens looked exactly the same as of many years before. I went into the house and called up to her. She answered, "You know where I am, godson Petey-boy." I went upstairs. Though the lights were exceedingly dim and objects heavily shadowed, everything was the same as the last time I had been there. Corinne was in her usual place with the cards of fate on the table before her.

"I knew you would come to me," she said.

I was taken by her youthfulness. she had to be eighty. In the obscure light I made out her soft round ripened fragile beauty. When she kissed my mouth in greeting the honey and lily of the valley smell of her flesh maddened me sexually.

I sat opposite her. The parrot on the top of the back of her hold his sexual superiority against him.

"Then you were jealous of your wife's dead husband, Harry. You're outraged that Harry robbed you of her virginity. You could never go to bed with your wife without seeing Harry in bed with you two. You wrote your novel LUST WILLS ETERNITY to get back at your wife and Harry. That is why in that book your self-moraled hero, Paul, dug up Harry's grave and desecrated his corpse, and caused the fictional wife, Isa, to go mental.

"After your wife recovered from *her* breakdown and told you she had had men before and after Harry and you, you went to pieces and could not write. You searched and did not like what you found.

"When your two sons grew up taller, stronger and better-looking than you and easily acted like your father towards the many girls, as much as you love them you were burningly jealous of them.

"In your middle age now you have gone all the way with masculine ego of jealousy. You believe you are the only man in the world who should have intercourse with women. You are frustratingly jealous of the Bible's Adam and the Bible's God Who created him. Your jealousy is driving you insane and impotent.

"I am not saying these things. The cards are saying them."

She studied the cards.

"I cannot quite decode certain symbols in full. There's something about you and your stepdaughter—also, when you're in serious trouble you return to your religion and present two faces in the confessional."

"I don't say I believe or disbelieve the cards," I said, "There's more than one side to a story and perhaps the cards mirror my life in an imperfect glass and darkly—I swear I never did anything really wrong—I have been more sinned against than—"

"The cards are not corruptible like humans. They only tell the truth. The cards say you came here out of sexual curiosity and not to know your future. You dread knowing. You love having a sense of guilt. And at the same time you want to take your father's place with me. Well, come to bed. Age adds to lust and bed resolves some things."

I followed her gropingly in the shadows. What my father did I tried to echo. I was immersed in drugging honey and lily of the valley.

Destiny and sex enveloped me like passionate death. There was the feeling of my life being drained by a vampire, and I kept hearing paesano voices shouting, "The Cabala! A la Franchese! A la Franchese! Always a la Franchese!"

Before dawn I barely had the strength to arise. As I departed she drawled, "Tonight the cards will give you the Answer—if you have the guts to come."

Back in my hotel room the enticing smell of Corinne was gone. My sleep was a nightmare reaching for consciousness.

In the evening I was in Eden and went to the opening of the Passion Play to see my half-brother, Jerry, enact the part of the Messiah. I wonderingly debated if I should go that night and learn my fate from Corrine's cards. Was it better to know, or not know, where one's life ends?

After the play I went backstage and introduced myself to Jerry Williamson. He looked like my father so much that it seemed he was my father talking to me.

There was a phone call for him. After he hung up he said, "That was the coroner. An hour ago a neighbor found mother dead. The coroner said she died yesterday at about midnight."

I knew there was a mistake about the time of her death and did not tell him about my visit to his mother. I went with him to her house. I could not equate and comprehend what I saw. The garden had been long gone, and the house terribly rundown. Inside, the place was worn, discolored and smelt sourly. Corrine's cards were still spread on the table. Unnoticed, I pocketed the frayed red and black cards.

I accompanied Jerry to the morgue. The body there before us was that of a whitehaired, shriveled old woman; dried, wrinkled and faded like a once–lovely flower. I told myself I could not trust my impressions. But, then again, appearances in the nocturnal shades and those of daylight are worlds apart.

Last night my dreams were a spectrum of disturbances. When I awoke this morning I phoned Jerry at his police station and was further puzzled. He was surprised to hear from me.

"I sure would like to see you," he said, "Shirt-tail relatives it's about time we met. I've a fair idea what you look like—I've seen your picture on the back of one of your books—you seem to be holding up pretty good for an old fellow." And he invited me to the opening of the Passion Play this evening. I pretended to overlook the fact that we had been together yesterday and said, "I want to repeat how sorry I am about the passing of godmother Corinne."

He asked in a shocked and amazed voice, "Jesus Christ, man, how the hell did you know about mother? —I just received the news of her death from the coroner a minute ago!"

I was silent. What was I to do with that kind of a guy? As I slowly hung up he said, "Hello?—Hello? Have we been cut off?"

There's nothing wrong with my mind because at this moment I'm holding in my hands Corinne's red and black cards.

Locked in these cards is the secret of the Answer for me. Maybe godmother Corinne "The Cabala" will reach me and tell how to read these cards.

In the meantime, I still have to go on in the dark until—

The House

The vegetables were on stands outside the market. Anne let other customers push ahead of her. She happened to look up; at the top of the tenement a boy threw a cat off the roof. Anne closed her eyes . . . on the way down the cat was crying . . . she felt for the cat. . . she had been hurt as far back as she could remember . . . diseases, wounds and curses . . . her father was picked up on the street by J. Edgar Hoover's anti-foreigner Red Scare agents and manacled and jailed after World War I and she was terrified when she went to see him behind bars.

She was brought from Italy to Hoboken as a kid and wasn't a citizen and the sight of cop paralyzed her . . . at seventeen she worked in the lace mill—the son of the Swiss boss was in love and wanted to marry her—never even touched her—her father followed her in the rain and as she tried to telephone the nice Swiss her father beat her head with his umbrella and called her a goddamned no-good hoor.

Her bricklaying father was killed on the job and she went to the police station around the corner from the job—the desk sergeant shouted, "The wop is under cardboard in the wheelbarrow out back! She recognized only the Bloomingdale's Christmas tie she had given him. Since then her nerves jumped at everything and made her heart pound and she was in dread of accidents from cars, planes, trolleys, subways, burning, drowning, bullets and bombs, bills, doorknocks, cancer, people, her teeth falling out and going bald and jagged objects piercing her eyeballs and hard solid things threatening to cut and crush and bash and break her and hurl her into the darkness.

Joe, the immigrant tailor she had married was timid—so were her three kids.

Now she expected the cat to squash on the sidewalk—but it

landed in the stack of rhubarb and it was a young male the color of the rhubarb stalks.

The cat began his graceful four-footed walk. She called him, "Rhubarb," and asked where he was going. Rhubarb turned and mewed for her to follow. He led her up the ramp of the Palisades to nearby Elysian Avenue on the Heights. One side was the park and playground, on the other, overlooking Hoboken, the Hudson River and New York City, was the row of three-story, vacant, dilapidated attached frame houses. Those were the houses that had been condemned for the proposed highway coming up from an additional tube to the Holland Tunnel. They were of the mid-nineteenth century, sixteen feet wide, the ground floor cellar-living quarters of brick, and a long wooden stairway to the high porch and first floor.

Rhubarb went familiarly through a hole in the wall and appeared at the window, standing upright on the sill and stretching his paws in welcome above his head against the pane.

Just then a real estate man came and nailed up a sign saying the houses were for sale at bargains—first come, first served. Anne let the man coax her to look through the house because she wanted to be with Rhubarb. In the backyard was a granite marker monument with a bronze plaque telling it was the center-line of the proposed highway. Rhubarb sprang and perched on the monument. The real estate man said jokingly that the cat was a good omen and wanted her to take the house. Anne thought the man was serious, and believed him. The price was a steal. She had the strongest feeling Rhubarb was urging her to live in the house with him. She asked Rhubarb if she should dare to try to buy the house. She was positive Rhubarb nodded . . . and her goose pimples determined her.

Anne's son, Tony, had returned from Vietnam. Between Tony's nest-egg, borrowing on the life insurance policies, a loan from Godfather Vincent, and Tony's GI mortgage, Anne became the owner of 390 Elysian Avenue. It was cagey to put the house in Tony's name and use his GI benefits—the government would never know it was really her house—you bet!—screw the government—God helps those who help themselves—and who better than Tony, a high school graduate, to look after the mysteries of mortgage payments, home-owner's liability and taxes? In this world you've got to use your head!

Anne rented the small apartment on the third floor to her daughter, Mary, and became "the landlady." As Anne said, she was reaching her "plateau." Her husband, Joe, was a union tailor; her son, Tony—God bless him!—a drugstore clerk who gave her half his paycheck; her retarded son, Mike, was an errand-boy and also shined shoes in Tony's drugstore—who would have believed that she who had been anemic and fearful was becoming rosily buxom and confident? You see how the wheel turns? Every dog has his day—knock wood!

Anne set the pace in the competition on the block to renovate. At first, changes were done on the exteriors front and rear—for all to see. Rotting shingles were replaced by pink and blue asbestos and chrome edgings. Anne put a pole and the American flag out front—and of course, soon, the neighbors did the same. Anne had the ace in the hole—redhead Godfather Vincent the bricklayer! Vincent had a wife and children in Italy whom he had not seen in thirty years (he supported them). He had a furnished room and lived as a sporting bachelor. For Anne and Joe, he built a trellised summer house in the backyard and planted grape vines for a shady retreat. He put a fake fireplace in parlor and put fancy bricks wherever possible.

The Sicilian widow, Ophelia, next door, operated a hot dog stand on the corner and made money hand-over-fist. Grateful to Heaven for her business she put a life-size white cement Lady of Fatima and grotto in the front of the house and outfitted it with twirling spotlights at night.

Anne went Ophelia one better. Godfather Vincent removed the rickety gingerbread porch and put up a stunning precast simulated-marble stairway and brass balustrade that led to a balcony porch held up by four limestone voluptuous caryatids that he rescued from a demolished mansion.

As Anne said, who the hell were the people on the block anyway? One worked in the Tootsie Roll plant, another in the mustard factory, a fourth was a garbage man who worked in the sewers like Art Carney's Ed Norton . . . go ahead—let them bust their balls copying all they wanted to. Her house was the incomparable gem of Elysian Avenue. Why lower herself to get chummy? Let them show off with their motorcycles and hot rods. Who needed those headaches? It was the house alone that counted!

The family's earning went into paint, wallpaper, tile converting the coal stove to kerosene, tiny lawns—and Joe on hands and knees snipping the grass around the two pink concrete flamingos with tailor's shears. And they stopped going to Holy Mass so that they could devote Sundays to the house.

Anne never left the house except for a momentous occasion—like to take Rhubarb to the vet. But what did she need "out there"? The world was the mountain that came to her through the radio, the *Enquirer*, the *New York Daily News*, the telephone and television. She didn't care for color TV—she said the actors looked like they were made up for their coffins. To behold her property becoming more valuable with the nylon clothesline, aluminum storm doors, screens and windows, kitchen cabinets from Sears-Roebuck, Frigidaire, vinyl floor, washing machine, steam iron, toilet off the kitchen, (with deodorants), was a thing of joy forever.

On Fridays, smiling freckled redhead Godfather Vincent, wearing his jaunty wide-brimmed Stetson and fashion-plate clothes, brought fruits of the sea—fish, lobsters, crabs, conch, periwinkles—or varying surprises like zucchini, chicory, spinach, broccoli-rabe, escarole. Sundays he brought shopping bags filled with fingerlicking gifts and wines. then in the evening on Sunday night Godfather Vincent would go to the Irish saloon, hob-nob and shoot pool or play shuffleboard with what Anne called the corned-beef-and-cabbage Archie Bunkers. Walking home, drunk from a lot of beer on top of a lot of wine, Joe and Vincent would argue and philosophize—Godfather Vincent was cheerful around the clock; he said, "take it as it comes." Joe would roar, "the best thing to do is work hard, eat hard, drink hard, crap hard, mind your business and worry about nothing!"

Celebrating the Fourth of July away from the house was more pain than pleasure. They went on an outing to the Long Island North Shore . . . hunting for mushrooms and dandelion Anne got awful poison ivy and was chewed by chiggers. The men sluiced their feet on oyster shells digging clams. The other holiday journey was to the picnic park by the Statue of Liberty. They went loaded with food and drink by subway to the Battery and by the ferry to Liberty Island.

They found a sanctuary away from the blacks, Puerto Ricans and out-of-state sightseers. With Lady Liberty untiringly holding her torch and looking on them they ate a gargantuan lunch dotted with ants—and got badly sunburned.

Ellis Island could be seen close by. Anne remembered arriving there in steerage with her young mother. They had had tags: "Italians. Husband Geremio will get them." Now corroding deserted Ellis Island was a visible ghost.

At 390 Elysian Avenue, Rhubarb was number one. All of Anne's affection went to the cat. She held personal dialogue with it: "Where oh where were you last night?"

Joe, would fume, "That surly bastard's stink makes me vomit—does his nibs bring money into the house? *Porca Miseria!* have you lost your bovine brain that you talk to a parasite animal like that—what is Christ's world coming to?"

Anne would flaunt, "I'll talk if I please to my love . . . and yes, if it comes to choosing between you and Rhubarb—you know what I mean? If Rhubarb hadn't led me there at precisely the right moment there would be no house, Mister J." That would bring Joe's "O.K . . . . you repeat yourself!"

There came a year when nothing more could be done for the house. 390 Elysian Avenue's mortgage was free and clear—thank you! How many home owners could say the same? No living beyond her means for Anne. She and Joe received their Social Security checks on the third of the month. They had their Medicare cards . . . and Joe got his tidy pension—not much, but better than nothing—from the Amalgamated Clothing Workers' Union. Anne would read aloud, "United States Treasury . . . Pay to the order of Anne so and so," and puff with pride. Life was on the good track.

Reading gossip columns, listening to soap operas, learning from talk shows and female shrinks on TV made Anne smug and superior.

She developed an uncanny knack of analyzing and criticizing that fascinated her family. "Hey, the Prez is going to speak from the Oval Room—what a crock!—get the enema can and put on your hip boots." "Here comes that beauty, the Secretary of State, Dr. Bullshit!" "Look at the satchels under Barbara Walters' eyes—she's wearing contacts—her eyes are bulging—she's not pretty this morning!" She was convinced all people were liars, schemers and rip-off artists. She picked her neighbors apart to the amusement of her family.

Anne's ears were her bugging apparatus. She'd pretend to be asleep on the sofa in the parlor and soak in the secret dirt. She heard Ranieri, her son's burly raucous pal, brag to Tony about Angelina, the divorcee daughter of Ophelia, the hot dog vendor next door. And Anne caught every word of Ranieri's description—"Wow"! that's a hot one!"—Ophelia with the spotlighted Madonna in the front yard that attracts weeping derelicts—oh that mealy-mouth religious hypocrite. Her husband died in the mental ward. And that prize daughter divorced from a jailbird has two married daughters and is seducing young Ranieri! Boy oh boy if Ophelia gets huffy she, Anne, will let her have the info word-for-word about Angelina with both barrels—over the phone!

Tony took to going out nights and returning very late. Anne thought there was nothing to worry about. After all, he was forty and his hair streaking grey. In the mornings she noticed his blanched condition . . . and the expression of thinking—figuring. She simply had to say, "Tony your lips are big and cracked and burned like you've eaten five pounds of salty *baccala*—and son—you're gray and green as if a vampire worked on you." And this was her Tony who had taken his vitamins, chest expander and punching bag to the front lines in Vietnam!

It was a hot brilliant Sunday morning. Joe came down into the kitchen, gave Rhubarb his broiled lamb chop and let him out.

Then he went out to the sunny back yard and watered the fig tree.

Anne was at the second floor window calling out orders to Joe—who kept nodding and mumbling obscenities under his breath. Mary was at the third floor window hanging the wash of the family's underwear. Anne gazed from her widow with the style and contentment of a rich opossum . . . the sights and sounds were beyond anything on television, beyond imagination. Below the Palisades lay squat Hoboken with its weathered shabbiness endearing and peculiarly glorious, evoking the nostalgia that is felt for crumbling mortar joints, peeling paint, tarnished tin, tired walls, leaning chimneys, drift-glass, the faded, the worn, the lived-in mute testimonials of another American time.

She had seen Hoboken wear the blizzard's icicles and snow, be hosed and scoured by spring showers, bake and bask in summer's torrid smiles. and she studied on tenements' ornate bricky faces the tristful dancing light-and-dark shadows. She never ceased to be startled breathless by the broad silvery Hudson that bore giant toy ships—and the continuous placenta of vehicles gushing from the steel uterus of the Holland Tunnel. There was the phantasmagoric Manhattan skyline that in fancy she reached out and caressed from the George Washington Bridge to the Statute of Liberty—which her father had archly dubbed, "The much screwed Madonna of U.S.A." Within Anne was the mute poet. To her, life was feeling.

The enthralling view from the house was never twice quite the same, and night came down on the river changing the ziggurats of Babylon into bejewelled temples and patterns of light. The hidden, fine, deeper Anne sensed that people wished for greener pastures, a someday happy Hollywood ending place, a chicken farm, avocado groves or mink ranch, a cottage or trailer on a lake, Leisure Village, castles in Spain, pipe dreams . . . but 390 Elysian Avenue was the nook of privacy and Macy's window on the world, her Shangri-La.

It was like any Sunday . . . Natty Godfather Vincent was the male *duenna*, bringing *provolone* and *Locatelli* cheese, *prosciutto*, salami, olives and wine. It was as though he were visiting Buckingham Palace. He treated Anne as if she were Empress, Joe her consort, and Rhubarb, the cat, the princeling of the realm.

As always Joe and Vincent helped Anne mix, knead and cut the *fettuccine*, arrange the antipasto, stuff the artichokes and eggplants and with appropriate Italian toasts—to thee for a hundred—nay—a thousand years!—launching the day's wine drinking effectively under way.

Vincent was the pin-cushion Joe could fondly prick with impunity. Heady from Zinfandel he would chide Vincent for having abandoned his family in Italy for the many years, and admonish him for his show-off extravagance to the women of Hoboken, Union City and Jersey City. The the weekly flagellation was a sop to Vincent's conscience. He would grinningly sigh and attribute his remissiveness to Destiny. Anne would put her two cents in.

"People who live in glass houses shouldn't throw stones—Mister J., would you be willing to put a gun in my hand and tell me to shoot you through the heart if I found out the truth about your sleeping with Puerto Ricans in Union City, too?"

Mike, thirty years old, was a cretin, but no problem. He was addicted to kissing everybody in a gentle, wispy, patronizing way. He would say in his adenoidal penny-whistled voice, "Would you believe—That's for sure—You can say that again . . . !" He could crack his knuckles back and forth in perfect time to Kate Smith's singing *The Star Spangled Banner*. He loved to ride buses; he'd tell you over and over that the man said, "Leave the driving to us" . . . and mimic all the sounds of bus riding so that you'd swear the Greyhound was coming through the house; and Sundays with a hand full of schedules, he was off on bus excursion specials to God knows where.

That Sunday morning Tony spent an hour before the mirror over the sink grooming and preening. When he left he casually said he was bringing a friend to dinner.

It was two o'clock in the afternoon . . . dinner began then and went on for three hours. Mary and her family came down to the big oblong kitchen table, and they all waited for Tony.

When Tony arrived, bringing Angelina the ageing divorcee daughter of Ophelia, mouths fell open. Anne knew Angelina was playing around with Tony's pal Ranieri, and now had the brass to entice Tony and come into her house acting as virgin as Doris Day. Just dig her ton of make-up and perfume and that chain around her neck with the gaudy cross with a Christ on it big enough to hang a midget! Anne would make *scungilli* sauce out of this nervy bum Angelina!

Anne pretended to be gracious and unconcerned, the while pointedly pumping Angelina with embarrassing questions to spoil her appetite and put her to flight.

"Angelina's husband was already out of jail—oh on parole?—and remarried? How interesting!—Angelina worked in a drugstore too—as a cosmetician—oh yeah?—Hey—cosmeticians make good money—by now Angelina must have 'piles'! And her daughters were married and she was a grandmother—how . . . nice . . . why Angelina must have been married when she was a baby—oh was she really fifty? Did she have her change of life?" If Angie thought she was going to hook her Tony, the scummy Sicilian woman was barking up the wrong tree!

They put the heat on Tony. Bringing Angie into the house made them suspect he had a fine taste for dung. What the hell did he see in that black slimy Sicilian ten years his senior, dressed like a gun-moll from the mafia with her teased, dyed, smelly hair, chandelier earrings, mangy white angora stole, beads and junk jewelry, harem skirt with the slit up the leg, spike-heeled platform clogs, slave bracelet on her boney ankle and around her neck a Woolworth's economy-size crucifix—now come on!—who did that broad think she was kidding!

Tony took it without a word. See, he knew in his guts his mother was right. No one could pull the wool over Anne's eyes. If Tony got married it should be to a young virgin with dough. Why doesn't he marry his Jewish boss' daughter and end up owning the drugstore?

One morning towards dawn a month later, Anne awoke and heard Tony's Lawrence Welk music. She sneaked down to the parlor and spied on Tony. He and Angelina were making love on the sofa. Anne was flabbergasted by what she witnessed—and immobilized for minutes like an innocent dove hypnotized before writhing snakes . . . .

Godfather Vincent, always well, suddenly became seriously ill. It was cancer. The operation was useless. Within weeks he wasted away in St. Mary's Hospital in Hoboken, and died smiling . . . that he had been screwed by Destiny. A strangeness set in 390 Elysian Avenue. Fridays and Sundays came and went and no Vincent bringing fish and greens, cheese, cold cuts, olives, bread and Gallo wine. Now there was an irritability in the house. Anne and Joe were not sufficient to themselves and each other and could not fathom it. The rituals of Vincent's company and the ever-driving impetus to doll up the house were gone. Anne's exciting no-holds-barred campaign against Angelina and her mother Ophelia—via the telephone—had simmered to a halt. The danger of Angelina winning Tony seemed done with. Mary had her hands full upstairs; conversation with retarded Mike was impossible. Rhubarb was his own person and only came home to recoup his energy for fights. Tony didn't talk but went about humming grimly. Only Godfather Vincent had made Anne feel she was a lady. He had been charmingly complimentary and appreciated every trivial thing she had done for him. Did Joe ever seat her to the table before he sat to gorge? Or hold her coat, open the door for her, direct poetic phrases to her? She had taken Redhead Vincent for granted. He had been the respectful cavalier in her house, and though he never over-stepped the line, perhaps he was secretly in love with her—of course—that's why he never sent for his wife—you see! And didn't she just automatically dress and pretty herself only when he visited! Vincent was manly and rugged like the Marlboro ad—and he smoked Marlboros. He seemed forever young, whereas Joe had become shrunken, yellowed and acrid like an old Chinaman. It was Joe with his unfair Italian ideas who kept her a human snail in a shell! She wasn't going to let him get away with it—better late than never. It was time to train her guns on Joe!

Her war with Joe seemed necessary to establish her ultimate superiority in The House. It began jestingly as a game of can-you-top-this insults. One snide word led to another. She ridiculed his bunions and Charlie Chaplin walk, his long fingernails, broken English . . . confounding him and relishing his frothing retorts.

The daily skirmishes of sarcasms, revilings and imprecations became exercises that rounded out the surfeit of time. If she called him Mister Halitosis or Señor Goat's-Armpits he retaliated with obscenities. They vented every wounding thought that came to mind, he finally accusing her of infidelity behind his back with Godfather Vincent, and she chortling and goading him to guess the worst—speaking of a Mexican divorce, dieting, a face-lift, gambling and "boy-friends" in faraway places.

Then the bomb was dropped—Mary told Anne that she had it from the horse's mouth that deceitful Tony had been seeing Angie night and day and was positively planning to marry her. The news electrified and reunited Anne and Joe. They had to save Tony. The common mortal enemy was Angelina. Anne felt invincible. She would devil Angelina to her knees and destroy her guts and feathers! She could do it right from the kitchen by telephone. At all hours she phoned Angelina's mother, family, friends, ex-husband and boss scathingly painting pictures of sodomy, piles and so forth.

Tony silently packed a bag and moved in with his promised bride. Anne was nervous—but sure he'd think it over and return. Weeks and many months passed. Tony wouldn't let Mike shine shoes any more in the drugstore. He refused to communicate with Anne and Joe nor care to be further regarded as their son. When his father went to the drugstore where he worked and doggedly and tearfully insisted upon speaking to him and giving him love he summoned a cop. Angelina had put the curse on the house—she had the *fattura* done to Tony.

The house was Anne's touchstone of being, its floors, roof and walls, her magic well. The House was her reality, her love, the past, present and future . . . The House was her womb, her eternity and paradise beyond which all other things were non-existent and inconceivable. Now, a piece of paper—the deed with Tony's signature—would collapse and disintegrate her cosmos.

Then Anne's main weapon, the telephone, worked against her. it would clang eerily in the bowels of the night. When she lifted the receiver she would hear Angelina's cackling triumphant laughter. She had the telephone disconnected. Mary got a shyster lawyer for Anne who took her savings as a binder and allegedly prepared suit to claim The House.

Joe broke every damn one of Tony's Lawrence Welk records and threw them into the garbage can. Joe wandered the area buttonholing strangers and telling them his son had the evil-eye stuck on him by Angelina . . . and that his son had stolen The House and was putting them out to die in the gutter . . . and he ran yelling through the streets that he was going to shoot Tony and Angelina and burn The House to ashes.

The Court ruled in Tony's favor. Tony's lawyer sent Anne and Joe the dispossession papers.

Anne was swirled back to her childhood and years of hurt and hopeless fear. Was there a God? She had not given her love to God, Joe, the children or society, but to The House, and Rhubarb, because the cat brought her to The House. But perhaps The House had a spirit of its own and had wanted to die and not be made over to live on . . .

Anne and Joe could not eat. They neglected themselves waiting for their son to relent through pity and transfer The House to Anne's name. During the severe winter they got the Asiatic Flu. They did not care to resist Death. For it was the comfort that freed them from Final Notice.

At the funerals Angelina and Tony wept and said they would not have put Anne and Joe out of The House—it was just that they "wanted to learn them a lesson."

Inflation and Recession came. Men were taken off welfare and put to work tearing down Elysian Avenue, and the long-intended highway was realized. The proceeds of The House were held in escrow . . . and consumed by lawyers. The only thing left of The House is the refurbished monument in the backyard which designates the exact centerline of the great new concrete expressway.

When the weather is sunny you'll see a beat-up old Tom cat crouched in front of the monument like a proprietary red sphinx.

The Broken Scaffold

Most of the men on the job hated me because, only a kid, I was the fastest bricklayer.

That day in the Shanty I had finished lunch and began to read. Tough Shorty Groves who stopped at nothing for a shocking laugh, growled, "You and your goddamn books. Books guys become dick lickers or priests. What shit are you readin' now?"

"Oh," I said, "just something called, Renan's Life of Christ." "Does it say he ever licked a dick?" I decided not to read on the job.

We were on the hanging scaffold at the thirtieth floor. Above, the steel frame was being riveted. A dozen piers separated window openings along the wall; a bricklayer to a pier. Mason tenders stacked brick, and shoveled mortar into tubs. The derrick was raising girders from the street. Sometimes a rigger rode a girder, seesawing them for fun. I paid no attention as the great I-beams rose and swung past the scaffold.

I ran out my pier ahead of the rest. We would have to go inside and back up the outside brick with terra cotta shoe-block for the binding header course. I took my tools, stepped off the hanging scaffold and went inside onto the floor. Mr. Nicks, the foreman, was by the elevator shaft, watching. He smiled, I smiled back. I was in good with Mr. Nicks. He had said he would make me one of his deputy-foremen someday. Shorty Groves banged his trowel on a brick and said aloud, "Pilin' up points, huh kid?"

"Honest," I said, "I'm not trying to put anybody in a hole—I jumped in to take a leak."

Mr. Nicks turned and walked away.

As I was doing it against a column Shorty hollered, "Kid, if yuh shake it more'n three times yuh're jerkin' off!" The men on the hanging scaffold broke out into laughter. Then it happened. As a load of girders reached the fortieth floor the cable snapped. It happened quick as thought. The girders smashed down on the hanging scaffold. I was buttoning my fly. I saw Shorty Groves shoot into space. There were no cries. There was no time. There was only the profound concussion of men and material meeting the concrete street.

Scaffold cables, drums, and angle brackets holding shattered planks, dangled.

I didn't follow the cursing, praying, trades who ran down all those flights of stairs to see it. I took off my overalls, dropped them on my tool bag, went to the ground floor of the skyscraper, and out another way.

On the subway to Brooklyn I trembled. My father had been crushed to death on a job. I missed his fate by seconds. If I hadn't gotten off the hanging scaffold to piss—another policeman would be coming to mama's kitchen door, knock, and, respectfully remove his cap. Mama could not speak English. She would not know about falling girders.

Until that derrick cable parted I was absolutely secure in the belief that Christ put me on earth for a mission.—Mama, and Mrs. Miller, the spiritualist, told me so. Sundays Mama and I went to mass, and to Mrs. Miller. Mrs. Miller needed a dollar, a white rose, and the caressing of mama's wedding ring to contact the other world. I knew each of the men who went down with the girders. They joined father.

Why didn't God or Father communicate to me directly?

A conviction that life and death depended upon blind chance, and that I was fragile, mortal as father and the men who had just been killed, hallowed me, terrorized me.

The Company has a job in Helmetta, New Jersey; a one story industrial building. Bill Browning was the foreman. Brownie, the master of masters (Mr. Nicks had said, "Every brick Brownie lays is plumb, level and neat as a diamond, but, he's as slow as the Second Coming!") had taught me a lot about brickwork.

I told mama the Company had no more jobs in the city, and that I would have to go to work in New Jersey and come home weekends.

I had an extra set of tools. Mama packed a bag with underwear, socks, a sweater and overalls; and added a St. Christopher medal to my Scapular.

I told Brownie why I quit Big Steel. In his toothless chuckling voice he said, "Where and when you're gonner get it is in 'the book.' You can't run away from 'the book,' kid. You took a leak because it wasn't your time to be stiffed."

The job was on country land. It was different laying bricks on a fresh air job that flattened out and not piercing upwards; laying bricks on broad weight-bearing walls, and surrounded by fields, and hearing the sound of birds, and a distant cow lowing and a cock crowing.

After work Brownie introduced me to a bricklayers, 'Jingo' Johnson, a wiry Texas Irish-Indian. "Jingo will take you to the boarding house."

It was a Colonial farmhouse by the railroad tracks. On the wall to the left of the entrance was a plaque that said George Washington had slept there. Across the street was the George Helm Copenhagen Snuff factory. The woman who ran the boardinghouse was named Ursula. She had an enormous bosom, the widest and fattest ass, slender shapely legs, very light blonde curls to her shoulders, a doll face, and a beautiful soprano voice.

A heavy scent of Lily of the valley perfume came from her. "Honey," she said, "I love your musical Italian name. You're such a nice young man—I'm giving you my own special—George Washington's room, and bed." Her southern drawl was full of honey.

There were construction floaters, a freckled 'Reverend' Ross, and a one hundred year old man in a wheelchair.

At the table the minister said grace. It was the first time I was having dinner away from home. Everyone grabbed. It wasn't the food mama made.

Fed, the boarders hurried out of the dining room as if being chased. The hundred year old had to have a listener. "Sonny, been here all my life. Ain't been more'n ten miles from Helmetta. Ain't been married. Bought the milk but never the cow. Frigged 'till eighty.

"Raised mushrooms, lived underground like a miner babyin' mushrooms with a candle in the dark. Seen the immigrant Polacks come to work in the snuff factory. Polack girls chew snuff. Did you know they fill condum with snuff and steal it out inside their twats?

"Did you know snuff juice and raw mushrooms makes you horny . . . Makes peckers poke and twats twitch. Sonny, you've come to the Garden of Eden. More good friggin' goin' on here than any place.

Polack girls frig free and natural like swans on a pond. Did you know the Helmetta is the snuff, mushroom, and friggin center of the world? Did you ever see an ass like Ursula's? Some ass!"

Main Street was three blocks long. The town smelled of snuff. I walked the three blocks back and forth. In a Salvation Army junk shop, I paid five cents for a rare biography of Edgar Allan Poe.

The snuff factory had a social club. I watched young Polish American play pool, bowl and dance. Home-bread and apple jack was sold. The girls did chew snuff. Maybe I could have picked up one of the sturdy girls, but I didn't try. I didn't have much of a boyhood, and I had forgotten how to play.

The job was my temple. Nothing can sully construction or make it stale. All its members come from the earth; stone, steel, lime, clay, lumber, glass, tar, pigment and sand. Sweet, open air, the sansons and crafts of building purify the vulgarity and profane gestures of man. I looked forward to each day on the scaffold. At night the walls of bricks I had put up were clear as photographs. In my mind's eye no picture could compare to precision brickwork; its uniform bond and crisp vertical and horizontal lines.

Jingo Johnson was top trowel. He worked like a house on fire and set the pace.

As a foreman gaffs the gang, the mason who lays the few extra bricks and beats the men by him, grins smugly, figuring he'll be kept on when others are canned. We had a long stretch of wall. I held back and let Jingo get ahead of me, while taking his measure. He was a slasher, sluggish bricks into the wall with chesty energy, but, making false moves. I know I could take Jingo.

Brownie sent Jingo and me on opposite corner piers. We were using common red brick. They had to be laid up in Flemish bond with thin joints. The secret of masonry is in knowing how much moisture the porous brick will absorb from the mortar. The amount and furrowing of the mortar cast upon the wall determines the ease with which the brick is laid. The swift gauging of the mortar spread allows the brick to bed themselves.

I glanced at Jingo's activity. His trowel was too big for tight jointed work, and he was spreading for too many bricks. By the time he covered the mortar with brick the drying mortar resisted the bricks.

I had a laborer wet the brick, and add water to the mortar and temper it. You should not have to fight the mortar; mortar should be silky, plastic and obey the trowel. The pointed Rose trowel was right for my wrist; it had a balanced, true ringing blade, and the wooded handle fitted my grasp, seeming an extension of my hand. My method was a rhythmic continuous dipping for mortar with trowel in one hand and picking up the brick with the other. I had trained my sight to put a brick squarely in place for plumb and level instantly. I topped out my work before Jingo finished his.

My room looked out on the backyard. It was early evening, warm, and sharp daylight. Ursula was hanging sheets. Bent over, taking one from the basket, a breeze lifted her dress. She had nothing beneath. Between the great round cheeks was the large and small openings adorned with bushy black fur. I had never seen that part of a woman. The sudden exposure magnetized me, and stayed framed in my mind.

That night I had a wet dream. Laying bricks, the view was with me and I could not discourage erection.

In my sleep Ursula's naked ass loomed and backed up towards me.

I was preparing to go home for the weekend. Ursula came into my room. From the immense woman came an overpowering sexual fragrance. She took the sheet off the bed. Our eyes met over the tell-tale spots. I blushed. She said singingly, "My Honey, what a waste. I've got a better place for all that good love cream. It'll be a pleasure, and easier on my washing . . ." Frozen, I nodded.

Arriving home, it seemed I had come to another boarding house. I had a new and wild urge for far unknown places, and not to be answerable to anyone, anything. I saw the church as a theatrical building, the mass as primitive mumbo-jumbo, and Christ and the Saints as painted plaster statues. Mrs. Miller was a ridiculous con woman, and her messages from the 'next' world, vaudeville. I was forced to act in a play I didn't want any part of. But I had to keep thoughts to myself; I could not disillusion and hurt mama.

The girders carrying death was reality. Ursula's white full moon of an ass and thick black bush was real. And I kept hearing Ursula's beautiful gay voice laughing at my wet dreams.

When surpassed, a top trowel loses heart. My outspeeding Jingo demoralized him. On the job he drank apple-jack. His work was slow and sloppy. Brownie warned him to get sober or be fired. He drank in the boarding house, muttered threats.

I was on the bed reading the life of Poe. Ursula came in. She kissed me, sticking her tongue in my mouth, her huge soft breasts swarming over me.

"Honey," she whispered, "Hollis works the railroad nights. Come anytime." She gave the bulge in my pants a squeeze. "Honey, we'll get rid of that . . . it'll be more fun than your hand and the sheet."

My throat parched. I managed to say, "Yes. Thank you very much."

I could not get to sleep. Trains pounded by, roaring as a frantic belling, whistling, phantom giant through the house.

I was a network of erotic expectations, a pyramid of erection. A few doors away drunken Jingo let out Indian war whoops for my benefit. There was music from the snuff factory social club punctuated by the crashing of bowling pins.

Should I sneak into Ursula's room? What would I say?—Or just get in bed with her and do it like a grim silent animal? Then should I stay and see how many times I could do it? I had never seen her husband, Hollis—What kind a guy was he? What would he do if he found us in bed? If I got into trouble how would I explain it to mama?

Finally, exhausted, I began to fall asleep, protesting the inevitable wet dreams.

The following night I got as far as her door. I stayed there congealed. I didn't have the guts. I returned to my room.

Laying bricks and thinking of her I came in my pants. That night I couldn't stand the torment, and was headily resolved. Life was curtained and brief—What the hell was I waiting for?

I'd do it and get it over with. It was late and dark. I tiptoed through the hall to her door. As I turned the doorknob I heard her bed jouncing, springs creaking, and a man's grunting exertions. A cold sweat came over me. Surely the man was her husband; and I almost walked in on them with a hard on.

I planned that when she came to my room with the soap and towels and to change the sheets I would quickly do it with her.

Jingo kicked open the door. He had a bottle of apple-jack. His wife tried to pull him out. "Goddamit, Jingo," she said, "Let the boy alone. You crazy Indian, the boy's done nothin' to you."

He brandished the bottle in my face. "You make Jingo Johnson look like an apprentice? I'm the hottest trowel from LA to Philly! An' you little wop bastard got the balls to give me the shaft?—make a fuckin' fool outta Jingo Johnson? I'll show you I'm more of a hundred percent man than you'll ever be—Drink"

His wife said, "Boy, drink to please him 'cause you never know what he's likely to do when crossed."

I took a mouthful. He snatched the bottle. "Wise guy kid kin you do this?" He drank down the whole quart. He went into a war dance, cartwheels and acrobatics, and with each feat shouted, "Kin you do this?"

He ripped off his clothes, and yanking and waving his big prick shouted, "Are you a true American like me? Did you fight for our country under Roosevelt and Pershing?" And as his prick enlarged, "Have you got this on *your* cock?"

Tattooed on it was the Flag, and under it "GOD BLESS AMERICA!"

Towards dawn I was awakened by an explosion followed by screams. It had come from Ursula's room. With other boarders I rushed there.

Ursula's husband had trapped her and the minister, Ross, and let them have it with a doubled barreled shotgun. Ross lay wounded by the window where he tried to escape. Ursula was moaning on the bed, her great big fat ass half blown off, shredded, spurting blood in all directions. The great wonderful ass and thick black bush that had been printed in my mind, was then ugly, grotesque, like a bloody great piece of liver.

Smiling, tall, foreman Mr. Nicks folded his hands. "Kept your tools and overalls for you. Missed your slick trowel and masonry without tears."

Brickwork on skyscraper had reached the fortieth floor; thirty more floors, and months of steady inside winter work on partitions to go.

Many strange faces made up the bricklaying gang. No one mentioned the accident.

The new safety regulation was that when girders were being hoisted the men were to get off the hanging scaffold and stand inside doing nothing.

The job towered over the Battery area. There was no other view like it. All of Manhattan island and the rivers were at our feet. Below on the street people and cars were insects. You could almost reach out and pat the Statue of Liberty on the head. Big Steel was King of construction.

We were waiting inside for girders to sling overhead. Mr. Nicks pointed to a spic and span ocean liner being tugged out through the narrows.

"Here we are," he said, "putting brick skin around Big Steel. You might say we're in bondage to Big Steel. But people on that ship are going somewhere."

"That's true, Mr. Nicks," I said.

"Don't you daydream, and wonder, about pretty girls, divine girls, on that ship; what it would be like to make love to them; who they are, what they're doing now, and what they're going to do with whom and where?"

The steel hoisting was over. The bricklayers started to clamber back onto the hanging scaffold. "Yes, Mr. Nicks," I answered, "I daydream, and I wonder."

Hicky Nicky The Floatin' Bricky

Mister Nicks, the tall, new bricklayer-foreman, was very difficult from the run of hard hats; he was educated and was a gentleman. What set him apart also was that he was happy with building; the average hard-hat is miserable—he thinks little and curses and drinks much and prattles about that "dream someday" of hitting the lottery, the someday when his particular special ship will come in and he'll throw his tools off the George Washington Bridge with a grand gesture. But this Mister Nicks had an affair with building; he loved construction the way a guy idolizes a woman.

Mister Nicks said, "Peter, you are different from the building slaves. You are probably the only apprentice bricklayer in the United States who comes to the job site with *The Divine Comedy*, the *Golden Bough* and Lampriere's classical dictionary under his arm."

I was embarrassed and said apologetically, "Well, you see, during lunch and when we're held up by weather, other trades or material, I like to read—I must read—I can't help it. Somehow, what I read seems more real than life." He said zealously, "You've got to read about architecture; construction reveals the essential history of man; Christ himself laid many a brick, and he was critical about the jerry-built tower of Siloam that fell and killed eighteen Hebrew workmen—I expected it to collapse—" "You 'what?'" I said. He skipped my question; his strange sunken big eyes glowed. "Peter, do you know that every landmark project has a 'genius' and is a shrine?" I said in confusion, "A 'shrine?' A shrine to what?" He smiled, "To the reason for life." There was something morbid, disastrous, in his smile. Then he laughed and said jokingly, "A shrine to anything. Let us say, a shrine to Mister Construction . . ."

While I was laying bricks rapidly around the Big Steel many floors above the city street he'd magically appear out on the swinging scaffold by my side, and say odd things: "Peter, don't you feel the building as a growing stalk, and you one of the chemicals urging it upward? Listen to the music of its heartbeat; the building is a plant with concrete roots, steel fibers, and skin of burnt clay. The skyscraper is like a great child, either ugly or beautiful, ashamed or arrogant, and sometimes relaxed and noble; it's a being throbbing high and naked in the elements—don't you feel it, see it?"

He was the boss; so I nodded and said I guess so. But he wouldn't let me go and he'd go on: "It's the offspring of the earth and water and fire; and like all things it tires and dies and dissolves and returns to the Great Earth Mother." I said, "Isn't there anything that remains? In my Catholic religion, if we're good we go to Heaven. What's your religion? He said, "Occasionally a few ponderous corpses like the pyramids and the Chinese Wall remain, but the spirits of the monuments return to the site like golems and vampires seeking sacred human blood for reincarnation because all things must die in order to live."

It would always be something like that—"life-death," "death-life," and suggesting the possibility that skyscraper was the "true" being and man its synthetic by-product, and so forth, making me uncomfortable, and finally saying it was a bit over my head and very interesting but that I had to concentrate on bricklaying and not fall behind the other brickies.

Hard-hats run to repetitive muscle behaviorism and are peevish children bitchily envious of anyone in the foreman's good graces. That the HH is practically a robot is not his fault; he is a product of our compartmentalized times. The challenging intricacies of past craft forms have been discarded; the improvised artistry of the building individual is not required and has disappeared; the rigger—eagle of the tower—puts together steel members like a kid with his Erector set—it is all modular; the bricklayer lays one brick upon one or two other bricks upon one or two other bricks ad infinitum; everything comes in prearranged marked sections from the kiln, foundry, mill, plant and factory; the HH is a belt-system putter-together; building today is an automatic process obviating the mind. The construction job, like the army, the insane asylum, monastery and prison is an unnatural, womanless, all-male society that evokes both subtly and blatantly the utter baseness of the herd.

The English bricky, Norman Parker, was favored by Mister Nicks. It's nice to be considered above the rest of the gang, assigned to corners and light work, treated before the men as an honored bricklayer, spoken to respectfully in dulcet appreciative tones.

There are countless personal worlds within the vast dizzying world, but your own local little world usually, eventually, is your whole world. At that time the goal on my horizon of Job was to be the star trowel and have the lord of my bread and butter, Mister Nicks, say with patronizing voice in front of the brickies, "Peter, please take your tools and put up the main corner. I want it dead plumb; that's why I send you to put it up."

Norman Parker told me, "There is something uncanny about Nicks. I was with the International Firebrick Company; we travelled the world puttin' up smokestacks for electric plants. Now, you're gonner think I'm crazy but I am ready to swear on my mother's grave I seen Nicks in Istanbul and Peking and Rangoon and Tierra del Fuego and Magnitogorsk as bricky foreman, and he was called 'Hicky Nicky The Floatin' Bricky.' An' would you believe it, kid, in the Himalayas an old Lama priest said to me pointin' to Nicks, 'My son do you know who he is?' I said, 'No, who and what is he?' He said, 'That person whom you think is of contemporary flesh and blood like you and I is—'"

Just at that moment Mister Nicks called Parker, "Oh Norman, I have a chore for you in the basement; follow me, Norman."

In the afternoon Parker returned. His rosy face was pale, chalky. He looked as if a mortician had drained his blood vessels, and his expression was as vacant as if he had been debrained. Mister Nicks sent him to another corner. Parker scooped mortar and bricked up the corner with the movements of a zombie. Mister Nicks said to me enthusiastically, "Peter, look at Parker's brickwork; every brick vertical as a plummet and level as the sea; neat and clean as diamonds."

Mister Nicks exuded an odor that made me blanch—I don't know—it was like the dank air of a tomb and the stomach-turning smell of the crematorium.

But, I must have had fever that day and imagined that Parker had come back from the basement; Parker's unwitnessed, accidental death in the basement must have shocked me so that I rejected its reality. They say he was putting a few bricks under a huge boiler that was suspended by block and tackle, and the boiler slipped its sling and crushed him. To me it did seem a stupid avoidable accident.

Mister Nicks said, "Our next job will be the tallest edifice in history." The burning light came into his eyes. It will be ten times higher than Babel!" He took me into his shanty-office and spread the blueprints of his job. The Morris Tower was to be also the most beautiful skyscraper in the world; it was to simulate a gigantic lily; a circular stem faced with white glazed brick one-hundred-and-fifty stories high with a great gold-faced with a flaring cap. He said with a grim smile, "Oh the thrill of constructing a pile that reaches the clouds and defies heaven!" His smile chilled me. He said melodiously, "Peter, you shall be my ace bricky!" I said, "But Mister Nicks, I'm only the apprentice."

To be number one bricky on a Wonder of the World kept me in a state of elation. I laid the first ceremonial brick. Mister Nicks spoke of the pyramids, and of the slaves who quarried the huge slabs and chiseled them into blocks; and how the slaves ferried them down the Nile and lived on onions, bread and locusts and a few mouthfuls of precious water; and how they obediently worked themselves to death; and how it was the highest honor for the workmen to die for the spirit of the pyramids.

Mister Nicks treated me as though I were king of the Morris Tower. My ego was pleased beyond description; the job was paradise, and Mister Nicks a sort of beneficent diety.

I had The Dream: Mister Nicks makes more work on dams and tunnels and bridges and the Morris Tower is the ferris wheel at Coney Island and I lay bricks on the revolving wall and my trowel is all wrong and the mortar is decayed garbage and the bricks are vegetables and bundles of rags and I'm in stocking feet and can't find my tools and work clothes and I'm far behind the men and Mister Nicks looks at his watch and berates me in front of his brickies and says he is going to fire me and he takes me to one of the cabs of the ferris wheel and it is his narrow dark dirty furnished room and he gives me nuts and raisins and it is very late and I'm tired and can't remember where I live and there is one bed and we sleep back to back and then his painted fairy face hovers lecherously over me and his breath stinks of onions and locusts and he puts his cold hands between my legs and I shout queer sonovabitch what the hell are you doing? Let go of my prick! Mister Nicks becomes dignified and says Peter bring up the fluted section on the south side and he leads me to the door and says it's safe and he pushes me out into space and I am falling from the one-hundred-and-fiftieth floor and in my terror I awake.

We were up near the top; it seemed you could reach out and touch the Hudson, the East River, Jersey, Westchester; and when the sky cleared bright you could see Riverhead sixty miles out on Long Island. Mister Nicks appeared. He spoke about the ships that looked like toys, and how glorious it was for men to raise a structure that tall. "Peter, I had an interesting dream about you." He peered at me. I remained silent. "Well," he said, "dreams may be of consequence—or—chaotic folly; don't you think so?" I felt guilty and ashamed for having that disgusting dream; but nevertheless I began to feel an uncontrollable revulsion for Mister Nicks. From then on he said little, but watched me constantly with a cloying smile; and when he gave me orders he spoke with a maddening, lilting nicety.

By day he concentrated on me like a confident, patient vulture awaiting certain surrender, and at night he was the incubus of my dreams, sucking my breath, encircling me, blocking my path, seeking me from beneath my feet and from over my head, and cornering me into the diminishing end of the tunnel. I simply could have quit and walked off the Morris Tower job; but curiosity as to what that man was up to and, further, my instinctive abhorrence and growing aggression, were lividly animating conditions; the crepuscular aura of unnamable danger that he cast made me acutely aware of being alive; amorphous demonic fear being a passion magnifying the senses and compressing livingness in a closer space and time; also, I felt, or preferred to feel, there was a profound or historical significance to my laying bricks—each brick a key in the mysterious code of the cosmos; and that what mattered was not the endurance of one's life but the quality and intensity—for example, the brief existence of Christ the construction worker; perhaps no one was actually sane, and Mister Nicks had to play a game: perhaps threatening, troubling and harming were eternals in the Scheme that dreaded the vacuum of common sense regularity.

And was Mr. Nicks just an erudite fellow trying to elevate me above the usual bricky who has his head stuck in the mortar tub and his ass pointing at the azure sky? He said, "Peter, if you're building a cesspool pretend you're laying brick on a cathedral. There's a genius in everyone if only they will call it forth, like Faustus summoned Mephisto—and who knows but that death is superior to life in sensual satisfaction!" Was I fated to have a clandestine rapport with the imago and psyche of the Tower Morris, a preordained belonging? Was Mister Nicks a male impersonator? Could I have erotic union with a skyscraper? Could there be final truth and justice in the man-job blood rites Mister Nicks hinted at? Were architecture and flesh and bones synonymous (structurally the church was the body of Christ—and flats and apartments were post-wombs) and was the building the receptacle and keeper of the soul scheduled for reincarnation like Ark and altar? And was the skyscraper God, and Mister Nicks its prophet—and was there a High Mass without the celebration of Sacrifice? If I hadn't mused fancifully while laying bricks, I would have gone mad or withered away.

Suddenly questions about ordinary everyday things posed importantly: all brickies piss against the wall right where they're working like self-unconscious animals in the street—and I never saw Mr. Nicks piss—never saw him drink water or eat lunch—did he have a wife, children where did he live—why didn't he attend meetings at the union hall—where was he from—who was he?

The more I thought of Norman Parker the more I was convinced he was murdered. Intuition told me that Mister Nicks was a goddamn nut who imagined each job was a separate sacred entity that had to be propitiated and consecrated by the violent death of a hard-hat. All signs indicated Mr. Nicks had chosen me as his next immolation—at least, I had to believe that in order to be on constant guard against the possible. I cryptically told Mister Nicks about the voodoo who salvaged and pampered a bushy-haired drunken white derelict so he could trap the derelict and add him to his fine collection of shrunken heads. Mister Nicks grinned.

He sent me to lay bricks on a stairwell by myself. Next to my mortar tub was a pail of water. I supposed it to be for tempering mortar. I don't know why, but I happened to look up and saw a steel worker about to cut holes in a beam with an acetylene torch; and I moved away from the stairwell.

Within moments a shower of molten steel fell upon where I had been; and what I had thought was a pail of water exploded and spread great flames; someone had put a pail of gasoline where I was to lay brick. In my mind's eye I visualized Mister Nicks stealthily placing the gasoline there, knowing that after I arrived there the steel worker would burn steel with his torch above me.

I saw myself hunted and destroyed by Mister Nicks: knocked down a chute and buried in fresh concrete, tricked into space and being squashed onto the street, mashed under a falling wall. My physical being—body, limbs and countless considerable parts—was my problem; only and all of that was in jeopardy; my ineffable soul could not be touched: My duty was to keep alive and intact. If anything was going to happen it would have to happen before the Morris Tower was completed. I was determined to watch Mister Nicks' movements from starting to quitting whistle.

Day's work was over and the brickies left the scaffold and rode the hoists down to the shanty. I had a premonition and hid behind a section of air duct. There was no one on the floor. The Tower was still. A few pigeons soared up and rested on girders above, looking at me. Mister Nicks appeared, carrying a wrench. He looked around, then went out on the swinging scaffold where I would be working in the morning. He loosened the inch-thick bolts holding the cable drum and scaffold brackets to the suspended cables. He did it very carefully, like a thief calibrating the tumblers of a safe.

After he was gone I examined the scaffold. The nuts were holding on to the bolts by a hairsbreadth, connecting with about one-half a turn on the last thread.

In the morning, if I went out onto that scaffold, between my weight and the burden of a full tub of mortar and more hands of brick, the vibrations would soon dislodge the nuts and bolts and brackets, and the planking under foot would give way and I'd plunge down one hundred stories. I fetched a wrench and tightened the nuts. There's nothing like being certain; Mister Nicks was my worst enemy in my life and world.

Next morning, I saw him at a distance. He must have assumed that the scaffold man or the safety inspector had found the defective bolts and routinely fixed the scaffold. He came to me and said it was a lovely day. He was affable and solicitous. His whorish acting did not succeed; I kept seeing him tamper with the scaffold in the private manner of an assassin to have me die for his insane job symbolism. I agreed that it was a lovely day but added that lovely day or not each day was a tremendously exciting lifetime because no one knew what might happen. His smile made me loathe him more than ever.

It was a murky, humid afternoon. Mister Nicks was away from the job a few days and Cockeye Lynch was running the work. I had unconsciously relaxed my vigilance. Finished with my stint, I had to go to the opposite side of the building. Carrying my level and tool bag I started across the inside of the building. As I came by the open elevator shaft I saw mirrored in a big stainless steel sheet crazy Mister Nicks coming at me from behind, and before I could turn around or move away from the elevator shaft, he shoved me.

In the split-second that I had seen him mirrored my reflexes operated with electronic speed to save my life; in that untimable flash I noticed the elevator cable and as I was thrown I dropped the level and tool bag, and, thrust into the open shaft, I lunged for and caught the cable with both hands and twined my legs about the cable and shouted for help with all my might; workmen responded immediately; one pushed the elevator button signaling the hoisting engineer not to run the hoist, while others threw planks across the shaft and brought me back onto the floor. Mister Nicks had disappeared.

Escape from seeming sure death cannot be justly described; the feeling is that of having been taken to the world beyond and rapidly returned. And there are circumstances that inalterably and morally make it mandatory to kill—to preserve your life.

A couple of days later Mister Nicks was again very much in evidence. I saw him as my prey. I was transformed. Had I missed the elevator cable I would have gone to the bottom of the shaft and become old as time. His conjuring the shadow of death had matured me.

Death is not to be equivocated; its triumph over the ambulating fruit called flesh is total and without redress throughout ever-expanding infinity; and that deceptive fiend, Mister Nicks, wanted my one and only life on earth to be offered as a sort of spiritual mascot to the skyscraper god, Morris Tower.

We reached the final story, and the bricklayers' scaffolds were dismantled. There was some masonry to be done overhand, and the great capping that would resemble the flaring fulcrum of the fleur-de-lis, which would be constructed by the steel workers and faced in gold-limned sheets by the ornamental metal men. If the Morris Tower had had a Corinthian capital it would have been the Grecian column of the ages.

We had one day's work left, closing the openings where the outrigging I-beams had protruded to hold the scaffold cable. At noon there was a little rooftree party on the hundred-and-fiftieth floor-top with tycoons, politicians and clergy, and free sandwiches and soda.

Mister Nicks had the goddamn nerve to speak to me, saying man had come a long way from the tree, cave and tent. He thanked me for my dedicated bricklaying. Then his hellish eyes looked into me and he said fanatically, prayerfully, "To build! To build! The noblest art of all the arts! All the other arts are merely abstractions cast by outward things . . . Architecture exists in itself and surpasses all man's accomplishments as substance shadow!" As he walked away I thought he said, "One must follow one's heart; obey impulse unthinkingly; act on the moment for good or evil!"

The work whistle blew; four hours more of bricklaying and we'd receive our pay envelopes and discharge slips. Filling the parapet openings was a fearsome task. It meant working on our knees, bending down and laying bricks overhand; one slight loss of balance, one false move would be the irreparable, irreversible end. We brickies warned each other to be extremely careful. We were alert and in full view of each other, and it was not possible for Mister Nicks to sneak behind me and nudge me over the brink—unless he were a phantom.

Below, no larger than an ant, I saw Mister Nicks emerge from a manhole and step out onto the street bridge; he had on the luminous yellow hard hat of the foreman. We always cautioned anyone who happened by beneath us. I checked the brickies on either side of me; they were not near, and were too occupied to see Mister Nicks. I did not cry out the usual, "Watch out below!"

Who was Mister Nicks? Was he the legendary Semite shepherd king, Hyksos Nyksos, who fashioned the first brick for mankind from the alluvial bed of the Euphrates in the Ur of Chaldees twenty thousand years ago? Was he Hiconium Niconium, the restless eternally wandering hermaphrodite of the Sacred Forbidden Architectural Mysteries? Or was he just that cabalistic snake oil doctor and Industrial Worker Of The World, Hicky Nicky The Floatin' Bricky, the invincible champion master mason from the parched clay lands of pueblo Western Americana who came east to erect high-rises, live in smelly furnished rooms, eat dried apricots and sunflower seeds, and molest and make improper advances to apprentices?

I had a trowel of mortar in my right hand and a glazed white brick in my left; I wanted to pull back the brick and put it on the concrete floor but nervousness and the rich sweat in my palm let the brick go from my grip—I swear on The Cross that I would never have purposely dropped that brick . . . The sheer of the round Tower streamed under my vision looming hypnotically in invisible aerial space—true plumb never seeming perpendicular to the plane of the horizon—and the fleeing brick described an appealing beautiful long-curved flight scudding about a foot or so from the gleaming cliff-wall down through the water like shimmering waves of heat and went uninterruptedly through Mister Nicks' hard hat and vanished home inside his head.

The Fireplace

In 1939 I was no different from today's healthy young fellows who chase girls and do and get away with what they can. My girl-hunting pal and patron was Dr. Dave Lieberman. He was a hot shot. We had a good set-up. His wife, Kit, taught school in the city and came home to Long Island weekends. While Kit was gone Dave and I had a ball with girls in his comfortable home. Kit wasn't wise to the goings-on. To her I was a serious promising writer who could do no wrong. In a sense, I was part of the family, and I got to know Dave's and Kit's orthodox parents and relatives.

It was nearing New Year. Dave said to me, "Pete, wait till you meet my sister-in-law, Kit's brother Max's wife, Leda!" "What about Leda?"

"She's a dream. You haven't seen a doll until you've seen her."

"Chances?"

"Absolutely nothing doing. Not stuff for you. Leda and Max are the perfect marriage. They'll be at my New Year's Eve party. Look at Leda, but don't touch. If you get ideas, you'll be wasting your time."

Dave held his New Year's Eve in the village's best restaurant. There were Dave's brother and sister and their mates, and Max and Leda.

Dave had not exaggerated about Leda. She was a stunning black-haired Hebraic beauty. Solomon had described her in the song of songs. Her husband, Max, though short, was handsome. They looked the ideal couple. Leda had an uprightness that discouraged approach. I managed one dance with her.

She would not let me press her to me. At midnight, when everybody got silly and slobbered kisses I pecked Leda's virtuous cheek. If I have my eye on a married woman, I always butter up the husband. Max and I got chummy. He and Leda taught school, and lived in Flatbush, Brooklyn. He collected butterflies and read science-fiction. They had a summer camp with Leda's mother, Sarah, in Provincetown, on Cape Cod.

"Come and visit us there next summer."

I assured him that I would.

"Leda and I are not going to have children until we're financially secure. How about that?"

"Max, you're both using your heads."

We were all Dave's overnight guests. When I went to the bathroom before retiring, Leda was in there. She came out in a flimsy nightgown. The way I scanned her made her uncomfortable. I envied Max's going to bed with her. It always seemed to be that the woman I hungered for belonged to some other guy.

Dave and I sat up in the den for a while discussing the pros and cons of seduction. Dave was an old hand, and certainly not the faint-hearted kind. He combined business with pleasures. More than a few of his conquests began right with the horizontal of gyniatrics, "The modern woman," he said "makes her own laws about morals. Under the right circumstances—boredom with household drudgery, a two-timing husband, sexual curiosity—flattery, a few strong drinks—romantic atmosphere—just about any woman can be had. But Leda is the exception. In her case you're up against religion more than anything else. She and her mother, Sarah, are women out of the Bible. They live by the old Law. To them, "Thou shalt not Commit Adultery" has teeth in it. Leda's modest behaviour is consequential to religion. The B of her virtue follows the A of her God. Pete, you're not going to get in." I accepted Dave's dictum. Nevertheless, I availed myself of every opportunity to feed my eyes upon Leda. I saw her at the Bar Mitzvah of Dave's boy. It was not until Dave took me along to her seventh wedding anniversary at her apartment in Brooklyn that I met her mother. Leda did not take after her mother in looks. The widow, Sarah, was plain and severe of face, a veritable female tabernacle with austere dress and the black wig of the Matriarch.

At the gathering, a rabbi blessed Leda and Max. He extolled Sarah as "a human inviolable island of the true faith in our Babylonian and

Faustian times," and "the Lord God's handmaiden and exemplar maternal rock."

The sentiments, refreshments and ceremonies were in the orthodox manner, amidst all of which, Sarah and Leda stood out as shining columns of womanhood.

There is a defective, remiss quality about an attractive loose woman. But about a beautiful. religious, good woman there is a most desireable something, a forbidden fruit aura that is maddeningly exciting. Leda's virtues heaped more fuel upon my flames.

I could feel Sarah's eyes going through me. I wondered whether the eagle-like woman could read my sensuous thoughts. At the table, by the light of the seven-branched silver candelabra, Sarah made me think of occult theosophy, the Dybbuk and the all-designing Qabbalah. I felt there was a mystic ruling bond between the voluptuous Leda and the stark Sarah. Sarah said little, and studied me.

Max showed me his butterfly collection, and explained how he went about finding, capturing and preserving them. I had to pretend interest.

In June I was building a patio around Dave's pool. Sarah and Leda visited. Sarah watched as I laid the slate in mortar. After I had a backstroke workout in the pool, Sarah ran her hand over my shoulder muscles and complimented me upon my physical ability. Leda as usual, remained proper and remote, I was surprised by Sarah's friendliness. During the few days at Dave's, Sarah favored my company. She read the galley-proofs of my novel, and discussed it with me. She had a wide knowledge of history and ethnic strains. I don't know how she found out that my parents had come from rugged, poetic Abruzzi region of Italy, but she knew more about the background of my people than I.

"You imagine yourself to be of Italian blood," she said "That is partly true. Originally the area of your people was settled by the Greeks after the fall of Troy. Then throughout the centuries followed the mixtures of other invading bloods, the Romans, Semitic, Saracens, Normans and finally, the Spaniards of the House of D'Avalos. Your face tells the story these races and cultures."

I asked her, "Sarah, is that good or bad?"

She smiles, and answered, "School ends in two weeks. We are going to the Provincetown cottage for the summer. We have a fireplace. would you come to Provincetown as my guest, and build a fireplace? I'll pay you."

Before I went to Provincetown, Dave asked me, "Did you ever have a physical check-up?

I told him I had never had anything wrong with my health. He badgered me into letting him examine me. the result was just as I thought. I was in first rate condition.

It was the end of June. Sarah and Leda arrived at Dave's in a Buick coupe. On the side Dave said, "Remember, Leda is my sister-in-law."

"I give you my word of honor," I said, "Don't worry, I'll behave."

Leda did the driving. We took the Port Jefferson ferry across the sound to Bridgeport; I asked Sarah why Max hadn't come along. She said he had to officiate for the Butterfly Society and would join us the following week or so.

The cottage was an ocean-dune outside of the village of Provincetown. Sarah and Leda slept in the bedrooms upstairs, and I had the one bedroom on the ground floor. I did not entertain hope of romancing Leda. Sarah wanted a stone fireplace. I ordered the materials. The stone delivered was sea-worn glacial-deposit rock of varying colors. Sarah and Leda helped me put in the concrete base, and mix the mortar for the masonry. After I built the hearth, firebox, smoke-shelf and throat, I split the stone for the face and chimney. As I sledged the stones, Sarah commented with admiration. But Leda stood at a distance. It took me four days to layup the stone and complete the job. As an act of frustration for Leda, I deliberately chose and built the face of the fireplace above the mantle, two stones shaped and symbolizing the male and female procreative organs. Neither Sarah or Leda said anything about the unmistakable effect.

We picked up driftwood from the shore and in the evening lighted the fireplace. We sat in silence before the entwining blue, yellow, green and red flame.

Sarah said, "The fire is writing the ancient Hebrew words, The forest and sea is burning with strange, passionate, leaping tales."

"When is Max arriving?" I asked Leda. She shrugged. It seemed that my presence disturbed or displeased her, from the moment we left Long Island she had been tight-lipped and tense toward me.

Having nothing to lose, I said, "There's no denying that you're a very beautiful girl, Leda. Perhaps I don't understand you or you don't understand me. You do not talk to me. You are not friendly. I get the impression that you think I'm some sort of a dangerous corrupting demon. You sit and look at me mutely, and frozen, like Lot's wife facing Sodom and Gomorrah as a lovely pillar of salt. Am I not right?"

An undefinable little smile escaped her. She lowered her head.

Sarah went to bed. Leda remained. It was the first time that I was alone with her. It could only go one way or the other. If she became shocked and insulted, I would pull in my horns, apologize, and leave in the morning before she and Sarah arose.

I sat next to her. She did not move away. That was heartening. Every stone and diamond has a grain cracking. Instinct warned me not to taint the situation with logic. Biology and reason do not mix well. Talk under the potential circumstances would have been worthless. I snapped off the light without explanation. Leda gazed intently into the smoldering fireplace. I put my hand on her hand. Kissing a girl's hand is a deferential key, opening doors. There was neither a positive nor negative response. I kissed her lips. She received that kiss as strickenly as one who expects the guillotine to fall. I proceeded smoothly. She lay as if under hypnosis. I whispered, "Leda, go up to bed, undress and pretend to go to sleep. I'll wait for you in my room. Come down quietly. For God's sake, make sure you don't awaken your mother." She nodded and arose.

I waited. She came softly down to me. She was reserved, embarrassed. It seemed I had to teach her. In bed she was a pulsing statue. At dawn, she blushingly covered her nudity and left.

I felt neither remorseful nor cynical. I was melted by her chaste aspect. I was in love with her. For her to break her moral barriers and give herself to me convinced me that she was in love with me. I had visions of her divorcing Max and marrying me. And I intended to bring that about.

Sarah treated me royally. She bought steaks, lobsters, clams, fresh fish, hot Portuguese bread, and just about anything I wanted to eat and drink. She made each day a gourmet occasion for me. I was extremely careful not to give her a clue or reason to suspect that I made love for hours every night in my bed with her daughter. Leda played her part also. Though naturally she had become warmer towards me, before Sarah, she did not betray the shadow of a sign of our intimacy. During the day she stayed by Sarah's side. I grew to like Sarah very much. I was sorry for being such a hypocrite, but what she didn't know could not hurt her.

One thing amazed me. The first three or four nights Leda was in bed with me, she was so passive, I felt like a rapist. By swiftly mounting degrees in bed she became a different Leda, wild with a Dionysian intoxication, making love with a sexually religious frenzy like the orgiastic maidens of Euripides' Bacchae, seeking to drain and consume my life away. Some things can be too good. The second week she couldn't get enough. In Paradise itself, too much would be too much. I was the hunter who had become the prey. I was not made of wood, but certainly not of iron. By the third week I began to wonder when her husband Max would arrive. She grew radiant, lovelier than ever, and I, weaker.

With the excuse that I wanted to wander for characters and possible stories, I spent the days by myself in Provincetown. The homosexuals had not claimed Provincetown yet. I met bohemians from Greenwich Village, the old eccentric poet, Harry Kemp, who had had an affair with one of Upton Sinclair's wives, and wrote with a seagull's quill and his own blood, a deaf and dumb time and space painter, an excommunicated alcoholic impotent priest, Johnny Craig, who was living with a female lion tamer, and a famous aged Portuguese sea Captain, Vadi. But more often—than not, I would go up the beach and rest at the foot of a dune to regain strength for the night with Leda.

After the fourth week, Leda suddenly reverted to her former closed self. She did not come to my room at night. At first I thought she too had become quite satiated. She and Sarah went about with a strange smiling happiness. Then I wanted her back in bed with me again. I could not get to her. Sarah became less solicitous. I began to feel unwanted in the cottage.

When Sarah told me that Max was definitely arriving in a few days, I knew I had to leave. I did not care to be under the same roof with a man whom I had so splendidly cuckolded.

Leda sweetly, but formally, bade me farewell, without even a token kiss. Sarah walked me to the railroad station. While waiting for the train, Sarah looked me in the face, and asked, "Did you enjoy Leda?" I was nettled by her tone and asked, "How do you mean 'enjoy'?"

"Having sexual intercourse with her every night for thirty days."

I stuttered, "Whatever gave you that idea?"

"I can tell you now, Pietro. Poor dear Max is sterile. I was not going to be deprived of a grandchild."

I got the message immediately. She continued, "I liked your mind, face and body, I chose you to sire Leda's child."

"What about Max?"

"Why do you think he agreed to stay away from you and Leda? You did not answer my question. Did you enjoy Leda?"

"Very, very much."

"That's nice"

"But tell me, Sarah, why did she suddenly turn cold and avoid me?

"Because my Leda is a good girl. When she missed her period and the medical examination proved she was pregnant, there was no further need of Leda's going to bed with you. That would have been sin. We are old-fashioned. To us marriage is sacred."

"I see. Why didn't you find someone of your own race to help Leda instead of me?"

Sarah ran her fingers lightly over my face and said softly, "Because there is so much about you which told me you had the soul of a Jew."

My train was about to pull out. Sarah put a roll of bills in my hand and said, "I did not want you to build our fireplace for nothing. You have made us such a wonderful fireplace."

My Uncivilized Past

It was a real fucked-up day in March 1939. I was a twenty-six-year-old Italian-American bricklayer who had written a novel, *Christ in Concrete*, that was ready for publication. That was the day the Book-of-the-Month Club judges were to choose between my book and John Steinbeck's *Grapes of Wrath* for the September selection.

There were seven brothers and sisters I was taking care of. We lived in a rented house on the hill in Northport overlooking Long Island Sound. I hated like a sonofabitch to leave home and the symphonic radio music in the kitchen on that cold depressing morning and go all the way to the Flushing Meadows to lay brick on the new World's Fair, but jobs were scarce and men were sucking asses for a day's pay.

Before I drove to the station the radio broadcast a bulletin that the Nazis had invaded Czechoslovakia and Hitler had arrived triumphantly in Prague. A few months before, when the United States recognized the Franco dictatorship that had been put in, by the fascist armies. I had written letters to Chamberlain, Roosevelt, Hitler, and Mussolini, calling them every kind of a cocksucker I could think of. I was madder yet when the criminals neither answered nor got the FBI after me.

Of course the lousy Long Island Railroad got me to work an hour late. The foreman was pissed off and I had words with him.

He said "Wise guy, if you're smart why are you slinging brick? Now I see why they call you 'Pete the Red.'"

"Red your mother's cunt!" I said, "Fuck you!"

Having to work outdoors in winter weather for your fucking bread makes you wish you were never born. Wind came up through the snow in a crazy gust and sent an ironworker off the high steel. I saw the dying man go into quivering sleep cradled into eternity on the concrete floor by a pile of brick. His rugged hands, his athletic body were divorced from things that remained to be done. No one stopped laying bricks. It was just another case for the Workmen's Compensation death claims.

All day I could only think of the judges of the Book-of-the-Month Club. Was it possible for me to have some goddamned good luck? As a counter-evil-eye Italian, with every brick I laid I said aloud, "Fuck them! Who needs them! Fuck them!"

At the end of the day, sure enough, I was fired. that was the evening I had to go to the publisher, Bobbs-Merrill, then located at Fourth Avenue and 28th Street, to find out whether the Book-of-the-Month Club had a chosen Steinbeck or me. Being laid off I had to take my four-foot level and big white canvas toolbag with me. I hated to carry tools in the street and subway—it made me feel like a goddamned robot slob.

I was furious about my insecurity, there was nothing glorious about being poor. The fucking Book-of-the-Month Club could change my life in a minute. A story is an author-rigged thing, but reality is a 100 percent unpredictable whore. I swore that if fortune smiled on me I would tell the world to kiss my ass.

In the novel I gave labor a soul. I made family an intimate, sacred community. I theatricalized the fable of religion, placing each scene within the framework of ritual, instinctively patterning my work after the morality plays of dark mystic times gone.

Was it possible to be an artist without prostituting oneself? When I had finished laying bricks and a building was complete, I wanted to demolish it and return it to the dust it came from. I looked around me in the subway. Why try to bullshit myself? The truth about the common man was as obvious as the sun at high noon: the mass man was just the blinding incontinent will to propagate; he was the jerk who endlessly bred jerks. Da Vinci had said he was a human sack who took food into the top hole and let it out at the bottom hole, and I saw that from the sack, from Joe Blow, came all the power and evil in society.

As the train pounded along, the nice looking kid next to me was reading *Moby Dick*. Suddenly, he burst out laughing and said to the black woman on his other side, "This sailor rents a room that he has to share with a stranger—and do you know what? His bedmate turns out to be a cannibal with a bone in his nose and wearing a silk top hat!"

I looked ridiculous myself, wearing a beret, a Prince Albert dress coat with a velvet collar, Lee work pants, and Sears-Roebuck's best cement-stuccoed work shoes. I had bought the formal coat at Rogers Peet at 41st and Fifth Avenue with a part of the money Arnold Gingrich had sent me for *Esquire*'s purchase of my first short story, "Christ in Concrete." William Saroyan, with Armenian acumen, had taken me to the young men's department where the prices were lower. My Prince Albert, and a pearl grey homburg, gray gloves, and spats, were to provide a proper literary appearance at the Plaza party given for me by Gingrich and Meyer Levin.

Hemingway had come to the party, thinking he'd see a gorilla-like, swarthy, Hoboken-Italian laborer (I was born and raised in Hoboken). But I was slender and aesthetic; I didn't smoke or drink. He said to the blonde with him, "He has the writing juice, but this bricklaying Donati cocksucker ain't so tough!"

I told him my name was not Donati but Di Donato. And I'll swear that squeaky-voiced, beady-eyed Hemingway had the most disgusting, dirtiest mouth I had ever heard.

Then Clifford Odets, Ben Appel, Millen Brand, Mike Blankfort, Louis Adamic, Louis Bromfield, and other famous authors of the day came out to Northport, like visitors to a zoo, to look me over. They came from curiosity, expecting to see some horny-handed phenomenon and found instead an angry, articulate, self-appointed missionary. I felt like Jesus about his cousin, John the Baptist, when he said to the sight-seeing gawkers, "What did you come out to the wilderness to behold? A reed being tossed by a wind? Really then, why did you come out? To see a prophet?"

I wrote because it is impossible to communicate directly and honestly with people. I was at war with society, and I said as much to the well-intended pilgrims, "You fucking scribblers, though you write with the cunning of journalists, the erudition of professors, and the privileged advantages of angels, yet have not a scorching hard-on for justice, you're full of shit and your books shall vanish like a fart in a storm!"

I came up from the Lexington Avenue subway a couple blocks from Bobbs-Merrill. It was dusk—sleeting, and gloomy. Tired and hungry, I went to a restaurant. At my table was a Greek. He told me that he never traveled without his own special garlic, lemons and olive oil. He ordered a dish of something and gave the waiter the three things. The waiter, bringing my soup, tripped and spilled the whole bowl of god-damned chicken gumbo right down the front of my Prince Albert. He promptly took hot black coffee and doused it on me to cut the soup.

In the publisher's building the elevator operator was about to close the door. He had a woman passenger. I stopped the door with my foot. The greaseball runt looked at my level, toolbag, chicken-and-coffee-stained coat and mortar-caked shoes; he barred my way and snidely said, "Where do you think you're going, Pal? Pal, use the stairway or the service elevator, Pal!"

I dropped my level and toolbag, grabbed him by the throat and thrust him up against the wall of the elevator. "Don't 'Pal' me, you guinea prick! No, you're not even a prick—a prick's part of a man! Now move your ass and take me up to the editor's floor!

He started the elevator and mumbled, "You don't look like an author or talk like an author."

"Fuck you" I said.

He said. "There's a lady here."

The woman was behind me. Without turning I said, "Fuck her too!"

The woman also got off at the editor's floor. She was probably old enough to be my mother, but she was perfectly curved, beautiful. She smelled of cool, fresh-crushed Concord grapes. She smiled. I felt foolish.

The editor, Lambert Davis, a Southerner who had left the *Virginia Quarterly* to come to Bobbs-Merrill, and pink-cheeked, mustachioed Ross Baker, head of promotion and sales, hurried from their offices as though God had arrived and greeted her with fawning respect. Mr.

Davis introduced me. She was the widow of President Woodrow Wilson. I had been a tiny kid when he was President, Commander-in-Chief, and all that jazz. I remember looking at the Hoboken newspapers after the end of World War I and seeing Wilson with Pershing in the victory parade. But all I knew about Mrs. Wilson was that she ran the government after the President became a vegetable and the old joke—*Question*: "What did Mrs. Wilson say when President Wilson asked her to be his wife?" *Answer*: She fell out of bed.

She read the apology—and something else—in my eyes.

"Charmed," I said. "Mrs. Wilson, it is my particular honor and pleasure to meet you." I thought that the prissy old horsefaced Presbyterian Princeton prude had sure snared himself a succulent cunt.

Mr. Davis said, "The First Lady was written for White House memoirs, a treasure for literature a human document, a landmark in American History."

I said laying it on thick, "To think that I, the son of illiterate pagan mountains of Abruzzi, am in the presence of the lovely wife of a towering president of the greatest nation on earth is truly wonderful, completely overwhelming. . . ."

Mr. Davis said, "Mrs. Wilson, Mr. di Donato had to leave school at the age of twelve to become a bricklayer picking up his father's bloodied trowel to support his widowed mother and three brothers and sisters—"

"Seven brothers and sisters," I said.

"Yes, yes, I know, Pietro, but three sounds less incredible than seven. Mrs. Wilson, Mr. Di Donato is a creative diamond in the rough—he doesn't write with mind or discipline, he with his flesh. Pietro is the Hoboken Wordsworth—'Strange fits of passion have I known' and 'dear imaginations realized . . . up to their loftiest measure, yea and more.'"

I didn't even know that there had been a Wordsworth. and just then I didn't care. I was too busy wondering when the bastards would say something about the Book-of-the-Month Club and if the judges had gotten off the pot.

Mrs. Wilson said, "I have reason to believe Mr. Di Donato speaks impressive English. Mr. Di Donato, if your book is a success will you continue to lay bricks?"

I'd like to lay you, right here, I thought. I said, "No, my dear Mrs. Wilson. My being a mason is a socioeconomic circumstance. I disdain bricklaying, it is beast of burden stuff. Monkeys can put on hard hats and be taught to lay bricks—better."

Davis said, "You don't mind waiting do you?"

I said, "Take your sweet time."

As he led Mrs. Wilson into his office, he said, "Hitler has now violated the Czechs."

"I heard it on the automobile radio," she said, "It's deplorable! Our dear, dear boys will be going 'over there' again. May God help them all."

The Bobbs-Merrill place was musty as an attic, with a few additional touches it could have been something right out of Dickens, or maybe vintage *Saturday Evening Post*. I actually saw cobwebs in the ceiling corners and wondered why spiders would settle for such a dingy location. The clerks both male and female, all seemed to be octogenarians in a printing house wax museum. In the small, uncomfortable sitting lobby, there were photos of fuddy-duddy Frank Baum who wrote *The Wizard of Oz*, Bruce Barton author of *The Man Nobody Knows*, and that famous guide for armchair adventures, Richard Haliburton, who only a week later was to go down with his do-it-yourself junk in the China Sea. They had not yet put up either Mrs. Woodrow Wilson's sugary, smiling picture or my own in a Byronesque pose from the waist up, wearing soiled Army-Navy Store winter underwear.

A phone rang, and a minute later Ross Baker ran out shouting, "We made it, Pietro! We made it! They've turned down *Grapes of Wrath* and chosen *Christ in Concrete*! The Book-of-the-Month judges are taking you to lunch tomorrow and will hand you a certified check for twenty-five thousand dollars!"

'*We* made it!' That was a belly laugh. The graceless buggering ambitions, the mediocrity and double-mouthing of the publishing carnival make about as much sense as a one-eyed black Hasidic jug-fucker. Originally, Simon & Schuster had possession of the manuscript but they threw it back in my lap, saying with compassionate profundity that it wasn't a book and couldn't ever be a book. Bobbs-Merrill sent Mrs. Woodrow Wilson's expensively printed and bound proofs to the Book-of-the-Month Club. My novel only got there by a fluke. My sister was managing a dress shop and met a woman there who needed medical help for her husband. I got a doctor pal to treat the guy for free, and his wife, while expressing her gratitude, told my sister she worked at the Book-of-the-Month Club. My sister said that her brother, Peter, had written a book called *Christ in Concrete*; the woman said she'd get a proof copy through her job and called Bobbs-Merrill. That copy got into the hands of the special readers who recommended it to the judges!

My life was transformed immediately. I was ushered into the sanctum sanctorum, Mrs. Woodrow Wilson dear-boyed me, the champagne was brought out, and I was accorded the full goose-who-laid-the-golden-egg treatment. One moment I was a day laborer and the next moment I was a rich guy. In a flash I became a careless phony like all the self-loving celebrity shits—I had been surfeited with character, but now it was going to be fun being no fucking good. I was soon to fully understand the rich; they are a breed unto themselves. There is the animal kingdom—the insect, the fish, the winged creature, mammals, the family of man, and the rich.

The Aladdin's lamp of wealth makes for elegantly long torsos and limbs, darling straight noses and close-fitting shell ears, equine skulls, teeth as unmarred as dentures, skin like living porcelain, and the frigid eyes of a fish. The rich have the transparent all-seeing orbs of the great horned owl—gem-clear eyes like the beautified, except that they do not mirror immorality. Their bodies do not cast shadows and their stance obviates soul. The unharassed young have an air of maturity, they are as insolent and confident as the planets, while the old have an ageless semblance of youth.

To die is a merciful escape for the disenfranchised who live only in hope that never fruits, but death for a millionaire is Greek tragedy—an irrevocable farewell to ego, power, *la dolce vita*, lovely orgies, a myriad pleasures, drinks, servants cute deviations, multiple lives, and—most of all—gourmet cuntlapping.

F. Scott Fitzgerald delineated the anatomy of the leisure class—but not quite completely. The rich have super style; they're the exquisite ones, gods on earth and positive that their shit is ice cream. But they sadly lack one thing; a caste mark made by a bullet—Pow! —precisely between their motherfucking eyes.

Mrs. Woodrow Wilson and the publishing people quaffed the champagne—the fucking beautiful Book-of-the-Month Club bonanza champagne! The editor conveniently forgot that he had recently told me, "We're going to spend a pile promoting the First Lady's memoirs, so—I've got to be frank with you, Pietro—aside from token ads your novel is going to have to sink or swim on its own. You see, the story of a primitive Italian laborer killed in construction work can't in a thousand years compare with life in the White House." Then he got witty: "But, of course, if you shot the President of the United States, say, the publicity would automatically put *Christ in Concrete* on the bestseller list." The prick!

I called my friend Saroyan at the Great Northern Hotel, where he was staying, and told him about my jackpot. He got me a room. Then I took a cab to Brooks Brothers and outfitted myself from head to foot with the best they had. At the hotel I showered, shaved, and changed, Saroyan invited me to see parts of his two Broadway hits, *My Heart's in the Highlands* and *Time of Your Life*, and then go out and do the town and get a piece of ass.

There was something I had to do. I made a bundle of my dirty sweat-stinking work clothes and shoes. I took the bundle, my four-foot level, the bag of tools, and an empty Coca-Cola bottle and went by cab to Saint Patrick's Cathedral. I told the cabbie I'd only be a minute. Inside, I signed the cross, genuflected to the Madonna, and thanked her for influencing the Book-of-the-Month Club judges. On my way out, I stopped at the font and filled the Coca-Cola bottle with holy water.

Every poor, tawdry, ball-busted, daydreaming bricklayer has cursingly vowed that—when his ship comes in, when a rich relative in Rangoon dies and leaves him a fortune, or when he wins the Irish Sweepstakes—he's going to throw his fucking tools off the Brooklyn Bridge.

I directed the cabbie to the Brooklyn Bridge and had him pull over to the railing near the middle of the graceful night lit span. I pissed into my tin hard hat and poured the Coca-Cola bottle of holy water into it also. Then I sprinkled the sacred liquid over both the cheap, soiled, unlovely clothes of my recent past and the tools and said, *"In Nomine Patris, et Filii, et Spiritus Sancti*—fuck you forever!" And I threw, one by one, the hard hat, the large Rose trowel and the pointing trowel, my ordinary Stanley six-foot lock-joint folding rule and my brand-new-brick-course Lufkin spacing rule, the hand-square and the carborundum rubbing stone, the brick hammer and the lump hammer, the scutch hammer and the chisels, and all the lines and line-blocks and pins and slickers and tape measures and canvas gloves and brushes and the Johnson & Johnson first-aid kit and my fucking Union card stamped with a twenty-five cent photo of me . . . and with each loss I cried, "Fuck you!"

Shake the dust from thy feet. That which offends thee, cut it off and cast it from thee. Let's settle something once and for all; I've spent most of my life laying bricks. and I know what I'm talking about when I say unequivocally that so-called honest character-building toil is a crock of shit. Straining, dull, repetitive, treadmill labor does not enhance, encourage, ennoble, or edify; it simply just fucking-well degenerates, brutalizes, and beats the mass robot into a zombie. And that's no shit!

The irremediable crime of my existence has not been ravening sensuality, incest, betrayal, broken promises, prejudice, lies, violence, obscenity, or just pettiness—but simply staying too long at bricklaying, putting up stupid walls proving nothing, like a fucking idiot fool. My crime was not being true to my only self—by squandering priceless hours, weeks, months, and years that Christ himself can't bring back—when I should have put all my brothers and sisters in an orphan asylum and freely wandered the fucking beautiful world, screwing to the hilt and writing about it all. Kiss and fuck and tell. Beware of deadly habits like daily work—fuck that slave habit! I want "WASTER" chiseled on my tombstone.

*

Going uptown to rejoin Saroyan I regaled the cabbie with my fantastic day.

He said, "We're all jerks and slobs until we get a break. So today you got rich and famous! Well, I'm glad a working stiff is getting a break for a change. How come to a writer so many interesting things happen?"

I told him the truth, "Because the writer can't help putting his fucking nose and tongue and prick into everybody's business."

"You should hump the president's wife you met—it will give you status and you can tell your grandchildren about how you banged someone from the White House."

I said, "No kidding, do you think I should fuck the wife of a president of the United States of America?"

"Vy not?" he said, "Mrs. Woodrow Wilson—I remember her. Who doesn't? So what if she could be your mother? The Talmud Torah says, 'More better an old hen for the best chicken fat.' Give her a bang for me too. I can't get it up no more . . . like trying to shove a wet noodle up a tiger's asshole in flytime. At my age now it's no more with the pisser . . . only with the kisser. You wanna do me a favor? Bring me a souvenir from the president's wife—maybe a pair of her panties . . . used . . . unwashed . . . all nice and goppy in the crotch!"

Saroyan and I went to the Copacabana, where the manager took us backstage to the showgirls' dressing room. The girls were breathtaking. Bill brought out a small fancy rug from his coat pocket—an Oriental prayer rug. He took off his shoes. Knelt on the rug, and praised Allah and the girls.

Both Saroyan and I fell for a gorgeous dancer, Tamara. After the floor show we wined and dined her and took her to her Greenwich Village apartment to listen to classical music and to bullshit. I wanted to lay Tamara in the worst way. Saroyan wasn't a bad-looking guy in the Armenian manner, but I felt quite sure she favored me. I figured I'd ditch Bill and then come back and fuck her—if I could.

I yawned and said that between bricklaying, the weather, suspense, Mrs. Woodrow Wilson, and the emotional stress of my *Christ in Concrete* winning over John Steinbeck's *Grapes of Wrath*, it had been a rough day—and that I'd have to be in shape to meet tomorrow with Heywood Broun, William Allen White, Henry Seidel Canby, Dorothy Canfield Fisher, and Harry Sherman, my good angels of the Book-of-the-Month Club.

We didn't know what to talk about, so Bill tried to make literary conversation asking me what I thought of Steinbeck's sophomoric, sentimental, simulated, self-serving sympathies were just a lot of lamp-smelling *tour de force* shit. As a boy, Steinbeck had lived in a twenty-six-room Victorian mansion in Salinas, California, while I was housed in a fucking cold-water railroad flat on the Hoboken Dardanelles, companioned by immigrants, lice, bedbugs, roaches, and rats. I said that Steinbeck was a reactionary idealist poseur who milked the pathos of the downtrodden for gain. (And remembering now that this "friend of mankind" ended up hawking in the front ranks of the cowardly gung-ho Vietnam war criminals, I wasn't so wrong back then after all.)

Saroyan finally said that he'd better call it a day and go home and have his yogurt and sleep. We said goodnight to Tamara and took a cab back to the hotel, where we bade each other an over-friendly good night.

Later, I sneaked out of the hotel and took a cab down to Tamara's place. In the hallway I heard Tamara screeching, the crashing of furniture. and other unmistakable sounds of the chase. I turned away and walked back down the hall, for I knew only too well what I would find if I opened that door.

September came and Bobbs-Merrill and the Book-of-the-Month Club brought out *Christ in Concrete*. There were full-page ads in the *New York Times*, and some very flattering reviews (the best was by the tragically fated movie star, beautiful Frances Farmer, in the Communist *Daily Worker*). As a smash bestseller it was the subject for pulpit sermons, and before long I was classified as a leading writer—almost a theologian! Soon I was an asshole buddy of all the big shits at the top of the heap—the glamorous ones like Mayor La Guardia, Bennett Cerf, George Balanchine, Rube Goldberg, Nathan Milstein—and then there were meetings with Pearl Buck, Professor Albert Einstein, Eleanor Roosevelt—oh hell! I could go on and on. Getting to know writers was a joke; they were all homely megalomaniacs who looked and acted as though they needed a good buggering enema. And as for authors being tough brave guys—well, Hemingway, Mailer, Breslin, and all the rest of the writing slobs lumped together couldn't punch their way out of a paper bag.

Once I got my head above the tide in the anonymous human cesspool and became a Name, life became an excitingly different flesh-and-blood movie every day. Most of my fan mail avowed: "Oh, what I've been through . . . my life would make the greatest book!" Each writer had had some deathless original experience like incest, sexual relations with an animal, or perhaps been given a blow-job by a denizen of outer space. One correspondent, a Catholic prelate to the Vatican, well known for work and youth and morals, insisted that I meet him in the city to allow him to tell me how much he appreciated *Christ in Concrete*.

This Monsignor took me to the Copa for dinner. His teeth were too white, his lips too red, and his eyes too bright. He was the traditional Irish-American baseball nut. As I was gnawing a turkey leg and salivating over the dancing showgirls, he said with brio, "I know Jumpin' Joe . . . After the games at the Yankee Stadium I take showers with the sluggers in the locker room. Why, Pietro, some of those guys have got pricks like baseball bats!"

Clifford Odets—and, by the way, what kind of an aborted concoction is 'Odets'?—well, anyhow, Odets gave me a newspaper clipping about a guy in Philadelphia who left a copy of my book on his bed opened at page 286 (which described a bricklayer falling off a skyscraper), with the following lines underscored: "Paul looked over the scaffold rail and through staring mouth and eyes sent his soul to catch his Godfather who flung out his arms and rested on the speed of space that sucked him down . . ." The Philadelphian then made an expert jump from his tiny toilet window on the twentieth floor.

A doctor phoned me from the Bellevue morgue to come and see a hood encased in a good concrete mix—with a missal and a gaudy rosary in his crossed hands—all in a carpentered plywood box dug out of the East River muck by sandhogs. This Brooklyn romantic had been garroted with baling wire. As I watched the skull-sawing brain-scooping autopsy, thoughts of both steak and cunnilingus became most extremely unappetizing.

Collecting the hood's cadaver for the 'Boys' was Big A, king of the riverfront and an honorary associate of Murder Incorporated. We met and he displayed a propensity for culture by admiring me. The next morning, he took me to the Waldorf to have breakfast with Frank Costello, who was *elegantissimo* until he opened his Italian accented "dese, dem, and dose" trap.

Later, I was a guest at Big A's estate in the Hamptons, and I learned that the Wasp millionaires there didn't dare complain about Big A's wife's freshly manured vegetable garden, or her pigeons, chickens, nanny goats, and clotheslines.

Big A told me the whole inside mobster-syndicate story while fat little Mrs. A gorged me with homemade ravioli and wine, repeatedly kissing holy pictures and blessing herself and Big A. She insisted that Big A never transgressed the law, but that all the *capos* he mentioned were *male carne*, that is, "bad meat." The word "Mafia" was never used by us Italians.

Big A had been brought as a snot-nosed kid from Palermo, Sicily, to the Brooklyn docks. I asked him how he summed up the New World.

"I'm a 100 percent true-blue American," he said vehemently. "I believe in the Stars and Stripes. Lemme tell you—other countries stink! This fuckin' America was made for Me—Big A. I got it by the balls!"

Bennett Cerf, Harold Ross, of the *New Yorker*, Dorothy Parker, Walter Winchell, Arthur Kober (Lillian Hellman's ex-Husband), I.F. Stone, at that time editor of the *New York Evening Post*, and I—as a group—attended the opening night of Lillian Hellman's *Little Foxes*. Later, backstage, before a large adulating congregation of the precious and famous, the star Tallulah Bankhead asked me how I liked the play. I told her honestly that it put me to sleep.

Tallulah shouted. "You goddamned greasy wop bricklayer! What could you *possibly* know about the theatre!"

Then on to the party for Lillian Hellman at the mansion of the, Jewish-Swiss international Midas, Frohnknecht. I was sentimental about Maggie Frohnknecht—well, either about her or her gold mines? Maggie's plain sister was married to Erich Leinsdorf, and what stands out in my mind from that evening is the memory of the pallid, bald, bespectacled, guttural Leinsdorf spitting into his wife's face while saying, "Bubbee, what do you think of me now?" In the embarrassed hush that followed, she looked up to him with a beatific smile and answered, "Erich, you are wonderful!" I whispered to Maggie Fronknescht, "This conducting character has never heard of the Madonna," and dark neurotic Maggie said, "Oh Shit."

Bennett Cerf and I made a strange tomcatting pair. I asked him the secret of his success, and he said, "Pete, I know how to listen." Bennett had been divorced from the actress, Sylvia Sidney, but his secretary was an exact look-alike for her and was madly in love with him. But Bennett fell in love with Ginger Rogers's niece, Phyllis, and I was forced to go pussy-hunting alone.

The night of Bennett's marriage to Phyllis, I wore a custom tailored tux, patent-leather pumps with imported tan bows, and tan imported French-pleated shirt. Leonard Lyons said I was the tops in formal clothes, and Dorothy Kilgallen flattered me by saying I was one of the best-looking men in America.

The brownstone townhouse had an interior court, complete with trees, bushes, flowers, statues, and fountains. I ran into a couple who latched onto me and helped me get drunk. He was tall and patrician and she glittered passionately. To this day I don't know how I ended up in bed with her in their St. Regis suite, but in the middle of the night I awoke there. She had her back to me and was snoring, I automatically let her have it—and she screamed, "Wrong place!"

In the daylight she was a withered, toothless harridan, as ancient and decrepit as the Cumaeam Siby! I had to vomit.

The last thing I recall is the three of us in the elevator descending to the lobby, and the old, old man weakly protesting. "There is such a thing as people!"

Envoi: The public wishes to believe that the creative artist comports himself with *the mystery and poise of God.*

NUDE OF AN AUTHOR

(The Profane Apotheosis And Sacred Damnation Of Peter Damiani.)

In the golden Roman sun there was no mistaking the classical profile of Peter Damiani. He was seated at a Piazza Navona sidewalk table by the Fountain of the Four Rivers. Middle-age Damiani, an indifferent American author, had recently become the owner of the foremost men's magazine, *Man's Way*. Damiani was conducting the MW Publishing Company in signorile Renaissance manner from his table of the Four Fountains.

While secretaries took dictation and sent and received cables and phone calls from all over the world he entertained people. My table adjoined his. I had the feeling he knew who I was, and carried on for my benefit, hoping I would be the medium of his posterity.

Damiani who had never been a literary success, was pontificating in Italian to the authors, Ignazio and Alberto, how to write for *Man's Way*.

"Be absurd. Have improbable plots—such as a story tongue in cheek with facts and figures how Superman has replaced the Father, Son, and Holy Ghost. Use cartoon execution. Avoid sense. This is the age of the importance of the artificial and nothing; the era of the surreal obscure. Mix the religion of sex and the lasciviousness of spirituality. Scatter in some maudlin social cellulose; ventilate it with the relief of accidental, unmeant, natural farce; vein, artery, organ and muscle it around a backbone of exquisite inevitability; ask questions; don't bother with answers; cap it with the hook of a mysterious, unrelated title, and send it to me. When you think of me hear in mind there is no one more impertinent and tyrannical than a frustrated author sitting on the publishing throne."

Then there were the fascist journalist, Rossi, one-eyed, communist Senator Dononi, who had once taught romance languages at Columbia, and a gross, influential Cardinal whose name cannot be mentioned.

Damiani said ostentatiously, "Where else but in the Eternal City and at the table of Peter Damiani illustrious emissaries of God and the devil congenially sit and drink Lacrime di Cristo?"

During a mock duel of words with the cardinal Damiani compared the Cardinal to a red-bereted Mephisto, and pityingly to himself as the haplesss Faust. The Cardinal promised to write an article suggesting revolutionary changes in the Church. Rossi wanted the world run by dictators. Dononi was for a United Europe and a eugenic cross-breeding of communism and capitalism. Damiani thought America should take over the entire Western hemisphere and become the Federated States of Pan-America. He claimed *Man's Way* the 'Raphael' of magazines, serenely assimilating without fear or favor every possible style, talent and idea.

Damiani was alone with Professor Diomede. I might have been imagining, but it seemed Damiani began revealing his innermost self in Diomede purposely for me to overhear.

"Diomede, what do you think of me?"

"When you were young you were poetic, unpredictable. Now you are a sage."

"In the field of truth the mower scythes off his own legs. Youth in itself is lyrical. Wealth has made me wise; and success is not to be argued with."

"That's bread for any tooth."

"The truth is a luxury."

"As Pilate asked Christ, 'What is truth?' But when one knows the truth where does one go from there?"

"I refer to the truth which is conformity to reality."

"You mean the truth is a drama of dissimilar characters; all are at odds and no one is wrong."

"Yes, and a state wherein the conditions are impossible to negate. The truth is a trinity: *enunciationis, cogitationis, voluntatis.*"

"Despite yourself you're saying the truth is moral rectitude."

"Did the body make the soul for the soul's use, or, did the soul make the body for the body's enjoyment?"

"How could we live without the question mark?"

"Let us be content then with resemblances."

Peter Damiani was the person I could possibly have been. I suspected that beings outside of ourselves were the chalices containing our correct images and destinies; like the primeval belief that one's vulnerable life and perpetual spirit was hidden in the pod of an inaccessible plant.

Though I was a stranger to Damiani, with my creative interest in him, I was both the acolyte and postulator of his artistic cause.

From my objective position I knew more about him than he himself knew. He was the Virgil to my Dante. Let us say that I was his witness.

Peter Damiani, the antipode of my entity, unresigned, and all too human, had the potential of a modern saint. His noble struggle with sins complemented and qualified him for a certain sanctity. The catalogue of the "Whole Ones" is filled with such as he.

I can testify that he received cruel blows: the stigma of being a conscientious objector, bearing the cross of a sadistic wife, pulled down into the mire by a degenerate stepdaughter, denied by a public blind to his inspirational works, harnessed with poverty, and trodden with the burden of his wife paralyzed by an accident.

Because of his genius for literature he won the publishing company. Calm seas and prosperous voyages are before him, and someday the grace of God will come upon him.

He is justly embittered and one must not hearken to what he says at times. He still mortifies himself, as he is doing now—that is his greatness—saying things which are "keys" and directly opposite to his feelings. Listen:

"Diomede, alleged evil is closest to nature, and is the vaulting element of society. I remind myself of the young fellow who posed for the Christ of The Last Supper; many years later DaVinci had him model for Judas."

"Children of mothers all. Better if we remained kids—but no, an acorn becomes an oak, a worm changes into a butterfly, and so wearingly on; endless permutations, and each drop of blood a storied universe."

"I'll give you the argument of my being with broad brush—details are so middle-class and for the myopic, the Lilliputians."

"Being your confidante is a profound responsibility."

"I'm above the laxatives of Purgatory, but do herald from the lofty plateau of soliloquy. Perhaps a shadow ambitious to nominate itself as my soul may get an earful."

"Damiani's manifesto as it were, or Testament?"

"Not the Mea Culpa but the Mea Summa."

"Why do I smell the incense of liturgy from your words? Is this going to be a lengthy novena?"

"It wasn't you who said that. I will expose the corrosive folly of virtues and prove that the worst enemy of the soul is the soul's righteousness; and try to do so without losing the essential in the circumstantial.

"When hairy down appears upon the lower part of the hypogastric region and life urges to reproduce itself the human story begins. The genital's mind is the bio-theological absolute and our true parent. The spoory organs, without eyes see, earless and tongueless, they hear and speak."

"Damiani, you're quite the prophet of privates. Somewhere you should say, the mortal and the divine are the parallel lines that meet and become one at the point of infinity. It's sophisticated to contravert oneself."

"—Work is unnatural, and the next foe of the cosmic scheme is marriage. Let thoughts fall where they may: My youthful first novel was meant as a symphony of the oppressed. Lifted above the masses I discovered that the book was an aria of personal rebellion and self-pity. My Christ-like common man I then saw as a sheep dangerous by his ever-multiplying numbers. I despised the earthbound herd and envied the winged rich."

"A predicament to be sure."

"With rational planes of the intellect I geometricized God out of the universe."

"A formidable feat, like Carnot's Principle of progress to disorder."

"It proved to be a pyrrhic conquest as it left me weightless in the vacuum of logic."

"How awesome."

"Without God sin is sterile. I enjoyed sin now as the sensual realization because I have come back to God. If there were no God, I would have invented Him."

"I decipher your cryptogram as follows: 'Without opposites we are done for. Man has God and animal nature. God does not have animal nature in him. He is 'senza testicolo.' Sin is all that which God is incapable of. And religion is the electronic nervous system that blesses us with the ability to feel the delight of sin-pleasures."

"Diomede, I choose to love God, and fear women, because women were made to not be trusted."

"Your return to God is a reversal of Time, a prediction of the Past, an implosion wherein your volitional consciousness streams back to the ever-enlarging planet, God. Enlighten me; does woman have a soul?"

"The day of her creation woman became the discover of the phallus as a filler, because she had a famished, fructive, hollow chamber, the womb, in lieu of a soul. That which makes, bears and discharges life does not require a soul."

"Then the male would be happier if he too had a womb?"

"Indubitably; he would be the complete centripetal and centrifugal unit."

"Perhaps science—"

"The admirable woman is the prostitute. Giving herself to all she gives herself to none in goddess fashion. Democracy and peace are found between her thighs. She lays and does not lie. She sells the needed commodity without fables. She is a Holy of Nature."

"Why do we live?"

"We are brought here by the Original Author who is curious as to how we experiment and evoke the ultimate product of human situations."

"*Va bene*, but are we free?"

"The subconscious travels at will in the fourth dimension of the cosmos."

"And the unconscious?"

"Has its own premonitions."

"That leaves the conscious as the inferior state."

"At best the conscious pimps for approvals."

My attachment for Damiani was wavering. I deplored his damaging vagaries. How far from the Right Path would he stray? I prayed.

Damiani's wife was brought in a wheelchair by the nurse to her table. Damiani nodded to her. Diomede shook his head and exclaimed, "Her accident—terrible; Paralyzed and rendered deaf and Mute—Ah, Elaine—*che bella donna . . . che peccato!*"

"Damiani, forgive me, but it occurs to me that you shift moral standards mercurially, like a planetary bee savoring myriad orbits."

"Not so; I am consistent in that I champion the specific. Let all parts sound off. If the subject is food I invite the digestive to speak; If sex, who better than the excitive zones to mount the rostrum? What we call, 'I,' is the plural and ceremonial master of diverse individuations."

"In that case your wife's infidelity was not committed by her sovereign being but by the autonomous office—and confederate self-governing parts. To blunt the sting tell yourself you've been behorned by her independent particulars."

"I have the queasy feeling the total was jubilantly involved. Look at her: Late autumn of Medusa. That face had me turned into straining captive stone and was indelibly printed on my brain: the serpentine head, small burning green eyes, large straight haut nose, luscious vulvar mouth and intaglioed cheeks—except for her daughter, Candy, no other woman has her coraline skin and perfected form. Now her once mink-titian hair is an argent aura. Behold, Diomede, her silenced tristful mask that touches me."

"The intense way she peers at you is frightening. I detect a death-wish behind that mask. You are mirrored in her eyes as a corpse."

"Nonsense, Diomede. She's a penitential flesh statue. What you see is deepest sorrow for the insult to my honor. Sir, she is the living example of daily immolation.

"Her love for me has become pure, boundless, now that there is no more sex between us. She is the trophy completely under my spell. This is what I had hoped for. I tell you her suffering is beautiful!"

"She could be the tragic heroine of an opera called 'Medusa Agonistes.' What a waste of desirable woman. If only she had not missed her footing and plunged down the stairway!"

"That version was pap for the public. This is the way it really was: She had returned from a pretended weekend visit with a girlfriend in Mystic. I received a reliable report that she had not been with her girlfriend but with a man all day, all night, and all the next day, on his boat at sea.

"I studied her closely. She was over-solicitous. There was a heady joy about her and the heightened tone and reek of the cat who had swallowed the forbidden cream. It takes one to catch one. I confronted her. Though there was no squirming out of it, she stood up to me scornfully, defying me with the taunting questions, 'Were you there? Did you see me in bed with the man?'

"At the moment her affection and the truth could have switched my fury onto a side track of philosophical consideration—a few slices from a loaf needed not be missed—who knows, I might even have been strangely excited by a bestial account.

"It was the demeaning contemptuous look of the adversary on her face that I smashed at. In trying to avoid my hands she tripped backwards down the cellar stairway."

"Had she been wise she would have feigned tears and shame—begged your forgiveness—taken you to bed—and swear you were the better man, nay the best. But though a crushed flower has more fragrance the horning of a husband still stinks.

"You should have lived on the island of Chios between Lesbos and Samos; there was no adultery committed there for the space of seven hundred years."

"I would rather have been ruler of the ancient Andromachiadae who brought their king all the nubile virgins."

"Are you sure your wife is deaf and cannot hear what we are saying?"

"Positive. Notice how her facial muscles never change."

"Of course you did not want her to be in her dire condition; yet everything happens from God's will. Sexologists establish that the majority are unfaithful. Is there enough room in the sulphurous gloom to contain all adulterers? Perhaps the subject is what you choose to make of it: excretory trivia or socio-spirito cataclysm. Is it possible that Eve was God's Galatea and Adam cuckolded the superbeing, God, and we are ever paying for Adam's presumptuous phallus?"

"God's wrathful sentence was fair. Only artists have the right to passions. The rest, in not creating, not singing the romance of being, must accommodate to the yoke and stupidly pedal the treadmills. But the human race got off to a messy start with Cain and Abel putting the horns on their father."

I was shocked by the sacrilegious two, Diomede, the yea-saying mind to that apophatic errant heart, Peter Damiani. The vile attitudes must lead Damiani into the Abyss.

Damiani pointed to his wife.

"That silvery-haired sphinx with her green stare fixed upon me was a glamorous widowed libertine with arrogant vaginal confidence.

"The night we met we went to her bed, as the large tinted picture of her fat, elderly, bespectacled, whitehaired husband, wearing a red carnation on his lapel, looked quizzically on.

"The following morning her little blonde daughter, Candy, came running in, naked with doll in arms, and gazed at us with electric blue-gray eyes; a child who was a race apart, such as the chrysalis of a saint, or demon.

"Through the healthy frankness of lust we readily agreed that marriage would not become us. She revelled in a compulsion to tell me the intimacies that she had had with her hotel-manager husband, Harry."

Similar to a St. Augustine I kept saying to myself, "Peter Damiani, tomorrow you must and will depart from This Woman!" Could it have been that the eerie, magical, promising cold-fire eyes of her little daughter held me?

"Crossing a street in a snowstorm Elaine said, 'I've told you the unimportant stuff about my marriage. The reason Harry drank himself to death, the big thing, the secret was—' A minute later I slipped on an icy spot, fell and hit my head on the curb. I was dazed for a while. That blow knocked out from my memory whatever she had told me. I knew she had revealed a startling truth, but I could not recall her 'secret,' nor get her to repeat it. Her face hardened shrewdly. To my coaxing she answered, 'Pal, it's just as well that you don't remember what I said.'

"After our marriage my mind became a theatre constantly running the film of magnified close-ups of her coitions with Harry. I was entranced in their bed between them, smelling and hearing them. In those sickening dreams he was the incubus and she was the succubus. The ghost of good old Harry was always vanquishing me. There he was, ever about, my genial grinning host, the white Eskimo handing me his salivated Elaine cud.

"I couldn't take anymore of it. One night I drove to Harry's grave, dug up the coffin, and opened it. His remains looked the same as his picture: the grandmotherly white hair, the red carnation, the prissy, benign, artificially smiling Rotarian hotel-manager's look of 'At your service, Damiani.' I tricked Elaine into coming to the grave, and cast the light upon her husband.

"Instead of being shattered and breaking down as I had expected, she chortled. 'You sure hate it bad! For Christ's sake shovel back the dirt before they catch you and take you to the bug-house!'"

"Damiani, the cross was not that another Man had preceeded you but the irreconcilable warfare between your Holy Roman Catholicism—The True Church, and her worldly, unconfessing, unredeeming Protestanism."

"I should have left Elaine, but I was powerless in her magnet. Paradoxically Harry's daughter provided my retribution upon the phantom of her father and the antidote to her mother's gorgonic enchantment.

"That little girl with the crystal blue-gray amoral eyes of a hypnotic creature from the depthless sea took me to bed and led me into a fantasia of eros."

"What tender sub-teen age was she?"

"Her instinct and imagination for libidinous explorations and satisfactions was consummate—as though she had practiced throughout the centuries. In comparison her mother was an amateur.

"As she grew older her interest in girls developed strongly. During her college days she left no doubt about her rabid lust for her own sex."

"Then she used you as a substitute until—"

"My writings were failures. Candy became a calculating adventuress amongst the rich girl-loving women. She did not go through any torturous complexes about being homosexual. She told me starkly that she would stop at nothing to obtain wealth to live her way."

"Can your wife lip-read? I think she knows what we're saying. It would be sad if she does—what mother can accept the fact that her daughter is perverted? Wouldn't you like to know what's going on in her mind?"

"Three years ago I sat here looking at the Fountain of the Four Rivers. I did not know where my next dollar would come from. I thought of Genesis and the four rivers that flowed out of Eden to water the Tree of Life.

"In the triangle of Elaine, Candy and myself, Candy, free from contradictions, was the strongest. I was middle-aged and hopeless as an earner. Life is selling and buying. Between the three of us only Candy with her youth and stunning beauty had something of value to sell.

"If reality would obey my wishes, reality would perhaps be snared by my fiction. With the novel *Four Rivers* I exorcized my wishes. I had moved through the paradise on earth of the rich; they were of bone and flesh and died also; wealth cannot be taken along into the darkness; riches remain behind for the stewards or spoilers.

"In my fiction envisioned Candy giving herself to the highest bidder and eventually acquiring an immense inheritance. The book had a happy ending: The unheroic author-main-character and his stepdaughter pensioned off his difficult problem-wife, and the two hedonists lived royally, hunting and sharing hymens.

"It was not chimerical; fiction is the mother of religions, laws, wars, sciences, fortunes and fashions; sensuality is the husband and sower of fiction, and, not love but fiction sustains the celestial bodies.

"Needless to say the book was unpublishable. Then Heaven beamed upon me. Danny Sharp, the owner of *Man's Way* magazine—who thought he was God—died. His lesbian wife, Jody, met and fell desperately for Candy. She became Candy's slave. Last year, today, Jody conveniently died, and left her millions and *Man's Way* to Candy.

"So you see, so-called evil and ill winds do blow good. God pampers me, and thus I reciprocate with my respects of belief—one hand washes the other. Without inner conflicts I am now the perfect man."

"After your hardships and humiliations you did well," said Diomede, "Better the *Man's Way* wealth in your worthy hands than drained by the undeserving."

I was praying for Damiani and his abetting apologist. Damiani had disappointed me miserably. If I could have reached him I would have shown him that his heart and mind were infected and the nemesis fatal to his blissful eternity.

The notorious bloated, painted, bejewelled procuress, Madam Palestrina, brought in the form of prey, a ragged little girl with the eyes of a fawn to Damiani. They spoke clandestinely, then the Madam raised her voice and said proudly of the little girl, "*Ah, Signor Damiani, tutta questa bella freschezza é per te!*"

Damiani turned to the child and stroked her hair and looked at her fondly. "Precious angel, if you are a good girl and play with my nice American daughter and me you can bring home to your dear hungry papa and mama money and gifts."

The other side of Damiani's face was grotesque, a half mask eaten and mutilated by mortal sins. The Madam led the girl to Damiani's palazzo across the piazza.

Reassuming his Apollonian pose Damiani said emphatically, "Curses on that witch, Madam Palestrina! There should be a special hell for the procuress who lures destitute little virgins to the rotten beds of aging satyrs!"

Diomede commented, "You do have noble sensibilities—but to arrange delectable assignments it is necessary to have the competent services of a ruffiana like Madam Palestrina.

"As for the nymphet; is it not better that she bestow her chaste membrane upon a gentle benefactor than have it ripped in squallor by a rash young lout who will stain her with a venereal or a bastard? The plucking of virgin honey must be weighed in the balance according to the quality of the bee." Damiani answered grinningly, "I like you. I could say that you are my celebrated alter ego, my practical reasoning computer."

I had had more than enough of Damini. Too much. That expressionist was beyond redemption. The time was nearing for the reckoning.

Damiani burst into a fit of laughing, exaggerated hysterical laughing. Whom the Ideal Spirit would destroy it first makes mad.

The nurse took Damiani's wife home. As she wheeled her away she lamented, "Signora, though you cannot hear me I suffer for your saintly self. I heard everything your husband said—He is the mouth of evil—Afflicted woman, that husband of yours is abominable Lucifer incarnate. Oh that a miracle would restore you! Have faith for there is the Buon Dio."

I was alone, streams of water gushed from the spotlighted Fountain of the Four Rivers. Late evening mass was being celebrated and sung in the church of the little martyr of purity, Saint Agnes. Diomede came by, clapped me on the back and said, "Damiani, you still here? Why are you dressed as a priest? Is there a masquerade tonight?"

"You have mistaken me sir," I said, "for that dissolute, renegade, hypocrite and damned person."

"If you are not Peter Damiani, you are his identical twin, or I have lost my wits. Tell me, Damiani, what character in what role does it please you to parade at the moment?"

"For certain I am not Peter Damiani, nor could ever care to be!"

"Then who would you be?"

"With credentials I am Father Dionysos."

"What!—the absolutist Doctor of the Church, the trouble making priest threatened with excommunication and anathema who would revive even by violence the impossible virtues of the fanatic Fourth Century Bishop of Carthage, Donatus, who demanded Christians behave like Jesus?! Listen Damiani, if Donatism prevailed there would be a dozen Christians left in the world—churches would mold and the human race would vanish. Come, Damiani, a joke is a joke!"

"Nevertheless, I am still Father Dionysos!"

"Seeking God and The Answer has overwhelmed you. All right—do not look at me so severely—if you are not Peter Damiani, then I am Damiani. But my friend it is not a serious matter whether one is Damiani, Dionysos, Diomede, Pope, God or the devil—you are whatever you think you are, for life is all in the head anyway. *Pax vobiscum et cum spirita tuo!*"

Madam Palestrina and the little girl came out of Damiani's palazzo; theprocuress smiling smugly, the violated child white and trembling as if having been plied by vampires.

I prayed that Damiani would make one laudable gesture against the irreparable pollution of his shameful existence.

He finally appeared; pale, distraught. I followed him into the church. He looked wildly about, and entered the Confessional.

I was prepared, and advised him to shrive himself to Creator with all his heart and his mind and his soul."

He said fearfully, "Your voice—the emanations—you seem familiar—a presence without tense—and yet—"

"There is relativity."

"I'm acquainted with statistics of heart and mind—but what is the experience of the soul?"

"I am praying you in that direction."

"I feel the force. Other hands hold me. I follow. Will this be good for me? My salvation?"

"Asking is not yours; you did not make the world nor yourself."

"Why anything? What is it all about?"

"Are you here to purge, or lecture and boast?"

"I confess to Almighty God, to blessed Mary, ever Virgin, to blessed Michael the Archangel, to blessed John the Baptist, to the holy Apostles Peter and Paul, and to all the saints, that I have sinned exceedingly in thought, word, and deed, through my faith, through my fault, through my most grievous fault.

"May the Almighty and merciful Lord grant me pardon, absolution, and remission of all my sins. Amen.

"Forgive me Father for the following sins: I married Elaine in order to possess her daughter, I deliberately and wrongly accused my wife of infidelity to offset my guilt. I planned fall and perversion of my stepdaughter for selfish ends; and did it with seductive means.

"My revulsion for Elaine's former marriage was an elaborate sham to screen my affair with her daughter. I wanted riches, luxuries and position even through the prostitution of my stepdaughter."

He became very agitated; then shouted, "My conscience refuses to dissemble! The gnawing truth is that I have tried to be like other people and believe in the soul and God but honestly cannot! I do not have faith in you to whom I am confessing! I despise your act! If there is God, He has much to answer for! I cannot bow to He Who does not show Himself!

"The truth! The truth is that I am now sorry for the harm I have done to my wife and her innocent child! I desecrated a dead man who had sincerely loved my darling before me!

"I resent and do not love the maddening abstracts of God and the immortal soul! I want this life and no other! I adore the flesh of woman and fear God and the idea of God! I care not for any God to patronize and forgive me! My heart begs for my dearest wife to forgive me!" I could not find the grace to intercede for Damiani.

He cried, "I rebel and can't go any further! What shall I do—Oh, what shall I do for peace?"

He was not with me. I did not have to tell him what to do.

He waited, I gave him no response. "I'll do it!" He screamed, "Goddamit, I'll do IT!" He shot himself and fell out of the Confessional.

Damiani lay dying. His wife was brought to him. She sprang from her wheelchair and talked eagerly with the doctor who assured her Damiani would not survive. Her sudden recovery was not a miracle. The wicked woman smiled victoriously upon Damiani. He whispered chokingly to her.

"Crossing the street in the snowstorm—the message comes to me now—I recall the 'secret' you confided to me: 'In the beginning Harry's "thing" was gorgeous! When he couldn't perform anymore I wished him out of my life. Harry obliged me by drinking himself to death!'

"That's what you said—that's exactly what you said—I can still hear you saying it!

"I was amused and called you a black widow spider—a devourer of the male—Then when I became impotent you put the horns on me and wished me dead—Omphale! Omphale!"

Mrs. Damiani shrugged carelessly and walked firmly away.

I knelt by Damiani, administered Extreme Unction, and intoned The Prayer For a Happy Death.

With his last breath he spat at me and hissed, "I did not commit suicide, sniper—I've been foully assassinated by you—the fiendish

Castrato—Inquisitor—The Jealous Soul!—What are you going to do without me? Soul go fuck yourself you impossible pietist cocksucker!"

Damiani, neither successfully good or evil, spurned by heaven and disclaimed by hell, must lump with the undecided in Purgatory.

I've used years on him. Poor Damiani. I will yet seek the heart and mind of an author to distill and inspirit . . . But! blood is pouring from my temples too! . . . And why am I turning into frozen wood?

The Overnight Guest

The summer of 1928 my swimming pal, Fred, and I decided on a two-week vacation. From newspaper ads I picked a "Camp-Do-Not-Worry" in the Berkshires. We arrived by bus in the evening, and then found out it was a Socialist camp. Fred was 19, I, 17. What counted was that the rates were cheap, the menu good, the tent nice, and here was a splendid lake for swimming.

The next morning we headed down the hillside to the lake. Up the path came a barefoot girl wearing shorts and a white linen Russian blouse. She had long brown braids, a child's face and the body of Venus. We introduced ourselves. Her name was Wanda Sloan. She said her parents were Rumanian Jews and progressives. From then on we were with her constantly. Fred adored her openly; I, secretly. I was like a kid brother to Fred and Wanda. We would spend the nights in Wanda's tent; Fred and I clothed, lying on either side of her; Fred holding her hand, and I keeping space between her and myself.

The two weeks went by. I chose to stay another week. Wanda and I walked Fred to the bus. After the bus left, Wanda hooked her arm into mine. "Your tent is sloppy. It needs a woman's touch." When she got through fixing up my tent, she suddenly embraced me and kissed me. I pushed her away and slapped her. She was startled.

"Are you crazy? Why did you hit me?"

"Fred's in love with you," I said, "and he thinks you're his girl. You let him think so, then you turn around and kiss me minutes after he's gone—you whore!"

"I just felt like kissing you—there's nothing wrong in that—oh, you'll never understand a girl!" She began to cry, and ran out of the tent.

Later, as I was on my way to the concert, she was waiting for me on the path. Her tent was at the top of the hill, and we sat half the night on the grass outside it. Then we lay in each other's arms on her cot until morning. Every night we were on her cot, silently and innocently kissing.

My vacation over, I hastened to see Fred. He was painfully lovesick for Wanda. I didn't want him hurt by her, so I told him how Wanda and I kissed and petted on her cot every night for a week. But sure enough, the following weekend Fred had Wanda out to our canoeing and swimming club at City Island.

Wanda let me know that Fred had told her everything I had said to him. She laughed, "You're a kid with weird Old World Ideas about girls."

During the winter weekends Fred, Wanda and I swam in the salt-water pool of the St. George Hotel. Then Wanda did not show up with Fred anymore. Wanda had been swept off her feet by an Englishman named Daniel Cummings and married him. I didn't meet Dan until the beginning of the Depression, a year later. Wanda's husband was tall, handsome and suave. I had to give up my dream of ever having Wanda for myself.

I moved my family of brothers and sisters from Brooklyn to a village far out on the north shore of Long Island. I lost contact with both Fred and Wanda. Years passed and the Depression deepened. During my long period of unemployment, I read a great deal and contemplated writing. I was compelled to write the story of my father's death and call it *Christ in Concrete*. After I finished it, Wanda loomed in my mind very strongly. No matter how many girls I went to bed with, there was always the vision of beautiful Wanda. I wrote her a long love letter, and also told her about the story I had written, I was surprised by her prompt answer. Her letter looked as if it had been scrawled by a little girl.

Accompanying my second love letter was the carbon copy of *Christ in Concrete*. In her return letter she said the story had made her laugh, then it shocked her and made her weep bitterly. She wanted to see me. I was to meet her in Milano's restaurant on 42nd Street near 8th Avenue.

On the appointed day it was snowing. I took the train into the city. Wanda was waiting for me in Milano's. She was breath-taking, the dark-brown hair, the small fine forehead and ears, the deep warm brown eyes, the slightly upturned nose, the rich mouth and lovely teeth, the sparkling skin, the short slender neck, the short arms and high hips above the long graceful legs. She gave me a modest kiss. We had a light lunch with wine and coffee.

"I have only bourgeois news to report," she said wearily. She and Dan had no children. Dan was a sporting-goods salesman at Gimbel's. She still modeled dresses and furs on 7th Avenue. They had a Yonkers apartment. Her parents lived around the corner from her. "A few years after my marriage I became disillusioned. Dan is not an Englishman; his father is a poor Bronx rabbi. In the beginning his cane, spats, monocle and handkerchief in his coat sleeve snowed me. He talked a storm about fabulous deals, but the best he could do was to be a salesman with a carnation in his lapel in department stores, and now he's a sporting-goods salesman at Gimbel's."

Without preliminaries she said calmly, "You are coming to bed with me tonight. Dan must think you dropped in unexpectedly. You will miss your last train and be our overnight guest. I've got it all worked out. Dan is going deer hunting at Greenwood Lake with pals. His pals are picking Dan up around two in the morning. After Dan leaves, you come to my bed. Tonight I am yours."

We left the restaurant late in the afternoon. It was a long ride by subway and bus to Yonkers. We shopped for dinner. She made me feel as though I were her husband by her side as we purchased the food and carried the bags to her apartment.

Dan arrived soon after. I was uneasy from the moment he came in. He was surprised but glad to see me.

"Dan dear," said Wanda, "a little while ago I heard a knock. I opened the door and there was Pee-ate-trow di Donato!"

Wanda took Dan his smoking jacket and slippers. In his superior manner he said, "Your *Christ in Concrete* is not too bad a piece of scribbling." He was the same bull-fuzz artist who knew all, had been everywhere, and could do anything.

During dinner Wanda talked about the Camp-Do-Not-Worry days, and then asked me, "Pietro, do you still have your hell-and-heaven ideas about girls? Dan, to him a woman is either a Madonna or a prostitute. You're twenty-six, Pietro, and still virgin, I'll bet."

Dan said with a patronizing air, "You'd better do something about your virginity." He reached over, ruffled my hair and said, "We're only pulling your leg because we're fond of you."

Wanda bubbled about in high spirits. Dan puffed his pipe with smug pride. The hours passed. Finally, Dan's eyebrows went up and he said to me, "You've a long trip home. What train are you catching?"

"The last train. What's the right time?"

"It is exactly ten to eleven."

I fumbled for my schedule, then handed it to him. He read it and said, "Your last train from Penn to the Island leaves 12:01. You'd better move fast."

"Do you think I can make it?"

"I don't know. Give it a try."

I rose to leave, "Wait a minute, Pietro," said Wanda. "Dan, how long does it take you to get to Gimbel's from here?"

"Well, darling, about an hour and ten minutes."

"At this time of night the buses and subway trains are few and far between, and his last train leaves in one hour and six minutes. It's impossible for him to make that train."

Dan looked at the schedule again. "There's the first morning train for the island that leaves Penn at four-thirty A.M. Benny and Hal are picking me up after two. We will drop Pietro at the Van Cortlandt Park subway station. He'll get to Penn three thirty or so. He can have coffee there, read the newspaper and get the four-thirty out. How about that, Pietro?"

I nodded.

Wanda said decisively, "I can tell that Pietro is coming down with a cold. He's going to sleep on the divan in the living room!"

"Thank you, Wanda," I said, "but how about my sleeping over at your mother's?" I did not want Dan to suspect me in the least.

Dan said quickly, "I'll give her a buzz for you—I know she'd love to put you up!"

"You'll do no such thing," commanded Wanda. "It is late and mother is an invalid." Then she went on heatedly, "Dan, you're trying to get rid of Pietro because you have a dirty evil mind and do not trust his being alone in the same apartment with me after you leave with your pals! Isn't that the truth?"

He took her in his arms and protested that he had never mistrusted her nor ever would.

After Wanda had her bath and went to bed, Dan said, "You take your bath now. I'll fix you a glass of warm milk and cookies. I'm worried about that cold of yours coming on. I'll give you a half dozen sleeping pills. You'll sleep like a baby and sweat out the cold . . ."

In the bathroom I threw the sleeping pills down the toilet. I had my bath and went out into the kitchen wearing a pair of his pajamas. I drank the warm milk and ate the cookies, although I hated milk and sweets. "Gee," I said, "those goddamn pills work fast—I'll have to say good night—I wish I hadn't missed that last train . . ."

"Will you be here when I get back from hunting?"

"I guess so . . ." He squeezed my hand, drilled his eyes into mine, and said, "Well then, kid, be good!"

I went to my divan bed in the living room. The glow of the corridor night light showed through the glazed pane of the door. Their bedroom adjoined my room. Dan took his bath and went to the bedroom. He wound the clock. Sleep was out of the question for me. I simply had to bide my time. Dan's clock ticked interminably and finally went off with a clatter. I heard Wanda tell him he was crazy to go off at that hour into the ice and snow. He kissed her and said, "I love you, Wanda. Remember that."

"I will," she answered sleepily. He dressed in the kitchen, then got his hunting gear out of the corridor closet.

A car with a broken muffler roared to a stop out in the street in front of the apartment house. I distinctly heard two pairs of heavy boots clomp through the hallway. Dan opened the door and let his pals in. They gathered in the kitchen with a boy-scout enthusiasm about hunting deer with bows and arrows. Dan checked the bows, twanging the strings, and also checked the side arms. One of his pals said, "The deer aren't going to wait for us. Let's go, boys!" The light was snapped off in the kitchen, the hall door opened and shut. I thought my ears were deceiving me, but again I distinctly heard two pairs, and not three pairs, of boots along the hallway. I did not hear the car motor start. Was it possible the car took off without my hearing it? I could hear Wanda snoring lightly, and the alarm clock. I had the feeling that Dan was hiding.

I prayed that Wanda would not awaken. I counted seconds into minutes, five, ten, twenty. If Dan was hiding in the kitchen that long, why wouldn't his pals get annoyed and come noisily back for him? Otherwise they were in on the scheme with him to catch me doing something with Wanda. A half hour had gone by. I figured I had let my imagination throw me. Dan was miles away on the road to Greenwood Lake.

I had always wanted Wanda. I was bursting with lust. I started to get up to go to her. Just then I heard an unmistakable creaking of the parquet floor in the corridor and saw a shadowy form through the glazed door pane. I didn't hear Wanda snoring. Was it Wanda on the other side of the door? The door opened slowly. I saw a figure with swelling hips. Wanda, of course.

In the instant I was about to exclaim "Wanda!" I realized it was Dan. The swelling hips were his hunting trousers billowing above the puttees. He tiptoed toward my bed with an unlighted flashlight and a revolver. I froze in pretended deep sleep. He felt me, reached over and felt around the bed. Then, to make sure, he flashed his light. I sat up and mumbled. There was a tormented dangerous expression in his eyes. I rubbed my eyes and growled. "Hey, Dan—what the hell's going on?" The crazy mask fell from his face.

"My pals and I are just about to take off—I came in for cartridges—thought I'd see if you had enough covers." He went to the closet, picked up some cartridges and tiptoed out, whispering, "Good night. Sleep tight." I heard his boots through the hallway. Seconds later the car out in the street churned and churned, started with a coughing bang, revved up and then roared away into the night. Then I wondered if he had sent his pals away and had removed his boots and sneaked back into the apartment. I couldn't get myself to leave the bed. I heard Wanda get up, go through the corridor, bolt and chain the hall door, go into the kitchen, snap on the light, go into the bathroom, flush the toilet, run water and then turn out the bathroom and kitchen lights.

She opened the door, came in and turned on the floor lamp. She was in a black negligee. She blinked her eyes, yawned, smiled and asked me, "Did you fall asleep, too?"

"That bastard, Dan!" And I told her what had taken place.

She yawned and shrugged, "How should I know what Dan would have done if he had caught us in bed? I'm no mind reader. If I'm not afraid, why should you be? I looked through the apartment. He's gone. The hall door is bolted and chained and the windows are locked. He'd have to be a Houdini to sneak up on us."

I made love to Wanda until five o'clock the following afternoon. After we got up and dressed she put on horn-rimmed glasses, looked at me sweetly and said, "You must forget we were in bed. I mean like it never happened."

About six o'clock Dan came in with his pals. They were jubilant; each had gotten a deer; Dan's had the biggest antlers. Wanda fell all over Dan. "Dan, my Dan!" Dan looked at me. Wanda had taken everything out of me.

"Pietro," he said, "boy, are you pale!"

I said, "Dan, you know that goddamn cold I had coming on? I got that goddamn cold!"

In The Wide Waste

Recently I participated in an evening symposium at Yeshiva University on the subject of minorities writers with Philip Roth and James Ellison. After the lectures, questions and answered we mingled with the audience. Rose Bentley, a friend whom I had not seen for years, came up to me. I had known Rose early in my writing career. At that time, she was a divorcee with a beautiful blonde ten year old daughter, Lenore.

I asked about Lenore.

Rose said: "Lenore is dead. She committed suicide three months ago. My darling Lenore is dead. . . forever more." The way she said it did not surprise me. I recalled that Rose had been romantic, a dreamer, different.

I accompanied Rose to her Riverside Drive home. It was a large old apartment. She took in roomers. There were about six women living there. On the walls and tables of the dining and living rooms were many pictures of Lenore. Though she was in her teens and twenties I recognized her, she was the shapely, happy blonde, winning girl. One picture in particular was interesting. On a grassy plain she was posed against a lone mistletoe entwined oak. Beneath she had scrawled with red ink, lines from Byron:

> "In the desert a fountain is springing,
> In the wide waste there still is a tree,
> and a bird in the solitude singing,
> which speaks to my spirit of thee.
> Leonore"

Rose brought out a bottle of blackberry brandy. "No fiction I know of," she said, "can equal the story of the life and death of my Lenore. Her father is involved at the heart of it. Did you ever happen to meet Max?"

Rose's ex-husband, Max, is a noted psychiatrist and cosmopolitan intellectual. I had read some of his books, heard him on radio, and had watched him quite a few times on television.

"To see him on those television panel shows you would think Max was thirty instead of fifty-five," she said, "Max is apparently ageless. He is like Dorian Gray.

"We met in teachers' training college. He had an inferiority complex. His father was a rabbi working in a kosher poultry market. Max looked Nordic. He was tall with blond hair, blue eyes and a sensitive face. It wasn't his fine looks that got me. Believe or not, it was the way he read poetry. Edgar Allen Poe was my bible, and *The Raven* my favorite poem. *The Raven* always made me sentimental. When Max read *The Raven* to me I fell in love with him. He gave it a thrilling, sad, mystical meaning. I can hear Max's hypnotic voice reading Poe's *Lenore* '. . . a dirge for her the doubly dead in that she died so young . . . the life upon her yellow hair . . . . but not with her eyes.'

"How I wept! Oh Max, I said, when we marry I hope our child is a golden-haired girl. We'll name her Lenore. We'll bring Poe's beautiful Lenore back to life!

"My widowed mother, Rhea, believed in communism. Though she spoke of revolution she wouldn't hurt a fly. We had a summer cottage in the Catskills. Max and I got married and went to work teaching English in a Manhattan high school.

"The first summers we spent in the country were idyllic. We studied Marxism and Leninism, played the guitar and sang songs of social justice around a camp fire, ate shish kebab and drank tea. I became pregnant: and had the little yellow-haired, blue-eyed girl of my dreams, Lenore. We planted a white oak tree in the open field symbolizing Lenore's being.

"Max developed an expert knowledge of communism. He joined the Party. A few years later he was looked up to as an authority and leader. In the schools he organized communist cells amongst the teachers, and directed agitation, propaganda and strikes. In those days we even talked of going to live in the Soviet Union.

"I noticed a hardening change in Max. He called it growth. Being a communist gave him a dictatorial sense of power. Party members obeyed him blindly. Max was the leading light of the communist summer camp, Unity, at Wingdale in the Berkshires. He was important with the Broadway theater group, and wrote articles for the *Daily Worker*. Comrades who were teachers were investigated and lost their jobs. Max's path was charmed. He would talk himself in and out of any situation. He read Nietzsche and Freud, and became more and more superior. In spite of his expanding ego Mother and I were proud of him and adored him. His brilliance was overwhelming. He quit teaching to study psychology. I kept on teaching. Our apartment in town and the country cottage were crammed with his books on religions, superstition and human behavior. During World War II he managed to stay out of the service as a conscientious objector. Following the war he was summoned to Washington for un-American activities. He got off clean. But it was suspected that he had betrayed comrades who were his closest friends.

"He left the party and set himself up as licensed psychologist, explaining to me that the rank and file comrades were sheep, and that psychoanalysis was a power that suited him better and more profitably than communist ideology. Right from the beginning he was a successful psychologist.

"All seemed to be going well. Lenore and the white oak in the country were growing tall in beauty.

"One night in the cottage, in bed, he said something that almost drove me out of my senses: 'Rose, we don't belong to the conscious image of ourselves but to the mysterious stream of blood, to the primeval god from the dark past within us. Conscience is the weakness of our Judaic race. When we were premoral and performed human sacrifices we were invincible. Idolatry was the true strength of the Jewish character. Gods feed on blood. Jehovah commanded Abraham to offer Isaac to him upon the altar at a high place. And the Almighty Father sacrificed His son, Jesus.'

"Max went on about how the ancient Jews were only too ready

to make dread sacrifices; placing their children into the hollow metal image of El and how the children rolled down into flames below; of the Ammonites who killed their children for Milcom, and Agamemnon who immolated his daughter, Iphigenia.

"I said, 'Max, I don't know what you're talking about. Just why are you telling me all this?'

"Though it was hot summer night he was trembling with chills. Finally, he said in a queer, strained voice, 'Rose I am not a man in a universe of chance. There shall be no gods before me. I have a compulsion that gives me no rest. Something in me tells me I must sacrifice Lenore. You will help me. There will be no danger. It will seem accidental. Then I will secretly have the power of God!'

"I was wide awake and knew I was not having a nightmare. I could only tell myself that Max had gone insane. I had often read in the newspapers of demented parents who had slain their children. The man in bed with me was no longer the Max I married but a maniac. I pretended I was going to the bathroom. I rushed to the bedroom where Lenore and my mother slept. I quietly got them up and out of the cottage; put them in the car, and drove to the State police. I couldn't tell the police what Max had said. They would have thought me crazy. I said that Max had threatened me, and that Mother and I wanted him out of the cottage.

"When we got back with the police Max was gone. Max had terrified me beyond words. I was positive that he had lost his mind. I did not wish to hurt him in any way or try to have him committed, but I did go ahead immediately with divorce proceedings. At the divorce hearing it was the old business of mental cruelty and incompatibility. Max's record as a communist was against him. He did not contest, but he did win the sympathy of the court with smooth psychological talk, inferring that it was I who needed treatment. The judge set alimony and permitted Max to see Lenore twice a month.

"I was always nervous when Max came to take Lenore out for the day. On one occasion he laughing said that he had told me horrible things that night in an experimental sort of way to just to see what my shock register was. But I had the unshakeable feeling that the man was a throwback from some bloodthirsty barbaric world of the past and grimly meant what he had said. After he brought Lenore back one evening, Lenore wonderingly related that he had brought her into the men's room of a deserted restaurant and had exposed himself. I did not doubt the child.

"Whether Max were brain-sick or not I could not tolerate any further experiences. I took him to court, and charged him with the exposure incident. It was shameful.

"Because of her tender age Lenore was not permitted to testify. Max was the perfect actor. He shook his head compassionately and said I was imagining things.

The court did not know who to believe. I said I would forego alimony and support Lenore on the condition that Max be forbidden to see her. Max shrugged and assented. The court approved.

"Happy years followed. I was not interested in remarriage. Lenore was my life. Mother and I never mentioned Max. As Lenore grew she forgot her father. I taught school and took in roomers.

"Mother and I never had a religion, but we were fascinated by odd inspired people. This stretch of Riverside Drive on the Hudson from the seventies to the eccentric apartment tower, the Rorich Museum, has drawn white believers of oriental religions and has been known as the 'Ganges' of New York. Disenchanted with communism because of Max, and also the cynical Soviet actions, Mother and I took up with vegetarians, pacifists, Rosicrucian's and what not. In these rooms we had followers of Baha Ullah, gurus with flowing robes and turbans, voodooists, yogis and bearded avant garde poets and artists. Lenore grew up in that atmosphere.

"Max married Polly, a doctor. She helped him get a medical degree. He then became a Park Avenue Psychiatrist. They had a daughter, Annabel. Friends kept me informed about him. Like other former communists that I knew personally, Max loved wealth. He began piling up a fortune. I was told he did shylocking, abortions, and preyed on senile women who believed in spirits and ectoplasm. Most of his patients were homosexuals and alcoholics. They swore by him because he adjusted them philosophically to their perversions. Max was an all-round operator. But he was out of my life, and for that I was grateful.

"What I feared eventually came about. Lenore learned that Max was her father. Max was going high up in the world and getting a lot of publicity. Celebrities attended his Saturday night penthouse parties. Max's daughter, Annabel, was a debutante featured in glamour magazines, showing her in the Park Avenue apartment, on Max's yacht and at Max's Southampton summer place. Every now and then Lenore expressed her longing to meet her father but I discouraged it without explanation.

"Lenore had a lovely natural voice and played the guitar. Her music scholarship put her through college. At a college party she met her half-sister, Annabel.

"Annabel was proud of Lenore and became attached to her. She raved to her parents about Lenore. Lenore brought Annabel here. She was not as pretty as my Lenore. But she was sweet and guileless. She begged me to allow Lenore to be her guest at her home. I had to think it over carefully.

"It would be as though Lenore were meeting Max for the first time. It would be the meeting of an attractive man and a young woman. What kind of an influence would Max be? The public considered Max a great mind. Was the public right and I wrong? Had Max changed? How long could I expect Lenore to be content with the penniless zanies of my circle? Was I denying her a successful father's association and sponsorship? Could I say to Lenore: Your father, the famous psychiatrist, wanted to murder you—wanted to sacrifice you when you were a child. You probably don't remember—you were eight years old—you came home and told me he took you into the men's room of a restaurant and exposed himself?

"Had I had the foresight and courage to tell her those things she might have been alive today. I couldn't get myself to do it. Though Lenore was of age and free to do as she pleased she would not go to Max's house without my sanction. Polly phoned me, introduced herself—said we should have known each other long before—and graciously asked me to let Lenore visit.

"I could not make a decision. That evening I was surprised by a phone call from Max. We hadn't been in communication since our day in court many years back. He said he was anxious to see Lenore, do all he could for her, and that there was nothing for me to worry about. He invited me to accompany Lenore. He wasn't superior or professional, and sounded sincere. He said he would be at my service for anything I wished, including money.

"I thanked him, and agreed to let Lenore visit. But I had no intention of seeing him. To me he was a living spectre. He was my conception of Mephistopheles. Ugly faces suggest the comical. Max's extraordinary handsome face completed the portrait of evil.

"Yet, he seemed a normal husband to Polly and father to Annabel. That I could not understand. Sometimes I thought it was I who had brought out the grotesque in him.

"After Lenore met Max it was as I had anticipated. Max gave her a car, charge accounts and luxuries; things that would dazzle any girl. He openly favored her above Annabel. She came back from his lavish parties excited and with stars in her eyes. I knew Max was subtly estranging her from me; making me look foolish; proving to her that I had been neurotic, and because of imaginary things he had said and done, I had left him, and deprived her for many years of a father.

"Polly befriended me and came here often. It was obvious that she was absolutely slavish to Max. Polly was a plain woman. I could not figure out what he saw in her."

It had gotten late. Rose prepared the divan for me, and went to bed. I looked at the picture of Lenore. In one she was posed with a young man, a Riccardo who really looked like Max. In another, with the well-known conductor-composer, Leo Bronstein. There was one of Lenore with Max in swim suits on his yacht, Fantasy. Lenore's bookshelf contained Kafka, Camus, Sartre, and books by Max on hypertension, deviations, and psychoanalyses of the prophets. Max's books did not say *from Dad*, or *to my daughter*, but were autographed as if to a lover.

In the morning I heard Rose's roomers leave. On the walls of the bathroom were Rose's instructions as to personal cleanliness and admonitions to pay the weekly rent promptly. In the kitchen were small individual padlocked refrigerators. The telephones were also under lock and key. Rose wore Chinese pajamas. For breakfast she served me vegetable juice, tea, honey and yogurt.

"While Lenore was singing with Leo Bronstein's orchestra touring South America, my mother passed away. The white oak Max and I planted at Lenore's birth was struck by lightning. From the trunk of the dead tree sprouted mistletoe. And in Brazil Lenore fell in love with Riccardo. Riccardo was a wealthy German-Brazilian. He was very much in love with Lenore and followed her back here. His resemblance to Max was startling. He believed the Germans were the super-race. With all his looks and qualities, to me he was another version of Max. Riccardo set a date for the marriage. Lenore bought her trousseau."

Rose lead me to a closet and displayed Lenore's bridal gown, veil and slippers.

"Something was bothering Lenore. She began to confide in me; not speaking to me but at me; as one who talks in her sleep. I asked her if she were sure she loved Riccardo.

"'Yes,' she said, 'as a reflection of my ideal.'

"'Reflecting whom,' I asked.

"She answered: 'Mother, you'd be the last person in the world to understand and see it my way if I told you.'

"She related the meetings of Max and Riccardo. It was a duel of minds; Max's communist dialectics against Riccardo's haughty Nazism. Max finally overcame Riccardo by telling him he had indisputable knowledge that Hitler was a Jew and that Hitler's mystic strength and appeal came from his sanguinary Old Testament ancestors.

"Lenore became increasingly moody with alternating periods of elation and depression. Max phoned me and said that Lenore had worked herself into a state of nervous tension because she did not love Riccardo and could not go through with the marriage. That she was emotionally confused and her unhappiness had affected her metabolism. He recommended glandular treatment and was only too glad to assume the responsibility and expenses. I tried to reason with Lenore but she would not listen to me. She signed herself into the Parkness sanitarium under Max's care. Max convinced Riccardo Lenore was a severe manic depressive case. Riccardo gave up hope of Lenore being his wife and returned to Brazil.

"After a month Max had Lenore released from the sanitarium. From then on she practically lived with Max's family. Lenore liked to ski. Max bought a Vermont farm and converted it into a skiing lodge for her. He took her along on all the vacation trips he made with Polly and Annabel throughout the states and Europe. It did seem as though Max was trying to redeem the past. Lenore never referred to him as her father; it was always, Max. I could never feel that theirs was an ethical father and daughter relationship. There was no law for Max. With his attitude of mental supremacy, he was capable of any abomination.

"For Max, Lenore had given up all her boyfriends. I knew Max as a cannibal of the mind. No one could be close to him and retain their own mind. I wanted to but didn't dare ask Lenore if Max had ever tried to be physically intimate.

"One winter's day Lenore came home to stay with me for a few weeks. She felt blue. Max had taken Polly and Annabel on a trip to Acapulco. They had left in the Cadillac. Polly and Annabel wanted Lenore to go with them. It was the first time Max did not invite Lenore along.

"Max and his family hadn't been gone two days when we received a call from Polly's relatives. There had been a tragedy. In South Carolina Max's car hit a truck. Polly was killed, and Annabel was mortally injured and in a coma. Max was the only one wearing a safety belt. Max, with minor injuries, was in the hospital.

"Polly's relatives wanted to ship her body back to New York for burial. Max told them that as Annabel was surely going to die they had better wait for her where Annabel lay dying and Polly's corpse was in the morgue. Then they could bring back both bodies at the same time. Annabel died the next day. Max was not upset. From his hospital bed Max told a reporter that the living must go on—that he had a healthy view of life and would remarry a year from the day of his accident.

"Lenore and I attended the double funeral. Max wasn't there. As I looked at Polly and Annabel in their coffins I thought of the night Max told me of his compulsion for human sacrifice. What the true story of the accident was I don't know.

"Max was free. And Lenore spent more time than ever with him. Then began the gayest time of Lenore's Life. On her infrequent visits home, she would tell me about Max's fabulous parties. I was on the outside, remote from it all.

"Someone else came into the picture. My cleaning woman, Adrilla, had gone back to Haiti. The employment agency sent me a girl named, Jane. Jane had long curly chestnut hair, but eyes, and a serious, rather pretty face. Jane spoke with a lisp. She had two little girls and had separated from her husband who was having an affair with her younger sister. She was intelligent and studious. Lenore felt sorry for Jane; gave her clothes and money, and talked Max into giving her a job. Jane learned the routine of a psychiatrist's office rapidly, and made herself valuable to Max. The girl was self-effacing and grateful to Lenore.

"The months went by and nearer to the date Max had vowed he would take a third wife.

"A definite change came over Lenore. She was highly exhilarated. Though her eyes glowed, their pupils grew smaller. Her laughter bordered on hysteria. She let drop clues that left me no doubt. Max had told her that the best way for her to communicate with him was to lie with him on his psychoanalyst's couch.

"She seemed to want to tell me everything. I shuddered and shunned away from possible details. She said they both took something that transported them to sensational magical worlds. There was the intimation that Max was going to move to South America and change his and her identity and that Max had made her a certain binding promise.

"She had to tell me at last that Max was the only man in the world for her and that I had the right to guess what took place between her and Max on the couch. As she talked her face had Max's weird, mesmeric expression. It was as though Max in feminine form were addressing me. I feared her. I was shattered.

"A week before the day that marked a year from Max's accident Max and the girl in his office, Jane, disappeared. Lenore's fraught inquiries brought no results. She came home. From morning to night she didn't say a word. That was the time I should have gotten competent doctors for her."

Rose went to a desk and got out a batch of newspapers. They were dated a year from the day of Max's accident. Each newspaper carried the story and pictures of Max's marriage to Jane. Max had even formally adopted Jane's two children.

"When Lenore saw these newspapers she calmly said she was going to fetch her belongings from Max's home and store them in our Catskills cottage. I wanted to go with her. She said she wanted to be alone and that she was not going to do anything wrong.

"I no longer had reason to keep the truth from her. I told her that Max who was treating people for mental disorders was himself a depraved, incurable madman. I spared her nothing. I repeated word for word what he had said to me in bed in the cottage when she was a little girl, of his frighteningly insane desire to kill her; to have me do it with him; sacrificing her in a manner seeming accidental, so that we two could be as gods of life and death. I told her also how after we were divorced he took her out and in the men's room of a restaurant disgustingly exposed himself to her.

"Without emotion she said she remembered it throughout the years. When she left she was distant and cold. She phoned me from Max's penthouse and said she had collected her things and would soon be on her way, driving upstate to the cottage.

"'Mother' she said, 'I'm going to stay overnight and get the good long sleep I need. Please don't phone me. I will not answer. I've got something to do. Then everything is going to be as it should be.'

"The following afternoon a state trooper from the Catskills came here, Lenore's body was discovered hanging from the bare, blackened, white oak beneath live mistletoe. Max's offspring had murdered the Lenore of my dreams. The undertaker found this note clenched in Lenore's hand:

"M. dearest,
In the desert a fountain is springing,
In the wide waste there still is a tree,
And a bird in the solitude singing,
Which speaks to my spirit of thee, dearest M.

Forever more, Lenore.'

"So by killing her life Lenore became a goddess."

Rose opened her copy of *The Prophet*, and read:

"The robbed is not blameless in being robbed. The righteous is not innocent of the deeds of the wicked.

"After my divorce I gave Lenore my maiden last name. The people who read about the lovely girl who hanged herself from a tree never knew she was the daughter of the celebrated Park Avenue psychiatrist. Lenore's death did not interrupt Max's honeymoon with his third wife.

"Max cannot harm me further. I have nothing left for him to destroy. I envy people who have faith and the one eternal god bigger than man. Perhaps if I had religion things would have been different.

"Max has had his human sacrifice. And not without first staining his victim with incest.

"Max is now the god he wanted to be."

Mask In The Cage

Joe, the parakeet, seemed ageless. He would escape the cage and flutter against the picture window trying to join the wild birds in the dogwood tree. As Jacqueline or I put him back in the cage he would chirp furiously and bite. He was the only responsibility left in the house. Our two sons had married, my mother-in-law had finally gone to live in an old ladies home, the sheep dog, Shaggy, was stolen, and then we had to take the sick senile black mongrel, Cleo, to the vet and have her put to sleep.

Joe changed. He sang less, and when we opened the door to let him fly he would refuse to leave, and we would have to clean the cage with him in it. One morning Jacqueline uncovered the cage, and found him dead. Jacqueline had wept when the boys left home, and sobbed with the loss of each pet. Those cares gone, she went more frequently to the beauty parlor and dress shops.

For years we had battled, sexed, condemned each other, and threatened to separate. After the parakeet went we became courteous, formal, and uneasily friendly. We saw a TV movie about a housewife and a doctor who met at a railroad station. They were perfect for each other. In the end, when they had to make a decision of breaking up their contented homes and running off, they parted and went back to their mates. I said to Jacqueline, "It's sad when a couple meet too late." She said ingenuously, "Jerome, is it *ever* too late?" I asked, "What would you do if I fell madly in love with a girl and left you?" She answered, "What *could* I do?" I said that after all our years together I would never dream of a new life with another woman.

I was always concerned about creating fiction. My routine was to write stories, help with housework, mow the lawn, gather wood for the fireplace, shop in the supermarkets, walk along the beach, and dig clams. Jacqueline had a few girltalk pals. They collected antiques, swapped recipes, and had little cocktail parties. Occasionally Jacqueline would drive with our neighbor, Myra, to Myra's old folks in Connecticut. After one of our trips Myra said, "Jacqueline and I met an awfully sweet and handsome fellow in a restaurant.

"Charlie Walsh—his sister was with him—he insisted upon paying for our drinks and dinner—he said he had bought a boat that sleeps ten—" Jacqueline added, "He was so kind—and dear he loves your book, *Take My Wife*—" I said, "I'm glad you enjoyed yourself—and with the sport paying first for the evening, you saved me some money." Myra had to say, "Charlie thought we were beautiful, made us feel, and the flattering compliment he gave to Jacqueline!"

I told Jacqueline about my idea to live in the city a while to get material for a novel about skyscrapers. I expected a long face and suspicion of my motives. She said, surprisingly, "You need a change. My poor dear, I've tied you down, and have been on your back. You should have privacy and seclusion."

I had my elation, and said, "I'll be busy studying the city and making notes, reading up on architectures; but, darling, what will you do with yourself?" "Don't worry about me," she answered, "I won't even disturb you with telephone calls. You'll write better." "I'll miss you, lovey," I said. She said, "That's nice."

My Greenwich Village apartment was on the first floor of a renovated old building behind the street building. The living room looked out on a small court, and the bedroom, on an alley. The place was a sanctuary. I set up the typewriter, ream of paper, carbon sheets and reference books on a card table. I vacuumed, rearranged the furniture, stocked the refrigerator, and bought a supply of beer and whiskey.

Jacqueline had a friend in the city, a sexy widow. Over the phone she exclaimed, "Jerome, come to spend the night with you? I wouldn't do that to Jacqueline. You shouldn't have any problem—the city is full of girls—No, I won't tell Jacqueline you called—happy hunting."

The woman in the basement apartment was too fat. A Philippino woman, Betty Corazon, rented the apartment above. She was slender and dark with bee-stung lips and an intriguing monkey-like face.

Jacqueline also had that tight-foreheaded, eyes wide apart simian face. I knew I would fall in love with Betty, and decided to cultivate her slowly. She worked for my publisher, and thought I was a great writer. One night we would have dinner in my apartment, the next in hers. I made no passes. We talked books, and she appreciated my respect.

On a hot overcast Sunday morning I walked to the nearby Hudson River. There was a girl at the end of the pier. She has long yellow hair, a classic face, and wore sandals and a shabby cotton dress. She was talking to the river. It began to rain hard. She started to skip back to the street, I followed. The soaked dress showed her high-breasted, high-hipped figure; the kind that never failed to excite me. I said, "You're getting a rain shampoo." She said, "The rain knows me."

I got her talking. She was Vicky, from Detroit, and lived on east Tenth Street. I thought her an odd one, not difficult to get, and asked her to the apartment for breakfast and drinks. I said, "I can't help noticing your amazingly pointed breasts—are you wearing falsies?" She blushed and answered, "No they're mine." She had come across town to have breakfast with a guy she had never met. I walked with her to a corner tenement on Bedford Street. Before she went in I wrote down her address, and gave her my address and phone number. Curious, I lingered in an opposite doorway. Half an hour later she came out into the rain with a grimy beatnik.

She remained in my mind. I visualized getting her some decent clothes, taking her to Chinatown or Little Italy for dinner, then to the apartment for heady doubles on the rocks. I wouldn't rush the sex part; I would kiss, fondle, caress, and let the fruit fall by itself into my hands. She would stay nights with me. I would have a triple life between Vicky, Betty and Jacqueline. I certainly would not blab my extra lives to Jacqueline. Having the three would give me the stimulating morale and tone to write a bestseller.

The following afternoon I was anxious to be with Vicky, and headed for her place. I saw her buying grapes at a vegetable stand. The sun was shining, and she was barefoot. I tugged her hair. She turned. Her smile was outer-worldly. I paid the Italian woman for the grapes. As we walked through a park, a teen-age beatnik with a knapsack on his back, handed her a scribbled poem. She read it, and her face lighted. I looked at it; it was gibberish. "Do you know him?" I asked. She shook her head. Her street was a Puerto Rican slum. The beatnik trailed us to the door of her flat. She asked him where he lived. He answered, "Like everywhere and like nowhere." "You can stay with me," she said. He pointed to his knapsack, "I've got like an air mattress. It's like I'll see you later."

He took a half-eaten salted pretzel from his pocket and offered to share it. I thanked him and told him to get lost. He saluted me and backed out of the hallway. Vicky had a two room rear flat on the right-handed side of the ground floor. Her bed was a lumpen mattress on the floor. There was a lamp, record-player, a step-ladder, a folding table, and boxes for chairs. By the bed a bony white cat was being suckled by seven famished kittens. Other thin dirty hungry cats were in the room, and more cats were outside the two grated windows, looking in. I was startled by the appearance from the other room of a half-naked bloated man. In his trembling hand he had a beer can filled with whiskey. Vicky introduced him as 'Father Craig.' Tears rolled down his face. He shuddered, "Please don't call me, 'Father.' When I betrayed God I forfeited that right!" He sobbingly told me he had been a Jesuit priest, a teacher of Latin and Greek, author of moral and theological works; but fell insanely in love with a parishioner, and left the church to marry her. After a few years his wife ran off with a girl.

He had me look at the document of his excommunication, and cried, "I am anathema and in purgatory!" He drank the can of whiskey, became incoherent, and passed out. I carried him to his room.

A little Puerto Rican boy came to the window. He asked timidly, "Lady, may I watch the kittens?" Vicky nodded. "I come to see them when you're not here," he said, "Kittens are so pretty and soft. They're not mean like people. My mother lets me bring them home. but when they grow big she throws them out because she says they eat too much." Vicky opened the window-grate and asked him in. They knelt, stroked the kittens, and told each other of their love of stray cars in child words. The boy left, promising to see her and the kittens every day.

The beatnik came back, inflated his air mattress, and put it on the floor in a corner of the room. I gave him a dollar and ordered him to leave the flat and not return until after I left.

In contrast to the filth of the miserable flat Vicky's person was sparkingly fresh. In my youth I despised a girl who gave herself to a middle-aged man, but I felt that should Vicky go to bed with me it would be natural and proper. I was sure I could have her. The waste of conversation was necessary, unavoidable. Her father worked in an auto plant, and her mother was a trained nurse. She had me read a letter from her kid sister, Beth. Beth said home was stuffy and boring, and wanted to come and live with Vicky in New York—to express herself.

Vicky said tonelessly, "My parents worry about sin, bills, neatness, and the clock. I'd rather die than live like them. I left home three years ago when I was sixteen. I've been in many cities. There is no place like New York. New York is beautiful." I said, "I suppose you've had a lover here and there, a normal girl is bound to." She answered without emotion, "I can't count the men I've had sex with." "How is that? What do you mean?" "I was a prostitute for two years in San Francisco." "On your own?" "No. I was in a house. The men were brought to me in my bed in my room—about twenty a day." Shocked, I asked why she did it. She said ecstatically, "When you throw yourself away you have no self to suffer about." "Were you ever diseased or pregnant—weren't you afraid of that?" She shook her head. Well then she was clear so far. Her limpid confession aroused me. I pulled her down onto the mattress. She backed away and got to her feet. "I don't want to do it with you," she said. I had not expected to be denied, and asked her, "What's wrong with me—don't you like me?" "Yes, but I fear you." "Fear me!—How can I hurt you?" "You 'care'; that's why you're an author; and to me caring is worst than death."

I said, "What the hell are you talking about? You've laid for thousands of slobs. All I want is just a little bit of 'it'; come on, be reasonable." She gave me the exasperating answer, "You're the kind of person who thinks. Thinking makes trouble; there is no evil without thinking. People who don't think can't hurt or be hurt. I want to live in a world of people who don't care about anything; who live as though they were never born; who want only the world of nothing."

"Come on, Vicky," I said, "what difference would it make if we have sex for a few minutes? You'll enjoy it." "I probably would," she said, "but you might make me think, and I don't want to think. I want to stay like that cat on the floor. All pain comes from thinking." "Now that you don't work as a prostitute, who do you give yourself to?" "To things that cannot be hurt or demand discipline. I can only give myself to men who are dead to life before they die. The dead do not judge and torture. Your mind frightens me, and our worlds can't mix." I tried to get her to do it for money at least. "I'll buy it from you," I said, "that way it will not involve sentiment and the mind." She would not. She said money was part of the world she feared.

Her face was that of an innocent child. The blue-gray eyes were distant and without light; eyes of a very old woman. They seemed eyes of the dead.

Having compassion for the broken priest, I went afternoons to Vicky's. He couldn't be taken off drink suddenly; I brought him a bottle each time. Having me as a sympathetic audience, he delivered critical orations on the absolutism of the religious hierarchy, and proclaimed histrionically, "At the Last Judgement our Lord will choose between the Vatican's Machiavellian grand inquisitors and my all-too-human sinning self!" As friend and author, I was entitled to go through the cartons of his personal papers.

There were spicy letters from the divorcee, Bertha, who had seduced him from his ordained calling—she said she had a 'certain' magical wand, and signed herself, "Your Golden Girl." Many of his written sermons inveighed against sexual immortality and drunkenness. It was evident that Bertha's 'certain' magical wand drew Father Craig down into the cesspool of damnation. I was thankful that sex did not dominate.—Of course, I was offended by Vicky's nonsensical obstinacy towards my persistent approaches.

One can't help seeing pretty, desirable girls in New York. I did not look at them through the mask indigenous to middle age, but with the prerogative of the author's objectivity. The cunning dimpled knees and cute legs of the small redhead, buying salami and Portugese bread in the unkempt grocery store on the corner, dangled preciously in my vision. The girls who moved me were mine. The fragile Japanese girl sipping beer in the Black Horse Tavern belonged to me and not to the smug balding intellectual escorting her. That went for Beautine, the colored girl, shopping for fresh pike in the fish market, and includes the Chinese girl, Joy Luck, who waited on me in the restaurant. The girls I noted possessing feminine mysteries were blessed by my mental ravishment. It was important only for me to kindle that truth.

I was determined to rehabilitate Father Craig. How he allowed himself to go off balance because of a woman was beyond my comprehension. One of the letters to him read: "Dear John: I can't imagine that you have been really happy—you are too intelligent for that. And there must be down deep a yearning to put things right between God and yourself. You must not think the situation is insoluble. The big thing in life is the salvation of your soul, and that is yours to save, no matter what has happened.

"I shall make this my intention in my daily Mass. Infinita est misericordia Dei.

Sincerely in Christ,
Adam Mann, S.J."

It took me a month to transform Father Craig, and Vicky's flat, and get rid of the beatnik-parasite and his air mattress. When I got through, Father Craig was sober, and the place clean, catless, painted, and furnished pleasantly, In the process Father Craig and I worked to change Vicky into a socially reliable girl. He had taught the deaf and dumb, and accompanied his words with enthusiastic sign-picture gestures. I said to the priest who was groping his way back, "Father, it's our duty to convert Vicky from an immoral existentialist into a proper penitent. We must make her develop a cathartic sense of guilt for her numerous sexual sins so that she will learn remorse, contrition and order." He said I had the Biblical soul of a man of God—which was near the mark. We tried to impress upon Vicky the potential rewarding life held in prospect for her after death. "You know, Vicky," I said, "churches and billions of people throughout history can't be wrong in their belief of the reality of the next world. If we do right in this world we will harvest happiness after we die."

Going past the Women's House of Detention in the Village I saw a very appealing face behind a barred window. The winsome features lingered with me. I went by a few times, but the girl was not there. On Sundays pretty girls came from church services. And there was a percentage of enticing well-shaped girls in subways and on streets. In the meantime my relationship with Betty Corazon in the apartment above was coming along fine; in fact, better than I had hoped—perhaps that was because she was virgin. To improve her grasp of modern literature I gave Betty my copy of *Histoire d'O*.

Vicky responded confusedly as Father Craig and I went about reshaping her mind and values; in our complex day a girl must have some sort of standard. I coaxed her to have dinner at my place. As we walked, an expensively dressed blonde sitting at a Village sidewalk cafe table definitely smiled to me. Her smile was vivid with possibilities. Had I been alone I would have made the stunning blonde's acquaintance. It was just one of those missed opportunities. I shopped at the markets and pushcarts on Bleeker Street and got the makings for a gourmet meal. While I was preparing dinner Betty Corazon phoned. *The Story of O* had furthered my cause. I said I regretted being occupied but that we would get together the following evening.

During dinner I was fascinated by Vicky's high, durable, pointed breasts. I steered the reluctant girl to my bed and undressed her. She was passive; it was like stripping a doll. Her body was more magnificent than I had imagined. She lay supinely, sacrificially, and said in an opaque voice, "You said a girl's flesh is sacred; you said I should marry and have children; you lectured to me like a priest; you said the moral life is the archway to the world to come; and then you do this." "Yes, dear," I explained, "I am different from the ordinary animal man; I am special, and my affection is not without regard and honor and admirable qualities; so you see it is good for you to do 'it' with me only, until—You understand, don't you? I deserve your intimacy as I am changing you into a splendid girl." The contrary creature said, "I don't think I understand you." I told her her cooperation and our mutual relaxation would benefit her. Girls have to be taken and not talked to. Sex is the lily itself, and art, the gilding. I acted. But nothing happened: I was ineffective; and try as I might, hopelessly incapable.

I walked her home, and forcefully pointed out that the negative phenomena was due to my knowledge of her awful promiscuous past, but that I would find a way to circumvent the fact.

The next morning a policeman came to my apartment. He said a girl on East Tenth Street had jumped from the roof. On her body was a note addressed to me: "You were compelling me to begin to care. Care degrades. Care is suffering. Care is intolerable."

The policeman took me to the morgue to identify Vicky. Viewing her corpse, I could only conclude that she had been mental, and that my well-meant efforts would have failed in any event. I thought it would be interesting to watch the autopsy, and received permission. I was struck by the face and form of the young female doctor who assisted at the autopsy. I have noticed that girls who wear glasses generally have good legs. She wore glasses and had fine legs. She did have a certain winning look. I started to leave after Vicky was eviscerated. A decomposing male corpse was brought in. I overheard the orderly say the dead man had been a writer. I was curious to look at the corpse, but the stench coming from it was hideous; and I left wondering who he had been. From there I went to visit Father Craig. He was in his room, drunk, and babbling idiotically. The Vatican knew what they were doing when they dropped him. I realized I had to give him up as a lost cause too.

Betty Corazon had dinner with me that night. I never did tell her about Vicky. People talk too much. What Betty didn't know wouldn't bother her. Betty's voice was the falling of flower petals. Her dainty monkey face was wispy figure delicately expressed nuances of the delectable feminine. She had that exquisite Philippino something. Being with her so easily and justifiably erased my twenty five years bondage to Jacqueline.

Jacqueline? How intelligent nature is out of my sight Jacqueline was not in my mind. I told Betty she was the love of my life; that I would divorce Jacqueline and marry her; and that the disparity of age did not matter as I was not a run of the mill person, but an author. I cited men much older than I, such as Crosby, Picasso and Chaplin. Betty agreed that age was no barrier to love. I knew it would be a cruel blow to Jacqueline, but one's happiness came before anything else. The decision to have a new, pleasurable life was up to me. Betty truly understood me. We would spend much time making love, and travel; she would type for me; we would live selfishly for each other and enjoy life. Betty and I embraced, and kissed. We petted gracefully as we should. I went so far and no further. My restraint endeared me to her.

She was not to think I was a liar and hypocrite leading her to gratify my lust. I even gallantly considered not consummating the physical until we were man and wife in the eyes of God and the law. I wanted her to be convinced of my sincere character. Our mating was to be without the usual masks. It was time for me to become a different man. Then again, if it were fate for us to go to bed before marriage, there would be nothing wrong with that . . . my own mind recognized that reality does not function according to tidy schedules.

At night I was awakened by the neighing of a horse. I could not believe my ears. It seemed the horse was in the kitchen. The neighing came shrill and piercingly three times; each time higher and louder. Then I distinctly heard the urgent stamping of a hoof three times.

I arose, put on the lights, and looked around the apartment. There was nothing to be found. I couldn't get back to sleep for hours. My conscience about leaving Jacqueline was probably playing tricks with me. Getting rid of Jacqueline was going to be an unpleasant bit of business. There would be tears, pleadings, recriminations about her giving me the best years, and then dooming her to loveless loneliness. I thought of delicious, simian, young Betty Corazon, and steeled myself.

Betty had a week's vacation. I told her that as we belonged to each other forever it would not be amiss to enjoy it as a sample period of a husband and wife relationship. She blushed demurely but didn't say no. How wonderful was a new love with a pristine girl; to say, "Betty, you are beautiful; I love you," and melt together in kisses and hot, exciting pressings. After many years of being caged by Jacqueline I was living the way I had secretly wanted to. Every young-minded middle-aged man should have the courage to free himself and live again!

We went to Chinatown, Lincoln Center, art galleries, museums, and took the excursion boat ride up the Hudson. I must admit there were pretty girls in all those places. At night we lay side by side in bed. I did not want to violate her sensitivities; that is to say, I left the anticipated, inevitable moment up to her; as an honest man should. The second night, while holding her in my arms, I heard the horse neighing and stamping out in the kitchen again. "Did you hear that?" I asked. She said, "You mean the fire engines out in the street?—they go night and day—is that what you mean?" "No," I said, "skip it."

The third night, breathing heavily, she silently pulled me atop her. To my utter chagrin, I couldn't do anything.

I apologized, and mumbled that I had had too much to drink. Three nights in a row I failed. I was dismayed, ashamed; I had become as impotent as the grave. I hastened to assure her that there were other ways—sophisticated methods—and began to elucidate. There was disgust, disillusionment, revulsion and pity in her face. She said, "I think we've made a mistake. But let's remain friends." She dressed furiously, and went up to her apartment.

I looked long in the mirror. Graying hair and wrinkles looked back at me; a man who was a caricature of the handsome, romantic image I had refused to depart from. That was all right; I had my Jacqueline. In Jacqueline's eyes I was still the sexy goodlooking guy. Thank God for Jacqueline. To hell with the city—to hell with pretty, young girls too stupid and foolish to value an author; I wasn't going to lower myself to them anymore; unless—. I saw country living in another light—and my darling slave, Jacqueline, too; my always available Jacqueline. Home, and Jacqueline, was my heart. I hoped Jacqueline wouldn't ask me what I had done in the city. If she found out she'd understand—an author should be forgiven many things—I would be Ulysses, worse for the wear, coming home to re-discover dear old Penelope—for it's true-true, marriages are made in heaven, I hoped.

I telephoned home. There was no answer. I got our neighbor, Myra, on the phone. She exclaimed, "Why, Jerome, fancy hearing from you—we thought you went to the great beyond. Jacqueline is just fine—never looked better—has stars in her eyes—the sabbatical has done her a world of good. I really don't see much of her. She's been driving to Connecticut with me, but staying at a motel instead of with me at my old folks. When I see Jacqueline I'll surprise her by telling her you called." I phoned the motel, gave them Jacqueline's name, and asked for her. There must have been some mix-up. They said no one by that name had ever registered or stayed at the motel.

I awoke that night in severe distress. My heart was an immense bird trying to break out of its prison. I could hardly breath, and had shivering pains in my shoulders and arms. I called the operator and gasped that I was having a dreadful heart attack. In my agonized condition I missed my devoted Jacqueline terribly. The two internes who came by ambulance from the hospital were the same doctor and lovely-legged girl I had seen doing Vicky's autopsy. The girl recognized me. She probed me from head to foot. I was embarrassed.

They found nothing wrong with me. My heart-beat and blood pressure were normal. I was indescribably relieved. The girl-interne's name was Irene. There's something suggestive about an 'Irene' who wears glasses.

She said, "Mr. Brooks, your heart-attack was psychosomatic, a nightmare; a result of sub-conscious imagination. It's related to your waking imagination. You're the first author I've met. Oh, if I could only write! I'd give anything to live with an author—it must be fascinating." I said I was sorry for having them race through streets on a false emergency, and made rounds of stiff drinks. On a side I asked Irene, "When you get off duty, why don't you come back—we'll have drinks and fun." She whispered, "You bet—that's a date."

I awakened in a state of peculiar sensation. The bedsheets smelled of an unfamiliar erotic perfume. I could hear the TV in the adjoining room. I thought I had a hangover and was home. The bathroom door opened, and I discerned Jacqueline's trim form. Jacqueline came through the dark to bed. It wasn't the first time I had come out of a drinking spell not knowing what I had done, said, or where I was. But I never felt more electrically virile in my life. After a glorious sex performance with silent Jacqueline, I said, "Jacqueline honey, I behaved myself and thought of you all the time."

She did not answer. "Don't by cynical," I said, "You've got to believe me—who would want an old man like me?—furthermore, you can't possibly prove I've played around." What I said made no impression; it was as though I were not there. A TV commercial blared annoyingly.

I snapped on the light. Not Jacqueline, but an extraordinarily pretty nude woman was lying beside me with her eyes closed. The place wasn't my home in the country. It was my Greenwich Village apartment; but the furniture and color of the walls was different. I heard my name clearly mentioned on TV. I went into the living room. There was a man asleep in the armchair. The eleventh hour newscaster was saying, "The outspoken widow of the author, Jerome Brooks, married the millionaire yachtsman, Charles Walsh the Third." Then followed film shots of my Jacqueline, and this guy, Charles Walsh, gaily taking off for their honeymoon on his boat, the Jacqueline I. The newscaster continued, "Life does go on—last month's tragedy-stricken Mrs. Jerome Brooks is today's rich, happy, smiling Mrs. Charles Walsh the Third. In a recent candid interview, the new bride advised girls not to marry authors—she said they were impossible and that their romance was all in their heads.

"You may recall that the decomposed body of author, Jerome Brooks, was found in his Greenwich Village apartment—death apparently due to a heart attack." So 'nice,' 'kind,' Charles Walsh the Third was the reason Jacqueline blithely let me have privacy and freedom in the city!

Anyway, I had been released from the cage of the flesh without knowing or feeling it. The After-Life is great—like me, everyone will find that out. The woman in the bed shouted, "Milton—remember it's you who has to get up early and go to work—The goddam TV is driving me crazy—and sleep on the divan—all of a sudden I'm bushed—and I rest better alone." The man shut off the TV. I wanted to get back into bed with the beautiful stranger, but I began to diminish, and disappear in the glowing, receding eye of the television tube.

Win A Kewpie Doll

'Curly' Chambrun was a thin bachelor with wavy dyed hair, dentures and a waxed mustache. He had a kewpie doll stand in Coney Island. Customers put their dimes on the numbers painted on the counter; he spun the wheel of chance; the winners had their choice of dolls, and he picked up the coins. It was more pleasure for him than work. In his French-accented pitch he spoke of his dolls as if they were lovely live girls. Being a bit of a ventriloquist he would hold amorous conversations with the dolls for the entertainment of the crowd.

Kewpie dolls flourished in the carefree Valentine era of the 'teens and 'twenties, and were not easy to get. That was no problem for Curly. He had come from a family of doll makers. When Coney Island closed down for the winter, Curly made dolls in his house behind the stand. Every doll was his Galatea, or what girls should be; as he said.

"Saucy, voluptuous, with frills and spangles, ribbons, beads, jewels, lipstick, rouge, mascara, with a touch of perfume; wearing dresses to enhance their breasts, callipygian rears, and cunning dimpled knees, yet suggesting a chaste soul."

Curly was a lover of love, and liked to think he was all the great lovers of the ages combined. The walls of his stand were decorated with hearts and girls' kissing lips. There was a rapport between whores and his dolls. Whores came from far and wide to his stand, melted by the sight of his dolls. His dolls found affection and homes in many a whorehouse. He worshipped at the shrine of prostitutes—"Courtesans," he called them; and they revered him as a patron saint. "Man," he would say, "comes from the lowly dust, but woman, ah! she was created from flesh! Eve taught Adam the delights of love before she became his wife. She was the first courtesan, and the story of the human race is built around her bed." He was the knight errant of whores; a Dante who uplifted every fallen woman to the vision of a beatific Beatrice. Curly honored Rahab and all the harlots of the Bible as though he had known them personally. His unique partiality to whores wasn't quite just a whim of traditional French chivalry.

As a youth, after he had landed in America, he fell dangerously ill, starving and freezing on a Bowery sidewalk. People passed him by. But, an old whore took him to her room. She nursed him back to health, and provided him with sex, clothes, money and courage.

Curly never bothered to seek male companionship. His social life in Coney Island consisted of a harem of three courtesans. These adorants came without fail on their weekly pilgrimage to his house. Muriel and Beautine were free-lancers, and Vicky worked in a whore mill. They were strong stout girls, much taller than Curly. None was actually pretty.

Muriel and Beautine, bleached blonde widows who had seen better days, shared a Manhattan apartment, and were third rate call-girls for the visiting firemen of hotel conventions. Beautine had two children who lived with her mother in Queens. Vicky worked in a cheap Greenwich Village house.

The interior of Curly's house was furnished in 19th century French style, elegant and cosy. He would exclaim to the girls, "You are now in Paris, the true Paradise of ladies."

With him there were none of the ugly terms and realities of their profession, He shed for them their whore-identities. He bestowed upon them the names of celebrated courtesans. Muriel became Phryne, the mistress of Praxiteles; Beautine was Manon Lescaut, the light of Chevalier Desgrieux's life, and young Vicky, Lesbia, beloved by Catullus. They never arrived in 'Paris' empty-handed. Despite his protests they brought their epicurean host vintage vines and gourmet foods. In 'Paris' behind the doll stand he was not Curly but 'Monsieur Le Comte Honore de Chambrun,' and the girls, 'Le Comtesse Phryne, Manon and Lesbia.' Each visit was a memorable holiday replete with delicate manners, dining, music and poetry, not to mention lessons in French. The following soiree was more or less typical: While Debussy music played the Countesses set the silver, china and linen around the candelabra on the table. As the fine dinner was leisurely eaten the Count reminded them of the enchanting personalities.

"Comtesse Phryne, after Apelles saw you on the seashore naked with disheveled hair he painted his Venus Anadyomene, which was placed in the temple of Apollo at Delhi. When you were accused of impiety and about to be condemned, you unveiled your beauteous bosom, which so influenced your judges, that you were immediately acquitted."

"Manon, mon cherie, though Desgrieux has been told of your alleged infidelities he says to you, 'Je T'aimais d'autant plus.' He loves you the more."

Then, pretending to be Catullus, and Vicky, Lesbia, old Curly said fervently in poetic voice, "Let us live and love, my Lesbia! Give me a thousand kisses, then a hundred, then another thousand, then a second hundred; or as the many stars that in the silence of night behold men's furtive amours; to kiss you with so many kisses is enough and more for your madly fond Catullus."

To cap the night came Curly's specialty, the feast of eros, in which he was supreme.

How girls who had worked hard on their backs the week long could thrill to aging Curly in bed may seem incredible. It was not so much Curly as it was Curly's little black bag. They didn't know about the little black bag. In that little black bag was that with which Curly delivered the joyous coup, the certain master-stroke so dear to womankind. Curly had guarded for many years the secret of the black bag.

As a gentleman, he sooner would have died than let any girl in on that mysterious black bag.

Curly was an accomplished romanticist. There was none of the disgusting modern one-two-three with him. To him a 'courtesan' was a divine organ of which every complicated key, chord and stop of her senses had to be duly played upon with irresistible virtuosity. He thought like Michelangelo—the beauty, the passion, was in the supine stone; it was up to the artist to bring it out. His preparations for love were as artistic as the approach to French cooking, with one measured and effective consideration after another.

"Miladies," he said, "the heart, the mind and psyche, must revel simultaneously with the bones, flesh and blood in the symphony of love."

Where else in the world but with Curly could a 'courtesan' be so rapturously elevated in feminine value? Under his roof they were nobility and had souls. There was no jealousy. They vied in their generosity to share him.

Curly knew that women should be given beautiful illusions; not deprived of them. His little black bag was his Pandora's box, and it was best for the girls to remain totally unaware of that holy of holies.

His oriental bedroom was a temple of love. The fortunate courtesan admitted could have by the light of candles, choice lingerie, panties and perfumes. Before the exorcisms of the silken-sheeted soft bed strewn with fresh flowers, she had to ritualistically drink a full portion of Curly's sacred 'elixir of love.' The elixir was Curly's own concoction of old-fashioned cough syrup spiked with a powerful dose of illicit aphrodisiacal drug. Soon after, Phryne, Manon, or Lesbia—no matter which—it affected them all the same—lay on the bed in erotically triggered euphoria. In the semi-obscurity old Curly would steal open his precious little black bag, and reach for one of his assortment of huge, propitious phalli.

The girls thought surely it was Curly himself who sent them to heaven and back. And they would leave Curly's 'Paris' with stars in their eyes, and another Kewpie doll, to face the next prosaic week of hustling. Last winter Curly decided to take the girls to Bermuda. They were excited as if instead of a three week cruise they were going on a trip around the world. There was much shopping for clothes, swim suits and baggage. Curly bought the girls to the pier in a hired limousine. Passengers were awed by the French Count and his nieces who were respectfully directed to their first-class luxury staterooms. The Captain insisted they dine with him at his table. The ship's doctor and officers danced with the girls and sought their company. By the time the Victoria Regina arrived in Bermuda the girls had received marriage proposals from various of the smitten passengers. In Bermuda, as on the ship, Curly and the girls changed their clothes three times a day. They were the prize guests of the hotel. The girls wore modest swim suits and frolicked like kittens in the hotel pool. At the manager's table they let fall innocent little French expressions that Curly had taught them. Under the azure sky they went in horse-drawn carriages to the churchs and historical sites, bought native souvenirs and packets of postcards.

They had been in Bermuda only ten days, but as the Victoria Regina's departing whistle blew there was a small but impressive crowd of friends to wave them farewell. Upon the calm sea the weather was perfect. The band was softly playing nostalgic native music. The girls, tanned and happy as in a dream, were relaxed in deck chairs by Curly. Suddenly he gasped and clutched his chest.

Curly lay dying in his stateroom. Phryne, Manon and Lesbia wept. They said they would give up their professional careers and come to live with him in his Coney Island 'Paris.' Oh, they would care for him and the doll stand and be one happy family forever. The Captain, doctor, and a minister stood by sadly. Curly had two last requests; the will said of giving the girls his cash and property, and, that a certain little black bag among his effects be buried with him.

In his coffin he resembled an aristocratic sparrow. After the girls went to their cabin there remained the task of closing the coffin and sending it down to the baggage hold. The Captain felt it his duty to know the contents of the little black bag. He took it to a side and looked in. He then placed it in the coffin with Curly and sealed the coffin. The doctor and the minister were curious about the bag. He answered with a wink, "It was a handy kit."

And Your Sister Too!

His card read, "Hollis Nicky . . . . Investigator . . . . Real Estate . . . . Mortician . . . . Church Of The Second Coming . . . . Little Rivers, Florida . . . . Home of Mother Nature."

It was 1944. Dolly and I were on our Honeymoon, planning to winter off the beaten track on Florida's lower west coast.

We had seen him outside the office, and made inquiries. "Been here all my life," he said, "They call me 'Hicky Nicky.' Little Rivers sure is God's own paradise." Chesty Hicky Nicky had black-dyed hair, a blotchy complexion, moved like a dog walking upright, and spoke with a toothy, lisping-hissing animation. He wore a seersucker suit, ventilated shoes, a loud shirt, bow tie, and an imitation Panama.

"I traveled this State inside and out with my pa sellin' snake oil. Little Rivers can't be beat.

"Best shrimpin' and fishin' in the whole world. We got citrus and pecan groves and mighty nice folks. You're in the garden spot of the U-nited States, and I have the lace you want."

Hicky Nicky drove an antique Packard hearse. We followed "Pussycat," as he affectionately called the hearse, to the four-unit house on one of the rivers. The pink and cream modern stucco building was scheduled among Palm and Moss trees a few minutes walk from the Gulf. Dolly liked the apartment. I unpacked our car, and went with Hicky Nicky in the hearse to the office.

On the way back he confided. "Last tenant was a movie star. Ole rich husband was a jealous soul. After I gave him my hell-fire pitch on Babylon the whore he hired me to keep her from the sin of adultery. One night his Cadillac wouldn't stir. He called me to taxi her. I pitched her a sermon that had her weepin' . . . an' then whoooeee! I dicked her here in Pussycat where the coffin sets."

He stopped by a shanty-houseboat on the river. A sign said, "Fanny Fuggs . . . Fish." He introduced me to Fanny, a hearty, redheaded amazon. There were children swarming about.

As the hearse purred along he snickered. "Thems my kids. Every time Joe Fuggs sails out after fish I dick Fanny. Fanny's powerful. Like dickin' a gorilla. Yes siree brother, the Good Books says a dickin' a day keeps the doctor away. That's how I do."

Dolly put her hair brush on the window still to air. The next morning it was gone. I told her to forget about it and buy a new one. She insisted upon making a big deal out of the incident. That particular brush had the bristle that suited her best; the handle had the right feel; a woman's hair was her crowning glory . . . she was very upset . . . what would men do if women had no hair? . . . no man could possibly realize how much the care of her hair means to a woman . . . and on and on and on about hair and brushes. I spent hours searching for the damn brush. To her the disappearance of her brush from the window sill was a great significant mystery. She harped on that hair brush until the mystery was cleared up . . . which was a month later.

Cynthia, the leggy blonde next door, invited us for drinks. She had a toddler son, an elderly sweet Virginian mother, and a schoolteacher sister, Elizabeth.

There were many pictures of her husband, Clay, a captain in the Air Force. He was the model homo Americanus from Frank Merriwell to dashing young Douglas McArthur at West Point.

My Patriotic D A R bride almost drained her kidneys admiring the eagle of the football and battle fields. We had missed meeting him by a few hours. He had been home on furlough and had left early the morning after we moved in.

Dolly studied Captain Clay's pictures. "Oh, Cynthia dear," she said, "Clay's gorgeous hunk of man! He's Cary Grant, Clark Gable and Gary Cooper rolled into one! How lucky you are . . . you must be mad about him . . . I don't blame you!" I couldn't stomach that crap. I would have liked to put horns on the tall, handsome bastard.

Cynthia had one of those faces wth a permanent expression of surprise. She talked as though she were running. "Clay flies the hump in India. I was pregnant. We had a house on Miami Beach. He brought home monkeys, parrots, snakes and codamunda bears . . . my backyard was a zoo.

"I poked the food into their cages with a long stick. They were males. All the nasty things did was eat, fight, mount each other, and play with themselves.

"There were hurricane warnings. People boarded up their houses and left. I was worried about Clay's awful creatures and stayed on. The hurricane hit and broke open the cages. My labor pains came. I called the police. There was murder going on in the backyard. The bears were after the monkeys. I picked up a broom and swatted at the bears. The police car barely made it. Two policemen delivered me while the bears ate up the monkeys . . . nuts . . . guts . . . and feathers!"

Cynthia wanted to know why she nightly dreamed she was in an outhouse when from the empty seat beside her would rear up the head of a snorting white stallion.

There was the greasy, sullen fellow who had the apartment above Cynthia. "He came weekends with a dame," Cynthia said, "He doesn't even say hello . . . he's either with the mafia or the FBI. I hear her kick off her high heels . . . a minute later his shoes hit the floor . . . one . . . two . . . then the bed sounds like it has asthma . . . He ought to oil the springs."

She told us of a society woman she met at a bridge party.

"I visited her. She said, 'Cynthia, take a shower with me.' I told her I just came from the shower. 'That's alright,' she answered, 'Have one with me; then we'll go to bed, darling.' I didn't want another shower. Now, what did she have in mind?"

Cynthia was scrubbing the ceiling of her car. She explained, "I was driving along the highway . . . picked up a babyface sailor . . . he worked his hand onto my knee . . . I read that when rapists are crossed they kill . . . didn't say a word . . . turned on the radio . . . Roosevelt was making a speech . . . he played with himself . . . enormous . . . then he buttoned up and said, 'Do you mind if I smoke?' . . . shook my head . . . shook my head . . . when he got off he tipped his hat and said, 'Thank you, kindly, Mam' . . . Why do men play with themselves . . . ?"

Hicky Nicky dropped by, trying to make Elizabeth. He was full of odd knowledge: the population of Rangoon, Egyptian embalming methods, signs of the zodiac. We went shrimping with him at the end of the pier. The shrimp leaped and skimmed the water in the glare of our lights as we netted them.

He tore off their cockroach-like heads, slipped off their shells and ate them raw. He considered himself a Floridian gourmet and offered to cook us raccoon, opossum, the giant tree-climbing river crab and alligator sweetbreads.

Hicky Nicky took me to The Church of the Second Coming. It was a long drive inland to the pine woods and glades of the hidden cracker world. In the moonlight the territory reminded me of the eerie landscape of the Krazy Kat cartoons with its lumpen shapes and brooding spaces.

On a clearing near a turpentine mill was the church, a barn. About three dozen groups arrived in pick-up trucks, by foot, and in jalopies. They were a sallow, squint-eyed, towheaded lot seeming from another planet. But there was something inbred and weirdly sexually appealing about the thin, high-hipped, high-breasted, hunched, ratty-featured girls.

Congregated on benches in the barn they began slowly and innocently enough, singing, "Happy Am I with My Redeemer," clapping and stamping.

Hicky Nicky went into his shout-preaching. He plunged through the Bible back and forth, confusing the Testaments, dates, characters and events. He had the Bible's harlots plying their wares in the Garden of Eden, St. Michael at the battle of Jericho, and Moses changing the Cana wedding water into wine, while the crackers continuously cried, "Hallelujah!"

Gallon tins of moonshine appeared. I joined in the prodigious drinking. The corn liquor had the taste of anti-freeze. Everyone became his own minister, holding incomprehensible dialogues with God. They shook and shimmied, jumped, danced and rolled in the dirt. There was an uncanny build-up of contagious rhythmic hysteria producing the most aphrodisiacal sensations.

The lights went out.

Hicky Nicky shouted, "Brothers and Sisters, Gee-zuz Kee-rr-eye-st wants us to love and dick each other for His glory AND OUR SALVATION!"

Then began the wildest sex free for all, accompanied by an orgiastic baying of pornographic words. In the shadows possessed fathers, mothers, husbands, wives, sons, daughters, brothers, sisters, relatives, friends, neighbors and strangers drunkenly had no ages or identities.

My head was pounding from the moonshine. I was whirled in the erotic vortex. I screamed the delighting obscenities with the rest. A female form lurched against me. I grabbed her. She might have been one of the little public girls with milky corn silk, or a sour sibylline crone. I'll never know. My senses were expanding and racing through the cosmos. I passed out cold.

I came to in Hicky Nicky's hearse. He had placed me in a casket. It was dawn. I was nauseated and covered with vomit.

As he drove, Hicky Nicky was whistling, "Praise the Lord and pass the ammunition."

My wife was a regular Medea towards other attractive women. I suspected that her cozy patronizing of Cynthia had some subconscious connection with Captain Clay. Her honey-tongued curiosity about Cynthia's Star-spangled superman bugged me. The only women I'd trust were the unborn and the dead. Why should I trust a woman when I didn't trust myself?

Cynthia's mother, Mammaw, told Dolly the kind of crap she loved to hear: Clay's boyhood on the adjoining plantation, Black Ankle, in dear old 'Virginny' how; good and charitable young 'Mars' Clay was to the homely 'negras' who would have laid down their lives in an instant for him; Clay 'ramrod straight' in his Southern military school uniform 'a-courtin' Cynthia; gentleman Clay the champion athlete, Beau Brummel, ham radio operator, Rhodes scholar, shining and promising light of the State Department in 'Washington Dee Cee,' and Clay the spit and polish do or die fearless 'Air Force aviator.' An' my wife did think Clay would make a stunning President in the White House, and what the hell not!

Cynthia was notified that Clay's plane had not returned from a mission and was presumed lost. Dolly wept and went to church with

Cynthia to pray. She had never seen the guy, but the way she carried on one would have thought it was I who was among the dead and missing in a far land.

As fed up as I was with the Captain Clay business I had to keep my feeling to myself and pretend sympathy as the guy had sacrificed his life for our country.

That wasn't the blessed end. A week later news came that sounded like a scenario for Gung Ho. Clay's plane had been shot down behind enemy lines. He was the sole survivor. He killed a whole Jap patrol and made his way over mountains, through jungles and across a desert, and was being flown back to the States very much decorated.

Wasn't there anything that manly charming bastard could do wrong? Did my wife have to exult and say, "I knew God would save Clay . . . he's too fine to die!" Was I going to have to wear horns on my honeymoon?

Clay came back, but not to his family. He stayed in Miami Beach, and made it plain that he did not want to see Cynthia.

Then to my joy I discovered that Clay wasn't perfect! Dolly, Cynthia and Elizabeth were on the patio outside my bedroom window. I had slept late, and awakened to hear Cynthia saying to Dolly,

"I've only had sex once with Clay . . . on our wedding night. . . we were both virgin . . . and he was stoned . . . that's how I became pregnant. He never came to bed with me since." Astonished, Dolly said, "Once in three years? What is he, a century plant?"

"Night after night I expected it. You'd think sex didn't exist. I wouldn't dare bring up the subject. Clay is so dignified. He made me feel as if my bedroom was one of his offices in the State Department. Lord, no one has more fastidious manners than Clay."

As the conversation went on, my wife, the self-appointed psychologist, hinted that perhaps there was something wrong in Clay's background, or with her, that deterred him from his sporting duty. What crap I heard!

Did Clay have a trauma about his mother? Maybe he was trying to protect her from a venereal disease acquired from a toilet seat. Cynthia should avoid asparagus as it creates a disagreeable odor you know where. How about breast-building exercise? Season his food highly.

Entice him when he has hangover lust. Maybe the lights should be on . . . or off? Why not try for matinees? Perhaps she's too anxious? A girl should hold something back. Use separate bathrooms and hide soiled undies to maintain the delicate romantic illusion.

Cynthia checked herself for bad breath and B O. She had tried suggestive French panties, Hindu lingeries, had every facial, shampoo, perfume, lipstick and powder; attempted telepathy, hypnosis, and wore sheer stockings and fancy garters to bed. Nothing worked.

"There's another woman . . . or women," concluded Dolly, "It's the nature of the beast." Cynthia didn't think so, and hesitated to tell why. Elizabeth said eagerly, "Dolly, you'd never guess in a million years what Clay did instead of going to bed with Cynthia!"

Cynthia said, "I'd buy a hair brush . . . use it a few times . . . and never see it again. I asked myself, 'What in heaven's name happens to my hair brushes?' One night I would have sworn Clay had a woman with him in his room. He was making all the noises. I was afraid to find out. The next morning my hair brush was gone. I bought one of those electric scalp massaging hair brushes. Another night I heard funny sounds again and thought he either had a woman or was in distress.

"I went to his room and snapped on the light . . . Clay was whanging away with my electric brush! Do all men play with themselves?" My Dolly was stumped and wondered how Cynthia could ever compete with a hair brush.

So, I take the trouble to go to Bergdof's in the ice and snow, select and buy Dolly an expensive English hair brush as one of her wedding gifts . . . drive it all the way to Florida . . . and that character, not even knowing us, and leaving early in the morning to go off to war, steals it from our window sill to get his disgusting rocks! Dazzling Captain Clay wasn't perfect!

Old Mammaw kept asking, "When is Clay coming home?" Clay had no intentions of coming back to Little Rivers. Dolly was positive that Clay had a mistress in Miami Beach. Cynthia was becoming a nervous wreck, and Elizabeth along with her. Cynthia hired Hicky Nicky to tail Clay and find out what he was up to.

After a week Hicky Nicky returned triumphantly. We were having drinks on the patio.

"Tracked loverboy down like a bloodhoun'. Clay has a hotel room . . . but shacks up with a gash . . . Elaine Henry . . . divorced . . . goes to her place at night . . . gets in the saddle and rides for ole glory . . . clocked him . . . bet he rides the range five times in a row . . . then goes back to his hotel lookin' like the cat that swallowed the rat . . . This Elaine Henry's got a beauty shop . . . but can't figger it . . . an alligator's prettier than her . . . now we'll bust in, get pictures of him in the saddle and the case'll be in the slot." Cynthia's eyes opened wide. She exclaimed, "Beauty parlor! Hair Brushes! He doesn't touch the woman . . . He goes to her apartment to have sex with the used hair brushes that she brings him from her beauty parlor . . . that's Clay's love affair!" Hicky Nicky didn't understand. I explained. He peered at Cynthia and shook his head. "Mam, there's somethin' radically wrong here." Hicky Nicky pondered deeply, and finally arrived at the solution.

"You know what you need to straighten this mess out, Mam?" Cynthia asked anxiously, "What, mister Nicky, what?" He answered emphatically, "You need a good fucking." Then he pointed to Elizabeth. "An' your sister too!"

Sugar, Spice And Everything Nice

I was in front of the Manhattan Hilton with the Italian television crew who were to do a documentary about me, and what I thought of the land Columbus discovered. It was the afternoon of the nation-wide protest against the undeclared criminal American invasion of Vietnam and Cambodia.

My eyes were on the police. I am profoundly interested in, and concerned about, the weapon-bearing civil guardian species, particularly in view of the fact that the mark of the beast is still clearly discernible in all the mental and moral faculties of the will-less, faceless, non-genius, common man, the herd man.

The term *police* is from the Latin, *politia*, meaning, broadly, policy. Policy in turn implies social sagacity, statecraft, prudent conduct.

The man privileged to use lethal arms, whether upon orders, or according to his own discretion, has localized within the entity of his physical being and cerebral consciousness awesome, godlike power.

I demand to know the physiological and psychological realism about police. I've observed them individually and collectively (there's insufficient rapport between the armed servants of the people and the people) (one is usually ill at ease with a cop—something important is lacking) (cops just don't look right in civilian clothes; seem misbegotten, misplaced and profane) (and, seriously, cops have told me that there is a very fine line that separates them from the enterprising criminal).

I feel for the underpaid, frustrating situation of the lawman, I want to empathetically follow him into his home and realize the clinical truths about his cultural and spiritual exercises, and witness for posterity his intimate actions as husband, father, and member of the religious community.

The police should be college graduates, and paid three times more than they now receive. The policeman should be versed and at home with the humanities, the classics, the great composers, history and the social sciences. The police and the National Guard should be on television in intelligence comparisons with the campus boys and girls. But the shocking abyss between the IQ's of the cop and the student he tries to kill is what it's all about, too.

Christ said, "Ye have eyes and ye see not."

My eyes were on the police, and I saw. The ordinary cop (who would never get anywhere, and have to moonlight and do "tricks" for their families whom they love) were champingly fingering their clubs, awaiting the signal from the brass.

I knew exactly what was going to happen; knew it as though it were a movie about to be shot, and I had written the scenario.

The marchers carried coffins, the names and towns of the young American dead soldiers, babies, and blown-up pictures in color of the My Lai massacre. My attention was diverted from the police by the never-to-be-forgotten picture by photographer Haeberle of the Vietnamese kid who pushed his tot brother to the ground and covered him with his beautiful frail self to shield him from American bullets. It was no use, as True Grit John Wayne said, American soldiers are expert riflemen.

Cops looked at their watches. It was time.

There is a time for dishonor.

Fear-spreading sirens screamed. Cop cars and vans converged. The marchers were crowd at that point. Stocky, anxious, armed, rednecked hard-hats from crime-infested unions jumped joyfully from the vans. (Oh, why are they tattooed?) They and the obvious cops charged into the marching booklovers, kicking, cursing, punching, and swinging clubs and blackjacks in their stellar utmost . . . to kill.

They did not attack singly; two, three or four worked on one protester, digging their clubs into his or her stomach, bashing faces and heads; and the blood of pacifists was as red as the blood on the fallen My Lai posters.

I had been through it all as a youth. The stout, muscular type, that become cops, asylum and prison guards, were the same. And I had not changed in my no-quarters, furious, inner reaction to cowardly brutality.

It reminded me that I had an experience with cops to tell. In that experience a cop ended up dead. I often thought about that incident. I guess it was a question of how to write it. (I remember what the dying author in "The Snows of Kilimanjaro" said about the stories he had planned and didn't put on paper: "Maybe you could never write them, and that was why you delayed the starting.")

I admitted to myself that the cop story was one of the many I had laid out with an honest, straightforward direction—only to play the imaginative artist with it and screw is up. So I said to myself, "Pretend you're dying; then recall the ideas, characters and incidents that could have made short stories. Write them in a straight line and fast as you won't have the time to meander off track and screw up. When you have nothing to lose because all is lost anyway, you don't have to kiss trend-asses, and you think tough and hit hard . . ."

Beholding the police cause bloodshed I remembered that long ago my young, sweet love of the sex act with girls was responsible for the death of a cop. Well, no, perhaps not actually responsible, but my lust was the A that led to the unforeseen tragic B; my uncontrollable need for sex that night sent the cop to his appointment in Samarra. Maybe it was just God's will that that cop died violently.

It was 1927, the tail end of Mitchell Palmer's Great Red Scare, that launched young short-nose, fawn-eyes J.E. Hoover on his quest for the Holy Grail. And the night of the mock funeral for Sacco and Vanzetti in Webster's Hall near Union Square. That's where I first saw lovely, leggy Susie Goldstein. She looked at the wall poster showing the two Italians behind bars, and Vanzetti's words to hell-damned, craven Judge Thayer about the shoemaker and fish peddler who loved humanity and were heroic enough to live at peace with their fellowmen.

A phonograph was playing the "Internationale." To the eye Sacco and Vanzetti were really corpses in the coffins. The loveliness of Susie Goldstein bent tearfully over the coffins and kissed the foreheads of the two electrocuted dreamers. How sensuously appealing is a beautiful "cause" girl at the wake of martyrs! In somber setting transfiguration becomes the vagina; of which much can be said.

I was wearing beret and trench coat; so was Susie. She liked the way I sadly smiled—fitting the occasion—and said tenderly, "Hello . . ."

Cops and patriots desecrated the funeral; they charged about madly tearing down all signs of propaganda. Then they destroyed the flimsy imitation coffins; and the marvelous death masks of Sacco and Vanzetti were left scattered bits of painted clay.

I was going to write now that Susie and I went for Russian-Yiddish food in the radicals' co-op where there were modernist revolutionary murals; and she told me her father deserted the family and that she had tried suicide when she was ten—putting her head in the gas oven—and a neighbor smelled the gas and came in and prevented the suicide. But Susie wasn't the girl, and the place was not in Webster's Hall and the mock Sacco and Vanzetti funeral.

I was going to swear and say it was Stella Eiderlon, the Romanian-Jewish Venus who lived at Eight Landscape Avenue in Yonkers—but I had used Stella in a *Playboy* story. (No girl could approach Stella's perfect beauty. When I did make up my mind to marry Stella it was too late—I learned she had married a pathologist and they had gone to live and be citizens in the State of Israel.)

All right, I'll confess then that the girl was Liz, a tall svelte black. That's not true; in the Twenties Negros seemed light years away from any participation in a progressive movement; and anyway, Liz was the German caretaker's wife on the Isle of Pines.

The girl of the cop's death episode was Myra, the juicy Irish Catholic virgin Communist who signed her letters to me, "Yours in Comrade Christ!" I would have done anything to have her. To get in good with her I joined the Communist Party that night; under an assumed name, of course; I think I put myself down as Peter Phillips (my father's foster-father's name was Di Phillipi). The Communist Party and the *Daily Worker* were in the building now occupied by Kleins' Department Store. The Communist Party office was small, looked like a storeroom for trash, and was run haphazardly by stray volunteers. So no one knew what the hell was going on, and no one cared what name you signed under—as no one believed anyone else.

The Italian saying goes, "If it's not true, at least it's well said." And that was the spoiler, imagination, butting in again. Myra wasn't even born then—she's young enough to be my daughter; she's divorced, has two kids (what would I do with them?) and is supremely delicious. Myra—ah, wishful thinking.

When fancy—which is the conceited, peculiar conception of what is "literary"—fails, and the story resists and eludes, I relax and tell the truth.

I was laying bricks for the Turner Construction Company on the Cadillac building by Columbus Circle. Three nights a week I attended engineering classes at the City College of New York. After work I'd change my clothes in the masons' shanty; and I'd go to Union Square for a bit of dinner; listen to soapbox orators like Anna Louise Strong, Carlo Tresca, Elizabeth Gurley Flynn, Jay Lovestone, Robert Minor, William E. Foster, and crackpots of all kinds, and then give myself time to get uptown to C.C.N.Y. by subway.

Well, social protest is not the answer to being oversexed. The God's truth is that I went to Union Square hoping to get some of the Communist alleged "free love" and that's it. Unfortunately, the sandaled, leather-jacketed, Russian-hatted-and-bloused, red-reputed "free lovers" were hairy, greasy, onion-and-herring-smelling, unkempt, misshapen frights. Granted that they were courageous, social-minded, class-conscious, visionary girls and women, but—!

The girl involved with the happening of the cop getting killed was at the co-op serve-yourself bagels and lox counter. We both had berets and trench coats, and took to each other. She spoke with a German accent in a strange, guttural, off-tone voice; an eerie voice, like another-world voice coming through a medium. Her name was Arletta. (That's not true—Arletta was the landlady of my Perry Street, Greenwich Village apartment, many-many years after the night of the cop's humiliating death.) She was Lottie. (That's a twist; Lottie is the statuesque white-haired housekeeper of a rich friend.) The girl was Vicky. (Dammit no; Vicky was the weird, fey, hippie I recently tried to cunnilingue and lay in the clandestine Perry Street apartment while I was trying to write an impossible book about skyscrapers for Doubleday; nor am I going to bring in the Playboy bunny I knew who had gotten the clap from a junkie.)

I give up; I can simulate no further; the unexciting fact of the matter is that for the life of me I cannot recall the girl's name, although I remember every detail about her physically, the dialogue, the cop's fatal wound and his corpse, and the rest.

The date I cannot forget, as it was the night of the execution of Sacco and Vanzetti, August 23, 1927. I could tell that under the belted trench coat and the girl was sleekly built. Her sandals showed long, slender feet; she had sparkling, fresh-rubbed skin, dark gold hair; but in the clean, perfect face were old, faded-blue eyes; eyes discharged of light, eyes that seemed the dispassionate eyes of a mummy, the released, equipoised eyes of nirvana. She spoke in a Trilby voice of disturbing contralto enchantment.

I knew how to talk to mother, sister, aunt, and nuns, but I never knew how to talk to the girl I wanted. Perhaps it's that nature and talking don't mix. Also, as much as I fought against being a hypocrite, the Catholic soul-saver, the Holy Roman moralist in me always came out and intruded upon the scene. I could not have sex without my spying watching. I don't think I'd want it any other way.

I paid for her tray; we sat at a table and I'm sure I talked nonsense in my sex-wrought voice.

There must have been a hundred thousand people in the park across the way. The Union Square crowds were looking at the floor above the co-op where the office of the Communist newspaper, *The Daily Worker*, ran huge bulletins about Sacco and Vanzetti. The people received the news that first Sacco, and then Vanzetti had been put to death in the electric chair. A hush fell over the people. Then there were murmurings. The murmurings grew and wrathful cries broke out against Capitalism. Cops on foot, horseback, on motorcycle and in motorcycle sidecars went berserk attacking the people. It was surrealistic to sit comfortably watching the bluecoats try to kill. Quarter-inch Pittsburgh plate glass separated me from the pandemonium. But the awful sounds came through the window front; the noises of pain, police sirens, hoofbeats, screeching brake, auto horns, pounding feet, gunshots, prayers.

There is only one obscenity: violence upon the unarmed and defenseless. The faces of men following orders to blindly kill are disgusting, pornographic, and grotesquely funny. I've seen the faces of murderous police in the violent and incontinent wards of mental hospitals. And I've also seen such faces on the soulless, cold-blooded fish in the mad predatory depths.

The girl became inspired and said, "Let's go out there into the magic circle of danger! Let's court the beauty and success of death!" "Out there" wasn't for me. She talked about luring fate, cleansing storms and wars and divine catacylsms, going "all the way," throwing yourself into the bottomless pools of shame and finding redemption through sin and destruction. I didn't know what she was talking about. All I knew was that crazy hell was going on "out there," and I wanted her in bed in the worst way. She got up and ran happily "out there." Like a fool I went with her out into the madness.

Someone running from the cops stuck a placard in my hand. With that a flock of cops attacked us. I was terrified. Clubs, fists and feet came at me from all directions. Had I a machine-gun I would have used it with all my mind, body and soul.

We darted through a small opening among the cops and ran. We went to a drugstore on Fourteenth Street and received sympathetic first aid. The girl's nose was broken, and her beret was gone. I had black eyes, swollen lips, bruises and lumps. I had not been aware that the cops in trying to hold me to kill me had ripped off my trench coat when I pushed and dashed from them.

When we left the drugstore the crowds were heading towards us, hysterically stampeded by cops on horseback and motorcycles; and the people were hoarsely shouting, "Cossacks! Robots! Murderers!" I grabbed the girl and pulled her into the movie-house next to the drugstore. *Mother*, a Russian film, was playing. We had come in from a pogrom on the streets to a portrayal of the futile, bloody 1905 Russian revolution. As the pathetic Gorky story precipitated itself with a kaleidoscope of masterful camera art the girl and I kissed and kissed. God willing, the girl would spend the night with me. I planned to take her to an unusual set-up, the Greenwich Village apartment of Father John Francis Craig, a derelict Jesuit. She'd hear him read the document of his Excommunication and there would be his wrenching sobbings and—No! I met the priest a decade later.

I had a bricklaying pal, Benny Portnoy, who was taking the same courses with me at C.C.N.Y. Portnoy had told me that he had a "clubroom" especially for shacking up.

At the time older Portnoy was my idol; he was a hot bricklayer, an athlete, intellectual and Communist. He taught me to swim, paddle a racing canoe, box, and gave me books to read like *The Economic Theory of the Leisure Class* and *Dialectical Materialism*.

As I was thinking of Portnoy's pad the girl asked me if I had a place we could go for the night.

I found Benny Portnoy playing ping-pong in the recreation hall of C.C.N.Y. Benny ogled the girl and said the clubroom was in a vacant house taken over by the City for taxes. It was a room nobody knew about; a hidden room. He knew the house inside-out because he had worked there for the eccentric owner when he was a kid. The owner had been a sex-obsessed, famous, old Italian sculptor. Benny said the dirty old boy used to have group orgies with little girls in the secret room. He told me where the house was, and how to get in and find the clubroom. Benny gave me the key.

He said, "You have to do a half mile backstroke with me tomorrow at the Sixtieth Street pool. In the ice-box there's heavy raw cream and eggs. When you're through screwin' drink a pint of egg-nog. The condoms are in the top dresser drawer. By the way, you'll have to screw in the piano. The release lever is on the left side of the keyboard."

I nodded but I didn't have the slightest idea of what he meant. (It turned out that the "piano" was a tricky, folding Murphy bed.)

The house was a Victorian brick mansion on the East River. I followed Benny Portnoy's instructions: alley to door of basement kitchen, up servants' stairway to pantry, to dining room; pull aside large false bookcase; enter rope-manipulated elevator; work rope until elevator came to top floor to the old Italian sculptor's "statutory-rape-nest."

The room was a sex maniac's dream. The floors, walls and ceilings were gold-mirrored, and there were thousands of photos of the old goat with sub-teenage girls in every possible and impossible position.

We had found our way from the basement to the dining room by the light of the moon through the large windows. Benny's clubroom had no windows, but Benny had hooked into the power line, and the room had all kinds of suggestive lighting. Benny had also told me where the dummy panel was that slid open onto the huge studio.

I was so bound with lust that I did not know what to do first. To this day I'm moralistically awkward about the initial moves—even with my wife. I grin and hem and haw and prance. There's a ritual starkness to sex. Sex did not come to me through my intellect; sex came to me as an over-whelming beast in my groin, and later as an insatiable, salivating animal in my tongue.

I kissed her standing and not gracefully. She took off her trench coat, and was naked. I had not known she was wearing nothing but the trench coat. I had never seen a girl naked. Seeing female nudity all at once was a little too much. Her high, pointed breasts protruded firmly at an amazing length. I haven't seen such breasts since. I would rather have discovered her perfect body, reddish crotch hair, crack of behind, and immaculate flesh bit by bit. (And I unreasonably wish to feel that a girl has not been seen nude, nor been touched before—me.)

I had trouble getting my clothes and shoes off—and my own nudity embarrassed me. She tickled my thing, and said in her hypnotic voice, "These boys' things are made of eels, toads, snails and puppy-dog tails."

I didn't know what to say, so I stupidly said, "And what are pussies made of?" She said, "Didn't you know? Sugar, spice and everything nice; that's what little girls are made of." She pulled me down atop her on the bed. No-no-no, there weren't any secret compartments or elevators or my wishful-thinking mirrored room of Eros . . .

We came in from a back room on the ground floor of the stately house, and in the dim light of the moon to a locked bedroom door. It was a massive, cruciform mahogany door with tarnished, weighty, brass hardware. The aristocratic house of many generations spoke to me—well, not literally; I sensed a personality of architectural time, a house soul. It had been the town house of English gentry. Founding Fathers had partaken of its Colonial hospitality. Its roof had smiled upon illustrious American Americans. Later, candelabra lighted the faces of Henry James and Walt Whitman; and its walls heard Whitman recite.

The gracious ladies and gentlemen disappeared, as though called to embellish a better world. The dignified house, the stalwart protector, the faithful comforter, lived on; stayed, keepsaking the refined ghosts of rare music, the classical library, high language, births, graduations, marriages, ranking officers of wars not shameful, gladsome festivities, somber, wordless moments, and revolving seasons.

The usurpers came: boorish merchants, the unreal who are politicians, a medical charlatan, a spiritual fakir, the Italian sculptor who did cemetery work, and finally, the artist who left the muse for bread and butter and manufactured artificial limbs. All the invaders died miserably.

Someone knocked on the door and said, "Open up in the name of the law!" I thought, "My luck to be jailed for trespassing City property and immorality!" I hastily put on my pants and lit the candle with the last match. The lock clicked; the door opened: I was about to say, "I'm sorry, officer, I didn't mean to break any laws—you know how nature is—" It was Benny Portnoy and two snickering pals, hoping to sidle in on a quiet little gang bang.

I said to Portnoy, "This is not nice . . . !" He said, "You shouldn't begrudge a friend construction worker—and comrade." "I'm not a 'comrade,'" I said, "and suppose I fall in love and marry her?"

The girl, covered by the blanket up to her chin, looked at Benny and his pals in a curious way—that I didn't like. Benny said unconvincingly, "Aw, I was only kidding." They left. The girl said, in a baffling manner, "Why did you let them go?" We drowsed off.

I was awakened by her getting out of bed. It was very late and dark and humid. She looked for matches, and I said we were out of matches. She put on her trench coat, unlocked the door, and went out into the big living room. The last occupant must have passed away suddenly and left no heirs, for the large living room was stocked with artificial, flesh-tinted feet, legs, hands and arms suspended from the ceiling, the place looking like it was in full swing. The limbs were for white, and black and yellow people, and seemed living members.

There was no more moonlight. Outside it was the irritating quiet before the storm. She must have been groping around as I heard her bump into things. It never occurred to me what she was up to; girls were still "sugar, and spice, and everything nice."

Thunder ramblings sounded. The skies then eliminated purging rain and raging lighting. The house took it calmly. The girl came sighing back to bed. It had gotten chilly, and Benny's coarse brown Army horse-blankets, though scratchy, were a solace. We returned to sleep.

We were awakened startlingly by the loud blows of nightsticks against the door and wall. Two cops were checking. I thought maybe Benny Portnoy was sore at not getting laid and had sent the cops as a practical joke; or, the great old mansion was on their beat and safeguarding it was routine; or maybe it was just a matter of coming in from the storm.

One was a loudmouth. He had a flask and offered the other cop a shot. The other cop spoke in a soft voice. They were fumbling about by matchlight. One of them slipped, and fell hard. He must have been heavy. There was a breathless silence. Then Loudmouth said unbelievingly, "—Oh no! . . . Oh my God!" He rushed out.

I'm tempted to write that I sneaked into the next room and saw the cop's temple smashed on a durable object with brains and blood oozing, and so forth—and he was the guy who had clubbed me earlier in Union Square and in his death throes, as I bent over him, he caught my hand and begged, "Save me—don't let me die. . . !" Nothing of the sort. I didn't dare move from the bed, and I wasn't about to leave that room and house until all the nonsense was over and I could get the girl and myself out safely.

The girl said, "Why did you let Benny and his friends go?" You'd think that nothing had happened in the next room. I'll never understand the female sex.

"What?" I said, "Do you mean to say that you would have been 'willing?'"

"This is supposed to be a free country," she said. "Why not? No one owns anybody. If three girls came in, wouldn't you do it with them? You would."

I said, "But a man is different. You say the strangest things."

"I'm man-hungry," she said. "I've been a prostitute in houses, I've had as many as twenty men, even colored, make love to me in one night. I'm a saint because prostitution is sacred."

I couldn't believe my ears. I moved away from her; and from that moment on, being confined to that bed and room, until the business of the cops was over and done with, was Chinese torture.

The storm got so violent that it seemed the world was ending. Through the storm I heard the sirens of the police cars and the ambulance. There was a fire engine also; what for, I don't know.

Then the absurd, though very real, took place. What happened and how it happened was batted back and forth, and it was so goddamn funny that I almost choked with laughter under the horse-blanket.

In the dark by the fireplace my girl had heartily relieved herself both ways, and covered it neatly with the Communist newspaper, *The Daily Worker*. In the dark the soft-spoken cop stepped on *The Daily Worker*; the mess gave way under his foot and weight, catapulting him backwards and striking the base of his skull on the brass spearheaded finial of the footrest on the hearth. The intern said he was killed instantly. Noting *The Daily Worker* he said, "Communist brutality."

There was quite a group: a Captain, cops, two priests, a reporter-photographer, and a female intern. Looking through the dead cop's wallet the Captain said in a wondering voice. "Here's a message—like a request—on his identification card: 'In case of fatal accident please do not have a witch doctor of a priest perform last rites. Mr. Whitman gave me a new life. His poems are my Gospels. I always have his bible, *Leaves of Grass*, on me. Whoever you are, please, please read over my remains, "Give Me the Splendid Silent Sun." "I, like mute millions, dream of the rainbow beyond the horizon. I but advance a moment only to wheel and hurry back in the darkness." Thank you.'"

The intern said, "This is not my department, and I'm not about to try to guess who and what the real God is—if any—but I think the dead man's request should be honored." The female intern—they called her Muriel—cried emotionally, "Don't listen to him! He's not even Christian—he's one of 'those!' Fathers! This dead, straying Catholic's soul may not have departed yet—don't let it go to hell! It's your duty to give it the one and only proper Holy Last Rites!"

They all argued ridiculously on and on. Finally, the priests, bored, tired, and impatient to leave, said the matter was out of their hands as they had to respect the departed's last wish.

Mass For Unknown Soldiers

I guessed that he had been a prize-fighter, and like many little ex-pugs, Petey Roman, was a bloated owner-bartender.

His tavern, a beery neglected affair, was hidden in a quiet village far out on eastern Long Island. I was summering there. Except for native farmers smelling of fertilizer, and ruddy thick fingered clam-diggers, there hardly ever were patrons. Close-mouthed Petey was a bachelor and didn't need much business. I used to go there and put away a dozen ruminating beers . . . even though the glasses were dirty and the beer flat. Once in a while it's a relief to be in a place like Petey's; a couple of strangers silently drinking, oblivious of each other; each guy kind of noiselessly gliding around in his very own psychic asylum.

Swarthy Petey, with the battered noise and cauliflower ears, would stand behind the end of the bar blinking his dark baggy eyes, weaving his head, drumming his fingers on the bar, with the look of a man who was somewhere else; then he'd know you'd want another brew, and with the quick movement of a startled toad, would run the tap and serve.

One evening there was a local plumber and an itinerant farm equipment salesman at the bar. The salesman, a voluble redhead, had just sold a tractor. He ordered Carstairs for us, and began telling stories: selling an Ohio farmer 'up hill' axle grease; how he bettered a shrewd Amish farmer and made love to his daughter in the bargain; and he rattled off the list of States to which he travelled. It seemed Petey had gotten to all those places at one time too. You could tell because he'd smile and grunt.

Later, when Petey and I were alone, he studied me, and said decisively, "You say you're a story writer. I'll tell you the story of my life which I ain't never told nobody, not even in confession to a priest."

Many people have told me, "My life would make a book," only to proceed to bore me with a dreary domestic catalogue. I nodded. He fetched a card-board shoe-box and emptied it on the bar. There were newspaper clippings with pictures of him in the ring, and accounts of his boxing career. I was impressed. He had been a popular name in sporting circles, and almost made the flyweight championship. Among the mementos were horse-racing sheets, steamer and railroad ticket stubs, and a diamond engagement ring. In his froggy voice he said, "You're sayin' to yourself, 'So what? Is this a big deal? Leather-pushers are a dime a dozen. Publicity and twenty cents gets you a ride on the subway.' I show you the pitchers to give you an idear what I wuz doin' before the war in 1917. The diamond ring ties in with the racin' sheets. I wuz engaged to a nice kid named Rosie. But I wuz nuts for horse-bettin'. My fightin' dough went to the bookies. I'd set a weddin' date with Rosie . . . lose a bundle at the track . . . borrow Rosie's ring an' hock it . . . that's the way it went alla time. I'd swear on the Virgin Mary I'd quit gamblin' . . . no go. I got sore at myself and said I'd go to the end of the woild where there wuz no horse tracks. I took a boat to China . . . like a horse-bettin' cure. I arrive in night in Shanghai . . . goes to a hotel . . . wakes up inna mornin' . . . pulls up the shades . . . looks out the winder . . . whaddo I see? . . . a goddamn race track. That's not the story. Yuh can dump the pony habit . . . yuh can live with a dame or without a dame . . . but yuh can't get away from somethin' like what I'm gonner tell yuh." He put the stuff back in the shoe-box, drew beers for me and himself, and continued. "I was drafted in the service, and shipped to France. In the ring I wuz good . . . on the battlefield I wuz lousy . . . as a shot I couldn't hit the side of a barn with a banjo." He made a deft sign of the cross. "Guys were blown to bits all aroun' me. I said my Hall Marys and waded into the crap. The Blessed Mudder musta had her eye on me; I come through all the crap without a scratch. With armistice I wuz brung to Paris. Guys usta laff at me 'cause I didn't go with hoors an' drink an' smoke. I kept in trainin', and boxed exhibition matches for the sojers. Yuh wanna join me in a snak?" I said I'd appreciate it. He filled my glass, and went into the kitchen. After some time he returned with a tray of garlic-pizza pies, a bowl of hot peppers, pickled conch, and a platter of tripe. As he ate he went on in a matter of fact tone. "Then I wuz brung to London to get onna transport for the States. My manager had fights lined up. I had it in my mind to make champ and marry Rosie. There wuz a couple ships I coulda took—I had pull. I got into a fast crap game, and teamed up with a Brooklyn Eyetalyun guy named Johnnie. We couldn't lose for winnin'. We racked up four grand between us. I wuz suppose to board a ship, Dixie Belle. Then I remembered I once dropped a wad onna sure-thing nag named, Dixie Belle. I figger it would be bad luck so I axe to go on anudder ship leavin' the next day. That night Johnnie axed me to go pub-hoppin' with him. I says, 'I don't drink,' he says, 'That's awright, jus' pal aong,' so I says, 'O.K.' But I shoulda never went. London wuz like Times Square on New Years. Sojers and sailors and dames wuz havin' a time all ova the town. We stop in a pub. Johnnie has his booze an' I axed for milk. They didn't have no milk; so I takes ginger ale. Two floozies next to us were kinda high an' havin' a argument with two big 'Merican sojers; they looked like tough New York West Side guys. One of the girls says to the two guys on the make, "Go to a hotel with youse? That's a laff—get lost youse Irish bums!" Then she gives me the come-on wink and says, "Hello, baby-face . . . would youse and your goodlookin' buddy buy us girls a drink?' The other says to Johnnie, 'Youses are Eyetalyuns, ain't youse? I love Eyetalyuns.' Johnnie says, 'Merican Eyetalyuns . . . whadda you dolls drinkin'?' Johnnie says in my ear, 'If they get rid of the other guys it's in the slot . . . pushover.' I says back, 'Hoors is trouble.' 'Don't worry, we'll be on the boat inna morin'' he says, 'maybe they ain't hoors an' nuttins gonner happen.'

"We bought them a lotta drinks while the two big sojers kept woikin' their points an' makin' a play for them stubborn-like. The girls rubbed it inna sojers how wonnerful Eyetalyuns like me an' Johnnie wuz; gettin' the sojers madder an' madder. About twelve the girls say they hadda go home to their husban's and kids. They gives us a goodbye kiss, an' spit on the floor by the sojers. Johnnie says, 'I wuz afraid nuttin' would happen. They're teasers an' they ain't hoors.' We thought that wuz that. When we leaves the joint the two big sojers follows us. They're boined an' got it in for us. We wuzn't lookin' for no trouble. We run inta anudder pub. These guys come in too. We're

wise to them; as long as we're where the action is they won't try nuttin'
. . . they wanta rough us without witnesses. The more we moves from
pub to pub the more these guys get idears. We figgers we make believe
we go to the gent's room, skip from the winder and get back to the
billets outside town. We thought sure we give them the slip. We wuz
onna dark road an' you couldn't see nuttin' in the fog when we hears
the buggers paddin' behind us. Johnnie says disgusted-like, 'what the
hell kinda crap is this? I'm sick of those guys. Let's stand up to the
one way or anudder.'

"'No, Johnnie,' I says, 'they're out for blood an' we gotta make that
boat inna mornin'; let's leg it; it ain't that I'm yeller . . . I jus' want no
trouble.' I have did a lotta road woik, but I never run so much in all
my life. What a helluva a screw for us . . . there we wuz, all set to go
back to the States with bankrolls in our pockets big enuf to choke a
horse, and runnin' like crazy for our skins. We run an' we run an' we
run. We gets to what wuz like a bridge. Johnnie says, 'I can't run no
more . . . this is it.' I says, 'Mee too.' Now we sees the two big bums
comin.' Johnnie hollers, "What's eatin' youse guys? We're 'Mericans
like youse. We ain't done nuttin' to youse . . . yuh want money? . . .
we'll give yuh lots . . . fuh chrissakes I got a wife and kids inna States.'
Now they ain't far from us an' one guy laffs like he means it, 'Say yuh
prayers . . . yuh wop sonuvabitches are good as dead!' I says, 'Johnnie,
that bastud called our mudders hoors.' 'Yeah,' says Johnnie, squarin'
off, 'Like callin' the Blessed Madonna a hoor.' Me an' Johnnie see red
an' the rumble begins. I weighed one-twelve an' Johnnie was stocky,
but the two sojers had easy a hunnert pounds apiece on us.

"I duck, I swing, I jab, I uppercut, I hook, a right cross, a left cross
. . . I musta trowed a tousand punches . . . my knuckles bounce off the
guy like I wuz hittin' a brick craphouse . . . his fist was bigger'n my
head . . . I don't get knicked on the battlefield an' this guy bangs and
bust my nose and ears . . . I'm punch-happy . . . I'm arm-weary . . .
like fightin' inna bad dream where I go to move an' ain't got no legs
. . . go to punch an' ain't got no arms . . . it wuz like I wuz fightin' the
guy aroun' the clock since I wuz born . . . I weave an' dodge an' roll
with his haymakers . . . I'm winded an' he keeps bulldozin' on an' on
inta me. I'm fightin' by memory like in what they say, a nightmare

. . . I'm bushed an' ain't got no more feelings . . . I got maybe one more punch left . . . I see a openin'. . . I don't know how I done it . . . I connected on his button . . . I broke my hand an' he dropped cold. The udder guy is got Johnnie against the railin' an' chokin' him . . . Johnnie looked like a gonner all blue inna face . . . even without tinkin' I scrambles behind the big guy, gets my shoulders between his legs an' up under his crotch an' heaves him with all my might over the railin'. When he goes over he screams . . . the scream went down-down-down, an' he hit soundin' like a watermelon squashin'. Me and Johnnie look over the railin'. . . it's one helluva way down . . . he's smashed acrost railroad tracks . . . there wuz a train comin' an' yuh could see the guy from the train light. We looked at the guy who was knocked out on the bridge. Me and Johnnie wuz tinkin' the same . . . when he come to he'd put the finger on us . . . nobody's believe our story an' we'd hang. I didn't say nuttin' an' Johnnie didn't say nuttin . . . we hadda do it . . . there wuz no way out . . . I got the big guy's feet an' Johnnie got his shoulders an' we dump him over the railin'. . . we didn't look over but we hear him hit the tracks like anudder watermelon squashin' . . . we wuz runnin' when the train come under the bridge . . . we come to a cross-road . . . without sayin' nuttin' he took one road an' I took the udder. The next mornin' I wuz on the transport back to the States.

I had a busted mitt . . . my ring days wuz over. Rosie, God bless her, married a barber in Brooklyn. I didn't wanna see noboby an' talk to nobody. I come out here an' bought the saloon. Would youse believe it . . . I ain't never went outside the saloon . . . I been in here like a mushroom . . . an' me who wuz nuts about travellin'. I ain't never forgot those two sojers . . . I axed myself a million times, 'Why they wanna kill me? . . . who wuz those two guys?' All these years I been payin' The Mudder of Forgiveness church in Brooklyn for special prayers for the souls of 'two unknown sojers.'

I asked him, "Why do you risk your neck telling me about the two deaths . . . why trust me with the secret . . . what if I wrote the story?" I nodded towards the tap. As he drew and watched the beer he said slowly and relaxedly. "I trust nobody. Since 1918 I been expectin' the law to come through that door an' catch up with me. You could give me away but it's too late . . . nuttin' could hoit me now . . . I got a good reason not to worry no more." He pulled a hospital report from his pocket, "Read it an' you'll see there can't be no more trouble for me." The report said he had inoperable cancer of the prostate in the terminal stage. He handed me the flat beer, said, "It's on me . . . tanks for listenin'," and became a toad again, blinking his eyes and drumming the bar with his fingers.

The Lily Pond

It was so comfortable to be dead. Her feelings were now an elastic non-shatterable murky glass. Maybe she was the white palping roots at the bottom of the lily pond. Her eyes could look up and be somewhat aware of objects that came and went. But her eyes were not curious. Desire had returned to the water-bag of Time. There was no wanting. She was a periphery of nothingness. Her clock had no marking hands and the numerals had been erased. It was only that there was a streaming. She might be the sun sifting through the barred windows. She might be or not be anything. Yet, when you're dead the dictionary is a book of blank definitions. It was just that care had dissolved itself.

"Here's your lunch, Miss Cooper," said the attendant, Mary. The eyes of a corpse can cut and burn. Corinne Cooper's food-tray remained untouched. Time did not molest the dead of its passage.

Corrinne was alone in the corridor that opened on many cell rooms.

Streaming is a level flowing independent of adjectives. Streaming could have a body. It could claim any content and form and measure itself against infinitesimal or boundless proportion. Streaming could be a part or whole, one thing and all things without registry. Streaming could be an ego, or nowness, or futurity. It could be a was, an is, or a never be. The court and policing was beyond order, beyond good or bad. Beyond. Perhaps hands to wrest the victory would never be.

There were the voices of patients playing in the yard.

Laughter ran on the track of streaming. Blood ran through Corinne. That was the blood's own business. It couldn't matter what the blood did. She didn't wander in and out of the rooms. The rooms came to her. If you're dead and other things move, it's their fault. Something is always doing something to something. Labels outside the mind make labels in a mind. Maybe she was in the process of being born. And her eyes were older. And her eyes remained from lived lives.

Richard Dean focused blurringly in her detached line of vision. He was searching. She could remember time ahead but could not remember the moment she walked up to him.

He turned and was startled by her silent presence. She was clothed in a shift. Loose white cotton stockings hung down over her ankles and slippers. Around her smooth neck was a small golden cross suspended from a fine chain. Her limbs were bruised, her heavy auburn hair matted, her cheeks pale, and about her hyper-red lips was perspiration. The whites of her gray-green eyes were dilated and her pupils diminished to black points.

The lean face with the large nose and olive skin opposite her was looking intensely and speaking. Even though a character is dead she can hear the sounds of the author's voice. She died because of a secret. Nothing is serious. All is equal, all is understood and forgiven in the gelid, opaque repose of death.

"Corinne——how are you . . . ?"

'How was she?' What else did he expect?

She stared at him for a long, long time.

What could she say but, "Are you satisfied now?"

He suddenly felt terribly guilty for being sane.

Within her removed camera he faded to a blob.

"Corinne, don't you know me? I am Richard."

Her speech was to stare. The signal was lost.

The kindest thing he could do then was to leave her. ". . . I'll see you, tomorrow, Corinne . . . "

What is tomorrow? Tomorrows might be mashed pasts and futures.

He disappeared in the streaming.

Corinne. Corinne was a word. Words were dead things, ghosts that went through walls.

"Alright, girls!" shouted the attendant out on the grass, "Playtime's over! Let's go to dinner!"

There was a slushing clatter of shuffling women's shoes, and mingled with it were songs, speeches and imprecations. Keys unlocked and locked doors. To Corinne they were frequencies that tuned in and receded. "Hey, Cooper," said the burly attendant, Mary, "Chow Time."

It was useless to order a catatonic about, but Mary had heard that sometimes when they are in that state they understood everything and noticed details. So with a patient you never knew. You were supposed to be surprised when they didn't surprise you. "Anyhow, kid, what are you doing in the corridor? You must not elope from your room, you bad girl. Seven is your room.—Why do I bother to talk to you. Come along, Cooper."

Mary pushed Corinne to the dining room. The patients lined up and received their food in trays from the worker-patients at the steam-wagon.

It was exquisite to be dead. The better life begins with death. The dead are not assaulted by smell and hunger. And there are so many hungers.

Corinne stood in a corner, forgotten. Maud, a colored patient, took Corinne to her room. She undressed Corinne and put her to bed. She patted the welts on Corinne's wrists.

"Honey, I'm glad to see you out of them straps. They tell me I had them on when I took sick. My man Bernard says I was tied up in the awful violent ward too. I don't remember."

Night in the asylum was a chrome gray-black nocturne. Corinne's eyelids stayed open.

Mrs. Finerty, the night attendant, smoked a cigarette at her desk in her cage in the ward. Now and then she called out to the ceaselessly chattering disturbed patients, "Quiet, girls! Get your beauty sleep!" Cacophonic voices went on and off from their uncharted islands of delusion, raucously smiting the darkness. The dynamos in the powerhouse whirred, and smoke from the stacks poured against the stars. There were a few lights showing from the nurses' home. A hilarious party went on in a doctor's cottage. Two wide-awake guards drove slowly about the grounds. Out on the main highway the Interstate bus roared by. A faraway plane sang and blinked. In the operating room of the infirmary an emergency appendectomy on a patient was being performed. In the underground tunnels worker-patients wheeled carts of linen towards the laundry. Into the commissary straggled weary attendants for coffee.

Corinne lay inert. Corinne lay gazing through the barred window at the moon. The moon was a dead planet shining. Lonely frigid moon. The moon was also uncaring of its orbit. Corinne in the moon. She was being swallow in cold whiteness. The moon was drowning her. Her lungs screamed.

Mrs. Finerty stirred. The scream had come from number seven. They'll do that for no reason. Then all was as before. Asylum nights drag and exhaustion finally makes for quiet. Mrs. Finerty continued to doze.

Doctor Berg discussed Miss Cooper with Richard Dean. "Mr. Dean," he said sympathetically, "Why don't you stay away until we can bring her back to the point where she will be able to recognize you and make sense."

"If you don't mind, doctor, I'd like to visit her every day."

"She may remain this way indefinitely."

"She will awaken."

"We hope so. I've seen them in this retarded form of death snap out of it as though nothing happened, and yet we've had others go through all the stages of progressive deterioration and be shipped from the incontinent ward to the morgue."

"I wish you would permit me to be near her."

"Love?"

"No."

"What makes you think you can help her?"

"I feel it."

"Ego," smiled Dr. Berg, "It's unorthodox for us to permit a layman's therapy, or speculations rather, but in our profession we do not exclude any possibilities."

Corinne lay immersed in a tub. First the water was hot, then cold. She was a lily in Richard's pond. The seasons were changing from summer to winter. Dr. Berg looked sown upon her. He told Mary to prepare her for shock treatment.

A water lily can spy. The doctor was Richard pretending to be someone else. Now he was going to put electricity into her body.

She could tell him the truth that she had no body. The body had been trouble. She was a pure element. Virgins are pure. Nothing is lost in nature said the physics teacher or was it scientist Richard Dean? Let Dr. Richard Dean do as he pleased. She was his idea. Dr. Dean was God who created her. The dead are human too. She had a tickling to laugh. Because of vowels and consonants. Was there anything in her contract with Dr. Dean about laughter? And now it was something about electricity. The dead are sly. Now they were going to wire a water lily.

Mary rubbed her dry and clothed her in a shift and slippers. Mary brought her to electro-therapy. It wasn't pretty to watch patients convulse and turn blue. There were others before Corinne. Corinne was without emotion. Corinne was a statute of flesh.

"Trust Mary," said Mary, "We're not going to hurt you one tiny bit."

What were these people doing to Dr. Dean's house? Were they ghosts also?

Two worker-patients strapped her onto the table. Dr. Berg ran his hand over her thick auburn hair. "There's a lot of beautiful woman here going to waste." He clamped a padded tongue depresser into Corinne's mouth and bent over her with the electrodes in his hands.

How could Dr. Dean do this to her? Let him. It seems he was never satisfied.

The electrodes touched her temples.

The dead can be divided into atoms. There was the crackling streaming that was magnified, and the trilling. She was a network of singing glass through which multi-colored neon flowed. Even the dead can't escape. What was the song? Her hearing was in a cathedral forest of tall whistling trees. And then the long high belling. For how many years did it play? Monsignor Richard Dean soared vastly from a great pulpit. She was frozen in a glacier and her eyes were iridescent rays beneath the surface.

It was Christmas morning. Next to the tree in the ward was a portable common altar. The patients looked about vacantly as the priests gave blessings.

The priest was surely Dr. Dean. And so was Santa Claus who passed out presents. Then there was Dr. Dean who had been coming to look at her and hold her hand for a thousand years. Or had his visits transpired all in a second? She was a bit worried because she seemed able to worry about it. And now her body was fretted by being dead. Because death could not last forever.

Richard Dean sat by her in the crowd of visitors and patients surrounding the lighted tree. Her fingers clung to his hand.

"Corinne, look at the Christmas tree. Try hard to think. Remember the night we met; you registered for my evening drama class at the high school. It was Christmas week too. The village and countryside was covered with snow. Remember that I had you over to my house on Christmas Eve? I drove you in the Ford. The car window wouldn't close; the snow came in and down our necks. You held a lighted candle to the windshield to melt the sleet. You met my brothers and sisters. You said our tree was perfect. Remember that bushy Christmas tree, Corinne?"

Of course. What a foolish question. Dr. Dean's sister was sweet to her, and admired her hair. One of his brothers had cut the tree down from the golf course at night and skipped home with it. They were chuckling about the robbery.

It was cozy roasting chestnuts and sipping creamy egg-nog by the fireplace. She wished she could live with Dr. Dean and his family. "I knew you'd like my sister, Anne," he said, "you remind me a lot of Anne." That made her happy because she thought it brought her closer to him. She didn't want to leave his home that Christmas Eve.

For a moment it seemed to Richard that behind her impenetrability there was a shadow of cognizance. Was she smiling behind her mask? Was she going to weep? Her lips trembled, and her fingers tightened on his. "Corinne, you do remember the pretty stolen Christmas tree."

Her wan transparent face flushed, and then went pale again. To her his words ran late each other and his speech became a jumble. The reel had swiftly changed. She was in a foreign theatre.

Going to the asylum each day had become a ritual for Richard. The institution no longer seemed to him the ultimate limbo where all human dignity was violated. The employees and patients accepted him and looked forward to his visits. During the months he pondered over the only sentence Corinne had uttered, "Are you satisfied now?"

Mary, this attendant, was reading Richard Dean's novel. Corinne saw his picture on the dust-jacket.

Why——she was a character of his. That's who she was. And she had either strayed or was lost from his fancies. There he is——sitting at his typewriter in the cottage. "Corinne, I can't write. The truth does not want to go on paper. I'll lose my mind trying to say real things." Now she's telling him he can't fail; his book will be a success. "You won't know me then, Richard." Oh no, he'll always be Richard. He's speaking on the radio but it is not his own voice. His pictures are in the newspapers and it's so hard to walk into the pictures to him. His face is on the back of the book—no it's mirrored on the lily pond—no he's standing on the little bridge pointing out the lilies to her—no she's looking up from the muddy bottom and his face is laughing and shimmering down and he's not Richard no no no she doesn't know who he is. Nothing is true. She doesn't exist She's a reflection in his brain.

She was aware of the aroma of coffee. It would be wonderful to drink coffee.

When Mary brought her the breakfast tray she reached for it.

"Don't you want me to feed you anymore?" asked Mary.

"How silly," she muttered.

"Good for you!" chortled Mary, "We'll have to celebrate——this afternoon I'll fix you up nice and lovely for Mr. Dean."

"I haven't seen Dr. Dean for ages. Why doesn't he come? What have I done to him?——I can't imagine . . ."

"Now-now, Corinne, you saw him yesterday . And he's not a doctor. Get that out of you head."

Mary was a liar. Dr. Dean was Dr. Dean. Was Mary deliberately trying to confuse her?

"Mary, you know very well that he's her doctor."

"Have it your way; just so's you keep talking. I thought the cat was going to keep your tongue forever."

Poor Mary; did she think she was talking to a child? Why did Mary have to dress her? Was she that helpless? She must be in a hospital. Maybe she was in an auto accident.

Mary brought her before the mirror in the washroom. It seemed amusing. The old black and yellow flowered dress was baggy on her. She must have dropped a lot of weight. "You have voluptuous lines," he had said, "When you come out of your shell you'll be glamorous."

Where had he said that? It was frustrating not to be able to remember. She tried not to remember and the next sentence followed, "The lily that is closing into meagre identity——in the morning when it opens——will be a gorgeous woman. A woman is not a sex or a gender or a breed: a woman is an art. A woman is God . . ."

Sunset on his lily pond. Somethings cannot be forgotten in this life, or any life.

Hunchback Nancy, Maud the colored girl, Granny Smith, the Duchess of Windsor and a dozen other patients had helped Mary care for Corrinne during her catatonic months. Mary passed the word around that Corinne had begun to talk. "I recall how she spoke before the King in Buckingham Palace," reminisced the Duchess.

"Corinne Cooper is a real lady," said Nancy. Then making wheels against her head and motioning towards the Duchess she added, "She ain't loony like some people in this joint. And Miss Cooper's got a swell gentleman with a Buick."

She heard them discussing her. That could mean that she had an identity. Or were they forming her into an identity. Or were they forming her into an identity through their own eye? Part of it made sense and some of it didn't. But they were kind.—Like a harmless babbling crowd in a meaningless dream.

When Richard Dean's car arrived Maud ran through the ward and shouted, "Whoopie, Corinne——here's your boy-friend!" At the entrance to the reception room Nancy greeted him. "Oh, Mr. Dean, you know what?——Miss Cooper ain't sick no more!"

The patients trailed him, calling out his name and giggling. Mary led Corinne to him. They had dressed her, rouged her cheeks and painted her nails. The red ribbon was a winsome touch in her long rich auburn hair."

"Ain't you gonner kiss your sweetheart," tittered Nancy.

He regretted that pity came to him. It should not have been that way.

Mary scolded the patients and herded them to the day ward. On the way they sang, "Mr. Dean loves Miss Cooper!"

They sat together as usual. The late afternoon dusk of departing winter softened the huge empty room. In the distance could be heard the ravings from the men's wards. Spoons and plates clinked in the adjoining room.

"Corinne, Spring will come soon," he said, "We can go for walks. There's a farm, a golf course, and even gardens here . . ."

It would be truly strange if the spell were evaporated and she spoke. He had gotten used to and contented with just sitting with her and holding her hand. It had become religion to have her mutely near, and then to leave and enjoy the women who were sure of themselves. And purifying to return to her each day.

She was embarrassed, but couldn't remember the word embarrassed. Dr. Dean was a real living person. She wasn't. It wouldn't be right of her to ask him if he'd stay always. In his presence the fingers of her knowing could grasp a fraction of substantiality. She strove to ask him why he had deserted her. Where had he been? Or maybe it was: where had she been? Her tongue was not connected to her questioning.

"Corinne, Mary tells me that you think I'm 'Dr.' Dean."

She peered into his eyes and said, "You are the only friend I have. You would not fool me. You are Dr. Dean."

He dropped his eyes. Her eyes could convince. And her newly-found voice thrilled him. He told himself it was because of his empathy; yet he was grateful for the sensation. What had gone on in her mind before it stunned itself? Did she realize why she was there? It was too soon to ask. He'd speak of Spring instead. It might re-seed her will to fully awaken.

His words came through to her in spots. Somewhere in the blotted pages of her mental book Spring showed her Pluto, Persephone and a pomegranate. Dr. Dean changed shapes before her eyes. Her head was numb in places. She needed glasses again. She wore glasses in parochial school. The rites of Spring in primitive times was a pagan festival said Sister Sebastian, pagan from pagano, meaning countryside, and there was a coal-man down the street named Pagano.

She couldn't control the fast-flipping picture-pages and the captions bunched and jammed. Why didn't Dr. Dean give her medicine for her headache. It was all no use.

Mary tip-toed in and whispered, "Sorry, Mr. Dean; Miss Cooper's bed-time. I've saved some hot dinner for her."

Mary was perverse; calling a doctor, "Mister."

As he was leaving Richard said, "I'll see you tomorrow, Corinne. Don't worry about anything. Be a good girl."

Mary put her arm around her. "Corinne Cooper is always a good girl."

This must be a hospital. It could be a hotel. Hadn't she seen a movie about a women's prison? Figuring things out was tiring. She ran her hands over the sheet. She could feel her limbs. Feeling was a pleasant discovery.

Mr. and Mrs. Cooper, Sis and Harold paid their weekly visit.

"My poor dear child!" cried Mrs. Cooper, "Thank the Lord you've come to! If you only knew how hard it is without you!"

"Everything is going and nothing coming in——"

Dr. Berg took Mrs. Cooper aside. Corinne heard her mother. "Of course, doctor. I wouldn't upset my daughter for the world. Who knows better than I what her condition is!"

What condition? Even now that she was sick she couldn't get away from her family. Mother. It was unfortunate that she could never love her mother. The sharp colorless face had been upon her since her childhood; the jarring voice, the constant plaint of better days in the past, her domestic puttering, her perpetual gabbling, downing and criticizing, her clichés and flights of sentimentality. No, mother didn't soothe the pains in her head. Nor could she get close to Father, Sis and Harold.

Sis pecked at her cheek. Gangling moody Harold didn't speak. He stood by with a Jehovah's Witness Bible in his hand. Mr. Cooper, a heavy flaccid man with small hands, cleared his throat and said weakly, "You'll be alright . . ."

They were a trap shutting her in.

After Dr. Berg left Mrs. Cooper screeched, "At night I go through the agonies of hell thinking of you in the asylum. But it was best to put you in the State Institution—you might have done something awful to yourself like your brother Alvin——I was afraid he'd go off—and he did!

"The trouble with our blood is that it is too fine—no fetlock stock in our strain——your great-grandfather's statue still stands in Memphis——if Tracy Todd had not been swindled by his partner we would not be living in abject proverty today——I told you not to stay up nights writing Lord-knows-what——you needed your strength for the dress-shop—how humilating for a Cooper!——you overworked yourself——I told you not to, dear——I thought I'd die when the doctor said you were insane."

Insane?

"Mother," admonished Sis wearily, "that Gone With The Wind mouth of yours would hang anybody."

Insane?

At the end of the ward a hallucinated patient shouted n terror, "Help! Help!"

Help! Help! Oh my God, help! Alvin shot himself! Harold is crying from the top of the stairway. She's running upstairs all unstrung. There's Alvin dying on the bedroom floor——insane——She's insane!

Her eyes dilated. She screamed hysterically.

Dr. Berg cautioned the Cooper family not to visit her in the following weeks.

The grueling tension slackened. Her body was burningly fatigued. She floated in restful lethargy. Her slowly resurging mind delicately reached threads over the black questioning chasms, building of itself fragile pathways to thinking.

Richard Dean consulted with Dr. Berg as to her diet and vitamins. He sent her tasteful foods and relished watching her eat. She improved physically and became more conscience of her appearance. It was then that he sent the dressmaker to fashion her attractive clothes, and the beautician to care for her shining auburn hair.

During her showers she felt a growing exuberance in the awareness of her body. And to Corinne there came a newness of being. Who said the body was that sacred flesh temple?

The Spring rains played day after day. She stood at the open barred windows and responded to their wetty freshness. Her mind fastened on relatively insignificant things, and her speech was simple but more articulate.

She sat with Richard, studying her dress and stroking her dress.

"You like your dress more than you like me," he said.

"I worked in a dress shop."

"Good, you remember. You used to wave to me when I waked by."

"You were a poor doctor then."

"Why do you say that?"

"I see you. You're wearing corduroy slacks, sport shoes, a navy blue trench coat and a grey fedora with the brim turned down. The girls said you wanted to look different, look like a genius."

"Did you agree with them?"

"I told them you were a genius."

"Am I still a doctor?"

"You're special doctor. and you did something mysterious to my mind."

"Why would I do any harm to you?"

"Oh, I don't resent it. You had to do it. Like an author who makes a character do things. You did it so that you could cure me. I didn't object."

He looked at her wonderingly.

She bent to him and confided, "But the secret will be between us alone."

He did not know how to answer. After a silence she said," I went to the movies in the recreation hall this morning."

"What picture did you see?"

"I saw you in a romance. I tried to get your attention. You were too busy making love to her. I didn't think she was much, but you looked very handsome, indeed!"

He commanded her eyes and said firmly, "Corinne, I was not in the movie. Perhaps the actor resembled me. Now listen carefully——try to follow me. I am not a doctor. I am your firend. You must have faith in what I tell you." She removed her hand from his.

"Please don't call me 'doctor,' Corinne. Call me Richard, as you did before you fell ill—please believe me."

Faith.

"How can I have faith in my scribbling when I've hardly faith in myself?"

"Those were your words, Richard. What's wrong with your mind, Richard——don't you remember that I said, 'Nothing can change my faith in you.'"

A week later he found her exhilarated.

"Richard, guess what! I'm a worker-patient! I was assigned to the infirmary today. I made beds and cleaned patients. I toted breakfast trays, and helped the nurse give out medicine. I fed oatmeal to a blind old woman who sits in a crib and thinks she's a baby. The patients call me 'nurse.' Oh, how I'm needed here! At noon Dr. Berg took me to the Commissary and treated me to a soda."

"Did the boys ogle you in the Commissary?"

"Richard, you're teasing."

She enthusiastically tried to accurately relate her impressions of the pathetic and humorous incidents of her day.

"Tomorrow we're going to scrub and wax Dr. Berg's offices."

"I miss not being your doctor anymore," he said with tristful lightness.

She held her hand to her forehead and said, "I must have said quite a few funny things when I was in 'that' condition."

"No . . . your words were magnetic keys and spiritual allegories. Someday when you're mind is strong enough I'd like to go over some of them with you."

"Must I answer all your curiosity then?"

"Why not?"

"The same instructor Dean of the Adult Education drama class."

"I see you're getting snippy again . . . !"

"What do you do when you're not with me? Or am I not supposed to ask? What do your girl-friends think of 'Corinne Cooper'?"

"I spend a bit of my time hoping to get you out into the world."

He was sincere. But couldn't he have said more than that? Wouldn't he ever go further than friendliness? Didn't he know what her illness was? Was he going to play his game until she was no longer a lily in his pond?

He said impressively, "I talked with the staff. They believe that in about a month you'll be able to go home."

Her loquacity ceased. She immediately became depressed.

He had taken her heart and mind. That didn't hurt too much. But after she would leave the asylum his interest in her would die. He'd go out of her life——as he had done before. That dreadful tremor shock her. It frightened her. She'd become ill again. And would she arise from the dead again?

She turned her head from him and said in a whisper, "I don't want to go home. I agreed to come here because you told me so. You wanted me to help you write your second book. That evening on the lily pond you said you had a story in mind about a man who could only fall in love with a water lily type of a girl——that he suffered in the night when it was closed and hidden in darkness. But that you couldn't do it because it didn't happen in your life and therefore you were creatively lost."

A chill went through him.

She said softly, "I can't leave here until our story is finished. Finished."

He gripped himself and stared at her.

It was the day of the annual Spring picnic. The picnic ground was the grassy field behind the superintendent's cottage. Nearby was a stone Quaker meetinghouse, and to the west was the blue-green sea.

Cooks broiled frankfurters and hamburgers. Under the shade trees were tables with refreshments. When the patients, employees, and visitors were congregated the asylum band played Hail, Hail, the gang's all here.

Corinne was proud of Richard and clung to him.

After the games and contests they sat on the benches for the open air stage show.

He thought of his drama pupils——the evening Corinne entered the classroom——she sat up front between Higgins the Linqua-phone salesman, and the French seamstress, Madame Vitu. It had been impossible to fit the class into a suitable play. He hit upon the idea of having them act out their problems, and called it improvised drama.

"Ladies and gentleman!" bellowed the master of ceremonies, "With the greatest of pleasure I call upon Miss Cooper, the songbird star of Ward D. Miss Cooper will graciously sing for us her favorite song, Apple Blossom Time. I give you Miss Cooper!"

Richard pressed her hand. She arose and went up on the stage. She sang as one hypnotized.

She would be with him——in apple blossom time . . .

The mass of patients did not make a sound. Her low voice captured the stillness. Her eyes were upon his face as she sang.

To him came the lily pond. She was by his side on the log bridge connecting the tiny island and the sloping green bank. They were leaning on the railing. The single tree on the island was a crab-apple in bloom. The evening breeze hushed the blossoms down upon the darkening water. He recalled being saddened by the slowly strangling lilies struggling for light. "Look Corinne," he had said, "the apple blossoms are kissing my lilies to sleep . . ." And in a spate of poetic inspiration he had told her that he wouldn't be happy until the rosy cavalier of the dawn had heralded them back to life and beauty.

The band struck up a popular tune. Almost everybody mingled without question and danced.

It was the first time she was in his arms. He asked, "Why . . . Corinne, why did this happen to you? Just what is it you want?"

"I . . . want . . . you!"

"——Was it——because of me?"

She had said it at last. She was tense, praying that he wouldn't say it shouldn't have happened——that it was all tragically wrong——a mistake——that he was terribly sorry. He stood speechless.

In asylum night the haunted bayed and cursed and groaned to the bland white moon. Corinne's eyes spoke to the moon. She had wanted Richard. That was it and it was no sin. She had wanted his person, his name, to be his wife and mother of his children. And finally she had said it. She could look into the past; it was no longer held from her.

"I'd do anything to get that feeling where a story lives and writes itself. I'd do anything to get that magic!" Those had been his words. Under the pretense of improvised imagined drama he got his class to reveal their shame and passions.

One night as he walked her home he said excitedly, "I never let on that I know their little acts and monologues are not fictional. Their portrayals of the hidden truths about themselves is the show of shows. What material for my writing——a gold mine!"

But he kept his own truth clandestine, denied. There were his alternate extremes of religion and cynicism, his indiscreet risky affairs, and then his high-flown excoriation of the immoral. He lived in other people's lives and fled from the damaging consequences at the climax. She knew he had to do it. He was an artist and she understood him inside. He did not believe himself inside and feared the instability of his mind and character. But she believed in him.

It was only a few weeks after her brother Alvin's suicide that he had said to her in class, "Miss Cooper, do you think you can improvise for us the part of girl who knows there is insanity in her family and fears that she is losing her mind?"

She played the part to please him. She shuddered as she played out her real fears. He was enthralled. And she was grateful to be able to affect him.

She could not go on forever working in the dress shop to support her burdensome family. Her mother fidgeted and gabbed about maids and mansions. Her father sat about the house dressed up, concentrating on an outdated World Almanac or poring through newspapers reading stock quotations, obituaries, and personal notices.

Morose brother Harold ate ravenously, showered many times a day and shut himself in his room. Sis kept the radio going from morning to night.

She used to pop in at Richard's house, chumming with his sister and kid brothers. He'd read his writings and have fits of doubt. She had prevented him from tearing up his manuscript.

When his book was published and became the bestseller he disappeared.

She made a scrapbook of his clippings, and heard him on the radio. His answers to her letters were few and formal. In the dress shop a wealthy customer said to her, "Do come sailing with us Sunday dear. You're pretty; the air will do you good. You'll meet the famous author, Richard Dean."

She fought to keep her composure when she saw him on the yacht. He was surprised and somewhat annoyed to meet her. He had brought a movie actress. He avoided talking about the old days. He said he had bought the big stone house with the lily pond.

Her long walks to the dress shop in the village were idylls filled with thoughts of him. One morning a sports car pulled up. "Hey dreamy!" he called, "Get in. Were you sleepwalking?" "Yes," she answered, "ever since I met you!" Naturally, he thought she was kidding. He drove to the seashore. His lean dark face showed ravages of dissipation.

He spoke bitterly about himself and his work.

She told him, "You said your second book would be about the girl who sacrifices her sanity for love."

"Someday," he sighed, "someday when it hits me right."

"That will be *our* book," she said, pretending to joke. He then looked directly at her. She was ashamed of her thinness, anemia and faded clothes. She flushed under his objective eyes. "What does the x-ray read, measles or a fractured heart," she flipped at him in defense.

"You have good bonework, skin with possibilities, sexy hair and gray-green eyes authors write about."

"I gather you approve of the architecture and the chemicals," she had said. "No ulterior motives behind the observation," he answered politely. "Well then, author, would you mind giving me back my bushel; it's chilly and I prefer to hide my light." "You know, Corinne," he continued patronizingly, "you're a sleeper. Some day a smart guy is going to take you over, fatten you, put roses in your cheeks, dress you up, and have a stunning good wife." She had wanted to cry. Instead, she laughed.

"A girl resents being labelled 'good.' It's almost eight-thirty. Now you may return Cinderella to the salt mine."

On the way to the dress shop he said soberly, "Don't you feel it's about time to let your family shift for themselves, and begin to live your own life?

"You rate a normal life; a husband, home and children." She remembered saying, "That's unromantic. I'll lie in my cardboard castle sleeping until you send Prince Charming——or come yourself. I might be a story for you."

He looked at her quizzically. She knew he was pitying her.

In front of the dress shop he turned to her. "Steer clear of men like me," he said sincerely, "I'm trouble and not husband material. My success has made me a vampire. I'm full of promises that I hate and will not keep."

"How awful!" she had exclaimed mockingly. "I'd never let you love and ruin me!" How could she have told him that she would have loved and lived with him under any circumstances and regardless what he said or did? He said affectionately, "You do remind me of my sweet sister, Anne, as I told you long ago. But you've a spritely lip. If you could only write the way you talk you'd make a pretty author." She stepped out of the car and chuckled, "Then I'd be your ghostwriter and you could devote all your time to 'bad' girls." "That's a promise, Corinne," he cried, and raced off.

He had noticed that she was a woman. She had hoped then that it would occur to him to take her. She was all too willing. She envisioned herself at the typewriter by his side, weaving stories, being needed, and part of him. Then there was her visit to his big stone house. He was alone, but he treated her as though she were a nun. He played symphonic records, and as the evening reds and purples seared the sky he walked her down to the lily pond. His words were poetic, but not about her——and she envied the lilies.

Night after night she lived in a fantasy writing the book he could not write——because a heroine had not lived it for him. The sleepless hours mounted her excitement until exhaustion trailed her off to flashes of restless slumber wherein she saw him looming towards her. In her waking hours she began to imagine him before her and spoke with him. He was on the street, in the skies, and in her room. At work she fainted. She was discharged and sent home. Everything slipped and moved away from her. She hardly recognized the people who spoke to her. Richard's face was with her but he eluded her touch. Dizzily she forced herself to go to the private hospital in the village. She told the doctor she was ill, that she would work for her keep and care. She remembered seeing Richard at the window of the hospital and running to the window calling, "Richard! Richard, save me!" She was sitting up feverishly in bed. He quietly opened the door. Somehow he had been notified. He stood there, not knowing what to do or say.

She had a rosary. She said, "You haven't just come Richard, you've been with me." She remembered telling him that she had died at five that morning and knew the answer to all things for his sake. He nodded as though he believed her. The doctor who controlled the hospital entered and talked with him near the window. "Miss Cooper is a psychopathic case. We cannot keep her here. She'll have to be taken to the State Institution. Her parents have already signed the necessary papers." Richard seemed greatly interested. Probably it hit him right; the story. He stood at the foot of the bed. He didn't come to near. "Corinne," he said carefully, "you're a sick girl. Things will seem very weird to you for a while——don't fight them——don't take them too seriously——do as you're told——please."

Yes, she would do as he wished.

Later, the doctor, the nurse, and two men in white uniforms came in. They dressed her. She asked them if Richard had come to take her home. They said Richard was outside waiting to take her home. They led her to the rear of the hospital. When they carried her into the asylum ambulance she screamed Richard's name over and over, wanting him to save her, telling him that she couldn't go through with it.

She had said it now, "I want you." And he remained speechless. She could only have said it in the asylum, for it didn't matter what the insane said. Surely she had frightened him away. Who could love and marry a girl who had once been declared insane? Richard visited her as an author, he did not love her. Alvin did kill himself. Richard did not want her. She'd have to die again. And stay dead. She saw the turgid swirling dread murky bottom of the lily pond.

Corinne did not touch her breakfast, nor did she join her fellow-worker-patients.

"You've got to be a good girl," cautioned Mary, "As much as we love you we want you out of here. Then you and Mr. Dean can drop in on us—for old time's sake. You wouldn't forget your friend, Mary, would you?" Corinne smiled wistfully.

What home? She had no home. This had been her home. She had gotten used to it. By now one didn't notice the morbid smells, the noises, the grotesque. This was home; the labyrinth of the unaccountable, the sanctuary of the faithful to passion, the temple of true lovers. In this her home solids were new unrepeated music, flesh was a flaming ghost, and walls were screen of metamorphosis.

Here the silent grandeur found place, here were they who had exceeded life. She was the stronger. She had descended into the underworld for him. She had redeemed him. And would he awaken and traverse the same path to her? This was her home.

He came that afternoon. It was the afternoon of gusts and greys. The skies were fraught, broken. She saw him from the barred window. He stopped on the path and talked with Dr. Berg.

She met him in the visiting room. She tried to print his face on her mind. Her only prayer was that when he left her forever his face would always be with her, and forever precious be.

He did not seem an author. He came with decision in his face. There read no curiosity.

They walked to the sea. What more could she say to him? They sat on a boulder. Gulls shrieked over the incoming tide. She felt united to him and torn from him by the heartbeat of the pounding waves. He turned from the view of the profound horizon and looked into her.

"Harold," he said evenly, "admitted that Alvin's death was not suicide. He and Alvin were handling the rifle. It went off accidently. He didn't have the courage to tell the truth.

"There is no insanity in your family. You broke down from overstrain. I'm taking you out of here today. You're going to live with me——as my wife. I've got your release. You're cured——and so am I. Our car is in front of the Administration building. You don't have to say a word. I want you and that is that. Let's go."

Farewell To Brahms

There is no accurate census figure on the cuckolds in our great nation, but it is conservative to say that if I had a dollar for every horned American (present company excepted) I would be a multi-millionaire. My purpose is to make the behorned see himself in an enviable light (a man does look crude and incomplete with nothing on his head.)

I postulate the cause of cuckoldry. It is a precious and civilizing contribution to our society. As a sincerely dedicated horn maker I am appalled by the widespread ignorance of its intrinsic and humanitarian worth. (The fame of Biblical kings rest securely upon their horning accomplishments.) How many cuckolds know that venerable St. Martin is their patron saint—and how many of them who have been informed, respect religion and are thankful for St. Martin's favoritism? And what is this one-sided idea of the masculine ego that only men have the privilege of sporting horns—doesn't it occur to thinking people that when a man has dalliance on the side he places a bonnet of dainty prongs on his wife's head?

I became aware of the magical significance of horns early. Over the entrance door of our house, Father nailed a pair of wicked-looking bull's horns. On a string around my neck I wore at least six amulet horns of coral, gold, silver, and olive wood, to ward off the evil-eye and mishaps. With every epidemic Mother added another horn. Mother physicked me with Pluto Water; on the label was a dashing red devil with horns. When I was ill the paesano witch, 'La Smorfia,' made me swallow a mixture of kerosene and powdered ram's horn—perhaps it always cured me as I was born under the sign of the ram's horn of Aries. My people referred to the male procreative organ—among other things—as "the horn of life." According to the Bible horns are symbols of strength, glory and pride. I read in the Good Book, "The Lord—is the horn of my salvation." Holding the Ten Commandments, Moses is portrayed with durable stubby horns. What would Jewish New Year be without the Shofar? And there is no doubt that horns are becoming.

I cannot claim to learning the age-old practice of horning all by myself. The late president of the International Association for the Advancement And Propagation Of Cornutos, Professor Marcello— whole place I have assumed—was of aid to me on my way up.

"Rafael," he said, "coronating husbands is an art. Successful horn-making and putting requires originality and finesse. As with fingerprints, no two sets of horns should be the same. The design, size, texture and color should be custom-made to fit the personality of the cornuted.—Contemplate cornucopianly: How would mooses' horns look on rhinoceroses? Snails' antennae on giraffes? A good seducer does not plagiarize; he makes crowns for husbands in his own inimitable style like a Da Vinci or Michelangelo.—Thus, when you 'nature' a man's wife—aside from soothing her nervous system—you honor him. For example: You take John Doe's wife to bed—you compliment his marital taste—a man should feel insulted if other men think so poorly of his wife that they disdain to sleep with her—After you've had John Doe's–wife—John Doe being a figure of speech—you have given him something he may never have had before: a lovely first edition of antlers "a la Rafael," to embellish and warm his noggin. Endowed with glittering personalized horns, he is no longer a bare-headed run-of-the-mill mortal; he is god-like, and entered into the realm of mythology. But you should be wary as a toreador—do not trust him—he may gore you with your very gift."

I asked Professor Marcello the goose and gander question, "Suppose one sweet day you look in the mirror and see Lucifer's nob poking from *your* forehead?"

"That can't happen. My silvery curling hair will never hear that decoration."

"Why?"

"No wife."

My mentor came to an untimely finale, curiously enough, not through an ungrateful berserk husband, but because of a virgin-spinster he was satyrically spoofing.

She met him in full daylight on Mulberry Street and weepingly accused him of deception. In his compulsive operatic manner, he pulled a pearl-handle revolver from his pocket, gave it to her, and declared, "Bernadette, you are the only woman in my life. If you don't believe me, put a bullet in my heart!" And she did.

The burden of his hornological genius fell upon my small shoulders. He left me his notes, and the drawings of the unfinished, CUCKOLDS' BEASTIARY. His inspired observations are a treasured trove. I quote at random:—'certain' hairs of exhibit #3,243 (Beautine S. Murray Hill O-IIIII) tied with chartreuse ribbon and stored with collection—

—what kind of mammal, fish or arthropod likeness is the woman in case mated to?

—virtue is a sexual deficiency symptom—

—why not, intimate horns prevent cancer?

—lovers are heroes—husbands are comedians—

—horns protect a man on the battlefield—

—life expectancy of cuckolds exceeds that of the hornless—

—unbranched horns—French horns—cusp of the moon—bony or skin-covered—the kind that shed and renew annually—it is no manly deed to love without danger, as with a single girl, prostitute, widow or divorcee; the bona-fide hornist essays the Garden of Eden itself!

—put 'mental horns' on men in highest places by e.s.p. over television—

—comparison of horns with the hat fetish; the premier and derby, President and sombrero, General and beret, Admiral and baseball cap et cetera—

—root-bound horns—phrenology—skull contours—visual horn-planting and arrangement over wigs—

—if you do not know husbands or have photograph you must design his set by intuition—

—Eskimos offer wives to guests; horns of hospitality—
the arts did a disservice to man by undressing girls—whereas, the

heights of esthetic thrill was to dress a girl from head to toe, and then make love to her!

Walking back to camp Myra told me she and Igor were born nudists, having been raised in Canada as Dukhobors, the Russian sect that believed that as Jehovah had no clothes man should be naked too. I asked her what she thought of nudism. She answered, "Boring, and so bourgeois . . . !" To me, when a woman stressingly uses the words, 'boring,' and 'bourgeois,' it is unmistakable invitation to fashion horns for her husband. "You couldn't be more right, Myra." I hastened to affirm, "It denies the mystic soul of romance, discourages imagination, and leaves nothing to the element of wonder." With a Venus di Milo modesty she buttoned the top of her blouse, and said, "Rafael, your honesty, intellect and culture is fascinating."

She stroked my seersucker coat sleeve sensuously, and blushed. We silently understood each other. The covering over of nudity, as the true path of passion, was our mutual clandestine secret. We would be the camp's tacit rebels.

As we entered camp stark naked Igor hailed us. Myra and I stripped with alacrity—to avoid suspicion. I asked Igor and Myra to come to my tent and listen to Brahms. I put on the E minor symphony. We sprawled on cots Myra said enthusiastically, "Brahms does something to me!" I explained the movements, especially the allegro energico e passionato. "Brahms," I said, looking meaningfully at Myra, "liberates the life forces and jubilantly unites the yin and yang. We adherents of his feel there is no God but E minor, and the Fourth of Brahms is his prophet." Myra said she could listen to Brahms forever. I pointed to my ten albums, "All his works. I'll play a different album for you two every afternoon or whenever you like." "Thanks," said Igor, "—I'm tone-deaf; do you mind if Myra comes alone?" I told him I would be glad to teach her Brahms appreciation.

The following afternoon Myra came to my tent, carrying a shopping bag. The bag was filled with clothes. I was so pleased that I decided to play the Festival Overture. "Myra, darling," I said, "quick—let us put on clothes, and love!"

Oh, the joy of article by article, garment by garment donning rituals—the exciting dressing prelude!

Later, it was saddening to have to undress and return to dull naked reality of the camp.

The afternoons were paradises of Brahms, the erotic excitement of dressing, and love. We exchanged long letters, lucidly recapturing and singing the details of each love-session. I scribbled the usual in-heat promises of having eyes and dreams only for her (much of which I copied from Madame Bovary) and of someday taking her with me to the enchanted far horizon. She wrote that she would not let Igor sleep with her or touch her as she was undyingly faithful to me.

In the meantime, I was exhausting both the Brahms music and myself. How much honey can a bee get from a flower? The summer was closing. Labor on The Cuckolds' Bestiary was dragging. How much time could I devote to the page on Igor's horns? An extra page doesn't make a book. Dissolving an affair is the most difficult part of hornology. I had a premonition that something nasty would happen.

Myra and I were in bed, fully clothed. Suddenly, the naked colossus, Igor, was towering over us. He had the terrifying grimace of the idealist. I looked up, and simulating calm, said, "Igor, let's talk this over . . ."

He waved the tell-tale bundle of letters. "Try to seduce my wife away from sacred nudism?! You snake in the grass—you subversive—you Communist!" He deliberately and methodically piled and straddled all my Brahms albums on two chairs breathed heavily, and with one karate chop cleanly broke every one of my blessed Brahms records—right in half—precisely down the middle. He turned to Myra, and said gently, imploringly, "Myra, dear, remember, once a Dukhobor always a Dukhobor. Please make yourself decent—get up and take off your clothes."

New York's Little Italy

On Manhattan's Lower East Side, Little Italy begins and stretches north to south from Prince to Bayard Streets, and east to west from Elizabeth to Baxter Streets. I have memories of going with father to Ellis Island to greet *paesanos* arriving like tagged sheep from Italy and of escorting them to their first lodgings in America on South Mulberry Street, overlooking little Mulberry Park (now Columbus Park), the notorious Five Points, the Miserable Tombs, and "Bye-bye Bacigalupo".

The tenements are still there, standing in continuous rows on narrow streets. They are a brick and stone and tin poem to the architectural conceit of the mushrooming metropolis of a century ago. Irish, English and Italian masons laid up the intricate patterns of bonds, fretted jambs and stately sills, the curved and flat arches, the showy quoins and stone balconies and stoops. Smiths molded and soldered seamless sculptured shapes of tin for baldachins before entrances and for imposing roof cornices. Iron shops hammered and joined the fanciful wrought-iron of fire-escape landings, and railings and ladders. Never again in American construction will be seen the imaginative postures, the flaunt, daunt, myth and craftsmanship of the mask of Tenement.

Behind the mask were dark, airless, disease-breeding cells with few taps for water and a single latrine in the hallway, basement or backyard. In the 1890's Little Italy was a soul-crushing quarter of mud, dirt and filth. In doorways, on stools on the sidewalks and out in the streets, women nursed their young, sewed, cleaned the withered greens which were the only ingredient of their soup, washed their clothes in grimy tubs, untangled and arranged one another's hair. They chattered, not in the happy and playful mood of the old country, but in an angry importuning way that stung the heart.

Everything was old and poor—the clothes the people wore, the displayed merchandise, the fruit, the herbs, the yellowed meat that hung in the butcher shops, the furniture in the open stalls, the sordid Italian and American bank notes in the windows of the banks, even the huge pictures of King Victor, Umberto and Garibaldi, and the tri-color flags that fluttered from the entrances of the small shops. The flags evoked a sense of tenderness and of national shame.

Today the interiors of the tenements have been made fit for humans, with electricity, adequate and sanitary plumbing and central heating. My immigrants have come a long way in their struggle to attain self-respect.

Recently I fulfilled a life-long dream. I visited Italy. The author Carlo Levi showed me the treasures and monuments of Rome. One moonlit night outside the Vatican, he put his hands dramatically to his heart and said, "Rome is my *amore* until I die. You have no such mistress in the New World. Your world is a nation of immigrants. You have the despotism of the immigrant, by the immigrant, for the immigrant. Your land was built by prejudice. The degrading prejudices between immigrant nationalities stimulated the aggression and competition that made your new Babylon rich. But we are fifty million Italians who will never emigrate. The immigrant is not a national but a species in himself. The true national loves his womb-land so that he would never abandon it; only the emigrating type who can wed himself to another sovereignty does. The flower of the Italians never thought of emigrating to America. The majority of Italo-Americans are the children of the lowest strata of Italian intelligence, and no matter what their achievements they are unformed social quantities who reflect the crudities of their illiterate parents. The Italians in America are hybrids. My dear Pietro, when your America has three thousand years of illustrious history and is the Holy Seat, then come and talk to me."

It is June in New York's Little Italy. I am having lunch at Ballato's on East Houston Street. Pier Donati's *ristorante* on the Via Della Conciliazione near Saint Peter's Square is not superior to Ballato's. There is another as good, Angelo's at 146 Mulberry Street, but I have known Ballato's for twenty-five years; it is the mecca for discriminating Italian gourments. Fiorello La Guardia and I ate there together many times. Ballato's intimacy, the soft classical music, the wine closet, the framed scenes of Rome on the green, charcoal, rose and yellow cloth-papered walls, the subtle cooking smells from the immaculate open kitchen, the temperate, leisurely, relaxing atmosphere make me feel as though I am back in the Old World. I find there my sweet, elderly friends of the La Guardia days—Edward Corsi, August Bellanca and Onofrio Ruota. There are times when it is priceless to be Italian. Shall I have a glass of St. Raphaele or Cinzano? Should I partake of *cozze* (mussels) *reganate*, or *bordetto di pesce asortiti marichiaro*, or *cotoletta di vitello parmigiana*, or *osso buco milanese con risotto*, and for dessert shall I have tortoni or zabaglione with my espresso? The food is cooked to order, and is worthy of being painted by a Tintoretto.

We old friends of Fiorello La Guardia affectionately recall him. To the Italo-Americans Mother Cabrini is the heroine, and Fiorello La Guardia is the hero.

Sentiment is a powerful trait of my people; it is life to them. As great an American as was Fiorello, his warmest love was for his Italians. After a meal at Ballato's he would sneak the left-over chicken or *polenta* or bread into a napkin to take home. The night he lost a big election he didn't care a damn—he was more concerned about the spaghetti sauce he was cooking for us. He had a penchant for roasted goat's head and salami made from horsemeat. After he became Mayor of New York City, a team of us went about with him inspecting the run-down City Hall. In the rubbish in the basement we found a statue of Columbus.

Fiorello screeched, "Our dear Columbus in the cellar? If it wasn't for this guy none of us would be in America. Get him out of here and scrub him up. We'll put him on a pedestal in Mulberry Street Park and call it Columbus Park."

In 1944, after joining Helen and me in civil matrimony at City Hall before sculptor Attilio Piccirilli and artist Onofrio Ruota, he wagged his finger at me and shouted, "Di Donato, remember, when I tie a man and woman together they stay hitched—don't do anything to embarrass me." Helen was a head taller than little Fiorello, and to kiss her, he hopped up upon his desk, then reached down and embraced her.

Like most Italians, he revered the arts, and he would often say, "Politics stink. I'd give it all up in a minute, jump out of a ten-story window and dance with joy in the streets if I could sculpt statues like Attilio Piccirilli or paint as good as Onorio Ruotolo."

Francesco Barilla's candy store adjoins Ballato's. Children are clamoring to "Uncle Frank" for service at the penny-candy counter. He nods smilingly, "One at a time, my darlings."

"I have nothing of interest to tell you," says short, stocky, eighty-year-old Francesco. "I am a Calabrian 'hard-head.' I have had this store and lived above it for sixty years. Come upstairs and meet my sweetheart—my lovely wife—she is from Sorrento. She has had a stroke."

Mrs. Barilla sits at the front-room window; she is listening to an Italian program on the radio. On a wall there are religious pictures and a photo of Francesco as a doughboy of the First World War. She tells me in Italian, "God comes first in our family. Francesco sent our three sons to college. He is the only one in New York who still sells a good cup of coffee with cream for five cents.

"We knew Mother Cabrini. We filled her oil-cloth shopping bag with candy for her orphans. She has answered my prayers. I am recovering from my stroke, God bless her.

"But we have nothing exciting for you. Our sixty years in Little Italy have been without trouble or disturbance."

A pigeon coop is visible atop a tenement. I climb the seven flights to the roof. A group of girls in bathing suits are lolling on a blanket and applying sun-tan lotion to their limbs. By the coop a handsome man is directing the flight of a pigeon flock with a long, whirring bamboo pole. He is wearing swim trunks, and about his neck are a chain and crucifix.

"Brother, you want to know why I stay in Little Italy? I was born here and lived all my life on this block. There's *something* about your own block. After my old folks won the fight over hatred of Italians and lousy conditions for us kids, are we supposed to run out on them and the place?

"You see the pigeons on the next roof? My birds won't mix with them; they know this coop is their home. Our kind of people are clannish too. I got my parents—thank God they're in good health—my wife, three girls, relatives and *real* friends in this building—and the TV brings the world to me. I don't have to knock myself out worrying about a mortgage, car installments and then end up in the bug house.

My rent is cheap, and I got a lot of time to fly my birds.

"Sure, the outside of the building looks crummy, but in my flat I'm just as well off as the guy on Park Avenue. There are rich guys commuting four hours every day to New York—four hours a day they'll never get back. I'm a teamster, and in ten minutes I'm at the garage.

"We got security here, and there ain't no safer place to live. There's no mugging and rape like in other sections. Our boys are on every corner and look out for the girls. My daughters can come home at any hour and no one can lay a finger on them.

"I stay in Little Italy because I'm proud. We were despised for garlic and pizza and spaghetti. Now the Americans eat more of that stuff than we do. The tourists are crazy about our restaurants here. American singers change their names to Italian to get into the opera, and the biggest names today are like Como and Borgnine and Sinatra and the swanky stores feature Italian-style clothes."

He invites me down to meet his family. There is newish furniture, an air-conditioner, TV, radio, a small piano, a modern kitchen, holy pictures and a glass-encased statuette of the Madonna—all a far cry from the bare, verminous dank flats of my boyhood.

His wife and teen-age girls greet me.

"My girls can even read and write Italian," he says.

His wife tells me that the girls attended the Church of the Transfiguration Parochial School on Mott Street. She points to a picture of a nun and says, "That's Mother Cabrini, my favorite Saint. She started the school. The Maryknoll Sisters are in charge of the school now. We donated a statue of the little saint of purity, Maria Goretti, to the church, and my girls carry her picture in their pocketbooks."

I am given glasses of Strega, introduced throughout the tenement of old folks and relatives and invited to dinner. I am made to feel completely at home.

One of the questions my new friend asks me, "Why do the movies and TV show so many gangsters as Italians? The people I know don't watch trash like *The Untouchables*; only hood punks look at that program to see what they can learn. Why don't TV show how immigrants raised families and sent kids to college? And what about the boys of Little Italy who died fighting for this country?"

I visit my dear, aged, ill but still spirited artist-friend Onofrio Ruota on the fringe of Little Italy. His studio evokes memories of celebrated Italians in America. There are photographs of him with Marconi, Toscanini, Caruso, Valentino, La Guardia. He had been a long-haired, flowing-tie idealist of the Arturo Giovanetti and Carlo Tresca days, but now he thinks of Christian mystics, the stigmatist Padre Pio, the martyred child saint Maria Goretti and Papini.

"Little Italy!" he says. "My boy, it's watered wine now, and made from second and third pressings. You were born too late. You should have been here at the turn of the century. Immigrants crossed the ocean for ten dollars. They were thick as ants on Mulberry Street, and exploding with life. The women had cheeks tight and ruddy as fresh red apples and suckled infants out on the street from magnificent breast for anyone to see and enjoy. The killings and stabbings were wonderful because they were inspired by romantic passion. Emotions were liberated in the New World. Life on Mulberry Street was a night-and-day opera from Verdi. The immigrants brought with them the love of ritual, music and drama.

"On Spring Street, in the back of the saloon, there was a theatre. The stage was a platform on top of beer barrels. The Italian actors played nothing but Shakespeare, and in the room above were Chinese prostitutes.

"In the store at 188 Mulberry Street Papa Manteo had his puppet theatre. The favorite play was the *The Paladins of France*. Papa Manteo and his family worked the puppets and simulated all the voices. The immigrants ate *lupino* beans while they watched the drama. At the climax one of the Manteos in the audience arose and fired a bullet into the head of the puppet villain.

"Then there was Clemente Giglio and his melodramas at the old Thalia theater. The audience was as much a part of the play as the actors; they would shout and warn and curse and advise the characters on the stage. Giglio, who wrote the plays, always had himself killed off in the first act so that he could jump down into the orchestra pit and relieve his son Sandrino at the piano.

"Prohibition spawned the criminal element. With the gang battles came the costly funerals. I made fat money designing mausoleums and tombstones, and received cases of hi-jacked whisky for painting noble portraits of murdered gangsters.

"At a ganster's funeral his widow was eulogizing the corpse and crying, 'Tony, you were the best gunman that ever lived. My Tony, you were the best-looking and slickest dressed. Tony darling, you were the toughest and didn't take sass from no one. You were the smartest. You could shoot the quickest. Tony, there will never be another professional like you.' The attending gangsters became so annoyed that they lifted the 'wonderful' dead gangster from the coffin and hurled him out the window.

"The gangsters were strangely religious. They had a society for a Saint X. One year the priest refused to let them borrow the saint's statue for their feast. They came at night to the church, threatened the priest with a machinegun and kidnapped the saint. The priest had to send to Italy for a new statue. From then on, after their feasts the gangsters stored the saint with their special undertaker.

"The man you should write about is Pati the banker. In 1908 Pati appeared on Mulberry Street in a chauffeur-driven Cadillac which created a sensation. He opened a bank for immigrants. He walked about dressed like a lord, with a high silk hat and cane, and advised the Italians to beware of American crooks. In the window of his bank he displayed a brand-new ten-thousand-dollar bill. The daily sight of that single bill overwhelmed the immigrants, and soon they were pouring their entire savings into his bank.

"An immigrant became suspicious and wanted to withdraw his account, Pati invited the immigrant into his office, shot him through the heart, put another pistol in the dead man's hand, then ran out onto Mulberry Street screaming 'Hold up!' The police congratulated Pati for saving the bank, and Little Italy held a parade and hailed him as their hero. A few days later Pati disappeared with a million dollars and was never seen again.

"You should mention detective Joe Petrosini, the master of disguise. I was walking along Mulberry Street and asked a bum for a match. As I was lighting my cigar the bum whispered, "Ruotolo, it's me, Petrosini. Don't come near this corner tonight. Angelo So-and-so is marked by the Black Hand.' That night the killing took place, but Pertrosini got his man.

"After the Mafia killed Petrosini, 'Treat-'em-Rought-Mike' Fiaschetti became head of the Italian squad. He sent one hundred men to the electric chair."

It is eight o'clock of a June morning in Boccie Park on East Houston Street, and some two hundred old Italians are there. To the *boccie* devotees it is "the countryside," for around the alleys and giving shade are seven plane trees and seven maple saplings.

The enthusiasts gather, sides are chosen by the throwing of odd and even fingers, and the sturdy faces become intent and profound. The small white lead ball is tossed. The team that gets their ball nearest the lead ball make points, and the score is noted on a pegboard. The balls are bowled to roll carefully, or daringly looped into the air to plummet down between close balls; or when the adversary's ball obstructs the lead ball, the desperate cannonading shot is made with a bellow, and the player weaves about to follow each throw with suggestive directing body English.

The old man next to me explains, "It's like American shuffleboard. Those guys aren't playing the game right. Without rules there is no dignity to the game. Play for money? No, Money? No, Money in sport makes bad blood.

"I came from Anzio sixty years ago. I was a track hand on the railroad. I got my pension, and I can ride the railroad free. Here, see, my railroad pass with my name and picture."

A group gathers about me. They are retired on pensions and old-age security. It is Italian to expound, to not agree. Among them are a former waiter, a stone-mason and a businessman.

The waiter looks at me dubiously. "You a writer? I bet you haven't the guts to write the truth I tell you. The Italians in America are turn-banners; when Mussolini was the man of the hour, they were on his side. He said, 'Follow me. If I lead you forward, immortalize me; if backward, kill me.' He made the world respect Italy. He made only one mistake—declaring war on America. All right, no one is perfect. But don't believe the propaganda that he begged for his life; he died like a man. It was a disgrace to hang him by the heels in public. Don't ask my name because I won't tell you."

"War did not ruin Italy; war makes progress," says the businessman. Then he adds lamentingly, "What ruins Italy is religion and the flesh. The hand of the priest is too heavy, with church here and church there. The other thing is that the Italian closes his business at noon, runs home to his wife or to his mistress, eats, drinks and makes love like a pig. Where would America be if Wall Street had that habit? The Italian thinks he is a cock in the barnyard. Yes sir, carnal sport in the afternoon is the downfall of Italy."

"That was done away with by Mussolini," persists the waiter, "but with the Christian Democrats in power, sex with lunch has returned. As for the Communists, they are careerists and rose-water revolutionists. Tomorrow they'll be something else."

What about immigrants who dream of retiring in the homeland?

"I was one of those who tried it," says the stonemason, "but it was not the bread for my teeth. Returning to my village in Bari I found myself neither large intestine nor small intestine. The dream was nothing more than a dream, for where one spends his youth and strength, that is his country. I walked the two blocks of the village back and forth. My wife and I were disgusted and longed for Mulberry Street. It is more Italian than Italy, and these markets have more and better food than all of Italy.

"In Bari I met returnees who gave up their American citizenship and then cursed themselves for it. If you think America is crooked, corruption and monopoly is ten times worse in the 'good old country.' Only beauty and the art of poverty is left to Italy.

"Then there are those who left wives and children in Bari. When they went back after ten, twenty or thirty years they were bitter strangers to their families. Money is not worth such woe.

"Many went back to find themselves beautifully cuckolded. And what about the illegitimate children their daughters had with German and then American and Negro soldiers?

"To go back is only good for childless couples who want to die there, and widowers and ugly bachelors who can snare themselves juicy young wives. Once you've lived in America the old country is out of the question."

I am in the rectory of the Church of The Most Precious Blood. Father Victorio is one of the ten children of a ditchdigger. The sandals on his bare feet are worn thin and his brown, woolen Franciscan cassock is frayed.

"With his pick and shovel, my father sent ten children through school. I'm the only poor one in the family.

"The young Italo-Americans are too materialist-minded; they discard principles of the old world, cannot replace them with vital qualities, and consequently struggle in the vacuum. All in all, though, they are a credit to the purpose of life. They still retain filial respect, make solid parents and do not subscribe too much to the sick ideas of our time.

"On the other side of the ledger, we're cursed with some criminal—there's no use denying it—but really not as many as the alarmists say. What burns me is that whenever an Italian gangster is dying he hollers for a priest. 'Get me a priest. I don't want to die without a priest.' I will not profane the sacred Mass by celebrating it for the sake of a gangster. In this parish the hoods know where I stand."

His swarthy, strong-jawed face relents.

"Not all the bad sheep stay lost. There are those who have reformed and earn an honest living. Now and then one calls up anonymously, offering food and help for the distressed."

Our conversation is interrupted. The phone rings. Dates are set for baptisms, religious instruction, marriages, a funeral. A woman wants a Mass said for the soul of her husband.

People ring the bell and are admitted. "Be seated," says the sacristan. "Father Victorio will be with you."

Problems are written on their faces. They have come to the right place. They sit and wait.

Father Victorio accompanies me to the door. I ask him if he ever gives himself a rest.

"Three more years to go. That will make twenty-five years since I was ordained. And then, O boy, the wonderful two months' vacation in Rome. I can hardly wait."

Filigreed arches span Mott and Grand streets. The Society of San Antonio of Padua is in a store on Grand Street. The "big pieces" are in the headquarters and out on the sidewalk. They are wearing swallow-tail suits, red silk *bandoliera* and belt sashes: silver medallions on ribbons around their necks; and badges on their lapels that say Pres., Sec., Treas.

The musicians look like Grand Marshals. Men, women and children crowd about, and I hear the *bel-canto* cadence of Italian speech on all sides. From the headquarters are brought brass-rimmed glass lanters fixed on poles, banners, the richly colored flag of the House of Savoy and the American flag.

Three wizened musicians jauntily improvise melodies with fife, drum and cymbals.

An old-timer says to me with a Western accent, "I'm thoroughly Americanized—third generation, and I'm a red-hot fan of San Antonio.

"My grandfather sailed around Cape Horn in 1852 and settled in the Napa Valley, California. He brought grape and fig and fruit cuttings with him from Sicily. He owed his success to San Antonio. My sons and me run the orchards—5,000 acres—we get along. I come from the Coast every year for this feast."

The procession is forming: flower-bearers first, lanterns, little girls, one dressed as a bride and others as bridesmaids, then the banners and band. The band initiates the feast with the old Italian national anthem, the *March Royale*, which raises all hearts, and follows with an automatic *Star Spangled Banner*.

Nearby, in the window of an *espresso* café, is a sober sign: THIS IS RAIDED PREMISES. POLICE DEPARTMENT.

It had been a bookie pint. The two policeman in the raided café are interested onlookers of San Antonio's glory.

On the corner of Grand and Mott, up against the tenement, is the tabernacle of painted cardboard enshrining the statue of San Antonio. Above him are fire escapes with potted plants, beach chairs canary cages, mops, brooms and wash.

San Antonio, holding the naked, crowned Infant, stands in a grotto of fresh flowers. The pedestal-and-statue is hoisted onto a litter shouldered by four men.

The procession begins, preceded by a police prowl car. Every few hundred feet the litter-bearers are relieved by others jealously seeking the honor. Thousands flank the procession from the sidewalks. The band is expert; their horns and fifes and cymbals make feelings quiver. No matter what song the musicians play, they return to the *March Royale*.

A man growls, "There is no more monarchy in Italy. They should play Mussolni's song—what are they afraid of?"

At each corner the police block off the traffic for San Antonio.

The procession crosses Canal Street and goes into Chinatown. A little spry octogenarian directs the way. I ask him why they take San Antonio into Chinatown. "The Chinese give us contributions for good luck," he answers. "The Chinese syndicate own the buildings in Little Italy. They will crowd us out and Little Italy will go bye-bye Bacigalupo."

At Bayard Street the procession makes the turn to go back to Little Italy up Mulberry Street. Dollar bills are thrown from windows to be picked up and pinned to San Antonio. For a coin or bill you get a holy card of the saint, and you kiss it.

As we go past Bacigalupo's Mortuary, the processionists do the horns of counter-evil with their fingers.

Father Victorio is in front of the Church of The Most Precious Blood. As he sprinkles Holy water upon the statue and blesses it, the litter-bearers give San Antonio a forceful rocking. I ask Father Victorio why they shake San Antonio.

"To urge the statue to come to life and walk among us."

A Bowery derelict trails the musicians, weeping, skipping and shouting, "Beautiful, Jesus, it's beautiful."

San Antonio's solicitors go into the stores: the meat market displaying whole furry rabits and woolly lambs, brains, sweetbreads, tripe, coils of hot sausages and bloody, eyeless, scalped goat heads; the fish market that overflows with sand shark, crustaceans, winkles, squid, octopus and all fruit of the seas; the herb shop; the dried bean and nut shop, the bakery; the grocery with baskets of Moroccan snails and cans of Mother Mine and Peace O My God olive oil; the novelty shop with Italian kitchen utensils, calendars, a religious articles and fortune-telling cards; the book store with musty classics in Italian—*The Wandering Jew, The Count of Monte Cristo, Uncle Tom's Cabin*, and exposing prominently the complete words of Ezra Pound, along with guitars, tambourines and sheet music; and the few hoody, questionable *espresso* cafés and 'social' clubs with signs that read MEMBERS ONLY where sharply-dressed, sallow, indolent, cruel-eyed fellows lounge—and will not answer when spoke to.

It is hot, and the tenements are blazed with lilac sunshine. At Mulberry and Grand, San Antonio is set on stilts, the litter-bearers and musicians step into the corner bar for that cool beer and wine.

I hear music in the distance and wonder if San Antonio has two bands.

"The other band belongs to San Vito of Mott Street." says the bartender.

"Two saints and feasts on the same day?"

"Better feasts than bad times," he responds.

Hearing the forces of San Vito, the San Antonio champions accept the challenge and gaily remuster. The armies of San Antonio and San Vito meet and march past each other on Grand Street, both playing the Italian national anthem with all their might.

San Vito is young and comely, in a hunting costume of the Middle Ages; in his right hand he upholds the cross, and in his left are the missal and the leashes of the two dogs sitting at his feet. The crude, boxed, wheeled affair on which he rides is being unsteadily pushed along.

In his procession the women wear veils over their heads and carry lighted candles and rosaries; the children are dressed as nuns, peasants, kings, queens, *carabinieri*, Italian soldiers and sailors, and all are chanting in Italian, "San Vito martyr, amiable youth protect and remember, O remember us."

A Neapolitan by my side looks upon the two processions pityingly and says, "This is corny. San Gennaro is the 'big piece' of Little Italy. Come in September to his feast. We raffle off new cars, put on concerts with opera stars and shows that make these second-hand saints look sick!"

It is night. The multi-color-lighted arches from sidewalk to sidewalk make the tenements glow with important life in their old age, and the streets and buildings and crowds look like a great open stage set.

The warm air is felicitous with Italian tongues of many dialects. From a loud record player soar tarantellas and songs of nostalgia. Smoke brings the smells of sausage over charcoal, burning pepper and onions, roasting nuts, fish frying in olive oil. Families stand at pushcarts and eat raw clams, pickled conch and steamed, garlic flavored mussels. The man with the balloons and talking crow tells fortunes for ten cents, and the organ-grinder and money compete with him. Children ride the carrousel and tumble-car. Bright-eyed lads try to entice me to their shell game of pennies manipulated under bottle caps. There are nickel-pitching games where you might win a cocktail shaker or a plastic Madonna.

The funning, noisy wane, the tenement dwellers return to their intimate flats, the music is a memory, San Antonio and San Vito are unceremoniously put in storage, and the laughing lights disappear.

What keeps Little Italy there? Cheap rent? Choice of any superlative food? Family ties? National pride? Social life of the tenement? Or the personal patron saints? In my heart of hearts I belong there too and not among chilling other races and in a mixed neo-community that my soul disdains to digest. I remember what the pigeon fancier on the Mulberry Street roof said, "Sure, I like it here. Why should I leave, I'm with my own people—is there any place better?"

A Rinascimento On L.I.

"Festa Italiana!" "Festa Italiana!" "Be Italian This Week" proclaim the red white and green banners. Red is the fire of love, white is the joy and purity of the soul, and green is hope. Il rosso, bianco e verde gonfalons, posters and flags crowd the eye! Where are we? Are we at the Palio in Siena's Piazza del Campo watching the races on buffaloes, the bullfights, and swarthy knights jousting? Are we in the Colosseum where gladiators bloody the sand and die for real and toothy lions keep vigorous on a diet of Christians? Are we with a million devoted religious at St. Peter's where the Fisherman lives Vaticanly? Are we on Mulberry Street, maybe at the Feast of San Gennaro?

Stop wondering, we are on Long Island, pushing a shopping cart loaded with pasta linguine, prosciutto ham, goat's milk cheese, broccoli-rabi greens, and squid sauce with the Pope's picture on the label in Setauket's King Kullen supermarket in rhythm to the Muzak's "E La Luna A Mezz U Mare!"

Splendiferous festivals in marts and malls are never held for other nationalities; but only for gli Italiani. Long Island has a heavy fall-out of Italianismo; bel canto names outnumber all others in the Suffolk County telephone directory, from Andriola's Cesspools to Signore Zuzzolo. Right now descendants of immigrants from the Adriatic and Mediterranean are the most attention-getting group on the American ethnograph.

Italophilism is endemic on the scene of melting-pot metamorphosis and its boffo-burlesco profile has passed on to the silent majority as the True Coin . . . per esempio: a fatted Mafia soap-opera novel, and a Sicilian gallows-bird's who-dun-what—it's family chit-chat-trivia belaboredly hacked out in Sanforized Victorian-treatment as non-fiction is all the lucrative mod.

*

Come va?—excuse me, I mean, How Come? Va bene—that is to say, Very well: Pause. Reflect. O times!—O manners! Yesterday my people arrived in America with umiltà and modestia. They were exploited and reviled as something outside of the pale, and called garlic-stinking anarchists, wops, dagoes, guineas. Today Americans eat garlic like bon-bons and scatter it in their gourmet cuisine by the handful—and the immigrants' progency charge about like Orlando Furioso with clamorous pompa and superbia.

How did the Di Donatos and their paisani get to flood Brooklyn, Queens and Long Island? Migration is an outstanding feature of human life, changing the ethnic composition of lands as prehistoric glaciers once changed their physical composition. Overpopulation and the disparate ration between the number of inhabitants and the resources at their disposal were the determining factors in the great migratory trend that brought yearly a quarter of a million emigrants from central and south Italy to labor-hungry America. The uprooting reminds us of the Bible's story of the separation of Abraham and Lot: "The land was not able to bear them, that they might dwell together."

My people had no notions about democracy; coming here meant work and escape from starvation, conscription and crushing taxes. I saw them in steerage packed no differently than livestock. I went with father to Ellis Island to meet relatives. The poor, tagged, mustachioed men with their rag bundles were from the lowest class in Italy and had the perspective of the medieval vassal. The paisano brought his fig and vine cuttings, the Holy Roman Catholic religion, his village patron saint, his virtues and vices; but of all the qualities he transplanted to the New World the most significant was the pride and passion centered in the concept of family.

The glory and perpetuation of la famiglia superseded everything: "The family that holds together is the State, the Nation, and the Church that holds together." The family was the shrine, the citadel that outlasted all aspects of history; the family was the living fruit-bearing, seed-sowing tree.

In our Mulberry Street, Bronx and Brooklyn neighborhoods the ruling powers and keepers of legends and mores were the venerable matriarchs. Material things and social distinction meant nothing, and onore, virtu e verità was the All with these ancient women; their eyes were judging fires and their tongues rods that smote.

From infancy girls and boys had responsible godfathers and godmothers; as they grew they were familiar with the members of every paisano family, and it was unthinkable that they would someday marry barbarians—that is to say, Americanos.

A girl was taught to wash, sew, shop, make wine and preserves, and second-mother her younger brothers and sisters. Her parents had an important say in the choice of her mate. The mother of a son was in a premium position because she controlled his pay envelope; the prospective daughter-in-law had to attend her with "white gloves" of high circumspect. Occasionally there was a Montague-Capulet situation with envenomed families trying to break the forlorn lovers with threats, violence, and disenchanting cabalistic exorcisms calculated to undo the 'fattura' each claimed the other committed upon the bewitched.

Il Nozze, with solemn High Mass, and reception in the bride's tenement flat was an event to be recalled for life. All night long and far into the next day was a cornucopia of exotic foods, sweets, wines, liqueurs, folk music, Tarantella dancing, unabashed vulgarity, tearful memories of the Old World and pagan hilarity. The family was built around the nuptial mattress. Looking down upon the child-breeders were the Crucifix and the Virgin Mary. The Italian Christ was no neurotic esthete, but a muscled laborer, and the Madonna resembled the stalwart peasant. The child was born in the bed in which it was made; it was delivered by the levatrice and its entrance into this fantastic world was reverentially witnessed by relatives, . . . and the father. The new mother was then permitted the confidence of the seasoned mothers.

The woman handled her man's pay judiciously. There was no waste and she would never dream of spending above means. "Ugly as debt" was a bitter truth. Her bank was her corseted bosom, or between her upper thigh and stocking—and dollar bills in those days spoke of an exciting cloying fragrance. Saturday evening was for the trip, family ensemble, to the church and purgation of the soul in the Confessional; usually that night they partook of the flesh's confession with a dose of castor oil, epsom salts or Pluto Water (a nun told me her Neapolitan father drank a lot of Pluto Water and lived to be 103). When illness befell the counter-evil-eye was invoked, and medicinal methods of the Dark Ages prevailed with leeches, rancid socks seaweed and herbs. The hysterical wife or child was quickly cured with the applied psychology of isolation and a sound thrashing.

Circa, the early nineteen-hundreds, Italians came to "Longa-Eye" estates as cooks and gardeners, and as master stone carvers, masons and marble setters for the castles of the tycoons. They came on outings to la campagna by horse and wagon, the L.I.R.R. and Model T peddlers' trucks to hunt the magic mushroom, to pick dandelion, poke weed and wild grape, and to dig clams and mussels and conch and fish and spear the darling eel.

They acquired plots and built summering vine-draped gazebos; and then, resorted to roofed-over foundations and outhouses; and little by little, like the camel moving into the Arab's tent, they hop-skip-jumped and inched their appreciative way to the Green Country, leaving behind New York's warrens and towers of Babel, bringing with them to both shores and the scrub pine hinterland the trowel and concrete block, the cobbler's bench, the barber's scissors, the tailor's needle, the fruiterer's touch, and the cement Madonna in her grotto for the front lawn. I came to Bay Shore from Bensonhurst, Brooklyn in 1929 for the Turner Construction Company to build the Pilgrim State Hospital.

In the last few generations different reasons contributed to the transformation of Italian family living, but the prime mover was the potency of the dollar, which seduces gods and men alike. The immigrant and his forebears never had anything but the stark necessities. In America mechanical servants gradually became available to him, beginning with the gas stove and gaslight, sewing machine, hand-wash wringer, linoleum carpet, coffee-grinder, Victrola, player-piano and crystal radio set.

To the have-not peasant and proletariat was opened the Circean age of private possession. America emerged from World War I as the wealthiest and leading nation. The sense of a hastening time and material expansion was contagious for the Italian immigrant also. His lush opportunities came with the vast building boom and Prohibition.

Italians were the only minority in the suddenly dry land making large amounts of wines and liqueurs for home use. Thirsty Americans implored them for alcohol at any price. Many immigrants and their sons then knew they did not have to strain their backs with pick and shovel when they could make easy money bootlegging, and thus the Italian gangster was spawned.

Mixed marriages and exodus to the suburbs added to the altering of the family. Education, travel, ambition and big earnings caused the young to become contemptuous of the old. Children born on holy days were no longer named after a saint but for some celebrity and fated to go through life as Debbie or Candy or Tuesday or John Wayne Puzzo, and many have anglicized the surname so that a Fabbro becomes a Smith, and Bruno a Brown, a Garibaldi Panatieri becomes Gary Baker.

The wonders wrought by Christ have been overshadowed by the miracle-performing genii of electronics and automation. The chain discount stores of the copulation explosion, and the pregnant prairie split-level ranch house colonial mansion cubist-butterfly Plasterboard Desert (the Levitt-Man Cometh) are the temples of the functional commodities of the New World Covenant.

The raised elbow and the plastic highball glass has taken the place of the sign of the Cross. TV is the madding votive light. Conversation is the jargon of wigs, falsies, ball games, car and appliance makes, and worse-than-death clichés. Music is no more live songs, arias, madrigals and symphonies but unceasing electrified deafening jungle grunts of ugh-ugh-ugh directly into idiocy.

O shoots of the Roman Empire in the Frankenstein American Dream Machine, Quo Vadis?

All values are not lost—it's just that they have been misplaced. The pendulum swings, society's tail goes full circle and meets its mouth. The sun also rises and I see the rosy-fingered rays of redemption and salvation beyond the smogged horizon. More students are studying the Italian language and history. Latin sacerdotes salivate for their Eyes and are militant war protestors. Giant Italian-Americans are looming over Long Island like my friends Dr. Edmund Pellegrino, who is building the most advanced medical complex in the world at Stony Brook University and Vic (Sue the Bastards!) Yannacone of Patchogue, a lawyer and the nation's first environmentalist. Italo-Ams are now in positions of power on Long Island, men like Nassau County Supervisor Ralph G. Caso, Glen Cove Mayor Andrew J. DiPaola, and Judge Mario Pittoni, or are nationally famous, like Perry Como. Others united strongly and loudly for respect, civil rights, and long overdue political power. (I'd love to see a member of the Italo-Am Civil Rights League become President and jail J. Edgar Hoover! I'd love to have the paradisical odoratus of garlic, olive oil, snails and tomatoes perfuming the White House!)

At a recent meeting of a Long Island chapter of the Italian-American Civil Rights League an elegant tigrish member with a Ph.D. and a rosary of college degrees and big diamond ring on his pinky, said through his teeth:

"Hoover's prejudice and discrimination against our race goes way back to 1917 when he was 24 and aide in charge of Enemy Alien Registration. He wooed Mitchell Palmer, the Attorney General of the infamous and discredited 'Great Red Scare.' Those lousy Rover Boy persecuted—to make points—thousands of penniless innocent immigrants, and framed and murdered Sacco and Vanzetti. I am investigating The Investigator's mysterious private life. When the truth about him hits the fan he'll stop 'alleging' and curse the day he ever tackled a wop! We emotional 30-million gutsy Italians will not rest now until we have Italian-Americans heading the F.B.I., the Supreme Court, the Cabinet, and the Office of the Chief Executive itself! Why not? We're not kidding!"

We short dark dolichocephalic Italis are leading the nation back to the good old trieds and trues with a rinascimento of the spirit and the flesh. We are nostalgically returning you to the supremacy of the family which is the heart—we aerate your brain with our incomparable arts and fashions—and we show a reflection of your soul on high which generously beckons you to blissful infinitude. But first we win you gastronomically.

How about the maccheroni dell'Abbruzzo alla chitarra (macaroni guitar style)? Or coscetto di castrato alla Chietina (mutton leg Chieti style)?—Well then, place mutton leg in casserole. Add half a glass of olive oil, bacon, celery, carrots, pepper, salt. Sauté gently, then add garlic and white wine. Later add tomato sauce, parsley, oregano and broth and cook slowly until done. Remove all fat from top and strain sauce. Pour sauce over meat and serve.

So ave festa Italiana! Salute! Buon appetito! Kiss me—I'm Italian!

New York Chinese World

On Manhattan's lower East Side the compound of 15,000 Chinese reaches south from Canal Street and Little Italy five blocks to Worth Street, and six blocks east from Centre Street's Criminal Courts buildings to Chatham Square, the derelict-strewn Bowery and the Gate of Heaven monument commemorating the Chinese-American War Dead.

The Buddhist Temple is at 68 Mott Street. Upon the altar is a statue of Kwan-Yin, the Virgin of Compassion, upholding Guatama, The Buddha. On another altar is a portrait of the late John F. Kennedy enshrined with votives. An incense spiral, suspended from the ceiling, burns continuously.

Deh Chun, recently from Hong Kong is seated yoga-fashion, to lunch. He is fifty, with shaven head, clear black eyes, and wearing a saffron robe and rope-soled sandals. With chopsticks he points to the rice bowl, snow-peas, bamboo shoots, bean curd and teapot, and asks me to share.

"So you want to realize the Chinese? My friend, to observe as a tourist you are in the larva stage. To question with sincere heart you will begin to depart the cocoon of ignorance and become the inquiring caterpillar. Then with the truths of the inner Chinese being achieved you will blossom into the knowing butterfly." "Reverend Deh Chun, is the late President a new god that you have his portrait upon an altar?"

"President Kennedy symbolizes a protecting ancestor to the little people of the world. We consider him 'Bodhisattva' which means, a man who gives his life for the salvation of others."

The streets teem with files of tourists gazing wonderingly at the Chinese.

"Is it as dangerous as Harlem here?"

"Do they still have opium dens and hatchet wars?"

"They look so quiet and sinister."

"The children are such dolls!"

"Is it true about the Chinese woman?"

They gawk into the grocery stores. There are white roots, strange greens, fatty glazed ducks hanging by the neck alongside of smoked parts of pig, and on shelves in the window, duck eggs, dried fungi, and withered fowls' feet wrapped with intestines.

At the fish counter an employee scales, guts, and filets the carp with a half-moon-shaped razor-sharp cleaver. The head is saved for soup. There are cod, dogfish, butterfish and heaps of squid and shrimp.

The tourist will buy oriental knick-knacks, a good-luck charms, a dragon-blazoned silk robe, pajamas, a sexy slitted dress, incense pot drawings, teakwood tea table, or a five hundred dollar screen in one of the many gift shops.

You exult when you see Lychee nuts and recall that as a boy you went to get your father's shirts and collars and the Chinese laundryman put aside his steam-iron and gave you a crinkled-shelled sweet-tasting Lychee nuts.

Chi-Min Tan and I are before the Community Center Building on Mott Street. A hundred youngsters of the Chinese Public School Drum and Bugle Corps are in the street. The girls wear white boots, short red silk skirts, blouses and shakos. Most of the girls are natural almond beauties with petal smooth skin, tight figures and eye-catching legs. Forty year old Chi-Min Tan, educated in China, is editor of the China Times.

"Tonight is the festival of the August Moon. Kublai Kahn and his mongols took over China in 120. In 1368, during the season of the August full moon, the Chinese overthrew Mongol rule and founded the Ming Dynasty. Tonight we celebrate that even with eating the happy August Moon Cakes."

A Cadillac arrives, flying the American and Nationalist flags, bringing a Taiwan official.

"My father-in-law was the right arm of Dr. Sun Yat-sen. This pompous Taiwan statesman used to be a minor bootlicking clerk in my father-in-law's office. Times and men change."

The youngsters' band greets the Taiwan official with, "America The Beautiful," "Onward Christian Soldiers," and "Roll Out The Barrel," and then marches through the streets playing patriotic numbers with thundering drums, trumpets, fifes, cymbals and gongs.

A cloudy afternoon. The drizzle becomes a downpour and the guided-tour customers are discouraged back to the Chinatown sight-seeing bus, Chi-Min Tan and I go into the Pagoda Theater and elude the rain. The Pagoda shows movies made in Hong Kong and Taiwan, with sub-titles to bridge the dialect difference. Whole familes come in. No charge for the little ones. The adults sit entranced and the kiddies run up and down the aisles, around the lobby and up to the balcony.

The themes of the movies are set in the days of paternal dynasties: feuds between good and bad nobles, brigands and knights, elders and postulant youths, a prince's love for a peasant girl, and the triumph of virtue. With the dissonant music and the crashing of temple gongs the actors go to song and ballet gestures. The musical instruments try to express the articulations of nature, to suggest the sound of stone, metal, silk, skin, vegetation, earth, sky and sea.

Competition among the numerous restaurants of Chinatown is very keen. Employees obediently work long hours for low pay, and are non-union. There is something forbidding about Chinese dignity that deters outsiders from intruding upon their ways. The restaurant business gets along on service and volume. The food is fresh, exactingly cooked, respectfully served, and inexpensive. Few restaurants have bars. Diners may bring their own bottles.

Chi-Min Tan and I eat at Stanley Chin's on the second floor of 22 Mott Street. Chin has been head of the Chinese Merchants' Tong, and is President of the Chin Family Tong of America.

"I always try to urge upon the diners the food we Chinese eat at home," says Chin, "and not the un-Chinese American concoctions of 'Chop Suey' and 'Chow Mein.'"

Chin, director of the China Times, says enthusiastically, "The difference between our newspaper and the other four dailies? We are the Chinese equal of the New York Times!"

The China Times is at 105 Mott Street. In the printing shop behind the office is the frame containing the thousands of lead type mysterious characters. I say to Chi-Min Tan that Chinese writing is baffling, more so than Hebrew. He chuckles, "The less a man has seen and studied the more he has to wonder at."

With brush and ink he quickly draws his characters in columns, from the top downwards and from the right to left.

"The characters are ideograms, devices based on a natural association of ideas. In China the Communist effort to introduce the Western alphabet failed. We treasure our system of characters as a thing of beauty. Painting, and handwriting, all done with brush and ink, are synonymous, done with the 'Grass hand.' Think first and then express the heart of the matter. As we say, 'The idea is present even where the brush has not passed.'"

He shows me some paperbacks from his book shelf.

"These are translation of Pearl Buck and Faulkner. If you could read them you would be delighted. The translator has surpassed the original and made every sentence a work of art."

In every Chinese home and business within a fifty mile radius of New York is a loudspeaker playing Chinese music, melodramas, and giving news of the Far East and the world. It is sent out by wire for a fee of ten dollars a month from the China Broadcasting Company on the second floor of Canal and Mott Streets.

Chinese youngsters are playing baseball in the courtyard of Mott Street's transfiguration R.C. Church of the Maryknoll Mission. A sister is talking to a pretty Chinese girl. The Pastor, white-haired Father John Mulcahy, and husky Father John Mihelko are by the doorway of the rectory making picnic plans with a group of Chinese.

Both priests spent many years in China.

Father Mihelko brings out the musty records. In the 1800's the section was English and Germany, and the church had been built for the Protestants. When Irish and the Italians flooded the area the Protestants moved and sold the church to the Catholics. The Chinese began to trickle in around 1900. Catholicism with its saints, elaborations, and a purgatory from which the sinful atoning souls can be raised to heaven by the prayers and merits of the living, was more in consonance with the Chinese religious orientation than Protestantism. Their universal system of belief is still ancestor worship. The conduct of the living affects the welfare of the dead, and the actions of the dead in the spirit world continue to help the living.

There is a Chinese catechism on Father Mihelko's desk. The first illustration depicts all the races of mankind genuflection and looking up with adoration to the Creator, a Chinese elder.

The oldest import-export house is at 32 Mott Street. In 1884 two Lee brothers came from San Francisco and started the business. It became a communications center for immigrants. Five generations of Lees have been managing the store. For years the store provided letter-writing and mailing service, advice, comfort, and was also a pharmacy with ancient herbs, drugs and cure-alls.

The interior is redolent with tea, incense and age. Overhead are antiquated wood-blade fans. One of the two worn counters is arcaded with open-wood carvings of laquared serpents, chimera, fruits and flowers. A half dozen venerable bearded Chinese sit on tea crates, smoking, immobile. A patrician Lee with gold-framed spectacles weighs out the herbs on the same hand-balanced scales used centuries ago. Young Lun Lee is doing his bookkeeping with the abacus. I cannot follow his fingers as he flips the beads along the wires.

"I have an IBM, but for me the beads arithmetic of the good old abacus is faster and more accurate."

The shelves are loaded with canned and jarred foods, teas, fancy matting, restaurant supplies, porcelain, silk handkerchiefs, and plain and ivory chopsticks.

"We drink tea because it is better for the health than coffee." The most costly tea is 'monkey-picked' tea. The rarest teas grow wild on inaccessible heights and cliffs. The Chinese train smart monkeys to climb and pick the tea. Packaged sharks' fins resemble bunches of plastic strings. They are the soft thin bones of the fins. They sell for eight dollars a pound. I think they are bought only by the rich.

"Oh no," Lun Lee assures me, "the poor Chinese buy sharks' fins often. They use it in soups, stews and sauces. The gelatine it becomes in cooking contains the life-giving secrets of the seas that make for delicious flavor and sexual potency. The Chinese spend money first for the stomach, seconds for clothes and third for living."

A customer comes in for a chopping block. The pine chopping

block he ordered is six inches thick and two feet in diameter, and comes from Taiwan. I mention to Lun Lee that we have no end of native pine. Lun Lee shakes his head and smiles.

"The food tastes better when it is chopped with an imported Chinese cleaver on a 'special' Chinese pine chopping block from Taiwan. Every Chinese home has a chopping block. At the table no knife, spoon or fork is needed when the food is cut into bite-size pieces, cooked, and ready to be picked up with chopsticks. The Chinese word for chopsticks is 'kwai-tez,' which means, 'nimble hands.' Chopsticks were invented under the occupation of China by the Mongols when the Chinese were forbidden knives and forks as possible weapons against the Mongols. Things were changing. Now, when an offspring gives up chopsticks for the knife and fork it is the breaking point between the past and the present; the act symbolizing modern revolt. Another thing saddens me; now all my 'Chinese' merchandise is stamped, 'Made in Japan.'

"The old days were better, more human. A man's character was his life and soul. The word given was the word kept regardless of money and circumstances. Today, a fast buck by any means, lying, cheating, is admired."

There are ancient medicine men and the 'needle doctor' who claims to fix all ills by tracing the morbid humor to a spot on the body and puncturing it away with a large magic silver needle. But nevertheless Chinese die.

In our society morticians have won high position. But Chinese undertakers are regarded as pariahs. The Chinese simply do not cotton to those who by profession handle the dead. To them morticians have the essences of their dead clients clinging to them. The Chinese severely avoid such contaminations.

There are a cluster of three undertakers, or "Funeral Corporations," one next to the other, discreetly tucked on Lower Mulberry Street away from the main stream and notice of Chinatown.

Belief in spirits, whether Christian or otherwise, is vivid. On "The street of the three undertakers," rentals for living quarters are cheap, but there are many vacancies because proximity to the spirit-polluted undertaking stores is anathema.

Young Tung To, who will return to Hong Kong after completing university studies in political science, works during the summer for one of the undertakers.

"To the superstitious Chinese," he says, "undertakers ae not socially acceptable. This funeral store was occupied by an Irish undertaker before the Chinese settled here. He moved uptown. No Chinese would rent this building.

"A foolhardy Chinese opened a grocery store. The suppliers would not set foot in the store. They dumped the merchandise on the sidewalk a block away. No Chinese came in to buy. They called it "The store of ghosts." They did not want to eat food radiated by the spirits of dead barbarian Irishmen. The groceryman gave his stock to the garbage collector and went out of business. From then on this store has been Chinese Funeral Corporation".

Tung To is proud of Hong Kong's importance, and tells me of the American correspondents there; of their drinking and ignorance. "The news you get is tailored to the ego of Washington. If you want the real truth of Red China and Viet Nam I can give you the inside dope. I belong to no parties. I believe in the Savior Jesus Christ." He points upwards. "I talk directly with Him. No go-betweens for me.—You want to make money? There's a lot of Chinese in Los Angeles and not one undertake. Take my tip—open up a Chinese Funeral Corporation in Los Angeles and get rich." In the Chapel is a male corpse. At a portable altar Deh Chun, the Buddhist monk, performs the sacred rites with incantations as relatives and friends loudly emote.

Pallbearers carry the coffin through the street of Chinatown followed by musicians who ride in splendor as others walk. Banners of the Tongs, wreaths and flags are in procession.

On flying ribbons are written the virtues and failing of the deceased. The burial takes place in the Chinese cemetery in Cypress Hill. At the graveside is placed a sumptuous repast for the dead. His spirit will have more than sufficient food for the three day journey to heaven.

No Chinese ends up in the Potter's Field. When a destitute Chinese dies the plight is immediately circulated, and ample funds raised for a nice funeral.

Chi-Min Tan tells me, "In some ways we Chinese feel we are more advanced than the bulk of your confused society. In Chinatown you will not find gangsters, Juvenile delinquents, drug addicts, derelicts, drunkards, homosexuals, prostitutes and welfare cases. We are a very old and conservative people. The unusual discipline in Chinatown is based upon the open mind and the establishment of the Family as the dominant social unit. First place goes to filial piety. In comparison with the family the individual counts for little. To the family he owes implicit loyalty. We Chinese are a family civilization rather than a national entity. Here in Chinatown each family is the prototype of the community, and all the families are members of the overall Tong family which is the Chinese community.

"The wives of the wealthy are educated, exquisitely groomed, and have expensive apartments and servants. The wives of the common men are simple village women who do not use cosmetics, and wear clothes that they make themselves. Many work in the dress factories and earn more than their husbands. They will not buy anything on the installment plan, and put money in the bank every week.

"Until World War II and the Korean War the men outnumbered the women twenty to one here in Chinatown. Chinese rarely marry outside their race. Chinese G.I.s sent to the Orient brought home wives and now the ratio is about five to one. Many older Chinese who have saved money for years go to the Far East and bring back young wives. Some of the brides fall in love with handsome young Chinese-Americans and run off with them. Others do nothing but pine and weep. In many cases it is not so much being married to an old man but the contrast of backgrounds and cultures between the beloved good earth of the homeland and New York."

In the city people of every nationality and color and creed lend themselves to interviews and sound off their opinion. Not so in Chinatown. The Chinese value decorum and the privacy of his views. Before he reveals what he thinks on vital matters you must prove your character and earn his confidence. Once he becomes your friend he will tell you what is in his heart, and he expects the same veracity from you.

In Chi-Min Tan's Apartment are the restaurant owner, Sing, his two sons, Jim and Roosevelt, and Wang, an intellectual from Hong Kong. "We feel that we are guests in an alien land," says Chi-Min Tan.

Other races were invited to America, and the Chinese denied entry. Here those races are involved in syndicated crime, corrupt politics, anti-Americanism and riots. The Chinese do not cause such troubles." Sing says, "I've nothing to complain about. In China I was the hungry child of a hungry fisherman. In America I'm rich. There's nothing preventing us from being highest quality citizens here. We ourselves have built an invisible wall around Chinatown. How can the rest of society know us if we don't get out and mix with them? There are those in Chinatown who wish a miraculous peace and justice happening on the mainland and returning to a safe utopia. Others yearn for Hong Kong or Taiwan. America with all its petty faults is my country."

Roosevelt Sing admits to liberalism, while Jim Sing agrees with his father and stands on conservative ground.

"Washington," says Roosevelt, "second the motion that the tiny Nationalist force will sail from Taiwan and retake the mainland. That is a fantasy that no one here in Chinatown believes." Wang, slight, alert, smokes a cigarette rapidly, darts his head about and speaks in bursts.

"I'm returning to Hong Kong soon. I can say what I please.

"Americans have never suffered invasion, partition, martial law, famine, and millions of war dead. Many people of Chinatown have seen loved ones beheaded by contending sides, have fished dead animals out of rivers for food. World-shaking power and socialist state are not new to China. The Chinese have always had communal life and organizations."

Sing shouts, "I cannot forgive the Communists for trying to break up the family!"

Wang shouts back, "They are replacing supremacy by elders with rule by dynamic brotherhood!"

It is a February evening. At midnight will begin the Chinese Lunar New Year. Moon blow and starlight are over the cold and neon brightness of Chinatown. Families go into the Church of the Transfiguration. Families go into the Pagoda movie house. Many store windows have signs emphatically stating, "We do not sell fireworks please!" Policemen walk relaxedly, safely. An old Chinese is making a call and pulling chewing gum from his shoe in the pagoda-roofed telephone booth. As every night it is the scene of bazaar. Along the street walk the Chinese income, the tourists. They arrive by bus, subway, cab, auto; and of course there are the inevitable Rolls Royce, other chauffeured limousines and the sports cars.

Glass mobiles tinkle like ice in highball glasses on the outdoor stands of novelty shops only to be overcome by the vesper chimes from the great bell in the tower of the Transfiguration Church. The tourists are from all classes, races and parts of the nation. They've got the "yen" for "Chinese food" and go into Stanley Chin's, Lung Fung's, Bobo's Wah Kee's and the dozens of other restaurants. Someone never fails to say, "Chinatown is the cheapest and best place in New York to eat. The food is divine—so different—fills you up—but a couple of hours later you're hungry again."

Tourists pause curiously before the window of the Buddhist Temple. From their expressions you would imagine the Temple to be the inner sanctum of oriental mysteries. Some dare to enter, get a whiff of the incense, give the Chinese madonna, Kwan-Yin, the once-over, and hasten out.

I go in to see Deh Chun. At the reading table are Hindus, Negros, Japanese, Chinese, and a young serious white couple. Deh Chun fetches me an orange from the fruit offering basket on the altar of John F. Kennedy. I ask him how he feels about the Nationalists and Red China.

"They both torture and kill for their ends. That makes them the same devil in different disguises. Buddha teaches us peace. Buddhism is faith based upon experiences verifiable by one's self. Buddhism does not deny or affirm the existence of God. It is merely indifferent. Impermanence is a law of the universe which nothing can escape, from the mightiest of astronomical systems to microscopic forms of life. The pure and the impure stand and fall by themselves. Man is completely free to destroy himself, or mold his good future from actions based on rational judgment."

Having gotten in his missionary work he comes back to the mundane. "I am here on a visa. I wish to remain and become an American. Do you know someone important in the Immigration Department or Washington?"

Before I leave I tell him about my family, and also about the big shaggy sheep dog who came to my house from nowhere and refuses to leave. Deh Chun rubs his shaven head. His eyes light up. "You cannot send him away. He is an honorable ancestor reincarnated and returned to you as a loving shaggy dog."

It is near midnight and the Lunar New Year, the Year of the Dragon, is about to begin. The Dragon is the emblem of guardianship and generosity, a legendary Santa Claus to the children. At midnight a dozen huge Dragons, Lions and Unicorns will be roused from their sleep to thwart any evil spirits lurking in Mott, Pell and Bayard Streets. Merchants will give them gifts for the poor. Dollars, attached to heads of lettuce symbolizing the good earth, are fed to the greeting Dragons.

In the streets the Chinese Public School Drum and Bugle Corps assembles. I have not eyes for the decorations, dignitaries or fire-breathing monsters but only for the lithe-limbed, short-skirted, young amandine beauties.

A Chinese woman picks up a face-down playing card from the gutter. She turns it over. It is a Jack of Diamonds. She carefully puts it away in her purse.

At the stroke of midnight firecrackers explode in every direction, the Lions, Unicorns and Dragons leap and dance gaily, and that joyous crowds cheer, and shout, "Gung hay fat choy!" (Happy New Year along with prosperity) "Gung hay fat choy!"

I have promised Chi-Min Tan and Stanley Chin an Italian dinner. I meet them outside the Buddhist Temple. We make our way through the hilariously happy crowds and head for my old Italian haunt, The Luna Restaurant, three blocks away on Mulberry Street in Little Italy. Stanley Chin says seriously, "Tonight I want that good old authentic Chinese dish, meatballs and spaghetti!" As we cross Canal Street and enter Little Italy, behind us, on Mott Street, fireworks rage, and the Drum and Bugle Corps makes the night reverberate with "Chinatown My Chinatown."

My Beloved Mafia

Nero was below medium height, had black waving hair, reptilian visage, iron lips in a redoubtable jaw, level white teeth, and deep-set black eyes, cold and positive with lethal Sicilian attraction. His ways were ascetic and he dressed conservatively. He considered that he became a man at eighteen after killing his fellow-gangster, Leone. At twenty five he was second in command to his godfather, Vito, the Lord of New York's mafia.

Nero Siciliano was the visionary who foresaw a syndicate with control in the nation's productive and commercial endeavors, including politics, and eventually the might to select a President; a complex plan to establish himself as the first pontiff of organized rackets on a sound insured monopolistic basis. In his rise to the top he wove his webs and built his traps perfectly, leaving nothing to chance. In 1933, with Prohibition over, new and original rackets had to be devised in labor and other fields. It was time for drastic change. There was definite need for a syndicate and Nero knew that if he did not found it some progressive gang leader would. Vito was the limited past, and he, the brain of an ever-expanding future. Vito who had been more than good to him was his problem. A number of times he had suggested to Vito a national congress of gangs and the formation of the syndicate. Aging sickly Vito, with the cadaverous little body and shadowy menacing lantern of a head, obstinately refused and made it plain that his sole joy was not money and the future but to remain to his final hour the parochial autocrat of New York's mafia.

Nero held a serious cabal with his brother, Al. "It's no use talking syndicate with godfather Vito. He's an old shark who loses his sense of direction and hard-headed swims over a reef, and when the tide turns can't make the deep and has got to die on the beach. We can't wait until he dies for me to take over. It's now or never. The guy won't listen. He's in my way. He's holding me back. Well, he's got to go. Too bad."

Vito had only one child; a daughter who was a nun. He regarded Nero as a son and his heir. Since Nero was a gutter kid he had schooled him in knife and gun, to collect bets, monitor whores, run dice games, and deliver narcotics with the caution of a cat. He let Nero drive his bullet-proof Cadillac, and took him to his upstate farm where the gang did their gun practice. Vito's bodyguard, husky tattooed Leone, was jealous of the favoritism shown Nero and overtly contemptuous of his small stature. Nero knew Leone was having an affair with Vito's wife, Luna. He would eliminate Leone. He told Vito he had seen Leone molesting Luna. Vito did not suspect his wife. He instructed her to entice Leone to her bedroom while he pretended to be up at the farm. Terrified, Luna complied. As he had planned, Nero, with Vito, caught Leone undressing in Vito's bedroom. Nero shot Leone. The frenzied Vito dismembered Leone's corpse screaming, "Put the horns on Vito?" Then Vito had the feeling that his wife had been fucking with Leone and had enjoyed the fucking, and to keep Sicilian face said to her, "If you have been faithful to me prove it now; cut off Leone's prick and eat it." He handed her the cleaver. She promptly cut off Leone's prick, took it to the kitchen, fried it in olive oil and ate it. The honor killing of Leone solemnized young Nero as a high priest of the mafia. It made him a Little Italy. When he walked the streets people took particular note of him. With his short slender legs and small feet he had the curt measured, inexorable step of the matador. Besides his godfather Vito, Nero had also Vito's longtime lesser partner, fat Spino, to get rid of. Spino's move to Brooklyn led to a rupture with Vito. His absence from Vito's Mulberry Street headquarters brought about alienation. Though Spino had no thought of displacing the superior Vito, Nero's cunning flattery and the enthusiasm of the young rash Brooklyn Sicilians pushed Spino up to a posture rivalling Vito's.

The Depression challenged the mafia to think. There were sparse monies to be extorted from the masses whose Welfare and Home Relief doles allowed only survival. People made their own intoxicants. Prostitution suffered severely as sex between the unemployed became a free pastime and daily tranquilizer. The social and economic system having failed, many aggressive youths were drawn to crime. The dollar's all-importance was impressed upon a non-working new generation. Mores, ethics and principles, let alone religion, did not pay for needs and pleasures.

The Sicilian youth who committed themselves to Vito, Nero or Spino did not care for a distant utopia but quick money at any risk. They saw the mafia as the only determined groups in the country. The mafia did not speak with pretty promises but with the profane language of the streets. Motion pictures portrayed and unwittingly glorified Nero's type as men of certainty, taking what they wanted from a jungle society with colorful unsentimental brute force. The youths who joined the mafia had nothing to lose but their lives and a possible Nero-like life to gain.

Spino's lieutenant was Joe "The Cardinal" Gazzo. Accompanying Joe on missions were his brothers, Johnny "Guitar" and Frankie "Chariot." They were known as "The mad dogs." Before entering the rackets, they had been bricklayers. Joe, a master mason, had studied blueprints and had hoped to be a foreman. Unemployment and destitution embittered him, and he and his brothers became Spino guns. After that the thought of honest labor seemed ridiculous for as Spino men they earned more without manual efforts in a month than at an arduous year of bricklaying. Joe "The Cardinal" called his gun, "my magic wand." While the average hood had a subnormal mentality Joe was quick-minded and perceiving. Crime and murder to him was a sport and practical joke. He sustained a morale of ruthlessness with a humor of cruelty and tortured his victims horribly to keep his brothers in garish laughter. He despised fat indecisive Spino. To him Spino was a pompous bluffing mustachio who shrank from blood and whistled in the dark. Joe respected Nero for his fearlessness and criminal genius.

Through disguised actions Nero precipitated the strife between Vito and Spino. Their patrols collided into arguments over the splits from warehouses, petty domains, bank and payroll hold-ups, muggings, pilfered and forged Home Relief checks, waterfront rights, stolen cars, store robberies and dope-pushing. The contentions led to swollen wrath, curses and loud-mouth threats, and from warnings to beatings to ambush and killings of incensed underling against underling. While to Nero it simply meant the necessity of too many little fish devouring each other to prove to themselves how tough they were, old Vito and Spino fanatically could not brook any diminution of status. They lived to destroy each other. Vito ordered death for Spino and all his men of Palermo on sight. Spino had no recourse but to breathlessly decree death for Vito and his men of Castellamare. This suited Nero. The rackets were at ebb. There were superfluous old-timers and unqualified new-comers—"wop-clowns," as he termed them. It was a time for trimming. He regarded Joe "The Cardinal's" efficient savagery, and wanted him and his brothers for his own future purposes—and then some day rub them out too when they got heady.

Nero managed to play one side against the other without showing his hand. The Vito-Spino war became a no-quarter-given battle buoyed by profitless ego and revenge. The homes of Vito and Spino men were fortresses, the men and families hardly daring to venture out in the daylight. The newspapers provided the avid public with grotesque photos of bodies fished from rivers, buried in cement, and burned with gasoline. The rackets came to a standstill. Editorials lauded the conflict and said the mafia was wiping itself out. The people of Little Italy knew the murdered and the murderers and kept stonily silent. Few suspects were arrested but none convicted. Within a year there were over a hundred dead, with Spino the heavier loser by far. The "Mad Dog" Gazzo brothers worked with Nero, informing him where to snare Spino's faithfuls. Nero in turn let them know how to trap the Vito men he wanted killed. When Spino began to mistrust the Gazzo brothers they openly changed over to Vito's side. Spino despaired. He knew that his wife's pleas to her sister, Vito's wife, would be useless, nor would his fortune offered to Vito, or attempted flight, save him from Vito's thirst for his death. He prayed for a miracle of salvation. Each Sunday, with an encircling wall of trigger-men, he and his family went to mass. Nero was ready to make the two moves necessary to pave the way for a syndicate. He rented a top floor flat a block from Spino's church. Through binoculars was visible an open transom in a stained-glass window that looked down upon the altar rail. On a Sunday morning Spino and his family were in church. Nero had his high-powered rifle with the telescope sight, silencer, and automatic camera attachments. The telescopic sight brought the altar rail within touching distance. Communicants lined the altar rail. Kneeling gray-headed, jowly, mustached Spino's face came into view. As Spino clasped his hands, raised his head, opened his mouth, closed his eyes and stuck out his tongue to receive the holy wafer from the priest, Nero centered Spino's head within the cross hairs and fired three times.

Looking at the photos, Vito smiled with satisfaction, proud of his godson Nero. He became somber, crossed his fingers to counter evil eye, and said, "Having a daughter who is a blessed nun I feel strange about hitting Spino in the house of God." He shook his head and made the sign of the cross twice; once for his own well-being, and for the consideration of heaven for his former sub-partner's soul. The feast of San Vito was nearing. Vito celebrated his birthdays and the Saint's by having dinner in Scaputo's on Mott Street. Upon Vito's arrival Scaputo would place him at a table away from outside gunfire range, and bolt the door. Hotheads from Spino's broken gang were still a threat. If nuns came to the door the chances were good that Vito would admit them. The unpleasant job could be done by two imported gunmen made up and dressed to pass for Italian nuns. What the two stranger guns would not know was that they would have to die, not only as Nero's mark of gratitude for his godfather but also to not have the onus of treachery pointed at him. The killers were to wear the habits of Vito's nun-daughter's order. Nero hated the unknown killers he was contracting by phone.

San Vito's day came in October. That evening Nero, the Gazzo brothers, and Nero's bodyguard, "Pete the Pimp," escorted Vito under the arched street lights, and past the festive booths to Scaputo's. Along the way people nodded to Vito and Nero with deference. Scaputo had seen to it that only a few gentle old immigrants were in his place. Vito went to the familiar paesanos, shook their hands as they wished him hundred years of life, and bought them wine.

In honor of Vito, Scaputo had placed on the table a figurine of San Vito.

"Pete the Pimp" posted himself inside by the bolted door, and the Gazzo brothers were the outside sentinels. The gaiety of the street pervaded the restaurant. In nostalgic mood Vito told Nero the feast brought him back to his boyhood days in Sicily. The statue of the hunter-saint, with cross in one hand and bow and arrow in the other, with a brace of dogs at his feet, was carried on a litter strewn with money. Behind the band marched the followers of San Vito dressed as old world peasants, carabineers, ladies and knights of the Middle Ages, all bearing lighted candles.

A seedy priest tapped at the door seeking alms. Scaputo waved him away. Nero emptied the wine bottle into Vito's glass. He and Vito drank a toast and put their arms about each other's shoulders. As the fireworks went off in the street two dark-faced Italian nuns came to the door, keeping their heads meekly bent. Scaputo went to the door to discourage them. Vito recognized their habits. He signaled questioningly to the Gazzo brothers outside. They pretended to look the nuns over closely, and then motioned to Vito and Nero that the nuns were real. "Let them in!" commanded Vito, "They are of my daughter's order." "Pete the Pimp" unlocked the door. Nero arose and told Vito he had to go to the men's room. Vito shrugged, "Godson, I can't do it for you."

The nuns approached Vito. He dug into his pocket, and counting out a handful of bills said, "Sisters, you were lucky to come to me on my birthday." Looking up he immediately saw they were men and that he was being sacrificed. He tried to reach for his gun. They opened up point-blank fire from under their robes. In that moment he saw Nero watching from behind the latticed alcove. He had taught his protégé too well and not wisely. The bullets tore through his chest, head and face, ripping out an eye that dropped into is spaghetti; another left his head and shattered the San Vito ceramic on the table. With the killers firing, Nero, Pete the Pimp, and the Gazzo brothers gunned down the killers.

In his coffin, with rosary in hands crossed on his chest, Vito seemed a stunted dummy with an old over-large vulture's head. His passing ended the immigrant mafia era. Vito's will was in keeping with his hell-paradise Sicilian character. He left his wealth distributed amongst his wife, relatives, the church, and left the farm upstate to his godson, Nero.

Nero gave Vito a funeral never before seen in Little Italy. The area was in emotional mourning for it was Vito who had made the lowly Italian immigrant into an image to be feared and regarded. It was given out that Nero had heroically punished his godfather's assassins.

As the ordinary people filed past Vito's bier they were given a card with Vito's picture on one side, and on the other a religious picture and a prayer for his soul.

By chance a sepulchre was available. Nero bought from an Italian sculptor the huge white marble Winged Victory of the Fascist Roman Empire that was made on commission for Mussolini who never sent the money.

Nero went successfully on to become a living legend. His dream of syndication worked out as he had expected. Throughout the year's vain attempts have been made upon his life. Hollywood begs him for permission to do a whitewashed take off of his career-showing him as only a former bootlegger and gambler, but he will not tolerate such nonsense. Today Nero plays golf, goes to the races, and quietly directs the land's second government—the richest private combine in the world. He is in excellent health and will prevail for years. His fond hope of the syndicate placing their choice in the White House is not impossible. He created the criminal institution as a permanent American way. Nero is an historical circumstance of the greatest of fables, reality.

Sicilian Vespers

April 13, 1895, at ten in the morning the Trapani courthouse was crowded for the trial of the Mafia monks.

Three Capuchins and a Cretan youth had been apprehended as the ring that had terrorized the Trapani, Sicily area.

Curious outsiders, Italian and foreign, had come to take in the trial, conviction, sentence and execution.

On the mainland this trial would have made for a commercial and festive atmosphere welcoming the tourists and their purses, but, the people of Trapani regarded the visitors as impertinent intruders upon the scene of a strictly private Sicilian affair.

The courthouse and jail had been a small mosque, recalling the days of the Arabic domination. Except for the section set apart for dignitaries and the nobility, the squalid Court of Assizes was packed with peasants, fishermen, salt and sulphur mine workers and their women folk.

The Court was to be presided over by the King's President and jury from Rome, as the case involved also the murder of a Carabineer, one of the King's Dragoon Guards. Furthermore, it would have been impossible to have assembled a Sicilian President and jury as the local authorities well-respected and knew the vengeance of the Mafia.

The high and low studied each other, the society ladies, painted, powdered and perfumed, wearing the latest Parisian fashions, and their gentlemen in British suits, impeccable linen, cravats and polished boots, and the native women all in plain black cotton and mantillas, and their men in homespun black woolen suits and hobnailed shoes, many of whom had heavy golden pendants dangling from their ears. Some of the Trapani women were tall with blue, clear Norman eyes, others with faces seen on Greek coins, a few with flaming red hair and slate-colored eyes, descendants of Phoenician pirates, but most were dark with ebony curled hair, deep-set eyes like African olives, aquiline nose, even white teeth and perfect red mouth of the Saracen.

Before the trial began the closeness was intolerable. The sirocco, the burning southeast wind hailing from the deserts of Africa, was blanketing the air of the courtroom. A thick stench, a mixture of stable and sweat, a stink of goats, a fustiness of filthy animals, and the throat-drying acrid smell of sulphur, was filling the room. The Trapanesi hardly noticed it, but the outsiders, the nosey busybodies, were uncomfortable and could barely breathe.

Catalano of Trapani, lawyer and avowed Siciliophile, had chosen to represent the accused though he knew it was hopeless and would end in a public hanging, except possibly for the young barefoot defendant, Manuzza, who was not a monk but an orphaned ward of the Capuchins. Catalano dreamed of an independent Sicilian Republic, and was the author of the anti-Monarchy diatribes signed, "Sicilian Gadfly."

The Carabineers, with their double-breasted dark blue, brass-buttoned uniforms, belted sabers and Napoleonic hats, led the chained prisoners, white-bearded Father Superior All Saints, greybeards Brothers Crucifix and Blessing, and young Manuzza into the caged dock. Sixteen year old Manuzza, dressed in peasant clothes, was short and swarthy with sunken eyes and a square fierce face. He was called "Manuzza" because his left arm was considerably shorter than his right. Some of the women, shading their eyes with mantillas sighed, "Ah, the poor motherless child . . . !"

Behind and above the solemnly robed President was a painting of a dark breasty Madonna suckling a fat Arab urchin.

When Petrosilo, the Inspector who had prepared the trap for the monks, appeared, the people looked at him coldly and made the sign of the evil eye against him. Petrosilo had been a puppeteer in Trapani, afterwards an actor, and known as "the man of many disguises." Then, pretending to study theatre in Milan, he became one of the King's secret police. Amongst the spectators, Petrosilo's brother, Nunzio, a police-hater like the rest, spat contemptuously on the floor in his direction, and the people nodded approval. A woman whispered, "Someday God will pay that Judas, Petrosilo, for this!"

After the first formalities, the jury sworn in, the prisoners identified, the President ordered the Clerk to read the charges. The prisoners were charged with having committed gross violations of human law and offenses against the sovereign state with acts of willful and deliberate deception, intimidation, extortion and murders.

Petrosilo, witness for the State, related the anatomy of the web of circumstances, clues and actions that enmeshed the criminals. In secrecy he had gathered facts from Mafia-victimized owners of olive, almond and grape estates, salt works, sulphur mines, commerce and tuna fishing fleets who fearfully and reluctantly confided to him.

Throughout the years the extortions were of the same pattern; a note wrapped around a stone, thrown through the window after midnight, with a message written in blood demanding an exorbitant sum of gold, or kidnaping, torture and death, and signed, "The Thirteen."

"The Thirteen" were reputedly the brigand Titta Marulla and his twelve "disciples." Whereabouts in the mountain fastness were "The Thirteen"? Had the people seen Titta Marullo? Living persons and not legends commit crimes. Whenever questioned the people withdrew into their shells. Many of the poor when in dire distress mysteriously received the help of money and would not reveal from whence. The people obeyed the code of "Omerta"—that is—"the turning of the back" upon police interrogation. Certain victims, recalcitrant and refusing to pay the demands of the mafia, disappeared. The leg and boot of wealthy La Rosa was found by fishermen in the belly of a shark; the skeleton of the landowner Corsi was discovered in a lime pit—rosary in hand. A consistent characteristic of the pattern was that somehow Padre All Saints' aid was sought and he always played the heroic, compassionate, endangered intermediary; alleging to meet the mafia in the obscurity of the deep woods blindfolded to prayerfully negotiate for the wellbeing of the victim.

Petrosilo testified, "I consulted with Dr. Cesare Lombroso, the noted criminologist, and his suspicions tallied with mine regarding the apparent 'good samaritan' monks of Trapani."

Petrosilo painstakingly traced marked gold pieces back to Padre All Saints, and uncovered that ransom monies had gone into investments and properties on the mainland in the name of one "Antonio Soma." The hushed description of "Antonio Soma," though in secular garb, was identical with Padre All Saints. Petrosilo realized that the only way to nail the monks was to catch them in an actual deed. He had to bide his time. The opportunity came when young Orza, an impoverished noble, returned to Trapani with a greedy, elderly, rich wife, Gesualdina. While Orza spent his time as a playboy she bought and acquired the monopoly of the irrigation system and heartlessly raised the price of the scarce and precious water vital to the small farmers. The Orzas received a 'note' with the dread circle and centered dot from "The Thirteen." Gesualdina contacted Petrosilo. He told her to pretend to comply—to beg Padre All Saints to intercede and bargain down the sum demanded—to play his "most Christian" part and see that she saved money and that no hard came to her and Orza. When she visited Padre All Saints and threw herself in distress at his feet, Padre All Saints was pleased by the seemingly evident prospect of easy success, and bestowed upon her his reverent blessings.

With his usual consummate acting Padre All Saints plied back and forth from the Orzas to the pretended "Thirteen."

He informed them that God had heard their prayers—"The Thirteen" would accept a lesser amount and not hurt a hair of their heads. The date was set for Padre All Saints to pick up the gold and placate the terrible "Thirteen."

In reflecting, Padre All Saints felt it had all gone too smoothly, for he knew Gesualdina valued money above all things—above life itself. He sensed her duplicity—decided to take no chances—to go an hour or so earlier—destroy the Orzas, and rifle their riches to the tune of more than that which he had sought.

He, the two monks and Manuzza arrived at the Orzas at dusk, before the time they were anticipated by Petrosilo.

They swiftly cut the throats of Orza and his wife, and were eagerly about to search for the gold. Hearing the Orzas agonizing screams, Petrosilo and his Carabineers came upon the monks through the door and windows. In their desperate attempt to escape, the monks succeeded in killing one of the Carabineers. It took six staunch Carabineers to overpower and bind the white-bearded Padre All Saints.

The monks loot was found in the Capuchin catacombs cached among the hooded, seated dead. Prodded about other crimes and of Titta Marullo and the "Twelve Disciplees," they remained silent.

"You hooked your fish," said Padre All Saints, sermonlike, "The weir you fashioned, worked. You netted us in the act of murder. With your God-given eyes you saw us suppress Christian lives. The rest follows, as litany. I played with the fires of hell. I got scorched. You will hang me. There's no more to be said except, that I will not hang easily or in a pleasing manner as since birth I have never had a neck."

Standing in the dock, not bothering to flick the swarms of flies from his head and face, Manuzza drew pity from even the Court. As foundlings he and a twin brother had been abandoned at the entrance of the monastery, and raised by the monks.

"I obey what I am told. I was told that God Almighty is my father and Mary the Madonna is my mother. At the feast of Santa Rosalia, before the fireworks, for a penny a gypsy told me my brother and me came from two almonds placed in the belly-button of a virgin—but I am too stupid to understand. The Brothers order me, "Manuzza, be humble like the ass, and stamp on your forehead 'Silence—Obedience.' They say my brother, who is dead, is a saint. I believe just what I am told, and yet, when me and my brother slept together on straw he wet me." His words provoked laughter that irked the dignity of the Court.

In the rear of the courtroom, her beautiful face hidden by a mourning veil, was Rosa Maria, the clandestine wife of Padre All Saints, who had fathered her three girls. To her he was "Papa." For years he had lived the dual life of holy man and devil. Twice a month, on donkey back, and attended by Manuzza, he left the monastery and went up to the mountain wilderness, supposedly to bring the sacraments and charity to the isolated shepherd and goatherd families. It was said that Padre All Saints went like Moses up the mountain to talk to God.

In the distant past upon this mountain, among the gigantic bleak limestone rock, the shepherds worshipped Venus Erycina, who by moonlight was adored in erotic mysteries.

High on the dizzying slope, scanning the African sea, under the parching sun, amongst the sprinkling of almond trees, aged, gnarled oaks, olive trunks, sage and wild mint, caper and liquorice and tall poplars, in the side of the mountain, part cave and hut of dry rock walls with roof of thatch, lived Rosa Maria, her daughters Stella, Luna and Terra, and her mother Maragrazia. Originally, widow Maragrazia serviced the monk, but when Rosa Maria became fourteen Maragrazia relinquished her position and ordered Rosa Maria to go to bed with the monk.

When Rosa Maria was unwell Maragrazia would bathe herself and get in bed with "Papa."

In Maragrazia's skyey roost there was a surplus of the good things of life and not the stark traditional want that had been her lot before "Papa." With his visits his ass was laden with salted fish, flour, olive oil, wine, condiments, delicacies, fine petticoats, dresses and gold; for which Maragrazia counted her blessings. Upon arriving "Papa" would fondle Rosa Maria and their three daughters, help Manuzza unload the sacks from the ass, and change from his brown hood and cassock and sandals to the shepherd's easy rough wear.

The nearest neighbors, an arduous half hour's climb away, were gentle young shepherd Lollo Zirafa and his wife Arabella. In Rosa Maria's eyes Lollo was comely as the morning sun.

Lollo and Titta Marulla had been felicitous little godfathers to each other since childhood. Titta Marullo, the feared Mafia brigand, the dangerous man of hairtrigger cock's temper, knife and gun, had an unswerving brotherly affection for Lollo and trusted him with his very life.

"Papa" was the haloed boss of Titta Marullo and his men. He was infallible. Absolutle respect and obedience was accorded him.

Titta Marullo's hideout was farther up the mountain near the snow-line of Mount Venus in the large "Cave of the Ear," a cavern almost inaccessible and so formed by time and nature that footsteps and voices from far below could be distinctly heard.

"Papa" reveled as a pagan on the mountain. With Rosa Maria and his band he conversed in a dark emotional tongue spoken with ancient melody. Away from monastery and chapel; removed from the social order of Christianity's Judaic conscience, with Venus' mountain as cathedral, and baldachino the blazing blue sky and mystic opal night, "Papa" lived life's true vehemence of early man. For "Papa" whole lambs were spitted, dressed with mountain herbs and roasted over the glowing ashes of almond wood, and wine was drunk from goatskins.

Rosa Maria was revolted by "Papa" in bed; like having a horny, virile old goat atop her. But "Papa" had Satan's power that fascinated, conquered and ruled and made her have climaxes—as her heart and flesh and dream said, "Lollo, Lollo."

"Papa" lectured her as though she were an understanding postulant. His thoughts were as real and cruel as birth pains, burning brush, jagged rocks. On the mountain he was the Anti-Christ, his own God, the solipsist saying, "The Gods are unicorns whom no one has ever seen, nor has a single soul come back from the dead. We are all children of the incest of Eve and her sons, or the issue of monkeys.

"It is a life of eat or be eaten, as in the jungle, sea, and on field of warring men. What else does the good shepherd care for and raise his sheep if not to shear them for wool and then butcher them for his belly's meat? My world begins and ends with me." To Rosa Maria he grinningly said, "The face is the index of desires. The eye betrays. Titta Marullo burns and erects for you. But you lust for Lollo. There was only one way: Titta Marullo will not kill me to obtain you because I am his brain. After I die Titta Marullo will take you. Then his life will be in jeopardy for you will undo him as your thighs and belly and fig ache for Lollo."

There was "Papa" in his hooded brown Capuchin habit, chained hand foot, sitting on the bench in the caged dock. With death imminent he still wore his chuckling enigmatic mask. Rosa Maria's sole feeling was of obliged gratitude for the security and daughters he had provided. She fingered the many gold coins sewn in layers in her petticoat. She would be released soon from "Papa."

Bloodthirsty Titta Marullo would immediately claim her. With Lollo in her breast she would be Titta Marullo's chattel, living the uncertain life of the hunted. Titta Marullo had blind faith in Lollo. There was only one way: if Lollo would have it; to violate the code and betray him and "The Twelve" to the police, and flee to America.

Defense counsel Catalano addressed the court.

"If you depart from our island without having realized the mentality, passion and psyche of the Sicilian, you will have defeated the aspiration of your ethical, moral and universal aim."

"Bravo," shouted a peasant. "We don't know what the manure you're talking about, but give the mainlanders hell anyway!"

"Sicily had been the victim of tyranny longer than any people on earth. The Sicilian has borne the oppression of the Greek, Carthaginian, Roman, Byzantine, Arabian, Norman, Swabian, Angevin and Spanish swords. For my repressed, socially crushed people the mafia evolved as a secret government with an honorable code of silence, family structure, blood rites and inner society of their very own—"

The President reminded Catalano that they were not in a university.

"Mr. President, I do not condone the crimes of the accused, nor do I suppose the Court will mercifully spare their lives, but this is a circumstance of Italians judging Sicilians. The men of the mafia come from and are abetted by the impoverished masses. The illiterate Sicilian instinctively knows more about the poetic realities of life than the educated and cultured. He sees the God-created soil, laws, advantages and well-fed police in the hands of the rich. He knows he has been the hapless pawn of popes, emperors and insolent nobles. He dwells with gnawing hunger from the womb to the grave. Either he cowardly submits and starves, or manfully plays the brigand." He reasons, "Is there a difference between soldiers and thieves? As the King's soldier he is exposed to maiming and death without recompense for his family, and so as a fisherman, toiler of the earth or miner. Thus he asserts his fearless masculinity, experience and exhilaration within the romantic adventures of the mafia. The good people in this courtroom do not feel sympathy for the murdered Gesualdina. Orza, a userer, an outsider who acquired the irrigation system by stealth and doubled the price of water, crucifying the small struggling farmers. Illustrious sirs, the common folk present are the very same souls of the Sicilian Vespers!"

The elegant people could not bear the heat, insects and strong smells. They left, content to sightsee until the hangings before departure.

Catalano, desirous of being the number one author of his beloved Sicily, lyricized the lowly Sicilian.

"He is not persuaded by logic but by surges of emotion. He is jealous of his independence and intolerant of any interference, has pride and disdain and when crossed by circumstances takes refuge in violent and terrible reaction. His woman must live cloistered in funeral black from head to foot, with baby at breast and rosary in hand. Our people, though fatalists, make a fable out of reality, in an atmosphere of sorcery, in a climate of satyrs, of Genesis and Apocalypse where man reveals his elementary and primordial impulses, the present being everything, and all life as an improvisation, encompassing and easily living between the pendulum of beatitudes and beastialities, and appreciating the devil out of respect to God who saw fit to create and perpetuate the devil."

Why, asked Catalano, had Garibaldi, upon liberating the island from the Spaniards, opened all the prisons and let loose the convicts to roam and settle at will? Why had the Kingdom established in Sicily penal colonies for criminals from the mainland? After serving their sentences thousands of men of heady bold blood remained and married. All factors combined, what else could the world expect.

The following day, Holy Thursday, the President advised Catalano that neither God or the King were on trial but callous Mafia killers. He forbade him further irrelevant rhetoric and commanded him to sum up the defense; the King's Court, Jury, and professional hangman being anxious to return home to the mainland for the Easter feast.

As a final gesture on behalf of the accused, Catalano appealed to the jury's Christian sensibilities.

Was not evil the other side of the human coin and related to good as night to day? Were not all happenings according to God's will? Were not all things and events predestined by the Creator for His own reason?

Catalano told how much Padre All Saints had done for the once run down monastery and of his many compassionate and generous deeds for the poor. The spectators wept and cried, "Benedictions on him—it's true—the gospel truth!" But when he related of Manuzza's sickly wraith of a twin brother who had visions of the Trinity, was training for the priesthood, and called himself "Little Brother, Fool of Christ," and of his malingering, sacrifice of self, angelic thoughts, and pathetic passing, the people broke out in furious lamentations.

Nevertheless, Manuzza was sentenced to thirty years at hard labor, and the monks were condemned to death.

By evening, Manuzza in leg and hand irons, with newly shaven head, and wearing the ill-fitting coarse striped suit of the convict, was carted off to the coast town penal colony of Noto.

That night by torchlight the gallows three were erected in the Piazza of the Saracens opposite the Church of the Most Precious Blood. The next morning, Good Friday, a regiment of the King's marksmen, the Bersaglieri, arrived to maintain order.

The people, to show their contempt for the Law stayed away from the proximity of the gallows. As usual on Good Fridays they performed "The Road To Cavalry" the Via Dolorosa; men and boys inflicting superficially upon themselves "The Five Wounds," and with bleeding stigmata, and arms outstretched as though in crucifixtion, trailed the "Procession Of The Mysteries," the carrying from the church and through the streets the life-size images of The Stations Of The Cross.

Padre All Saints and the two monks were confessed and given the last sacraments. Soldiers, sailors, the elite, the police, photographers, and foreign tourists assembled around the gallows.

From a distance Rosa Maria watched through her veil. As the death drums rolled, the old cleric she called "Papa," his hands bound behind his back, was led, grinning, up the steps to the scaffold. The two monks paralyzed with fright, had to be dragged and carried. The hangman placed their feet upon the trapdoors, and looped the nooses around their necks.

When the drums stopped rolling he sprung the trap-doors. The necks of the two monks snapped. Padre All Saints dangled and squirmed. Hanging could not kill him. He swung about like an acrobat gasping. Minutes passed with no results. The spectators were aghast and cried out for a merciful ending. The captain of the Bersaglieri consulted with the President of the Court; hastily formed a firing squad; and at the fall of his saber they sent a roaring fusillade in Padre All Saints' heart.

Rosa Maria mounted her ass and rode toward the rugged mountain. That night Titta Marullo would take her. She had had respect for "Papa" but could not possibly have for Titta Marullo. He was the son of the deceased weird old shepherd, "Sheep-dung," who had lived highest up the mountain than any shepherd in a cave near the edge of perpetual snow where nested the eagles. It was surmised that "Sheep-dung" had had Manuzza and his twin brother by his own teen-age daughter, dark, brooding hairy Venus, and after delivering her himself left the twins at the entrance of the monastery.

Titta Marullo with his face of a vulture, ignorant and savage, tortured and killed victims for amusement. Would her growing daughters also be despoiled by Titta Marullo and the hunted men, and bear their marked and murderous children?

With all his cunning and lofty wisdom "Papa" had been caught and put to death. Surely, sooner or later the King's police would close in on the band at the mountain lair. She would either hang along with them or rot the rest of her life in jail.

She yearned for Lollo Zirafa. Lollo loved her and not his sterile wife, Arabella. Why shouldn't she and Lollo live like Christian human beings among the Sicilians in faraway America? Yes, she would give herself to Titta Marullo and artfully service him, and appease his moods and demands. At the right time she would take the great risk of making a bargain with Inspector Petrosilo. She and Lollo must go free at the price of the heads of Titta Marullo and The Twelve.

Where town met countryside was the fountain of Diana. Women and children awaited to fill their pitchers. It was said that the waters of the fountain would not mix with wine when drawn by women of doubtful virtue. Rosa Maria drank from the fountain and watered her ass. Past the fountain, alone and safe from recognition, she removed her veil. Her straight jet black hair, her face of slender Spanish cast, with deep-set eyes, incomparable lips of the Saracen, and black mole starred on her cheek above the right side of her mouth, was piercingly lovely.

The road led up to an arid clayey plain shaggy with seared stubble. In the useless land were the bleached bones of an ass. Above her the unkind sun, and beneath, the brimstone earth. It was the high noon, that brought the "fiachezza" the weighting inert drab weariness, the feeling of indolence, or irritation, of hate that simmers and smoulders, and that cries for a sudden unrestrained violence of mind and flesh. At the foot of the mountain among the tangle of rock, thorny scrub, mulberries and cactus, her ass found the secret path.

If Titta Marullo were ever to suspect in the least her plan he would kill her as though she were a fly. In her world the informer was lower than Judas Escariot. With the riddling of Titta Marullo there was one place she and Lollo could escape to, America, and the seat of the Sicilians, called, "Mulberry Street." She had heard of the wretched woeful hunted of the Mafia; sometimes sought by both police and Mafia who were in the haven of America waxing fat and rich.

That night Titta Marullo would celebrate with wine his rise to "Papa's" place. He would get drunk, drag her to bed, rip off her clothes, bite her breasts, and rudely clutch her hind and thighs with his iron hands. She would play her game. She would gasp and bite him with feigned wildness, joy and laughter. And he would pay for his pleasure with his blood.

Titta Marullo spent the nights ravishing Rosa Maria and the days gaming and carousing with his men. He talked of migrating to another region, of joining and taking by force greener pastures of the Mafia. But that was impossible with Petrosilo's Carabineers about, waiting to pounce on him. He learned that a wealthy Calabrian builder, Bellanca, had come to nearby Segesta with contracts for public works. He waited until Bellanca left for the mainland, then at night came down from the mountain with his band, broke into the villa and kidnapped Bellanca's youngest son and a nephew who was a religious novice. Signora Bellanca's screams and tears were to no avail. He gave her a week in which to provide the ransom. The hostages were blindfolded, gagged, tied to the backs of asses and brought to the Cave of the Ear. When Titta Marullo's men came for the money Signora Bellanca gave them half, bewailing that it was all she had.

The Calabrian rich were to be taught that the Sicilian Mafia were not to be trifled with. He commanded the novice to write a note to the effect that until the entire sum was paid, plus the penalty of a new outfit of clothes and shoes for himself and his band, he would send back the hostages piece by bloody piece. Signora Bellanca sent the other half of the gold promptly, and set about to sew shirts and trousers for Titta Marullo. At night, after Titta Marullo had had her, and he and his men were sprawled in drunken slumber under the trees, Rosa Maria crept to the side of the hostages in the cave. She fed them and confided that she too was a victim and weepingly deplored her hunted life. "I swear on the heads of my innocent children that I will risk my life to be freed from Titta Marullo and live as a Christian. After you are returned to safety, reach Inspector Petrosilo and tell him to meet me the following Saturday, disguised as a priest in the Confessional of the Church of the Most Precious Blood."

In the shadow of the Confessional Rosa Maria conspired with Petrosilo the fate of Titta Marullo. It was Titta Marullo's habit to dine Sunday evenings with his soul-trusted little godfather, Lollo Zirafa. And it would be there in the hut of Lollo that the betrayal would take place. Under the veil of the Confessional Petrosilo gave Rosa Maria the packet of powder with which to dope Titta Marullo's wine; for, even when drunk Titta Marullo and his men were as formidable as a company of Carabineers.

The time and signal for ambush would be the moment the light in Lollo's hut went out.

At Lollo's table Titta Marullo and his men were festive. Between courses they beat their cups and plates with their forks and sang. Rosa Maria served roasted sheep's heads, figs, cheese bread and wine. At dusk she lighted the oil lamp over the table. The lamp burned poorly. The sentinels, who had taken turns were reeling from the copious wine. Unnoticed, Rosa Maria drugged the skins of wine. The lethal wine soon took effect. Petrosilo and his many Carabineers had come stealthily up the mountain and were hidden close by. One by one Titta Marullo's men left the hut and fell asleep on the ground. At the table Titta Marulla drooped his head. In the darkness Petrosilo came behind the open door with a long stiletto in hand. Rosa Maria and Lollo watched Titta Marullo in the flickering gloom. "Titta Marullo," said Rosa Maria loudly, "I must put out the light and refill the lamp." All was hazy to Titta Marullo. He mumbled senselessly. Rosa Maria stood on the bench and blew out the light. Petrosilo rushed in and plunged his stiletto up to the handle into Titta Marullo's back. Rosa Maria relighted the lamp. With animal strength Titta Marullo arose and tried to wrench the stiletto from his back. He cried, "Lollo, dear Lollo, be my salvation!"

He began to fall, and pressed his blood-dripping hands against the lime-white wall in the effort to stand and remain alive. As he lay dying he whispered, "May Christ forgive you, dear Lollo . . . curses on your treacherous cunt, Rosa Maria . . . !" The following day, as a warning to the Mafia, Titta Marullo's corpse and the twelve prisoners were hanged in the public square.

Petrosilo honored his pact with Rosa Maria. She, Lollo, her mother and daughers were taken under cover to Naples and put aboard a ship sailing for New York.

Thinking that she had thwarted the hated law, Rosa Maria's fame spread among the common folk, and they composed a song that began, "*Rosa Maria pronto e lestra—semenao pé la fenesta—*" "Rosa Maria ready and nimble escaped the kill—by leaping away out over the windowsill—."

The other story circulated with melody trist, called, "Our very own Titta Marulla's veronica," sang how the bloody prints of Titta Marullo's hands on Lollo's walls protested and refused to be covered by coats of lime, and that finally the shepherd who took over Lollo's hut removed the wall and threw the stones down the mountainside.

Petrosilo's few victories over the Mafia was his death warrant. He was assigned to track down the Mafia in Palermo but never got there. Older heads had advised him that wiping out the Mafia was to empty the sea with a pitchfork. While urinating in the outdoor public toilet he received a bullet in the back of his head. The crime was never solved. The people said the Mafia had the courtesy to let Petrosilo finish relieving himself before firing the bullet into his head. A song soon became laughingly current that went: "—with sighing relief in hand doomed Inspector Petrosilo departed our land—"

The killing of Petrosilo was superstitiously regarded as a just act from Above that miraculously broke the spell of the curse occasioned by the hangings of Padre All Saints and the two monks. From that event on a disastrous drought had set in the brought hardship to Trapani. All the age-old practices failed to conjure rain: praying to, beseeching and propitiating the saints; threatening the plaster saints with degradation and violence, and finally punishing the mute angels of God by tearing off their wings and dragging them through the dust of the waterless baking streets. Even resort to the pagan ritual of sacrificing black goats at midnight in the forest did not work.

But scant hours after Petrosilo's murder the skies became fraught with raging clouds, and the life-renewing rain fell for days.

Where The Mafia Goes To Die

Padre Arcangelo Giordano and I were in the rectory. The window framed the plain and the tan walls and red-tiled roofs, of Tor San Lorenzo, a village within the *Provincia di Roma*.

"I was Fascist soldier," said the peasant priest, "ready to obey Mussolini's orders. As I witnessed the Nazi massacre of the hostage youths in the great cave of Rome, the Lord called me. It was the answer. I threw away the gun and embraced the cross.

"Tor San Lorenzo was swampland; it didn't become a village until the Pontine marshes were drained after the war. When I came here there was no church. I rented a stable and celebrated mass. Don Ciccio Coppola, whom the newspapers now call 'gangster Frankie-Boy Coppola,' and the tenant farmers built this church. The nobility and the fat cats of Rome did not contribute a lira. It is the poor who maintain the house of God. Don Ciccio, who has just been deported from America, brought building materials with his truck and helped mix the mortar and carry and lay the bricks."

I believed him because the masonry looked as though it had been done by children.

"Don Ciccio provided boards and nails and worked to put up the altar. The local baron had a sweet Madonna in his barn gathering dust. I begged him to loan it to us until we had money to acquire our own. He lied and said it had been promised elsewhere; but one word from Don Ciccio and the Madonna found her home here."

Padre Giordano showed me the register with the baptisms at which Francesco Paolo Coppola presided as godfather . . . and the notation of the death of Coppola's wife, Emma.

Then the priest said, "Good and its opposite are relative even as the sun and the moon, light and darkness. If there were not evil, Christ's mission would have been superfluous—tourism. The Garden of Eden without the father of lies is unimaginable. Categorically, we can say that Satan was the first *mafioso*."

I stopped at the California Snak Bar, talked with toothless peasants, and treated them to *caffè* and aperitifs. Today they spoke well but reservedly of neighbor Coppola. One said, "Frankie-Boy Coppola gives everybody nicknames. He called me *Pasta Asciutto* (dry noodle). Now you know he's got only three fingers on his left hand—and I told him to his face, 'Don Ciccio, even though you break horns, if you call me *Pasta Asciutto, Porca Madonna*, I'll call you *Tre Dita* (three fingers)!' At least my skin is still in one piece."

(In Italian folk culture, "horns" denote shame. Thus, a wife who acts disrespectfully to her husband is said to have given "the horns." To "break horns" is to avenge.)

I went to the house of Frank Coppola's daughter, Pietrina, and her fast, mod son, Joe. Young Joe took me around in a small Innocenti, though hiding in the garage was a $20,000 Mercedes-Benz.

I admired Pietrina's big kitchen and the wood-burning oven; she gave me bread, hot from the oven, and homemade wine from Frank's grapes. Then she brought out portraits of her father in his prime as *capomafia* of Kansas City and friend of Harry Truman. Handsome Frank Coppola wore tailored tweeds; the left hand with three fingers was in his trousers pocket and the other held a cigarette.

Two years ago I was in Rome working on a corny film script called my *My Brother Anastasia*, and I got to know Father "Sal" Anastasia, the priest and youngest brother of the former head of Murder Incorporated, Albert Anastasia. Father Sal, Albert, Lucky Luciano, Joe Adonis, Joe Profaci, Gambino, Nick Gentile, and just about all Italian and American VIPs of the Mafia attended Pietrina Coppola's wedding in Rome. It was Father Salvatore Anastasia who first introduced me to Coppola. Frank was small, deep-chested, and genial, with young gray eyes and a Vandyke beard. His presence was commanding. We liked each other right away.

He had read the Italian translation of my book, *Christ in Concrete*.

He said, "I was born 75 years ago on a farm in Partinico, Sicily. I started life as a peasant. When I left the big town Kansas City and beautiful America, I came back to the farm. I got land here and in Sicily. We Sicilians are mad about land; we want land as far as the eye can reach and more."

At that time, he lived on a farm, and his 100 acres were covered with grapevines, the rows carefully staked and trellised. Around the farmhouse and stables were a lot of dogs and cats.

"In Sicily," said Frank, "got mules and horses and jackasses, chickens, pigs, sheep, goats, and ducks; and I'm nuts about hunting game—my two fingers were shot off in a hunting accident . . . We got a way of life there that's different. That's what makes a Sicilian stand out, his style." Then he ruminated. "I wonder whether I made a mistake by coming to live in the province of Rome." I asked why he had. He said maybe it was because he'd gotten used to being near the center of things.

It was hot summer and the vineyard was an ocean of white grapes and green leaves sparkling in the sun. Peasants with heavy hoes cultivated the reddish volcanic earth at the roots of the thick vines.

A good-looking niece, Giovanna La Spesa, ran the farmhouse. Italians don't know what breakfast is. In the morning it's just coffee and a bun. But lunch and dinner in Don Ciccio's farmhouse were feasts with aperitifs before eating, wines with various dishes, and fruits, cheeses, and desserts. Also *Centerba*—a hair-raising liquor made with 100 herbs—and demitasse. Following lunch you had to nap because everybody disappeared to bed—and not just to sleep.

Arriving in Rome this trip I learned that Father Sal Anastasia had died of cancer in the town of his birth in Calabria, and that old Frank Coppola was in the formidable prison of Regina Coeli (Queen of Heaven) in Rome on a charge of attempted murder.

With all that's written about the Mafia by self-appointed experts, when I contacted the Department of Justice and the Immigration Bureau in Washington for the whereabouts of deported Italian-American *mafiosi*, they could only come up with Frank Coppola and Nicolo Gentile as internationally known *capos* residing in Italy; the rest were uncelebrated soldiers named Cucchiara, Barese, Catalanotte, De Chiara, and Badalamenti, and they've apparently vanished completely.

For two tiresome weeks I had solicited faceless authorities in the Palace of Justice, the Palace of the Carabinieri, the Palace of the Police, and finally the immense Palace of the Courts, Il Tribunale, in an effort to see Frank.

Ministro Rompipalle of the Tribunale told me, "Your well-meaning friends of *Variety*, *The New York Times*, and the *Rome Daily American News* called me on your behalf regarding your desire to consort with Francesco Paolo Coppola in the Carcere Regina Coeli. Signore Di Donato, in Italy the law is the law, and the following dictum has never been violated in the entire history of our prisons: Unless one is close family or lawyer, before trial not even Jesus Christ himself is permitted to interview a convict!"

I sought out Frank's lawyer, Giuseppe Mirabile. He'd just come out of a courtroom for a smoke, wearing the elaborate Hallan legal costume of cape with robe and tassels. Mirabile, from Agrigento, Sicily, a relative of Luigi Pirandello, said, "Patience, even cardinals find out that there is more than one way to bugger a cat . . . Nothing is done here without politics and wiggling—bureaucracy in Rome is like the virtuous Italian woman: always no, absolutely no-no-no—until the right vein is touched. And then the three openings are yours."

In Italy you do better with your enemy. Mirabile introduced me to his arch adversary, Prosecutor Nessuno. Calls and documents were arranged, and before I knew it I was a noted criminologist. But the ritual was for me to first "inspect" the model prison city of Ribibbia—for there is no straight line with Italians—and then, lo and behold, I would be asked to do them the honor of scurrying through the antique Regina Coeli jail, where, by strange coincidence, dwelled one Frank Coppola.

On the Via Delle Lungara near the Tiber is the Carcere Guidiziario of Regina Coeli, on the site of the temple of Venus. Constantine converted it into the Christian Chapel Regina Coeli; then following the unification of Italy, the place became a prison.

The lobby is a 12-angled rotunda soaring to its dome. High on the balconied concave walls is a great Madonna, and opposite, her huge Italian son on his cross.

The chief guard, the *maresciallo* guiding me, said, "This is different from America, is it not? America is Babylon; there the prison is a bestiary—Noah's ark in the madhouse. Here we are all Italian with one culture—God and family."

He showed me a plain portable altar that is brought into the rotunda for the chanting of the mass. "Pope John came here often. He bathed and kissed the feet of criminals and ate spaghetti and drank wine. He was people."

Each prisoner had his own cell—with a touch of home: pictures, radio, books, hobbies, a sink, toilet, a one-burner electric stove for cooking if he didn't want to go to the mess hall. Most were young and poor.

"All the guards have children," said the *maresciallo*. "We feel for these trapped youths."

Frank Coppola came along the corridor escorted by a guard. Don Ciccio wore a Molotov sable hat, a long old-man's overcoat, and dark glasses; he used a cane and walked with ailing steps. Once inside the private chamber assigned to us and with the door closed, he removed the hat, coat, and glasses and put the cane aside. After Sicilian kisses we sat. He was smart in his tweed jacket, Brioni slacks, custom-made shoes, and cashmere turtle-neck sweater.

I said, "Frank, how the fuck did you end up here?"

He lighted a Marlboro and slowly shook his head. "Pete, it's a bad movie for real. I pulled a lot of fast, risky ones in the States and here. I had a charm going for me—nobody could prove nothing. And now, when I go legitimate and grow grapes like I love to do, all of a sudden I'm arrested, handcuffed, and put into jail for something I *didn't* do."

"When I heard you were in Regina Coeli I wrote you a letter."

"I never got it. The Italian postal service is a joke. This ain't America." He stroked his Vandyke beard with the three-fingered left hand. "Like they say in those cops-and-robbers movies, 'I'm a victim of circumstances.' Everything in Italy is bossed by the holy trinity—Vatican, Politics, and Police.

"Politics is in my blood. I was steering Christian Democrats, Socialists, and Communists; through Frank Coppola a lot of slobs were made senators, judges, ministers, and what have you. They're all whores—everybody's happy until a nut like this Roman police commissioner, Angelo Mangano, comes along who'll shove it in his mother's ear for a buck. This guy Mangano made a name with Interpol and the Antimafiz and then got on my back about Luciano Liggio. Liggio was a *capo* off Corleone territory in Sicily, next to my territory, Partinico. Liggio knocked of rival *capos* and government guys—never bothered me—and took off. And Mangano claimed that *I* was hiding Liggio.

"Mangano bugged the phones in my houses in Partinico, Pomezia, and Tor San Lorenzo. Lots of times he came to my villa in San Lorenzo to fill his gut, and he had a tape recorder on him. I wasn't born yesterday—do you think I'd say anything that would hook me? Then Mangano pulled a Nixon. He fucked with the tapes—cut out the truth and phonied my voice. Then he comes to me and says, 'Frank, I got you by the balls. I can have you put away for five years in Regina Coeli. You're 75 and rich. Could you last five years in jail? Your freedom is worth at least $50,000!' (Mangano denies this vehemently.)

"Well, anyway, I was a sucker for the first time in my life. I didn't want trouble—my wife had died—I just wanted to grow grapes. I went to my Pomezia bank and drew out cash for this wise guy.

"Two Milanesi shot Mangano. His wounds healed and he put the finger on me. That's a joke because if I'd wanted him out of the way I would have used my own people, Sicilians. You can always depend upon them to do a thorough job."

On the top floor in the sick bay was Frank's spacious, high-ceilinged cell containing only two beds. He had every accommodation, and on a stand at the foot of his bed was a new supersize TV. He said that, technically, Italian television was the best in the world.

"This country's wild for movies and TV. I remember when they began by imitating the American shows, but now they beat the States for class, musicals, and pretty girls,"

The old cell door was four-inch-thick wood with a small rectangular peephole that could be shut and bolted.

Frank took me around the community cells and introduced me to convict-patients who offered us *pasta a la carbonara*—spaghetti with a sauce of minced prosciutto, olives, and slightly cooked egg mixture, covered with mozzarella cheese, and hot peppers. The food and the bottles of beer had been paid for by Don Ciccio.

Frank said, "These kids are in for murder, rape, robbery; they ain't had enough dough to live decent like you see advertised. *Alma perduti*, lost souls, I feel for them . . ."

Prisoners, guards, and officials had an appropriate sense of respect and deference for Frank; he was more than a *padrino*—a godfather—he was the veritable *signore padrone* in the Queen of Heaven prison, a bona fide "great father." Later, I asked the compassionate *maresciallo* what Frank's chances were. He said with an ironic smile, "The rich don't die in jail—only the miserable poor."

On the wall over the bed next to Frank's, and evidently scratched by a suicide, was *"Libera d'ogni peso e canone"*—"Freed from every burden and regulation."

From Frank's cell window is seen the nearby Città Vaticano, Castel Sant Angelo, and beneath, the Tiber and its bridges. The bulk of St. Peter's oppressive majesty dominates the Tiber and Regina Coeli, and more than a few times Frank and I mutely watched the December early golden sunset hover over Peter's place like a hope. And we passed time making out the graffiti scrawled with aerosol paint on the splayed embankments of the Tiber: *"Vaticano dico no—Divorzio si,"* *"Yankee go home,"* *"Vive Allende,"* *"Cile e Vietnam libero e morte a Nixon."* By a fascist symbol was *"Fuck Christian Democracy—Maria, Paolo ti amo!"*

On the Feast of the Immaculata, the Pope leaves the Vatican by horse-drawn carriage to bless the Holy Virgin in the Piazza di Spagna. People come from all over the world; the streets are decorated and flaming torches hung, creating a medieval atmosphere. My hotel, Sorriso, is a block from Piazza di Spagna. Looking for a taxi to go to Regina Coeli, I was caught in the human jam behind the policed barricades of Via dei Condotti and I saw the Pope go by—I could have touched him—and saw him again on his return. Half an hour later I was with Frank Coppola. Frank was in bed resting. Brought in on a stretcher and put in the other bed was a bruised and bloodied drunk.

Soon he got up and went to Frank and said he had seen Frank's pictures in the newspapers. "I salute you. My name is Aldo. Death robbed me of my wife. My two sons are policemen in the Senate House. I am the wino of the Spanish Steps and they call me Barabbas. The middle class has a terror of gypsies, demonstrations, and Barabbas—the only true Communist in Italy!"

It seems that as the pontiff was going through his motions before the effigy of the Immaculata in Piazza di Spagna, Barabbas broke through the crowd and bawled the hell out of him for living like a kept woman and not selling the church's jewels to feed the poor. Barabbas was arrested and beaten. What he said was printed in all the newspapers. Frank said, "It takes all kinds to make a horse race." We laughed, and Frank treated us to bread, cheese, salami, wine, and chestnuts.

He didn't mind my asking a lot of questions. "Pete, at night I dream I'm back in Kansas City with pals—Tom Prendergast and Governor Rolfe and Harry Truman . . . People didn't like Harry's guts, and when Harry made important political trips he'd call me and say, 'Frankie, you and your boys get your ass to these places and soften up those goddamn sons of bitches.' How many times we drank the best bourbon in the Muehlebach Hotel! You know, Peter, I'm Sicilian, but I always dream in the American language.

"Harry was running for re-election against Dewey and it looked bad for Harry and a sure thing for Dewey, but Harry was a guy like Nixon who didn't know how to give up. Harry sent for me and laid out a plan, and I contacted all the loyal Families from coast to coast. Now, Bill O'Dwyer was mayor of New York and everybody knew his connections and takes with mob operations, and the investigations on him were getting too hot. Harry called O'Dwyer and promised him an out as Mexico ambassador with immunity. Bill worked with me and Costello and Lucky's soldiers, and all the Families stuck together for Harry, and we squeezed Harry back into the White House. Pete, those were glory days—and me a Sicilian farm kid!"

In 1974, Don Ciccio's pal, the former President of the United States of America, was dead. Prison and a serious charge of attempted murder were his reality. His lawyer urged him to reveal to the Tribunale Penale Procura Della Republica that Mangano had been trying to blackmail him. Frank was confused. "I never ratted on anybody before," Frank said. "I never even squealed on guys who tried to knock me off!"

It was night and we were at the window. On both sides of the Tiber and traversing its spans were torrents of headlights and red taillights. The monotonous hum of the traffic counterpointed the screeching sirens of the Carabinieri's agile Alfa-Romeos. Above it all was the confident aura of the leonine dome of St. Peter's.

"No words can tell you what a lousy, closed-in, choking feeling it is to be jailed. I envy the beggar in the street. I'm 75 and I ain't kidding myself about the time that's left me—a couple of maybe good years—and then back to being a baby . . . and over and out.

"Italy's not the place for me no more. I'm bored being the famous American gangster for newspaper publicity and cops and lawyers and the jerks in the street." Still, he had $3,000,000 if he did get out.

Lawyer Mirabile came in with a draft of a statement declaring Frank the victim of political and police corruption. Frank was still reluctant to sign; he said he wanted to think it through.

I had to go to Sicily to try to find the *capo of capos*, Nicola Gentile. Neither American nor Italian authorities would admit knowing his exact whereabouts. Frank said there was nothing to it; Nick was where he always was, Realmonte, Sicily. Lawyer Mirabile said he'd call his brother Guido, in Agrigento, to look after me.

Frank had said, "In the Sicilian way we call Nick Gentile 'Zu 'Cola'—Uncle Cola. He was the best *consigliere*, advisor, the society of honor ever had. You can ask Meyer Lansky. If arrogant hotheads like Capone, Anastasia, and Lucky Luciano had followed his advice, they's still be warm."

In Palermo, Vittorio Nistico, editorial director of *L'Ora*, and his tall, svelte editor, Kris Mancuso, and Sicilian authors Leonardo Sciascia and Michele Pantaleone were my hosts, taking me through the mysterious city and feeding me at the Ristorante Charleston, a dreamland setting with large, soft-green, tasseled lampshade chandeliers, aqua walls, and linen and silver from a forgotten time. Michele Pantalone gave me his book *Mafia e Politica*. Pantaleone's tracings indicate the sadomasochistic

Sicilian labyrinth of good/evil and the fascinating, macabre isolation of this ancient island people.

L'Ora—The Hour—is a firebrand communist daily that battles Italy's healthy, extant fascism and the perpetual Mafia with quixotic abandon. It sustains casualties, the most recent being ace reporter Mauro De Mauro, who was kidnapped in front of his house with his daughter looking on, whisked away, and murdered—allegedly by the *Grand Madre Santissima*, as the Mafia is sometimes called.

I was surprised at how little these Sicilians seemed to know or care about their exclusive export, the Mafia. I, a stranger, found myself telling them where Zu 'Cola Gentile was.

"But," said Leonardo Sciascia, "that is our style; our obsession is form. *Sicilianismo* means fixation with the obscure, the intensely predatory combined with lordly diffidence. No one is more sure of himself than the Sicilian—everyone is a prince.

"Myth is our *anima vita*; without myth there is no art to being. We keep darkness intact in the white glare of the midday sun; if we leave the shadows and become an 'open' public we will lose our image— the only thing we really have—and no longer be a separate nation of Sicilians, but numbers like the robots in Italy and your America."

On the two-hour train ride to Agrigento along the African sea, I read the newspaper *Giornale di Sicilia*. The news of the moment was the Coppola-Mangano case, crimes of passion, bank holdups, the Vatican on divorce versus the government mosaics of rights and lefts and in-betweens, cinema, TV, a massacre at Fiumicino, austerity, and a humorous story about how the U.S.A. has run out of toilet tissue and should discover the bidet. The editorial page asked the furious question, "Why should we, friends of sheiks, be deprived of oil because of the Pentagon-Kissinger maladventure in Egypt?"

Franks's lawyer's brother, Guido Mirabile, and his father-in-law, Count Guglielmo Cavallaro, met me at the Agrigento railroad station. They drove me in a red Ferrari up a steep hillside to their home.

The time-worn palazzo Cavallaro was severe and the tan stucco was flaking from the three-foot-thick walls of tufa, but inside it was luxurious; one salon maintained its 17th Century origins and the other was ultramodern. Guido's wife Inez, wearing diamonds and a Paris pants suit, was stocky and lively, with green eyes and titian hair. The servants placed a feast on the table; Sicilian hospitality, whether of the rich or the poor, has no equal. And they are kissers.

I was anxious to find Nick Gentile. After various phone calls we confirmed Frank Coppola's information that Gentile was in Realmonte.

"It's only 15 minutes from here," said Inez. "We'll go in the Citröen 1220 and be less conspicuous."

Realmonte was only 15 minutes away because Inez averaged about 100 miles an hour over the mountain roads and curves, saying, "Don't worry, I'm a capable driver."

The church of San Calogero was intoning the *Ave Maria* as we entered Realmonte, and dusk was falling. I saw a *carabiniere* with his Napoleonic hat, white gloves, and saber.

Inez said,, "He won't tell you where *capomafia* Gentile lives. The law dodges involvement: they say nothing that may bring woe to their wives and children, so they practice the tight lips of *omertà*."

We parked by the town piazza that overlooked the sea. I accosted peasants but got nowhere. Impatient, Inez took over. A burly peasant with a shotgun slung from his shoulder was approaching; he was leading an ass loaded with fragrant hops, and strung behind the ass was a milk-laden goat, her kid, and a beagle. Inez's *signorile* aspect of the nobly born made the peasant diffident.

"Yes, milady," he said, "his honor, Zu 'Cola, lives in that house with the green door and brass knocker."

The street was Via Grande, and the number was 76. No one was there. A woman appeared from an adjoining doorway. Inez haughtily said we were relatives of Zu 'Cola. The woman called her husband and told him to walk us about the village to find him.

Later we realized that the man knew all the while that Gentile would be either at the Società di La Virgine di Realmonte or the Società di San Calogero, but he asked villagers here and there, and each, studying Inez and me, had an ambiguous idea where he would not be and why. We circled the town before ending at the Società di San Calogero.

The clubhouse was a bare store with a chipped statue of the mountain village's patron saint. A naked bulb hung from the ceiling, bleakly lighting a table at which grizzled old men were playing cards. Nick Gentile was the clean-shaven one, wearing a pearl-gray homburg and dressed in an expensive formal overcoat and city clothes.

Our escort removed his hat humbly and said, "Zu 'Cola, illustrious, this man and this woman seek thee."

"I am the daughter of Count Cavalaro," said Inez, "and this gentleman is a most *simpatico* Italo-American artist who brings you greetings and salutations from Don Ciccio Coppola."

Ramrod old Gentile kept perusing his card hand.

I told him who I was and that I was sorry my Italian stank.

Without looking at me he said in Sicilian-accented New Yorkese, "I know who you are—you think I can't read?"

Finally he played his card and turned to us.

"There isn't anybody important in Agrigento whom I'm not aware of. I was a friend of Count Cavallaro, and the Prince of Lampedusa, who wrote *Il Gatapardo* (*The Leopard*), and Dottore Luigi Pirandello, who wanted to write a theater play about me. Inez, your husband is head of the Banca di Sicilia, and your father is a fine Fascist. And you, Pete, what's on your mind?"

I asked if I could visit him in the morning. He nodded, and as we left he peered at Inez's hips.

In the morning, after a drawn bath, orange juice, Sicilian pastry, and an espresso with anisette, my hosts insisted the red Ferrari was mine during my stay.

On the ground floor of the building where Gentile lived was the Banca di Agricoltura; the second and third floors were the old man's quarters. Zu 'Cola opened the door. He had on long woolen underwear and a nightcap and was barely awake. Over his cot was a crucifix, and on a small bedside table a Madonna with a votive candle; there were also medicine bottles and empty fruit-juice cans. An American electric heater warmed the room. I apologized for coming too early and said I'd be back.

You can do the town in one hour. Most of the ancient houses of the narrow twisting streets never had their crude tufa-and-rubble walls plastered yet they have balconies. On the street level are the kitchens with strips of rags in the open doorway to delude flies. Solid shutters serve as windows, and on many doors are black-edged signs of remembrance: FOR MY WIFE, FOR MY BROTHER-IN-LAW, and also up-to-date announcements: YESTERDAY AT THE HOUR OF 13:59 WAS SPENT MY HUSBAND, TITTO MARULLO.

Four old guys with wine jugs and bags of bread and cheese and onions were waiting for the bus to Sciacca. They said they shared some acres of olive trees and prickly pears, almonds and limes, and stayed weeks at a time working the soil and pruning; they lived like children, eating and drinking and sleeping under the trees. Dozens of peasants were leaving for the mountainsides with shotguns, wicked knives, pouches, and dogs. I asked one what his gun was for. He mimicked the sawing-off of the barrels to hide weapon under his cloak and said smilingly, "For men . . . and even wolves, at *bruciapelo*—point-blank." Herds of sheep and goats and buffalo were being marched by boys and girls with long whirring sticks to distant precious grazing. The huge square pavement stones laid in diagonal patterns promised that the streets would endure additional anonymous centuries. On the wall of the stark church meeting hall was a hand-written poster by the Realmonte Communist Party advertising two films: "Underground documentary of the CIA's running dogs, the Chilean Fascists, torturing and killing Marxists" and *Fellini Satyricon*. Beneath the posters in vigorous letters was painted, NIXON ASSASSINO!

A peasant was shoveling manure into his mule-drawn cart. As I was jotting notes about this typical heavy two-wheeler with its fabulous designs and carvings of pagan gods and Christian angels on the body and spokes, women spied from windows and doorways; they made questioning gestures, and I heard one say, "What's that dumb prick of an American doing?"

I went by the cliff road to the sea. A rock-rough, white-haired, white-mustachioed mariner beached his gaily painted bark, and with block and tackle fastened to a stake pulled the boat above the highwater mark. He had been out all night and had just a few baskets of sardines, octopus, and tiny swordfish for his trouble. He was 'Brosio (Ambrose) and he said, 'Yes-a, I speak-a Americano." He'd been a salmon fisherman on sailing schooners for the canneries off the Alaskan coast. He'd saved a pile, come back to Realmont, and, according to local standards, was propertied.

I told him my business.

He said laughingly, "I know your two *mafiosi* since they were barefoot starvelings; you see, 'Cola Gentile and I are the same age, 90. And I know Sicily like the palm of my hand. Coppola was always a presuming type, a grabber, a gladhander. I can tell you all his maneuvering in Alcamo, Corleone, Partinico. A regular *figlio di puttana* (whoreson) of the first water.

"Gentile is another breed of serpent but a *capo figlio di puttana*, too! At 90 he brags that he can still break horns—tell to him that 'Brosio said for him to break the antlers his wife and five daughters put on his head!

"Let's compare. Zu 'Cola was a Ulysses in America for 40 years, scheming and killing, stealing, spreading drugs, and exploiting whores, and now he is despised by his own children and lives alone like a leper. I'm an illiterate fisherman and peasant, but I have land, livestock, a family, sea, sun, health, and teeth that can crush stones. I don't know the written word, but one would have to be an imbecile not to be able to read life with the good eyes God gave him. Write in your tale that the world is one village and that 'Brosio said the Mafia exist because the common people are sheep who love to be fucked in the ass, sheared, and butchered, and there is no end to sheep. Say also that the mean character of the Sicilian does not permit occupation and opportunity for young men and they must emigrate; that our towns have only women, the old, and children. If it were not for employment in Germany, France, and Switzerland, and the money sent back, thousands of Sicilians would die of want."

'Brosio wrapped up the sardines in newspaper for me to take to Zu 'Cola for breakfast.

I told Gentile about 'Brosio. He said, "Grandpa 'Brosio is *prepotente* and has the obstinate head of a Calabrian. He is one tough old *figlio di puttana*."

Gentile was proud of his house; he had it built in 1919 with $100,000 of mob money. He was born in the next town, Siculiana. The Siculians and the Sicilians were the original people of the island before the invasions of Carthaginians, Greeks, and other races. His wife was a Realmonte peasant. He used the salon as his bedroom; the plastered vaulted ceiling depicted heaven, and the cherubim in the center held three varicolored balloons on strings.

From the street came the Moorish-Sicilian cadenced cries of goats' milk, eggs, fish, snails, and spinach vendors—the greens seller pronounced it, "*Spinuchududo!*"

Gentile admitted he's been cool to me the night before because he suspected I might be an FBI bastard. He is above medium height, balding, has some of his teeth and the rest bridged, a fair complexion, delicate hands, and a patrician face, but it's his eyes that get and hold you. They seem black but are of the deepest, hardest, purest brown. He will never use glasses. Saints have those eyes; they never swerve or falter. Later he told me that often in a mortal showdown with a Mafia enemy the steadfastness of his glance would safely resolve the issue.

Gentile puts on freshly laundered socks and made-to-order monogrammed shirts twice a day. While he slowly dressed, I wandered the rooms. On a table were heaps of letters and cards from Families in America . . . and of all things, William Saroyan's *The Human Comedy* in Italian, a U.S. Army overseas edition. I said I'd take a walk if he needed time to himself.

He growled, "Can't you stay put?" He commanded me to relax, to read something—look at newspapers, magazines, or listen to the radio. I said, "I see, Nick, commanding is still with you."

In Mafia Sicilian dialect he said "*Cummannari é megghiu ca futtere*"—"To command is better than fucking." He made very strong espresso and insisted that I drink some with him.

In the street the women bowed their heads and the men tipped their hats to Zu 'Cola. He entered the barbershop. There were faded nudes of the *Playboy* Marilyn Monroe and plenty of flies. After he was shaved and massaged he ran his hand over my face.

"Pete, your face is not neat. Get in the barber chair."

It was no use protesting that I cringed at the thought of being shaved with a straight razor; but then I did enjoy it and almost fell asleep. Barber Giuseppe Impera gave Gentile two perfumed 1974 pocket calendars with colored pictures of desirable naked girls. He tucked one into my trench-coat pocket.

Gentile took me into the hungry church of San Calogero. There was the musky smell of incense and the stubby old women in black with black shawls and black rosaries. The low organ music was superb, other-world creating, eye-misting. The priest nodded to Gentile and said "*Laudata a Gesù, Don 'Cola nostro*" ("Praise Jesus, Don 'Cola our very own), and continued, "The hearts of those that err may repent and return to the unity of Thy truth. Let us pray also for the perfidious Jews . . ." On the way out Zu 'Cola and I lighted candles . . . for different reasons.

As with Coppola, Gentile and I conversed in Italian and English, sliding in and out of both for immediate facile and particular comprehension. He wanted to visit Inez and her father, Count Cavallaro. During the drive he made me stop and see the 2500-year old remains of Agrigento's Grecian temples of Jove, Diana, Venus, etc. Some were practically intact; they were all built of the natural red-brown concrete, the *pozzolana tufo*, which is the measureless bed under the rich blanket of Italy's soil. Then he insisted that we go to the adjacent home of Luigi Pirandello. A peasant and his wife, caretakers, live in a section of the mansion. Reeking of garlic and with steaming sheep dung on his boots, the peasant displayed Pirandello's Nobel Prize, citations, letters, manuscripts, and photos of his actress-loves.

The grave was on a promontory, under a tall pine tree. On the monument was an inscription Pirandello had written about his birth: 28 GIUGNO 1867. UNA NOTTE DI GIUGNO CADDI COME UNA LUCCIOLA SOTTO UN PINO SOLITARIO IN UNA CAMPAGNA D'OLIVI SARACENI AFFACCIATA AGLI ORLI D'UN ALTIPIANO D'ARGILLE AZZURE SUL MARE AFRICANO. He'd left the world in the same place he'd entered it.

I brought *capomafia* Nicola Gentile into the palazzo Cavallaro without warning. Cavallaro's wife, the countess, mother of Inez, was affronted but, though displeased, graciously made Gentile feel at home, ordered food, and excused herself.

In the period salon, while we sipped coffee and cognac, the count sat at the piano and played "music of the soul"—arias from Puccini, whom he had known as a youth—then went into best jazz I ever heard . . . and this in Sicily's bright midday. Soon Zu 'Cola's 90 years told; I drove him back to primitive Realmonte for his siesta.

In the morning Inez's maid awoke me. Gentile was on the phone. He wanted me to bring Inez to his home for lunch.

"Can you imagine," said Inez, "he didn't ask whether it was convenient. He told me imperiously, he actually commanded me to be his guest—without fail! And he said he would tell me of many *cosi nostri* (*our* things)."

Gentile was fashionably dressed and smelled of imported after-shave. He had done the marketing. He removed his jacket and vest and put on a white waiter's apron. Inez opened the French doors of the balcony and let in the sea air and sun. Despite his testy objections she went right ahead helping him in the kitchen, and as they argued over how things should be done, he caressed her face and said, "You're a beautiful doll . . . a living doll!" Inez pretended not to understand, and I translated, "*Tu si na bella bambola—na vera bellissima bambola viva!*"

Gentile said, "In America, when I was a column of a man, I had so many beautiful dolls . . . now all dead . . ."

Zu 'Cola had made the fettuccini before we arrived and had it drying on coat hangers. In the tomato-sauce pot he put the stuffed rolled beef and then the fresh-made sausage containing parsley, hot pepper, and cheese curdled from buffalo milk. He made Sicily's specialty *pasta con sardina*: fillets of morning caught-sardines in olive oil, butter, garlic, black olives, a touch of fennel, ferns, capers, and pine nuts. There is no better sauce. For verdure he cooked artichokes with long tender stems and my favorite, *broccolo-rabi*, and mixed a salad. I had noticed a bottle of rare champagne on a catchall table in his bedroom. He sent me to get it. He opened it, poured, and, said, "I saved this for happy-time occasion. It's been on that table for I don't know how many years."

He wouldn't let us be until we had finished all the food, dessert, and coffee, and he said what every Italian in the world says. "It's a sin to throw food away." Inez started to clear away the table, "You're my guest," he said, "and I command you not to lift a finger!"

Inez said, not unkindly, "To whom do you think you're talking? Zu 'Cola, you'd do better to command the wind." She pushed him aside and went to work. As she rinsed, he dried.

Gentile said, "In the Mafia the most despised thing is weakness. I have masked with much attention my terrible weakness for women."

In the next room—with poet's license—I lifted papers that were of better use to me than to Nick: sentimental letters from various Families and a sensational full-page article about him and Lucky Luciano and other startling names in *L'Ora*, dated Sunday September 12, 1965, by the murdered journalist, Mauro De Mauro. I hid the material in my coat and walked the brief distance to 'Brosio's house on the sea cliff. 'Brosio was feeding hops and artichokes stalks to his ass while piglets scurried and guinea fowl pecked.

'Brosio said, "So the big-a–shot-a is going to regale you with the miracles and wonderful adventures of his life, eh? Let me tell you, the day a *cafone* (lout) of a *malecarne* (rotten meat) doesn't shoot a friend or competitor in the back like the fearful coward he is—that day it will snow in hell and Christ will be seen on the streets of Realmonte.

"Gentile appears to you a gallant Christian now? Old age makes any *mafioso* a philosopher. The tiger changes his stripes, but in his heart, not his vices. Zu 'Cola was born a bad *figlio di puttana* and will die a bad *figlio di puttana*. But I love him as a fellow being in this mystery of life and feel sorry for him. Have him tell you of the treachery of his wife and daughters."

Gentile said he had given up smoking two years before when he'd stopped driving his Alfa Romeo. Inez stuck a Marlboro in his mouth and said, "At 90 what difference?"

The dispassionate eyes focused in the past. "My village, Siculiana, next to Realmonte here, offered a boy famine, physical slavery, ignorance, and violence. Men killed over a pig, a goat, a handful of eggs, or an insinuation. It was the life of beasts—just to get enough to eat to stay alive was an exhausting struggle . . . and much worse in time of war when dogs and cats and rats were not safe from man. Relatives and peasants commented about my strong personality. I educated myself a bit, and at 18 I knew I had the power in me and I wanted to give an account of myself to the world. That made me dangerous.

"I stowed away on a ship from Palermo, and when it got to New York I skipped. A mariner took me to a Sicilian family at 91 Elizabeth Street in Little Italy. The way of the *onorata società* was in my blood; I found the Mafia that had come from the province of Agrigento. I was a *paesano*. They accepted me and that was fine."

He learned the extortion-protection racket—forcing successful storekeepers to let the *mafiosi* allow them to ply their businesses *"tranquillo e in santa pace"*—"in tranquility and blessed peace." He was superior to the run of *mafiosi* and at 20 was promoted to his first responsible assignment, "to eliminate a certain troublesome, dangerous, unscrupulous man. The plan was prepared by me . . . I want to illustrate an action of justice for the Family." He enlisted the two closest friends of the condemned. On a certain evening he was having dinner with the *capo* who ordered the killing. "After the spaghetti I left for the appointment with the condemned. I met him and as I shook and held his hand his two friends fired from behind and ran. I stood over him and pumped his head with lead to make positive that he had been chilled.

"Onlookers evaporated. I went across the street to a bar, drank a whiskey, and returned to resume dinner with my *capo*. The whole turn took about ten minutes. As I began eating the meat course the *capo* whispered nervously, 'How did your mission go?' And I said, 'All good.'"

According to Gentile he was the brain, the balance wheel of the founding fathers of American organized crime.

Inez was racing the Ferrari back to her *palazzo*. I said I had been disturbingly hypnotized by Gentile's recital and liturgy of his associates, Capone, Costello, Cuciano, and so on, and the numerous acts of justice on Masseria, Maranzano, and others, and even by how he took credit for pleading and saving various of the condemned.

"You come from working people," said Inez, "and those *mafiosi* make an impression on you. One looks at those things from the position of one's class. My breed fostered the Mafia as private armies to safeguard our privileges and interests; to us the *mafiosi* have been, are, and shall always be expendable, low, grasping peasant animals."

Gentile fixed up a bedroom and had me stay with him. On Christmas Eve we went to mass, listened to the shepherds sing carols and play bagpipes in the street, met 'Brosio, and went to the bar for drinks. Gentile went to the telephone and called his daughter in Porto Empedocle. After he hung up I asked him what happened. With no expression he answered, "She shouted, '*Murderer*, evil man, why do you stay on earth? Why don't you die?!'" And he mumbled, "I thought *Natale* was the time for pardon, to forgive, at least for a day . . ."

'Brosio's son-in-law, grandchildren, and great-grandchildren came to fetch him for the traditional Christmas feast. 'Brosio made a sign with his head for me to follow: he took Gentile by the arm and said, "Come, Zu 'Cola, tonight I command!" And we paraded to 'Brosio's home over the livestock-smelling stable for wine made with his grapes, honey balls, raw sea urchins with lime juice, and sardines, octopus, and giant eels fried in bubbling olive oil.

Gentile asked how my wife and two sons were to me. I said there wasn't a day that they didn't hug and kiss me.

"You are fortunate," he said. "American dollars were my *cafone* wife's god. I was not attached to money; to command is my god. When I was pinched for passing ten pounds of heroin in Palermo for the New York market, I thought I was frigging the law by putting my bank accounts and property in my wife's name—if you can't trust your wife and children then who can you trust in this world? But I got off easy with a fast $50,000 'fine.' I came home happy; I wanted to surprise my wife, so I came into the house quietly. My wife didn't know I was there, and I overheard her talking to the godfather of my daughters . . . this *figlio di puttana* had put the horns on me because I couldn't expect her to sew up her hole while I was in the States for 40 years . . . and she said to the *buon padrino*, 'They should not have let Nick out of jail. With his return the evil *mafioso* will ruin our happiness. We have his money now, so what do we need him around for?' Thank God I had funds cached. But she confiscated the lion's share. The daughters clutched it with her. Do you know they spat on me? I mean they spat right in my face and pushed me out of the house!—knowing I'd rather die than sue or harm them. They kept the wealth for which I risked my skin a thousand times. To them the money was good and I was bad. Pete, I won every battle to the death in the Mafia but was defeated by my loves ones. The wife died and left the girls millionaires. They are more realistic, more cynical, more *mafiosi* than me. They have the cursed cruel Arab blood in them."

Gentile told me to drive him to Palermo.

"I'll break your arm if you try to pay anything. This trip's on me. When I can't be a sport no more I'll call it quits."

He took me to the Grand Hotel et Des Palmes. In the dining salon he demanded the last table on the left.

"This table could tell stories about me and other guys—like Riccardo Wagner writing *Parsifal* on it and *Sicily's* capos, Don Calogero Vizzini, Cenco Russo, and Liggio eating on it. Us members of *Madre Santissima* called this hotel our Vatican. I'm serious. We held a big *schiticchiui*, 'banquet for men of honor,' here in October '57 that would have knocked your eyes out; all of us were kings of *capos, tuti pezzu di 90*, the piece of 90, which is the loudest, biggest fireworks bomb shot off at the end of religious holidays. This meeting was a few months before the American Mafia shit all over themselves at the villa of Joe Barbera in the mountains of Appalachia when the cops flush them. Joe Bonanno was here—Lover-Boy Bananas who kidnaps himself like a Sinatra movie star and gets a book written—and Luciano and Adonis. One important point of business was the restructuring of the entire European organization of the handling and distribution of '*ceneri*'—'ashes,' meaning drugs. Also on the agenda was our Supreme-court verdict and sentence: '*Freddandolo a bruciapelo*,' 'to be chilled at powder-burn range,' for that puffed-up Calabrese, Albert Anastasia.

"Me and Frankie Coppola was the only ones who didn't look like wops. He carried himself tall for a little guy. A lot of 'brothers' thought we was the best of godfathers to each other, but I got to tell you something because there ain't no secrets nowhere. I don't like to quack-quack, but behind my shoulders *Tre Dita* Coppola talks and has got me marked as a traitor—'*nu spiare pi sbirri*,' 'a spy for the fuzz.' It ain't that I want to criticize him now that he's down, but it's not saying much for how smart he is that at 75 he's '*pizzicatu e convittu*,' 'pinched and detained in the government boarding school.'

Zu 'Cola left a 5000-lire tip. He looked around with nostalgia.

"Upstairs in suite 351, you wouldn't believe how many beautiful dolls—some imported from New York—I ate and banged. Now? I'm the sun gone down, a cracked old piss pot out the window. The worst sinner, the worst criminal, the worst *mafioso* of all is . . . old age."

Franco Rosi's film, *Lucky Luciano* with Rod Steiger, Edmond O'Brien, and the real narcotics agent, Charles Siragusa, was playing at the Cinema Edison (400 lire a ticket: 70cents). Rosi had the run English version in Rome for me and Hank Werba of *Variety*, but I wanted to see it in Italian and I coaxed Gentile to go.

Italian *mafs* pronounce Lucky Luciano 'Loka Lootch.' Gentile said, "The Siragusas are a dime a dozen, and showing Loka Lootch as the *capo* with the strength and wisdom of the Pope is a laugh. Loka Lootch was a greasy, arrogant *cafone*; a vain, stupid guinea imitating Hollywood gangster movies with his obvious clothes and the *'fagiuolo'* —bean—on his pinky. Loka Lootch loved himself. Now let's take count of how smart he was.

"Me and him were arrested for white slavery by Dewey. On bail I skipped back to Italy and paid Mussolini personally $100,000 to protect me. Loka Lootch was given 50 years. After nine years—and you know what nine years is with bars and bungholers and other things—a political comedy was cooked up by Dewey in Washington that got Lootch deported.

"They say he died from a heart attack. *Cafone* Lootch was strong as a bull. He took pep pills. Among them was sneaked poison pills. At the Naples airport he picked the wrong pill and was quickly chilled."

I asked who put the poison in his pill container.

Zu 'Cola grinned grimly, "Friends, best friends. How else?"

In the morning I stopped to say goodbye to Leonardo Sciascia and Kris Mancuso at *L'Ora*. The day's paper headlined Frank Coppola's charges of police and political corruption. Returning to the parked Ferrari and Gentile I bought the *Giornale di Sicilia*, and that had a front-page picture of dapper Frankie with the caption, "*Condannato a Morte Dalla Mafia?*" It was the beginning of Italy's Watergate scandal, complete with tampered tapes, attempted bribes, threats, cover-ups, and counter charges. At this writing, the case has not been settled.

Gentile said, "Like mushrooms in the quiet and dark, we prospered. Silence in any situation was our power; *'gumitu,'* 'take the liver and not ask help.' It was our magic over people.

"Times have changed. A lot of crazy green *mafiosi* give themselves airs at any price; the '*sbirri*,' 'fuzz,' is the legal Mafia. They want most of the action and they can chill anybody and get a medal for it—especially an old guy like Frank."

Gentile said that in Sicily ten *mafiosi* make a "leaf" of an "artichoke," and on the road to Realmonte we visited the artichokes that fill the country from Palermo to Agrigento. These villages nest on mountain flanks and from the real patterns of Mafia organization. They are old and squalid in the violet sunshine—Torretta, Belolampo, Montelepre, Partinico, Trappeto Castellammare.

Montelepre has been the stronghold of the dazzling young Salvatore "Turiddu" Giuliano. I saw his tomb. On the marble was his own prepared epitaph: LIFE AND DREAMS . . . AS POOR LITTLE BIRDS IN THE FOREST SQUANDERED.

Gentile chuckled. "Turiddu was a wild Turk; he gave Frank Coppola a plum without meaning to. He machine-gunned Leonardo Renda, secretary of the influential Christian Democrats, and Santo Fleres, *capomafia* of Partinico, just at the time that Truman was out of the White House and turned his back on Frank. The heat was on Frank, so he switched countries and came home to his town Partinico and took over as the 'genial' *capo*."

I had heady wine with Zu 'Cola's friends—iron-faced descendants of Giuliano's famous band of "*picciotti*," "dear little fellows." One kissed his hand and said, "A friend gives all for a friend, even his blood."

It was the only time I saw Zu 'Cola moved. He said somberly, "I repeat what honorable Don Calogero wrote on the wall of his cell in Palermo's Ucciardone prison, '*Vicaria, malattia, e nicissitari si vidi lu cori di l'amicu!*'—'In prison, sickness, and necessity is seen the heart of a friend!'"

We had driven to the heights behind Borgo Trappeto and the Centro di Formazione per la Pianificazione Organica, a utopian, modernistic prototype complex for a new Sicily, planned by humanist Nobel nominee and social theorist Danilo Dolci. From there you could see the Mafia towns of Partinico, Montelepre, Mussomeli, and Corleone, and to the left, the Mount of Venus.

Gentile said, "Me and Coppola tangled horns with Danilo Dolci long ago. He doesn't mind his own business and makes trouble for the honored society. He's got some strange ideas. I'd like to know who's laying out all the money for his operations. Tell him Nicola Gentile said he's a phony *figlio di puttana*."

We drove to Dolci's home. Gentile waited in the car. Danilo invited me to stay with his big family: there was to be a concert that evening. I said I would go after I took Nick Gentile home. At first he thought I was being funny, but when he learned I had Gentile in the car he threw up his hands and said, "What are you doing with that killer?" I told him I'd befriended Coppola and Gentile for literary reasons and found them to be extraordinary men.

"You wouldn't find them so interesting if you knew the horrible struggles the peasants, fishermen, miners, and I have fought with Coppola and Gentile. They are *mafiosi figlio di puttana*!" He gave me one of the anti-Mafia books he had written, *Inchi esta a Palermo*.

As I drove Gentile home, the small villages were toy blocks of pink and white and gray and brown in the moody sunlight of early evening; the enfolding mountains were phalli and breasts and horns and buttocks and vaginas of original gods; the live sea and the light and shade of the male and female slopes, rises, and dropping contours explained Sicily's violence: It was no place for a new religion, no sanctuary for confession and fear and remorse, no setting for a utopia.

In Italian I said to Gentile, "What is stolen can be replaced. When you destroy a man you destroy a world, and the echoes of that destruction never stop. And if you tried throughout eternity, you could never bring back the man and replace his world. Tell me, Nick, does it bother you that you have taken the lives of men?"

"We're losers from the moment we're born; no one's got a chance. It's destiny to kill and die. When you die, that's it, there's nothing. '*Chisti é la vita*'—'This is life;' '*Chisti fu la mia vita*'—'This has been my life.'"

"What is the one thing left that you want to do?"

"I miss the wide-open loose manner of America. I dream of crawling back there to die . . ."

Sicilian Aristocracy

Godfathers of the Mafia

Sicily is Circe: she subjugates conquerors and keeps them at her feet. Each invader—Mycenaeans, Phoenicians, Greeks, Romans, Goths, Byzantines, Arabs, Normans, Spaniards—contributed an original facet to the Sicilian nobility, a style more than a class. The Egyptian culture aside, the Sicilian aristocratic style has prevailed longer than that of any other aristocracy.

The Normans introduced feudalism to Sicily in the Ninth Century. Since then the nobles have neither known nor experienced good government or bad. Only the divine right of force has prevailed. The aristocracy had faith in cold intrigues, luxurious machinations and megalomania.

When Sicilian barons tired of wives, uxoricide was not merely practiced, but considered quite acceptable, provided, of course, that it was accompanied by religious rites. Usually the dear woman was given *acqua di Palermo*, a slow-working aperitif with an arsenic base.

For a baron not to go all out and into debt for a family funeral— even a murdered wife's—was to lose face. An incomparable funeral was the most important act of existence. The leading houses attended in a lavish carriage cortege, while thousands followed on foot: monks, nuns, orphans, vassals, workmen's guilds, torches, flowers, floats, effigies, bands, choir. All the church bells rang. At times, the dead were embalmed. Today, more than 7000 mummies can be found in the convent of the Cappuccini.

Among other Sicilian extravagances was the "Feast of Carnival," with its drunken masses, brawls, and *corsi di bagasci*—foot races run by prostitutes for a prize of embroidered panties. The barons looked down disdainfully from palace balconies, but later the nobility held naked wife- and daughter-swapping orgies by the light of the Sicilian moon.

The seed of the Mafia originated within the inner sanctum of the Holy Inquisition under the Spanish Dominican, Torquemada, who introduced his *Bianchi Frati* to Sicily in 1487.

The Sicilian Inquisition was a colossal entity capable of not only destroying political adversaries but of giving bread and work to favored followers. This was an authorized Mafia, a state within the state, carrying weapons and not paying taxes. From it came the White Brotherhood of Saint Francis de Paul, the *Beati Paoli*, underground partisans against the Bourbon aristocracy—allegedly religious Robin Hoods but actually self-serving murder-for-hire terrorists.

The modern Mafia began when the Sicilian barons fostered the Constitution of 1812, an anti-Bourbon document modeled along English democratic lines. It cut off the legs of the hated Bourbon rule, but also eroded the barons' own powers. King Ferdinando, who had left Sicily in 1802 calling the Sicilians cannibals, returned in 1806. In 1815 he abolished the Constitution of 1812. The middle class, having tasted free movement, conspired with the *Carboneria* (freemasons) and the burgeoning Mafia.

The armed attempt of the barons in 1820 under Prince di San Cataldo to take over Sicily—stupidly burning the huts and killing the livestock of the peasantry—turned the people toward the Mafia for leadership. The Mafia, coming into its own, collaborated with judges and police, guaranteed results of elections, controlled public offices, defended their new property privileges, and maneuvered personal and banking credits.

The rise of the Mafia and the decadence of the nobility was termed among the Sicilian *cognoscenti* "*Il suicido dei Gattopardi*." All went well for a time, but when, like the Junkers hiring Nazis as bully boys, the *Gattopardi* got the bright idea of fostering criminal peasants and descendants of the *Beati Paoli* as private armies against the free peasant class, they marked their own doom. Step by inexorable step, the greedy and ambitious *mafiosi* became the aristocracy's police, judiciary and executioner, tax collector, and then '*Gabellotto*'—exploiting rentor, subrenting to helpless tenant farmers. Finally the *mafiosi* terrorized the nobility that fed them. They ended by hijacking the impotent barons' vast farms.

A few aged aristocrats survive, such as the families Spadafora, Bordonaro, Giardinelli, and Di Vincenzo. Soon there will be none. Still, for the present, they are comfortable. The old palaces that remain to be seen are Lanza di Mazzarino, Ganci, and Lampedusao Villa Niscemi. Surrounding the palaces are stores, markets, apartments, TV antennae, and the noises of radios and cars. Within is the dreamworld of the past.

The gallery of Lampedusa palace is a filthy ruin, raucous with voices of vendors and the children of fishermen, but past the majestic door and threshold there are still porters and butlers in white jackets and gloves. The grand vaulted frescoed rooms contain archaeological treasures and Renaissance embellishments, marbles, silvers, golds, and oil paintings of illustrious ancestors.

It was here on a night in 1956 that the aristrocracy had its final moment of glory. The huge kerosene lamps with the stained-glass shades were lighted. On the shelves of the rich library stood Sophocles, Vergil, Dante, Goethe, Proust, Stendhal, Croce, D'Annunzio, and thousands of precious books. Handsome Prince Giuseppe Tomasi di Lampedusa read to his wife, Baroness Wolf-Stomersee and friends. Then he modestly announced that he had written a novel about his family and the aristocracy, entitled *Il Gattopardo*. He handed the manuscript of *The Leopard* to Elena Craveri Croce with humble doubts as to its literary worth and wondered whether she would approach some publisher. Soon after, Prince Lampedusa died without knowing that the world would proclaim his book a masterpiece.

A Gift From Dottie Ryan

"Gee, Honey," said Dottie to the Boss in her "southern" kewpie-doll voice, "you done a lot for me; I wish I could do something big for you!"

Boss Marino smiled sentimentally.

"You jus' keep yuh nose clean, baby; that's good enough for me."

The big swarthy Italo-American racket king was as happy as he ever could be. He had a quiet wife, and children, a mother he loved, millions in deposit boxes, and Dottie. The Boss picked them young and liked to think they were virgin. His romantic preference had always been show-girls, peroxide blondes of Anglo-Saxon origin. It kind of set off his Latin oiliness. He acquired Dottie Ryan from the floor show in his night club the Bluebird on the first night she appeared there. She was a small sixteen year old curvy dancer with neat legs, a large mouth and breasts, and bleached platinum hair. He put her up in a ten-room suite, with a chauffeur, Cadillac, maids, and took her to the races and night clubs. Saturday nights he spent in Dottie's apartment; Sunday with his family, Momma Marino and the many respectful relatives who lived off of him. He wore around his neck the Scapula that Momma Marino had sent from Rome—blessed especially for him. Throughout the United States the Boss's name had a magic fascination: many people admired him, and Hollywood gave him infamous but lasting identity.

"You boys just stay in with the Boss and you'll always be in the clear," he told them.

But he was beginning to have his own troubles.

He was treated circumspectly by governors, mayors, labor leaders and the newspapers, and he was proud of it. He owned the Italian section, Manny Goat Hill, half the city, and enjoyed three palatial winter homes. His henchmen distributed food baskets on holidays in Little Italy, his donations to the churches were huge, and his undertaking establishments buried the poor gratis. He was not ashamed to tell the boys that he had come up the tough solitary way.

Not long after the Boss had taken over Dottie he had private complaints of a purulent nature, although he had been faithful to Dottie. At length he called in old Dr. Archimedes Vitone. Dr. Vitone hated the Boss—and he had good reason to. Dr. Vitone remembered Philly in its halcyon days before the Boss Marino rule, the time when he had come from Italy an idealistic medical student who married an Irish girl and brought her to the Italian section. For years he had hopelessly railed against the Marino mob in secret, and on many occasions had had a gun held to his back and been forced to operate and save the life of a bullet-ridden Marino man. Besides having had to deliver the Boss's children and attend to his family, he was a victim of the Boss's shakedown protective association.

"Mr. Marino," announced Dr. Vitone after having examined the Boss, "some woman has made you a present of gonorrhea."

"Yuh mean, now I'm a man?" laughed the Boss, "Hell, that's nothin' but a cold in the nose—I ain't gonner let a little thing like that bother me!"

Dr. Vitone, not too encouragingly, suggested a blood test.

"My good wop blood'll keep me a hundred years!" thundered the Boss. And he was really infuriated when Dr. Vitone said he thought Miss Ryan should be looked at.

That night Dr. Vitone was in high spirits. He confided to his wife: "I've just seen Marino's death warrant under a microscope. I found gonorrhea in him. He was amused and will probably treat himself with hot peppers and wine like all the tough guys. What I didn't tell him was that he has syphilis also—Heaven will forgive me! It may cost me my old life, but I'll see to it that his syphilis is not discovered until it reads four-plus, and then it will be too late! That spirochete has been sucking the blood of decent America—but right at this moment he is filled with minute silent gangsters!"

A few years later Momma Marino was worried about her favorite son. The Boss wasn't well. He neglected the intricate machinations of his rackets. He wandered off in an amnesic state for days. He did not sleep for weeks at a stretch. He turned upon his trusted gunmen and punched them for no reason at all. Instead of making his hard-hitting ruthless decisions he scribbled dadoes and laughed. His brothers Mike and Tony found it impossible to interest him in the rackets. His dark oily eyes glittered with a grinning light. They thought it was because Dottie Ryan had run off and left him, but they were sure he'd snap out of it and be his old kingly self. Momma Marino told Dr. Vitone that the evil-eye had been cast upon her son. Dr. Vitone readily conceded that it was possible. Momma Marino assiduously performed incantations and administered old-world potions to her son. The Boss had become unapproachable. He accused his brothers and henchmen of planning to kill him. Word got around that Boss Marino was slipping. But his gangster rivals decided it was another cunning dodge, a typical getaway stunt. When the Federal government queasily mustered the courage to convict and sentence him for a short term on a comparatively bland charge, the Boss didn't seem to care to get out of it. In court his attention strayed and he gave silly giggles as answers. It pleased the public to think that the Boss had arranged to be sent to jail to save his life from gangster enemies and so did the hoods, at least for a while.

But, in prison the Boss's behavior was extremely schizophrenic. He attacked his cell mate sexually, addressing the frightened fellow as Dottie darling. The prison doctor's Wasserman blood test of the Boss explained his unintegrated actions of violence, perversion, maudlin streaks and days of stupid disinterested silence. The silver bullets of science could not rub out the tiny hi-jackers that had corkscrewed into his brain. Now and then the newspapers gingerly ran contrasting photos of the Boss's big winter homes, the Boss in his hey-day, and the Boss in drab prison clothes, with careful intimations that after the government had caught up with him he couldn't take it and that the change in his fortunes had brought him to the point of nervous breakdown. The Boss was automatically remanded to an asylum.

When Boss Marino was marched in, Hymie Finkle, a worker-patient, surveyed him and remarked to Charlie the attendant: "So dot's the Big Shot Marino mit siffliss—vell, vell, Solomon said: 'Vun hair from a voman can trample a man more den an army mit swords and horses!'"

Another patient who was admitted the same afternoon, was a tall gaunt anemic young man with glaucomous eyes, named Stanislaus. He had a pale yellow beard and long locks down over his shoulders. He carried a Bible and wore a sack-cloth robe and sandals. He was committed after he had picketed the White House night and day with a placard demanding from the President immediate cessation of bloodshed throughout the world. It was inevitable that he be nick-named "The Messiah" by the patients as well as the attendants.

The Boss made a troublesome patient. His paretic mind could not realize that this was not his palace on Sea Island nor his guarded sumptuous hotel suite. He wandered about the milling ward excitedly. Something in him compelled him to turn on the showers, knock over mops and pails, unravel rolls of tissue as though it were very important to do so, scatter bed-pans about the lavatory and toss sleeping patients from them cots. "I wanna talk to Joe Louis and Franklin D. Roosevelt!" he shouted, "I'm gonner strip every sonuvabitch in the world and walk all over them! My boys kin lick the United States army! Mike! Tony! Turn the typewriters on these jerks! What are they doin' in my place! Here Dottie, take this ten grand and buy yuhself a new brassiere! Get yourself perfumed up sweetie, put on yuh silver fox an' we'll burn up Philly! I told yuh city hall bums to lay off my snow peddlers or I'll but yuh! Tony! What's the take on the Washington cat-houses! Yuh not working the polack bims hard enough! Git that newspaper guy that's riding me! Rub him out!"

Charlie the attendant shook his head. "Hollywood and the newspapers oughta get a load of this." Charlie took a drink from his pint bottle and muttered through his teeth: "If yuh don't drink on this job so help me Jesus yuh'll end up buggy yuhself!"

The Boss rattled away to a catatonic negro and then bellowed: "Where's Dottie, yuh black bastard!" The negro remained motionless. "Wise, eh!" shouted the Boss. He punched the negro to the floor and kicked him. Stanislaus came up to the Boss. "Brother," he said softly, "Love thy neighbor . . ." The Boss babbled insensibly and rushed away. Stanislaus helped the wounded negro to his feet.

Charlie the attendant said to one on his worker-patients: "Pete, did you see that? The show goes on twenty four hours a day—no wonder I don't go to the movies no more!"

Pete paused with the bed-pans in his hand. "Yes," he agreed, "this place is full of lunatics. If it weren't for my secret love affair with the Queen of England I wouldn't have been framed and sent here."

At mess-time Charlie brought the Boss his tray of food that the Boss's family arranged to send in three times a day from an expensive restaurant. The Boss accepted it and without warning slammed it against Charlie's head.

"Alright! you wop bastard!" said Charlie under his breath, "From now on you'll eat the regular crap and I'll treat myself to your tray—who'll know the difference! You're no Boss Marino here! When they put you in a place like this you've lost your ticket! Anything goes! You're just another nut and we'll fix your little red wagon here!"

When Charlie handed the Messiah his cup of bean soup and boiled frankfurters, Stanislaus gently refused it.

"No thank thee, brother," he said, "it is my bounden duty to fast until there is peace on earth. Thou shalt not kill, saith the Lord God Jehovah."

"You can do what you like with your own belly, son."

Night in the asylum behind the barred windows as an eerie heart crushing fascinating chrome gray-black nocturne of driven unpunctuated voices. Men who had once been free members of society raved raucously against dreams in the darkness from their abandoned lighthouses of illusion.

The Messiah walked the dim wards singing psalms and carrying water and bed-pans to patients. Men cursed, laughed, prayed, groaned and called for their wives and children. The night attendant sat in his cage drowsily smoking his pipe. A hilarious party was going on in a doctor's cottage. Two hospital guards drove slowly about the grounds. Out on the main highway the Greyhound bus roared by. In the operating room of the infirmary a young patient was having a gangrenous leg removed. In the tunnels connecting each unit of buildings worker-patients pushed loads of soiled sheets and clothing to the laundry. At the power-house smoke poured from the tall stack and within the building huge dynamos whirred ceaselessly. In the morgue ice-box rows of bodies were carefully kept at the right temperature. On the shelves in the laboratory glass jars were labeled with their contents of hearts, lungs and brains. On their cots thousands of patients slept, soon to awaken to the nightmare of day.

Boss Marino knew neither night nor day. He paced his room shouting in great agitation: "I tell yuh nobody's rolled Dottie Ryan but the Boss! I'll murder the bum who says Dottie ain't clean! I took you outta show-business honey; no more hoofin' for you! Yuh kin have anything in the world, sugar! Meet me at the Bluebird. Them slugs from the west side ain't gonner muscle in on my cathouses! Line 'em up and turn the heat on 'em! I run this lousy town! Cops are two-penny jerks! Make 'em and break 'em! Go git yuhself the best skins, baby. Fifty thousand from the waterfront unions or they'll git their heads pushed in! City Hall's on the payroll. Stay with the Boss and yuh'll be in the silk. Tony keep after the boys. Hot rods. Lay offa Dottie. She's mine and nobody ain't goner have her but me, savvy! Marino's the law! Yuh hear me yuh sonuvabitches; Nobody kin touch the Boss! Yeh! Hahaha! An' I was a poor wop kid! Slashed a cop in the old country! Yuh gotta know how to handle a sticker and a gat! I know what I want! I git what I want! I knocked off an old dame on the Titanic and lifted her dough! Yuh can't buck Marino! I'm tough! Nothin' kin kill me! 'Fraid of nothin' and no sonuvabitch in the world! The jerks want whores and geegees and happy dust and alky and numbers! I'm the guy to give it to 'em. If I'm sucker not to do it some other wise guy will! I'm the law in Philly! Wipe out the small-timers! Take care of the wops in Nanny Goat Hill! Give the sky-pilots some dough! Don't be cheap! Hand out free lunch to the quiet slobs! Jesus! That blonde hair sends me, Dottie! Meet me at the races, honey!"

The Marino clan pulled up to the hospital each day in an imposing cortege of bullet-proof Cadillacs. Mike and Tony though flashily dressed entered the hospital somberly. With them came their bleached show-girl wives. Momma Marino brought hot dishes of spaghetti and meat balls. Mike and Tony talked out of the sides of their mouths to the Boss about the rackets, but the Boss stared directly through them, not understanding. The Boss wasn't getting any better. He did silly things while the mobsters earnestly tried to communicate with him. It began to dawn upon them that the Boss wasn't pulling an act.

One day the Boss said to his family and pals: "I wanna talk to Joe Louis and Franklin D. Roosevelt. But they gotta get naked first!" He busily began to strip. When his brothers attempted to stop him he punched them ferociously. Then he ran about nakedly waving his arms as though he were flying. Momma Marino sobbed her way out of the hospital. Someone had put the evil spirits into her boy.

Dr. Beckman and the staff knew cause and effect. The rapidly dividing and multiplying spirochetes were eating away at the capillaries of the blood vessels of the Boss's brain, developing the inevitable lesions that closed off the blood supply lines with inflammatory reaction, which disconnected the mental faculties and left each chamber a sloughing irresponsible agency.

At another time, in the presence of his visitors, the Boss suddenly attacked and seriously injured a nurse. The staff fearfully explained to the Marinos that they had no other choice but to transfer him to the violent ward.

Stanislaus, meanwhile was a patient less easy to diagnose. His actions frustrated Dr. Beckman. The doctor examined him, found no organic distrubances, and was forced to rate his I.Q. as unusually high. He decided that Stanislaus was faking Christian ideals to evade military service.

"Send the 'Messiah' along with Marino," he ordered, "Ward B will snap any pacifist out of his ivory tower!"

On visiting days in B ward Boss Marino would tolerate no one but Momma Marino. For that she was grateful and hopeful.

It seemed that when she was near him he calmed down. She kissed him and held his hand. "Gigi, son of mine," said the illiterate old Italian woman, "do you know your mother?" The Boss nodded dumbly. "I am making the Novena for you, Gigi. Enemies have cast a fatura upon you and the devils have stolen your head—but your mother will bring it back to you." She spat on her finger and signed Cross on his forehead and temples. "I pray for you, your wife and children pray for you, your brothers Mike and Tony pray for you, the priest says Mass for you each morning, and all the paesanos pray for you."

The tautness in the Boss's face loosened. For a moment he was coherent. Tears came to his eyes and he lisped: "You're the only one that's ever loved me . . . God bless you Momma . . ."

B ward was jammed with ganglionically tense inmates; former boxers, cops, dancers, laborers and men from all walks of life. There was a morbid self-perpetuating stimulus in the air; the turmoil was never-ending, and the large room smelled acidly of hyper-active flesh.

Most of the time the Boss kept apart from the uncontrollable mass. He stood with his hat and coat on at a window breathlessly in the hallucination that Dottie and his gang were conversing with him.

The masculine vigor in the ward was extraordinary. A wiry one-legged men perched on a bench near Marino jerked his head about and lashed out at anyone within reach. A big ex-detective sat barefoot on the concrete floor dealing out cards to an invisible player; an acrobat did somersaults until prostrated; a white-haired homosexual pursed a blank-minded boy; a thick-limbed stevedore with a pair of drawers wrapped around his head chortled gaily in German, "Yah-yah-yah-yah-kartufel" on and on; a starkly wild blind man in restraint pulled at his bonds until his wrists were lacerated to the bone, and crying, "I want an operation! Cut me open! Cut me apart!"; virile men shouted cacophonically, swinging at the air, and almost every patient bore blackened eyes, broken noses and injuries.

Two whiskey-loving Irishmen with clubs in hand kept the patients barricaded behind a row of metal park benches. Jo-Jo, a tremendous asylum-born imbecilic negro who could utter none but guttural sounds and yet understood simple directions kept himself posted by the attendants like a nubian Cerberus awaiting their commands to rush over the benches and punish troublesome patients. At messtime the attendants and strong-armed worker-patients clubbed the men into line through a narrow passage that led to the mess-hall. With the evening quietus of exhaustion upon them they were corralled into dormitories, some chained to their cots, and many sent to double-tiered cots in the basement.

In the other patients the Boss imagined that he saw the hundreds of men whom he had had murdered and that they had come back to life and were closing in on him. He spent his waking hours in frothing fury, punching, kicking, gouging, and strangling the patients about him.

His brutality passed itself over to the more vicious of the patients and they in turn attacked the weaker men, keeping the ward's physical hysteria at a constant pitch. Each day more of the Boss's victims were carried off to the infirmary. One afternoon as his family were entering the visiting room of ward B they were treated to the sight of the bloodied body of a small man whom the Boss had stomped to death; and in their gangland minds sunk the fact that their great Boss was hopelessly insane.

None of the attendants dared take the responsibility of restraining him. But Jo-Jo the imbecile whose physical supremacy of the violent ward had been challenged, glowered for hours at the Boss and lived for the moment when the attendants would permit him to tackle Marino.

Stanislaus' safety in the violent ward was miraculous. He went amongst the raging men unharmed. It seemed the tormented insane by an inexplicable process received a spiritual message from Stanislaus who possessed peace, as though somewhere in the exploded labyrinthes of their minds his dignified biblical appearance established an inviolable altar.

The attendants, incredibly underpaid State employees, and for the most part of undeveloped character, having a very real power of life and death over the mentally afflicted, could not resist sadistic entertainment, based on their assumption that the patients were the living-dead anyway. In their boredom they set one patient against the other and promoted satyrical scenes of perversion.

One evening, though decimated by fasting, Stanislaus was changing the soiled bedsheets for a sick patient. Mulkeen the attendant was drunk. He interrupted Stanislaus and questioned him about his beliefs.

"Have yuh ever had fun with a dame?" leered Mulkeen, "I mean a hot no-good babe?"

"I know no evil woman in this world, brother," answered Stanislaus, "Whatever the Father creates is beautiful."

"Is Killer Marino beautiful, yuh sap?"

"Marino came from the hand of God also."

Mulkeen struck Stanislaus. "I'll smack some sense into yuh! Ain't that beautiful?" Stanislaus fell to the floor.

The Boss watched the attendant hit the Messiah and came towards them. Stanislaus arose and smilingly offered his cheek for the next blow. Mulkeen was taken aback. He blurted in comtempt: "Yuh goddamned fool, yuh *are* nuts!"

"Yes, brother," said Stanislaus blissfully, "a fool for Christ's sake."

The Boss collared Mulkeen. "You're the dirty rat that made a play for Dottie!" The attendant was terrorized. He reached for his whistle to summon Jo-Jo. With one blow the Boss broke his nose.

"Jo-Jo!" cried Mulkeen, "Jo-Jo! Let him have it!"

Jo-Jo charged the Boss with an inarticulate roar. For a few minutes it was the fight of two crazed jungle beasts; the Boss with quick short blows and Jo-Jo with animal strength. The Boss staggered Jo-Jo again and again but Jo-Jo kept coming into him with his head lowered. Finally Jo-Jo caught him full in the stomach. The Boss stood helpless. Jo-Jo kicked him between the legs, choked him and smashed him up against the wall, lifted him high above his head and sent him crashing to the floor. As the Boss lay there dazed and open-mouthed, Jo-Jo held his legs up and apart and stomped upon his groin. He got down astride the Boss's chest and battered his head upon the concrete until his face was a gory pulp.

The doctors relayed Mulkeen's report to the Marino family that the Boss had attempted suicide during the night by repeatedly running his head against the brick wall in the lavatory.

The lesions in the Boss's brain increased, and produced an amnesic state. The once most-feared man in America staggered and fell about the ward in idiotic bewilderment. At night Jo-Jo delighted in pulling him from his cot and beating him mercilessly. Within a month there no longer was any semblance to his face and his body was bruised and swollen.

Momma Marino knew she was going to lose her son. When she spoke to him he slobbered and mumbled, "Ga-ga-ga-ga, ma-ma-ma-ma . . ."

The Messiah tended him and was his only friend. Something in the Boss's brain clicked and for a week he whispered Stanislaus' words: "Don't kill . . . don't kill . . ."

Johnny Ricci, an egocentric youth who imagined that he controlled the world from inside his brain but who in reality was doomed to live out his life in asylums, made the rounds of the wards for diversion.

While the Messiah sat reading his Bible to the Boss who was now like a one year old child, Johnny cheerfully philosophized:

"You'll die soon of starvation Stan and go straight to Heaven. Maybe you'll save the Boss from burning in Hell—but I've decided not to die. I'm going to stick around and keep the world rolling. People work, struggle, study, kill each other and have to pay to be buried. The people on the outside are screwy, I get all I want here without work or worry. I got the jump on everybody because I know how I'm wired. I say don't drink the cup of life; bring it to your lips and leave a kiss in the cup.'"

Johnny patted the Boss's head. "Keep smiling Boss—it's never so dark as before the dawn. It's all in the head. You'd a been better off if you were satisfied selling bananas. You were a big shot—where did it get you?—right in the pleat. I'll dash off a note a la literati to your maternal relation."

In a lavish script hand he wrote on a wrinkled paper bag: *Dearest Mom: Having wonderful time. Am well and happy. I have seen the light. Honesty is the best policy. A poor law-abiding citizen is infinitely richer than a wacky millionaire. I have made many fine acquaintances, including Johnny Ricci. This is a divine place and I recommend it for the rest of the boys. The food is excellent and all are so kind to me. Stanislaus the true Messiah has taught me the Bible which I can quote verbatim. I look forward to a quick recovery from my trifling indisposition and the trip home. Signed, your loving son Louis Marino.*

Before he ambled off he fashioned a paper dunce hat for the Boss and hung a cardboard nameplate over the Boss's head that read: *Mr. Durance Vile.*

Stanislaus and the Boss were taken to the infirmary for shock treatment. They were strapped upon cots, padded tongue depressors stuck sideways in their mouths and electrodes clamped to their temples. When the nurse threw the switch they were shocked unconscious; their limbs were convulsed and their faces turned purple. For days they lay in unknowing stupor. Then followed insulin treatment. They were held face downward while a doctor pierced the lower spinal column with a large needle and injected insulin. The Boss screamed in agony. Stanislaus sweated and murmured prayers. Week after week they lay wasting in the infirmary. Stanislaus, a physical wraith, was propped in the cot next to the Boss's.

The Boss, dying bit by bit in a silly disgusting manner, irked the two new gang lords Mike and Tony. They hoped he would die immediately and get it over with. The king was worse than dead and it was to their chagrin that the mob and the police and the public knew that a couple of bugs a thousand times smaller than a bullet that the Boss picked up while having a good time and not the law nor competing gangsters were rubbing out the Boss.

To simple Momma Marino it was not the colossus of American crime who was dying—it was her son Gigi—a baby that had issued from her—a baptized Christian for whom she had suffered to bring to life. Stanislaus' wan face smiling kindly to her son came as the sole balm to her. This strange sweet young man with the beard whom she reverentially called the Holy man aided her in her mother's distress. She knew that the Holy man shed the rare unworldly aura of pity about her son. In her heart she took him to her as her son also. She said to him in Italian: "May my son be by thy side in the world to come." And she went to him and kissed his hand.

In phases of delirium Stanislaus thought he was truly the Son of God. He saw himself on the Mount and upholding his mission of peace before Pilate and Herod. He resisted forced feeding and intravenous nourishment. "In my name give man peace on earth!" he said over and over. Emaciation had rendered him almost transparent.

Dr. Beckman, whose conscience perturbed him for having psychoanalyzed Stanislaus as a religious imposter, sent for a local priest.

"Do you not remember," said the priest to Stanislaus, "'they cry peace, but there is no peace'?" The Messiah smiled forgivingly. "We were created in His likeness. We have the flower of peace within us to bring forth with the second birth—that of the soul."

"Yes, yes," affirmed the priest confounded, "that sounds lovely, but he put us here to live as man with all the faults of man not as God, and He equipped us as he did all forms of life to defend and preserve ourselves!"

"Thus spake the very Pharisees at First Coming, but the Master was above defense."

"In destroying yourself," persisted the priest, "you are destroying His work. You are committing murder, the same thing you decry. Do you not fear that you will have to stand trial for it?"

"Thou art the one who with eyes refuses to see. He died for us peacefully. Can we do less?"

"But you have done no wrong in your life," continued the priest, "you owe yourself; you are not like the men about you here who have feasted upon their own damnation."

"They too are the children of God. It can be no other way," gasped Stanislaus. "They seem alien to thee because . . . in my Father's house there are many mansions . . ." Stanislaus' lids wavered, and he closed his eyes happily.

The spirochetes sucked deeply into the walls of the vessels of the Boss's brain, severing the organization of the impulses. Locomotor ataxis partially paralyzed his legs and he lost the natural discipline of his alimentary functions.

Upon beholding him fouled from head to foot Momma Marino wept and besought God to take him out of his misery. She stayed with him for hours trying to clean him and get him to recognize her.

It was necessary to remove him from the infirmary and wheel him over to the incontinent ward in A building.

Within building A there was an overwhelming yellow-brown miasma of man's worst possible putridity. It was a male stable with a thousand naked white and colored men and boys. Through insult to the brain by venereals, trauma, arterio-sclerosis, encephalitis and senility, men who had been fathers of families, clergymen, businessmen, artists, intellectuals, politicians and fastidious individuals, were reduced to infantilism wallowing ravenously in their own and each other's bodily voidances with which the unwashed floors, walls, doors, ceilings, and windows were splattered and caked. The stench was that of the oceanic slime from which in the beginning of Time the fauna of man slowly assembled. In A ward man was an oozing intestinal cell, a urolagnic and scatological primate.

The hospital authorities shied away from A ward, and the ward was shut off from public eyes.

Iconoclastic Ivan Matchek and a small faithful group on

institutionalized worker-patients were the custodians of A ward. Matchek was a morose man who looked at the ground and talked to himself. The doctors agreed that he had worked too long in the incontinent ward. For twenty years he had tried to quit and live a normal life, but the bottomless sour smell and degradation of A ward had soaked into his senses and soul. The daily hourly vision of men scavenging human offal and indulging zoophilia was so vast a proof of man's hapless fragile transiency and so terrible a living picture of God's imagination and man's suffering that to him it transcended fecal reality and was profound, and before it he humbly bent his head.

Boss Marino, skeletal, his battered head shaven, his nose bashed, his ears misshapen, his face puffed up black and blue, his teeth gone, and his legs rollng spastically, was escorted into A ward by Matchek.

"Ai, ai, ai," sighed Matchek, "What does it matter who you were or what you ever did, poor devil, you are coming into the last Hell."

The Boss slept on a rubber mattress in the basement. During the night a negro patient near him had an epileptic fit. When he came out of it he abused the Boss in an animal act. The Boss did not know. In the morning he was dragged up to the mess-hall. He fumbled with his bowl of slops and poured it over his head. After breakfast he was pushed in line down into the basement where open stalls with drains in the floor served relief purposes.

On hands and knees he crawled and avidly devoured filth. Lice and vermin scurried in troops over the unsanitary half-living bodies. Some twisted hanging fragment of his brain told him that a huge fat roach on his knee was Dottie Ryan. His paralyzed fingers tried to grasp it in desire. The long unfeeling days he spent huddled against the mire-smeared flesh of other patients in a corner of the ward. Soon he became blind and catatonic. His body was rotting with pus-running sores, his formless mouth and face was matted and infected with ordure, and greenish-white fungi grew on the soles of his feet. The triumphant luetic virus invaded every major organism in his body and brain.

On a bright sunny morning Momma Marino and his wife and his children prostrated themselves in church praying for his soul. He lay expiring under a pile of patients in a basement stall, his decaying limbs contracting him into a stinking bundle. Large blood vessels in his brain blew out, gushing blood over the remnants of his brain tissue. On the rapidly vanishing mirrors of his memory were discordantly refracted scenes from his dangerous life.

The liberated blood pumping within the rigid brain pan screamed for outlet, crushing his brain cells, compressing the billions of minute islands down through the foramen magnum and obliterating the cardiac and respiratory centers in the medulla oblongata.

Momma Marino, dressed heavy black, lent tears to her personal tragedy behind the shuttered wealth of the Marino home. Mike and Tony Marino, wearing black ties and arm bands, impatiently awaited Federal permission to remove the Boss's remains.

The Boss's shrunken corpse lay in the morgue. The Messiah lay on a table against the wall as though sleeping peacefully.

The pathologist, a short fellow with thick-lensed spectacles, peered at the identification tag on the Boss's foot. He put on his apron and rolled up his sleeves. His assistant, a tall pretty redhead, handed him a cleaver. He took the cleaver and hacked open the Boss from the crotch to the chin; quickly hollowing out the cadaver. He weighed, measured and sliced the viscera, and the efficient pretty redhead jotted down the data. The pathologist drew a chalk-line across the Boss's forehead, slit along it with a knife, peeled the scalp down over the face, and began cutting into the bared skull with a stiff-backed saw. As he energetically worked the saw and ripped through the bony shell, the Boss's head thudded from side to side on the marble slab.

The gift had been delivered—the present from Dottie Ryan, whose full name was Dorothy Ryan Vitone.

O'Hara's Love

In 1927 I was a 16-year-old bricklayer trying to support my mother and seven brothers and sisters. We were living in a buggy flat above a grocery store in the Bath Beach Italian section of Brooklyn. My father had been killed four years earlier in the collapse of a New York building under construction. Mother had not received a cent for Father's death, because the contractor and the insurance carrier were in litigation as to liability. But Mother had positive faith in God and spiritualism and knew somehow that she would get the insurance. Mother and I went once a week to the medium, Mrs. Miller, and communicated with Father. We believed he was in heaven guiding us. And Mother genuinely believed I was her pure champion and her son-saint on earth.

When Mike O'Hara, an investigator for the Workmen's Compensation Board, came into our lives, there was happiness for us. He took up our cause. Through him Mother obtained her due insurance money and bought a sweet, spacious old one-family house with a garden and peach trees in quiet Bensonhurst. We were convinced that God and my father had answered our prayers by sending Mike O'Hara to us. He was about 28; a tall, broad-shouldered, handsome man dressed in tweeds; an Irish-American who could have posed for collar ads. After we moved into our nice house, he came to see us and share our joy. In the cellar we had four barrels of chianti and muscatel wine and some 100 bottles of liquor made by my father and practically untouched since his death. Mother put the traditionally splendid Italian dinner on the table before O'Hara, and timidly wondered if he would be offended by the offer of wine. In all my life, I had never seen anybody who could drink like O'Hara. He only nibbled at the food, but by midnight had drunk a quart of grappa whiskey and two gallons of wine. It was as though he were drinking water. He chain-smoked and drank and drank. When I accompanied him to the subway, he walked erect and unwavering. Mother and I were so grateful to O'Hara. The wine and whiskey in the cellar were of no use to us. We were glad we had it to give to him.

O'Hara came often. We looked forward to his visits. Though Mother could hardly speak English, she and he talked about God and family in the language of the heart. He told us about his parochial school and college days, his hitch as a Marine, his adventures as a Pinkerton detective. He was very fond of us, and assured Mother he would always be a big brother to me.

Mother was anxious to have the pleasure of meeting Mrs. O'Hara. She imagined Mrs. O'Hara to be a great lady. Surely, Mr. O'Hara must have married a fine woman. But he kept finding excuses for not bringing his wife to our house in Bensonhurst.

My older sister, Mary, was going to be married to a *paisano*. We were fixing an apartment on the second floor for her. Mother begged O'Hara to bring his wife to the wedding party to be held in our house. He brought his wife to the wedding party. Milly O'Hara was completely different from what Mother had expected. Milly was a sloppily dressed, overgrown hoyden. It was a strange night. The house was full of rollicking non-English speaking *paisanos*. The wine and whiskey flowed. The musicians played the tarantella over and over. O'Hara sat at a table drinking, a perfect gentleman winning the respect of all. The *paisano* men, mostly bricklayers and hod carriers, got drunk and whirled Milly around in the dancing and blatantly ogled her and ran their hot hands around her. The men were like so many bulls in heat after her. The *paisano* women whispered that the American woman, Mrs. O'Hara, was a shameless *puttana*, and Mother had to admit it with chagrin. Mother was awfully disappointed in Milly and felt pity for Mr. O'Hara. *Sotto voce* the men made raw, drooling comments about Milly's buttocks. Milly guzzled an unending stream of wine and whiskey and laughed, her big black eyes shining wildly. O'Hara constantly filled her glass and tended her as if she were a helpless innocent child. After the party, Mother shook her head and said, "Our dear friend and savior, Mr. O'Hara, has an alcoholically incontinent woman."

From then on, O'Hara brought Milly with him. They made a practice of dropping in on Saturday nights. To our amazement, Milly outdrank her husband. When I went close to voluptuous Milly to fill and refill her glass, I could feel Mother's shrewd eyes. I did not betray the lust for Milly that was mounting in me. Mother wished that O'Hara would visit without Milly. They would stay drinking until past dawn and then get back to the city in time for early Sunday Mass.

One Saturday O'Hara did not appear. I received a letter from him. He was seriously ill and going to St. Matthew's Hospital. The news inflamed me. I had been thinking night and day about Milly. I had overheard Mother tell my sister, "O'Hara's wife is a *puttana*. I feared she'd get Pietro itching for his first taste of woman. Her kind, the legs open easily and wide just for a bottle."

Mother's opinion of Milly would not leave me. Milly was a *puttana*—how could I miss having my first sexual experience? I was a battleground of faith and desire. My flesh would not give me peace. From my bedroom window I saw a woman across the way undress every night. In the subway I was jammed up against women and their rounded parts. Desire tormented me while laying bricks on the skyscrapers. The more I tried not to think of sex, the more desire pained me. My mind was in my groin and I could not get Milly out of my mind. Mother's words, "O'Hara's wife is a *puttana*," rang as a prelude to fate, like time turned about, an act that happened in the future. Masturbation maddened me. At night in my sleep, teasing, luring Milly gave me nocturnal emissions to my fury. The struggle to remain a "good" boy I could not seem to win—or was it a victory I really did not care to seek? A rainy day would do it. Can't lay bricks in the rain. It would have to rain before O'Hara returned home from the hospital. The rain came. Raindrops on my window were tom-toms drumming Milly, Milly, Milly, sex, sex, sex. My flesh between bed sheets was an unbearable flamboyant symptom. I tried to concentrate on my mother, my duty as breadwinner and head of the family, of Father in heaven, of Christ and the Madonna, of my debt of honor to O'Hara, but the rain knew what I had to do. I spent a long vacillating time in the bathroom, showering, brushing my teeth, shaving the few hairs on my face, combing my hair, flexing my muscles, hard all over, too hard, brittling hard. In the mirror I visualized my approach to Milly. "I came because—oh my—I didn't know Mike—I mean Mr. O'Hara wasn't home," or, "Good morning, Mrs. O'Hara, I don't mean to bother you—I just thought Mr. O'Hara," or would I rashly come right to the point?

I dressed, put on my beret and trench coat, and told Mother I was going to New York to look for some needed tools.

That was the first lie I ever told Mother. That lie seemed to liberate me and cast the die. It was heady and thrilling. Like going alive to another world.

The O'Hara flat was on the Upper West Side. I had the address from his letter. I might have hesitated and said no to myself had the building been imposing, but it was an uncaring tenement. The letter box in the vestibule that read M. O'Hara sent a pleasant shiver through me. Going up the dark stairway, I had the sensation of being all body in the middle. I felt I was a composition of flesh galvanically magnified, each organ alert. I stood before the door of apartment 4B with my heart pounding as though I had run a long race at top speed. It seemed that it was not my hand that knocked on the door. The scuffling of Milly's slippers came to me. Milly opened the door. She was wearing a near-transparent soiled shift. I was the last person in the world she had expected to see at her doorway. She gathered something from my tension, my speechlessness, my nervousness. From the obscure room behind her I heard the horny sound of dog's paws. A dirty little ragged poodle appeared and looked at me curiously. Milly said, "Come on in, Pete." The she slurred, with grinning uncontained eyes, "Mike's in St. Matthew's. I'm *alone*."

I followed her into the front room. I did not have the coordination to remove my beret and trench coat.

"Mrs. O'Hara," I said, "my mother asked me to find out about Mr. O'Hara—if it hadn't been for Mr.O'Hara—"

My knees refused to carry me. I sat down. The poodle licked my hand. Sex magazines and empty bottles littered the filthy room. There were smells of tobacco and drink. Under the divan, and tied in a knot, was a used white rubber contraceptive. That and the disordered sheetless bed in the next room quivered me. Milly squatted in a chair opposite me, giving me a view of her hefty round white thighs. I could not believe I was there alone with Milly. Frozen with lust, I could not utter anything. I sat there as if I had been struck dumb. I wanted to be honest and grimly tell her what I had come for; even expressing it in four-letter words. Her well-shaped Amazonian limbs churned about impulsively. My throat was thick. I had to have a drink of water. In the rancid bathroom I found an unwashed glass with lipstick on it. The lipstick smudges thrilled me. Clothes, socks and underwear were heaped on the floor. In the wastebasket was a used Kotex. I tried to urinate but couldn't. I washed my hands and dried them with a tired towel smelling damply of Milly O'Hara.

I returned to the front room. She was looking out the window. I managed to say stupidly, "Watching the rain, Mrs. O'Hara?"

"No, honey. I never know when that lousy Secret Service agent brother of Mike's is spying on me. He's got a key to this place and he pops in and out to see what's going on when Mike's not here. He's too goddamn good for this world—doesn't drink or screw. Raymond's a stuffy bastard. I always have the feeling he'd like to 'harpoon' me himself, the prissy bastard. Christ, what I wouldn't do for a blast! Honey, didn't your mother send a bottle with you?"

Mother's words, that Milly would give herself to any man for a bottle, echoed within me. That was it. I hurried elatedly through the rain to a bootlegger's address that she gave me, and bought a quart of whiskey. I figured that if she got dead drunk I could have her without her even knowing it.

I sat beside her with a trembling hand on her bare knee as she drank. Milly O'Hara; the unkempt straight black hair with the bangs, the puffed child's face, the loose large mouth, the sturdy undeveloped peculiarly pointed breasts, the acrid cloying sexual odor of her body, the free and easy air of the *puttana*. I kissed her knee and hand, mumbling, "Mrs. O'Hara, I love you—Milly, I love you!" She closed her eyes and offered me her mouth. I felt her body heave to an inviting resistless calm. She went to the bathroom. I followed, begging for "love," clinging, stumbling. After she urinated and stood up, I threw myself upon her. She lost her balance and we both fell awkwardly to the floor.

She handled me. She grabbed my hips and surged upward, saying, "Pete, honey, if you don't blab to no one, I'll let you have all you can take. Kid, you're built like a man!"

As my virginity departed, the poodle barked and gnawed at my shoelaces. When I arose, I blushingly told her she was the first woman I had ever had.

"You were cherry when you came here? You'll never forget cutting your teeth on me then, kid. You forget a lotta things, but you always remember the one who copped your cherry. Let me tell you, Pete, girls are only too glad to get rid of their cherries."

We sat in the front room again. I still had not removed my beret and trench coat. My experience had confused me. Sex was so toiletlike and different from what I had ecstatically imagined it to be. In reality it was the way of animals. It was a graceless, gutty, sticky, smelly business that repelled as powerfully as it attracted. My dreams of women being so many living flowers tumbled.

Milly was then as uninhibited as a jungle beast. She told me all she wanted from life was drink and men.

"Mike should have been a priest. He's a religious cardboard gentleman. His goddamn goodness kills me. Being in bed with him is like sleeping with an old woman. I hate marriage and housework. I'd rather work in a whorehouse where two and two make four. I have fun with the milkman and the iceman and Lou the mulatto janitor. As long as they bring me booze, I got plenty of ass to give—like throwing meat to dogs. Come back with a couple of bottles, Pete, and spend the night with me. Won't you kid?"

"What will I tell my mother?"

"You poor kid! Tell her you spent the night at a pal's house. I gotta douche. I don't want to get knocked up."

While she was washing up in the bathroom, I was getting excited again. I was thinking of stripping off my clothes and going to bed with her. But I had a fear, a premonition not to do so. I heard a key unlock the entrance door, and was afraid that it was Mike returning from St. Matthew's. It was Mike's brother, the Secret Service agent. He came into the front room. He was a big man with a pinched face and thin mouth. I nodded to him and huddled back into the chair.

He glowered at me. I looked down and saw that I had not rebuttoned my fly. I placed my hand over my open fly.

Milly came out of the bathroom and walked drunkenly into the front room. She brought with her the strong telltale douching odor of Lysol. Ever since then, Lysol reminds me of my lost virginity and that scent. She said, flustered, "Bill, this is the boy of the Italian widow—in Brooklyn—you know—that Mike helped in the compensation case—Mike and I visited them—these Italian people got big hearts—make you feel at home—"

Bill slapped her hard and spat, "Drunken no-good bitch!" He turned to me. His mouth tightened. He motioned with his thumb for me to leave, and said through his teeth, "You ungrateful wop bastard, beat it!"

I was scared. I left in haste. Then I was beset. I had lied to Mother, the touchstone of my being. I had laid a Samaritan's wife. I was no longer virgin. That morning I had become another person. My flesh won. The spirit lost. I had broken the magical golden string linking me to heaven. Remorse made me feel I had to immediately run to Mike, tell him the truth and save him from an evil woman. I ran all the way to St. Matthew's.

Mike O'Hara shared a room with an aged Passionist monk. He was propped up in bed, pale and weak. He greeted me as warmly as if I had been his son. He introduced me to the old bearded monk in the adjoining bed as "one of the best boys in the world." The monk was senile and quite deaf. He smiled and gave me his blessing in Latin. Mike asked me about my mother and family. He said we were not to feel obliged to him—that he had only done his Catholic duty in helping us, and so forth.

I was impatient to unburden myself.

"Mr. O'Hara . . ." I said. My throat stuck. My eyes burned. "Mr. O'Hara . . . There's something I have to tell you. I . . . I've 'been' with your wife . . . !"

O'Hara looked perplexedly at me for a moment then chuckled, "Peter, boy, that was fine of you to stop and see Milly. I'm sorry; the reason I never invited you and your mother was because we're kind of not settled in that apartment. Well, I mean Milly is such a child in many ways and not the world's best housekeeper, and our place always looks like a hurricane hit it. I thank you for dropping in on Milly. My being here is tough on her—all alone with the poodle. Did Milly say whether she's coming to see me this evening?"

". . . Mr. O'Hara . . . !"

"I want to help *you*, Mr. O'Hara—I want to help save you from— Mr. O'Hara—it's terrible—you don't understand," I shouted. "I've just had sexual intercourse with your wife!"

"You what—?!"

"I had—for God's sake, Mr. O'Hara—I screwed Milly!"

O'Hara jerked upright and repressed his breathing. His wan face flooded red.

I burst out into tears. "I'm sorry, Mr. O'Hara. I'm awfully sorry. Forgive me, Mr. O'Hara."

A headshaking tremor seized O'Hara. ". . . How . . . did it happen . . . ? Whose idea was it . . . did you go to my place—knowing I was here—looking for that?"

From then on, sex and lies had to go together for me. On that path there was no turning back.

"Oh, no, Mr. O'Hara. Because of the rain I couldn't work today. Mother and I were worried about you—she told me to visit you—I thought maybe you had comeback from the hospital—so I went to your place first—when I found out you weren't home I wanted to leave right away. Milly asked me to buy whiskey for her—I did—I didn't know how to refuse—you know I don't drink. She got drunk and grabbed me and excited me—you know what I mean—I swear, Mr. O'Hara—I had no intention—I wouldn't dream of it—especially after all you did for us—I never touched a woman before—I was *virgin*—then I couldn't help myself—she told me about laying with a lot of other men for a long time—that you were made of cardboard—I know I shouldn't repeat these things, but don't you see I'm doing it to help you save yourself from her—she's a bad woman—I'm so sorry—save yourself, Mr. O'Hara, please save yourself!"

O'Hara believed me and felt bad that Milly had taken my virginity. Tears came to his eyes. He patted my head.

"You're a good kid. Milly should not have done this to you. But

Milly is a kid, too. She's my responsibility, my love, for better or for worse. I'm a captain on a sinking ship. I will not desert Milly—regardless."

On the subway back to Brooklyn, I saw a pair of pretty legs. Desire fanned up and came to me like a giant wave. I felt foolish. If I hadn't idiotically blurted the truth to O'Hara, I could have returned to Milly.

Mother asked me if I had found the tools I had sought. I could not become an accomplished liar in one day. I lamely told her I could not find what I needed, then decided to go see Mr. O'Hara at the hospital.

"Did you see Mrs. O'Hara?"

"Oh, I forgot to tell you—yes—you know, I thought maybe he was home from the hospital—he lives near the hospital—it was raining hard—his place is near the subway station—so I went to his apartment first—I didn't go in—she came to the door. Mr. O'Hara's brother was there—I think he lives there, too—they were nice to me and told me Mr. O'Hara was in the hospital. Mr. O'Hara is pretty sick—he was glad to see me—he asked about you—when he gets better he'll visit us again——"

Laying Milly was my fall in the Garden of Eden of our home. And I would want more and more of that forbidden fruit. I rebelled against the idea of being watched by my father from the other world.

When I went with Mother to the old medium for the weekly spiritual communication with Father, I saw it all differently from when I was virgin. I wanted the wilderness of the truth. My future sex life could not bear to have heaven as an audience. My senses clamored for the smell and feel of woman and not for the sterile phantasmagoria of heaven. In the transformation I gained sensuous liberty and forfeited the assurance that all things were the will of God and death the door to the eternal true life.

As old Mrs. Miller went through the routine of bringing messages from Father, I saw her as a psychologist faker.

I had sought and gotten Milly's thighs and shattered the precious bond with Mother. From then on I would lie with many wives, and surely not blurt the fact to their husbands. I was to become a competent liar and deceiver like countless millions of men and women.

Mike O'Hara never came to the house again. Mother knew why, but never brought up the subject. I eavesdropped while she confided to my married sister. "My golden son has changed. He does not look me in the eye. He has added more horns to the head of good Mr. O'Hara. I knew it would happen the day Mr. O'Hara brought his wife here. Milly O'Hara is a *puttana*. What happened to my Pietro could not have been otherwise. The flesh is as nothing. It is what Milly has done to his soul."

Now I am 55. I have a son in Palm Beach, Florida, and a son in Hollywood, California. My wife is still with me. The attrition between sex and religion has worn away. Sex and religion have become one, and both accrue to the greater glory and sublime pleasure of the other. Material things, social systems and mores are trash to me. My spirit and flesh dwell indivisible in heaven and the beds of beautiful girls. I have united passion and heaven for myself.

For years I had dreaded ever meeting O'Hara again. Finally I felt quite positive that Mike and Milly O'Hara were dead. But recently, after leaving the bistro Tony's Wife, and while walking along Second Avenue in the 50s, I came face to face with Mike O'Hara. I tried to walk past him, but O'Hara's eyes would not allow it.

"Hello, Peter," he said in the very same soft tone he had used decades before, and he motioned toward a nearby bar. The bar was a popular scummy little dive frequented by editors, TV people, bums, prostitutes, fairies and lesbians. It was the place where fragmented lives started drinking in the morning.

Milly was sitting at a small round table. Her appearance was shocking. Only by her eyes did I recognize her; the magnificent big, bold, black, amoral eyes.

"Milly, dearest," said O'Hara, "you remember young Peter." Milly grinned and nodded. O'Hara said tenderly, compassionately, "My Milly has been through hell twice with two brain operations for the removal of malignant tumors. The Good Lord stood by her."

Milly smiled her wild smile and said with difficulty, "Hello . . . Petey . . . long time. I'm a goddamn mess . . . left side paralyzed—it's a sonuvabitch—arm and leg as dead as Kelsey's nuts . . . they can't kill me—still in the race—can still lay the Army and Navy—still tight where it's good to be tight——"

I've seen exhumed corpses look better than Mike and Milly O'Hara. Milly was bloated and shapeless, her skin was sickening, her hair, still lividly black, was cropped close and the frightening scars of her brain operations showed. She wore ridiculous big earrings, cheap rings, and a tattered vomit-splattered dress. The layers of paint on her face were awry. Yet she still radiated a bestial sex appeal. Milly O'Hara in her 60's horribly broken down, still flew the same colors. There was a weird insensible fascination about her; the crazy but never-ending magnetism of the *puttana*. She drank her whiskey straight, washing it down with beer, shakingly raising spilling glasses to her mouth.

I noticed O'Hara grimy black dirty ripped white shirt, shiny-worn frayed and stale blue-serge suit, the cracked beat brown shoes, his green denture. He handled his whiskey glass the same way he used to; the coddling touch with the ever-smoking cigarette between his nicotine-dyed fingers. He was a tall, bloodless, white-haired skeleton, a graveless Lazarus; and all that remained were the cloudless blue eyes, his faultless long hands and the noble bonework of his chaste face.

My "How've you been, Mike?" was as hollow as his gaunt dying cheeks.

"I've been just fine, fine, Peter. My ulcers kick up now and then. Certain foods don't agree with me. Milly's been bearing the cross, though. In and out of hospitals. Last year she fell asleep smoking. Set herself on fire. Bad infection. But skin grafts fixed her up. I'm thankful to God for Milly. I couldn't live without her. We get along swell."

I joined them drinking. O'Hara wanted to pay for the drinks. Said I was their honored guest. While we were drinking Milly urinated, and her urine formed a pool in the sawdust on the floor.

"I'm sorry we sort of lost touch with each other," said O'Hara. "Your first novel is very dear to me. I reread it because you describe your mother so lovingly. What year did she pass away to her reward?"

I shrank from the mention of the past. Guilt I could not stave off welled in me.

"Mike, that's been ages ago."

Milly was sodden. She talked profanely of her sex affairs and boasted that she was better than ever at it.

O'Hara smiled benignly. "She's my little girl Milly who'll never grow up. Dear God, I don't know what I'd do without her."

They drank until midnight, drinking intensively, profoundly, as though their drinking was the most sacred of rituals. When I rose to leave, Milly was sprawled face downward on the table. O'Hara, his eyes pure, his voice clear and steady, said, "Peter, I've been waiting for you. I knew we'd see each other again. There is something I have to give to you. I knew you'd be directed to me before I met my Maker, because I prayed for it."

He took my hand and pressed a weathered scapular of the Blessed Heart of Jesus into my hand; the very same one my mother had given him. I did my best to fight off tears.

I'll never forget the peace that was in Mike O'Hara's face.

The Roman Circus
Of Bernardo Bertolucci

Bernardo Bertolucci is tall, large-boned, soft-fleshed, with a long, equine, Periclean head and the identical face of Ninetta, his very handsome mother. Put a dress on him and he would be Ninetta (excepting her open, honest expression), what with his ample, straight thin nose, delicate Etruscan lips, fine chin, and small dark penetration eyes. The whole aspect tells of a consciously plumbed, integrated being. But one not without a certain unhealthiness. We are at the exhibit of Guerreschi's *Vietnam Suite* in Rome's Galleria 11 Fante di Spade on Via de Ripetta. "Dicki" and "Patty" Nixon, Coca-Cola bottles, the Stars and Stripes, and "With Love" in torn bleeding parts of Vietnamese baby bodies. Bernado is still smarting from the accusation of profanity and obscenity surrounding *Last Tango in Paris*. He tapped Nixon's head in the painting and said, "This criminal Nixon person is obscene not *Tango*. The comedian Nixon's bombing is pornography, and John Wayne's cowardly *Green Berets* is flat perversion, but positively not my *Tango*.

"The two protagonist forces today are Communist and Fascist. The clown Kissinger's detente is a bad, expensive Hollywood movie. There is no inbetween reality. The world scene is the idealistic left against the unregenerated right to the absolute death." He studied me and added firmly in his improvised English, "I am a Communist Party membership."

In his gentle hesitant way he wanted to know if I also was a "Socialist." I could have told him that I joined the American Communist party the night the United States murdered my *paesanos* Sacco and

Vanzetti in the electric chair. But instead I said: "Communism has become too fucking bourgeois and capitalistically cancerous for my speed. Revolution has missed the true boat and is left with the ship of Judas-mass fools. I'm out to destroy those who have the mark of the beast. I am the man who comes singing and dancing, healding the Apocalypse and Last Judgement."

Bernardo Bertolucci, the overgrown kid, looked at me perplexed.

Rome is a theater where life is a moment-to-moment drama. We went to Rosati's on the Piazza del Popolo for espresso. Gian Carlo Fusco, the writer with the monocle, said to Bernado, "Our Di Donato is laying the prostitutes. He fancies all the women of Rome, including the skinny one who frightens one into a hard-on, La Fallaci—I don't know how he does it." I said I wish it were so, and added that I had seen Oriana Fallaci in the Italian *Playboy* office, and that all we did was size each other up and nod.

Along the Via del Ripetta, by the Church of Santa Maria Porta Paradisi, is a mortuary. I convinced Bertolucci to go with with me. In a candleit chamber an old male corpse with artificial flowers tossed on his feet lay awkwardly and disgustingly on a sheeted table. A black-edged poster said the deceased had fought the good Marxist fight and was duly mourned by his staunch Italian Communist Party comrades. None of the assorted weepers recognized us—which was not flattering. The attendant asked Bertolucci if we were relatives.

"We are all related in the scheme," said Bertolucci.

"Ah, yes, *signore*," said the attendant, "today, with science, the whole fucking world is one village."

As we descended the steps of the cheerless *mortuario funebre* we bumped into Vanno Caruso, wife of the Venetian painter Giulio Turcato. She said she had lived across the street for years and had never entered the house of the dead. Bernardo said to see funerals was good luck.

Titian-haired Vanna—a movie director in her own right (is there anyone in Rome who isn't a movie director?)—is not impressed by Bernardo's brand of communism. Vanna Caruso's father was the Fascist police commissioner of Rome who blithely countersigned Adolph Hitler's order for the reprisal torture and execution of 335 young hostages held in the Adreatine Cave. Communist partisan summarily shot Caruso.

Bernardo's apartment lies on the Via del Babuino above Via Margutta, where the poet-painter Alfonso Gatto and Fellini live. To the left is Monte Pincio, the Park that begins Villa Borghese, and to the right, the Dedici palace. The Church of Trinità dei Monti and the exquisite Obelisk look down the Spanish Steps. All Bernardo's belongings were packed, mostly books and metal cases of film reels.

On the terrace commanding this old part of Rome he said, "I'll miss this panorama. There will be an emptiness. I'll have to abandon the plants I have so often talked to. My new place on the Via della Lungara does not have a terrace.

"Walls remember," Bernardo continued. "You yearn for change, especially in the morning. But when it comes, you want to stay. Departures always make one feel traitorous."

In Italy, elegance, the fruit of 3000 years, is the unwritten law tacitly obeyed by all except gypsies, beggars, artists, and saints. Bernardo was dressed in the predictable role of the precocious moviemaker who had "arrived"; sued jacket, silk shirt, gaudy neckerchief, Levi's, and Tooled cowboy boots. He wanted to go to Clara Schiavolena and ask her to rent him her duplex until his new apartment on the Via della Lungara was renovated according to his design. He, his girlfriend Fiammetta, and I came down to Via del Babuino, a raceway. Although we took precautions before crossing, Bernardo was almost run over by a speeding pretty girl motorcyclist. Bernardo shouted, "You almost killed me!" The girl turned and sang back "*Vaffa n'culo!*" ("Go get fucked up your ass!")

I told Bernado and Fiammetta we should go to Clara Schiavolena's by cutting through Via Gesu e Maria because there were wonderful posters of Fellini's lasted work, *Amarcord*. The night before, Fellini had put on a preview for the embassy of Red China and friends. I said to Bernardo that I loved Fellini dearly but that the posters were better than the movie. Bertolucci said, "That's the secret of our cinema; Italian film is not moving pictures, but moving posters."

We came into the farmers' market on Via Bocca di Leone, and the corner of Via Della Lupo, where Elizabeth Barrett and Robert

Browning loved and lived. Bernardo greeted the wrinkled Sicilian cobbler, Carmelo Sorbello. Eighty-year-old Carmelo from Catania, Sicily, is an abstainer and blames Italy's woes on alcohol and priests. He could detect on us the previous night's wine. Under his scrutiny, Bernardo confessed he had a bit of a Lambrusco headache, to which Carmelo shouted, "And you expect to be the number-one genius with shit poisoning your brain? *Puttana di la Madonna!* Being the biggest director in the world is a joke if you aren't man enough to master your vices. My child, I don't want to be annoyed by more vain resolutions. How many times have I told you that wine is man's foe? If you don't abide by my advice then *vaffa n'culo!*"

The greens vendors and the flowerwoman hailed Bernardo and wanted to be remembered to his parents. Some one said melodiously, "Hello, Bernardo and Peter." We turned; it was Federico Fellini. He had his pleasant white-haired cook with him; she was buying vegetables and fruits, and he a bouquet of roses. He said his Giulietta had been hit by a car on her way to the dentist and was in the hospital of San Giacomo with contusions. Shaking his head, he said, "Life is beginning to imitate my films—the damned automobile is the Frankenstein of Rome!"

Helping the flowerwoman was homely, graying, retarded Mario. Mario took Bernardo aside to show him a German porno magazine, *Vulva*. Bernardo kidded him, saying he was only 55 and far too young for sex and asked him what kind of a girl he preferred, blonde, redhead, or brunette. Mario made a pleat with forefinger and thumb, ogled it, licked it salaciously, and said, "The hole is all I need!" The flowerwoman made the sign of the cross.

Bernardo remembered that at that hour he was supposed to see Alberto Moravia in the Caffé Greco, so we continued along the Via dei Condotti center of gravity of international fashion Fiammetta paused to discuss pants suit with Nello the street sweeper. Nello has his hair styled at the one and only Pepppino's, along with princes, and Bernardo intends to cast Nello as Roman emporer. Nello knows the Ferragamos. Guccis, Puccis, Valentinos, and Schuberths. He gets discounts for friends and favors Schuberth's creation. That intersection is also the beat of four subteen gypsy sisters, seedling Lolitas. Filthy and barefoot, wearing tattered men's jackets and aprons, singing chortling, laughing, begging shamelessly, they psych the expensively dressed passer's by. The leader, a ten-year-old with a gold tooth, lifted her apron, flourished her dirty little hairless cut, squatted before Valentino's fabulous window, and pissed. The gypsyettes approached us confidently, saying to Bernardo and me, "Beautiful Marlon Brandos, thank you for your generosity," and calling Fiametta "Beautiful Jackie Kennedy," When I said I resented being called Marlon Brando, pushed them aside, and told them to get lost, they spat and cursed us, made the "fuck you" gesture and the horns of the evil eye, and cried, "The cunt of your mother! *Figli di puttani, vaffa n'culo!*" But when superstitious Bernardo gave them more money then they could have dreamed of, they lauded and blessed us.

In the Caffé Greco Bernardo said, "We moved from Emilia—'the meeting of the ways'—to Rome when I was 12. Father often brought my brother Giuseppe and me to the old place. Father wrote a poem about the Greco—It's here." Coming out of the Galleria ca' d'Oro across the street was Alberto Moravia with Dacia Marino, young daughter of a Sicilian duke, and Georgio de Chirico. They joined us for *aperitivo*. No one has the Apollonian stance of near-centenarian De Chirico in his vicuña cashmere polo coat; and Moravia more than makes up for his little whit crop, badly crippled left leg, and toothless maw with his frenetic mesmeric ceaseless chatter about—Moravia. Bernardo has reason to call him "*maestro mio,*" if only for Moravia's *The Comformist,* which Bernardo re-created and bettered as a startlingly brilliant film. Bernardo said his father regarded two artists as true geniuses, Modigliani and De Chirico. Girogio de Chirico, above impression, was bored. I asked him whom he considered the greats of filmmaking. "Greats?" he said. "You know absolutely nothing! You fool, cinema is not art!" And he disdainfully left.

With the pride of a little boy, Bernardo pointed to a framed portrait on a pilaster near an old gold-plated mirror. It was three stanzas in 12 lines of jeweled words, entitled *Piccolo Autoritratto (Caffé Greco)* and it was of course, a small self-portrait by Attilo Bertolucci. Bernardo told me that within the walls of Caffé Greco had been Casanova. Goethe, Gogol, Byron, Keats, future popes, even Orson Wells. As we were leaving a huge Fiat bus stopped, and Japanese tourists streamed out and scurried about the Greco snapping pictures.

From Clara Schisvolena's terrace, were it not for an occasional TV antenna, you would think you were beholding the tile roofs, chiminey pots, and attics of Michelangelo's day. Blonde, slateeyed Clara the Sicilian said, "Bernardo, you're going to Parma to prepare ypur film. Why bother to rent this place? If you suddenly find you need it, just move right in, and I'll go to the country house in Bracciano." She had leased it to *A Clockwork Orange* Burgess but had reserved quarters for herself.

Bernardo invited her to Caesarina's, which you could almost reach out and touch on Via della Croce. Caesarina has seven tables. You cannot tell from the street that it is a restaurant. High-ranking government officials and film stars feel fortunate when they find a seat.

Bernardo had chicken cacciatore, polenta, ricotta, and a bottle of Lambrusco just like a North Italian. I deliberately brought up the subject of success. Bernardo said success, having to do with quantity, was inevitably vulgar, something that had to be digested and gotten over with, so that one could go on. Clara said, "The truth about glamor and success is the whore at the altar, the policeman without his uniform, the bartender in the morning sunlight, and the body at the morgue. Art and artists are tawdry when it comes to character. As you know, I lived with Mino Paolello for 28 years. He used my flesh, he picked my brain. I was his courage, his dreams, his imagination. Carla, help me with the scenario. Whom should I cast? What do you think of this? And what do you think of that? He didn't make a move without Clara. Suddenly he abandons me and marries a young woman who will not even permit him to mention my name. Now he is a complete stranger. Film directors are cowardly ingrates, Why can't directors be *men*?"

We listened in sympathetic silence, although we knew all about it, and Bernardo Bertolucci had that disarming faraway look of a child.

I rode the train from Rome to Bertolucci's native Parma. Surely nothing could shock sophisticated Parma, city of the Etruscans, Gauls,

Goths, Byzantines, city of the despotic Farnese dynasty and also of the Bourbons. Parma is the temple of things rare and beautiful—theaters, musical, ballets. Now Parma is Marxist Red, the opulent *città grassa*—fat city—of North Italy's Emilia Romagna emblazoned with Bertoluccian conquest.

It was a cold night in the Piazza Garibaldi. The warmly dressed few dozen formed the nocturnal confrontation of factions—the literary club of the ripened well-off, the apostles of Parmesan culture—self-ordained devil's advocates, critics, and judges, all eager to lock horns over *Tango*. Among the reputables were priests, atheists, zealots of the left, right, and center, an antique dealer, a hotel manager, a restaurant man, lawyers, professors, a fag hairdresser, and three doctors—a dermatologist, a specialist in rectal cancer, and Bernardo Bertolucci's very popular pediatrician uncle. A journalist said, "Censor a film, even the very worst, and the idiot masses flock to it as to a shrine of miracles."

The priest admonished, "We are not treating reality. It is only a film of fiction from Bernardo's technical fantasies. There is no need to be sacrilegious."

Lofreddo, the Fascist journalist said, "We continually say *'Vaffa n'culo!'* and finally one of our townsmen has immortalized it in a cinematic form. The phrase *'vaffa n' culo!'* will now become as immortal as 'God will it!' and 'I shall return!'"

"We Parmesans," said the medical student, "are noted for cheese, violent perfume, and now unpasteurized-buttered-bugging——"

The dermatologist interrupted, "*Contraception a la Marlon via Bernardo!*"

"No, seriously," continued the young man of Parms's School of Medicine. "The cinema, originally called the bioscope, is the craft of visual duplicit. Pictures move and occupy the eye and do not allow the full play of reason within the context of sensible reality."

"I'll explain." the hairdresser chimed in "Marlon gets his erection into Maria's anus."

"The reaming is presumed," the rectal-cancer specialist corrected. "Pasolini is less refined than Bertolucci. He would have shown you the real thing, Marlon's prick going up the dirt road. Come on, are we thumb-sucking children?"

The medical student was off again. "All right, all right. Then under his direction she cuts her fingernails and manipulates *his* anus, without the benefit of a disinfecting, sterilizing suppository or the refreshing services of a bidet. All impromptu, yes? Of course. Where is the board of health in all this? Now elementary hygiene tells you that without thorough colonic irrigation, the terminal area of the large intestine houses feces residue that ferments from blood-temperature heat and is replete with it concomitant noxious humors. Right? Fact. Further Bertolucci implies Maria Schneider was a rectal virgin. Her yelling and pain under stallion Brando should have suggested anal bleeding. But anyway, *paesani*, we are dealing with scatological exercises by coprophiliacs! Fact!"

"I resent your vulgar values!" the antique dealer cried. "This kind of talk is enough to make one vomit! *Last Tango in Paris* is sheer high tragedy. The sodomy was symbolic of profound poetic suffering! You owe the truth an apology!"

"My wife and I perform 69 and fancy positions that make the Schneider-Brando dog act look like the efforts of novices," one of the lawyers bragged. "But, God forgive me, we do not call it art!"

A bearded queen with a female basset hound on a leash said through his eerie, battery powered larynx, "Butter to grease the way—salted? sweet?—better than oleomargarine. I simply love Marlon. He lived the part. Marlon has a prettier rump than Roman Polanski!"

A dignified man confided to me, "Don't get the wrong impression of the local street critics. Regardless of what they say, they are extremely proud of the Professor Attilio Bertolucci's sons. The boys, Bernardo and Giuseppe, were called the Gemini, Castor and Pollux. Did you know that the father is a famous poet?

"I can see Bernardino in shorts pants. With the least threat of bad weather, they bundled him up with earmuffs, gloves, shawls, and sweaters down to his ankles. He was addicted to the cinematic world of make-believe. He buried himself in movie houses. The tallish lad would come out of the theaters into the sunshine pale as a mushroom and blinking his eyes.

"Professor Attilio was also a film critic for the *Gazzetta*. Everybody saw Bernardo's father, his large craggy face and scholar's hunched shoulders, crossing the piazza, books under arm, wearing his wide-brimmed poet's fuzzy fedora on the hottest days. Or pedaling his bicycle fanatically like a long-distance racer in from the countryside, ritualistically stopping to admire the baptistery and mopping sweat. I remember when he made Bernardo read all of Gide under the family mulberry tree.

"If you find Parmesans a bit strange, its because we are descended from the ancients Celts and still respond to the call of the Druid,"

One said, "Art fights imperialism with allegorical booby traps. Deciphered, *Tango* is an utter denunciation of Western society."

A Maoist dissented "*Last Tango in Paris* is neither polemical warfare, Parisian chic, nor a South American dance. Besides the misnomer, it is flaccid perversion, literary intimidation. and cultural terrorism. In *Das Kapital* Karl Marx wrote that bungholing was revolutionary, nor does the *Communist Manifesto* recommend pricks in asses. The masses have been reamed enough!"

"Attilio has written old fashioned, authenitic poetry," the hotelier added, "clear streams from the Castalian spring. But his overeducated son produced false art with *Tango*. Though I am a Christian Democrat I can see Bernardo has not been true to his Moscow-Peking ideology."

"You all miss the mark," the antique dealer rejoined. "*Tango* is a beautiful film of the soul that requires preparation to absorb. But on a second thought I agree that Bertolucci is a cocktail of many people, nothing original, a confused intellectual and a superb technician."

Lofreddo the Fascist thundered, "Imbeciles go to the movies! I'll tell you about real life! I had a dream of a girl in a curtained stall of the world's most expensive restaurant in Paris. She ate and drank until I thought she would burst. I put my fur lined coat on the bench under her and was happily sodomizing her. She cried, 'Quick. Take it out. I must——!' and *Madonna mia* she backfired and covered me and the coat! Where is the movie that will show that? That sirs is life!"

Bertolucci's uncle, the hearty pediatrician Dr. Maurizio, appeared and they pressed him. "Of this splendid film," he said eloquently, "I cannot talk. All the critics of the universe have spoken with their best hosannas. It's a runaway success that speaks for itself. The people fly to it as to a bona fide poet and genius. Bernardo had nothing dirty or vulgar in mind."

"There are also mediocre poets."

Bertolucci's uncle was working up anger, and almost shouting said, "You only dare to attack Bernardo behind his back. History will vindicate my nephew. Go read the slander of Puccini's treacherous colleagues and see who today is thought of as one of the world's greats."

"Oh yeah? Fellini, Antonioni, even Godard have snubbed the film. Godard ran out in the middle of the movie, 'Too much, too much,' and Pasolini is alleged to have remarked, 'I'll never greet Bernardo again!'"

Bertolucci's kinsman said, "Envy! Fellini is a school child still sniffing at girl's bicycles seats. Godard is *nouveau* vague, Antonioni is a foggy roach in the woodwork, and Pasolini is old hat. Have they made millions on one work like my nephew? They are jealous. It is understandable."

With righteous indignation, though patently enjoying it, the Bertolucci relative started to walk away, saying, "My soul is free—I don't have to listen." Disappearing into the star-bright Emilian night, Bernardo uncle roared, "Fine townspeople! Love is never chaste. Marxist or no, moralist or no, only the pigs make chaste love. Strong cowardly blows from so small an assembly! Your frothings are invidious semantics. Results count! Money talks! Are you on the covers of *Time* and *Newsweek*? Have you been invited to lunch with Kennedy women? Pigsty? By God, *Tango* spells *love!*"

We all laughed, then decided to get out of the cold and go to the bar for drinks. On a street poster of Brando standing with his hands up, waiting to be prostrate-pronged by Schneider, someone had written with brown spray paint, "We want him naked," signed "Sex Power!"

In the bar, we made many fertile jokes about the subject and had a rollicking time. Before the Parmesans went home, they swore to me that opposite the great Giuseppe Verdi monument with all the statues of the four lions pulling a chariot, they were going to erect a 100-foot white marble statue of Bernardo Bertolucci holding a stick of butter made of 14 carat gold.

"Without clothes," said Lofreddo, "so that on hot summer days the breezes will cool and refresh his own controversial ass!"

*

The next day I returned to Rome. By the Bernini colonnage of St. Peters I took the 62 autobus that wound up the long slope of Monte Janiculum to the street named after the Garibaldean Red shirt, Giacinto Carini, an area built for the Fascist bourgeoisie during the florid prosperity of Mussolini's comic criminal opera *Imperium Romanum.* On the top floor of Via Giancinto Carini, 45, is the home of the Bertolucci family. They have lived in the same brown apartment since their migration from Parma 21 years ago. Spread before the Bertolucci terrace is Rome: its haloed hills, masses of russet tile roofs and clay colored stucco houses, Vatican City, Castle Sant'Angelo, the Colosseum, Baths of Caracalla, Villa Borghese, the Forum, the Campidoglio, Sant' Giovanni in Laterano, in numerable squares, monuments, and palaces, and directly below, along the Tiber, The Via della Lungara with the dread prison Regina Coeli at number 29, and Bernardo's new apartment in the Palazzo Corsini at number 3.

Evalina Bertolucci, 'Ninetta,' was born in Australia of Italian mother and wild Irish revolutionary father. She met Attilio at Bologna University where she was laureate with her thesis on the pagan poet, Catullus. She is a professor of English. Attilio Bertolucci came from landed gentry and was educated in Parma, Bologna, and Rome; besides being steward of the profitable terrain passed on to him, he made himself a literary critic, art sage, film reviewer, professor, editor of eclectic magazines, and—crowningly—noted poet.

Ninetta served tea with honied pastries from the oven; all was proper: family china, silver, and ivory napkin rings. As on other visits, Ninetta was at the fore in the conversations; Attilio admires her, grinning benignly.

There was the air of studied frugality that the ethical affluent indulge (orange and lemon peels converted to marmalade). The poet's gray worsted suit was painfully neat but exploited to a shine, and the cordovan shoes seamed, worn, affectionately saddle-soaped, and newly heeled and soled.

On the coffee table was Aubrey Beardsley's book with a faded oval photo of the exotic young Englishman on the cover. Near Attilio's armchair on a low bench were a bargain-store record player and albums of Glenn Miller, Benny Goodman, and Louis Armstrong.

Attilio said, "On his tenth birthday Bernardo asked for and received a 16 millimeter motion-picture camera. Ninetta and I knew he would be different from the general run of movie bugs who film jackanapes, soccer games, and meaningless things. He wrote a scenario, *In Search of Mystery*, and cast his three little cousins. His story was about four children who hunt through the forest for a '*teleferica*' that transmitted and received handwritten messages by beams of light refracted from the past, present, and future, revealing the destiny of mankind. They acted it out as though not knowing whether the *teleferica* was a remembrance from the womb and infancy . . . or a dream.

"From the savings of his five-dollars-a-week allowance he had the negative developed and ran showings for a fee. So you see I became Bernardo's first producer—which I had secretly hoped for. In his second movie he follows the semination, birth, nursing, brief happy life, amd butchering of a pretty female suckling pig for market, and his camera continues through to the meat being bought, cooked, and eaten by human carnivores.

"Our son is a dedicated celebrant of the movie camera, and the cinema has been his ordained order ever since he received his First Holy Communion and the simple Kodak gift that went with it."

From beneath beetling brows Attilio said, "Bernardo is a precise son; he figures out and plans everything backwards and forwards and leaves nothing to chance. Out Bernardo knows exactly what he is doing."

Bernardo was supposed to have been in the province of Parma for ten days, but it was three weeks before he got back to Rome. When I arrived for family dinner, it was raining heavily. A swarthy priest with sparkling black eyes and pronounced dimples came to meet me and have one of my books, *Tre Cerchi di Luce*, autographed.

"Father," I said, "forgive me my disease, curiosity. What made you become a priest—how and why did you decide?"

He said, "I have always been a priest, as 'God is always the same.'"

Ninetta asked him to stay for dinner. He obliged by drinking wine, thanked her, and said he had to press on to Clara Schiavolena's. Later I was apprised that he was far gone in love with a nun, and that they were wont to ritualize their agape in a neighbor's guest bedroom (God Bless!).

Ninetta came in from the kitchen.

"How is the rice?" said Attilio.

"The rice is perfect."

He took out his watch, put it to his ear, rubbed is apprehensively.

"Ninetta, why aren't the boys here by now?"

"How should I know? The boys will be here."

He said to me, "Hours ago Giuseppe called from the garage in the basement. He and Bernardo borrowed my car. I don't like driving. It's a good car, an honest Fiat, only 13 years old. You know, we keep cars going. But there's a first time for any machine to fail, possibly in a dangerous place. The traffic in Rome has become a nightmare, and when the sun goes down it is a scene from Walpurgis night. I could never understand mechanical things. I confess I am inferior to the violence of technological facts."

He fussed and fretted and walked about the smallish room. He had Ninetta check the time with the kitchen clock. Ninetta said patiently, "If either or both boys do not appear punctually as promised he immediately generates uneasiness. As minutes pass his worry increases. He never fails. I often wonder if it's a form of pleasure. In any event, Bernardo and Giuseppe are forever children to him."

"This doesn't make sense," said Attilio. "Have they had an accident? There must be something wrong. If nothing is wrong, why don't they call and reassure me?" The phone rang; the boys had been detained but were on their way.

"You see?" said Ninetta.

When Attilio heard the elevator and then his sons' footsteps, he beamed. Bernardo, 33 and Giuseppe, 30, embraced and kissed their parents, whom they had not seen for . . . hours. Ninetta Bertolucci is the queen, the great mother of the gods. But then, is there a street invenerable Rome that does not adore the Madonna in house corners and in wall shrines?

The *aperitivo*, prosciutto, port-liver sausage, sheep's milk mozzarella, olives, and wines had come from their Parma farms. Hostess Ninetta was her own cook and serving maid. The repast was obviously Parmesan: succulent veal knuckles, yellow corn polenta, gnocchi made of chestnut flour, long-grained rice with pine nuts, egg dripping, raisins, and capers. A large bowl held fresh raw artichokes, lettuce, radishes, carrots, celery, and scallions to be dipped in salt-and-peppered olive oil. The Bertolucci white wine was dry and casky, but the red was fragrant, dark, chewable crimson gold.

Attilio speaks like his poetry—in laconic complete autonomies; lifting a glass he said, "Hail to thee, too, Dionysus, abundant in grapes! Let us rejoice in the seasons . . . . And after the seasons for many years to come!" I said his was a wonderful toast; he said it was Homer's.

My grim proletarian past does not quit; the Bertoluccis, monied by heritage and strangers to toil, are *preziosi* who remind me of fascinating lush hot house plants. They are not the short, broad-jawed, callused, knotty-fingered Michelangeloesque peasants and brick layers like my South Italian *paesani*, and I never cease to marvel and be concerned at how people come into this world and live luxuriously without economic harassment, sweating and breaking their asses.

They were amused by my archaic dialect from the mountains of Abruzzi, and I found their crusty, crackling, gutty Parmesan speech peculiar. With espresso and Scotch we listened to parts of Verdi's *Macbeth* and Bellini's *I Puritani*, and a record I had brought from Abruzzi, *Lament of a Widow*, and Attilio fumbled the needle and ruined it. Then we enjoyed Louis Armstrong's trumpet.

On leaving I showed photos of my sons, Peter the doctor and Dick the actor. Ninetta tossed her head and proclaimed, "And I have two glorious sons!"

I pity the girl who tries to compete with the mother of the Bertolucci kids.

Bernardo's place is spacious and surgically severe in chalk-white. He does not greet effusively like Fellini, Zeffirelli and Pier Paolo Pasolini. There were young folk about—like wrought wraiths. Bernardo presented and praised his cameraman, an olive-skinned hook-nosed tight youth with an unwarranted fierce demeanor and a tense attenuated desirable girl who smoked desperately and looked as though she had been dipped in acid.

I said, "Bernardo, my editor wants to know if you are a homosexual."

". . . Oh . . ." he said with the expression of a surprised cherub, "that probably comes from reading Ingmar Bergman's reference to the homosexuality in *The Conformist* and the lesbianism of la Schneider. Let me tell you, a director who makes pictures that lose money dies quickly. What they call perversion is commercial today. Just look at the attention that your American media gives to gay lib. Now, sodomy is as old as the mold and the filler. Deviation is as popular as the drive-in and is expected and demanded as much as butchery and gore and psychopathy and hot—forgive me—'buttered' popcorn."

He inclined his head to one side and suggestively tugged at his earlobe. "In Rome they wink and say sighingly of just about every director—particularly the outstanding—'Ah, but he's an *orecchione*.' and indicate that he takes it in the 'ear.' Via Veneto gossip has it that his holiness heads the list."

Bernardo is familiar with the larva, the chrysalis, the imago of the cinema. He speaks calmly of *The Great Train Robbery*, D.W. Griffith, Mack Sennett, Pudovkin, Cocteau, Rossellini, Godard, and on and on. But he always ends with a hushed reverence for "*il grande* Luchino Visconti." He relates what Marshall McLuhan designates as "the reel world" to the influence of mysteries, superstitions, ideologies, religions, dreams, ideals, painting, music, philosophies, electronics, astral bodies, the occult, fads, sculpture, humanities, madness, and his fanatic endeavors for communication and communion.

I said, "What is an immortal film?"

He said, "You die in the theater . . . you are transfigured to something better and can never again be the same . . . you transcend and leave the theater a disembodied spirit . . . soul shriveled."

We agreed on King Vidor's *The Crowd*, a French film, *That They Might Live*, *Mother*, *Open City*, and touched admiringly upon *Trash* and *Mean Streets*—I said the only recent work that dug into me was Jean-Luc Godard's *Les Carabinieres*, and Bernardo said without humor,

"Yes, the two robot killers roaming the world and violating humanity were Nixon and Kissinger in *Les Carabinieres*." In talking about box-office smashes he was anxious to know how I, leading Italo-American author, felt about *The Godfather*.

I'd kiss a director's ass only if the director were a sweet-smelling young girl, so I said, "Young man, I'll put it this way. At lunch with JFK and Premier Fanfani in the White House I met a noted Washington psychiatrist. Later he took me for a tour of a private 'rest' home for the rich. I saw a patient, a former national leader, with what I thought was a big unlit Castro cigar in his mouth. Introduced to the politico, I was shocked to see that the cigar was a firm human turd. When I showed my horror and begged him to spit out the goddamn thing he got on his high horse: 'This is a free country—God's blessed democracy. Sir, who is eating this delicious stuff—you or I?' I backed off and said, 'Senator, that *delicious* stuff happens to be shit, and bad shit at that. With all kinds of good food available, why do you eat filth?'

"'You fool!' he shouted, 'I eat shit because I love shit!'

"So you realize, Bernardo, it takes two to tango—the movie and the audience. What the people pay five dollars a ticket to swallow is their problem, not mine." I didn't have to draw Bernardo a picture as to how I felt about today's vaunted box-office hits.

"For me interviews are artificial and demoralizing," he said. "This question-and-answer business is never spontaneous, involved, and organic, particularly when my mind is preoccupied with my new film, *Novecento (1900)*. Parma is the setting. I will probably use Robert De Niro."

He ran his long soft fingers through his hair, played with his hands while thinking, lit a Marlboro, and then spoke in vague tones as if soliloquizing, "What can I say about myself? I am a happy pessimist, a despairing optimist, a pansensualist. Women are better creatures than men. Women understand my work; they need and relish my type of film brutality for a new dialogue with the opposite sex. There's the anguish of seeking one's identity in front of the image of father—can one ever equal one's wonderful father?"

He paused, and Attilio's image filled the room. "If life is an inferno of cowards, liars, and assassins, and sex is vicious, urinal, intestinal, and anal, then the guilt, the sin, the crime, the fault is not Bernardo Bertolucci's. It is rumored that I am cunning and a pretender. I really try to be honest. I have the benefit of a combination of harmonious circumstances, background, tradition, family wealth. My home environment was full of the arts and world's literary classics. I knew Sophocles intimately at the age of ten, and I have obviated hang-ups, fears, distortions, and inferiorities. That permits me accurate measures, values, and ideals . . ."

He did more toying with his cigarette than smoking, and then continued. "Like Raphael, I absorbed the techniques of the greats into my crucible and fused a completely individual Bertoluccian style. There was the verism of Rossellini, the fecund endlessness of doctor Fellini, the sociorealism of Francesco Rosi, the vivid naturalism of Pasolini, the camera poetry of Antonioni—it is a shame that Antonioni's fine work of art, *Zabriskie Point*, was not understood and appreciated by Americans."

Bernardo glows under his halo of the missionary. He said, "Empathy and revolution are in my blood; the plight of the suffering poor, the disenfranchised, the oppressed has always summoned me. Pasolini helped me with my first professional film, *Accattone—Beggar*. At 21 I made *La Commare Secca*—the story of four crude and picturesque city youths affected by the death of a prostitute. My father, mother, brother Giuseppe, and a troupe of elated relatives escorted me to its showing at the 1962 Venice Film Festival. I left poetry for the cinema and imagined my Olivetti electric typewriter a motion-picture camera."

His dark, savage-looking young cameraman had to leave. Bernardo said with a strange reverence, "He . . . he is *my* cameraman!"

I said, "I know, you told me that before." Bernardo nodded, excused himself, took the uncommunicative fellow carefully by the arm as if he were made of thin glass, and accompanied him out to the Via della Lungara.

I went to take a leak. When I came back into the room Bernardo said, "The camera became my lyric instrument. I wrote scenario after scenario and pounded many doors without results. Nothing came easy. It took me two persistent years to convince old man Angelo Rizzoli, the publishing tycoon, to finance *Prima della Rivoluzione* (*Before the*

Revolution). The title is from Talleyrand, 'Only those who lived before the revolution know the sweetness of life.' It's about middle-class revolutionaries ten years before the liberation, about the sweetness of life in my Emilia, about the poplars with their heads in the mist. There is an incestuous youth who falls in love with and lays his bourgeois, pretty aunt. The boy could have been myself, an immature rebel. Drawing much from my own experiences, *Before the Revolution* was a proving ground indicating to me that I must later evolve a cultural hero. Every artist is instinctively his own hero."

The cunty-lean girl with the ratty eroded face brought Bernardo his choice Lambrusco. The kid, with her semblance of having been "distressed" or "antiqued," had insidious, overwhelming sex appeal.

"You see, Di Donato, to do the great living 20th Century alfresco chapel has been with me from the moment I pressed the button of my first movie camera. All my exertions have led to that vision. Now the millions from *Tango* make *1900* possible. Do you not agree that what we have to do has been with us from the beginning?

"In a few words the outline is this: On the same day in 1900 two babies are born near each other in the Parma countryside. We follow them for 95 years. They grow as friends, one rich, the other poor, eventually becoming Fascist and Communist and enemies. There is anarchy, strikes, patriotism, war, then fascism and the Second World War, the flight from the good earth, the catastrophe of agricultural civilization, the agony of the deserted land, the evils of our technological age, the mad pace, pollution, physical atrophy, abdication of principles, spiritual cowardly forfeiture to robot surrender, and a whole cataclysm of many, many things.

"Toynbee said recently, 'We have seen our last days of freedom. The economic siege of the West will lead inevitably to civil wars or to totalitarian governments.'

"Italy is again going to bed with fascism. Bankrupt Italy is dancing on the Titanic. It is all upside down. The intelligent rich are Communist and the miserable despondent ignorant have-nots are Fascist. The Mephisuphelean CIA is all over the world like rotten syphilis. We here may soon become Chile—Italia. It will come as a drugged dream, a plague, quietly, smoothly, unresisted, accepted with open arms as the merciful anticlimax to an unendurable suspense. Social responsibility and continence seem too much of a burden for the common man.

"I'll probably end *1900* as a science fiction spectacular. I must get this testament off my chest—before the H-bomb nullifies everything."

He had spoken resolutely with the limpid serene cadence of the crusading innocent. My first instantaneous impresson of Bernardo Bertolucci recurred: An Italian Prince Myshkin with an aura suggesting the Messiah. Actually, Myshkin was not The Idiot. He just had stuff going that was far ahead of the people he dealt with—and that's like Bernardo, too. His mother had said that the morning after he had run his first film, *In Search of Mystery*, she had found written on the kitchen blackboard, "THE BEST DIRECTOR EVER BORN!"

Attilio, who knows his son better than anybody—after all, he molded Bernardo—had said to me, "Bernardo follows Chekhov's dictum, 'If a musket is humg over the mantelpiece in the first act, it has to go off and shoot a character in the second act.' Every dot and title Bernardo puts into a film has a logic, a motive, a scheme, a purpose to an end."

I thought of how the big-shot director Paolello had left my friend Clara Schiavolena after enjoying her for 28 years, and I said to Bernardo, "They say *Tango* made you dizzy, that you couldn't take it and got a swollen head, that it broke up your last relationship."

"Oh no . . . " he said, "that simply is not true. Long ago my father and my mother instructed me to be above and beyond success. She became repressive. I became repressive. It is not good to be repressed. That prevented each of us from breathing, from bursting out, from seeking new ways."

On Alitalia to Kennedy, I was reading Professor Attilio Bertolucci's cleansing poetry. A Roman journalist was sitting next to me. He knew Attilio's work and said, "I recall Bernardo as a boy when he was an oblique curious fatted calf."

He inclined his head, reached for his ear, chuckled, winked, and said, "Do you know your precious Bernardo is . . ." Then he suggestively tugged at his earlobe.

Ladies Of The Roman Night

It was the day I moved into the pensione where the whores lived—close to the Piazza Di Spagna. I was in the armchair by the desk. A strangely beautiful girl with luminous bleached-platinum hair and a nervous, dignified middle aged man got out of the elevator. I thought they were husband and wife, and I could not help staring at her. The man rushed over to me and thrust out his identification card. Under the photo was the name of his wool mill in the Maiella mountains of Abruzzi. I said, in Italian, "Excuse me but I am not the proprietor." Then the proprietor's wife appeared and, without a word, took the man's 5000 lire and gave him the key to PRIVATO. The girl was Elena. Her face stuck in my mind. I have since followed Elena through the chic promenading evening crowds that window-shop at the elite stores in our Piazza di Spagna neighborhood. It thrilled me to watch her go into the hairdresser's and to see the fairies flit about her, or to trail her to a fashionable shop and to behold her, through the plate glasss, moseying about, lighting up and sighing over fine things. Her lovely face, with the high cheekbones and perfect lips, had a impid expression. men turned from their cives and peered, but she paid no mind, not even to those who were rich and handsome. You'd think she were alone in a chapel. In the dreams of night, I followed her, saying "Elena, you are a good girl."

Elena's parasite pimp (who hardly bothered to bring her men) was haughty Umberto. He was a greasy Bogart with baggy eyes, a jaundiced complexion, and a winningly dissolute air. I used to see Elena, Umberto and the baby, Giulietta, in a proletarian *trattoria*. The bar was up five steps in the front—with bread, *lupine* beans, cheese, salami and prosciutto for the seedy drunkards. Wine from the taps of giant casks was five cents a tumbler. In the rear was a farmhouse style dining room with a pregnant peasant waitress and a long unfinished table. In the center of the room, with nicotine-stained fingers and gaudy jewelry on his wrists, Umberto held court, judging pugilists and soccer champions and treating friends to food and drink. Elena hardly spoke. But back at the *pensione*, Anna, the crippled maid, spoke breathlessly and reverently of her as the lady of room four. Anna cared for Elena's room each afternoon; she put fresh flowers in the vase and took care of the marvelous baby, Giulietta. Elena gave Anna more in tips and costly gifts than Anna received from the *pensione* proprietor.

The proprietor and his wife treated Elena like a goddess. At noon, the wife would knock lightly on Elena's door, which was next to mine, and whispered, "El-e-na. Elena dearest. El-e-na treasure, are you ready for the tub and collation? Elena, if you are resting, do not disturb yourself. Let us know what you desire—at your pleasure."

After Elena left the bathroom in the corridor, I would go in to smell her ambrosial shampoo and bubble bath and kiss her towels and suck in the damp ghost of her mysterious female being. Often her door would be partly open and she would be wearing a Chinese dressing gown and rhinestone-heeled silk slippers, her hair up in curlers and a Marlboro in her mouth. She'd put the breakfast tray on the hallway floor by the head of the stairs. After breakfast, Elena would spend hours at her make-up table going through the ritual of embellishment that she didn't need.

Elena leaving the *pensione* at night and heading for the Piazza di Spagna was something else. Her platinum hair was soft and radiant; her handbag, containing such occupational equipment as condoms, petroleum jelly douch and antispetics, among other things, was slung efficiently over her shoulder. Her clothing was somewhat loud: She favored a shorish flower- decorated white imitation-leather jacket, and I guess she wore slacks because her cunning legs were thin. She was a Saint Joan of cunt, going fearlessly, relentlessly into combat.

On the lintel of the room next to mine was an enameled gaslight era placque that said PRIVATO. After ten P.M. the thick door to the street was locked; the outside bell had to be rung, and the proprietor's wife— on night duty did not ask "Who is it?" as she did in the daytime, but simply pushed the buzzer. And far into the Roman night, the buzzer sounded, as regular as clockwork, for the darling *mignotte* leading in their *clienti*. The wall between my room and PRIVATO was an improvised partition, and by putting my ear to the wall, I heard most of what went on. There was the guy's comical oohing and ahhing, and when his breathing slowed, I could tell he had shot his load.

Elena processed men rapidly. In order to get a look at her, I'd pretend to have to go to the toilet, but she was not fooled. She'd come out appearing brand new and look through me as though I were invisible. And there would be the pale john rinsing the corpse of his prick or battling the stuck zipper of his fly. Every other week, the middle-aged wool manufacturer came from Abruzzzi. He was lost, mad, gone for Elena: "Elena, angel of mine, oh, how I love thee! What good I feel for thee!"

Besides Elena, six whores thought of the *pensione* as home. Black Angelica worked the Via Vento from Air France to the American Embassy; plump Ursula, who carried a miniature poodle in her bag, the Trevi Founntain; leggy Gay, from the Via del Corso to the Piazza San Silvestro. Bespectacled Dorothea, called the teacher, worked by Valentino's shop in the Hotel Inghilterra and Via Condotti; and Cinzia with the child's face and streaked hair, Lisetta the Sardinian redhead (her pussy was dark religious hue of tomato paste—how salutatory are a flaming bush and speckled thighs for a change!) and unforgettable Elena walked the Piazza di Spagna. They could have graced a centerfold, which is what it is all about.

One rainy night, they were by the desk with the proprietor's wife. Their perfumes came up the elevator shaft in aphrodisiac bouquet. Neapolitan Anna, the lame domestic, brought in Elena's splendid one-year-old Giulietta for the girls to coo over. I didn't know if Giulietta was Umberto's child or if she had been fathered by one of Elena's clients. If I recall correctly, the proprietor once told me that Elena had found the baby when it was abandoned by an Irish-English hippie couple. Giulietta gleefully echoed what she had been taught: "*Mamma Elena bella! Mamma Elena bella!*" The childless proprietor and his wife fawned on the baby. The proprietor's tubby white haired mother appeared; I caught her quick shrewd glance at Elena, the baby and her son. The pimp Umberto came up the marble stairs with a boxer on a chain, took a wad of lire from Elena to bet on the horses and left. The rain stopped. The girls combed their hair, took out cosmetics, touched up and sallied forth into the streets.

In the Piazza di Spagna, they went singly to the middle of the block, and when men in cars approached, they communicated the availability of flesh and of every manner of orgasm—oral, anal, vaginal, manual, fetishistic. They employed the *gesticolaria*, a system of furtive signs from ancient Roman times. They put the middle finger to the mouth inviting fellatio and the ear inviting sodomy. Motorist slowed down and the whores approached them jauntily. "*Carissimo!* Dearest! Enjoy life. Let us make love!" On the night in question, I heard one man ask how much, although he already knew the price to be 20,000 or 30,000 lire; he felt he owed it to his family to economize. The girl said, "Everything is high today. Inflation caused by the Arabs' oil is frigging all of us. Darling, obey your prick. It has to live too. Make yourself courageous. Come. Where? To a family-style hotel nearby. It's safer than your own home. If not, to a hotel of your choosing."

A timid Swiss businessman followed the girls and stared, and when they beckoned, he first froze, then scurried away, then returned. He did this over and over. Finally, a girl took pity, grabbed him and pulled him along to the *pensione*. A couple of married wise guys from Milan gave the girls a hard time to demonstrate the superiority of Northern Italians over Central Italians; but when the girls got tough and told them, "*Stronzi vaffa n'culo!*" (Turds, go get fucked in the ass!), they became lambs.

Rome's first whore was Acca Larentia the wife of Faustulus, the shepherd of Ning Numitor's flocks who found Romulus and Remus abandoned on the banks of the Tiber and brought them up; because of her wantonness, Acca Larentia was called *lupa*, prostitute—whence the fable that Romulus and Remus were suckled by a she-wolf. The there was Flora the whore, who left a tremendous fortune for the amusement of the Roman people—whereupon followed the festival of the whores, the Floralian Games. The Games' motto: "If I can conquer with my cunt, why should I bear arms?" At the Games, the rich whores of Rome paraded from their houses with slaves, dwarfs, priests and fools, assembled in the arena of the circus and did a slow strip tease. The Romans applauded their lascivious postures. Then, to the blare of trumpets, nude men with astonishing erections burst into the arena, and there was a frightful orgy.

Ovid, Horace, Catullus, Propertius, Tibullus, Vergil, Petronius, all the Roman poets sang of their luscious whores. Horace screwed the prostitute Gratidia, then went for her daughter Tyndaris, saying to the kid, "*O matre pulchra filia pulchrior.*" (O you the more beautiful daughter of a beautiful mother.) And Petronius said, "Booze and whores destroy the health of the body, and yet the true happiness of life lies in booze and whores."

The prostitute was and still is called by a variety of epithets. *Bliteae* were the lowest of the low old whores; *bustuariae*, whores who work cemeteries; *forariae*, country whores; *delicatae*, high-class whores; *famosae*, patrician whores; *noctilucae*, nightwalkers; *quasillariae*, servant whores; *nanae*, dwarf whores; *paedicones*, pederasts; *unguentarii*, young male whores; *peripateticae*, traveling whores; *gallinae*, whores who are also thieves; *felatrices*, female cocksuckers; *fellatores*, male cocksuckers; *pergulae*, balcony whores; *carogni*, old whores; *intactae*, virgins. Eunuchs are *spadones* and *castrati*; homosexuals are *effeminati*; and bisexuals are *orecchioni*. Pimps are *lenocinatores*, *papponi* and *ruffiani*. Lesbians are *introversae*. Whores with large vaginas are *Pasiphaës*, after the wife of King Minos who couldn't get a human cock big enough, so shut herself in the belly of the temple bronze cow in order to be fucked by a bull.

At dinner at the home of an Italian political leader, I said, "I wonder how a woman can give herself to men simply for a fee."

The politician's very proper wife surprised me with her reply. "My husband, you, and all men, have promiscuous sex left and right with no more thought than that given to dogs in the street. Is there a woman in Rome who is not a potential whore, when it is simply a matter of the amount?" she said.

I questioned many other Italian women about their feelings toward whores. The sum of what they said was that they preferred the whore's ass to be sodomized, sore and bleeding rather than their own; let the whore take into her mouth the repulsive object that invariably spoiled one's taste for coffee in the morning. Also, the husband returning home form the whore's loins with his beastly satyriasis appeased was the cat who had stolen the cream and whose guilty conscience made him sweet and fit to live with—a better father and husband.

The Church, with its casuistical labyrinth of weights and counterweights, is circumspect about the oldest profession. Countless rich whores on their deathbeds have bequeathed their all to the Church for absolution.

A prelate of St. Peter's told me, "We bear in mind Rahab, the harlot of Jericho, who by faith did not perish: Mary Magdalene; and the woman of Samaria at the well with our Lord. You will look in vain in the *Osservatore Romano* for the Vatican's attitude toward prostitution; we are concerned not with the imperfect, polluted, ephemeral body but with the soul, with fidelity to the Holy Roman Catholic Church, with sincere confession and with contrition. Many prostitutes have forgone the world and joined the religious orders. Their Holinesses Innocent III and Gregory IX pronounced it a praiseworthy act to marry a fallen woman and uplift her. Remember, a whore was first at the Cross and first at the tomb!"

The Church views divorce with horror and alarm: it views the prostitute as a spillway for the animal needs of the father-husband. When I did research on the life of little Saint Maria Goretti, a cardinal in the Vatican told me that it would have been better all around if the sex-crazed young peasant, Allesandro Serenelli, had gone to a prostitute instead of trying to rape Maria. Also, it would have been better if the Goretti child had given in to Serenelli, so that she could have started a family. She would have lived, and the youth woud not have spent his life in prison.

Prositition is against the law. When the *carabinieri* and the police brass are driven about on inspection tours, the girls know beforehand and scatter in mock and terror. The police know that, unlike American whores with their drugs, alcohol and criminality, Roman whores have character. It is insanity to think that officialdom will ever enforce the antiprostitution edicts and stop the girls from milking tourists of the many millions of dollars they in turn put into the sick economy of Rome and Italy.

One night Cinzia was on the outlook for trade in a chiaroscuro of lamplight by the Palazzo di Propaganda Fide—stamping her feet and swinging her arms to keep warm. I watched her from in front of the heavily guarded Spanish Embassy and talked to an old cop.

"Look at that dear angel of a child," he said. "She probably has an invalid hero father who lost his legs in the war to protect the rich, or a widowed mother and a regiment of hungry mouths to feed at home. I don't understand the things God permits. I for one rebel against His cruel ways. If she were the daughter of Carlo Ponti and Sophia Loren or of the Fiat billionaires, she wouldn't be out here chancing influenza and suffering for the family bread. Capitalism is a sin. There is no equality in this country. Brother, why don't you do a noble thing? Patronize her. It will give you nature's delight and help her situation."

I pretended that I didn't know Cinzia and was afraid of disease.

"Our *mignotte* are wise; they go to doctors and use the bidet and douche. They take a sharp look at your sausage and squeeze the head hard to test that all's well. As for cleanliness, you could eat spaghetti off their pussies!" he said. I kept Cinzia company; I asked her what she would do when her youth was gone and she was no longer marketable. She tossed her head: "There's time yet!" I asked what had decided her to become a prostitute.

"What was your father?" she asked.

"My father was a bricklayer like his father."

"And what work did you do for most of your life?"

I told her I had been a bricklayer also. She said that both her mother and grandmother had been whores and that they had ultimately married workingmen and settled down to normal family life; that, perhaps, would be her destiny, too. According to her, it is rare that an Italian whore ends badly.

Romans, whores included, are highly civilized, moderate and practical. And as for the ideal women: Fellini, Rosi, Bertolucci, in fact all the top Italian directors have told me that actresses fight one another like wildcats to get to play the role of a whore.

With the Romans, there is no neurotic intellectual shit about sex; they put fucking on the level of breathing, but that doesn't mean fucker and fuckee will always commingle heart and soul. Love and spirit together are the exclusive prerogative of the King of the home, the husband. Among the 11,000 prostitutes of Rome are many housewives, veritable saints, who hawk the trinity of their orifices with the encouragement of their grateful mates so that the family can meet car, appliance and mortgage payments, send the kids to better schools and provide dowries.

Ursula with the white powder-puff poodle told me that, for her, prostitution was a filler, and pricks were really the last things in the world she wanted. "My true calling is the cinema. I have been in Doctor Fellini's films. As you know, he glorifies the overweight woman. I just want to star in a few movies and then retire to the seaside and live like a nun, tranquil and serene."

I took her to Franco Rosi's party; most of Italy's top directors were there. Fellini was glad to see Ursula and made her feel like a queen.

I asked him why his films were so crowded with enormous whores. He said that when he was 11 years old, he had caught the family's huge maid, a former prostitute, using his mother's bathtub and her imported soap. "If Mother had known, she would have fired the maid." The maid asked me to dry her back with Mother's Turkish towel, then her legs and so on. I had never seen a naked woman before and I got a painful hard-on. She weighed more than 300 pounds. Her breasts were bigger than watermelons. Her nipples were as big as your fist and smelled like potato peels. She made me swear on holy pictures that I wouldn't tell Mother, and she gave me a grand jerking off.

"I spun a love fantasy about her and made her promise to marry me when I grew up and became the world's greatest movie director. She taught me all the tricks. Each time she jerked me off, she would look at the Virgin on the wall and say, 'Mary is watching, and this causes her heartfelt displeasure. See her sad look? We must not make the Madonna unhappy. Here, I have the solution.' So she would grab my ears and jam my head into her big hairy bush, saying, 'Ah, Federico, the Lord's mother cannot see you down there. Eat it, my child. It will make you a genius. It will make you live forever.'

Hundreds of cathouses are advertised in the newspapers under the guise of massage establishments. They feature aesthetic, satisfying, relaxing, health creating manicures, spinal manipulations, foot treatments, muscle kneading, soothing exercises and also out-call services in your domicile no matter the place, the day or the night—during strikes, demonstrations, religious festivals and in all weathers and seasons.

One evening I was with Colonel T, an ugly sex-mad Greek who had taken a room at the *pensione*, and his French friend, Jean-Pierre, who was an international art dealer. Jean-Pierre warned me that T had supported the dictatorship. We walked along the Tiber by Castel Sant' Angelo and passed a clutch of stunning whores by the bridge. We made the mistake of seeming interested. The gorgeous cunts were men, more female than Eve, exotically gotten up with platform shoes, white silk stockings up to their tucked-in balls, earrings and clanking jewelry. As we left them, we turned, out of curiosity. That did it! They came after us, salivating like dragons in heat and making blatant sucking and anal-lingual gestures. The he-she bastards followed us for blocks, and we didn't shake them until the nutty Greek decided to hire one of the transvestites; and Frenchman and I escaped.

Another evening, I looked over the dolls on the Via Veneto. Whether because of the full moon or the bankruptcy of the nation, pussy was legion, and so were the madams and pimps. On such a night, the show is the best in the world—Fellini, Bertolucci, Visconti and Zeffirelli notwithstanding. Two old horned-toad Texas cowboys in boots, Stetsons and shoestring ties were kissing transvestites on their lipsticked mouths and fondling their asses. Lesbians were boldly accosting girls and even women tourists accompanied by husbands. One pregnant woman said maliciously to her confounded mate, "How she looks at me! It gives me a funny feeling. Honey what could she possibly want?"

I spotted Jean-Pierre and Colonel T. The cocky midget pimp who roosts at the corner of the Café de Paris by the newspaper kiosk said to Jean-Pierre, Colonel T and me, "Gentlemen, I have a deluxe cunt for you!" Jackie, the *mignotta* he called over, certainly was special; she was 19 and spoke smatterings of French, Greek and English.

"Only thirty thousand lire apiece," she said. "Don't hesitate. Make love now. Be brave!"

Fifty dollars apiece in a country with its back against the wall? I gagged and feigned reluctance, hoping that the price would go down. Jean-Pierre shrugged; he was neutral. But the swarthy bald Greek, Colonel T, was rank and ready.

She said, "Friends, I have my own apartment and machine and driver; you will luxuriate in fine drinks and food, music and smokes. I will give you a full happy hour each. Or I will take you all at the same time, if you wish. You'll see. Come, you are getting older by the second and never know when you may die. Let us make this a special occasion. Look then: twenty-five thousand lire apiece!" Jean-Pierre said, nodding toward me, "It's up to the maestro."

I said to Jean-Pierre on the side, "Let's bargain her down to twenty —maybe fifteen."

She heard and held her ground. People swirled about us. It was obvious to onlookers what was being transacted. Wives of milk-toast Americans gawked at Jackie in wonder and admiration as she pumped her pussy against me and, with my hands in hers, made me feel her hips, breasts and box.

The midget pimp drove us in a new Alfa Romeo; the young prostitute's apartment was lush, and the drinks and snacks she served were the finest.

I had my fun first. Then tall bearded Jean-Pierre mounted her. The Greek said he had to have privacy, but we opened the door of the bedroom and peeked: He was having seconds and thirds and whispering, "You are a thousand times more beautiful than Jackie Onassis. Promise you'll be true to me. Promise you won't fuck Jean-Pierre and Pietro!" Then he dove down on her—slobbering, slurping and growling like a famished dog. And that was the Greek hygiene fanatic who, in Jean-Pierre's kitchen, insisted upon washing the vegetables with soap and hot water!

Weeks before Christmas, a number of streets were barricaded to traffic and decorated with red carpets, poinsettia plants, pine and palm trees, cushioned wicker lounges and antique oil-burning lamps. On the first spacious landing of the Spanish Steps, a village with a wondrous manger was built. On cold nights, there was a precious family feeling, with Elena and the other regular girls plus new stray lovelies, a policeman, a couple of *carabinieri*, a night watchman or two and the beloved drunk of the Steps, Barabbas—whose real name is Aldo. He tells everybody that the evil mob freed him in order to have Jesus Christ crucified. Barabbas would make a bonfire and we'd broil sausages and roast chestnuts, and the generous *mignotte*, with hearts bigger than their sweet asses, sent for vintage Bardolino and plates of spaghetti—between fast fucks for clients.

An oddball mother and daughter prostitute team came while the girls were warming at the fire and passed out handbills for a National Prostitutes' Civil Rights Union. The girls shook their heads; they were not about to be suckered into Orwellian identity cards, photos, monitoring, overhead and taxes. The failed mother and daughter whores were sexually undesirable, a disgrace to the profession; eventually they were reduced to working as postal clerks.

At the *pensione*, the girls exchanged gifts, including holy pictures and amulets—they are devoutly religious. The proprietor's mother had baked the traditional pastries for them. As Elena prepared to leave to spend the natal feast with Umberto's folks, the proprietor took baby Giulietta from Anna the maid. He held the child tightly and said with tearful eyes, "Treasure of treasures!"

The week Elena and the girls were gone the *pensione* was a nicely illuminated tomb.

On a spring day by the Piazza del Popolo, I met Elena pushing Giulietta in her gocart. We walked without talking up to the gardens of the Pincio. Giulietta played on the grass with other toddlers. Elena and I rented the big telescope and inspected every part of Rome. Opposite the Villa Medici, Giulietta saw a woman feeding a cat.

I told the woman that my calico cat in the U.S.A., Miss Minnie Mascara, drove me out of my wits with her moody tastes. The refined woman said, "Your American young lady lacks the best appetizer:

hunger." We introduced ourselves. We knew each other through our books. She was Elsa Morante, the great European author and—something I didn't know—the wife of Alberto Moravia.

I visited Elsa Morante at her duplex. "This was Moravia's apartment," she said. "We are good friends because we have always lived separate lives. Moravia comes here now only to tell me of the problems his mistresses give him." I said shamefacedly that I was doing a magazine piece on Roman prostitution.

Elsa said, "If there's anything you want to know, ask me. I was a professional whore for years. I was one of the dependable prostitutes at the railroad station."

"Because of economic distress?"

"Yes."

"Goddamn the dirty fucking capitalistic society!" I said.

"Oh, don't say that," she said. "I found being a prostitute wonderful! I was from the Jewish ghetto; I had a terrible sense of vaginal inferiority; I felt unattractive and unwanted. To me, whoring was the spice of life. New lover's night and day. No lies or bourgeois garbage. Every woman has a fascinating whore in her. She should use it. It is the supreme school for living, marriage and writing.

"Before a woman leaves this world she should be fucked by Proteus, who changes himself into a different man every hour. What a grand and beautiful gesture against destiny and death!

"But when it came to money, I was the most stupid whore. Business transactions frightened me. I never charged enough. And now I'm the same way with agents and publishers. Oh, no, I was not a good commercial whore."

I said, "I was a bricklayer, and I still lay bricks. One's craft is never lost. If you don't mind—let's not be stuffy—I'll hire your services tonight and give you much more than you would ask. You see, I've never fucked a writer."

"Thank you," she said, "I appreciate your meaning. But I am no longer a woman on this planet. Elsa Morante is dead. Her soul and brain live in the idealism of paper and the typewriter."

*

There was a call for long-legged Gay. The proprietor of the *pensione* rang her room, put his hand over the mouthpiece and gave me the phone, saying, "You have to hear this!" It was Gay's pimp cursing her for not having made the payment on his Ferrari.

When Gay came down, she was upset. The proprietor led me to the room behind the desk where there was a window overlooking the street. A white Ferrari convertible, driven by Gay's flashy pimp, arrived. He pulled her hair, slapped her.

The proprietor said, "*Disgraziato!* Ingrate!"

The following week I saw Gay's pimp arrested. When the *carabinieri* silently closed in on him, he threw a plastic bag over the wall. A young *carabiniere* fetched it from among the orange trees and bushes. In front of the pimp, he opened the bag, revealing packets of dope and hypodermic needles. They put chains on the pimp and hustled him down the Spanish Steps to the Alfa Romeo police car.

Gay left the *pensione* to live with the pimp's mother and sisters. The proprietor bewailed his loss. He said he leased the *pensione* from Vatican Realty, and were it not for the whores, he'd starve to death. He took me into the dining room where he played piano ragtime and had me drink a quart of brady and sing with him. And I learned the details of his fucking the *mignotte* of the *pensione*—without cost.

"But Elena! For Elena, I would throw away my wife, the *pensione*, my soul!" And making that Roman sign of top quality, the forefinger screwed into the cheek: "If Jesus Christ made more ineffable cunt than Elena, the son of a bitch has kept it for himself!" He wept and said, "What I could tell you about me and Elena and my treasure Giulietta would make you the best book!"

The *pensione* was definitely not a whorehouse; in it, the girls were untouchable—you don't shit on your own doorstep. Pacts had to be struck outside. Then it was permissible to come back to the *pensione* and go through the routine of paying a day's rent for a few minutes' use of PRIVATO. They knew I was writing about them, and it was baby-face Cinza who put me on the spot: "Look here, doctor, your rich American magazine pays you but not me and you're taking up my time. If you don't care to fuck or can't get it stiff, be a big Yankee sport and give me the 30,000 lire for chatting with you."

When I was walking one day with my Roman niece, who was made up like a stage star with paint, powder, heavy lipstick, blond wig and false eyelashes, Cinza took her for a brazen competing whore, came over, grimaced and blew cigarette smoke in her face. My niece was flattered.

I had had the girls of the *pensione* one by one with the exception of Elena, who had avoided me. A motion-picture camera should have recorded how I spied on Elena's movements from about 200 feet away. It was weird. I can't imagine what she thought of my behavior. Also, I believe that my respect and civil kindness—thin masks for my infatuation—terrorized Elena, were a foreign body in her social stream, an invasion of her lifestyle.

One night I decided: There's a time for all things. I took Elena by the arm. She did not resist. In Rome, it is not what you do, but how you do it. In front of Bulgari's window, which was scintillating diamonds, rubies and sapphires, I put three new 10,000 lire notes in her hand. What an indescribable blessing it is that an aging Faustus can buy an edible Margaret, a pearl, and take her to bed for a paradisiacal spell. An hour with the dive whore is as 1000 years—without society and religion's lousy bulls!

In PRIVATO, the graceful way Elena undressed was entrancing. A girl denuding is the artist born. Without effort, Elena invoked all that is love. It seemed she was serving herself to me on an altar. After a quick appraisal of the thing and a cursory squeeze of the knob, she got a condom from her purse, tenderly unrolled it onto me, lay back on the bed like earth received the rain, spread and worked me in. Elena did something transfiguring for a man. It made him say and mean with all his being, "Elena, I love you!"

I had to go to Sicily for two months. When I returned, the proprietor told me that Elena was gone, Elena had found out from a doctor that she had the first symptoms of tuberculosis. The wool man had taken her and the baby to the Abruzzian mountains. He had set them up in the small village hotel and, for appearance' sake, he had given her a job in the mill as a weaver. His son, who was about Elen's age, fell madly in love with the girl; and Umberto, the abandoned pimp, tracked her down, assaulted the old wool manufacturer and was arrested and sent to prison.

"I miss that girl the way a man suddenly blinded missed his vision," the proprietor said. "I see Elena's face in the *Pietà*—and many duplicates of her face and profile can be seen on the reliefs in Augustus' tomb. Ah, who wouldn't love Elena though she's been fucked by thousands? A whore makes the very best wife. Elena will come back. There is something about her career!"

After he got over his reverie, he said, "Do not be offended—you know how women are: My wife wants me to tell you that your typewriter bothers our tired construction worker guests at night and by day, interrupts the sleep of the girls. We must think first about the comfort of our permanent guests."

One morning in the Piazza di Spagna I thought I was imagining things—but it was not a mirage. Giulietta, having learned to walk since I had last seen her was clambering up the steps ahead of Elena. The baby was rushing happily toward the great banks of azaleas. And Elena pointed out the various colors.

The next day, a messenger brought her an impressive gift box from the florist. Before the proprietor sent it up, he opened the package and showed me the espensive long-stemmed American Beauty roses and the card. He said they were from the wool man's son. Later we saw the tall, rich, magnificent young man call for her. The proprietor brought out the customary quart of brandy.

"Some of us dream," he said. "In this uncertain life, who knows what may happen? Suppose God in His mysterious ways and wisdom called my dear wife to heaven. Elena could take her place at this desk. You see—you have got to know—Elena's Giulietta is my child, my angel, my blood."

We drank on that.

"I guess we all dream," he said. "But, remember, even a dream is better than nothing."

I Killed Maria Goretti

Alessandro Serenelli, the killer of the girl-siant, Maria Goretti, had been hidden from the world for thirty years in the remote Capuchin monastery on the mountaintop of Marcerata.

Father Valenti, with whom I communicated through the Vatican, greeted me. "Sersenelli," he said, "is in bed. He doesn's give interviews, but I did persuade him to talk freely to you tomorrow.

"You know, he's eighty-five. Remarkable for his age. Throughout the world there are strange notions about him: that he is a priest performing miracles, that he is a diving devil. The plain fact is that he is a discreet, rational domestic of our Capuchin community, and a lay brother of the secular third order, with the privilege of wearing our habit for the first time, in his coffin."

I sat up late with the monk in the kitchen drinking wine and smoking. He was a down to earth priest and humanist. We philosophized: Nature was from God. Luigi, Maria Goretti's father, and Giovanni, Alessandro's father, had been life-long friends and share cropping partners. Young Alessandro was like a big brother to Maria. He became smitten with her. B follows A. After Luigi Goretti's death from Malaria in the Pontine marshes the thought of sex with Maria dominated Alessandro.

Whether for procreation or pleasure sex was nothing new. Sex was rampant in the Old Testament. Christ did not have a puritanical, damning view of sexual relationships—and so forth. Young Alessandro talked himself into believing he had a right to Maria. On a July afternoon he forcibly tried to possess her. She fought him. Frustrated he hacked her with a brush hook.

Was virginity worth being killed? Is death better rape? Must one live by absolutes at all costs? Had Maria given in Alessandro would have married her. Many girls throughout the world learn to love and live happily with their seducers.

Was purity more important than the denial of nature, the agony and loss of one life, the ruin of another, and the sorrow of two families?

What were the sensible values in life as it is? Did Maria Goretti merit sanctity for the refusal of a moment? Did God give anyone or group the authority to designate who is a saint and who is not?

Doesn't one have to take everything with a bit of salt and weigh which causes the greater damage and grief? Doesn't the rapist and killer lurk in most men?

"Father Valenti," I said, "Alessandro's ill-considered attempt to have his sexual experience sent him to thirty years of hard labor. After he left prison did he ever have a woman?

The monk shrugged and chuckled, "My Friend, who knows?"

I met Serenelli at breakfast. He was handsome and powerfully built, looking much younger than his years. Children coming to the Capuchin school hailed him as "Uncle Alessandro."

His room was piled with books; works of the great and classic authors. I noticed old newspapers with the accounts of the execution of Caryl Chessman.

"The crime I committed," he said, "does not seem real; as though it happened to another person who resembles me and has my name. I have read thousands of books and some how the stories seem more actual than the gloomy events of one's life.

"In Ferriere whenever Father went to Nettuno or Anzio he brought me something to read. He was proud of me; I was the only peasant who was literate. I read with out distinction magazines, halfpenny tabloids, horror and crime stories and romances. They said I pasted obscene picture on the walls of my room. That is not so. The isolated fret of the marches would not spare me. During the oppressive winter nights by lamplight I buried myself in reading, as the saying goes, 'just to kill time.'

"Though my character was one timid and apart, inwardly I raged aginst the stupid labor, poverty, and devouring solitude of the marshes.

"The farmhouse over the barn in Ferriere where the tragedy took place was my appointment in Samara. I was happy on the sea as a fisherman with my married brother Pietro before Father sent for me. I should have disobeyed Father and not gone to Ferriere."

He felt at home with the best literature and spoke of "—the sentiment of order and discipline of the writings of the Romans, that of grace and beauty with Greek works, wit and finesse with Italian, heroism with Spanish, melancholy with English and German, pity with Russian." When I complimented his erudition he said, "Books make for good or evil. In my reading youth I was like the majority of mankind: good sense sends them to sleep while paradox and passion enchant them."

The sensational author was the accomplice to my crime. Our actions depend largely on destructive or constructive conceptions we take in and digest.

"I didn't know then that the mirror reflects and that the Writer must select. I let the bizzare things I read inflame me: Stendahl's love of murders, the hideous and shocking . . . . stories that flayed moral responsibility. I read of Byron saying to Taine, "I should be curious to experience the sensations a man must have when he has just committed a murder." And a character in *The Possessed* proclaiming, "Murder is not a form of madness, but a sound doctrine, almost a duty, in any case, a fine act of protest."

"And how often did I read of a passionate here declaring to a girl, 'Be mine, or I will kill you! Love or death!'

"I had come to the pestilential marches of Ferriere when I was seventeen with Father and the Goretti family to sharecrop for Count Mazzoleni, and was discontented from the day of arrival. Peasants died like flies from malaria. Life wasn't worth a penny there. Fear of the death-filled air added to my desperation.

"I had left the sea and its free life and fresh salt smell. In Ferriere the five years I had spent at sea seemed a mirage. The sea was to my fancy; ever changing, beholden to no rules of man. I often recalled the tides and restless waves, the bells and whistles, ports, nets, and the briny smell of kelp and fish. The Mariners were not mute plodders chained to the stubborn soil. There ship was a roving home that took them to Pescara, Vasto. Termoli and new places where a man could go a shore and walk streets and see life without being censured.

"There were no churches at sea, and no Commandments to wall one in.

"The fishermen were a fatalistic lot, given to song, profanity and lust, without shame or remorse. The life of the sea was pagan. The sides of the cabin had suggestive pictures of the gallant women of the ports. I listened to the licentious talk of the sailors with an excitement I did not reveal. Captain Casparri had given me the nickname . . . hermit crab.

"As for the wants of the stomach, it was not like the peasant's slavish waiting for the earth to rear the wheat. At sea one picked mussels and snails from the rocks, and the nets were full of lobsters and crabs and myriad fish that were scaled gutted and flipped over coals of the brazier, or mixed in the accompaniment of hard bread and wine.

"On ship there was Daniele, a boy my age, who went to a pot with oil and herbs for a hearty meal that asked only for the bordelios. He tried to get me to go along. Maybe if I had gone with them . . . But when it came to taking such a step I was always paralyzed. I am sincere to say it was not from religious or moral reasons. A certain fastidious contradiction within prevented me.

"Since I was a child I was a stranger to people and families, a creature fated to be alone with ungovernable impressions and reactions. When I lived with my brother Pietro I would stay awake to listen to Pietro and his wife making love in the next bedroom. Dear mother of God what the heat of desire can do to a youth!

"Indelicacy both revolted and drew me. I asked myself why I could not be like the peasants who treated sex as casually as eating a plate of macaroni.

"At twelve Marietta was beautiful, with a perfect face and figure, with deep brown eyes and long chestnut hair . . . but she was not as developed as the newspaper alleged.

"Her widowed mother, Assunta, toiled with Father and me in the fields while Marietta did the home chores.

"I indulged the idea of visiting the prostitute in Anzio that the peasant men talked about, but shrank from doing it. I contemplated some girls in nearby Conca but their vulgar manners offended my image of myself.

"I wanted Marietta. I was in love with her and could not wait a few more years . . . ah, had she been older . . . I made awkward but gentle advances various times when we were alone. The girl was resolutely religious and with silent protest slipped from me.

"The need to have her became my mania. No matter what I said to her she refused to let me kiss her. Everytime I tried to embrace her she balked me. My passion increased the more. It is said the Italian is a man of uncontrollable amorous energy, of undue excitedability, and when thwarted becomes a fierce vindictive, uomo di cortello, . . . 'man of the knife.'"

On the sorry day, July 5th, of 1902, the heat was unbearable. Anthropologists say under a sky of flame men's sensualities are more urgent and rabid than under one of ice; the fiery desire is more often than not but the outcome of fiery suns.

"That day I arose from my abused bed of torment choking for Marietta and vowed, 'Today there must be an end! Marietta consents, or else.'"

He handed me an old newspaper clipping and said, "I do not try to exculpate myseld, but here is something to think about."

It read: "Canalintas entered the following plea for Alessandro in the liberal vein indigenous to the heady progressive currents of the times: Alessandro Serenelli's crime is distressing and humiliating to our concepts of what humanity should be and boasted civilization.

"Our vaunted authors who for profit have made passion and criminality glamorous to the masses are equally guilty of Maria Gorettis death . . . also, organized religion with it impractical uncompromising, dictate: 'Death rather than sin!' Would it not have better for all concerned if Serenelli were being charged with rape here rather than murder? The other partner to Serenelli's crime was Nature with its inexorable biological pressure.

"Along with the frenzied youth who bestially struck down Maria Goretti we must indict the absence of a mother's love and guidance, the social phemomena of the widespread popularity of pornographic and horror literature!

"Would it not be well for us to inquire, why does passion, capable of producing saints, heroes and the enjoyment of love, so often take the hapless to crime? The trail of Serenelli should be an example of a scientific exploration of the subject and the mystic secrets of good and evil.

"Our day and age creates crime by mental contagion through its newspapers, novels and magazines, and even our stage portrays wholesale butchery, infidelity, sexual pervision and unmentionable vices which we applaud. Our literature copies crimes . . . the crime of berserk outbreaks . . . just as crime of the same type in turn copies literature.

"Alessandro Serenelli drank into his limited and inflexible peasant mind the crimes daily elevated by literature, between the lines of which is the subliminal suggestion, 'Make a name for yourself . . . go you and do likewise.'

"Our literature, which glorifies passion and crime is a school of sensuality, teaching the ever pernicious lesson that crime is justified as flowing from an over mastering emotion."

The article concluded: "President Vitelli admonished, 'I wish the jury to bear in mind and beware of the sophistries the council for defense sees fit to exercise. Remember, literature is one thing, and the Criminal Assizes is another.'

"My lawyer wanted to plead insanity. He was the Clarence Darrow of Rome. Stiff-necked pride in truth and my intelligence made me spurn his advice. I wonder how it would have gone if I had co-operated with him: But when one is sizzling in the frying pan how could one know what is the wisest thing to do? Does brutal punishment by the law redeem a human being?

"But to pick up the thread again—. That morning, Father, who was sickly with a recurrence of malaria, said to Assunta, Today will be an inferno. The Cimarellis are going to trash the beans. We too will thrash beans in the barn. They were the carob beans called, 'St. John's bread,' which were used as fodder for livestock.

"Teresa Cimarelli, Marietta's godmother who lived in the adjoining farmhouse, came up into the kitchen with a red blouse and skirt sent to Marietta by the Casoni woman whose daughter had outgrown the garments.

"We all went down to the big barn below. Father and I hitched the two pair of oxen to the carts. The oxen were driven about in a continuous circle; the long dried beans were scattered on the earthen floor, and the hooves of the oxen and the iron cart tires shredded them. The pods and beans were scooped up into sacks. We took turns driving the oxen with harmless whips and shouts. Marietta placed her sister, Ersilia, who was four and baby Teresa in a corner where she could watch them while she worked.

"But I didn't share the others gaiety. The rehearsals of lust in my mind had been fiction for too long. The goading dreams, the carnal vision had to burst from the cave of my brain.

"'Today,' I said, 'Today.' Lust said the breathless air, the scent of sweat, the sticky heat and marsh gas.

"After lunch the sun was at its highest. Assunta went to her bedroom to rest. Father, not well, went down to the shaded arcade under the stairway and flung himself upon sacks of beans to sleep. From my room I heard Marietta making peace between her two quarreling brothers.

"For weeks Marietta had been avoiding me. I devised a plan that would keep her away from the others for a while. As Assunta and her children were about to return to threshing I said to Marietta, 'My only other shirt is torn and must be repaired now.'

"She did not answer. Assunta said, 'Marietta you surprise me Do what Alessandro tells you.' Marietta asked, 'Where is the shirt?'

"I answered, 'You will find it on my bed; and there is also a piece to patch it with.'

"Without looking up she said, 'Very well.' Marietta wanted Ersilia to stay with her. I held my breath until Ersilia said, 'There's no fun up here. I want to ride the cart and shout at the animals.' Marietta was left alone with baby Teresa asleep on a pallet in the kitchen.

"At three o'clock I decided that was my opportunity . . . I had no more sense that a foaming dog in heat. Father was still sleeping under the stairway. The shouts of the children, the stamping of the hooves, the creaking of the cart wheels and the popping of the beans would muffle sounds from above where Marietta was.

"I halted my cart and said to Assunta, 'I am bathed in sweat take over . . . I am going for a bit, to fetch a handkerchief . . .'

"Marietta was on the landing at the top of the stairway seated on a stool and sewing the patch on my shirt. By her side and asleep on a blanket was Teresa.

"Father was snoring under the stairway. When I went up the stairway Marietta moved her bare feet to let me by to the kitchen door. In the kitchen I picked up the brush hook to threaten and frighten her with if she resisted. I stuck the brush hook into my belt and went to the door. I felt like one stalking in a dream. She was about to pick up the baby and hurry down to the barn. I opened the door, blocked her way and demanded she come into the kitchen with me.

"'What for?' she asked.

"'Never mind what for,' I said, 'come into the kitchen for a few minutes!'

"She shook her head and made a move to go down to the stairway. I grabbed her arms, pulled her into the kitchen, and kicked the door closed. I thought surely she had no recourse but to obey me, and let her go. She backed away and begged me not to touch her. I caught her and tried to throw her to the floor.

"She struggled with amazing strength. I thought to terrify her to get what I wanted. I pulled the brush hook from my belt and pressed it against her breast saying, 'You do as I say this moment. You let me have my way or you die!'

"I didn't mean it, but when she cried out for help the alarm of her voice brought on an explosive fury . . . blindly I struck her again and again.

"As she lay dying she moaned, 'I forgive you for you do not know what you're doing . . . Alessandro, I forgive you . . .'

"The madness left me as quickly as it came. I asked, 'Why, Marietta, why did you not submit to me?'

"The peasants wanted to lynch me. The police tied my hands, and pulled by leather reins I had to follow them on foot while they were on horseback, the seven miles to jail on Nettuno.

"Marietta died the next day. I recognixed the fact that society was stronger than I. I had no will left and didn't care what became of me.

"I was twenty. Had I been twenty one I would have received life imprisonment. When the court condemned me to three years in solitary confinement, and the other twenty seven years at hard labor, the president asked Assunta Goretti if she had any final words to utter as the mother of my victim. Assunta arose, gazed upon me with pity, and answered, 'Yes, sir President . . . like Marietta, I forgive Alessandro.'

"Silence came over the courtroom, then many, recovering from the astonishment created by Assunta's charity, shouted indignantly, 'Never!' 'It should not be!' 'I would never forgive the beast!' Assunta faced those who had raised their voices and asked, 'And suppose in turn, Jesus Christ, does not forgive us?'

"Two things kept me from suicide in the long-long suffocating prison years; Marietta's and Assunta's forgiveness, and reading.

"I found refuge and lived in books and not life. When as a middle-aged man I was freed Assunta became my mother and gave me the tenderest love.

"I could have gone to America and changed my identity, but I feared reality. And yet reality seems to be the greatest fiction. Is there anyone who lives without doubts? Maybe I was wrong to withdraw into the monastic walls.

"The memory of most crimes wears away in to oblivion. The Church kept the tragedy alive and the drama went on like a serial. Some saw in me an Italian Rasputin, others an inspired visionary and holy man, others a penitent primitive with the soul of an ox. Who can keep up with the fancies of the public?

"I was bewildered and entranced by Marietta being made a saint. During the fantastic canonical process I was taken to Rome and given a proper raking over the coals by the Devil's Advocate.

"I have not seen the face of God and know not what makes a saint, but if anyone deserved that rare honor it was Assunta.

"Did you know a movie was made of the whole business entitled, *The Sky Over the Marshes*? I went to a city in disguise and saw it. There was much falsity. Story makers bend the truth to please the crowds. I do not talk about the portrayal of myself whom they warped in a thousand ways . . . as though I had been an ape-like Valentino . . . but they made my poor sick father appear heartless and a drunk. Lawyers were anxious to sue the movie people for defamation, but I told them, 'It is not a serious matter. The movie is not important as it is make-believe.'

I asked if he had ever been interested in writing. He answered bashfully, "I tried writing but it wasn't bread for my teeth. Lies came out of my pen. When I read what I wrote I saw that it was the theatricality of hypocritical confession that most are prone to. My lines were full of postures and apologetics, a lame masquerade of that honesty that is one's very own and collides with the outward shock. Talking and writing are two different animals. I found myself fashioning words and thoughts the world expected of me. I don't mean to be presumptuous, but must not one be inordinately egotistic and more than a little demented to dare to write?

"Today's literature is more morbid than that of my youth. Your modern writers aim to bring out insanity in their readers. It is the stuff of the slaughterhouse, the morgue and the mental asylum; stories brimming with violence, narcotics, adultery, criminals, spies, and degenerates. Mere boys calmly commit multiple murders and then explain they went about it according to the description of mass murders in a bestseller. Life contains enough sadness without authors increasing its intensity.

"In former days the object of lofty authors was the encouragement to the reader towards health of body and mind. Now the way to fame is through nervous disease and a disordered imagination. It is only in novels that bad men have generous hearts and philosophic minds.

"What the modern author does to the reader's brain reminds me of the cannibal story. A missionary was pointing out to a cannibal who was going to eat a human head, how odious it was to kill a man in order to eat a head that thinks. 'That is just why,' retorted the cannibal, 'it is so delightful to eat it.' Erotic writers think to excuse themselves by stating that their own life is respectable as Ovid said of himself, 'My character is opposite from my verse; my life is modest, only my muse sportive.'

"My destiny was to be a recluse while others mixed and lived to the edge of the cup. In my modest estimation every word we say, every act we do, exercises some influence over the words and acts of other people. I think each man is born for the salvation or ruin of some of his fellow-creatures . . . and the author more than anybody. The end of literature should be to ennoble man."

I was curious about a few things. Alessandro, after all, was a human being. I asked him, "When you were released from prison and out in the world again, did you obey nature?"

"What do you mean?"

"Sex."

"I was a man, but . . . Anyway, when the period of police surveillance was over, my brother Pietro said, 'Now that the law has finished picking the flesh from your tail, settle to a normal life with a woman.'

"The widow Valeria was not concerned about the furore of the past, need a man on her land and has proposed that you marry her daughter, Elena. And why not? The world will talk about you but not give you bread. Take Valeria's daughter and you will have land, a roof, and a robust wife in bed. Say the word and I'll arrange it."

"I couldn't do it. Marriage in the beginning would seem nice but then would come trouble as our children would have to grow under the stigma of a father who had killed a saint and had been a convict forever held suspect . . . And yet, perhaps I was wrong again.

"The irony was that men feared me, and women sought me. An old sharecropper took me in. He didn't care about my past and said, 'As long as you work hard and behave, I consider you part of my family.'

"But again ill luck dogged me. The young wife of the sharecropper became infatuated with me, or the exaggerated publicized image of me. One day while sickling grain by my side she offered herself in a manner that I cannot describe. It was something like Zola's *La Terre*. I told her to make her dress decent again and get up from the ground. She kept insisting. I backed away and begged her to forget the idea. She spat at me and said scornfully, 'You killed a saint for the very same thing I freely offer you. Have you been sanctified too?'

"Alessandro, what are some of your personal thoughts?"

"Deep inside, as present as my bones are scenes and wondering questions. I was in the prison in Noto, Sicily. It was five in the morning, December 28th, 1908. A tremendous earthquake trembled my cell and slipt open the stone walls; the floor heaved. The cell bars twisted. The hundreds of prisoners and even I cried to be let out before we were crushed.

"The guards led us out safely to the courtyard. Later the news came that Messina, not too distant from us, had been wiped out in seconds with a loss of seventy thousand lives.

"A Sardinian matricide said to me, 'My boy, enough innocent people to fill the Colosseum have been killed in Messina in the twinkling of an eye, and we men of evil in prison have not been scratched. I tell you, Alessandro, God loves us!"

"Regardless of circumstances one eventually learns to appreciate being alive and sound. I agreed with the Sardinian and we danced about joyfully.

"Then in 1914 came the World War. Each day I read of the conflict. Because I was a criminal I was kept far away from the battlefields. By my crime I was spared. In all truth it was a satisfactory feeling to be legally protected from the carnage and destruction. How could one feel otherwise?"

"And suppose you could live your life over?"

"I am not much of a one to speculate on fables, but ah, who doesn't dream? If I were to live my life over I would have a stout fishing boat and find a woman who would follow the sea with me.

"In my dotage I would sit with my wife—Ulysses is said to have preferred his old wife to immortality . . . with my children and grandchildren, content with a piece of fish, greens, bread and wine, and call it a day. But there, what I have just said is probably the product of reading."

"Alessandro, did you ever have a woman . . . even once?"

The strong, aged man blushed. ". . . No . . . Perhaps remaining virgin was self-imposed atonement. Or was it that when one has been bitten by a serpent he dreads also a lizard? But who knows . . . after my one misdeed and prison cross I should have grasped life by the horns and did as men do."

He thought for a long while. His face clouded. He sighed bitterly, stonily, "Why did it have to happen to me? Why me!"

Christ In Plastic

On March 16, 1978, Aldo Moro, president of Italy's ruling party, the Christian Democrats, was kidnapped by terrorists, an act setting off the greatest manhunt in history and seriously shaking the Italian government. On May 8 Moro was killed when the government refused to exchange thirteen terrorist leaders for him. *Penthouse* sent Pietro Di Donato, an Italian-American novelist and the author of Christ in Conrete to cover the story.

For months the Aldo Moro case called worldwide attention to the existence of the Brigate Rosse—Italy's Red Brigades—but for all of its saturation coverage, the media never talked to a BR member. Small wonder. Italians talk only to other Italians.

Five years ago, while writing a movie script in Italy, I met through a Communist senator (who would today like to forget the whole thing), a man whom I'll call R1. He was a successful businessman; he was also a revolutionary, though there was no talk of the then-non-violent Red Brigades.

Since I travel to Italy frequently, we kept in touch. When I began to believe that R1 was in earnest, was really involved in antigovernment actions, my interest deepened; I'd joined the Communist party on August 23, 1927, the day capitalism killed Sacco and Vanzetti; I was sixteen. Out of their deaths and the earlier death of my father, Geremio, came my novel Christ in Concrete. *Since then I've grown more sophisticated about the nature of all political groups—I'm no longer a card carrier—but I've kept on searching.*

Last May I returned to Rome for the Moro affair. I was prepared to try to use R1 and to let him try to use me, and I think the bargain worked out fine. Through R1 I met another man—I might as well call him R2—who had access to the master cell that kidnapped and executed Aldo Moro. I spent two months interviewing the two Brigatisti, friends of the Moro family, police, journalists, political observers, priests—whoever would talk to me. From the material I gathered I allowed myself the license to portray Moro's fifty-four-day ordeal and crucifixion.

The word sacrifice, *from the Latin, means "to make holy." R1 and I discussed the taking of life—the bloodiest and cruelest and perhaps the most necessary act visited upon man by man—from the little Jewish carpenter of Nazareth, to the never-ending bloodbath of war, to my illiterate bricklayer father, sacrificed in concrete to the Great God Job, to Aldo Moro, the synthetic savior of the Christian Democrats, the crucified politician, the modern plastic Christ . . .*

The killer of Aldo Moro will never be found . . . His mutual sacrificers will not permit it. —P.D.D.

ROME, MARCH 16, 1978

Aldo Moro, the Godfather of the ruling Christian Democrats, has espresso and pastry, shaves, dresses in a conservative suit, and listens to the cautionary counsel of his homely wife, Eleonora.

It is 8:30 A.M. The bell rings; the voice from the intercom at the street entrance is that of Marshal Oreste Leonardi, Moro's protecting shadow. Eleonora Moro tells him to come up with his boys for coffee. The ritual occurs every morning as though for the first time.

Hats in hand, the bodyguards enter. They wear civilian clothes. With the marshal are Domenico Ricci, the son of peasants and Moro's chauffeur for twenty years; young Giulio Rivera, from a Campobasso farm; chunky Raffaele Iozzino, a laborer's son; and Francesco Zizzi, also from a poor family. Zizzi is elated. It is his first day in the envious job; He is replacing Officer Gentiluomo, who has suddenly and inexplicably left Moro's employ (and who subsequently disappears). "My whole family lit candles to Our Lady of Fatima in gratitude for my being given the honor of guarding the precious life of the president of the Christian Democrat party," Zizzi babbles to Mrs. Moro.

*

In the Balduina section of Rome, four men of the Red Brigades (Brigate Rosse), wearing the blue hats, insignia, and uniforms of Alitalia pilots, pack machine guns in airline bags.

At 8:30 A.M. they are driven in a white Fiat 128, with a Diplomatic Corps license plate, toward Monte Mario, the Roman suburb where Moro lives. Simultaneously, from separate points of departure, three more Fiats, carrying seven men and a blonde, and a motorcyclist dressed as a policeman head for Monte Mario. The white Fiat stops at the curb on upper Via Mario Fani. The two men in front remain in the car. The four "pilots" casually walk one block to the intersection of Via Mario Fani and Via Stresa and stand chatting in front of a closed bar. The corner is a bus stop for Alitalia limousine service to Leonardo da Vinci airport. The three other cars and the "policeman" on his high-powered motorcycle park behind the white Fiat. Several other commandos, dressed as telephone workers, stand by to sabotage telephone lines.

Two housewives come out of the corner apartment building opposite the bus stop. One has a dog on a leash. They comment on the absence of a florist, Antonio Spiriticchio, and his wife. In any weather the two arrive in a van each morning to set up flowers on the sidewalk. Today is crisp and sunny. They should be here.

An old man on a balcony feeds and talks to his canaries. A police car filled with carabinieri races by, speeding dangerously for no reason, as usual. A few middle-aged professional men leave home.

The BR has worked on this operation for months. In Czechoslovakia they rehearsed the ambush to come with cars and dummies—each move laid out geometrically, pinpointed and timed. The night before, two of them had gone to Via Angelo Brunetti 38, where the florist Spiriticchio lives, and slashed the tires of his Ford van so that it wouldn't obstruct their shooting. (They planned to do a lot of it.)

Aldo Moro bids his wife and three of his four grown children *adio*. Eleonora goes about her chores.

The leader of the Christian Democrats leaves his house at Via del Forte Trionfale 79 and gets into his blue Fiat 130. Moro is a methodical man. People in the neighborhood are familiar with his habits and route. Each morning he stops to pray at the church of Santa Chiara, pauses at his favorite newsstand to buy the official organs of the six Italian political parties, and then goes on to government business. (On the night before, however, Moro had told Leonardi that, for safety's sake, they would use a new, devious way to get to the seat of government in the center of Rome. Then he phoned Leonardi and told him he'd decided to go along Via Mario Fani, as usual. The Red Brigades commandos were apprised of both changes. They also knew neither of Moro's cars was bulletproof.)

Domenico Ricci drives carefully. By his side is Marshal Leonardi; Aldo Moro is in the left rear seat. The official escort car, a white 130 Alfa Romeo "Alfetta" model, carrying Rivera. Zizzi, and Iozzino, follows.

Many aviation personnel live in Monte Mario. An airline employee, spotting the four Alitalia "pilots," stops his sports car and says he has room for two passengers. They thank him and say they'll wait for the Alitalia limousine, due shortly, because they want to stay together.

At the newsstand the vendor praises Moro for having shaped the new coalition—meaning Moro's "historic compromise" with Enrico Berlinguer and the Communists. This very morning a new government will be formed; forty-six elected officials, members of Moro's Christian Democrats and Berlinguer's *Partito Communisti Italiano* (PCI), will be selected.

The two Moro cars leave the newsstand at 8:55. Moro hates fast driving. He glances at *Paesa Sera*, the Communist paper, and *Il Messagero*, then reads about himself in *Il Giorno*. *Il Giorno* emphasizes the loyalty to Moro of Italian President Giovanni Leone, Prime Minister Giulio Andreotti, Senate President Amintore Fanfani, and Christian Democrat Secretary Benigno Zaccagnini. Moro has to smile. Fanfani is openly maneuvering for his job. They are all about as trustworthy as vampires.

At 9:00 Ricci drives by the landmark of Forte Trionfale; three minutes later he turns left on Via Mario Fani.

*

The commandos' white Fiat begins to trail the Moro cars. The other three BR cars follow it. Ahead, on the corner, the pilots unzip their bags and step into the street. A few yards from the intersection of Via Stresa and Via Fani, the white Fiat speeds up, passes Moro's car, swerves in front of it, and stops dead. Ricci jams on the brakes to avoid a collision, and the second Moro guard car bangs into him, shaking everyone slightly. Moro, engaged with the political news, pays little attention.

Before Moro's guards can react, the BR commandos open fire. The telephone lines are cut at the precise moment the shooting starts. The two men from the white Fiat and the pilots are blasting away from the front and street sides, the fake motorcycle cop and commandos from the other three cars from the rear. They fire hundreds of bullets, riddling each guard from head to waist. Only young Iozzino makes it out of the second Moro car, and the automatic-weapons fire nearly cuts him in half.

Moro, cringing, is spattered with the blood and brains of his guards. He is dragged from his car. In his fright he clings to his portfolio, as if it can save him, but in the street he drops it and begins crying: "Please let me go—what do you want of me?" The BR commandos abandon their white car, shove Moro into one of the others, then screech out of Via Fani, turning right at the corner, and roaring up Via Stresa. The motorcyclist brings up the rear.

The whole operation takes less than a minute.

The BR cars turn on Via Trionfale and race to Via Casale De Bustis. Two of the cars stop and transfer Moro to a waiting car. Then everyone goes in different directions.

Moro is held on the floor and drugged; taking him any distance is hazardous, despite the sabotaging of the telephone lines. The car containing Moro and two of the Alitalia "pilots," who have now ditched their hats and coats, slows down and pulls into the cavernous underground garage of a large apartment complex in Balduina, just ten minutes away. The garage attendants are BR, prepared to receive Moro.

There was an unnatural quiet in Via Fani. Then the residents came out to safely view the bodies. Young, fat Iozzino was sprawled in the gutter with outstretched arms, red openings in his groin, chest, arms, and face. A woman placed *Il Giorno* over him, but a breeze blew the sports section from his indifferent face. In the escort car, Zizzi and Rivera, painted with blood, looked like they'd been flung by the hand of God or the devil. In Moro's car Marshal Leonardi's head was pressed on driver Ricci's chest, and Ricci's bloody mouth was on Leonardi's forehead, as though kissing him.

Via Mario Fani became a Verdi opera: police, *carabinieri*, and the army came careening at breakneck speed, sirens screaming. Armed helicopters hovered, as though they could fight and destroy the Red Brigades at the scene of the crime. Then came Cardinal Poletti, vicar of Rome, reinforced by his monsignors and priests.

Eleonora Moro and her four children arrived. The poor woman went from corpse to corpse. She said to people: "I knew each. They were good boys. I would rather have wept the death of my husband than to see these so young dead."

Before RAI Telegiornale television cameras, the politicians came and held Eleonora's hands. They vowed fidelity and solidarity, love and prayers. They vowed all aid to redeem her kidnapped husband.

In his high voice, fascist Republican Ugo La Malfa said, "We are in a state of war. We need the death penalty returned!" Socialist Bettino Craxi brayed incomprehensibly. Prime Minister Andreotti, in his government building, vomited with excitement and had to change his clothes. Francesco Cossiga, minister of the interior and head of security, became hysterical. He called the Pentagon and the CIA, the *Bundeskriminalamt* specialists in Wiesbaden, Scotland Yard, the French Secret Service, the League of Private Detectives, and all departments of his police. He ordered thousands of *carabinieri, granatieri*, and *bersaglieri* from such distant places as Sicilia, Calabria, and Sardegna called out. "I want every telephone in Italy controlled!" he shouted.

The BR called the major newspapers, saying they had killed "Cossiga's leather-heads" and kidnapped Aldo Moro. But so did the Walter Alasia Column of Revolutionary Action, the Armed Proletarian Cells (NAP), the Group Action Partisans (GAP), and the Baader-Meinhof gang.

The little Sardinian duke and millionaire head of Italy's Communist party, "the father of Euro-Communism," Enrico Berlinguer, swore that it was all a plot by multinational conglomerates. According to "the cybernetics of probabilities," it was the "last psychological chess move of universal capitalism" that was subsidizing the "fake Communists" of the Red Brigades to commit atrocities in order to shock the good people of the world and turn them against his Italian Communist party.

The families of the guards came to Via Fani to identify the bodies. Detectives and reporter questioned residents. An old lady said a woman had been in command of the *Brigatisti*, a blonde who barked orders in German. The Secret Police received a call from a guttural female voice: "*Aldo mit uns!*" A man at a window said the leader had been a bearded fat man who shouted with a Milanese accent. A woman reported that she had photographed the ambush and turned the film over to the police, but it "disappeared." No two stories agreed.

The florist, Antonio Spiriticchio, and his wife were seized and given the third degree. A neighbor who had a grudge against him said Spiriticchio was a *Brigatista*. Another swore she'd taken her dog out at dawn to pee and had seen two men slashing the tires of Spiriticchio's Ford van. She'd called the police. They did not appear. Other neighbors spoke on the florist's behalf. Antonio Spiriticchio, then was treated as a hero. Mrs. Spiriticchio was even interviewed on television. She said she had seen the killings and the kidnapping of Aldo Moro and gave a stirring, detailed account—never mind that she was ten miles away, helping her husband remove the flat tires of the van, when the slaughter happened. Italians don't care whether a story is true or not so long as it is well told.

In his Turin prison, Renato Curcio, founder of the Red Brigades, and twelve other BR members under charges of "kneecapping" (shooting government officials and businessmen in the knees) and subversion, heard the news on the radio while in the exercise yard. They raised their fists, shouted revolutionary slogans, and sang "The Red Flag."

Pope Paul VI sent Eleonora Moro a telegram: "I desire to express my alarm and unity with you at the ambush that snatched your beloved consort and cut off the lives of five innocents . . ." Fanfani, Berlinguer, Zaccagnini, and the rest of Aldo's comrades and "friends to the end" called Eleonora in the night. Their messages were like that of the pope: saccharine hope and no commitment.

Eleonora talked with her children: Maria Fida, a journalist with the *Gazzetta del Mezzogiorno*; Anna, a pediatrician; Agnese, a librarian; and Giovanni, a law student. Each was a child of our time, an intellectual of the far left who had condemned the father's reactionary establishment. They spoke of the kidnapping in 1974 of the hated Genovese prosecutor, fascist Mario Sossi, in the BR's Operation Sunflower.

The BR had tried Sossi, sentenced him to death, and then said they would release him if certain BR prisoners were freed. Sossi and his wife implored the government to negotiate. It refused. So Sossi and his wife clamored to the newspapers that his fellow politicians had cynically signed his death warrant. The only moral government in Italy was the press. The BR in Genoa, having made their point and using the propaganda to gain sympathy with the people, released Sossi without condition after holding him for a month.

"But," said Eleonora, "the situation with Papa is different. Until now the BR has not killed anyone. With Papa, they went past the point of no return. Now they will go all the way. I had a chill from the ambiguous demeanor of Pope Paul and Zaccagnini and the others. They will stand, cowardly, on the mythical honor of church and state and become our mortal enemies."

It was Eleonora who had said in 1964: "To me the political world is inhuman. Within these walls [the Moro apartment] shall prevail only human sentiments!" Hard to believe, but Moro was forbidden to talk politics in his own home.

Security head Cossiga—who owed his career to Moro and claimed to love him with all his heart—overnight turned Italy into a police state. The police actually search the labyrinthine underground garage in the apartment building where the master cell held Aldo Moro, but their inspection was superficial. They chatted with the *Brigatisti* garage attendants, then cleared the place of suspicion. In a gesture of contempt, the BR drove back to within a block of the scene of the massacre on Via Fani and abandoned the three ambush cars.

MARCH 18

At noon the BR called Ezio Pasera, who is a reporter for *Il Messagero*.

"This is the Red Brigades."

"If you're the Red Brigades," said Pasera, "I'm Buffalo Bill."

But the caller was calm and serious: "In the underpassage between Largo Argentina and Via Arenual there is a booth with a Xerox machine. On top under a ream of paper is a yellow business envelope. In it you will find Communication Number One and a photo."

Pasaera hastened knowing that all press phones are tapped. He got there before the cops and found the envelope. The message was a declaration of war upon the system of "corrupt clowns" of the government and announced the beginning of a protracted trial of the prisoner before the so-called peoples' tribunal. Reactionaries subsequently said that the BR had already slain Moro and that the photo was a montage. But experts said it was an authentic Polaroid Moro with an open white shirt was seated before the big banner that said BRIGATE ROSSE, the BR emblem, a five-pointed star in a circle, was clearly visible. Moro had a querulous mocking, anticlimactic expression: lucid apprehension confronting grotesque destiny.

That afternoon saw the funeral of the guards in the church of San Lorenzo.

The Red Bridgades are referred to by the "Sbirri" and "Sgherri" the police and their agent provocateurs as the Bierre. The Italian phonetic pronounciation for the letters B and R. Italians like laconic labels and so the press and magazines always reduce "Brigate Rosse" to the simple "BR."

In its fledgling days the BR had no precise setup. But after two notable betrayals by alleged members Marco Pisetta and an unsavory ex-priest Silvano Girotto that led to the arrest of Renato Curico, the BR perfected an organic structure of autonomous cells. Each cell had three members. Six cells in a pyramid form a nucleus. The national pyramid is a foolproof construction of all the successive, autonomous pyramids. The BR is like a worm cut into many parts. It exists as separate entities. When police chance upon a cell, the captured don't know the whole BR operation and thus cannot betray it. The Sbirri *don't get blood from stones. So they content themselves with irrelevant units. For cosmetic reasons they falsify their findings.*

It is not easy to get into the BR. Leading members to include psychologist who critically evaluate prospective joiners. The traitors Pisetta and Girotto proved a lesson.

"Zucor"—not his real name—the director of the master cell in charge of the March 16 operation, received the president of the Christian Democrats with civility. The BR, Zucor told Moro, were not brigands like the bums kidnapping wealthy industrialists throughout the country. The BR was an as yet unrecognized political group at war with the "legitimate" régime. No matter what you called the régime, it was dominated as through the centuries, by family dynasties, landowners, corporations and foreigners—particularly American interests. Moro had to admit that, no? So Moro was not kidnapped for money; he was a political prisoner. Moro grunted at Zucor and asked if political prisoners needed to be trussed up like chickens.

The BR master-cell hideout in which Moro was to be held for the next fifty-four days had been a year in preparation. It was a soundproof dead-storage space in a huge, anonymous apartment building; entry was made through a false wall. It was stocked with enough provisions so that entries were minimal—once a day at most, at a prearranged hour that changed constantly. *Brigatisti* attendants working in the underground garage were on guard twenty-four hours. Zucor did not even chance an illegal telephone.

A doctor examined Moro. He was anemic and had a cyst of the thyroid and some degeneration of the left kidney. Otherwise, he wasn't too bad.

Italy is a small place. It turned out that Zucor and Moro were not strangers.

Zucor and Moro recalled meeting through the Communist writer, Carlo Levi. Moro had been minister of public education. Fanfani was president, and Angelo Roncalli had just become Pope John XXIII. Moro and Zucor, both attractive men (Zucor was a few years younger) had talked about their mistresses and then about the perpetual politics. Zuccor said he was a revolutionary: "When you were a young, compliant officer in the Fascist army, I was underground, hiding Communists and Jews and killing Blackshirts and Nazis." In 1970 he'd left the "corrupt Communists" and joined the Brigate Rosse, a younger, less "intellectual" group that purged itself regularly, and had come to believe in violence "when necessary."

Captor and prisoner now had graying hair. Moro looked at Zuccor and said, "Politics means life to me. It is my art, more a methodology than a system of ideas."

Zuccor said, "I had all the pleasures and a chain of infatuations, but I had an empathy for the deprived, and that became my sensuality. We are opposite parts, polarized forces but I feel for you and your family."

Moro watched Zuccor, who made a solemn ritual of cooking. The food was good, but Moro hardly ate and lost weight. He thought of his villa, "Three Geese," and little farm in Torrita Tiberina, where only recently Eleonora had planted fava beans, artichokes, tomatoes, peppers, greens, and herbs.

Eventually, Moro had the run of the confined space. He was given reading material, a television set, and a record player, but the sound on the latter two were fixed on low.

As time passed, Zucor and Moro developed a curious fraternity. Moro did not have to be pressured, just spoken to, He was not toyed wit. Zucor told him, "We are not your brutal Cossiga police. In your trial you will cooperate and give us the inner workings of the crimes your government has commited. If condemned to die, you may live, if exchanged for the BR prisoners in Turin. We would rather see you live. We expect you to help yourself and do hope you are saved by your friends."

Moro's trail was informal and grave. He thought of Raskolnikov and his affable prosecutor. There was nothing Zucor and his jury could tell him about himself. In thirty years of political juggling, the press had already caricatured him as the Levantine Clausewitz, the Latin Kerensky, the Trojan Horse of Clerical Marxism, the Pygmalion of Liberalism, the Machiavelli of Pasta Politics, the Theorist of Doubt, the Hamlet of Dialectics, the Last Bus for the Italian Bourgeoisie . . . Moro's irony asserted itself. He grinned at the avalanche: "You have presided at the councils that decided upon reactionary laws. You are responsible for the killings of striking workers in Scelba Modena, Reggio Emilia, Palermo, Catania, and many other places; and for the murder of Mara, Renato Curcio's wife, and the students Roberto Franceschi and Giorgiana Masi. You are guilty of involvement in countless scandals involving oil deals, coffee purchases, Lockheed, arms traffic. You've held every government post: therefore you're guilty of every crime."

The interrogation began, Moro's answers were recorded. His denials were futile. "Leone embezzled large sums, is it not so?" "No." "You lie!" "His wife, Vittoria, conducted sex orgies in the president's country mansion, 'Le Rughe,' is it not true?" "No!" "You lie!"

Moro was regularly inundated with radical literature: the publication "*Counterinformation*' and four books about the Red Brigades: *Criminalization of the Class Struggle, BR—Documents and Chronicles of the Red Brigades, Red Emergency and Never Again Without a Rifle!—Orgin of the BR*. He read about himself, the BR's analysis of the phrases of the Moro-esque style that was fashioned to "mesmerize the mediocre Senate": "linguistic modules sent into polictical orbit," "parallel convergence," "convergence of postures," "convergence of squared circles," "convergence of contrary rationales," "reciprocal comprehension of diverse fronts." Then there was that term so dear to him, *pluralismo*, used in combinations: "juridical pluralism," "practical and polemical pluralism." Moro had coined "interclassism," "centrism," "experimental caution," "operation without trauma," "fluid situational rapport," "angularity of confluent visions." In a circumstance beyond his control (the first time this had happened to him since as a student he'd learned the political poetry of duplicity), Moro was reading about another Aldo Moro. This one was the Father of Lies. He saw his words covered with flies.

At night in what he'd hoped would be merciful slumber, he began to dream of Eleonora and his children in the villa "Three Geese." But his wife was scowling, and the children were sneering. More and more often, he found himself in the realm of dormant phastasmagoria, wandering and conferring with grinning Zaccagnini and fawning Cossiga in the Palazzo Chigi, Montecitorio, the Viminale, the Department of Justice, or in Christian Democrat headquarters on the Piazza di Gesu. Moro dreamed of himself scheming without end: Malvolio, or as they called him in Naples and the south, '*Lenguanero*" (Black tongue).

He, Fanfani, Andreotti, and Cossiga in the name of democracy had struck laws more unjust that those of Il Duce. Moro had long felt the hate of the young but in recent years' hate seemed universal. Zucor and his jurors now reminded Moro of how indifferent the Italian masses were to his plight. He was far from a popular man. His kidnapping, like any other circus act, was welcomed as a diversion from the bleak boredom of life without work, money or dreams.

Moro and Zucor were both very Catholic, a fact overlooked by many commentators on the case including the shrill bitch journalist Oriana Fallaci. As Moro began to see how abandoned he was by politicians, religionists, and friends, he came to savor his imprisionment, the absence of power. Gradually, as he talked to Zucor and observed the BR, a curious romanticism, the basis of Moro's occult Catholicism, long buried, reasserted itself, perhaps reawakened by the stress that flooded him. According to Zucor, Moro seemed glad he was being punished . . .

At the BR's direction, Moro wrote letters in his scholarly, middle-class manner to each of his associates, trying to convince them that the peoples's court was serious, that the guerrillas of the Red Brigades were at war with the government, and that the international rules of warfare applied. An exchange of prisoners was necessary. He wrote nearly eighty letters. On the outside, people assumed he was being tortured and drugged.

Moro and the BR watched the news of their drama on Telegiornale. Automomous BR cells called in spurious leads, and the police raced madly through the streets and countryside to raid barns and cellars. They even searched congregations at Mass. The affair was made for television, and Moro began to see his life as a soap opera. Each day, following the exacting ordeal of his own trial, Moro watched the televised legal proceedings against Renato Curcio, Roberto Ognibene, and Alberto Franceschini, the chiefs of the BR. They were in chains, caged like birds in a Turin courtroom. Two of their lawyers, suave Guisa and falcon-faced Di Giovanni, questioned prospective jurors.

The process had been going on for a long time, since no one wanted to sit in judgement of the BR, Italian *Christiani* knew their Ecclesiastes: "A time to kill—a time to keep one's mouth shut."

Moro watched Cossiga, his former protégé, justify the Italian government's implacable stand against making any deal with the BR to save him. Cossiga, viewed by millions, mouthed a quote from the Catholic martyr Thomas More: "In our moral purpose we must proceed with utmost firmness not apparent to the public." Moro saw his iron-faced wife talking with the bizarrely attired, skinny old man of the Vatican, the absurd claimant to infallibility and intimacy with the Creator of the cosmos. Eleonora asked the pope for the deliverance of her husband. The pope broke wind on her burning heart; he bestowed pietist vaporings upon her. Moro, immersed in a fathomless moment of truth, reasoned: "The pope has a language difficulty—he does not know how to utter simple words: 'I, the spiritual guide of 700 million followers, can and will save Aldo Moro.'" And Moro saw Fanfani and Zaccagnini, protected by a small army, enter his home to warn his wife and children not to negotiate with the BR. He saw them then as false faces and the mirror of his soul told him that he too had been the master of masks.

Zucor told Moro that after a strategy of tension his life could be exchanged for the Turin comrades. However, in analyzing Moro's position, he minced no words. "You are an embarrassment now to church and state. Crucified, you may be of more use." This situation was exacerbated by Aniello Coppola's biography, *Moro*. It had been selling well before the kidnapping, and it brought to light the minutiae of thirty years of Mephisto manipulation of Italy—Italians called Italy, "*Italia Morotea*." Moro and his government had been mute about Vietnam, Chile, and the South America dictatorships manufactured in the White House. Worse, they had daily loused up Italy. In their weekly pre-Communion confessions, there was never the breath of *mea maxima culpa*.

At one point, Moro asked Zucor the significance of his being snatched on March 16. "Giangiacomo Feltrinelli [the GAP revolutionary] was murdered by your government and the CIA on the sixteenth," Zucor replied.

Feltrinelli and Zucor, very wealthy and of nobility, had long been friends. For a brief period Zucor and Feltrinelli had been playboys, sniffing coke with the industrial royalty. Zucor's father was a dilettante poet, and to their palazzo came Benedetto Croce and the towering thinkers and artists. By the time he was twelve, Zucor had read 2,000 books in his father's library. Zucor's mother wrote love stories under a pen name. To Zucor, she was queen of the universe. Zucor went to mass because his mother loved Christ. She died at ninety-five, a few months before the Via Fani venture. Zucor's space in the Moro hideout was hung with his mother's worn crucifixes and rosaries.

Brilliant Feltrinelli expanded his family's publishing house and founded an institute documenting the history of workers' movements. He joined the Communists, but uncompromising revolution was in his blood: in 1957 he broke with Palmiro Togliatti and the Italian Communist party, contending that it "pissed on the heads of the workers."

He visited Castro in the Sierra Maestra and went with Ché Guevara and Regis Debray to the jungles of Bolivia (where, ironically, only his fortune and status saved him). He later tracked down one of Ché's assassins, Roberto Quintanilla, in the Bolivian Consulate in Hamburg. The gun that killed Quintanilla was Feltrinelli's Colt Cobra.

The United States' military intervention in South America and Indochina convinced Feltrinelli that at any moment the CIA would turn Italy into another Chile. In Italy he went underground. Under many names he furnished seed money for various radical groups: the "Hammer and Sickles," "Italian Marxist-Leninist Party," "G.A.P.," "XXII Ottobre." In 1969 at the University of Trento and in the factories of Turin, Genoa, and Milan, through Feltrinelli, Zucor, Curcio, and Curcio's wife, Mara, the Brigate Rosse was born.

The soul and nucleus of the BR is now the imprisoned *Brigatisti*. Somehow they communicate with anonymous, sympathetic intellectuals, professional people, and workers, sending out guidelines to the molecular network of terrorism. Zucor spoke of articulation in "capillary circles" of "*simpatizzanti*"—adherents interconnected according to the sophisticated techniques of modern clandestine war. The BR has gone from minor to major bloody episodes relatively quickly. But the ruthless character of its attacks, Zucor points out, is in the great tradition of political killings in Italy—even the Jesuits claim the right to murder rulers who opposed "the will of God and the people." Power has its own logic.

Moro was the brains of the Catholic and dollar democratic hierarchy. "Go with the times and absord the adversary," said Moro, who had begun his career in Bari as a sycophant of the Catholic Fascist party. Systematically, the BR maintained, he'd brought the mundane methods of the Holy Roman Empire and the age of the degenerate popes to the modern Italian ruling class. Even now street cynics sneer: "The Holy Roman Empire can never die; if the BR wins, the Vatican will simply bless it."

MARCH 29

Moro's letter to Cossiga: "Caro Francesco . . ." After bourgeois amenities, he broaches the realism of a deal.

In the *Corriere della Sera*, Zaccagnini says, "Did the maximum leader and inspirer of Italian politics write it, or an Aldo Moro reduced to impotence in a vile prison, stunned by drugs and psychological brainwashing? . . . Surely the BR wrote the letter and forged his signature—or Moro has gone insane. The Christian Democrats extend their profound semtiments of moral and political solidarity . . . to Aldo Moro, but the government judges it unthinkable to have any dialogue with criminal enemies of the state."

In the Cossiga letter, Moro cited the agreement between Leonid Brezhnev and Augusto Pinochet for the exchange of renegade dissident Vladmir Bukowski and the Chilean Communist Leader Luis Corvalan. He also condemned the inflexible stand of Isreal and the Federal Republic of Germany for refusing to negotiate with the terrorist of the Black September group after their attack on the Isreali Olympic team.

On Easter, television crews focus long-distance lenses on the window of Moro's home, but they are curtained. Eleonora and the children have locked themselves away from the circus. Only steadfast friends come and go at Via Forte Trionfale 79. Nicolo Rana and Corrado Guerzoni maintain secret communications with the BR, negotiating for Moro's life. The police hound them.

MARCH 31

Moro's Christian Democrats formally abandon him. A statement is issued: "As long as the party stands firm against any negotiations, the killing of Moro will represent a spiritual victory for Italy and a definite defeat for the terrorists." Knowing that there are secret communications between the BR and the family, Attorney General De Matteo goes to the Moro home in order to grill Eleonora subtly. She considers him an enemy. Then the pope belches again: "The Church deplores Aldo Moro's predicament, but we do not despair; we pray."

Zaccagnini goes to Eleonora Moro and tries to persuade her that the honor and dignity of the state take prededence over her emotions. Eleonora all but throws him out.

APRIL 2

Now consciousness became Moro's nightmare. He often daydreamed. He was in a strange land, surrounded by menacing blacks; he couldn't find the police, and there was no way back to Eleonora.

Eleonora had often said that politicians were not human. He himself was not capable of compassion, only of the chess of statecraft. He rarely saw his family. Once, Eleonora found a love letter in his coat. From then on she went no more to the beauty shop, nor used cosmetics, nor bought dresses. She mourned his infidelity and linked it to his indifference to the fate of the victims of the powerful.

In some ways "Anna"—that is not her real name—the one female member of Zucor's cell (who wore the blonde wig at Via Fani) reminded Moro of Eleonora. She had her strength. Anna was part of the Trento University political larva of 1967-69 that evolved from the dialectial "*Universita Negativa*" into the BR. Anna had been Margharita ("Mara") Cagol's bridesmaid when she married Renato Curcio. Anna, Mara,

Curcio, Mauro Rostagno, and the German student leader Peter Schneider were the prenatal BR.

Anna had no illusions about a Castro-type victory. She had written, "This is our prerevolutionary moment. Italy's situation is not similar to the experience of the Russians, Chinese, or Cubans. We must adjust to a long period of bloody struggle. We must not be . . . intellectual voyeurs . . . who sit on the sidelines and 'interpret.' The capitalist enemy kills, as they killed my father in the police-provoked Milan riot of December 12, 1969. Either we kill them or they kill us."

By accident, Anna happened not to be with Mara when Mara was trapped and shot to death by the police. Anna could have passed for Mara Cagol Curcio: small, frail, soft spoken. But it was Anna who gave Renato Curcio his nickname, "Pippo," because of his big nose.

During Moro's trail, Anna brought the evidence of the charges, along with photos and films of police terrorism. She presented "proof" of government frauds, of its liaisons with the Mafia and the Vatican to "keep Italy feudal." She made Moro feel very old.

Once, feverishly, he dared whisper to Anna that if she would help him, he'd give his word to exempt her from prosecution "*Your Word*! As valueless as government treaties with Indians! As valueless as summit conferences with the unconscious! We will not hesitate to tear your word to shreds! Write your confession! Cough up your identity and restore the magical balance of memory and desire!" She actually spat at Moro.

They brought much—too much—against him. He no longer answered at all. He became as ingenuous as Prince Myshkin the *The Idiot*.

APRIL 10

Moro told Zucor he had a premonition of death. President Leone had cynically named his water spaniel "Moro."

APRIL 15

The editor of *La Republica* receives a phone call: Communication Number Six is in a certain garbage can on Via dell'Annunciata. It begins: "*L'interrogatrio al prigioniero Aldo Moro è terminato,*" and ends, "*Non ci sono dubbi. ALDO MORO È COLPEVOLE E VIENE PERTANTO CONDANNATO A MORTE.*" Moro's trial is completed. He is guilty beyond doubt and forthwith condemned to die.

Charity Italy, Amnesty International, and Kurt Waldheim of the United Nations immediately offer to mediate. The Italian government refuses. A clown sends an alleged BR message: Moro committed suicide; his body can be found in Lake Duchessa, high in the Abruzzi Mountains. The government doesn't hesitate to spend lavishly on a search operation that could relieve it of its Moro problem.

Moro's son, Giovanni, however, secretly in touch with the BR, knows his father is alive. He organizes a petition of antipapal prelates for an appeal to the government. It is ignored.

Choosing to believe him dead, Moro's comrades in government feel the relief of catharsis; they quickly begin their felonious chatter: "hero of the nation with grandiosity of soul," "genius of conciliation," "Aldo lives on in our breasts!" Via Mario Fani has its name changed to Via Martyr of March 16.

APRIL 19

A corpse is found under the ice of Lake Duchessa, but it is that of a local man. The disappointment in Roman power circles is palpable.

The BR strikes all over Italy, knee-capping—"turning powerful reactionaries into lame horses." They chill Lorenzo Cotugno, the sadistic warden of Curcio's prison.

APRIL 20

Communication Number Seven: Moro's death sentence can be

commuted if BR prisoners are freed. The government is allowed forty-eight hours. To erase any doubts about Moro's being alive, the BR calls the editor of *Il Messagero*. Nearby, on Via Tritone, is an envelope with a photo. In it Moro has a tranquil expression. Behind him is the Brigate Rosse banner; propped in front of him is *La Republica* with the headline HAS MORO BEEN KILLED?

The BR sends zerox copies of eight pages written by Moro to cities throughout Italy. Moro insists on the government's making a deal. He has departed from his old schoolteacher grammar; his words are anguished and plain: "You—Zaccagnini, Andreotti, Fanfani, Berlinguer, Leone, and Cossiga—are all guilty along with me and must rise to the manliness of sharing my fate. I am here for all of you, and should you not agree to the prisoner exchange, I shall hold you and the government as my murderers. Aldo Moro."

APRIL 21

The pope addresses an appeal to the BR: "I write you, men of the Red Brigades, and pray of thee on bended knees to restore to the common brotherhood of man our faithful son of the Church of Christ, the Honorable Aldo Moro, without conditions. Paul VI." But the following day, from his balcony, the pope squeals harshly of Moro's keepers. This does not help the Moro family's efforts. However, the BR does not act upon its deadline. The government leaders seem smug. Berlinguer, not to be outdone, pulls out all the stops. He shrieks against "the assassins of the Brigate Rosse." Berlinguer is particularly offended that the BR are calling themselves "the true Communists."

APRIL 22

The Bishop of Ivrea, Luigi Bettazzi, working with the Moro family, offers his life as hostage to the BR. The pope indignantly squelches the bishop's involvement. But the bishop defies the pope; he and anonymous rich friends raise $10 million ransom and pledge an additional $20 million. Church and state negate the attempt as an act demeaning to the government's inviolable stance. A statement is issued: "With the saving of Moro, the lawless BR will kill and kidnap continually."

The BR turn down the ransom offer. They are not interested in money. They want the recognition of political status.

A group of impotent actors, buffoon directors, narcissistic writers, and discarded celebrities, such as Federico Fellini, Eugenio Montale, Sergio Amidei, and Alberto Moravia, sign an anti-BR sermon. The Communist Bernardo Bertolucci keeps his mouth shut.

APRIL 24

Communication Number Eight: Thirteen prisoners are to be freed, including Brigatisti, Nappisti, and members of the October Twenty-second Group— "the flower of flowers of terrorism." If not, Moro dies.

Minister Marco Pannella wants the situation debated in Parliament. Cabinet President Pietro Ingrao says no. Ingrao takes his orders from Fanfani and Berlinguer.

APRIL 25

Moro's third letter to Zaccagnini: "Zac . . . we are at the moment of my slaughter. The DC must depart from its attachment to mythomania, admit to reality, and accept the conditions of the Brigate Rosse . . . I do not accept the inequity and ingratitude and the atrocious death sentence visited upon me by the Christian Democrat party, which is not the people but you, my friends of thirty years—and, as I see now . . . little men who will have to account to my family, the nation, history, and God for your participation in my murder . . . for what you have committed against us. I demand that no State authorities or men of the DC desecrate my funeral with their presence. I wish my corpse to be attended only by the few who in God's eyes were good and true to me . . . Aldo Moro."

As answer, church and state make imaginative gestures to show the people that they are aiding Aldo and Eleonora. The pope has a helicopter containing a beautiful statue of Our Lady of Fatima and a priest saying a Salvation Mass hover over Moro's home; the Air Force has six jets paint the red, white, and green Italian flag in the skies over the Via Martyr.

In Torrita Tiberina the white-haired pastor, Agostino Mancini, Moro's confessor, speaks sadly over Marlboros and wine: "In the twenty-five years that I confessed the Honorable Aldo Moro, God and I heard things about government that would make your hair stand on end. Signora Eleonora begged him to retire from what she called the inhumanity of his pursuit, but he had given his soul as bail to the state he designed. The common people unanimously say that Moro will be immolated by the fad of Italian democracy. I will not comment on the pontiff—he is not Pope John . . . but the BR prisoners could be released. Panama has offered them sanctuary, and after Moro is home, the government could do like Israelis and West Germans: track them down and 'justice' them. Poor Moro. He has not even picked out a tomb . . ."

APRIL 26

Privately, Socialist Craxi speaks of an "autonomous initiative" bargain with the BR. Zaccagnini goes crazy: "What the hell do you mean by 'autonomous initiative'?" Craxi suggests one or two prisoners be allowed to dig a tunnel and escape; then let others out on the pretended grounds of endangered health. The plan leaks to the papers. There is a furor among the fascists. Craxi modifies his plan: suspend a few sentences and give paroles; also, reform the Dark Ages prison conditions. The Communist party thunders no!

APRIL 27

Moro's personal secretary, Nicolo Rana, family friends Corrado Guerzoni and Sereno Freata, and Eleonora and the children come up with a scheme: BR prisoners could be transferred from the Turin jail to a provincial prison no more secure than a chicken coop; BR commandos could raid the prison and free the comrades, with the blame placed on the rural authorities. Moro is released, everybody is happy, and the government's face is saved.

Zaccagnini and his boys fiercely reject the idea. Eleonora appeals to Paul VI, but the pope clasps his ringed hands deploringly and shakes his head.

APRIL 28

Moro has never watched so much television. Along with 25 million other TV fans, he sees a series, "Madame Bovary." He discusses is with Zucor and his keepers.

APRIL 30

Il Messagero publishes another Moro message. As president of the DC, he wants a convocation of the National Council. "I want the impossible done to save my life! The Socialists have shown more humanity . . . I wish Misasi to preside in my place.

"My social views and the dialectics and ideals of the BR have hardly anything in common, but all my public life I have retained as humanely feasible the merciful exchange of prisoners of war. The Christian Democrats have judged that Aldo Moro must die." Moro repeats that he does not want the men of power, not even the pope, at his funeral. Then: "I see that my party wants my destruction—assumes that I am writing under the dictation of the BR. Why do you lie? . . ."

MAY 1

A satyricon begins: The Italian soccer team is eliminated from World Cup competition. Television shows the result of the defeat. All over Italy, there is rage, depression, drinking.

Zaccagnini, whose hobby is the study of Nostradamus, announces that Nostradamus prophesied the Moro ambush. This seems to comfort Zaccagnini.

The Society of Jesuits accuses DIGOS—the secret service—of effeminate weakness and muddling. Fascist Republicans Massimo De Carolis and La Malfa vow that there is undeniable collusion between the police and the BR.

MAY 2

Magistrate Mario Daniele of Milan proposes that in exchange for Moro, the government commute the sentences of all BR prisoners to a maximum of two years. Zaccagnini, no doubt thinking of Nostradamus, thunders "No!" again.

Yasssir Arafat defines the BR terrorism as "military operations."

Idi Amin Dada, over Radio Kampala in Uganda, says he will convince the BR to release Moro, since he believes, along with Jimmy Carter, in upholding human rights.

President Carter's representative, Joe Califano, who doesn't know his ass from a hole in the ground in Italy, applauds Zaccagnini's no.

Russia's *Pravda* calls the Brigate Rosse "Red Bandits" and bad-mouths Socialist Craxi for trying to save Moro.

An American novelist describes for an Italian magazine a *Sgherri* headquarters in Trastevere: ". . . in their bare rooms they wile away the time like cretins, playing with ball of paper, making airplanes, practicing fast draws like heroes in American cop movies, holding masturbation contests."

The Communist saint, Enrico Berlinguer, informs on "extreme leftists" who have left his party "to most likely ally themselves with the clandestine political terrorists!"

MAY 5

The ninth and final BR communication arrives: "The action initiated

March 16 is properly now reaching its climax with the fulfillment of the sentence to which Aldo Moro was condemned . . . The Moro battle is the first of many. This is only the beginning."

MAY 6

Eleonora receives a call: "This is the BR. You have a few hours left in which to save your husband. Aldo Moro, the father of your children."

The phone is tapped by Cossiga's police, but the message is just code anyway: deciphered, it means that a note from Aldo awaits. The daughter, Anna, leaves the house. Anna takes buss 446 to Ponte Milvio. She bides her turn patiently at a phone booth, enters, does not make a call, finds a letter in one of the directories, returns home by bus.

"Dearest Norina, This is it . . . they have told me that in a little while they are going to kill me. The DC and the government, had they wanted, could easily have saved me. This is the end. I am to die very soon. I kiss you for the last time. Kiss the children for me."

Eleonora immediately gives the letter to all the papers. They publish special editions.

The arch-reactionaries in the DC severely criticize Moro's farewell missive and pressure the pope to tell Moro that it's God's will for him to die and that he should face death happily, as have many Catholics before him.

Most government leaders have left Rome on their election campaigns.

The populace are fixed to their television sets as usual, watching an Agatha Christie murder mystery. The Aldo Moro show is getting boring.

The DC sends the unctuous paunch, Fanfani, to Eleonora, and Paul VI sends Cardinal Poletti. She is to resign herself to the martyrdom of her man for the ineffable glory of The Law and Jesus Christ. Eleonora Chiavarelli Moro, erudite daughter of a physician, Montessorian teacher, finally explodes with truths. In her rage, she calls the pope and the politicians charlatans, pederasts, whores, and cowards. They are traitors, who are soon to be stained with the blood of Aldo Moro so that Italy won't lose face before the rotten superpowers and stinking multinational corporations. In her wrath she curses man-made church and state and smashes a large vase filled with flowers against the wall near Cardinal Poletti and Fanfani.

The Christian Democrats had preferred Moro as a martyr prior to the regional and national elections. They had calculated that the shocked public would react emotionally for law and order, increasing the power of the DC and diminishing notably, if not disastrously, the standings that the radical parties had. Indeed, they were right. In the subsequent election, the DC picked up 8 percent of the national vote, raising its share to 46. The Communists, to Berlinguer's chargin, dropped down to 30 percent.

MAY 8

A BR source in police intelligence reports that a German criminologist has correctly deduced the area of the Moro hideout. At night the master cell vacates. Moro is taken in a van to a temporary hideout near the sea. It's an area of summer homes for the rich, relatively uninhabited until June, an hour from Rome.

MAY 9

Zucor tells Moro that this is it.

Moro admits that he is tired. He has been thinking of a message, sent by Eleonora. "You have been abandoned by the Church and man. Only Aldo Moro can help you now . . ." Moro thinks of defecting, then rejects the idea. "I'd look bad in khaki," he tells Zucor.

He doesn't eat his last meal. He refuses sedation. He just wants to pray; he has no other desire.

A priest is sent for, a young radical who will never inform. He is brought in a closed van, then blindfolded from the van to Moro's room. Moro softly confesses his sins, but his Act of Contrition is fervent. The young priest celebrates Mass and gives Moro the last sacraments. The priest weeps.

For collation Moro has a cup of water. Anna gives him a haircut. He showers and brushes his teeth, but he doesn't bother to shave. He dresses in the clothes he wore when kidnapped. He puts on his socks of midnight blue (which, he does not notice, are inside out), the white shirt with blue stripes made by La Ninarelli in Bologna, suspenders, the beige Swiss sweater, the carefully knotted tie with tiny, white designs, the dark blue suit, flexible shoes called "*mocassini*." He puts his scapulars, rosary as well as some medals of saints in his pockets.

Zucor tells him, "You will go now with Anna and Franco." Anna wears a red wig this time. Moro meekly follows them out of the house and along a driveway to a red Renault 4 station wagon. Zucor says: "Please get in and lie down." Aldo Moro obeys. The space in the back is so cramped that he has to fold his legs under him.

Zucor gives the following orders to Anna and Franco: "Park and lock the car on Via Caetani, in the ancient Jewish ghetto between Moro's Christian Democrats and the building of Berlinguer's Communists. Walk slowly away with your weapons in the shopping bag."

Franco drives, while Anna covers Moro from the front seat. The Renault, with stolen license "Roma N57686," is passed by a few cars and trucks on the highway by the sea. It turns onto an isolated, sandy road. No one says anything.

Franco and Anna get out. He holds a 9mm pistol; she, a scorpion machine pistol. Both are fitted with silencers. They lift the station wagon's rear door and fix the latch. Moro looks at them. To die in such a shabby way . . .

Eleven bullets slam through Moro's chest, leaving a path of punctures. They wrap him in a large sheet of orange-colored plastic and place him on a heavy, soiled overcoat. They put their guns in a STANDA store bag and drive back on to the highway toward Rome.

Not one bullet touched Aldo Moro's heart. It took him from five to ten minutes to bleed to death.

Tropic Of Cuba

At a table in Havana's Floridita bar, I sat with Hemingway. His companion was a mannishly dressed blonde with a magazine figure and a neoclassic but hard face. She would have looked just right astride a jumper.

Hemingway resembled an altered, jowly, tomcat with mouse clenched between teeth. From the massive, swarthy guy came a small high pitched peacock's voice. We exchanged amenities while instinctively not talking to each other.

A little beggar girl, leading her blind grandfather, came in to sell white roses. When she approached Hemingway, he shrugged and said, "Tiny daughter, I have no money for bread."

Tears of pity came into her eyes. She pinned her best flower on his lapel and said. "I give you this Maddona rose as a gift. You'll see; it will bring you good luck!"

Hemingway put a large bill in her hand and kissed her.

The waiter, who brought us platters of miniature ocean-salt oysters, addressed Hemingway as Don Ernesto.

Hoppy, the grinning, opium doped Chinaman, sold Hemingway paper cones filled with peanuts. Hemingway and Hoppy were old friends. They rattled away laughingly in a code that escaped me. It struck me that Hemingway was inordinately fond of his inferiors.

With my background of paisano blasphemy and years as a construction worker profanity had always been at home, like good bread, in my mouth. But Hemingway's scatological language was repellent to me and exceeded any verbal obscenity I was capable of.

He bored me with talk of big game, fish, boxing, and bulls. In my turn, I expanded upon the fine art of girl hunting and the incomparble joys of all love making positions.

Hemingway was annoyed and said my skull was crammed with cunts. I told him that if he thought it was all in my head, he should come along with me to a whorehouse and find out which of us was the better man.

Writers should be read and not heard or seen. To me Hemingway in person was the usual miserable disappointment. His thin voice was unpleasant and his piggish red veined eyes behind spectacles irritating. He expected me to be some kind of hulking wop; he said to the inperturbable blonde, "This cunt lapper ain't so tough."

I come from the sacred soil and sea and sun of volcanoes and slopes of the ovile and the vine dear to the human pagan gods; I come from the most aristocratic and accomplished people in history, the Romans, capable of the greatest good and evil, vice and virtue; and it is in our blood to read the reality of a person; to immediately and instinctively see the caricatures that most people are; to measure characters, to mentally go into entrails and sense and smell the many-faceted truth. So I said to him, "You're right, I adore tongueing cunt; and I'm right in saying you're a phony." And then the words went flying.

I said he was full of shit and he said his shit was better than anyone else's shit. According to him he was the champ of writing and of this and of that. "To me he was his mother with a mustache and hopelessly imbedded was his father's hysteria; and I felt his type was comfortable only with lesbians." He said I was a flash in the pan and could never discipline myself as a professional author; and what was funny was that he, a convert to Catholicism, called me a false Catholic. I got drunker and drunker and more specific. Yes, he had written some short masterpieces as an unknown hungry youth; but as far as I was concerned the rest of the stuff was posturing tour de force; THE SUN ALSO RISES was more of a travelogue and bill of fare than a novel, and FAREWELL TO ARMS mannered rhythm was suitable as moronic articulation: I told Hemingway, "The woman of your tales have rough hairy balls, and your one-dimensional men are 'Method' actor-grunters from lamenting play-it-safe social-injustice-deploring Fakir Steinbeck's OF MICE . . .

He said, "Writers try to imitate me, but every word I put down is gold on the market and the sale is the only decision that counts—Papa is King, you wop cunt-eater."

Our drinking reduced the observations, and epithets to the absurdity of truth. It is not that I was jealous of his success, for I would gladly and humbly kiss the feet of Sophocles, Homer, Virgil, Dante, the authors of certain parts of the Bible, Shakespeare, Whitman, Pirandello, Lorca and James Agee—But, Christ in concrete the bullshit that has been thrown about Hemingway!—oh the bullshit of the publisher and magazines and newspapers and movies and the bullshit of reviewers and self-appointed sacrosanct mumbling incomprehensible lecturing critics; and all the bullshit spells jobs, position, prestige, narcissism, which means Money which equals security, front, plenty of young cunts, gourmet food and drink, leisure, travel which means Success which means Fun-life all smiles no tears. Oh the bullshit Hemingway image of the Hollywood U.S.A. hero, the invincible stoic jerk American lout; the buddy-buddy speaking-out-of-the-side-of-his-mouth melting-pot mongrel sports buff, the dooming uncultured modern barbarian.

I told him Spaniards and Latins laughed at his pidgen Spanish stories. "Spaniards tolerated him as an overgrown boy, an artsy-fartsy graceless intruder upon the Spanish scene." One winging line of Lorca's puts the Hemingway Iberian pretentions to shame.

The blonde left without my noticing. Then we goodhumoredly shouted "You cocksucker!" at each other, shocking listeners.

The bastard had never really been a combat soldier. And what chance has a fish got against a man in a big boat? And how can any wild animal in the jungle win against native beaters and portable cannon? I had read somewhere that fat little Morley Callaghan had knocked him on his ass in Paris. In my alcoholic haze I said something like, "You yellow cocksucker—about your heroism and masculinity methinks thou dost protest too much. You write because you want to convince yourself and the world that you are a man—I write because I am Ishmael, a guy at war with a rotten fuckin' society. You've made yourself a legend and a fortune . . . by whistling in the dark . . ."

He punched me in the shoulder, sending me to the floor. He grinned and in that voice of fingernails scratching slate said, "A guy who jerks his mouth off like you can't be all bad. You got the juice, kid; but will you know what to do with it? Now listen to Papa about bullshit—bullshit makes the world go 'round—bullshit is as necessary and strong as the invisible gravitational forces that keep the planets pegged in space—the bullshit of the witch-doctor, the Pope, the Evangelist, rabbi, headshrinker, President, all politicians, artists, advertisers, and even Eternity is the bullshit of nothing—nada."

I saw Hemingway a few more times. He was staying at the Ambos Mundos, a hotel for Cubans. The sign of the Ambos Mundos was two globes of the world. It was traditional to gamble for the drinks at the Ambos Mundos bar. We threw four dice from a leather cup with the barkeep for double or nothing. The dice always came out right for Hemingway. I couldn't keep up with the hairy, big guy in drinking. I'm a menace when I've had too much. After a flock of drinks, I got drunk and critical. Anyway, Hemingway liked to egg a guy on.

My Havana pal and generous self-appointed host was Vito, the melonheaded Neapolitan New Yorker who was the produce monopolist of Cuba. Like the Cuban wags, he called the vagina *fruta bomba*. He would lecture me against the bonds of matrimony.

"I manured myself with three wives. No more wives! Pete, the dollar buys all the *fruta bomba* you want. If you get married, I don't want to know you!"

I was in his office overlooking the *malecón*, the mall. He was on the phone, ordering a shipload of tomatoes and pineapples to be dumped at sea because the A&P company would not pay the price he demanded.

Business over, he said, "Time for sport. You're coming to my favorite whorehouse, I phoned Prudencia, the *madre superior*. She read your book in Spanish."

With Vito's Rolls-Royce, we picked up Luis, society doctor, Juan, the world's sugar king, and the Harvard-educated playboy, Esteban.

Prudencia's *residencia de reunión* was a palace. A liveried servant showed us into the salon, which was splendid with rare paintings and coats of mail.

Madama Prudencia was an illustrious lady with a fine figure and the chaste mien of youthful abbess. When I kissed her hand, she said graciously, "Welcome to the *dulce vida de Cuba*."

The five girls *Madama* had arranged for us arrived.

She whispered proudly, "These girls are pristine, pure and virginal as diamonds. This is their first assignment in my establishment."

The nymphets carried school-books. I remember their names: Juanilla, Belita, Magdalena, Chuchita and María de Jesús. They were from upper-class families.

We were served a gourmet lunch and wines. I chose María de Jesús. She was small and thin, a sexy wisp with a rat-faced attraction. Maria said she was 16. She looked 12. Esteban told bawdy stories. The girls giggled and shrieked, In the grandiose salon, *Madama* showed pornographic color films accompanied by a Brahms recording. We danced with our girls and fondled them. *Madama* escorted each pair of us to a dreamlike bedroom. I felt her hips and whispered that I preferred her to the kid. She invited me to return later and spend the night with her. *Madama* told me to do anything and everything except actual entry with María de Jesús.

The vaginal halo is peculiar to Latins, sacrosanct virginity being a physiological dowry, the husband's inalienable right to consummate his betroth's mysterious hymen. Consequently, the virginal Latin girl must imaginatively resort to lingual, digital and anal delights.

Dallying with the naked nymphet brought me twinges of conscience. I could visualize her at the altar in the symbolic white of purity, dropping her eyes modestly as her husband slipped the wedding ring onto her finger. Her experiences at *Madama* Prudencia's would be discreetly forgotten, or perhaps vividly recalled. But other little girls would come to the *residencia de reunión* to accommodate rich men. It is not what is done. It is how it is done.

That night I was in bed with *Madama* Prudencia. We also talked. She and her brother Ramón fought on the side of the Loyalists. Her other brother, Rodrigo, was an ardent Franco officer. Her parents' hearts torn. Ramón was captured by Franco soldiers. Rodrigo watched the execution of his brother and of the poet Lorca. The sight drove him out of his mind. He hanged himself.

When Franco came into absolute power with the aid of the Fascist and Nazi armies, Prudencia gathered her wealth and fled to Cuba. She said, "You can see for yourself that the great United States is represented here by greedy businessmen, gangsters and perverts. America should offer Cuba statehood. But she is too blind to do it. The heaven of the rich will end in Cuba. There will be revolution and civil war, followed by a Communist society."

"What will happen to your establishment?"

"Nature will prevail. Aging men, whether capitalist or Communist, want little girls for sex."

I pleased her. She said with dignity, "Marry me. I will share my fortune with you. I will provide you with all the girls you desire." I often felt I made a mistake by not accepting her proposition. I could have avoided many hells. But the only thing constant about me is my God-given compulsive promiscuity.

Each morning when I awoke and the sea air and sun greeted me at my Nacional Hotel tenth-floor window, I looked forward to the adventure of another girl. There was, is and never will be anything better in the world than a swift passion with a lovely new girl.

The magnet of Havana's night life was the Nacional gambling casino. Natasha, the Broadway singing star of the floor-show, was my current. One night, sugar-king Juan took a shine to Helene, a doll in the chorus. He had the waiter bring her to our table. Juan said he wanted her to go to bed with him. She refused. He placed ten one-thousand-dollar bills before her. She looked hungrily at the money. I thought she was a foolish girl, and later tried to make her. She said the reason she had to reject Juan's fabulous deal was that she was painfully ill with a bad dose of gonorrhea given to her by a jerk Cuban musician in the band.

Pleasure had become routine. At night it was the Nacional casino and my girl, Natasha, on stage, reaching out her arms to me and throatily singing *Smoke Gets in Your Eyes*. We would leave at three A.M. with a group of the rich and world famous for the carnival park, Los Fritos, watch the drugged voodoo dancers, stop in at the waterfront fish-fry dives on the *malecón* and banter with the wise white and black whores, or go to peep shows and view the professional orgies of Lesbian and fag circuses, and end up past dawn in the lobby of the

Nacional Hotel drinking chilled Tropicale beer. Then upstairs to bed with Natasha and not arising until the afternoon.

Natasha was getting bourgeois. She annoyed me about having to find positive direction in life, ethics, fidelity, true love; she spoke about divorcing her husband and gave me that stuff about "Marry me or lose me."

I discussed this danger with Vito and Juan. Juan owned most of Camagüey. He wanted me to go to his vast estate and write a historical novel glorifying his Spanish ancestors who had settled there after Columbus voyages, their massacre of the natives, slave traffic and the founding of the family sugar empire.

"When I get there," he said, "I'll take you 'Red hunting.' Any bastard peon that complains about conditions—we make them run, give them a start; then we track them, flush them and shoot them down like dirty dogs. No sir; we don't stand for any Communist shit!"

When I was alone with Vito, he said haughtily, "Me and you; we're Americans. You ain't gonner be the guest of a goddam spick. You go to my Isle of Pines Planatation, Casa del Río, and take it easy. Buddy, you're getting too much *fruta bomba*. You'll burn yourself out. I'll have my pilot fly you there."

"I've never been in a plane. I don't want to fly."

"Ok, take the boat from Batabanó. My caretaker, Johannes, will meet you at the Nueva Gerona dock on the Isle of Pines."

It took hours for the bumpy, chlorine-smelling train to get to Batabanó. On the way, we passed an insane asylum with nightmarish drawings on the walls.

Batabanó was the port of the sponge and coral fishers. There was a fleet of their gaily painted shallow-draft sailing boats, most of them named after saints.

It was an overnight voyage in a small tired steamer to the Isle of Pines.

Vito's caretaker, Johannes, a grizzly, jaundiced German, met me at the Nueva Gerona dock. In the Ford station wagon, we drove the ten miles over the red-clay washboard roads to the plantation. On the way, I made resolutions: Isolate myself. Stop sleeping with women. Commune only with pencil, paper and typewriter. Hemingway in a better moment had said, "Pete, you got the writing 'juice.'" I was going to put my juice into writing and not girls. No more wasting.

Casa del Río was a wonderland of brilliant foliage, tropical trees, fruit and citrus orchards, pastures and the thatch-roofed *bohios* of the peons. My quarters were in the U-shaped Spanish mansion. Johannes unpacked my bags and said, "Mr. Vito gave me instructions that you were to be the boss here and have anything you want. Anything, positively."

I sat at a desk with sheets of paper. I got up, paced and squirmed. I didn't have a cause, an idea. Finally, I typed, "I don't want to write or worry or fight for anything. To hell with responsibility. All I want are women and fun. Period."

By late afternoon I had had enough of my own company. An edifying book has no breast and a typewriter no girl's thigh. I wasn't Onan. Nor could I conjure a woman from my ribs. Myself gnawed me. It was not before or after, but the fleshy moment that counted. I went to Johannes' *bohio* told him I'd have dinner with him. He was embarrassed. A master should be a master. I told him that writers were a classless breed who became the same as the people they were with. Vito's liquour cellar was under the *bohio*. I had Johannes bring up bottles of champagne.

"I can't drink alone," I said. "You've got to drink with me."

"Sir, I do what Mr. Vito's guest says. Absolutely."

He asked me what I wished for dinner. I told him to surprise me. He suggested marinated iguana, jellied black parrots, pheasant, wild rice, fried bananas and coconut ice cream. I agreed. He went to the doorway and shouted, "Liz! Liz!, come here, you jungle bitch!"

A tall, svelte, dreamy young Negress appeared. He gave her orders for the dinner. I had never been with a black girl. My desire for her was instantaneous, like a volcano erupting.

Johannes and I sat at the kitchen table. The champagne made him talk about himself.

Thirty years before, he had been an immigrant weaver in a Massachusetts mill. When he came home unexpectedly and found his wife in bed with his best friend, the Lutheran minister, he walked to Boston and boarded the first freighter he saw. The ship's destination was the Isle of Pines. He went to work for Vito and never set foot off the island.

Liz came in with a brace of pheasants. I could not take my eyes from her as she tended the charcoal stove, prepared the birds and moved sensuously about.

"Johannes," I said, "I want sweet Liz to drink and eat with us." He was startled. She looked at him questioningly. I poured her champagne. She did not accept the goblet as I held it out to her.

Johannes barked, "Don't stand there like an ape bitch! Obey the gentleman! Drink with Mr. Vito's honorable guest and drink jolly, by Christ!"

Night fell. After Liz put the strange dinner on the table, I had her sit by my side. Her nearness had me in a spiraling knot. I was drawn to her uppointing breasts, perfect ears, hands, and tight round black knees close to mine. I caressed her knees under the table. I barely touched my dinner. Liz was the food I wanted. My plan was to get us all drunk and then take Liz to my bed. I had Johannes open bottle upon bottle of champagne. Liz stood up and leaned over to clear the table. I could not resist running my hand up under her dress along the hard smooth thighs and firm, curved, polished magical buttocks.

Johannes watched me intently. Suddenly he asked, "Sir you like Liz?"

"Of course—she's wonderful!"

"Sir, you thinking of sleeping with Liz?"

"Why not—that would be great!"

Through my champagne haze, I saw him peering at me weirdly. He blurted, "Mister! Liz is my wife!"

I struggled to sober up and distinguish our positions.

"Now goddamnit, Johannes, why didn't you tell me in the beginning that Liz is your wife? I wouldn't touch another man's woman, but I'm no mind reader, godddamnit!"

"I thought a gentleman would be disgusted and insulted if I told him I married a nigger."

"Johannes, we're not in uncivilized, racial America."

"Would the gentleman still care to sleep with my wife?"

I didn't answer. His square head wavered. He read me. He gritted his teeth and sweaty purple veins stood out on his pale forehead.

"Liz," he glowered, "You heard the gentleman's desire?" She nodded. He bellowed, "On the phone, Mr. Vito gave me instructions that his guest, the gentleman, was to have quickly anything he wanted! What the hell are you waiting for! Go to the big house. Get your black-bitch ass and cunt in the tub with hot water and plenty sweet-smelling soap! Put on nice perfume and powder! Then come back with a fancy flimsy, *schnell*!"

During her absence, the thick gray German and I drank urgently in silence. Liz returned, in a saffron veil of negligee, exotic from bath, perfume and make-up. Johannes grabbed her arm brutally and shoved her toward me. "Go with the gentleman and see you give him the best time!"

Liz's straight features and mouth were childlike and sultry. Her body put to shame her sisters of other races. In Liz, God had designed the most desirable form and colored her deeply dark. With Liz I enjoyed the virtue of unconditional lust. I savored that animal pleasure closest to the truth of nature.

I caught the mad face of Johannes gazing through the window. I snapped out the bed lamp. Liz drawled confidently, "The ole man ain't gonner do nothing. Mr. Vito's the Lord to him. An' you is Mr. Vito's special guest."

Then we heard him stomping around the grounds of the mansion, howling guttural cries interspersed with shotgun blasts. After his drunken yawps ceased, the surrounding jungle became fraught with the screeching of peacocks, twittering of nightingales, chattering of monkeys, satire of parrots, hooting of owls and the confusion of other creatures.

I awoke to find myself alone. The moiling heady spoor of Liz was on the silken sheets. Johannes came to the door to tell me that Liz could draw the bath and serve breakfast at my convenience.

Liz was with me nights while Johannes, outside, made berserk noises and tore up the landscape. In the mornings, everything would be serene, Liz working with the servants and Johannes anxious to cater to me.

Nueva Gerona was a ramshackle river town with docks, bars, a church, bank, dance hall, gas station, farm-implements agency, telephone building, slaughter-house, filthy fly-laden restaurant and markets and unpaved streets. Off the thoroughfare were packed rows of thatch- and tin-roofed hovels with walls of dried clay. They were the same: earthen floor, sunless interior, fowl, swine goats running in and out, an unkempt father in the doorway, and behind, on the wall, the inevitable lithograph of Our Lady of Sorrows. When seeing a stranger roaming by, it was not unusual for the man in the doorway to bring out a ragged, barefoot, hardly teenage girl and offer her to the wanderer for 50 cents or less. On an occasion, I was tempted; the little girl was very pretty, all soulful eyes; but the hopeless sacrificial expression on the child's face shamed me. Or was it because I had been told that tuberculosis, leprosy and other diseases infested the peons?

Near Nueva Gerona, on a plain barricaded by marbled heights and dense forests, was the *presidio modelo*. Under the glaring sun stood the high lime-coated circular model prison. The commandant, a stout Batista army officer with sideburns and mustachio, was happy to show me the place. He took me inside to the center of the drum-shaped structure. From that hub, no movement could evade notice. Within the dramatic concave there were four tiers of unbroken balconies fronting the barred cells. A word from the commandant and all the doors opened mechanically. Convicts came out of the cells and lined the railing. The majority were Negroid, their blackness contrasting starkly with the whitewash of the prison.

I saw chained convicts working the marble quarry, in the forest felling ebony, mahogany and guayacan trees; others making cordage from the bark of the majagua tree. There seemed to be as many armed soldier-guards and dangerous dogs as there were prisoners.

"Most of these men were convicted of political crimes against the government," said the commandant. "They subscribe to foreign radical doctrines and therefore must be treated as vermin. Whoever escapes is hunted down and shot dead on the sight. Also those who give them refuge—even a glass of water. No one has fled the *presido* and lived."

The prisoners appeared to be nothing but simple peasants.

At a quay in Nueva Gerona was a sponge-fishing boat, the Santa Isidora. Next to it, a luxury cruiser, the Sturgeon. On the Sturgeon's deck was a slim blond sunning herself. The sponge fishers had brought a pig from the slaughter house. They cut it apart, salted the pieces away in buckets and gave the heart, liver, intestines and brains to a covetous policeman, who wrapped them in burlap and left with elation.

The racy girl on the Sturgeon and I smiled at each other. She beckoned me to come aboard. Her name was Alice. She made martinis of vodka and sake. Alice was from Cleveland. She was on her honeymoon. Her husband had been called away to negotiate a defense contract. The Second World War was in the air. He was making a lot of money. The Sturgeon belonged to her father, Dr. Farber. Alice said casually, "Dad is protecting me from sin until my husband returns. Mother Mary. I'm bored."

Without ado, we discussed sex.

"There's one way to get around Dad so that we can be together. He's nutty about Hitler. Play along with him."

Dr. Farber came abroad with pockets of mail. He was fair, with rosy cheeks, a Charlie Chaplin mustasche and glassy blue eyes. He was not about to let me get next to his daughter.

After a few perfunctory visits, I confided to Dr. Farber that I hated the Reds and loved Hitler. His eyes glowed. He expounded Nazi theology for hours.

I echoed everything he said. He trembled with joy.

"Your heart is in the right place," he said. "You are highly intelligent—fine, fine. I trust you!"

He took me to his cabin, showed me his two-way short-wave set and tuned in Berlin. On the wall was a painting of Hitler, daggers and a swastika flag. He asked me breathlessly. "Would you raise your arm and *heil* the *Führer* with me?"

I joined him in *heiling*. After that he asked me to do him the favor of keeping his lonely daughter company and to help him safeguard her virtue. When he left on an overnight hush-hush mission to a fellow Nazi's plantation, Alice and I spent the night and the following day on the bed in ravenous erotica beneath the portrait of Hitler. With Dr. Farber's blessings, Alice was my guest at Vito's Casa del Río for days.

I had only two other girls during my Isle of Pines holiday: short, husky, freckled Pamela, daughter of a Canadian clergyman who was obsessed with locating pirate treasure in the sea; and a Chinese girl, lissome, almond Cricket, whose father had a crude bar for peons off of Casa del Río in a jungle clearing where once flourished a village that was leveled by the 1926 hurricane.

I used to drive to the jungle bar and shoot pool and drink beer with the peons. The Chinaman never said a word to me. One night, after the peons left and her father retired, Cricket and I made love atop the pool table. She tasted like cloying litchi nuts.

On February second, Nuova Gerona delebrated the *candelaria*, the purification of the Virgin Mary. The main street was thronged. Peons came by foot, burro, oxcarts and trucks belonging to the plantation owners from McKinley, Los Indios, Punto de los Barcos, Santa Fe, Santa Barbara and San Pedro. German, English and Cuban plantation owners came either on horseback or in large expensive autos covered with the dust of the red-clay roads. There was no consciousness of skin color. Comingled were Spaniards, Indians, whites and blacks, with their children ranging from sepia to high yellow. What did stand out sharply was the distinction between rich and poor, master and vassal. For every 50 *macheteros* (peons toting cane knives on their sides) there was a stern-faced *capataz*—boss man, a veritable conquistador—wearing panama, embroidered shirt, white-linen jacket, cartridge belt and pistol.

Vendors sold fried chicken, fish, snails, rice, sauages, hot peppers and black beans. The delicacy of the peons was roast pork. Bristled greasy fat, meat and bones, blanketed with enormous green flies, were cut with a machete for sandwiches. The affluent drank Pepsi-Cola and Coca-Cola. Others wetted their mouths with rum, beer or fruit juices. The children sucked raw sugar cane.

Plantation owners and overseers sat in the cool of arcades gambling at cards. Peons grouped humbly about, amazed at the sight of mounds of pesetas. For those who wore shoes or boots, there was the status ritual of having their footwear shined—even though minutes later they were again caked with road dust. Within the one stifling dance hall, youths did the *zapateado*—the clog dance—and their sinuous samba and rumba.

The air was felicitously burdened with oven-hot sunshine, oily foods, tobacco, vaporous red dust, rum, colas and perspiration. Under the thatched dome of an open-timbered structure were held the cockfights. The raised benches around the arena were jammed. The arrogantly beautiful burnished, razor-spurred bantams strutted warily in deathly ballet and then lightninglike flew into each other, pecking, gouging, slashing and scattering their blood and feathers. The bettors cried encouragement with pleas and curses to their cocks. The cockmasters implored their champions to blind and kill the adversary, spoke to them in poetically endearing terms, picked them up lovingly, licked the blood from them, massaged them, kissed them and blew stimulating air up their behinds,

Night saw the procession of the *candelaria*. Behind the vestmented priest, soldiers, police and the gaudy effigy of the Virgin Mary, the mass carried candles.

Outside a hovel at the end of town, a cow was dying. Someone said the cow had anthrax. The cow was desperately trying to raise his head into the moonlight. The owner and his wife were wringing their hands. The priest and procession formed about the stricken animal, knelt and prayed for its comfort. Realizing that the cow was in its last throes, many set up lamentations, keening as to its life-sustaining value and the catastrophic loss to the penniless family. A policeman wept also.

Following the sanctifying of the candles and the observances paid to the Virgin Mary, the mayor lauded the government and requested all to bow their heads and pray thankgiving to General Batista. Blessings by the priest and an indifferent fireworks display concluded the festivities for the purification of the Virgin Mary.

The crowds were about to depart. In the distance sounded the ominous steam whistle of the *presidio*. It blew incessantly. There had been an escape. The soldiers and police drew their guns with much fanfare and ordered the people to remain. There was fright on the faces of the peons. The plantaton dons moved about with authority and organized their own posse.

Armored vehicles sped into town with bells clanging and sirens wailing. Following them were pickup trucks bringing bloodhounds. The peons were rounded up, told to throw their machetes into a heap and submit to the scrutiny of *presidio* officials and guards. Four political prisoners had escaped.

The commandant asked me to use Vito's station wagon to transport soldiers for the hunt. He told me, "The bastards took advantage of the *candelaria* to escape. They've been gone for hours. I hope we don't find them too quickly—it will spoil the excitement of the chase,"

As I went for the station wagon. I saw the priest speaking gravely to the commandant. The commandant shook his head emphatically. The priest looked sad and choking. I guessed that the priest was begging mercy for the prisoners or did not wish the prisoners, when caught, to meet death without Christian spiritual preparation.

The many hunters fanned out toward Santa Barbara, Sante Fe and the center of the island reaching to the low mountains of La Cañada. Reluctantly, I drove overfed soldiers with the central contingent heading for the range of La Cañada. Between the stops and searches at plantaions, the soldiers carried on as if on carnival outing, smoking big cigars and drinking wildly. The terrorized peons were offensively interrogated and manhandled.

At dawn the bloodhounds scented out the prisoners in a haystack of a tenant farm on a slope of La Cañada. I wish I had not been there. I had been praying for the prisoners not to be found. The prisoners, young peons, one white and three black, were herded at gunpoint into the open field, riddled with hundreds of bullets, spat upon, urinated upon and their bodies hacked to bits with machetes.

The peon tenant farmer was accused of harboring the fugitives. He screamed that he did not even know the prisoners had hidden in his haystack. The soldiers threw him upon the butchered corpses and shot him to death. His wife and daughters were dragged out of the farmhouse and raped by the soldiers. Back in Nueva Gerona, the drink-maddened soldiers went on a rampage.

As I packed my bags at Casa del Rio, Liz looked softly at me and said she was pregnant. Would I think of her once in a while? I would. And dearly.

Johannes drove me to Nueva Gerona. I thanked him for the good care he had taken of me.

"The best is none too good for Mr. Vito's guest," he answered.

On poles and buildigs, the police were tacking up posters with the death sign of skull and crossbones, warning of a new rabies outbreak.

I boarded the steamer for Batabanó. My soul welled with murder. I saw myself with a machine gun filled with neverending bullets shooting down Vito, the rich Cubans, Batista and his soldiers and police and, like a Jesus, miraculously bringing back to life the four prisoners and the tenant farmer.

In Havana, I sat with Hemingway again at the Ambros Mundos bar. The place was deserted. We were alone. We drank. But that time drinking could not make me drunk. I told him about the escaped prisoners, the tenant farmer and how I felt. I said, "In the name of Christ, how can you bear to live in Cuba and not write and protest about the goddamn things that take place here?"

Hemingway answered, "I can't count the people I've seen killed for an ideal. Kid, you've never been in a war. You get used to such things. It happens from generation to generation, like another spring, another harvest. Man is a mothering son of a bitch. The world could be a paradise, but the people hate God and themselves. The peons you saw shot yesterday would be on the other end of the rifle tomorrow. When the revolution comes here, then it will be turnabout and some other unfortunate slob's day in the barrel. You are green. You let sex, religion and social conditions overwhelm you. You're not a bad kid. You'll see it my way someday. We're all born to die. What's the difference if it comes sooner or later? All man's troubles come from his two heads. Perhaps the noblest thing a man can do is to cut off his lower head and blow his goddamn brains out. Now this advice will cost you a drink!"

I did not bother to look up my other playmates in Havana. With revulsion and impatience to get away from that land, I overcame my fear of flying and got on a plane for Miami. Aside from the memory of wondrous Liz, the sensual fruits of the tropic of Cuba had turned to acrid blood in my mouth.

The Flesh, The Devil And Santiago

Santiago Mezzanotte's blacksmith shop was across the street from our tenement. It had been there long before he acquired it, for on the red clapboards above the entrance was a wooden figure head of a horse and under it in faded lettering: Adolph Schotze . . . est. 1880. My earlist recollection was of certain rainy days when father had him forge out bricklayer's tools. I see the cindery dirt floor, iron rimmed wagon wheels, the hooded forge and bellows, the shoeing bench and battered anvil, and still smell the horses' leavings, the acid coke and the callous-gelatin order of hot horseshoes charring into hooves. The children called him Zio Santiago; we used to fashion scooters with roller skates and wood, and racing cars from discarded perambulators and soapboxes. We brought our problems to him; he pretended they were complicated and helped us with serious concern. Though past sixty and with a mane of white hair, he was proportioned like the Moses of Michelangelo. He had left Italy in his youth and toured the world with a circus, performing feats of strength, and had been known as Santiago The Great. He was slow thinking and spoke whisperingly, and had an open, amazed face. Santiago showed us handbills of his first wife, Christina, the bareback rider; he grimacingly demonstrated how he wrestled and vanquished the Terrible Turk, and prided to display his tremendous muscles. In awe we woud feel his coiling biceps that were hard as marble. "Become strong dear little ones," he would say in his hushing voice. "Match thy strength with gentleness and compassion, and injure not even the fly, for our almighty Father made him also as He made thee and me."

Partitioned from the shop was the stable; my huge beared Garibaldian uncle, Barbarosso, who was a dynamiter and hauled blasted rock from foundations with his dump-wagon, kept his beloved white mule, Mazzini, in one of the stalls near some drayhorses and Santiago's ebony stud, Africano. Above the stable was the hayloft. Out in the court was the ammonia-steaming manure pit; to a side were carriages, wagons, and an obsolete horse-drawn tramcar—Bergenline Rapid Transit—in which we played, yanking brakes and clanging the tram gong. In the rear was Santiago's vine-veined Victorian house with upper and lower verandas and widow's walk atop the flat roof. There with him and his young wife Stella, lived Stella's mother, Luna Ciucanera, Santiago's foster son, Pasqualino, and Santiago's mother, Adalaida. Blind, senile Adalaida could find her way about the house and yard; each day she fed and watered the chickens and the greyhound, Arrigo, who was chained within the doorway of the stable. Adalaida would it on the porch, taking snuff, and doing a monologue of Bible quoting and laughter. Pasqualino was splay footed as was his real father, Vincenzo (Charlie Chapin) Passalaqua, but he was animalistically handsome, with thick black curly hair and a dark olive color. Working as a smithy with Santiago he had grown man-sized before his time.

I used to wonder about various things: How did it feel being a man, and just why was a man interested in a woman? Why were people different from each other? Why this? Why that? I had an uncontrollable compulsion to observe, listen and compare. Two incidents made me fear and hate Pasqualino: When the iceman's horse was dying of colic, Pasqualino picked me up and trust me down upon the convulsing horse. And one afternoon as I was coming down the ladder from the hayloft he grabbed me and kicked me and said: "You li'l sonubithch if I catch you in the hayloft I'll break your gooddam sneaky neck!"

I was on the tenement roof paddling tomato *purée* in vats so that the summer sun would render it to paste; below was the well of backyards with their teetering fences, litter, crooked washpoles and clotheslines running to each kitchen window. I heard the Artichoke's wife carol to Mother: "Annunziata . . . ! Know thee the new of it? The nephew of Padre Onorio, Friar Gian-carlo, tomorrow arrives from the Italy upon the Duca Di Aosta!" "Conchettina, who apprised thee?" "Sebastiano, the garlic vendor, freshly from the rectory of San Rocco —Don Onorio was with Marconi message in hand."

Padre Onorio and Brother Gian-carlo bore the same surname as Mother, Cinquina, and we were related. This was an important occasion: Mother assisted by fat, crippled Rosa La Zoppa, housemaid to Padre Onorio, prepared dinner: *olives condite, caponata, provolone* cheese and *prosciutti, brodetta,* snail pie, stuffed octopus, roasted head of goat, fennel chestnuts, prickly pears, honey-balls, muscatel wine, *espresso* and anise-flavored *gelati.* Padre Onori, Santiago and Father went to fetch Brother Gian-carlo. They left West Hoboken maneuvered the steep road from the Palisades to Hoboken, boarded the ferry to New York and then to Ellis Island. Questing among the betagged immigrants, Padre Onorio found his nephew. "Bless thee, bless thee, dearest nephew and welcome to the America where with delighted heart kith, kin and kind receive thee." Our guests at dinner were Padre Onorio, Santiago's family, and Uncle Barbarosso. Mother had warned Uncle, "In front of the young priest I'll have no talk about thy boon companionship with Lucifer!"

Brother Gian-carlo wore a cassock buttoned from throat to ankles; he was tall and prematurely gray; he had a smallish head and spindly hands; his face was fleshy, his nose peaked, his mouth thin, his blue eyes sunken and his scrubbed skin had a monastic pallor. He stretched his fingers constantly and sat with a nervous deference that invoked uneasiness. "Was Vasto yet of surpassing Bellezza?" "Yes, very much so." "Did America seem alien from Vasto?" "Yes, very much so." Father whispered to Mother, "Our young 'undertaker' must be famished— bring food." Mother remarked *sotto voce,* "I'll gamble 'very much so' is going to be one to reckon with!" When Mother laid the table, Gian-carlo struggled to say, "Good cousin—it had been my usage to wash my own plate and utensils—is it permitted?" He excused himself and took his knife, fork and plate to the sink. He soaped and rinsed and wiped them again and again. He thanked Mother for each helping but declined the meat because Mother had cooked it in an aluminum pot, nor would he have wine.

Aside from the fact that Santiago was the sacristan of our church, Mother had invited him because my eldest sister Mary was smitten with his foster son, Pasqualino, his 'son of gold.' But when he brought his mother-in-law, Luna Ciucanera, Mother smiled ruefully and Father grinned. La Ciucanera breaking bread at their virtuous table—that was America for you—and the end of the world! In Vasto decent women were not allowed near the person of La Ciucanera—that was for men and the night. Pasqualino was ten years old when Santiago's wife Christina died. Soon after, Luna Ciuncanera and her daughter came to America; they were ostracized. Resourceful Ciucanera upon learning of the widower Santiago who was innocent of Vastese gossip and had house and *dennaro*, led her daughter Stella to the blacksmith shop and sat before him daily. She thew herself upon his mercy and offered Stella to him, convincing the simple ferrier, who was old enough to be the girl's father, that the Maddona had appeared in a dream to her. She was to tell him to marry Stella and merit God's reward for keeping spotless the souls of a mother and her virgin child. With the marriage Luna Ciucanera had vaulted into position amongst the *paesanos*. And now wouldn't she be lisping to Brother Gian-carlo how she had even considered the nunnery! With the *expresso* and brandy the men puffed La Contributor cigars; Santiago did not smoke, and neither did Gian-carlo, who was irritated and coughed. Mother, shrewdly perceptive, silently rolled pellets of bread; she did not push my sister Mary towards Pasqualino—as she put it: "There was the unique smell of carnality between Pasqualino and the woman of Santiago."

The *paesanos* came to greet Brother Gian-carlo; the Kaiser from the floor above with his speared mustaches, the Artichoke, Pass-water and his mate, Teresina the Meatball, from next door, and so many others that our railroad flat seemed a felicitous cattle car. Pasqualino's actual father, and brother to Pass-water, entered; properly he was Vincenzo Passalaqua, but he had been named Charlie Chaplin because of his antics. His wife, Gabriella, died giving birth to Pasqualino; Christina, the original wife of Santiago, took the infant to her babyless teats, and Santiago retained this son-through-milk. Charlie Chaplin took to the brothels and the stage of Zuccaro's saloon. Pasqualino dutifully arose and kissed his hand. Charlie Chapin took Gian-carlo's measure and smirked, "Ah my boy, it can be said that at heart I am a bit of a monk." With salacious winks he paid the floweriest of compliments to Luna Ciucanera. The more sanguine adjourned with Charlie Chapin to Pass-water's flat, and the rest went to the front-room to hear my sister play the piano. *The Burning of Rome* and *The Sunshine of Your Smile* did not move them. But when Father sat at the piano, the room tremored as Uncle Barbarosso, Stella and Rosa La Zoppa sang *Bella Figlie Dell Amore*, and the *paesanos* were lachrymose with the sad throbbing of *O Terra Addio*.

Midnight was the hour of epos. The building of our church was told about in detail. How the early Vastese *paesanos* chose the comfort of San Rocco, patron of pilgrims, as they felt they were 'Roccini,' peregrinous: foerigners, travelers. Then their aspiration to build a brick church. The women had said, "The trowels that make bread shall also serve the edifice of God!" Padre Onorio had mused: "Solomon truly ruled that one special hair of woman can draw more than twenty team of oxen." Charlie Chaplin designed the structure— *"una diadema"*—the first floor square, the *campanile* octagonal and capped with a dome. The materials had been pilfered from jobs, but blessed by Padre Onorio, such Friday meat is turned into fish. The *paesanos*, of course, had to manifest their trowel-cunning, and our miniature Vatican had Pass-waters pinnacles, Dainty-dainty's arches, the *rondelles* of the Kaiser, and the Confessional of the Artichoke. The dome which was molded from the master hand of Charlie Chaplin was referred to as "Charlie Chaplin's ball."

Also told was how Pass-water's woman, Teresina the Meatball, though big with child, wore overalls, smoked a pipe and spread mortar for her man and sons. Boasted she, "Why should I not sling the trowel when from out of my belly have come bricklayers!" The belated child had to be born right on the scaffold—literally in a mortar-pan. *"Finalmente!"* cried Teresina. And according to Pass-water's wish, Padre Onorio immediately baptized the baby with the name Finalmente Rocco Passalaqua. The picture taken by Mastrobellangini, the photographer, on rooftree day was brought out. The children were ranged in the foreground. I wore a cowboy suit and brandished cap pistols, Head-of-Pig's son, Gigi, was doing a handstand, the Kaiser's brats were astride Uncle Barbarosso's mule, Whadda-you-want's children were piled in Padre Onorio's motorcycle and side-car, some kids sat in wheelbarrows and others dangled from the scaffolding in the background. Dainty-dainty stood fastidiously aloof wearing a white roll-neck sweater and gloves; Charlie Chaplin was the only *paesano* who ever possessed a raincoat and he was showing it off although the sun was shining; Uncle Barbarosso was in his cape, beaver hat and leather puttees holding a jug of wine to his lips as Garibaldi, his beagle, crouched at his feet; Pass-water wore his wife's shawl and held the swaddled baby, Finalmente, while his wife, the Meatball, pipe in mouth, was plumbing his head with level and hammer; Mother was seated on a stock of brick behind me; she was pregnant with my brother Giogio. Standing behind her, and holding a glass of wine, was Father, in a blue suit, pork-pie hat, wing collar and polka-dot bow tie; in a corner of his mouth was a Royal Bengal Tiger cheroot. The white-haired Santiago had one arm about the waist of Stella and the other lovingly about Pasqualino; in the center was Rosa La Zoppa handing Padre Onorio the rooftree, a potted fig plant. The mighty Santiago had lifted Padre Onorio, tree and all, and carried him upon his shoulders up the ladders to the top of the dome. It was Santiago on the day of consecration of San Rocco who had unmuffled the tongue of the bell in the tower; the bell was ancient, and had been sent as a gift from the diocese in Vasto. It had sung o'er the hearths of Vasto for generations into centuries gone by, and in West Hoboken its voice was newly rich and clear.

In Pass-water's kitchen, Charlie Chaplin, drinking strega, regaled, evoking guffaws. "Recall thee the house inside the gate of Vasto? Since Testament it has been the 'shrine of fornicari' and what sights its walls have seen! There was always a mother and daughter with public thighs. There the mystic ministry of the harlot was perpetuated, and there aboded Luna Ciucanera and her mother, Sola—a constellation of *puttana*. My sire, rest his soul, was serviced by Luna's mother. Whenever Luna and her mother vacationed, Vasto was afflicted with masculine distemper. I 'cut my teeth' on Luna. We thought she was the grand lady of Vasto: parasol, high heels, a hat big as a mortar-pan and laden with artificial flowers, long gloves, a red dress, perfume and a gallon of paint on her face. Saturday mornings she posted herself at the fork of the road, leading to Ortona; Don Peppino, the olive grower, would come by in his cart lugged by the little black donkey and take her with him—for ye know what—and thus we called her La Ciucanera—'the lady of the black ass.' One night, dark as debt, when Geremio and I visited her, Gigi, who was sentinel in the street below, shouted '*I Carabiniere!*' And didn't leap we out the window, with only the moon covering our tassels!"

Charlie Chaplin rolled his head. "How the wheel of fate revolved—the lactal mother and woman of the ferrier who raised my Pasqualino dies. Luna Ciucanera and her delectable piece of a daughter come to America. The women held her at large—but Luna, like the gull flies forward into the wind, gives Stella to the wealthy Santiago. Ciucanera is a dessicated Maria Magdalena and her daughter is stepmother of my son." Drunken, drooling, he shook his finger and winked: "Like mother, like daughter; like father, like son! My colt has become a stallion; he will plant the horns and gallop back to me. Blood is stronger than milk!"

Stella Mezzanotte had sent me to the pharmacist. "Tell *Dottore* Caprio to give thee that certain article of female necessity. He will comprehend." I stood in the kitchen with the package. "I am in the room of the bed," she called. She was behind a glass-beaded curtain, wrapping on her corset. She asked me to come and hook her backstays. I had not forgotten the time I fell into the manure pit and how she bathed every part of me in the washtub. I did not know then just why I trembled with excitement. Stella was not stocky and buxom like most of the *paesano* women, whose bellies were ponderous and whose breasts were swollen udders. I fastened her corset and my eyes could not help seeking. She hugged me affectionately. A sweet fragrance came up into me and a twelve year old boy's first adoring love of woman burgeoned.

At night my pillow was Stella. By day I played in Santiago's yard, finding reasons to be near Stella, dreaming of being her slave. I would carry her shopping bag, hang washing and do other chores. When she noticed my gaping she would chuckle. She handed me a bundle of her clothes to throw away, but I took them to my hideaway in the hayloft and smelled from them her womanly musk. Santiago and Pasqualino were working at the forge. From the hayloft I aimed my cap pistol at Pasqualino and planned revenge for the whipping he had given me—torture like I had seen in the serials at the City Theatre.

Santiago looked at his watch; it was time for him to take his mother-in-law to visit Brother Gian-carlo; the three had become quite taken with one another. In the afternoons Luna would place herself in the grotto of the Madonna for passersby to witness her devotions, while Santiago worked the Rosarium, or played games of *bocci* with Gian-carlo. Before he could leave, Stella came in to complain about Pasqualino. "When thy fatherly presence is absent he is disrespectful." Pasqualino grunted he did not wish to be treated as a boy. "Calm, calm, my dear children," soothed Santiago, "this is not a thing tragic." "With regret I am not thy womb-spring," said Stella, "but as a lad thou wert as my own; of a sudden thou thinkest thyself man and art brute; thou needest wife, not mother." "Then 'tis not thy concern!" retorted Pasqualino. Santiago placed his massive arms about them. "In the household of Santiago I pray for love."

Santiago and Stella's mother left. Stella and Pasqualino did not move. After the horses clatter upon the cobblestones was gone Pasqualino said fiercely, "We're alone!" He embraced her, kissing her mouth and handling her intimately. He pulled her out of the shop. Stella called to Santiago's mother: "Adalaida, I go to the groceria . . . !" They came into the stable and climbed the ladder. Within a few feet of my hiding place Pasqualino spread a horse-blanket upon a mat of hay. With graceful alacrity Stella removed her shoes, dress, petticoat and corset and lay on the blanket naked as Pasqualino fumblingly undressed. Pasqualino's swarthiness and Stella's pink-white petal blazoned before my eyes. He sprawled his rude length atop her and with violence wedged to her. They rolled and contorted. A sickening flowered in the pit of my stomach. The greyhound below began to bark. Adalaida came and quieted him. She called for Pasqualino, then said to the dog, "Do love-birds rustling hay furiate thy envy?" Stella and Pasqualino passioned in a way that left no area unexplored. My throat swelled. I was suffocating. I told myself that I should not be spying. Prostrate and without shame, they lay relaxed in the sunlight that entered the gable window. I saw Stella's head with its tawny, low hairline and high cheek-bones, the tiny ears, and beneath the green eyes the rose-cream of face, the large, straight nose and flaring nostrils, the intaglios at temple, in cheeks and under her lower lip, the black mole above the full-pouted lips, the flawless mamillated pendants, the shy belly, the long hypnotic legs. I could smell the smell of her, and see fine bubbles of sweat about her lips and the private titian jewels, and I wanted to reach through the slats of the crib.

Pasqualino stood up. "Vest thyself," he said nervously. "Fear always comes to me when we've done." She lazily put on her clothes. "Why should you fear when I am not afraid?" "And if Pappa came back and trapped us?" "What is to be will be." His face clouded. "Why did you wed my stepfather?" he demanded. She shrugged. "I hear you and he get into bed!—What do you do? How can you let him, an old man, touch you after being with me!" "Thou wert a boy when I married . . . and there is the love of night and the love of day." He slapped her face and in grinding muffled breath shouted: "*Puttana! Puttana!* I see his white head in bed with thee. I wish him dead! . . . and at times thee too!"

At a post-prandial discussion at our table, Padre Onorio said, "My nephew has a mania for hygiene—not once but twice daily he bathes in the wash-boiler letting forth with 'Hosannah! Hosannah!' He laves his linen in solutions of brown soap and bleach until he smells like a laundry. As for my pipe and decanter, he views them as abominations. But he possesses intellect beyond my ken; he reads books and writes notations; he remains up by lamp until dawn studying and every so often sends out a jubilant 'HOSANNAH!' that startles me from slumber. My nephew is in the cocoon of priestly enthusiasm, when he emerges, 'tis possible he may surprise us." "It is understood," said Mother, "the pot with tight lid generates great heat." The women, though earthy, were moral, and Gian-carlo had made an impression. "How somber," said they. "He is austere and can outcountenance the blasphemy of our men." They were enthralled with celibate youth dedicated.

At the approach of Lent, Padre Onorio assigned Giancarlo to supervise the pageant of the Passion Play. The women welcomed the rehearsals as it excused them from stove and cradle. They and their men were obedient under Gian-carlo's direction. He cast Stella as the Madonna, Pasqualino as the Messiah and Santiago as Longinus. Everyone clamored to be a good disciple, and no one would accept the roles of the accursed Caiphus, Pilate and Judas. "You look more of a Judas than I!" "I'd rather receive a fusillade of bullet-balls in my head than simulate the Caiphus!" "I wash my hands of Pilate!" Charlie Chaplin volunteered Judas as he contended the betrayal was Judas' rash hope of the Messiah proving Himself right there. It was then that Padre Onorio became ill from hot peppers, dashed on his motorcycle towards the drugstore for Pluto water, collided with a brewery wagon and smashed his rib cage. Brother Gian-carlo had to take over as pastor. In celebrating the Missa Gian-carlo was as majestic as a patriarch; when he mounted the pulpit he seemed taller, overpowering. He transfixed all with a searching gaze.

"SIN!!!" burst from him. "You know what a brick is; a crust of bread . . . know you what is SIN? Sin is transgression against Divine Law! Sin is that which alone can assassinate the soul! The adversary is sin! Whence came sin? From woman, which was Eve! The devil came into the intestine of her mind; he looked out of her eyes in the form of *desiderata* and the lust of her eye was followed by that act which gave birth to sin! Lust was the filth that spawned sin! Without the first sin of the flesh there could not have come into the world other sins! And what is thy bounden task? To resist sin with body, mind and soul! I shall tell thee of temptation. I was boarding student with a family in Rome. One night the comely daughter of the house uninvited entered my room. She was distraught with desire. She removed her nightclothes before me and begged me to sink into the slime with her. I closed my eyes and began to pray. The room had become fetid with demons." Then pointing to the windows of Saint Justina. "To the wretched girl I said aloud, 'Saint Justina,' I implored, 'send the unicorn to guard this poor, weak girl from the devils of concupiscence!' The girl fell to weeping; she covered her shame and prayed with me. Then what said she? 'Brother Gian-carlo! I see him! He is here! The white unicorn has come and saved me!' The malodorous humors evaporated. 'Hosannah!' I shouted, 'Hosannah on high; Hosannah!'" Padre Gian-carlo brought a cataract of emotion to San Rocco. The women were transported. Father said wryly, "Padre Gian-carlo, when a field hunting sin with blunderbuss load, spares not even the lowly toad." Gian-carlo's influence upon the women exceeded their husbands' imagination: under his guidance they had a committee against coarse thoughts, the committee inveighing profanity, the committee for the pageant of the Passion Play, the committee governing all committees planning the observance of Lenten quarantine; it was Gian-carlo this and Gian-carlo that and rush rush to San Rocco. Masculine tempers fumed into choler. Passwater shouted to his wife, "Led by that eunuch Gian-carlo and Luna Ciucanera, the town whore of Vasto, you would virginize thyself? You go to the job and lay brick! Wear my pants and in it my man thing! I'll put on bloomers, petticoats and suckle the babies!"

The knife of emasculation fell on the first day of Lent when Padre Gian-carlo announced that "hearkening to the voice of Heaven" the women would vow sexual continence for forty days. Father said, "This Gian-carlo now has thrown all our meat into his fire!" The men gathered at Zuccaro's saloon and swore to grow beards and go unwashed in reprisal. The women held firm. Charlie Chaplin championed the cause of the men and organized "mushroom expeditions." They left arm in arm with bottles, lunch and bags, Zuccaro driving them in his touring car, and they would return late, drunk and rowdy, and without mushrooms. One night Father came home from mushroom-hunting, wearied, pale, smelling of cheap perfume. Mother picked up the hatchet form the woodpile and chased him down into the street. He spent the night sleeping at the head of the hallway stairs.

The crib in the hayloft was my paradise. I could not stay away from it. One afternoon I had been in the crib for hours watching Stella and Pasqualino. Between loves they had talked: Santiago would not suspect as long as they kept up their pretended dislike for each other. Blind Adalaida, Santiago's old mother, probably knew but would never tell. Stella's mother Luna Ciucanera knew from the beginning and for all her reformation decoyed Santiago to San Rocco to cover Stella and would stand by her daughter in hell itself. Should Santiago find out, they would run away. But no one had a contract with life; if Santiago died that would be an end to subterfuge. To my consternation I learned that they intended to stay until morning, as Santiago had not taken Luna Ciucanera to San Rocco, but had left to pick up iron stock, and could not return that night. I heard the quitting whistles blow from the silk mills; dusk came, and night. I could not see Stella and Pasqualino, but I sensed them; they alternately loved and rested, their combined breathings coming harsh and raspy. Then blending long and soft. My insides were pressing for release. For me there was sin, fear and sound; the bell of San Rocco, the loud voices leaving Zuccaro's saloon, wagons and cars, the trolley on Spring street, mice and birds in the loft and the horses in the stable below. Far in the night I heard my father out in the street calling, "Pietro! Pietrino! Where art thou? Pietrinnnno . . . !" Stella and Pasqualino were in exhausted sleep, and then there was nothing but Pasqualino's raucous snoring, and Arrigo the dog's low growling.

A wagon entered the courtyard. Footsteps approached the dog. It was Santiago. The dog stopped growling and whined happily and then was silent. Pasqualino's snoring vibrated the silence. Santiago struck a match. I saw the light coming up the ladder. His white-haired head appeared at the top of the ladder. He held a candle. In its flickering glow he saw naked Stella, and Pasqualino with his leg flung over Stella's hip. He stared and sighed. In his staring, his eyes became burned out sulphurous chasms, and his granite face dissolved. He descended and left with his horse and wagon.

At daylight Luna Ciucanera came into the stable and called her daughter and Pasqualino to breakfast. My frantic parents had been up the night drinking coffee. Father thrashed me before I could explain. But after I revealed where I had been, what I had seen, and why I could not leave, he grinned and kissed me. But then Mother lambasted me. "Twelve years old! and you know now the bestial practice! You sought it!" She grabbed me by what I cannot name, and tugging, screamed, "Wouldst be like thy father? And this green wood itching for the blaze? Wouldst pleasure thy tickling giblets at twelve? Take that! and that! and quickly-quick to the physic of Confessional!"

Before the sun had set, the news had travelled from scaffold to scaffold, market to market, window to window, kitchen to kitchen, and every *paesano* knew of the enormous horns Stella and Charlie Chaplin's son Pasqualino had made for the ferrier. Behind his back Santiago was crowned 'Il Cornuto.' Charlie Chaplin thought it justice because of Luna

Ciucanera's past and Santiago's age. At the saloon he entertained upon the subject of the behorned; bravoing his son's prowess. Santiago was passing the open door of the saloon and overheard Charlie Chaplin: "Santiago is old and without salt who will not injure a fly! I wouldst thank him for raising my son and tell to him he is honored by my son servicing the luscious fig of his wife!" Santiago relinquished his visits with Padre Gian-carlo; he left his forge cold and meandered about. When anyone greeted him he lowered his head. "Something must happen," said the *paesanos*. "Atlas himself could not bear the weight of such horns."

It was Sunday night at San Rocco. The pageant was to be given after Mass. The *paesanos* engaged in the play in Biblical costumes contrived of sheets, cement bags and sacking. Padre Gian-carlo stood in the pulpit, clenching his hands, smoldering, quivering. Santiago, Stella, Luna Ciucanera, Pasqualino and blind Adalaida were seated in the pew nearest the stained-glass window of Saint Justina and the Unicorn.

"Commandment Seven. God is more explicit against this vice than against any other. Against it He uttered His voice on Sinai, 'Thou shalt not commit adultery!' All the vices in the end cheat their dupes, but none with total disaster as this vice of impurity! If any of you possess this nameless shame, then thy heart is the dwelling place of more than seven devils of uncleanliness! Many have perished by the beauty of a woman, and that husband who condones his adulterous wife has been sucked into the lowest inferno wherein all goodness and all hope for him has been destroyed! I say more merciful would it be if adulterers had never been born!" Padre Gian-carlo pointed to the window of Saint Justina above Santiago. All eyes found the pew of Santiago. Luna Ciucanera had been smiling and nodding approvingly. Stella, dressed as the Madonna, kept her head high; Pasqualino was blanched and immobile. Beside him Santiago seemed a dazed mute. Beginning in a hardly audible voice and winding up to a thundering bolt, Padre Gian-carlo, said, "And I say that the foul antlers forged of lust must be destroyed by the chaste lance of Unicorn!" With the closing service, crippled Rosa La Zoppa, Stella and Uncle Barbarosso sang the Ave Maria, which momentarily obliviated the tensions caused by these trials of flesh.

We actors in the Passion Play received our final instructions from Padre Gian-carlo. I was a Hebrew beggar, Father was Peter; the unwanted parts had been settled; the convalescing Padre Onorio was Pilate, Gian-carlo as Caiphus, Charlie Chaplin as Judas, Teresina the Meatball as Veronica and Santiago as the Centurion. The church was darkened except for the moonlight that filtered through the stained-glass windows. With the organ music hovering from the choir-loft Padre Gian-carlo introduced each tableau; the *personaggi* stood statue-still holding lighted candles as he narrated the incident. The scenes though crudely postured held the *paesanos* spellbound; to them Stella's face was really the Madonna's and handsome Pasqualino was truly the Messiah. They commented, condemned and wept; they were there and it was actually happening. They were furious with Caiphus, hissed Judas, admonished Peter for cowardly denial but applauded him when he struck off the Roman soldier's ear, pleaded with Pilate not to listen to the High Priests and were wrung with pity at the agonies of the Stations. The Crucifixion scene arrived. Pasqualino was roped to a semblance of a Cross; Stella as Mary was kneeling by; disciples, Jews and Romans, all but Santiago were in position. Padre Gian-carlo took Santiago by the arm and led him to his place before Pasqualino. Santiago, holding a lighted candle in his left hand and a long smithy's file representing a spear in his right hand, wavered as though ill. Through glazed eyes he peered at his wife and stepson. His lips twisted and foamed. A hush came over the *paesanos*. They held their breaths. They were not hearing Padre Gian-carlo's narration. The pageant was finished. Santiago did not move. The *paesanos* were congealed. Padre Gian-carlo came from out of the shadows to arouse Santiago. The instant he touched him, Santiago raised his file. Pasqualino screamed, "Forgive—" With one voice the *paesanos* cried, "No!!!" And Santiago with an anguished moan drove the file through Pasqualino's heart. A fountain of blood gushed from Pasqualino's breast and rained down upon Santiago's white head.

Charlie Chapin reclaimed his son. He held the wake in Zuccaro's saloon. In his casket Pasqualino was a pretty boy sleeping. Delirious with grief and wine, Charlie Chaplin insisted upon entertaining the mourners with every role that flashed into his shocked mind; he lectured on the cosmos, religion, politics, and caricatured the *paesanos*; he sang and danced and his comedy only made our tears run faster. At the grave in the cemetery of San Rocco where Pasqualino was buried above his real mother, Charlie Chaplin threw himself upon Stella and shouted, *"Puttana di la morte!"*

Stella, thereafter designated as *'La Puttana,'* bloomed more beautiful than ever. She carried herself proudly, and her defiance made her more desirable. Santiago, acquitted, was as a Lazarus retrieved and shunned to rot in his shroud. Before a year went by, he and his mother Adalaida passed away. Stella married a young, good-looking and jealous contractor. Brother Gian-carlo departed from San Rocco and went unnoticed to a monastery. And Padre Onorio resumed his homely, reasonable shepherdhood.

Throughout the many years since, I have cared not to dispel the dream of Stella, my first supreme goddess of beauty, who for me could do no wrong. But always piercing that idyll has been the vision of the ugly red-dripping horns of *Il Cornuto*.

Border Episodes

Gloria, the young Mexican maid, was at the picture window of my brother's place in Los Angeles' Studio City on a high hill that overlooks Italian cypresses, green slopes, ostentatious cardboard homes, spiraling roads, cars and the San Fernando Valley.

Below was Ventura Boulevard, with the supermarket that also feeds neighbors Ernest Borgnine, Ralph Bellamy and other make-believers of the movie mills; the Sportsmen's Lodge Hotel; the Queen Mary, featuring female impersonators; massage parlors; porno flick houses; The Swing, where wives are bartered.

The mesmeric Tarahumara girl and I passed through yearning moods of day and weather—granular rain and the spectacle of a hailstone shower under the bursting sun. Gloria, with the jet Indian hair, coppery velvet skin, melting brown eyes and meaningful hips, said, "*Mira, mira*, this is not my village of Umira, OK? Mexico is in me, yes; Los Angeles, no. Your land has the cosmetic smile of a corpse, the unreality of a dream. That sun dying behind the skyscrapers and the mountain is from a postcard."

Mexicans shorten Estados Unidos to E.U. Gloria said, "I am here in the Ay Ooh to get the pesos for the security I will gusto where my heart is, sacred Umira above the Urique canyon. OK, gringo?"

The night we contemplated the myriad electric lights of Los Angeles she said, "It is the sea mantled in *las luciérnagas*, fireflies. No, it is the *candelaria* of the penitents in purgatory, each bearing a burning confessional taper."

With glowing countenance, she told me about her Umira—of a nomadic life in the mountains and of the mountains' incredible beauty, as far as the eye could see. The Tarahumara were never conquered by the Spanish. The girls married extremely young, brought in the firewood, wove wool blankets and braided baskets while watching the flocks graze. They made clothing and clay pots. The women bore children alone in the forest. When people died, the tribe feasted and drank much *tesquino*—a corn liquor—danced the *tutubi* and *yumari*, sacrificed animals and did the ballet of the matachinas.

"Los Angeles is not Umira. OK, gringo?"

Gloria, unasked, acknowledged herself an illegal alien without the proper *papeles*, papers. She was a *mojada*, a wetback and lived in fear of being apprehended and taken back across the border. In the *Los Angeles Times*, there was always news about border hoppers: "HUNDREDS OF COYOTES TRAPPED" (coyotes are smugglers of human cargo). "60,818 WETBACKS SEIZED." "ALIENS FEARFUL OF DETECTION ARE EASY PREY FOR UNSCRUPULOUS PRACTITIONERS." And on the Spanish-speaking radio, a commercial: "You never know when Immigration will come to knock on your hide-out door! Quickly call today to Carlson and Kaplan for a free consultation, before it's too late!"

Gloria did not return from her weekend pad in some chicano ghetto. Other wetback domestics along my brother's fashionable sun-swept drive hinted that probably she had been ratted on by a jealous rival or a spurned suitor and had been carted away to Tijuana, where Immigration usually dumps *los desautorizados*.

I went to the pleasant bracero-packed town of San Fernando looking for Gloria or information. No use. I searched the Mexican district around drab, industrial, bum-ridden Los Angeles Street and talked to the unemployed, to bartenders and to priests, who shrugged, feigning not to know English.

Gloria's meager worldly goods were in the maid's room. Under trim cheap slacks in the dresser drawer, I found her reading matter: photo *novelas* of seduced virgins, spurned by their beloveds' aristocratic families, who seek refuge with God in monasteries; of frustrated Romeos and Juliets setting themselves on fire with cleaning fluid. And there were sensational magazines such as *Vida Verdadera* and *¡Alarma!* with headlines blazoning: "¡DROGAS! ¡PLACER! ¡ALCOHOL! ¡ORGIAS! ¡CASA SATANICA! ¡PERVERSION! ¡MISERIA HUMANA! ¡VILEZA Y INFAMIA!"

Cause for wonder: There also were worn paperbacks of Jorgé Luis Borges, Léopoldo Clarín, Juan Goytisolo and Horacio Quiroga; Pedro de Alarcón's *El Sombrero de Tres Picos*; and *¡Venceremos!* by Ché Guevara. In the Borges book—*Labyrinths*—Gloria had marked passages with ? and !, particulalrly in "Funes the Memorious" and "Story of the Warrior and the Captive," which told of an English girl who had reversed the process of civilization and had become an Indian savage.

Letters stamped CORREO AEREO/ENTREGA INMEDIATA were trapped in perfumed panties embroidered with hearts and lips. She was Gloria Haydee, and the other last names she used were Davila, Gonzalez and Mendoza. The Mexican identity card said she was 25, *soltera*, single, lived in Tijuana on the Avenida Revolución and worked in a private office. There was her letter from Umira in the state of Chihuahua to a Rafael Mendoza on Flower Street, Los Angeles: "Remembered and unforgettable *señor*." The immigrant's communication was rife with concern for scarce *dinero*. There was trepidation; there was hope. And the letter ended with the imprint of her lipsticked mouth and drawn hearts joining their names, one containing the words *amor y paz*.

A ten-page letter from Rafael Mendoza, with the greeting "Remembered and unforgettable dearest little cunning heart of mine," gives infinite advice and directions from the bus stop in Chihuahua to the terminal in Tijuana:

> Engrave on your mind to take not the Flecha Amarilla bus line but the Tres Estrellas de Oro—the machines are newer and better. In this callous world, trust no one. In this devil's age, character, truth and principles are abominated! OK? Say with presumption undaunted that you are going to an uncle who is influential with the authorities—OK? Enclosed are 150 American dollars; change to pesos just enough for your trip. Watch even a centavo. Take *asperina* and peyote or calming pills and pray to our charitable patron, Señor de Esquipulas. OK? Tell the taxi to bring you to the Hotel Lafayette in Tijuana. I enclose the phone number of my employer in Los Angeles, the coyote who will smuggle you across the border, who will bring your ineffable treasure of a self to my loving arms. I regard your

three little children as though sprung from my very own seed. Our two hearts are eternally bonded.

Tu esposo,
Rafael

After Gloria's disappearance, two letters came from Umira, one written by herself, stamped REHUSADA—REFUSED. It was an ardent message to a young Edgar Oliverio Gutiérrez in which she expressed sorrow at being away from his embrace: She will be his, body and soul, until death—even though he is about to house himself with another. Will she kiss her children for her, provided no one suspects their carnal association? Making money in the Ay Ooh is not as magical as one had imagined.

The last letter, written in naïf peon's hand, was from Gloria's father, Antonio:

> Gloria, I tell you that your venture to the E.U. has gained nothing. It is better you return to Umira and the care of your three children. When you worked on the Sierra Madre slope, your children ate corn and beans and a blessed pit of pig. Now they are shrinking with hunger. What you have done to your old father and mother is a blight before God. Palaver is not needed. This letter should have been put together solely of the words Send money or come yourself to care for your children. I write no more.

The Southwest has a million chicanos who have sneaked over from Mexican border towns; many perish attempting a canal, river, desert—or are robbed or murdered by coyotes. Chicanos with papers, union power, unemployment insurance, welfare and civil rights are hostile to their wetback brothers who allow a rancher or a restaurant owner, a hotel, garage, construction or sweatshop boss to piss in their hands and deny workmen's compensation and all the benfits proletarian heroes have fought and died for.

A Los Angeles–born chicano said, "Jesus, man we break our humps in the lettuce and cantaloupe hassles to make and keep decent conditions and the naked wetbacks come in like termites and undermine us! All right, all right, we're the good guys and they're the bad guys; we're *auténticos* and the poor *paisano* slobs are los *transgresores*. The setup is like a lifeboat in a storm: Too many get in it and everybody's swamped! Ask the Saint. He'll tell you no different. The same. Ditto! OK? And you want to know something? The animals—Murder Incorporated in Washington, D.C.that zapped King and the Kennedys—they're going to kill *him*, too. Wait and see!"

The Saint is César Chavez. He and Peter C. Garcia subscribe to the traditional unionist line, buying themselves with the plight of their own workers, and all the workers of the world. Chavez complains that Immigration bends to the demands of the monster conglomerates that exploit the wetbacks, frequently closing its eyes to the illegals.

Then there are the chicano Idealists: Tijerina, Corona, Guttiérez, Gonzales and García. Reies López Tijerina, the New Mexico militant, organizer of the Alianza Federal de Mercedes, the Federal Alliance of Land Grants, told me that all chicano problems can be traced back to the days when Anglos cheated the Mexicans out of their land. Tijerina's Alianza seeks to reclaim those lost lands and to establish a confederation of free city-states in New Mexico.

He said, "You crazy arrogant gringos reinstituted the scattered Hebrews in Palestine at the cost of billions twenty centuries after they were forced out. Is it too much to request the return of the great southwest territories you recently stole from us?"

Bert Corona, the Texas activist, said "You ask me what I think of border places? All working people everywhere have common interests and must confront the oppressor. The so-called American-Mexican border is a dubious one. It is merely political—an arbitrarily drawn abstract wall. Corporations don't respect it. The economy is united; look at mining, cattle raising the agribusiness and the history of railroads in the area. If the border is to be closed to people, then why is it not closed to corporate goods as well? The economy dictates the flow of people across the border, but the immigration laws don't."

José Angel Guttiérez, youngest of the new leaders, founded La Raza Unida, The United People, in Texas. Fiery Rodolfo "Corky" Gonzales organized The Crusade for Justice in Denver; he advocates chicano nationalism and a revival of the legendary Aztec homeland.

*

In Brownsville, Texas, I went onto the bridge that spans the Rio Grande to Matamoros. Walking alongside me was a peaches-and-cream hippie nymphling with yellow-speckled eyes and the same color yellow hair. Her name was Robin. She was from, she said, "a place nobody ever heard of, a nothing town, the asshole of Montana: a good place to die." And she wanted to live it up. She was hitchhiking to Tijuana to buy $20 worth of dope and make $500 from it in the States. She did not have a cent and wasn't worried. Robin chewed gum and her nails; she was too young to give anyone a hard time. I didn't look the gift in the mouth. I assured her I'd see her to Tijuana and so forth.

Even on the bridge, the moment you leave the Stars and Stripes and encounter the handsome green, white and red flag with the golden eagle clutching a furious snake in its talon and beak, you are in a vastly different world. Mexico has its own sun; and the wind comes suddenly and violently from nowhere, kicks up the alkaline cementlike dust into the arid air and goes petulantly back to nowhere.

In the *central de autobúses* at Canales and Luis Aguiir Streets in Matamoros, I bought tickets for the 1500-mile trip to Tijuana. The ticket clerk had been reading the Spanish-language Jehovah's Witnesses Watch Tower Bible. I said it was a fucking good book and that I had a copy given to me by Glady Brown, my fish-market woman back home in Port Jefferson, Long Island, and that as far as I was concerned, the best part was the Apocalypse.

He said, "Brother, do you believe in Christ crucified and risen? Do you know the world will end in three years?"

I asked by what means. My bus was sounding the departure warning.

The Mexican Witness said placidly, "By the red horse and rider from the East." I told Robin.

The kid said, "Three years is a long time; you can have a hell of a lot of fun in three years and then—wow!"

We boarded a splendid made-in-Mexico DINA bus of Autotransportes Tres Estrellas de Oro. Signs said CLIMA ARTIFICIAL and SANITARIOS HIGIENICOS PARA DAMAS Y CABALLEROS.

Seats one and two behind the *piloto* were reserved for personnel—the relief *piloto*, always a good-looking young Indian absorbed in comics; or the drivers's wife and children, drinking Coca-Cola and watching poppa show off at the wheel. The best seats, then, are three on the aisle and four by the window—for leg room and the view.

The *piloto*'s section was a veritable chapel: The transparent plastic handle of the gearshift had an illuminated Madonna breast feeding a fat Mexican infant on it; there were scapulars and rosaries hanging from the overhead mirror; and an American Greyhound bus placard—

YOUR OPERATOR

SAFE . . . . RELIABLE . . . . COURTEOUS

—held to the wall by nails through the hands and feet of a silver crossless Christ.

Leaving Matamoros, we went past the new bull ring on the right and spacious fields of corn, sorghum and cotton. I bullied a peon out of seat three and maneuvered the pussyette, Robin, into the seat behind me, her Wrigley going like a suction pump. A Mexican grandmother was next to me: Luz Maria, born in Tijuana. She walked across the border as a girl and lived and worked in San Ysidro, where she could see the lights of Avenida Revolución.

"Put this in your story: You green-grow-the-lilacs greedy gringos killed, violated my people and stole our lands. Your guilty conscience makes you treat us the same as the Orientals you fear. You subsidize Negroes, Puerto Ricans, Filipinos and Vietnames refugees to live lazy criminal careers, and our chicanos, who are law-abiding and gentle, have to do all the hard, dirty, insulting labor the blacks disdain. The name chicano is a stigma: We goddamn well don't like it. The blacks act superior to us. My friend, do you know what we call in Spanish among ourselves the blacks? We call the blacks *moyate*—you know, the black bees that eat shit?

"I figured how to screw Uncle Sam long ago. I made sure my children and grandchildren became citizens of the United States. We earn our money on one side of the boundary and spend and enjoy it on the other side. We buy property around Tijuana and have nice *rancheros*; we work six months and collect six months' unemployment insurance and enjoy the best of *ambos mundos*—that means both worlds. I just got my Social Security, my company pension and Medicare—my husband too. OK?

"You gringos make your own obstacles; you don't know whether you're coming or going. Mexicans are Indians; Indians are rocks that don't change. We refuse to admit problems. We don't see them. So nothing bugs us. If you know one Indian, you know the whole secret of Mexico."

The highway was a concrete ribbon, sometimes an asphalt reel, in places a merely reddish hardpan path; and you didn't believe the oncoming tractor-trailers would get by. When buses approached, the *pilotos* flashed headlights, punked horns and gave each other a swift straight-armed hail.

The windshield was a Technicolor movie cyclorama bringing in terrain gashed with dry gullies and washes, stream beds, sunken deserts, dreary levels, bold buttes, picturesque mesas, bits of green valley and chromatic tones of ochre, brown, blue, purple, yellow, and white sandstone, shale and clay; and you found it otherworldly and weird, but you knew it was the happy, cozy domicile of iguanas, snakes, scorpions, cacti and Indians and—though the bus was air-conditioned—windows were open and let in hot calcium carbonate-tasting currents. Sheep, goats and cattle grazing along the edge of the road moved not a hair as our bus bore down. Peons tilling with crooked-stick plows hauled by oxen and burros aided by girls and women brought you instantly to a primeval time.

Outside one village was a pretty walled burial ground, where cheerful peons were drinking and dancing in celebration of the *Día de los Difuntos*. Near the entrance gate, there had just been an accident. A late-model Mustang had catapulted into the waterless irrigation ditch and was squashed; the police had enlisted a mule to pull it back up. The victim, a heavy set *padrone* wearing the fancy white-on-white shirtjacket of the ruling class, had been thrown clear, and was extended comfortably on the botton of the ditch amid broken bottles of the best tequilas.

Our *piloto* said, "*Mucha tequila, muy borracho, ahora muy muerto.*" People from the cemetery came over to the bus, eating candy skeletons and skulls.

In the desolate wastes, there occasionally are the remains of a horse, steer, dog or cow, never unattended, the repast of healthy vultures; but they are outnumbered by rust-bleeding, peeling, lonely, defiant cadavers of senselessly murdered Fords and Chevrolets. There is a radiance of soul in everything. The desert is without the ridiculous self-inflictions, bourgeois torments and masturbations of such meretricious and impertinent things as progress and civilization. It speaks of the nature god. It is calming and silence is its dignity.

The *piloto* played stereo tapes. He sang along with *Indiecita Mía, My Little Indian Maiden*, and the peons joined in.

At bus stops, we got out to piss, drink papaya juice with raw eggs and snack on *burritos* and *tacos* with chile.

Campesino passengers were regarded as famiy by the *piloto*; he patiently stowed their produce and small livestock in the luggage holds. *Campesino* men wore straw sombreros with tassels in the back and thongs to slip under the chin when the wind blew; they carried serapes—native blankets that are sleeveless cloaks. The women wore *rebozos*—eye-catching shawls with which they entwined their babies. Most everybody wore *guaraches* with rubber-tire soles, and socks were quite unheard of.

Ciudad Juárez, with El Paso staring at it, is a big city with the feel of a Latin Los Angeles. The Cordova Bridge connecting the two cities is only a gesture, inasmuch as the Rio Bravo, called the Rio Grande, Great River, is simply a concrete culvert. There are no Hollywood-movie waves; in fact, there is no water—just damp stains. Ragamuffins use it as a playing-and-pissing ground.

We were halfway to Nogales. It was midnight. The passengers were asleep; they did not snore the way gringos do. In the close quarters, the Indian body smell is assertive, like wet brown metals or the crushed bedbugs that I can't forget from my Hoboken tenement childhood—a smell that attracted and repelled.

We stopped in a small pueblo. I saw the sign of a hotel. I asked the kid if she would say over. She said why not.

The hotel was a stark affair—an adobe house with a few extra rooms in the rear. There was an urchin at a makeshift desk. He said he was the *administrador* and a room for two would cost 20 pesos—less than two dollars. We followed him through the kitchen. In the family room, his ailing pregnant mother was on a couch. Her ten children stared at us. Three of the girls were knocked up. The mother got my situation without ado and said firmly that the room would be 50 pesos in advance. I said I wanted to register our Mister and Missus and address—because one never knows. She ripped a piece from a gressy brown-paper bag and said I could write what I pleased, and she would put it in a safe place.

The room on a sort of open-to-the-sky corridor—like a painting of time and space. The bed was enormous and solid; an old light bulb hung from the ceiling. The door was of sheet iron and had an ancient lock and key. It would have been unrealistic to ask for soap, towels and toilet tissue. The kid wanted something to drink and said that, if I went and got it, she'd wait for me.

The Mexicans make night into visual, touchable life-size poetry. They were outside with their families and animals at open-shack restaurants, eating by the light of kerosene lamps; fried pork fat; black beans; soup with onions and shrimp; soup of male goat; tender baby cactus; fruits—sapote, mammee, mango, avocado; and tortillas—maize softened in warm limewater and then ground flat and thin on a stone called a metate and baked on an earthenware griddle over a wood fire. In the occult night, humans and beasts and eucalyptus and bougainvillaea and flesh cooking made you feel as though you were, are and shall always be. Clocks do not exist.

The Mexicans speak low, uncomplicatedly, and summon with a mellifluous "Sissst . . . ! Ppissssst!" I peered avidly at pubescent barefoot girls whose faces were naked shining jewels, and their elders casually comprehended. I said to myself this should be the *mea summa*; why am I dashing my fucking brains against synthetic democracy? Why don't I cut the crap and go native with these *campesinos*? And as the Mexican grandmother on the bus, Luz María, Light of Mary, said, "Live in a hidden Mexican village on your Social Security and writings and be a white god like Cortes. Take an Indian virgin. And her sisters. And then another little girlmate and her sisters, too." I saw not one expression of chagrin for living. Hideous worry does not fit their childlike faces.

In the shadow of the 17th Century Spanish church, on the corner of the arcaded plaza, was the village bar. You will not see a woman in a *campesino* saloon. Penniless young peons were drinking pulque and mescal, the offering of a richly attired silvery-haired don who was singing to the music of a hired *mariachi* band. The bartender shook his head, opened his mouth, rolled his tongue about and whispered, "*Mujercilla . . . afeminada . . . .*"

In the angle of the barroom was the toilet, a hole in the ground, closed off from the bar by a crotch-high partition. In that nook, on the wall above a peon pissing, was a votive light before the *Immaculata*, and looking directly at Our Lord's mother from the opposite wall was a fading page from a magazine: the gorgeous nude of Marilyn Monroe that was in the hymenal issue of *Playboy*. After a bunch of Tecate beers, I bought a fifth of Sauza tequila.

In the morning, I asked the kid from Montana her age.

"Fourteen," she said, grinning.

I accommodated her and put her on the first bus. The early sun rooted out the juices of day and the rural Mexican morning had a pervading vaginal odor. I went into a shabby barber's and, by God, the Indian gave me the best haircut of my life—a masterpiece—for seven pesos, 56 U.S. cents.

By nightfall, my bus had gone through the border town and desert area of the two Nogales. At Sonoita, the officious ("*¡Señor!* I spick Ingleesh!") Mexican customs officer raked unnecessarily through luggage and papers, hinting for gratuities. Some suckers fell for it. I wandered the few paces to the border, dubbed Gringo Pass, and rapped with a tired, disgusted border-patrol officer who said that trying to stop wetbacks was like counting grains of desert sand and that the border patrol had nabbed two donkeys loaded with bales of grass, nonchalantly traversing the border. It was the first time in Immigration Service history that two asses had been arrested and booked.

Along Mexico Highway 2, from Mexicali to the mountaintop pueblito of La Rumorosa, is the setting for Dante's ascent from the

Inferno: guts of extinct volcanoes, sterile Titans, eerie seas of lava and ashy pulverized rock. A lunar landscape.

As the *piloto* raced up around each tight hairpin curve, he kissed the rosary and made the sign of the cross. The driver of a bus coming toward us gave our *piloto* a message. Our *piloto* said over the speaker, "Accident ahead. Carnage and fire. One is not obliged to look."

A pickup truck and a camper had met head on. The driver of the camper had been sheared in half from head to foot. The pickup truck, packed with peon families and bringing home tins of gasoline, was all fire and smoke.

At the grimy Tijuana bus terminal, a sign read

> WELCOME TO THE MOST VISITED BORDER TOWN IN THE WORLD, AND ADMIRABLE MOSAIC OF THE REGIONS OF THE MEXICAN REPUBLIC. AT THIS FRONTIER BEGINS THE FATHERLAND. NUESTRA CASA ES SU CASA. OUR HOUSE IS YOURS!

You can walk along Avenida N. Unidas or Boulevard A. López Mateos to the border. On the way, there are vendors of pottery, leather, copper, shawls, no end of auto painters and repairers, and many lawyers' shacks with signs saying INSTANT MARRIAGES AND QUICK HAPPY DIVORCES.

Hundreds of young braceros in jaunty sombreros and pointed boots or sandals, their possessions in cardboard boxes or shopping bags, lounge longingly by that magical line they can actually touch—the border. The large concerte border marker proclaims

> BOUNDAY OF THE UNITED STATES TREATY OF 1853 RE-ESTABLISHED BY THE CONVENTIONS OF 1882–1889. THE DESTRUCTION OR DISPLACEMENT OF THIS MONUMENT IS A MISDEMEANOR PUNISHABLE BY THE UNITED STATES OR MEXICO.

They look at beacons in the gringo Promised Land of milk and honey, the big 76 gasoline advertisement and the huge McDonald's hamburger sign, and they can see the Valli-Hi Motel and the Valley Shadows Restaurant, and to them, the people who are permitted through the guarded passages and into the Estados Unidos de Norte America on the other side of the hurricane fence have divine privilege.

At night, particularly in fog, they'll try it—what have they to lose?—scampering like frightened chickens through the red shank and manzanilla brush by border marker 255 or through the concrete drainage tunnel under Interstate Route 5.

A border-patrol agent said, "We're all kids playing cops and wetbacks: Tag! You're it! We gather them, write down a lot of crap and put them up in hotels that charge the Government an arm and a leg; even the county jails soak us. We cart them back across the border, and the next night we catch the same poor bastards all over again."

My curiosity sometimes leads me on a fool's chase; on a sidewalk, written in chalk, was ¡ATENCION! SEGUIR LAS FLECHAS PARA LA VERDAD. Follow the arrows to truth. I followed the arrows for blocks; at the end, inside a chalk circle, was a pile of dog stool, and it was labled ¡PRES. GERALDO FORD DE LOS E.U.!

At a newsstand, I asked the guy for the best paper. He said, "*Excelsior, el periódico de la vida nacional.*"

I said, "Do you have a communist paper—or socialist one?" A terrified look came over his face. He was relieved that no one had heard me ask. He said, "*Señor*, do you want information or propaganda?"

On Avenida Revolución, the main street with all the folkware for tourists, is Woolworth's. At the lunch counter, I scanned the menu. The American sitting next to me said, "Pal, what you want is a cup of honest-to-goodness java and the old never-failing ham and eggs, without chili and *tacos*!"

He had been married five times—today's children were unpatriotic, downright subversive. He was in Mexivo to save the U.S. from enemies.

"Buddy, do you know what I did to Papa? I knocked the big fairy on his ass! You should have seen Hemingway's face when he came to!" The guy was smoking, drinking coffee and laughing hysterically at how Hemingway sat on the floor looking up at him; then he choked—and threw up the coffee and his dentures.

He flattered me about my novel *Christ in Concrete* and had me hooked until he said he remembered the story because it was all about Christ of the Andes statue.

El Moreno informed me, "Woolworth's is his beat. That character told me he was with the CIA. He's a fart in the windstorm. We call him John Wayne."

El Moreno is a timeless Yaqui with a hard, remote face and white-leather skin. He was born in the border town of Piedras Negras and went across the Rio Grande to school in Eagle Pass so he speaks Spanish with a Texas drawl; but he's been in Tijuana a lot of years and is the man about town.

When we first met, he declared that the wild, evil Tijuana was gone; today it is a model community with no crime to speak of; and if there were any whores and deviates and criminals, they were contraband people from other places across the border like Dago—San Diego—and El Ay. Just then a policeman and a porcine American came up to us; the cop prentended not to understand English. The fat tourist bellowed, "What the hell kind of place is this? I've just been ripped off in broad daylight, deliberately jostled and goodbye wallet with five hundred bucks and my goddamn documents!" Soon there were two more tourists who had been robbed. El Moreno whispered to the cops to get with it and see that the wallets were brought to him within the hour. The wallets showed up on schedule—without the money. Alone, he said the pickpockets had hungry families and more need for the dollars than did the gringos.

I wanted the formula for his longevity and tough condition. He said a man was what he ate, happiness was what you didn't eat, and his diet was the same as the ape's—fruit and vegetables. "And I chew the peyote cactus and damiana."

Peyote is a buttonlike cactus that grows only an inch aboveground; it is eaten by the Cora and Huichol Indians to cure sickness and during religious ceremonies. El Moreno said it would make me psychic—a better author—and protect me from Montezuma'a revenge, dysentery; damiana is an aromatic yellow-flowered shrub with aphrodisiac properties.

Having done his virtous Tijuana public-relations routine, El Moreno said he would take me at night to a house where no holds are barred everybody did the whole works before your eyes. Also, there would be a platform with a line-up of girls who brought their cunts mouth-high to the clients; you could go along as if blowing a harmonica, sampling for free—kissing, tasting, fingering, licking and sucking your heart out.

I inquired about cock-, dog- and bullfights. He said, "A man doesn't go; only cowardly overgrown kids go. In the Plaza de Toros, they sever the vocal cords of the picadors' horses, the bull slams his horns into the light padding on their sides and breaks their ribs and the innocent creatures scream their agnony in vain. With his lance, the picador cuts the bull's neck tendons and the bull cannot raise his head to see and gauge his reprisals against his tormentors, so the *torero* easily kills an almost-blind bull. It is rotten and one-sided; the bulls, cocks and dogs are the victims of the worst of all animals: the human spectator.

"You gringos are barbarians and don't know your asses from a hole in the ground about us. We were the Oriental Olmec civilization that migrated transpacific to Ecuador ten thousand years ago and moved north to the Gulf of Mexico—Veracruz and Tabasco—and west to Guerrero, Oaxaca, Chiapas and Guatemala. Our Olmec god, the were-jaguar, is the precursor of the Toltec and Aztec feathered serpent.

"You want to know when the Castro revolution is going to happen in Mexico? Probably never. Reds want to be capitalists, and reactionaries are communists turned inside out. *Amigo*, right and left are Siamese twins of technology—belt-system by-products. Our peon negates and defeats the age of science. We still come out of a female's wet vagina. The peon communes with night and is immobilized by day. He snacks, drinks tequila, puts chili in his Coca-Cola and fucks around the clock. By remaining a child, he has no social liabilities, no neurotic realities. The peon can do without the cancer of democracy and the constipation of a Red dictatorship. I got news for you: Castro didn't win by fighting; the old regime fell from the weight of its corruption, the way a leper's prick falls off. OK?"

We stayed out very late doing the night spots. He recommended the Cesare Hotel.

"Hector, the night manager, is my friend. I'll send you an Indian. She won't roll you; you'll be as safe as if you were at your dear mother's breast."

The room cost eight dollars. It wasn't too bad. But I was awakened by a woman crying, "¡Ayuda! ¡Ayuda!" I called the desk and said a woman was yelling for help. The desk said nothing was wrong; she was a drunk from Chicago who wanted to be screwed—the night porter would come up and take care of her.

It is the weekend and hygenic Norte Americanos in droves pound the beaten path, the ten blocks along Avenida Revolución. The Indians with flat copper faces, barrel bodies and stubby little hands and feet sell splashy paper flowers, balloons and knickknack souvenirs to them. And the *turistas*—astride striped burros with white rings around their eyes or in peasant carts with shawls and blankets and exaggerated sombreros or with gun belts and rifles and sabers and neckerchiefs posing à la Pancho Villa and his field women—have pictures taken with a Matthew Brady–vintage camera. They are steered through malls and bazaar to Woolworth's, Sambo's, Denny's and Sanborn's—bleached Bing Crosbys and Doris Days in polyester fabrics, Hush Puppies and sunglasses; they never left the bingo hall and Disneyland.

The Midnight Guitar and 77 Sunset Strip stand side by side, flanked by marriage/divorce factories. The one-armed pea-eyed scarface pitching for The Guitar goes "Pssissst . . . sissst . . . !" And says in oily pandering falsetto, "Hey, *señor*, beautiful pussies, girls topless and bottomless: Take a peep. You see heaven with the hair around it. Beer cheap, seventy-five cents; sexy music from U.S.A. Take a peep. Cost nothing to peep!"

After passing a few times, I thought I'd take the peep that costs nothing. The pimp was right: The nude girls were beautiful, all Glorias. They swarmed and battled over the customers, wrapping arms and legs around them, grabbing their flies, patting their wallets. And it was only midday.

Two blocks from the Tres Estrellas de Oro bus terminal and to the right on Avenida Revolución, running into Puente Mexico, the exclusive domain of the poor begins startlingly. At the edge of the world's worst slum, the sidewalks are jammed with carts and stands outside native bars and singing cafés.

Radios, TVs, generators, auto parts, broken boxes of Kotex, scabby medical supplies, battered chamber pots, sundry appliances, ragged clothes, shamefully worn-out shoes and items useless beyond redemption are tumbled with collectors' handmade adzes, picks, pinch and crowbars, chisels, archaic scutch hammers, planes, manly knives, embossed machetes, massive mattocks. And what made my throat catch—being symbols of my strange life—were a gleaming, exquisite 12-inch Rose bricklayer's trowel with a slick bicycle-grip leather-on-wood handle and an untouched ivory IBM portable typewriter without a case—both undoubtedly hot. I paid $6.50 for the lovely trowel and $35 for the typewriter. I said to Pietro di Donato, "Now, you son of a bitch, you'll write the novel *Elena* on that sweet IBM and keep the rust off that ringing Rose blade because you may have to rebuild the world!"

Like Antaeus, Mexicans have an affinity with the lowly earth—squatting, sprawling, as if on silken sheets. A woman sits askew on the ground peddling herbs, simples, potions, words on paper that will transform you into a *divinador*, seaweeds, dried insects, crystallized placentas and snake oils—all of which will cure cancer, piles, indigestion, ill humors, evil eyes, impotence, infertility or any disease or affliction you could name.

A young derelict with the butt of a joint behind his ear has just died of alcoholism. They walk over his body imperturbably. He had the right to leave all this in his own way, and in the meat store facing the dead youth, legions of fearless flies park on the pork. The sign says LAS MOSCAS VENCEN, the flies win.

Stands and booths just wide enough to seat one or two or three people are frying—in turgid simmering fat—lungs, brains, sweetbreads, intestines, clusters of shell-less eggs freshly yanked from chickens' bellies, animal feet, livers, gizards, testicles; roasting pigs' ears and tails and scalped goats' heads with gaping eyes on lively charcoal. Grown men bite the fiber off sugar-cane stalks and eat the cores with drooling pleasure. There are seafood stands with mollusks, thick glasses filled with cold shrimp, lobster, oysters, conch, crab meat and baby crawling crabs in chili, broiled shark steaks, cumbersome pismo clams with lime on the brown insides, saffron-steaming caldrons of *paella* Valenciana (disappointing), beans and peppers of many colors, melons, *garbanzos* in sticky verdant pods, a candy made from orchid bulbs and everywhere the cheesy groiny reek of tortillas. All foods without exception are lorded over fiercely, nervously, by fly squadrons.

This fabulous filth, destitution and squalor of the shack homes are so utter and organic as to be godlike. A genius could not assemble the collages of trash, the impromptu patterns and graffiti of junk, ideographs of contempt for order rendering the serious comic—a futile barrier of bedsprings, TV antennas, car seats, a Mercedes chassis, oil tanks, bottles, cans, crumpled auto hoods and twisted doors—exceeding in existentialism, nonsense and surrealism the best of today's scrap art. Shanties, contrived of moldy crates, pieces of truck bodies, thatch and wattle, sheet plastic, corrugated tin, mud adobe and papier-mâché, lean and hold one another teeteringly up in continuous rows. They are on lanes with grandiose, progressive names: Insurgentes, Victoria, Reforma, Idealismo. Each home is numbered and the inhabitant's name glaringly scrawled. There are simulated arrangements of inner courts and patios, and the alleys are so emaciated that you could piss easily into your neighbor's windowless sty.

Kids sit and yak in dishonored, abandoned cars that have forgotten motion, glass and wheels. Men are doing something to jalopies with a frenzy, as if fucking them. What woman isn't pregnant?

And what man works? Men recline in the shade with that peace that surpasses understanding, inscrutably watching little girls and boys and old women staggering determinedly under loads of brushwood or clay jugs or, with a shoulder yoke, five-gallon tins of sallow water from a streamlet, church fountain or town tap. The females wash clothes by hand in stone tubs as doggedly as Sisyphus and somehow they hang radiant laundry; their offspring are as clean as angels. Tykes lack covering for their behinds, but their gold and diamond-speck earrings sparkle in the sun.

*

I went to the address that was mentioned in one of Gloria's letters. The garden wall was an enfilade of bald bus tires. The shack had two levels. Above was a tiny wood-box balcony with children, dog, cat, canary, cans of flowers, a woman suckling a baby. Downstairs there was a crude sign: CUARTOS PARA ALQUILAR EN LA PLANTA BAJA—NO NINOS, lower quarters for rent—no children, and as an afterthought in small letters, economical—sanitary—attractive—secure.

Yes, of course they knew the romantic Glow-rree-ah. While trying to cross the border, she had been gang-banged by the coyotes. That was not nice. The police got them. The picture of the rapists was in *¡Alarma!* Of a certainty, Gloria of Umira is in Los Angeles.

As I stepped out into the foul rutted road, a woman pushed aside the rag curtain of a doorway and hurled a tin can of piss and shit, just missing me as I swerved—I'd rather be hit by a baseball bat. The pretty woman and children on the balcony laughed, and the woman called down to the hag with the dripping can in her hand. "*Gringo. A-mierda-cano. Muy delicado. ¡Mieda mierda!*"

Time and desert heat petrify putrescence into jewels of reconsideration. Mexico's cloacal spoors, anal/uterine/wombal aromas arouse taste buds; it is an olfactory experience you later miss. Human piss and excrement, old and new commingling, seasoned with food leavings and animal offal, baking, frying, broiling, toasting and pullulating in the passion of Montezuma's blazing sun is the most stirring and indelibly memorable queen of smells.

Around the corner, on Avenida Callejón Revolución, is a carnival, put on by Atracciones Alvarez from the state of Michoacán. The Whip and the Ferris wheel are being whirled as crazily as the Mexican drives his car, but the carrousel mares are still being screwed to the turntable.

A policeman is smoking a cigar and reading a Spanish Mickey Mouse paperback. I ask what holiday is it. He says, "*Santa Cruz, patrona de los albañiloes*," patron of bricklayers. Construction jobs are being blessed with food, drink and big flowered crosses.

Peons come in from the countryside by bus, on foot, in pickups— or trot in on asses' haunches. Any show or display is an incalculable treat. The peons watch openmouthed as the explosives hiss and boom and screech and twirl and racket. Monkeys and miniature alligators perform professionally. The hokeypokey man busily scrapes ice and soaks it with syrups. The air is thick with piglet roasts. The flies are enjoying themselves, too. There are Indians in their tribal outfits of beads and feathers and tassels and ruling dons and their *señoras* in stunning *charro* costumes on fine mounts, and these contemporary conquistadors sport loaded pistols and cartridge belts with real bullets.

Dwarfs from a visiting convention elbow and butt among people's legs; they permit children and awed peons to fondle their oversized heads and reticent little limbs, and they are wisely amused. Hurdy-gurdies grind and drone, and the carrousel calliope flutes nostalgic music. The peons look about like actors coming onstage for the first time, partaking with felicitous countenance of idiotic loving-kindly beatification. When Jesus Christ crosses the border and comes to this market place, these children will not let him down. He will pipe and they will dance.

I go with them from the carnival to the bars, and there is bar after bar after bar, each dark and overfilled, no bigger than the average room, and always without gringos—who fear for their hypocritical blanched skins. They begin with margaritas in tall thin glasses and alternate with beer from nearby Tecate. I drank mescal from Oaxaca in a black clay vessel with a pouch that contained salt and *gusanitos de maguey*—the white worms that are found around the heart of the century plant.

Within the broad adobe walls, the *mariachi* rhythms cut you open and fuse into your veins and arteries. The Mexicans dance hypnotized and slither like snakes, rubbing and rotating crotches into one another. And the girls have that genital, tongue-provoking, Indian smell that coats your mouth, nostrils and throat to pungent, cloying salivation. It is a sanctuary of entrancement; a fetal lair you should never leave. You say to the stupid absurd world, "Go fuck yourself; go shit in the sea!" Here there is no generation gap—because decrepit crones let their hair flow down to their asses like teenagers and they are painted and have all the dreams of youth, and no one condemns, and criticism dies on the vine, and care has no place. These folk are the obviators, the nonaccusers—each an autonomous planet serene in the ageless cosmos of innocence. They do not recognize sin, hate, repression. I saw not one bomber pilot. Something whispers into their souls and tells them no one fools nature or death, and all exit with less than when they entered. Sublime is the word.

Cocks on the hills of Tijuana are crowing. It is dawn at the border. The morningtide routs shadows; light floods the dew-wet galvanized wire fence that divides Americans from the children of the sun. El Moreno said his people played at being Christians and thought no more of the foreign Semitic God than they did of dolls. They were at home only with the ancestral deity; they worked it out from nature: the miracle of day drawn from the black bowels of night. They committed human sacrifice not for evil kicks, but because they believed the sun-god needed blood to give him strength for his daily return from the far region of death.

Sitting on the ground by the fence were a peon and his young daughter. Their faces were hunger. In their booths a few feet away, officers of the gringo border patrol were drinking coffee from a Thermos and eating doughnuts. The girl was looking at America. She put her fingers through the webbing of the fence and caressed America. They were a barefoot primitive pair. They needed a Samaritan, and I could not decide. What Indians were they? I know of at least 30 tribes. Were they Chinantecs who speak by making sounds with their mouths closed? Mazatecs who dance the *huapango* and the *bamba*? Cholutecans from the Holy City, Cholula? Zapotecs? The vegetarian, Otomis? Or, like Gloria, Tarahumara Indians from the canyon caves of the Sierra Madre Occidental in the state of Chihuahua?

I meandered some miles along the border, but the girl's being came with me—the statuesque shoulders, the way her sitting graced the earth, the nigrescent sheen of the high-cheek-boned wide lava face, the purest look from the wild doe's obsidian eyes.

Fifty dollars, four hundred pesos, would feed them and keep them alive for a month. Maybe they'd make it across the border and eventually become gringoized chicanos, and maybe she'd work for my brother Giovanni in the big house with the picture window and swimming pool in Studio City and we'd talk about the past. Or maybe they would flee and, with intelligent instinct, like birds, return to the rain forest, the sheltering cave, to nature.

When I mutely handed her the pesos, our finger tips touched and the world was created.

When Willy K. Vanderbilt Frolicked
And I Shoveled His Snow

During the Depression I lived on a Long Island hillside that overlooked Northport harbor and William K. Vanderbilt's baronial estate, "Eagle's Nest," in Centerport. Anchored in the harbor was Willy's gleaming white yacht the ALVA, as big as an ocean liner, and on the shore was the hangar for his world-spanning flying boat and smaller planes.

The Depression was a renaissance for the unemployed. Being on Home Relief you could sleep late, loll, read books, and seriously devote yourself to sex; sex as the topic, the art, the *raison d'etre* of life. Sex was the entertaining safety valve that saw America through the Depression's superfluity of time and obviated social disorder. Some ill winds blew good, some liabilities became assets. The memorable snowstorm of the early '30s was a boon; it gave us Home-Reliefers shovels, 50c. an hour, with a cozy berth for me on Willy K.'s estate. Digging out Willy's snow-packed private roads I was befriended by one of his host of caretakers, Nelson, whose hobbies were his trumpet and the servant girls. Nelson conjured work for me, some masonry, gardening, and odd jobs.

I'll never forget the head chef sending one of the chauffeurs and the Rolls Royce all the way into Willy's Park Avenue home for a box of iodized salt, nor peering into the window of the music room and seeking a drunken nude woman at the piano playing and singing the *Ave Maria*.

I had never met a rich man before, and beholding a real multi-millionaire in the flesh, Willy K. Vanderbilt, was like seeing God. Puttering around Eagle's Nest I came within touching distance of the rich. Money has a chemical effect upon the human system. A tremendous bank account can create a physiological metamorphosis. The Aladdin's lamp of immense wealth makes for elegantly shaped torsos and limbs, close-fitting ears, equine faces, skin of living porcelain, gem-clear eyes that do not mirror immorality, and a stance that needs not soul. The unharassed young are confident as the stars and have an air of maturity, and the old have an agelessly young semblance.

The help, living the life of lords on Willy's bounty, gossiped gleefully about him and the other Vanderbilts: that he seduced Rosamund Warburton from her husband, kept a French mistress named Nellie on Riverside Drive near Grant's tomb, she and Willy entertaining the President there, Rosamund's alcoholism, how Willy played Jekyll and Hyde under aliases and went slumming in the lower depths. At the time I thought it was shameful for servants to scandalize and bite the hand that fed them.

It was no secret that Willy K., then 60ish, was a swordsman of Aphrodite, a fabulousy rich Don Juan who lunged at every passing skirt regardless of race, color or creed. The provincials referred to his estate not as Eagle's Nest but as Wolf's Lair.

One summer's day I swam with a young Northport rake named Lidvig Rutter to the ALVA, sneaked up the ship's ladder and saw his lusty old nibs dallying with an exquisite high-yellow girl in an enviable but unmentionable position. I should have had a camera with me.

Willy K. and I had something in common: girls whose people were on Home Relief and smelled of kerosene lamp smoke in bed. A kersone-smelling clam-digger's daughter working in the kitchen of the estate went to bed with Willy by day, and by night with me.

Willy K., well past three score and 10, had to forfeit his earthly consolation in January, 1944, leaving behind $40 million and proving that all men are not born equal. But, if the Good Book deceive us not, Willy K. has been trying to shove a camel through a needle's eye since.

In many cases death is a blessed escape for the hard-up who live in hopes and die in despair, but death for a millionaire is a Greek tragedy, an irrevocable farewell to *la dolce vita*, lovely orgies, myriad pleasures, ego, power, divine foods and drinks, servants, cute deviations, multiple lives, and gorgeous young girls, a veritable paradise lost.

It would be a classic of justice if the poor had never been born and the rich never had to die. But I did not make the world.

The Guaranty Trust Company of New York was the Executor of the Last Will and Testament of William K. Vanderbilt, Deceased.

The will was dreary reading: Legacy of income for life and $2 million for this female relative, and two for that one, and so on.

The final accounting of the vast holdings did not materialize for judicial settlement and distribution until 1955, with interest accured.

Onto the stage of the Surrogate's court studded with posh legatees such a Phelps, Paine, Warburton, Gaynor, Pratt and Hutton, comes an elderly little gray-haired, bespectacled, quietly dressed woman of Jewish background, to softly claim one third of the $40 million. She comes into the proceedings like a character from a Pirandello play, with her petition:

> "To set aside the Final accounting of the Will of the Late William K. Vanderbilt, Deceased.
>
> This petition of the undersigned Dora Blowers respectfully states:
>
> That I was married to William K. Vanderbilt under the alias of Arthur Blowers on December 30th, 1925 by the Clerk of the Court in Stamford, Connecticut.
>
> That as a result of this marriage, three children were born to us, a son in September, 1926, named William Harris Blowers, a son in October, 1927, named Reginald Philp Blowers and a daughter in July, 1933 named Alva Esther Blowers.
>
> That I am the widow of the deceased William K. Vanderbilt.
>
> That in September, 1927, my husband revealed his identity to me as William K. Vanderbilt and stated he divorced his first wife, Virgina Graham Vanderbilt, to make good his marriage to me. That he was forced into his marriage to Rosamund Lancaster Warburton for "social misdemeanor." That Willian K. Vanderbuilt never legally adopted the two Warburton children, Barclay and Rosemary Warburton. That William K. Vanderbilt made a settlement of 2 million by a secret divorce from Rosamund Lancaster Warburton in 1932, and in 1933, asked for Catholic *demarches* from the Pope. That she was his wife in name only.

That mysterious fires with the love letters my husband William K. Vanderbilt sent to me and the fire with the furniture he bought for me and the disappearance of important papers, change of records and substitutions through the years pertaining to this claim, bear out my contention that many unusual occurrences to hide my husband's identity took place through the years.

That I never sought publicity having personally contacted Mr. Crooker of the Guaranty Trust Company in October 1947 and again by letter on June 1952 pleading for consideration of the legal rights of my children and me to avoid Court expenses and notoriety.

Wherefore, your Petitioner prays that an Order be granted directing the Will and Probate Proceedings of the late William K. Vanderbilt be set aside and a postponement be granted for the final audit of accounts of the late William K. Vanderbilt by the Guaranty Trust Company of New York, in order to give your Petitioner time to further her claim to the moneys due her from the estate of William K. Vanderbilt.

Dora Blowers."

Adding theatrical cast to the ensuing *Right You Are, If You Think You Are* drama was the surrogate, Edgar F. Hazelton, former Supreme Court judge, District Attorney, and defense lawyer for the corset salesman Judd Gray, and sash-weight murderess Ruth Synder—("Good God, Pietro, I had a deal to snatch Ruth from the chair but the lousy D.A. double crossed me!" "Ah, the past is a bucket of ashes, the sun gone down, a chamberpot out the window!" Years ago David Belasco used to go to court to enjoy the histrionics of the young criminal lawyer Hazelton, and offered him a fat storage contract.)

Gasser and Hayes Esquires, very proper patrician legal gentlemen representing the respondent seemed rather set against handing over 13 million to Dora 'Vanderbilt' Blowers and Willy K.'s possible three children, notwithstanding the casual coincidence that somehow or other William, Reginald and Alva Blowers happened to be living images of Willy K. At first they suggested that Dora Blowers was not of sound mind. That could not hold water; Dora Blowers was a federal government employee and if the court accepted Gasser and Hayes' version of her it would have meant that it pleased the FBI, the Treasury and the Air Force to keep crazy people in their ranks.

It behooved the Vanderbilt Estate to come up with an Arthur Blowers in the quick. They found four Arthur Blowers in the quick. The most suitable for their purposes was an *Of Mice and Men* one in Ticonderago, New York, a superannuated loner, floater and boozer who had been the periodic guest of various Veterans' mental hospitals, otherwise a willing and accommodating chap. His testimony was a hobo's odyessy. Woodenly he said he had been the husband of the gray-haired Dora Blowers present in the Surrogate's chamber. Was he the father of her three children? Well, he supposed so—he could have been—of course he did not know the names of his children. He bummed about the country here and there, and when East shacked up with Dora Blowers once in a while.

(Now the spotlight is on the character called Dora Blowers.)

Q. Mrs. Blowers, you realize you are under oath now. A. Yes.

Q. You must tell the truth. A. I always do.

Q. And that if there is a falsehood, you will be subject to the penalties of the law. A. Right. Q. What is your occupation?

A. I am a clerk-typist with the government for over 11 years, at present the finance contract desk of the Newark Airport Procurement District, a brance of the Air Force. I do secretarial, statistical and auditing work. I was with the Department of Justice from February, 1942, and in 1944 when my husband William K. Vanderbilt died I asked for and was given permission to be transferred to the office of Dependents' Benefits, a branch of the Treasury Department in Newark. (Before that she had been a memory teacher, taught handicapped children, and had been a teacher with the Central Commercial High School at 214 East 42nd Street, New York City.)

Q. You saw the witness take the stand who testified he lived in Ticonderoga? A. Yes. Q. And said he was Arthur Blowers and *the* Arthur Blowers who married you under that name. *Is* he?

A. No—Definitely no! Q. You don't need to call out loudly in a dramatic manner; just say so. Have you ever seen him before? A. I met him in 1953 in the office of Mr. Viscardi, when Senator Morritt, then my attorney, told me there was an 'Arthur Blowers' living in Ticonderoga. Mr. Viscardi called in this Mr. Blowers that is here now and asked him 15 intimate questions relating to our courtship and marriage, but he wasn't able to answer. How could he? There was no recognition—neither this 'Mr. Blowers' knew me nor did I know him. Q. When and where did you meet *your* Arthur Blowers? A. I was employed as the teacher for children at Camp Arcady on Lake George. In the evenings I went down to the camp entertainments at the foot of the lake and there met my husband—then my sweetheart. He took pictures of me but would never let me photograh him. Q. When did you meet Mr. Vanderbilt again after Lake George? A. Well, I came back to Jersey City and he said he took a job with the New York, New Haven and Hartford line on a new division that they were breaking in around Harlem on the far east side of the New York Central line. I used to telephone him there and he would telephone me at Jersey City at my mother's house.

Q. All this time you knew him as Arthur Blowers? A. Yes.

Q. You didn't know him as William K. Vanderbilt? A. No. Though he was many years older than I he was charming. On December 30th, 1925 we met at the Grand Central station. He had a white gold wedding ring for me with a wreath design. We took the train to Stamford, Connecticut. We both made application for marriage and that application was read to us by George R. Close, the clerk of the court. Q. Where did you go from there? A. We went to 48 East 92nd Street. That is where we set up house-keeping. It was a beautiful duplex; had a large living room with a spiral staircase, remodeled brownstone. Q. Did you become pregnant there? A. Yes. Our son William was born at home September, 1926. Q. Mr. Blowers paid the doctor? A. Yes, he paid Dr. McLean. I lived entirely on what Mr. Blowers paid. In August, 1927, my husband said he had to take a long railroad trip. I objected to that because I was expecting another child soon. While he was gone I saw in the newspaper his picture and a picture of my best friend and neighbor, Rose, together—

(The Court: it sounds fantastic—but the truth has often sounded fantastic.) A. (interposing.)—I had a neighbor that came in, by the name of Rose, and when my husband went on his railroad trip, both of them disappeared and then I saw her picture—I recognized her first, Rosamund Lancaster Warburton, just married to William K. Vanderbilt, and there was his round picture below her, in the New York *American*, August 28th, 1927.

Q. When did you have your second child with Mr. blowers?

A. October 5th, 1927. Q. Was this before or after the Rosamund—
A. No, she came into the house when we were there before the first
child was born and again later and in—Then my husband came back
to me at 48 East 92nd Street and he revealed his identity to me. Q. Is
that the first time you knew Arthur Blowers as William K. Vanderbilt?
A. Right. Up to that time I believed he was Arthur Blowers. Q. Had
he left his wife, Mrs. Warburton, at that time, when he came back to
you? A. He certainly did. He lived with me right along, and we went
to Jersey City, at Claymore Avenue, for the birth of our second child.

Q. Can you explain how your first son got the name of William?

A. I wanted to name him after my father Harris, and my husband
said, "If you are going to name him after your father, name him after
my father, too." so I was going to name him Arthur Harris Blowers, and
he said, "No, my father's was William," so, innocently, I named him
after both grandfathers, William Harris Blowers. After he revealed his
identity to me we named the following two children after his family.

Q. At that time were [you] ill in the mind? A. No, except for the
shock that my neighbor Rose had taken my husband and that my
husband was another personality, even regardless of the name.

Q. Do you recall anything about French's farmhouse? A. In 1928
my husband sent me up to French's Farmhouse at Lake Conega. I met
Gloria Vanderbilt, then five or six years old. My children and Gloria
and some other children were being boarded there—it is about 10
miles outside of Monticello.

Q. Did you receive love letters from your husband? A. Oh, yes,
when he went away to adjust his affairs. Q. Where are those letters?
A. I left a package containing them and my husband's officer's
gold pin with Alfred Ross, a lawyer, on Broadway, Monticello for
safe-keeping. When I had need of them to prove my relationship
to William K. Vanderbilt, Mr. Ross wrote back, "A mysterious fire
occurred and the package you left was burned."

Q. When was the last time you saw Mr. 'Blowers' Vanderbilt?

A. I saw him in the fall of 1943 in Virginia; he came to see our
children. He still insisted he would do right by me and the children.
Though he was always charming, he lied. I know it is startling and

unbelievable, but I swear again to every statement I made. All this did not happen overnight—I know that my husband was William K. Vanderbilt.

There were five hearings. Witnesses who had 'seen' William K. Vanderbilt with Dora Blowers as Arthur Blowers were subpoenaed but never appeared. Dora Blowers' request for trial by jury was denied. As witness for the respondent, Harold Vanderbilt showed his social breeding; he was courteous and sympathetic to Dora Blowers but stated that though quite familiar with his brother's many amorous adventures he had no recollection of the Blowers association.

The Guaranty Trust with blurred scraps of paper and handwriting experts fashioned a broken-down roustabout, Arthur Blowers of Ticonderoga, in place of Willy K. as Dora's husband. Whether Dora and Arthur Blowers of Ticonderoga actually knew each other became a problem for the grave to answer, for Arthur Blowers of Ticonderoga conveniently died during the hearings. Also, it was unexplainably strange that the signature of Willy K. on the will and the signature of an Arthur Blowers on a 1939 motor vehicle license from Huntington, Long Island where Willy L. lived, were the same.

Poor people try to ape the rich; why should the rich be denied the privilege of aping the poor? Why shouldn't Willy K. have been allowed to taste the peculiar glory of coarse bread and bed with Dora Blowers? The rich are waking up and fighting for their democratic rights; multi-millionaires want to be reclassified as human beings and savor all the kicks of our pluralistic society; now they beg to be boot-lickers of the common man, striving to be servants of The People, battling each other to work as mayors, governors, and President.

On the stage of Inheritance Law, a penniless, sweet, little old government employee is contradicted by a $40 million protagonist, and yet there is an eerie feeling in the chamber that Dora Blowers certainly knew Willy K. The Court, weighing all factors, decides Dora Blowers is not to receive $13 million and dismisses her petition.

If Dora Blowers fabricated her story why wasn't she punished for perjury or committed? Was her relaltionship with Willy K. a psychic miracle? Was she a dream character in search of an author? Was all this a hallucinated hoax, or a very great injustice?

I revisited the locale of Vanderbilt's estate and sat at the bar of Mariner's Inn on the Northport shorefront. With me was Ludvig Rutter, no longer young, but whose air still bore the gypsy earrings of the guy differently marked from the herd. Through the seascape window I again beheld Willy's place across the harbor, the baroque piles with the Spanish tile roofs the hangar vacant of its metal birds, and in the harbor where royally bestrode his floating city of pleasure, the ALVA, was the bourgeois armada, the bobbing bottoms of the newly affluent little man.

The area surrounding Willy's sexing fief has bowed its neck to the fickle, fretful deity, Change: Gone are the salty clam-diggers, the *Spoon River Anthology* rustics and the mannered master-aping servant class to the rich. The Levittized man hath come and his pregnant prairie runneth over. Breathing upon Willy's lordly domain are education mills, theatrical supermarkets, a technicolor maze of pizza-oramas, toilet-bowloramas, this and that shoppes, cat and dog sanitoriums, eating factories, surrealistic temples vending soul insurance, kegling lanes, roadside burger and spun candy shrines, drive-ins, discount bazaars, green thumb marts, Mephisto's heavenly loan companies and all the material carnivalia of the atom-goosed United Statesian.

Willy bequeathed his estate and $2 million for its maintenance to the county. Eagle's Nest, of yore paganly hallowed with Willy's sensuous revels, is now a decorous institution, a public museum; yet in truth, a memorial monument to his victorious, Olympian hedonism. Today common feet tread his Oriental rugs. Joe Jerk's eyes gawk at Willy's inactive bed, the palatial appointments, the gardens worthy of Louis XIV, with slavish awe. Joe Jerk is convinced that Mr. W. K. Vanderbilt, tycoon maker of railroads, was a lofty pillar of Democracy.

But Ludvig Rutter and I, downing gold Scotch, still vividly saw old Willy in his birthday suit on the sun-sparkling deck of the gleaming white ALVA entwined like a centaur with the nude exotic brown girl. To do justice to the past romantic age, that pose should be immortalized in marble alongside the stern bronze statue of Commodore Vanderbilt in front of great Grand Central station.

The Widow Of Whadda-you-want

Left to itself the mind is a rather honest functionary, but put people together—particularly my paesanos—well then, addio to facts. And yet, the magnified bubble of fiction can also become the mother of history. Let's go back to West Hoboken, 1922, a ten-cent piece, the number 99, and a buttonhole maker called "Carnivale."

I remember the day of Whadda-you-want's death. You wonder why: Whadda-you-want. My paesanos were perfectly illiterate, or as they themselves said: "—without alphabet." They hardly knew their own names let alone the spelling of the names. To them anything written on paper was magic; only in the archives of the city hall in Vasto, Italy, and on their passports would you find their actual names—if actual. What names did they know themselves as? By American nicknames, or by others they earned from some uncomplimentary characteristic or idiosyncrasy. A Vincenzo became a "Jimmy" in America, a Simone became "Harry," a Sebastiano "Jack." In the years Simone Whadda-you-want had been in America all the English he learned to say was a vociferous "Whadda-you-want?" And thus to the paesanos from Simone-to-Harry he became Whadda-you-want, his wife, the woman of Whadda-you-want, his nine sons, the masculines of Whadda-you-want.

One afternoon a voice raised itself like the call of a horn. Mother paused at the coal stove. The call was a low muted quavering summoning. Mother went to the window. Across the backyards and framed in her kitchen window was Rosamaria, the wife of Whadda-you-want. Mother respectfully made the sign of the Cross. The Black Angel had visited the house of Whadda-you-want.

The home of Whadda-you-want resembled a warehouse; it was stocked with the miscellaneous stuffs carried on freighters, for Whadda-you-want was a longshoreman on Lackawanna docks in Hoboken along the Hudson River. Whadda-you-want died by drowning. He had stumbled off the gangplank while leaving the ship for home. Whether he could swim or not was beside the point—when the police grapneled his body up from bottom they found some one hundred pounds of salt pork cached under his overcoat.

When our paesano mothers rushed to the scene of death, christening or wedding they scruffed along their entire brood. Picture the Whadda-you-want flat with its assembled dutybound keeners and their hordes of children ranging from breast-clingers to bashful young men and women. Rosamaria (the fair) Whadda-you-want was a simple Amazonian woman. For the women of my people procreation, aside from religious dictates and certain initial pleasures, seemed a blooming form of beauty treatments. Their complexions were baby-smooth, and their flesh had a sweet mammillary fragrance. Mother used to say: "The woman who does not have babies, fruits and purges soon turn sour." A buxom wife was at a premium. Any woman who weighed less than one hundred and eighty pounds was "wasting away."

As for paint and powder and short hair—that was the trademark of a shameless woman, a prostitute.

The lament of Rosamaria and her chorus of mourners began that afternoon and endured until the sun had set and arose again. This ritual which came to America with my paesanos and that had been performed with exact fidelity has since become lost in the fusing blends of the new composite creature, the America Man. But that afternoon, Rosamaria, sitting on the couch in the kitchen surrounded by the Vastese women, could just as well have been Rosamaria the freshly notified widow of Caesar's warrior drowned in the Rubicon. I sat on the floor pinned in with the children of "The hairy one," "The Meatball," "The Cheesegrater," "The Artichoke," and others. On the wall above Rosamaria was an outdated calendar in the Italian red, white and green, with the wistfully small King Umberto standing behind his seated queen, princes and princesses, against a background of belching cannon, gondolas, Mt. Vesuvius, the Colosseum, and the ruins of Pompeii. To the side of the calendar was a faded lithograph of Jesus, Mary and Joseph. Hanging on a hook between these two pictures was an object that I always beheld in awe whenever I was in the Whadda-you-want kitchen, a large loaded pistol, recalling Whadda-you-want's military service under the ill-fated Baratire in Ethiopia.

In this, the keening, Rosamaria was the Chosen; mother and the other paesano women were the Simulators. Here was the tonal fugue of grief, music raw from the flesh-embedded soul. In this vocal exorcism was the propitiation to the Death God; Rosamaria the deprived, and her handmaidens whom it behove to pretend they also had been robbed by the Death God, therefore confusing the Reaper that he might overlook their homes. Rosamaria's wordless song came throaty and lifted ever so slowly, even as a burdened bird. The paesano women followed her passage with synchronized dissonance. Hour upon hour it continued, the tenor and tempo increasing imperceptibly. By late evening the paesano men arrived—my father included. They watched obediently. This belonged strictly to the women; the women who had borne children, the high priestesses of bed and board. By dawn the keening had reached the highest possible peak of shrilling. Then Rosamaria spoke. "In God's will lies my peace." Catharsis had been achieved. When father and mother gathered us tired children to leave, Rosamaria was wolfishly eating a heroic portion of hot peppers and bread immersed in wine.

How fiction became a fact, how the abstract made of itself substance in the life of the widow of the Whadda-you-want, came about through a dime and the numerals 9 and 9—or if you please: "head to head." The paesanos played the "numbers" daily. Numbers were picked through hunches, combinations, dates, coincidences, but mostly decided by dreams, and the dream-form was called La Smorphia. "Chicken" Compitello, a roguish Neapolitan, was the numbers man. Every day for twenty years Compitello had collected ten cents from Rosamaria for the number she had faith in, 99, head-to-head. On the Friday after Whadda-you-want had been buried 99 came through.

"Rosamaria!" said Compitello with fanfare, "head-to-head has proven!" He did not bother to tell her how much, and if she had not been an incredibly simple woman she would have learned from him that she had won eighty dollars.

"It will take a little time to get the money; papers, signatures, letters, lawyers and so on—" Although "The Chicken" had the eighty dollars right in his pocket. The Neapolitan Chicken never spoke forthrightly; even in privacy he would work his sole listener into a corner and whisper from the side of his mouth, making of ordinary talk a secret subject, the while bobbing his head about to apprehend eavesdroppers. He confided to the Artichoke that Rosamaria had won eight hundred dollars; a stretching of fact that could only boot the paesanos to pursue more furiously the numbers. The Artichoke's woman immediately relayed to Teresina the Meatball that the widow of Whadda-you-want had "done the numbers to the tune of eighteen hundred dollars, or, more like twenty-eight hundred dollars." By evening mother informed father that Rosamaria had "taken the numbers for at least forty-eight hundred dollars." Through peddlers of pots, pans, needles, and holy articles, by word of mouth, rumor spread to the other outposts of Vastese colonials, from West Hoboken to Harlem to Baltimore to Cleveland. In Cleveland the figure was eight thousand dollars. Through a professional letter writer the news went trans-Atlantic to the ancient home village, Vasto, Italy. Between illiteracy and the mysteries of dollars and lire, the correspondence from Vasto back to West Hoboken leveled off the figure at eighty thousand dollars!

West Hoboken, aside from being a stew of nationalities, was a humming textile town; the Schwarzenbach Huber silk mill on Highpoint avenue and Spring street, dyeing mills, numerous small Swiss embroidery mills and clothing sweat shops. "Carnivale" Tedeschi had made millions of buttonholes since his steerage glimpse of the Statue of Liberty. Automatic buttonhole machines were rare in those days. Bent over his lumpy manual machine, he whistled incessantly. "Chinese" Giovanni alongside of him would mutter: "The bird in the cage sings either for joy or rage."

Tedeschi slipped a garment over the bedplate. Guided by the tailor's chalk marks he clamped the garment in buttonhole position; he pulled the lever arm and down came the small knife cutting the eye and slit in the cloth; his short legs push-pedaled the sprocket, shuttling the upper and lower threaded needles through the throat-plate to edge a neat chain-stitch around the buttonhole.

"Eighty thousand skins," sighed the Chinese, "eighty thousand American pictures!"

"What mouthing of 'eighty thousand' is this?" questioned Carnivale Tedeschi.

"How the wheel of fortune rotates," philosophized the Chinese. "One week the police drag Whadda-you-want out of the river on the end of a hook like a swollen stinking cod; the next week his widow hooks the numbers for eighty thousand fish!"

Upon hearing that Carnivale trembled and nearly put a buttonhole through the palm of his hand. Carnivale Tedeschi was not a true paesano, a blooded paesano. He had originally come from Ortona-a-Mare, a village to the north of Vasto. He was somewhat accepted by our tribe through marriage to Fiammetta, a withered unpleasant Vastese woman who bore him nine daughters. The clannishness of the Vastese was monolithic. Their pride in being Vastese was such that feuds, hatreds, curses, violence and murder were reserved only for their own kind. The Vastese ("Strong but gentle!") had their own special language—more like code; a woman was: La Mat, a man: U-Bitzuare, silent: A-Buzenai. Anyone not born in Vasto was looked down upon—and that took in the whole world. Tedeschi, like any outsider who married a Vastese, had to be circumspect and defer to the birthright Vastese. Vincenzo (Jimmy) Tedeschi was a short, stout, balding, middle-aged man with a florid cherubic face; his manner was mild and fumbling, and he had the habit of rolling his head, as if constantly trying to dodge the quick hands of his wife. The sallow, grim, attenuated Fiammetta was his antipode; and it was she who derisively dubbed him "Carnivale," which meant clown, shambling fool. "Carnivale! Your fat buffon face invites slapping!"

As though in revenge upon Nature for weighting her with nine daughters, Fiammetta was desperately penurious. The wine in the Tedeschi household was watered dregs, the meals, the very cheapest: dried beans, pasta, kale, stale bread, beef heart, pig's blood, knuckle bones, chickens' necks. She worked fiendishly at embroidery, cutting far into the night by candle-light, driving her daughters with their scissors scalloping the endless rolls of embroidery, blaming them for being female and lashing out at Carnivale whose only defense was to whistle—which made her bile flow faster. It was not uncommon to see Fiammetta pushing a scraggly baby carriage loaded with salable rubbish she had retrieved from evil-smelling town dump. It was on one of these scavenging trips that a large dump rat ripped her leg, and the very day Carnivale was apprised of Rosamaria's eighty thousand dollars, Fiammetta lay in bed hopelessly sick with bloodpoisoning. A sense of destiny struck Carnivale. Rosamaria had won the fabulous riches with 99; she had nine sons, he had nine daughters, Rosamaria was without man, and he—Fiammetta was in condition grave. Of course, it the lord saw fit—he shuddered to contemplate a second wife while the first one was still warm.

Fiammetta personally supervised the event of her passing. It was primitive scene of adjudication. The ceremony attendant upon a woman's death was in delineation distinctly unique from that of the male's demise. The male was the laboring deity from whose brow was wrought bread and shelter, from whose loins were sown the seeds of resurging life—the male was the crude muscular sacerdote and chieftain of the cave; his fall from the earthly world was heralded with elaborate anguished acclaim, attrition and mortification. But the female had ruled: "Better the father shall be taken from the children than the mother." The traditional and voluntary subjugation of the Vastese women was a surface rubric; beneath lay their complete correct power, perpetuated upon the rock-bottom base of fidelity, fount of birth and keeper of legend. It was for them to glorify the male, despise their own kind, and yet wield the true force. A paesano mother's death though establishing greater disaster to the institution of the home did not invoke flamboyance. That morning Fiammetta had sent her daughters to notify kith and kin of her approaching death. My mother promptly went to Fiammetta's side, sat on the bed, propped up the wasted buttonhole-maker's wife and held her in her stanch arms. Fiammetta was in her wedding dress. She looked a cadaver. She spoke gaspingly in her strident adenoidal voice.

"In the night dark as a hound's jaws, there came a lucid knocking thrice, and thrice repeated." She pointed to her husband who stood immobile at the foot of the bed. "Upon hearing it this carnival coward hid his cabbage 'neath cover. I arose and went to the kitchen, and inquired aloud: 'Who seeks to rob the poor?'

"There was someone in the kitchen. This someone lit the lamp. 'Twas a woman not of our time nor of the living; flames of light shone from her. She responded me thus: 'When I tell thee who I am thou wilt ken thy obligation. I am Zia Philomela.'" The antique women of West Hoboken recalled Zia Philomela, "The Sainted Nightingale," from their childhood. Zia Philomela had been dead the last seventy-five years, but since had been unofficially canonized by the Vastese.

"Zia Philomela swept the kitchen and set the table for collation:

"'Fiammetta, with the vision of dawn, cleanse thy flesh, don thy wedding dress, fire three scented candles, inform the paesanos, lay thee down in bed, make thy confession and holy communion; say thy farewells, for at three the Angels shall come for thee.'"

I remember the moribund stench from Fiammetta's infected leg where the rat had bitten her at the garbage dump; and the gagging lamb fat fumes that came in from the light-shaft window from the Armenian flats, the scarred and tattooed Armenians; the pungent winey smoke of the paesano men's di Nobili cigars (how I longed to grow up and puff sternfacedly , arrogantly on a man-full black di Nobili!); and the unforgettable wonderful natural woman-perfume of the paesano women with their abundant she-meat and voluminous hair; the room being crushed with women; the Pimpinellis from the Bronx, the "Cheesegraters" from "One hundred and seventeen" (Harlem), the Cinquinas from Mulberry Street, the Molinos from Brooklyn, the Sandrinos from North Bergen, and the "Pipe-stems" from West New York. Fiammetta gathered her final strength and hurled it at her husband.

"You shoulder-shrugging clowning skin-headed sack of pulp, hear you these parting excoriations—though inwardly you grin and rejoice—were it not for bitter scrounging Fiammetta your be-skirted offsprings would be barefoot in the streets. You dungeoned me with nine daughters in your gelatinous image. Sure, scratch securely the violoncello, dream of the opera and 'romance' while this fool of a wife scissored her blood away in embroidery! You buffoon of indecision, who will meet the landlord at the door after I'm gone? You never even had the courage nor the taste to beat me as every real husband does to a wife. And then the last cross: your infernal whistling, Phtt–phtt–

phtt!" Carnivale was looking at Rosamaria Whadda-you-want with cow-eyed simpatico.

"Carnivale Tedeschi," spat Fiammetta, "this is my prophecy: if you marry again you won't live long enough to lick your chops—and in the other world we'll see—we'll see if you continue to whistle!" Barely breathing Fiammetta could say no more. Padre Onorio, in vestments, and assisted by two altar boys, bestowed upon her the Last Sacrament. The paesano women, in their long black shawls, knelt to their beads. That was a tableau puppeted in the niche of memory; where are the women of shawls who knew not reading nor writing, the Biblical, who stylized emotion, who of their flesh and raiment made note, portrait and choreography of passion?

Fiammetta beckoned to her husband, and whispered: "Leaves of corn . . ." She then bolted back upright in my mother's arms and died with her eyes wide open, and though lifeless glared contemptuously at the man she had named Carnivale. Mother pulled Fiammetta's lids shut and laid her out. Pimpinelli's sixteen-year-old daughter decided to initiate herself in the estate of hysteria; that tantrumic erotica precious to the occasion of death She had no call to do so as that right was delegated to the married women, they who through God and law knew man. Her mother speedily thrashed her; while the Artichoke's wife serenely breast-fed her infant.

One stroke of fate had removed Fiammetta. The sudden rush of freedom and peace dizzied Carnivale. The scourge, the snapper was gone. The role of being wrong had long since become a well-worn coat that he had gotten used to. Sprung from his incubus of torment he found himself in a vacuum of loneliness.

As night follows day, the paesanos realized there was a "situation" in the clan; there was a widow and there was a widower. In our own little Vastese world of West Hoboken the direction of these two lives could not have taken any other course . . . it impinged upon a widow and a widower to join; the lame with the lame, the blind with the blind, the bereaved with the bereaved. We had our very own fashioned propriety. The possible and probable marital arrangements native and common to modern American society such as divorce, separation, mixed national or religious marriages, young unmarried men wedding older widowed women, were absolutely unthought of or tabooed. Let alone the outlanders from provinces in Italy beyond the sacred confines of Vasto, the creatures of other races and creeds were considered as strange and unbelonging as the denizens of the jungles, the cold fish of the sea or the unseen peoples of the moon. They were wont to say: "A Vastese who has not been washed all his life smells sweeter than an outsider." "The ugliest Vastese is a beauty compared to any outsider!" And come to think of it, Vasto being located centrally along the Adriatic shore of the Boot offers the classic head and face; Italy for centuries had been History's most important blending pot for the Roman empire. My paesanos were spared the long equine head of the North and the squat jaw of Campobasso.

"Leaves of corn," Fiammetta had whispered to Carnivale with her dying breath. Man and woman bound by Heaven need firstly leaves of corn—a mattress. Around that mattress they build a home. Vastese mattresses were made at home. The under-mattress that lay upon the bedspring (homemade: heavy hemp or wire knotted net-like and stapled to timbers that fit in the bedstead) was a bulk of corn leaves contained in coarse ticking. The top mattress was of fine strong cotton fat with goose down. Carnivale understood that Fiammetta's savings were in the bottom mattress. From amongst the yellow withered corn leaves Carnivale garnered a bushel of wrinkled, soiled, one dollar bills—three thousand.

The sight of money is a clandestine thrill; naked green denominations can make a middle-aged man's blood pound and plan, and stir his limbs to act. A man with a basketful of purchasing power cannot be chained to a buttonhole machine. Carnivale then had the courage to request of the Artichoke and the Meatball to "combine" for him the marriage with the widow of Whadda-you-want. The hierarchy of the elder paesanos deemed it Christian and salutary that Rosamaria have a mate; after all, she only had nine children and had at least a decade of fruitful years before her.

"Rosamaria, a walled city must open its portals. You are without man and Carnivale is without woman. Children need parents. Carnivale is honest and felicitous. One back will warm the other."

The wedding was quick and unadorned, as second marriages did not rate the orgy attendant upon the espousal of the new, the young, the untried, the innocent. Had Carnivale been a literate, or for that matter, a crafty man he would have investigated the facts of the eighty thousand dollars before he immured himself with another wife and her nine children. But he did not. Fiammetta's bone-scraping, scrimpingly accumulated three thousand dollars was the author of his successful campaign to become the husband of Whadda-you-want's widow, that he might share the eighty thousand dollars. He had Fiammetta's hoard converted into one-hundred-dollar bills—which he carried ostentatiously on his person and flourishingly referred to as his "lotsa casha moneys." Being a sensitive man he put off broaching to Rosamaria the business of her alleged fortune. He was generously willing to use up his thirty one-hundred-dollar bills before participating in Rosamaria's money. What was three as against eighty! Fiammetta's sweat-stained sacrifice started the avalanche of credit and goodwill that was heaped upon Carnivale. Carnivale's casha moneys, visible to all, determined beyond any doubt the reality of Rosamaria's numbers bonanza—convincing for once and for all even the simple Rosamaria—she imagining that he as her new master was dutifully ministering her interests. Real estate agents vied to sell Carnivale a house. A few of the one-hundred-dollar bills down and the multitudinous new family was ensconced in the big cream-colored brick house on the corner of Summit Avenue and Jane Street. In the memory of our colony in "the Vasto Hoboke" there had never been a paesano who did not have to work hard for an ordinary living. The leisure and opulence of Carnivale was a phenomenon. Salesmen came from Jersey City and as far as Newark to give Carnivale furniture and what not. They were discreet enough not to demand full payment. "A small down payment—it's yours—pay as you wish—no hurry—your credit is good—" The paesanos trafficked daily through Carnivale's house. When we visited our eyes popped out; real rugs—why, no paesano had more than shoddy linoleum in the front room! I think Carnivale and Rosamaria were the very first to have electricity, steam heat and a bathtub.

Father and mother sat gaping as Carnivale turned his battery radio and out of the horn-speaker we heard Caruso (who had returned to Naples to die) sing "I Remember Napoli in the Morning." Soon after, Caruso died and we heard on Carnivale's radio, "They Needed a Songbird in Heaven, That's Why God Took Caruso Away."

The sensation came when a sales-happy auto dealer sold Carnivale a gigantic secondhand yellow Pierce Arrow touring car that looked like a towering stage coach. Father admitted, "The America is paved with gold." Rosamaria and Carnivale were given the new appropriate names, The Millonaires, The Gentry. Rosamaria took it in her phlegmatic way; Carnivale lived in an aura of dazzling comets. Mention of "The Millionaires" was constantly on the paesanos' tongues; it was nice to have a Millionaire Vastese family. The playing of the numbers raged; dreams of pregnancy, birth, death, sickness, travel, accidents, love and the Evil Eye were turned into numbers to be gamed.

It was every paesano's ambition to own a grocery store. Carnivale opened one on Central Avenue. What a feeling of well-being to be the padrone in this hanging forest of edibles! —gourd-shaped cheeses, highly seasoned hams and salamis, stacks of dried cod, wicker baskets brimming with snails, bushels of drived fava beans, ceci, chestnuts.

The grocery store guaranteed alimentary security; subconsciously, instinctively, the paesanos worshipped at the intestinal altar. They lived jubilantly through the hot coursing vehicle of their bones and flesh; auto-negation, psychoanalysis were beneath them; such repulsive treasures belong to pallid, literate commercial man, the permanent tenant of Purgatory; my paesanos disdained navel-mucking Limbo; they were either in the raptures of Heaven or of Hell.

The grocery store was where the women gathered news and passed judgments. How rare fortune can change a man! Carnivale midst the women in his grocery store did not whistle and roll his head; he was jolly—nay, bawdy! He greeted his female customer with a familiar pat on her rump. When she asked for a pound of baccala (dried cod), he'd hold the saw upside down and pretend he was sawing his hand off at the wrist unbeknownst—to shrieks and howls, and then he'd throw in an extra pound free. Everyone blessed the extravagant Carnivale—no longer Fiammetta's badgered ridiculous Carnivale, but Millionaire-Rosamaria-Whadda-you-want's smiling, assuring, guffawing Carnivale—even though he laughed epileptically and in the wrong places. His Pierce Arrow parked in front of the grocery store was tagged by the paesanos as The Yellow Tornado; and his green driving terrorized West Hoboken.

An eager American insurance agent (oh yes, a William Kennedy III) dogged Carnivale, trying to convince him that a person of his importance merited a sizable policy. But none of my people countenanced life insurance. Any wife who would ever have dared mentioned life insurance would have been accused of wishing her husband's death; she would have been ostracized by the women and severely beaten by her husband. It was considered ill portent to discuss the subject or even listen to the overtures of an insurance agent—after all, was not insurance a posted reward for the death of the husband?

Carnivale was sucked into a vortex of momentous social life. Through appointed envoys he was invited to the wedding in the Bronx of Gennaro Sparafucil (starveling, freebooting reporter of the Italo-American Fascist sheet *La Verita*) to the daughter of the rich contractor, La Peppe.

It was potato-nose Sparafucil who arranged for the Italian Consul to have Carnivale elevated to the rank of "Commendatore"—a racket plied by the Consulate to bilk donations for Mussolini. Then the trip to Brooklyn as guest of Gaetano Impelliteri, the foreman of the spumoni factory. Impelliteri worked and saved the many years to go back to Italy and glory in the Nuovo Roma. They say after he arrived in Italy he was denuded by the Fascists, and his American-born children declared Italian nationals. Carnivale even voyaged to Mulberry street to accept the honor of becoming the twelfth "Disciple" in Il Cenacolo, a group of doctors, lawyers and undertakers, dedicated to arts, sciences and ideals.

Ere long, Carnivale was pressed against reality; the thick wad of casha moneys in his pocket had dwindled to four one-hundred-dollar bills. He finally mentioned to Rosamaria that they would have to begin nibbling at the edges of her eighty thousand dollars.

Said Rosamaria: "Husband, since we wed you have been master of wife, family and the common purse; continue to employ the lottery winnings. The money has been in your hands and shall remain in your hands."

Realization of the truth about the eighty thousand dollars came to Carnivale like the shock of a bomb bursting in the center of his head.

Everyone it seems, had said, had sworn, that Rosamaria had eighty thousand dollars. But Rosamaria herself had never said it. Then she, as everyone else, thought the casha moneys in his pocket was part of her winnings. And that was why Compitello the numbers agent eluded him, and left West Hoboken to work the Baltimore colony!

It was the week before Lent, and Mr. William Kennedy III, the American insurance man who was determined to sell Carnivale a juicy policy found him ripe.

"Mr. Tedeschi, a man with your wealth is only making another good investment when he takes this policy; six hundred dollars a year you pay; we give you interest and compound interest—better than the money you have in the bank. If you die of old age or sickness your family gets forty thousand dollars—and if, God forbid—ten minutes after you sign this policy, you break your neck, your family gets eighty thousand dollars."

"Eighty thousand dollars?" queried Carnivale somberly.

"God forbid—in case of accidental death Mrs. Tedeschi will be paid quickly and without question the sum of eighty thousand dollars."

Carnivale broke out into healthy jovial laughter. Agreed. He gave Mr. William Kennedy III three one-hundred-dollar bills, and put his X on the policy. Mr. William Kennedy III took Carnivale to a speakeasy, bought him a steak dinner, and brought him home drunk.

After secretly taking out the insurance Carnivale's openhandedness knew no bounds. If macaroni sold for two dollars a twenty-five-pound box, Carnivale with a philanthropic gesture said one dollar, and then pretended to put it on account. It was Utopia for the paesano women. "Benedictions on Carnivale; he squeeze my thigh and presented me with a bushel of peppers—let him squeeze on—may he live a hundred years!"

The Burial of Carnival ushers in the Lenten period, meaning that with this earthy rite frivolities and indulgences—all too human—cease until the glorious resurrection. To the delight of the paesanos, Carnivale Tedeschi proclaimed that the expense of the festivities was his treat. There had been memorable picnics to the Campagna; but the outing to celebrate the Vastese festival of the Burial of Carnival was more exciting than the triumphal march of Aida.

I wonder what the outlanders, the English, Irish, etc. (to us Vastese: foreigners, fish on legs) thought as we proceeded out of West Hoboken towards Weehawken and the Palisades? Carnivale and his Pierce Arrow jammed with his and Rosamaria's eighteen children, led the way, followed by a horsedrawn black hearse which bore the effigy of *Carnival* sitting up by the driver, Tony, The Meatball's son. (Tony was the Rodolpho Valentino of West Hoboken; he had played as an extra at the Fort Lee studios; a mail-clad knight run through by the hero's lance. The picture came to the Strand, and the paesanos attended; when the scene with Tony's vanquishment appeared, his mother, The Meatball, ran screaming down the aisle towards the screen to save him!) After the hearse came a mélange of wagons; garbage wagon, iceman's wagon, peddler's wagon, and beer wagon. Father was a bricklayer-foreman; young Patsy Manna who worked under Father, bought a Flint touring car, and we rode with Patsy; he was showing off the Flint chassis demonstration stunt—removing one of the disc front wheels and driving on three wheels.

We camped on a plain atop King's Mountain, overlooking the Hudson. The men put scaffold planks on sawhorses for tables in a grove, and unloaded the prodigious foodstuffs supplied by Carnivale from his grocery store; and the bellying wine casks were set up under shade trees. The big bowling contest got under way. Leather straps were wound around the narrow flat rim of large wheel-like hard black-wax-covered cheeses. With long underhand sweeps the brawny arms of the men sent the cheeses spinning over the grassy plain, down the slopes and up the hillsides. The object was to knock the other man's cheese out of its course—the while they refreshed themselves with great draughts of wine from wooden and goatskin bottles. Then came quoits and the rock-splitting game. Mighty fieldstones were designated as Hunger, Illness, Poverty, Mischance; the man who sledged them clean in half with the fewest blows won the laurel of grape leaves.

The women competed to see who could skin and prepare for roasting a kid goat the soonest. Then came the making of the community paschal wine—half of which in the spring was given to St. Rocco's church to be blessed and served by Padre Onorio at Mass. The women carried heavy baskets of Alicante and Barbera grapes from the wagon to the treading troughs. Barefoot men, women and children stamped and crushed the grapes while the old men sang:

> "Water can do thee harm
> Wine will bring thee charm.
> With water thou might chance
> Wine will make thee dance.
> What joy can water bring
> When wine will have thee sing!"

By the time the ceremonies for the effigy of *Carnival* commenced the men were reelingly wined, and paying no heed to the humid overcast sky closing in. Four male paesanos dressed as gravediggers, and with long reed-stemmed clay pipes in their mouths, and bottles of wine slung from their shoulder belts, bore the effigy of *Carnival* on a bier. Everyone carried a Radica, a root; and the women flauntingly danced the Saltarello. Teresina The Meatball elected to play the mourning mate of *Carnival*. She was shrouded in weeds and preceded the bier.

Carnivale Tedeschi was gaily drunk. He threw himself with tearful maudlin laughter upon the effigy.

"Brother-soul, that sour shrew Fiammetta joined us; she made you, me, and me, you. Birthed Vincenzo Tedeschi; in the America become Jimmy; by marriage become Carnivale; justly have I become thee; we live for nothing more serious than joy, and joy shall seriously do us in . . . poor, poor *Carnival*." And with that kissed the effigy.

"Right! Rightly put!" cried the paesanos with glee. They heaved Carnivale onto the bier and stuck the effigy's paper clown hat upon his head. Though impromptu it was in character with the Vastese; whether the clan gathered for weal or woe for a certainty there would be an original improvisation; this they had inherited from the dawn of man in the caves of Latium, ages before they had adopted as Father, Son and Holy Ghost, the Prince of Peace.

The cortege moved to the din of a blasphemous dirge made by pots and pans, bottles and horns, which stopped abruptly to permit

Carnivale and The Meatball to address the paesanos, pointing out the plight of frail man's and woman's desires and frustrations. With each complete round of words and counterwords the noisy music and march resumed. Leaving off the general nature of the occasion, Carnivale and The Meatball engaged in personal defections with grotesque parody, which the paesanos expected, relished and lauded.

"The Heavens must have found you savory to their liking," sang Teresina The Meatball, "they did in your shriveled scathing Fiammetta and put you to bed with the goose-fat pleasant lottery-lucky widow of Whadda-you-want, and thus have you been skipping like a drunken goat upon Fiammetta's cold dome since."

"Bravo for Carnivale!" approvingly shouted the men. The convivial funeral train halted with much fun-pomp at a huge bonfire, tossed the limp effigy of *Carnival* onto the pyre, and each threw his root into the first chanting: "*Carnival* is dead! Return, oh *Carnival*; come back to us with the Primavera! Thou wilt be as old wine for new barrels!" The gravediggers dug a semblance of a grave; a few shovels full of ashes represented the remains of *Carnival*.

"*Carnival* is dead! Dead with his joy in hand!" The wives pelted their husbands with chestnuts, and ran—the men madly after them, as though to commit outrage. The men were too heady with wine to regard the ominous signals of storm. The dusky calm of early evening was suddenly disturbed by swirling bellowing winds; the skies fired a lurid orange, lighting up King's Mountain lividly; the women's skirts flew up, showing their stout legs, garters corsets and petticoats; bolt upon bolt of lightning veined the sky and trembled the hills; the tethered horses broke loose, kicking and neighing; paper, burning sticks from the bonfire, dust, hats, leaves and utensils took wings, and the cries of the children were swallowed in the whirl.

In the eerie lumination globs of rain rifled down. Parents dragged their children beneath the wagons for refuge. Darkness clapped the Palisade and the rain rammed down inexhaustibly. Man, women, child and beast were drenched and shivering. Father managed to corral our family into Patsy Mann's Flint. The car had no curtains, and its three wheels were deeply mired. Mother prayed.

Father cursed through grinding teeth and found solace in repeating: "The unmentionable ultimate finish of the unmentionable infinite world!!!"

The abandoned chaos reminded me of the time—I was about five—my impulsive romantic young father took me to the construction job, and at the end of a day of bricklaying, and in his mortar-whitened work shoes, took me to the Metropolitan to see Caruso in *Faust*; we sat in the gallery seats tiered up near the ceiling; in a Hades scene with Caruso in the role of Mephistopheles all Hell broke apart with the souls of sinners spilling in flames and screams—and I had nightmares for years.

Carnivale Tedeschi's Pierce Arrow stood alongside us. He shouted to Father that he would drive Rosamaria and their 18 children back to West Hoboken, and return to try to relay the other paesano children. He accelerated the massive twelve-cylinder motor; the high wooden-spoked wheels spun mud and the Yellow Tornado roared away across the fields.

I'll never forget that night we had to spend on King's Mountain; by rights we should have all died of exposure; we eight children were plastered to mother's bosom. Mother's prayers surpassed Father's maledictions; the world did not end; the smashing rain had left by morning, which was Ash Wednesday. We scouted about and found cast-off heels of bread and scraps of food that tasted divine, while the men organized the trek back to West Hoboken; how clear our hunger, how caressing the bright youthful morning sun!

To succor the paesano children had been a legitimate pretext for Carnivale to return alone to King's Mountain after he had safely taken Rosamaria and the children home. He raced the Pierce Arrow back up the steep Weehawken hill in the blinding storm. There was not a penny left of Fiammetta's three thousand dollars, Fiammetta's grim efforts for security. He had secretly wished for Fiammetta's death and had aspired to Rosamaria's alleged fortune. He was guilty of mortal sin. But there was no fortune; it was all a chimera; he had believed the Vastese paesanos; the paesanos believed in belief; he should have known the Vastese; to them a jot was a continent; an invisible thread they wove into whole cloth; hearsay they fabricated into a structure;

for the Vastese, tongue and ear manipulated with enthusiasm, made grandiose fables which they honored as common fact; that was all well and good in Italy where there were peasants, poets and princes, and fables gained legs only amongst the peasants, but in the America there were no proper nobility who kept you happily in your place—the fantastic Americans thought him monied and forced many rich goods with credit upon him.

The Vastese had vaulted him to lofty height and had impaled him upon the glowing pinnacle of wishful thinking; he could not de-ascend to careless joking obscurity; the creditors would put him in jail; he'd never again have the faithful companionship of his buttonhole machine; Fiammetta's nine daughters and Rosamaria's nine sons would rue the name of Carnivale Tedeschi; so soon as the Vastese learned he was a fraud and destitute he'd become a silhouette for their exceedingly fine and merciless scissors. While the Pierce Arrow raged up toward the Palisades Carnivale's head rolled from side to side and the funny little phttt—phttt whistling escaped his lips. At the summit near the stone monument to Alexander Hamilton was the precipitous turn that led to the King's Mountain road. Carnivale pressed the gas pedal to the floor; the Yellow Tornado did not round the turn. The top-heavy touring car snorted through the iron railing and sailed out over the rim of the Palisades. In mid-air Carnivale relaxed; he belonged with Fiammetta; a man is eternally branded by his first marriage. And gods fashioned of men were made to be destroyed.

From King's Mountain the celebrants of the previous day, Shrove Tuesday, pilgrimaged to St. Rocco's to receive the blessed Palm Ashes upon their brows. And the hearse that had mockingly borne the effigy of *Carnival* to the festival, brought back Carnivale Tedeschi's charred body.

And how spoke the scissors of the Vastese?

"Rosamaria loses one husband by water—the other by fire."

"If God meant man to travel by auto He would have given him wheels instead of legs."

"Friday's winnings bear misfortune, and gold is the mother of sorrow."

"Better a live poor naked hungry man than a rich fried corpse."

"In Death's lottery three is favorite: Whadda-you-want, Fiammetta, and Carnivale Tedeschi add to three."

Fiammetta's sweated famished savings staked Carnivale's insurance premium; the insurance company punctually paid Rosamaria eighty thousand dollars double indemnity for Carnivale's "accidental" death. When Rosamaria affixed her X to the settlement papers and received a certified check for eighty thousand dollars she was positive that it was her numbers' winnings.

The paesanos were never wrong; they were right; ninety-nine, "head to head" had brought the widow of Whadda-you-want eighty thousand dollars. Who shall dispute the Vastese!

Lunch With President Kennedy

The day Senator John F. Kennedy had won the Presidential election, I had received from McGraw-Hill the special blue leather hand-bound copy of my newly published book, "Immigrant Saint," the life of Mother Cabrini.

I was supposed to send the book to Francis Cardinal Spellman who had given the work its Imprimatur.

Along with millions I saw the young Kennedy couple on television being celebrated for the presidential victory in their hometown, Hyannis, the following morning.

It was like watching a Rock Hudson-Doris Day movie. God gave man eyes to see, among lesser things, that rarity, a divinely beautiful young woman.

The President-elect's wife, Jacqueline, with her thick dark hair, sultry face, wide-apart eyes, bee-stung lips and Vogue figure was certainly the lovliest First Lady in the history of the United States. And also, she was the first Catholic First Lady.

So I authographed Cardinal Spellman's copy of Immigrant Saint to Mrs. Kennedy, and mailed it to her.

Had she looked like the wives of other Presidents, including the present, who should be veiled and cloistered, I surely would have sent the book to the Cardinal for whom it was meant; and even doubt whether I would have voted for Mr. Kennedy.

Soon after, Mrs. Kennedy wrote to me. On modest beige store stationery, the school-girlishly written letter read:

I don't remember dates, but it was the time the President had injured his back and using crutches that his telegram from the White House came requesting my presence at a stag luncheon to be given for Premier Fanfani of Italy.

I informed the White House by telephone of my acceptance.

Then followed the elegant White House card with my name in script, and the official pass for the main gate.

My wife Helen, and I arrived in Washington the day before the luncheon. It was July and very hot. We stayed with a friend, Veronica. Veronica, a publicity agent, promoter, charity fundraiser, believer in extra sensory perception, and ectoplasm, was part of Washington's inner sanctum of soiled linen smellers and tellers.

Veronica had a passionate genius for running down the Kennedy clan. She 'heard this' and 'heard that' from 'dependable inside sources.' 'Old Joe K. had a shady financial career that netted him a billion dollars—had had two mistresses and bought the Presidency for his son—like father-like son' and so forth.

Veronica also had knowledge about the White House future from her friend and patroness, a Washington socialite who supplied Veronica with predictions of events to come by reaching the spirit world through her cat.

Veronica said gossip with no holds barred was justified in Washington because the Capitol's boring provincial atmosphere.

Listening to her you would think Washington was the Florence of Machiavelli's day: every move plotted for gain, each act motivated and a web within a web; the White House referred to as 'the Palace,' and in the 'Top Drawers' surrounding the Palace were deadly, bitter, internal feuds, back doors, high living and rendezvous in Georgetown.

My Helen a D A R with her warrior-father buried in Arlington, resented 'the slander' of the office of the President and proclaimed haughtily that big people were human and had the right to live it up. I'm a would-be opportunist. I did not agree or disagree with either Veronica or Helen as all is possible and nothing surprises me.

The next morning we were out early. Helen wanted to drive by the White House on our way to visit her father's grave in Arlington.

We never got to the cemetery. In front of the White House a man was trying to get his old car going. He told us hysterically that he had to get to a finance company in Silver Springs to plead with the shylocks not to foreclose his home. We pushed his car for blocks. It wouldn't start. My wife was in character; she made me drive him the long distance to Silver Springs. The finance company turned him down. Helen gave him a check for his two months late mortgage payments. That was the last of him and the money.

I barely had time to get back to Veronica's apartment and change for the luncheon. Helen had outfitted me from head to foot; black mohair suit, Italian tie, fine handkerchief, shirt with French cuffs, and English shoes. She filed my nails, trimmed the hairs in my ears, plied me with under-arm deodorant, and then began her litany of do's and don'ts: *no drinking*—one drink and become Mr. Hyde—refuse drinks even if it kills you—address Kennedy as 'Mister President,' and his wife, 'Mrs. Kennedy,'—don't smooch or kiss her hand and don't make with the cute remarks and ogle her—you're so obvious—be proud not vain—no scratching, combing, spitting, nose-picking—no drinking—for once in your life keep your thoughts to yourself—no sounding off on sex, religion, ideologies and personalities—but do talk about your wife and children—no four-letter words—don't slap famous men on the back—don't be pushy—at the table watch others and do what they do—say 'thank you' to the waiters when served—and—above all, do not forget to bring me the luncheon menu!"

I chafed under the spurring and said, "who the hell do you think I'm going to be with—God in Paradise? Come off it; I've been around."

"Yes," she retorted, "The last time you were in Washington you went with some artist to the party at the Russian Embassy—got blind on vodka and love-dovey with the ememy and had the FBI on your tail for months!"

At the main gate of the White House Helen said, "I won't be with you to hold your hand. Go in and act as though you've lived there all your life. Remember your manners! No drinking! And-don'-forget-the-luncheon-menu!"

It's an edifying feeling to be known and expected at the White House. When your card is passed as something sacred and your name is correctly pronounced from uniformed flunkey to flunkey from the main gate—as your wife beholds it all—across the lawn to the portico, you dearly love your name—and other names announced strike your ears as comical. There is egotistical fluff in all of us; we're all jerks until we get a break.

The President arrived by helicopter which came down on the lawn near the portico. His suit was sadly wrinkled. Why did I take notice of the suit before the man? I thought of how the paesanos reacted when the runty King Emmanuel visited their village. They were disgusted because he had only one head on his shoulders.

The faces of the personages greeting the President were mediocre. Perhaps mediocrity makes for the greatness of a nation. They were a fawning litter. But those upon whom a President deigns to bestow the fat bread of office can only be grateful or envious.

Kennedy was a profusion of hair above puffy eyes and exposed teeth, radiating the conviction that it was the best of fun to be a rich, young, President. There but for the fancy of God went I.

As a President's image is magnified beyond good sense so is the White House architecturally and decoratively. The White House is neither a Greek Temple, the Taj Mahal nor the Vatican. It has no more romance than an Episcopalian hymn. In its Protestant puritanical rooms there are paintings of grim, be-wigged, hard-nosed Presidents of early, shipping, farming, mercantile and slave-holding America.

When tiny Premier Fanfani came in with his excitable entourage the White House band played O Sole Mio, and Return to Sorrento. That was the corniest. I blushed for the memory of Imperial Rome.

I had known Fanfani in Italy; "Ah, Di Donato!" he exclaimed, and kissed me on the cheeks. That gave me status among the guests.

Everyone was free to meet each other. Senators, congressmen and governors were standing about in the 'great I Am' pose. I fell in with friendly, un-self-conscious Senator Dirkson, intense, impeccable Edward R. Murrow, and the American ambassador to Italy. The ambassador didn't know one word of Italian. That figured.

Murrow, who had recently been made head of the Office of Information, was chargrined with his job, frankly saying that his hands were tied and his efforts frustrated by the lilliputians of Washington bureaucracy. Dirkson chuckingly reminded him that while the illustrious elected and appointed have their hour in the public sun and come and go it was the nay-saying clerks who kept the machines of Democracy and Government fueled, lubricated and going.

A negro butler brought a large tray of drinks. I kept hearing Helen: "No drinks!"

The silvery-maned Dirkson was put off because I wouldn't join him in double bourbons. As the tray kept coming back he said, "You don't drink? What kind of a writer are you?" I began to drink. We toasted each other. "Son," he said, "every drink is a blow struck for liberty. Aged bourbon increases pleasantry and is as fire to incense."

After a few more rounds I said, "Uncle Everett, you're younger and better-looking in the live flesh than on television. You could put all the politicians in your pocket. Uncle, you're the balance wheel of the government; the United States of America would be lost without you. We need you. Please take care of yourself." "My boy," he answered dramatically, "I'm just a simple old man watching the parade go by, hoping and praying for the good of everybody." I asked him about foreign policy. "Cato answered your question long ago. Rome picked three ambassadors for a complicated mission to Bythnia; one had the gout, one had his skull trepanned, and the third was little better than a fool. They made such a mess of things. Cato said, 'No wonder; the Romans sent an embassy on foreign affairs that had neither feet, head, nor heart.'" "Senator Uncle Everett, I say of you what was said of Aristotle, 'Among his many gifts he had that of persuasiveness.'"

The President was ready to receive the guests. Each had a number and was led to a place in the line. "Hello, Pietro," said Kennedy warmly, "glad you came. I'm sorry my wife's not here. Jacqueline is in Greece. I know she would have loved to meet you. I hope you enjoy yourself today. Let's talk after lunch."

There was the physical magnetism of a tawny brilliant-colored animal about him, coming through for the aura of burnished reddish brown hair and the most sparkling and vital of complexions. His voice and person said jubilantly, "Health! Aliveness!"

In an instant he could look into you, know your mind, and make you feel you and he were alone, one. That was the quality I described in Mother Cabrini; the same I felt when I was with Padre Pio the miracle-worker and stigmatist, the same sensation I had when I was with the humanist Pope John. The soul, the spirit, the mystique of a man is to me as evident and real as his physical being. I felt revulsion with Rusk, and uneasiness with Johnson. It was not prejudice (as I consider all politicans prostitutes and ham actors who should be flogged daily for the salutary benefit of the nation) but involuntary instinct. Rusk gave me the hand of a mummy to shake, and his artificial smile came from a white papier mache pumpkin.

Johnson extended his left hand. I, right-handed, unthinkingly reached and grabbed his right hand from his side. Johnson howled and jumped. I let go his hand. In pain, he displayed a bandaged splinted small finger. He should have told me first that the pinky of his right hand was fractured—or kept that hand behind his back. I apologized.

Kennedy was seated at the center of the horseshoe table a few chairs away from me. Opposite me was Edward Murrow; on my left, Count X, a Vatican representative.

My luncheon menu, to the left of my china and silver, was a splendidly printed thing, a work of art. Helen would surely be pleased with that trophy. The menu was better than the vaunted White House food. I have a recollection of cold lobster stuffed with peas and carrots, filet mignon, potatoes, salad, and a glace dessert, all tasteless. The superb wines, champagne, brandy and Havana cigars redeemed the food.

With the aid of his crutches Kennedy stood and spoke. "I'm part Italian," he said, "as the F in my name comes from my grandfather,

'Fitzgeraldino.' And no doubt I am decended form the Irish girls who married Caesar's Roman Legionaires . . ."

The purpose of the luncheon was to honor Premier Fanfani, things Italian, and Italo-Americans votes. He accomplished it with humor. It was not what he said but how he said it.

He made the incidents that Columbus gave us the New World, Vespucci mapped it and named it, the Italians built it, and Sinatra crooned about it, entertaining.

He delivered his jollity with what Latins call 'duende,' that philosophical exuberance for life that is not in the tongue, but comes up from inside, from the very soles of the feet.

From the corner of my eyes I saw Count X's hand creeping like a plague towards my luncheon menu. The bastard—his own menu for his wife—and mine for his mistress. Had I my wits about me I would have placed my hand on the menu—or take it and put it in my pocket where it would be safe—or when he got to it, said to him with icy politeness, "My dear Count, you're making a slight mistake; this is my menu—yours is on the other side of your plate." But I didn't have the nerve. Later, I turned to him. He smiled innocently. My menu, Helen's prized souvenir was gone.

Speeches by other members of the Government were the eternal stereotype statements about Italian culture and the American crusade for world freedon. Fanfani, who knew no English, nodded approval. When he got up and said a few words that were translated he causally pointed out, "Our aim in Italy is not to engage in mortal combat with communism but to survive it."

Kennedy drank, smoked and laughed heartily; enjoying life. Johnson sitting beside him with his sand-filled eyes and cold, lean lips, was sedately taciturn. I could see him as an admirable Macbeth. Amenities are one thing and insatiable ambition another. Is there a stand-in who does not wish for God in his wisdom to call the lead to heaven before the show closes? Any Vice President is a White House voodoo despite all protestations to the contrary. Were I President I would cover myself with amulets and make the horned sign of the counter-evil-eye each time the Vice President wished me health and a safe journey.

The ceremonies over, and free drinks abounding, groups formed, and vulgar expressions and the clichés of political shop talk hummed.

The President kept his promise to chat with me. What dreams one has during minutes of personal conversation with the most powerful man in the land—delusions that he will appoint you to the Federal gravy, fit you into the cultural program, send you to the Consulate in Rome.

Yes, he would give my regards to his wife, and both he and Jacqueline would look forward to my next book, "My beloved Mafia." Of course he would invite me again to Washington some time or other. "Good luck to you, Pietro." "Thank you, and long life to you, Mister President."

On the portico I bumped into Count X. The menu! I was going to say something about the menu. He said, "I am flying back to the Vatican. I have a horrible fear of planes. Signore, you have been most charming; would you pray for me?"

Driving out of Washington, Helen said, "I heard an awful thing. Veronica took me to the woman with the cat. She predicted that the President will be assassinated. She mentioned the place and month but not the day and hour." "Do you fall for that bunk?" "Veronica swears that other predictions the woman with the cat has made have come true. One Never knows." "The woman with the cat is nuts," I said, "And Veronica is nuts too. Veronica is the biggest liar I ever met. Jack will be in the White House for twelve years—I'd change places with him right now!" "You've been drinking, and the President is your old pal, 'Jack.' Oh, darling, I'm dying to see the luncheon menu."

I told her what happened. She was furious. "You failed me again—you got drunk, probably disgraced yourself, and you let that sneaky Italian steal my menu right from under your eyes—coward!"

I shouted back, "What the hell is a little thing like a menu!"

She shouted back, "You'll never grow up and understand a woman—It's the 'little things' that mean so much to a woman!"

She began to weep.

I cursed a blue streak.

About The Author

PIETRO DI DONATO was born on April 3, 1911, in West Hoboken, New Jersey. When he was twelve years old his bricklayer father, Geremio, was killed in a building collapse close to the Brooklyn Bridge in Manhattan. As a result, young Peter, being the oldest male, had no choice but to drop out of school in the seventh grade to support his family as an apprentice bricklayer, under the watchful eye of his father's *paesanos*. Though he had little formal education, di Donato discovered the French and Russian novelists when he was twenty-five years old. Inspired by the works of Èmile Zola and Leo Tolstoy, amongst others, he began to write, recounting the unusual and often brutal circumstances of his childhood after his father's death.

In 1937 the first version of *Christ in Concrete*—a short story telling of the father's death—was published in *Esquire* magazine. Met by immediate acclaim, and being encouraged by *Esquire*'s Arnold Gingrich, he expanded the short story into the full length novel which premiered in 1939, becoming a bestseller overnight after being chosen by the Book of the Month Club, beating out Steinbeck's *The Grapes of Wrath*. During the almost five decades in the home he built for his family on Strong's Neck, on Long Island, di Donato went on to write five more books and numerous popular short stories in the magazines of the day. His last great work, *The American Gospels*, written between 1969 and 1989, has yet to be published. He died in 1992 in Stony Brook, New York.

About The Editor

FRED L. GARDAPHÉ is Distinguished Professor of English and Italian American Studies at Queens College/CUNY and the John D. Calandra Italian American Institute. After writing the "Introduction" to the Signet Classics reprint edition of *Christ in Concrete* (1993), he devoted much of his career to teaching, writing, and lecturing on di Donato's work, as well as other American writers of Italian descent. His books include *Italian Signs, American Streets: The Evolution of Italian American Narrative, Dagoes Read: Tradition and the Italian/American Writer, Moustache Pete is Dead!, Leaving Little Italy*, and *From Wiseguys to Wise Men: Masculinities and the Italian American Gangster*. His latest study on humor and irony in Italian American culture, will be published by Penn State University Press

CAROSONE & LOGIUDICE. *Our Naked Lives*. Vol 87. Essays.

JAMES PERICONI. *Strangers in a Strange Land: A Survey of Italian-Language American Books*.Vol 86. Book History.

DANIELA GIOSEFFI. *Escaping La Vita Della Cucina*. Vol 85. Essays.

MARIA FAMÀ. *Mystics in the Family*. Vol 84. Poetry.

ROSSANA DEL ZIO. *From Bread and Tomatoes to Zuppa di Pesce "Ciambotto"*. Vol. 83. Memoir.

LORENZO DELBOCA. *Polentoni*. Vol 82. Italian Studies.

SAMUEL GHELLI. *A Reference Grammar*. Vol 81. Italian Language.

ROSS TALARICO. *Sled Run*. Vol 80. Fiction.

FRED MISURELLA. *Only Sons*. Vol 79. Fiction.

FRANK LENTRICCHIA. *The Portable Lentricchia*. Vol 78. Fiction.

RICHARD VETERE. *The Other Colors in a Snow Storm*. Vol 77. Poetry.

GARIBALDI LAPOLLA. *Fire in the Flesh*. Vol 76 Fiction & Criticism.

GEORGE GUIDA. *The Pope Stories*. Vol 75 Prose.

ROBERT VISCUSI. *Ellis Island*. Vol 74. Poetry.

ELENA GIANINI BELOTTI. *The Bitter Taste of Strangers Bread*. Vol 73. Fiction.

PINO APRILE. *Terroni*. Vol 72. Italian Studies.

EMANUEL DI PASQUALE. *Harvest*. Vol 71. Poetry.

ROBERT ZWEIG. *Return to Naples*. Vol 70. Memoir.

AIROS & CAPPELLI. *Guido*. Vol 69. Italian/American Studies.

FRED GARDAPHÉ. *Moustache Pete is Dead! Long Live Moustache Pete!*. Vol 67. Literature/Oral History.

PAOLO RUFFILLI. *Dark Room/Camera oscura*. Vol 66. Poetry.

HELEN BAROLINI. *Crossing the Alps*. Vol 65. Fiction.

COSMO FERRARA. *Profiles of Italian Americans*. Vol 64. Italian Americana.

GIL FAGIANI. *Chianti in Connecticut*. Vol 63. Poetry.

BASSETTI & D'ACQUINO. *Italic Lessons*. Vol 62. Italian/American Studies.

CAVALIERI & PASCARELLI, Eds. *The Poet's Cookbook*. Vol 61. Poetry/Recipes.

EMANUEL DI PASQUALE. *Siciliana*. Vol 60. Poetry.

NATALIA COSTA, Ed. *Bufalini*. Vol 59. Poetry.

RICHARD VETERE. *Baroque*. Vol 58. Fiction.

LEWIS TURCO. *La Famiglia/The Family*. Vol 57. Memoir.

NICK JAMES MILETI. *The Unscrupulous*. Vol 56. Humanities.

BASSETTI. ACCOLLA. D'AQUINO. *Italici: An Encounter with Piero Bassetti*. Vol 55. Italian Studies.

GIOSE RIMANELLI. *The Three-legged One*. Vol 54. Fiction.

CHARLES KLOPP. *Bele Antiche Stòrie*. Vol 53. Criticism.

JOSEPH RICAPITO. *Second Wave*. Vol 52. Poetry.

GARY MORMINO. *Italians in Florida*. Vol 51. History.

GIANFRANCO ANGELUCCI. *Federico F*. Vol 50. Fiction.

ANTHONY VALERIO. *The Little Sailor*. Vol 49. Memoir.

ROSS TALARICO. *The Reptilian Interludes*. Vol 48. Poetry.

RACHEL GUIDO DE VRIES. *Teeny Tiny Tino's Fishing Story*. Vol 47. Children's Literature.

EMANUEL DI PASQUALE. *Writing Anew*. Vol 46. Poetry.

MARIA FAMÀ. *Looking For Cover*. Vol 45. Poetry.

ANTHONY VALERIO. *Toni Cade Bambara's One Sicilian Night*. Vol 44. Poetry.

EMANUEL CARNEVALI. *Furnished Rooms*. Vol 43. Poetry.

BRENT ADKINS. et al., Ed. *Shifting Borders. Negotiating Places*.
 Vol 42. Conference.

GEORGE GUIDA. *Low Italian*. Vol 41. Poetry.

GARDAPHÈ, GIORDANO, TAMBURRI. *Introducing Italian Americana*.
 Vol 40. Italian/American Studies.

DANIELA GIOSEFFI. *Blood Autumn/Autunno di sangue*. Vol 39. Poetry.

FRED MISURELLA. *Lies to Live By*. Vol 38. Stories.

STEVEN BELLUSCIO. *Constructing a Bibliography*. Vol 37. Italian Americana.

ANTHONY JULIAN TAMBURRI, Ed. *Italian Cultural Studies 2002*.
 Vol 36. Essays.

BEA TUSIANI. *con amore*. Vol 35. Memoir.

FLAVIA BRIZIO-SKOV, Ed. *Reconstructing Societies in the Aftermath of War*.
 Vol 34. History.

TAMBURRI. et al., Eds. *Italian Cultural Studies 2001*. Vol 33. Essays.

ELIZABETH G. MESSINA, Ed. *In Our Own Voices*.
 Vol 32. Italian/American Studies.

STANISLAO G. PUGLIESE. *Desperate Inscriptions*. Vol 31. History.

HOSTERT & TAMBURRI, Eds. *Screening Ethnicity*.
 Vol 30. Italian/American Culture.

G. PARATI & B. LAWTON, Eds. *Italian Cultural Studies*. Vol 29. Essays.

HELEN BAROLINI. *More Italian Hours*. Vol 28. Fiction.

FRANCO NASI, Ed. *Intorno alla Via Emilia*. Vol 27. Culture.

ARTHUR L. CLEMENTS. *The Book of Madness & Love*. Vol 26. Poetry.

JOHN CASEY, et al. *Imagining Humanity*. Vol 25. Interdisciplinary Studies.

ROBERT LIMA. *Sardinia/Sardegna*. Vol 24. Poetry.

DANIELA GIOSEFFI. *Going On*. Vol 23. Poetry.

ROSS TALARICO. *The Journey Home*. Vol 22. Poetry.

EMANUEL DI PASQUALE. *The Silver Lake Love Poems*. Vol 21. Poetry.

JOSEPH TUSIANI. *Ethnicity*. Vol 20. Poetry.

JENNIFER LAGIER. *Second Class Citizen*. Vol 19. Poetry.

FELIX STEFANILE. *The Country of Absence*. Vol 18. Poetry.

PHILIP CANNISTRARO. *Blackshirts*. Vol 17. History.

LUIGI RUSTICHELLI, Ed. *Seminario sul racconto*. Vol 16. Narrative.

LEWIS TURCO. *Shaking the Family Tree*. Vol 15. Memoirs.

LUIGI RUSTICHELLI, Ed. *Seminario sulla drammaturgia*.
 Vol 14. Theater/Essays.

FRED GARDAPHÈ. *Moustache Pete is Dead! Long Live Moustache Pete!*.
 Vol 13. Oral Literature.

JONE GAILLARD CORSI. *Il libretto d'autore. 1860 - 1930*. Vol 12. Criticism.

HELEN BAROLINI. *Chiaroscuro: Essays of Identity*. Vol 11. Essays.

PICARAZZI & FEINSTEIN, Eds. *An African Harlequin in Milan*.
 Vol 10. Theater/Essays.

JOSEPH RICAPITO. *Florentine Streets & Other Poems*. Vol 9. Poetry.

www.ingramcontent.com/pod-product-compliance
Lightning Source LLC
Chambersburg PA
CBHW030910050726
47498CB00003BA/675

* 9 7 8 1 5 9 9 5 4 2 2 2 5 *